Brian George Brown
Who loved to read & is forever missed

England's Martyr

Book One of the Ironside Trilogy

Alfred Read

Copyright © 2023 Alfred Read
All rights reserved.

ISBN: 9781739504502
Cover design by ebooklaunch.com

To my grandfather, Silas Reginald Banks, 1920-2009.

A Few Words…

England's Martyr is a work of historical fiction set during the sequence of events from the Battle of Ringmere in 1010 to Svienn Forkbeard's invasion of 1013. Whilst some of the characters portrayed are indeed fictional, many are not, and their story sets the stage for the emergence of the English hero and legend, Edmund Ironside, who is, of course, the main focus of the rest of the (upcoming) Ironside Trilogy.

In writing this book, I wanted to make a couple of points. The first is that history matters. It really, really matters. In an age where we're inundated with so-called "historical" dramas and "shows", it seems real history has become more remote, or has at the very least struggled to avoid becoming warped and sensationalised by distinctly modern agendas. That's something that's always annoyed me, especially when the end result disrespects the lives of those who lived, or indeed attempts to portray their lives in a partial or dishonest fashion.

Narratives set during the so-called "Viking Age" seem to be particularly vulnerable to this. Whilst I'm not attempting to single anyone out for criticism, it is the case that modern portrayals of this epoch tend to focus on a glorified image of "the Vikings" that seems to imply their shocking violence was somehow admirable or justified. This is a problem for many reasons, not purely because of the obvious immorality of such a thing, but because the impression conveyed is inaccurate and, as I imply above, sensationalises an issue that should be taken seriously. I'm not remotely happy with seeing history so abused, and I don't think I'm alone. England suffered greatly because of these "Vikings" (itself a Norse word used to denote an activity, not an ethnicity, and one the English would have rarely used) and the reality of that needs to be properly understood.

England's Martyr is, of course, not written by a historian, nor is it an attempt to recreate a supposedly "pure" and objective historical narrative, something that would be beyond my capabilities. It does, however, attempt to portray an episode of English history in a serious manner, one that tries to address the complexities of a nation at war whilst still making room for the softer, more contemplative aspects of faith, family, and friendship.

It's also the case that Edmund Ironside, specifically, has not received the attention he's due. He lived, he suffered, he strove, all for the sake of saving his country from foreign dominion, yet there is not one statue of him in England, and most Englishmen will be unaware of his existence. This series attempts to shed some light on what kind of man he might have been, and this first book here introduces him as the troubled yet heroic individual I suspect he likely was. I hope it's of interest, to Englishmen and all others.

Alfred Read
15/07/23

Character list

(* after name denotes fictional character.)

Alaric*, Thegn. Son of the Ealdorman Ælfric. Husband of Æva. Father of Brandon.

Alfred, Aetheling, son of Æthelred and Emma. Brother of Edward and Godgifu.

Bana*, warrior.

Beorhtric, Thegn. Brother of the Ealdorman Eadric.

Bertram*, warrior.

Brandon*, son of Alaric and Æva.

Byrhtnoð (deceased), former Ealdorman of Exsessa.

Cenric*, captain of the Ealdorman Ælfric's hearthweru.

Cnut, son of King Svienn.

Cuthbert*, steward to King Æthelred.

Dobron*, priest.

Eadgyth, Aetheling. Daughter of Æthelred and Ælfgifu. Wife of Eadric. Sister of Æthelstan, Edmund, Eadwig, Eadred, and Wulfhild.

Eadred (deceased), Aetheling. Son of Æthelred and Ælfgifu. Brother of Edmund, Æthelstan, Eadwig, Eadgyth, and Wulfhild.

Eadric, Ealdorman of Mierċe. Husband of Eadgyth.

Eadwig, Aetheling. Son of Æthelred and Ælfgifu. Brother of Æthelstan, Edmund, Eadred, Eadgyth, Wulfhild.

Eadwulf*, Thegn.

Ealdgyth, wife of Sigeferth.

Eamon*, warrior.

Ecgberht*, Commander of the Lundenburg garrison.

Edgar (deceased), King of England. Husband to Æthelflæd, Ælfthryth, and Wulfthryth. Father of Edward and Æthelred.

Edmund, Aetheling. Son of Æthelred and Ælfgifu. Brother of Æthelstan, Eadwig, Eadred, Eadgyth, and Wulfhild.

Edward, Aetheling. Son of Æthelred and Emma. Brother of Alfred and Godgifu.

Edward (deceased), martyred King of England. Son of King Edgar and Æthelflæd.

Ælfgar, Thegn. Son of the Ealdorman Ælfric. Brother of Alaric.

Ælfgifu (deceased), wife of Æthelred. Mother of Æthelstan, Edmund, Eadwig, Wulfhild, Eadgyth, and Eadred.

Ælfheah, Archbishop of Canterburie.

Ælfhelm (deceased), Ealdorman of Southern Norþanhymbre.

Ælfric, Ealdorman of Hamptonscir. Father of Alaric and Ælfgar. Father-in-law of Æva. Grandfather of Brandon.

Ælfthryth (deceased), Queen of England. Wife of King Edgar. Mother of Æthelred.

Ælfmær, Abbot.

Ælfweard, Reeve.

Æthelflæd (deceased), wife to King Edgar. Mother to King Edward.

Æthelmaer, Ealdorman of Dæfenascir.

Æthelred, King of England. Son of Ælfthryth and Edgar. Father of Æthelstan, Edmund, Eadwig, Eadred, Wulfhild, Eadgyth, Edward, Alfred, and Godgifu. Husband of Emma. Widower of Ælfgifu.

Æthelstan, Aetheling. Son of Æthelred and Ælfgifu. Brother to Edmund, Eadwig, Eadred, Eadgyth, and Wulfhild.

Æthelstan, Thegn. Son of the Ealdorman Thored. Brother of Ælfgifu. Brother-in-law of Æthelred. Uncle of Æthelstan, Edmund, Eadwig, Eadred, Wulfhild, and Eadgyth.

Æva*, wife of Alaric. Mother of Brandon. Daughter-in-law of the Ealdorman Ælfric.

Godgifu, Aetheling. Daughter of Æthelred and Emma. Sister of Alfred and Edward.

Hereward*, Thegn.

Hemingr, brother of Thorkell.

Leofgifu*, cook.

Leofwine*, captain of Canterburie's garrison.

Morcar, Thegn. Brother to Sigeferth.

Olaf Haraldsson, associate of Thorkell.

Olaf Tryggvason, former King of Norway

Osbert*, personal steward of the Ealdorman Ulfcytel.

Oscar*, veteran.

Osgar*, merchant.

Osmund*, warrior.

Oswy, Thegn. Kin of the Ealdorman Byrhtnoð.

Richard II, Duke of Normandy. Brother of Emma. Brother-in-law of Æthelred.

Sigeferth, Thegn. Brother to Morcar and husband to Ealdgyth.

Svienn "Forkbeard", King of Denmark. Father of Cnut.

Thored (deceased), former Ealdorman of Euerwic. Father of Æthelstan and Ælfgifu.

Thorkell "The Tall", leader of the Jomsvikings. Brother of Hemingr.

Thurcytel, a captain in the Ealdorman Ulfcytel's army.

Uhtred, Ealdorman of Norþanhymbre.

Ulfcytel, Ealdorman of Eastengle. Husband of Wulfhild.

Wilfrid*, warrior.

Wulfgeat, monk and former Thegn.

Wulfhild, Aetheling. Daughter of Æthelred and Ælfgifu. Sister of Æthelstan, Eadwig, Eadred, Eadgyth, and Edmund.

Wulfnoth, Thegn.

Wulfric, Thegn.

Wulfstan, Archbishop of Euerwic.

Wulfthryth (deceased), wife of King Edgar.

Place names.

Abbendone = Abingdon.

Arewan = Orwell.

Aultone = Alton.

Bade = Bath.

Beamfleote = Benfleet.

Bebbanburg = Bamburg.

Bernecestre = Bicester.

Buccingahammscir = Buckinghamshire.

Cantebrigie = Cambridge.

Canterburie = Canterbury.

Cantwara = Kent.

Chipeham = Chippenham.

Cocheham = Cookham.

Corf = Corfe.

Dæfenascir = Devon.

Derbei = Derby.

Eastengle = East Anglia.

Esledes = Leeds (Kent).

Estreham = Streatham.

Euerwic = York.

Execestre = Exeter.

Exsessa = Essex.

Gainesburg = Gainsborough.

Gipeswic = Ipswich.

Hametuna = Ampton.

Hamptonscir = Hampshire.

Hringmere = Ringmere.

Humbre = The Humber.

Isle of Wit = Isle of Wight.

Lundenburg = London.

Malduna = Maldon.

Mideltune = Milton.

Mierce = Mercia.

Norþanhymbre = Northumbria.

Northantone = Northampton.

Noruic = Norwich.

Offetuna = Offton.

Oxeneford = Oxford.

Oxenefordscir = Oxfordshire.

Panta = Blackwater.

Porteceaster = Portchester.

Reddinges = Reading.

Remmesgate = Ramsgate.

Sandwice = Sandwich.

Sceftesberie = Shaftsbury.

Snotingeham = Nottingham.

Sūþsēaxe = Sussex.

Suthhamtunam = Southampton.

Tæseford = Tempsford.

Temes = Thames.

Theodford = Thetford.

Trente = Trent.

Wadetuna = Watton.

Westceape = Cheapside.

Westseaxe = Wessex.

Wiltunscir = Wiltshire.

Wiltune = Wilton.

Wincestre = Winchester.

Witenestaple = Whitstable.

Wirecestre = Worcester.

Miscellaneous.

Aetheling = A member of the royal family, title generally reserved for eligible heirs.

Breecs = Trousers.

Boss = Central point in a shield, usually fashioned from iron.

Cyrtel = A type of dress.

Ealdorman = Person of significant authority, appointed by the monarch and responsible for a specific region.

Fyrd = Militia forces raised in a specific locality.

Hearthweru = Elite troops answering to a specific notable, quite often an ealdorman.

Heregeld = Army tax.

Jarl = Scandinavian noble, loosely equivalent to an English ealdorman.

Kirtle = Long tunic fashioned from wool or linen. Word applies to garments worn by men and women both.

Reeve = Senior official, again appointed by the monarch to carry out a specific administrative task within a specific area.

Rönd (Danish) = Round shield.

Scir = Shire/district.

Seax = A short sword or knife/dagger.

Thegn = Nobleman, usually holding lands in obedience to the local ealdorman.

Witan = Council of notables, meaning "wise men". Generally made up of the monarch and his ealdormen/thegns for the sake of dealing with matters of import to the realm in general.

Prologue

The dream was always the same. He was a young man again, too young yet to have been compelled to take on the burdens of kingship. He stood alone in a small, draughty stone chapel, a place unadorned by finery or warmth, the night black and featureless outside. Before him lay the body of his older half-brother, Edward. Edward was dead. He was always dead, his pallid form lying motionless upon the altar, his sunken eyes closed and hands clasped up to his chest as if in prayer.

He tried to reach out to him, hoping to take his hand in his, imploring him to wake up. He never stirred. Part of him always wished him to somehow spring to life, to be the boy he was and spare him the burdens of what lay ahead. Edward never moved. He lay still, saintly in his repose, the faint, flickering candlelight playing across his ever-youthful features. He then noticed the wound, that jagged, ugly gash in Edward's side, a mark left by the hand of one who would kill a king. He felt alarm now. Somebody had done this. Somebody had killed him. Then the guilt. The heavy, suffocating guilt and anxiety. He was being watched. He turned around.

They were all there again. Staring at him, accusation in their eyes. Bishop Dunstan was one of them, long dead now, but here again tonight, placing blame with the others. That slippery bastard, Ælfric, was there alongside his son, Ælfgar, both of them looking straight at him, along with a younger man he didn't recognise. The valiant Byrhtnoð stood off to the side, not so brave tonight but ready to accuse with the rest of them. Bishop Ælfstan too. Ulfcytel. Ælfhelm. Thored. Sigeferth. Wulfgeat. They were all here and more, they were always here, crowding the chapel, staring at him, silent in their accusations. They all believed he'd killed his own brother. They all thought he'd killed the king. He hadn't. He was just a boy. It wasn't fair. But they wouldn't look away. If only they would look away.

Panic rose in his chest. From the shadows, always on time, emerged his mother, Ælfthryth. She moved towards him, ignoring the others, dressed in heavy, dark robes. She was always saying something, just quiet enough to be inaudible, but what was it? Why would she not speak up? And why would the others not turn to look at her? Her eyes, this night and every other, were fixed on Edward rather than him, a look of remorse etched upon her face, her lips moving swiftly as she repeated the same phrase, over and over, always too quiet. Too quiet. TOO QUIET.

King Æthelred opened his eyes, his nightclothes clinging to his skin and the bedsheets drenched in sweat. Another night with the dream. Always the same dream, going exactly as it had dozens of times before. Sometimes months would go by without them, and in their absence his sleep would be undisturbed, the memories of his troubled past seeming to finally fade into wishful irrelevance. Then they would return, and with them, strife across the realm. Dissent, treachery, and war seemed to be his lot as king, his troubles never-ending, a new threat from outside and within always looming on the horizon.

He sat up, prising the sheets from his body and shifting his weight around so his legs exited the side of his bed in one fluid movement. He rose to his feet and took a few halting steps over to his desk, working the strength back into his limbs as he did so. A splash of water from a hand basin drove the fatigue from his eyes, the cool sensation easing his mind back into focus. He stared at his hazy, shifting reflection in the water. Aged. Thinning, silvered hair reaching just past his shoulders. A short scrub of a beard. Dark, tired, mournful eyes. A troubled man. From the days of his youth onward.

He turned away, the sight doing absolutely nothing to lift his spirits. A sharp chill had worked its way into his bedchamber, his skin prickling against the clinging, soaked linen of his nightshirt. He tore the garment from his body, hurling it with disgust and frustration against the wall, the cloth impacting on the bare masonry with a damp slap.

Æthelred retrieved a woollen nightgown from the chest at the foot of his bed, taking a moment to savour the new-found warmth after easing his feet into a pair of fur-lined leather slippers. He knew it was useless attempting to sleep again. Once he was up he was up, and the fear of falling back into the presence of those accusing eyes always served to keep him fully awake. Something was off about the last dream, too. He couldn't put his finger on it, but there'd been something different about it, although precisely what had changed eluded him. That had not happened before. He would have to think.

The hall outside his bedchamber seemed more foreboding than usual, the flickering shadows cast by a line of stuttering torches moving as if they had a life of their own. Æthelred strode past the two figures standing guard at his door, both men instinctively falling into step behind him, the heavy treads of their armoured bodies echoing across the hallway and carrying into the passageways beyond.

After twenty or so paces, he turned left, his hand reaching out to grasp the ageing iron door handle to his study. He pushed with some effort, the heavy oak door easing back on its hinges, the welcome sight of what he sometimes felt was his one true refuge opening up before him. He paused in the doorway, a moment later turning to address one of the two guards immediately behind him.

"Bring Eadric," he said simply, the armoured figure nodding its head once before striding away down the hall, its expression hidden beneath a sheer mail coif that hung from the silver-plated metal of its visor. Æthelred ducked through the now open doorway, the single remaining guard stepping through after him.

The air inside was noticeably warmer, no doubt due to the wood fire crackling softly from an impressively wide stone hearth on the far side of the room. Stout shelves lined a good portion of the walls here, offering a wide assortment of tomes and curiosities that it still pleased Æthelred to keep around. A well-tailored crimson rug lay a short distance from the hearth, upon which rested a pair of finely carved chairs placed to accommodate any reader looking to take full advantage of both heat and light for after-hours study.

This was not the time for reading, and the king instead made his way over to his usual spot at the window. The guard behind him gently eased the door to a close before taking up a protective vigil beside it, his mail-clad form motionless yet potent in the dim firelight. Æthelred pushed the window's wooden shutters ajar and then open, breathing in deeply as the rich air of the Temes washed over him. The night sky hung stark and silent above, the stars sharp and lustrous in their heavenly splendour, the cobbled streets and stone buildings below veiled in darkness.

For a moment, he felt the vast expanse of the world stretching out before him, a thousand times a thousand places to go, far away from the pontificating, backstabbing futilities of his court. A breeze tugged at his robes, almost as if he were being encouraged to make that audacious step and just ride out into the city and beyond, free to make his own fate. But he wasn't free. He was the rightful King of England. He had responsibilities to the realm, and the throne was his until God said otherwise.

Yet if any other ruler had ever had as many enemies, he'd not heard it. Foes near and far wished to unseat him, and perhaps the most threatening of these was the Danish king, Svienn Forkbeard. This foreign savage had plagued his kingdom for years now, his hordes striking with little warning to loot and burn whatever they pleased and then escape from grasp before Æthelred could muster the forces to face them.

In desperation, he'd resorted to paying Svienn to leave his lands unharmed; a humiliation that weighed heavily on his reputation. This had also created a significant tax burden upon his subjects, leading to grumbling and dissent from ingrates unwilling to pay their due. Æthelred would have none of it, and the fact that Svienn had at last withdrawn back to Denmark was evidence enough his policy had been the correct one. Let his people complain all they liked; at least they were alive.

Unfortunately, that wasn't the end of England's troubles, and as Svienn returned to Denmark, another threat had emerged. Thorkell the Tall was his name, and after gathering an army from across Scandinavia, he was bleeding England just as Svienn had done, demanding hefty tribute to spare its people and then taking what remained through violence whenever it pleased him.

Thorkell was an unknown quantity to Æthelred. The word was he was the leader of some kind of association of warriors for hire, and that he'd won prestige and authority through martial prowess rather than statecraft or heritage. This may explain how he'd been able to recruit men from all corners of the North, promising renown and easy pickings preying on an England already weakened by the campaigns of Svienn Forkbeard.

Æthelred didn't want to admit Thorkell was right in his assumptions. England had been weakened, in more ways than one. In better times, it may have been a simple matter to raise a force to drive the invaders back. Yet rather than rallying to their king, plenty of so-called nobles could see no further than their own petty interests, second-guessing their rightful monarch and ensuring no cohesive defence was ever possible. In the past, this had repeatedly frustrated Æthelred's efforts to bring Svienn to battle, and the same was happening now.

Indeed, one of the direst of such incidents had occurred last year when he'd assembled an armada to do battle with Thorkell's invasion fleet off the coast of Cantwara. If they had won there, Thorkell's army would have been smashed before it could even land, thus sparing the kingdom the prolonged bloodletting it was presently enduring. Alas, it was not to be. Just as they were preparing to confront the enemy, Lord Beorhtric, a brother to Æthelred's own trusted Eadric, had accused the supposedly noble Lord Wulfnoth of treachery against the crown. Wulfnoth and his supporters had acted fast, stealing over twenty vessels from Æthelred's fleet and using them to make their escape. They'd then turned their ire on the innocent, burning and looting several settlements along the south coast and putting their people to the sword. Æthelred still couldn't believe Wulfnoth was capable of such vindictiveness. He'd always come across as so civilised.

Beorhtric had given chase, promising to deliver the traitor to Æthelred alive if possible. Yet as if part of some dark spell, an accursed storm had seen his force dashed on the shore, their ships lost and their men without aid. Wulfnoth had then attacked them, seeking to take revenge on Beorhtric for exposing his treason. Beorhtric had fought him off with great bravery, but the same storm that had assailed him had then caught Æthelred's fleet in its jaws, wreaking havoc and necessitating his speedy retreat to his capital, Lundenburg. Æthelred still wondered what had gotten into Wulfnoth. The man had always seemed loyal. Where he had escaped to remained a mystery.

In any case, the chaos had allowed Thorkell to land at Sandwice, debarking his thousands of warriors from his hundreds of ships entirely unopposed. The fiend had then spent the autumn of last year ransacking much of the south, reducing many a hamlet and village to smoking ruin. Even the great and holy city of Canterburie had been threatened, forcing the locals to hand over a vast amount of coin right into Thorkell's own coffers. That wasn't acceptable, and so Æthelred had bravely rushed southward to face the enemy, expecting to be joined in his campaign by his local thegns. He was to be disappointed yet again. Eadric had discovered at the last moment that the half-wit Ealdorman of Hamptonscir, Ælfric, had failed to raise the forces he'd promised, putting the king's army at a numerical disadvantage. He'd again returned to Lundenburg, reminding himself to deal with Ælfric at a later date. This had not been the first time the man had failed him.

Æthelred took some satisfaction from recalling what had happened next. Overconfident and drunk on his victories, Thorkell had been foolish enough to attack the capital itself. His savage horde had thrown itself against the city's ancient walls, losing many of their number to both spear and arrow shot from above. Thorkell had eventually been driven off, much to the elation of Lundenburg's people, but he'd then moved westward, sacking the great city of Oxeneford before heading back east into Cantwara. There he'd lurked all winter, licking his wounds or receiving reinforcements, Æthelred knew not, only to suddenly take to ship and head north to Eastengle with the first rays of spring.

Word then came that a large English force was gathering to oppose him, under the leadership of Eastengle's famous ealdorman, Ulfcytel. Æthelred had tried to be pleased. Six years previously, Ulfcytel had led a rag-tag force against another of Svienn Forkbeard's invading hosts and bloodied the bastards as deserved. Although it hadn't been a complete victory given the enemy had retained the field, Ulfcytel had won some renown as a leader of men, and the news that he was now moving to oppose Thorkell had uplifted many.

Yet in his darker moments, Æthelred was not so enamoured. A popular leader at the head of an army was not something a man in his position could afford to be complacent about. He and Ulfcytel had admittedly once been friends, and Æthelred had even allowed him to marry his daughter, Wulfhild. But that was before he'd won fame against the Forkbeard, and his influence had only grown since then to terrifying proportions. Would he move against him? It was not impossible, considering the level of treachery already on display from his supposed subjects, and should Ulfcytel even defeat Thorkell…

Æthelred was startled from his troubled thoughts by a knock at the door, the sudden, sharp sound cutting through the peaceful, contemplative ambience of his study. He turned from his view at the window, nodding once to the solitary guard to receive his guest. He knew who it was. Eadric was always prompt when summoned.

The king's guard moved from his post and slid the door back a few inches, peering through the gap he'd made in an attempt to spy any potential threats outside. Clearly satisfied, he heaved the door open entirely with a single movement, allowing two figures to enter. Æthelred recognised one of the newcomers as the guard he'd sent to fetch Eadric, his posture suggesting he wasn't entirely at ease, almost as if he didn't trust the man he'd been sent to escort. It mattered not. He had important business to discuss, matters which were best aired away from prying ears.

"Both of you can wait in the hall," Æthelred said curtly, his two faithful protectors responding immediately and exiting the study without a word. They were loyal men, and he trusted them with his life. Sadly, the mind of a simple soldier was ill-equipped to hear of the complexities of politics, and Æthelred wasn't inclined to share his thoughts with just anyone, even those charged with his protection. They could best fulfil their duties out of earshot, at least for the next hour or so.

If Eadric had been asleep he showed little sign, his face remaining free of any hint of lethargy and seemingly fully alert. His grey eyes retained their usual sharpness, his blond hair tied back as if he'd been at weapons practice. His short, no-nonsense beard also appeared immaculate, showing no trace of the disarray that usually came from prolonged slumber. His chosen attire of a hardened leather tunic and breecs was also unusual for the hour, reinforcing the impression he'd been engaged in some kind of martial pursuit. He bowed before his king, a perfectly executed manoeuvre.

"Did I disturb you?" Æthelred inquired, gesturing lazily towards one of the chairs by the fire.

"You did not, my king," Eadric replied neutrally, correctly interpreting Æthelred's gesture as an invitation to take a seat. He did so, a look of slight consternation on his face upon noticing the still-open window. The chill of the outside world had already made serious inroads into the previously comfortable warmth of the study.

Æthelred ignored him, crossing the room to claim his own place by the fire, the window left open. The two men sat in silence for awhile, the light cast from the hearth dancing erratically in the gloom. The king had become naturally suspicious in his time, his once youthful enthusiasm giving way to a certain bitterness as calamity after calamity afflicted his realm. It was not easy for him to speak his true intentions, let alone converse with another on his very dreams. Eadric did him a service by breaking the silence.

"As I understood it, my king had wished to hear my report on the present crisis after breakfast? Has something changed?"

"I had the dream again," Æthelred said quietly.

"About your brother?"

"Indeed, although something was different," Æthelred breathed, his mind straining to remember precisely how his all-too-regular nightmare had changed.

"Does my king take this as an omen?" Eadric inquired, his voice now hardly louder than a murmur, his grey eyes sharp and almost sparkling in the firelight. He was on to something, Æthelred thought. He wasn't a superstitious man, but he believed things generally happened for a reason.

"Perhaps," said Æthelred, his gaze lingering on a single ember that had escaped its brethren and was now glowing, ruby red, on the hearthstones. "The dream always comes when trouble lies ahead…this situation with Ulfcytel…"

His voice trailed off. Eadric seemed to read his thoughts. "You don't trust him," he said. "That's understandable. He has an army. He's popular. If he defeats Thorkell, he'll win even more renown. People may even start to see him as the man to defend the kingdom when Svienn Forkbeard returns."

Æthelred's jaw tightened at his choice of words. He'd hoped his policy of paying tribute to his Danish counterpart would be seen as a hard-won diplomatic victory, despite how many times Svienn had returned in the past to again wage war on England. To hear of his reappearance spoken of with such certainty was a sting Æthelred could do without.

And yet he couldn't disagree. Svienn would almost certainly return, again demanding payment and again likely to try and destroy everything in his path if he didn't get it. Such were the Danes. This would be an ideal time to prepare a defence of some kind, provided they could find a way to deal with Thorkell. But how?

"Are you suggesting that Ulfcytel could defeat Thorkell without me?" Æthelred asked, his pride wounded.

"Ulfcytel already has a capable force and is himself a capable fighter," Eadric replied, unperturbed by his king's tone. "And yet he's outnumbered. He'll expect you to move north with the garrison to attack Thorkell with him. You should remain here."

"Why?" Æthelred asked, irritated at the idea of again being seen as an indecisive, even cowardly, ruler.

"Because there is every chance that Thorkell could simply double back if he detects you and Ulfcytel attempting to trap him. He'd be a fool not to. And Lundenburg without your protection will fall."

That would be it, Æthelred knew. If he lost Lundenburg, it would take a miracle to keep the loyalty of any of his thegns and ealdormen; a task hard enough already. Thorkell could simply loot the city and return to his ships or, even worse, occupy it and attempt to stay, perhaps even declare himself king.

Æthelred's mind began to work feverishly, imagining a scenario where he'd be forced to lay siege to his own capital, the walls of his fair city manned by Norsemen intent on carving out the heart of his country. And Ulfcytel…the English would then look to him or some other bastard to lead them. It would be the end for King Æthelred. All his efforts up until now would have been in vain.

"That must not happen," Æthelred said firmly. "That cannot happen."

"It need not," Eadric assured. "You and your forces should remain in Lundenburg. But I will ask…you recall using Norse mercenaries in the past, yes? How you won Olaf Tryggvason over?"

Æthelred nodded, wondering where this was going. The mercenaries in question had initially been a welcome addition to his forces, although they were both expensive and unreliable, and many of them had gone on to betray him when opportunity arose. He'd made sure they'd paid for that in blood, and what was already known as the "Saint Brice's Day Massacre" had sent a clear message he would not tolerate the treachery of foreigners. His English troops had also resented them massively, for the hatred between the two peoples remained intense after decades of conflict and would not be eased through the mere exchange of coin. It was to be expected.

"How about we simply pay Thorkell to fight with us?" Eadric asked. This was an unexpected proposal. It was one thing to hire Danes on an irregular basis and in relatively small numbers, but to purchase the services of an entire army, their infamous leader alongside them, was quite unusual. And likely painfully expensive.

"That would drain my coffers further," said Æthelred, a touch of exasperation in his voice. "The realm is already overtaxed as it is. I could have a revolt on my hands."

"Possibly, but think on this," Eadric continued, leaning forward slightly as he spoke. "People will fear you all the more with Thorkell by your side, not just the English, but also Svienn. An English king able to command a Norse war host? That would turn heads. Svienn would take note. He'd take us seriously then. He'd be a fool not to, just as he'd be a fool to try and attack us with Thorkell in our employ."

Æthelred paused to properly digest his words. What was being proposed was quite novel, yet the amount of coin needed would indeed require more taxes. This would anger his subjects immensely, although he wondered how successful any revolt could be if he had an army of Norsemen ready to unleash. It would also most certainly make an impression on Svienn, perhaps even convince the cur to stay away altogether. Yet there were dangers. Betrayal could come at any moment, and Æthelred had learned that money was only enough to secure loyalty for so long. But given England's currently perilous state, did he have much choice? Perhaps Eadric's proposal would give them time to consider other options.

"Any attempt to approach Thorkell with such an offer should be done with the utmost care," Æthelred said thoughtfully. "I cannot be seen to be negotiating with him so closely after all he has done."

Eadric nodded slowly, becoming lost in his thoughts for a few moments. "I will be blunt, my king," he finally said. "If Ulfcytel attacks Thorkell, we can forget this plan, and Svienn will likely return anyway. If Ulfcytel somehow defeats Thorkell, his reputation will only grow, and considering so many are already moving to join him…"

"Who?" interrupted Æthelred, anger now rising in his throat. "Who else joins Ulfcytel?"

"Several notables have already promised troops or are attempting to join him themselves," Eadric replied quickly, a flash of concern entering his voice. "Your kin, Æthelstan, is with him, as is Oswy, kin by law to Byrhtnoð, hero of Malduna…"

That last name really set Æthelred on edge. He'd known his brother-in-law, Æthelstan, was in Eastengle, probably as a means to prove himself considering his father, Thored, a former Ealdorman of Euerwic, had passed on some years ago. He was something of an unknown factor, admittedly, and the king's real ties with Æthelstan's family had been severed following the death of his dear wife, Ælfgifu. She'd been a wise match at the time, the marriage securing the loyalty of Norþanhymbre under Thored and providing Æthelred with sons and daughters.

It was also very possible Æthelstan resented the rule of the brave and loyal Uhtred as the current Ealdorman of Norþanhymbre, perhaps thinking it was time his own family regained their former prestige. Æthelred was unsure if Æthelstan was even aware of the dark events he and Eadric had set in motion to secure Uhtred's position, but given his affiliations with Ulfcytel, it seemed very possible he was up to something.

Yet it was the mention of Oswy that was cause for real alarm. The man was a living reminder of the illustrious Byrhtnoð, and when people thought of him they thought of one thing: Malduna. It was almost twenty years past, but Æthelred could still remember first hearing of it; how the battle had lasted all day, how the English had refused to give in even in the face of Svienn Forkbeard's vast horde, how Byrhtnoð had been slain fighting to the last…the Battle of Malduna had become legend, and rightly so.

But legends could be dangerous, especially in the hands of those able to lay claim to them. Oswy was able to do precisely that due to his relationship with the martyred Byrhtnoð. The news that he was now preparing for war alongside the famous Ulfcytel thus made Æthelred more than a little uneasy. Was this simply coincidence, or were the two men conspiring against him?

"Why would you say Oswy has gone to join Ulfcytel?" Æthelred asked pointedly, now more than ever wishing Eadric would say something that allayed his suspicions. Unfortunately, he was to be disappointed, the very next words he heard sounding as if they'd been plucked from his own troubled mind.

"If Ulfcytel wishes to raise a formidable force, Oswy would be important to him in more ways than one. When people see him, they remember Malduna. They remember Byrhtnoð. They remember resistance. They remember their pride. Oswy could be useful for any man wishing to…"

"Wishing to what?" Æthelred snapped, his patience wearing thin.

"…use his prestige for political reasons. Political power. To become a leader of men. Impose his will on others," Eadric finished.

"Impose his will on me," Æthelred muttered. It was not a question, and he did not need clarification. He understood the situation. He could see the danger he now faced, and it wasn't solely from the foreign warlord, Thorkell. His own kind were not just unreliable, unpredictable, or incompetent. There was treachery here.

"There is more you should know, my king," Eadric said, a note of caution returning to his voice. Æthelred saw the man seemed almost fearful of his reaction at times, an observation that pleased him. Given all the disobedience across his kingdom, at least one man knew his place.

"Of those notables travelling to join Ulfcytel," continued Eadric, "there is one who I fear will all but confirm our suspicions as to what he may be planning."

"Who is it?" Æthelred asked, wondering how anyone at this point could make the situation worse.

Eadric inhaled deeply. "Ælfric. The Ealdorman Ælfric has raised what's left of the Hamptonscir fyrd and is marching for Eastengle."

Æthelred slowly got to his feet. He took a few measured steps forward towards the fire, holding his hand out over the stuttering flames. He noted how cold his study had become. He'd not really felt it before, perhaps finding the frigid air a strange comfort whilst he pondered his many troubles.

"Close my window," he said bluntly, observing with some satisfaction how quickly the young Eadric carried out his command. An authoritative response was what was needed, in small matters and large. Dealing with Ælfric would be no different. He should have done this years ago. It was all so clear now.

Ælfric's recent failure to raise troops to join Æthelred in his bid to confront Thorkell had been suspicious enough. The fact he had now managed to raise his fyrd but to join Ulfcytel marked him as a traitor. He should have been made an example of the first time he'd tried to betray Æthelred some eighteen years past. The king had been patient then. Not now. Action was needed.

"I have made up my mind," Æthelred said aloud, his back turned as he continued to stand over the hearth, gazing into the flames. "The presence of Ulfcytel, Oswy, and Ælfric in one place might have been innocent enough, but at the head of an army…it's too much. I am no fool. I can read the political situation. I am a king still, despite how much that may pain some."

Æthelred wished it had not come to this, but the realm was again in peril, and if he could not trust those who owed him obedience, he would have to look for support elsewhere. He continued to stare into the flames whilst he spoke, finding it easier to convey his grave instructions as if he were merely thinking aloud.

"You are to have your agents open up a means of communication with Thorkell. You are to impress upon him the good sense of gaining wealth through loyal service to me, King Æthelred, rather than throwing away the lives of his men in struggle and strife."

Eadric nodded slightly, his face unreadable whilst he listened.

"I also have an additional task for you, one likely as difficult as it is dangerous," said Æthelred. "I want you to go to Ulfcytel. You are to make the strategic situation clear to him and that it's impossible for me to leave Lundenburg undefended. He has no hope of victory without me, so his army is to move south. Tell him I intend for us to join forces or something akin to that. I can then deal with him as I see fit. If he will not cooperate, I want you to use the situation to eliminate Oswy, Ulfcytel, Ælfric, and anyone else who may be a threat to me. However you do it, we can blame it on the Danes. Is that understood?"

Eadric smiled grimly, untroubled by what he'd just heard. "I am pleased that my king has come to see the situation for what it is," he said almost appreciatively. "I will set out for Eastengle without delay and convey your desires to Ulfcytel. I already have somebody in his camp, close to him. Almost kin, you could say. So if he will not obey his king, the chaos of any clash between himself and Thorkell will open up opportunities for us to punish such disloyalty."

Æthelred liked the way he talked. He'd understood what was being asked of him, and he knew the dire nature of the task did not necessitate further elaboration. A victorious army headed by Ulfcytel, Oswy, and Ælfric would be a greater threat to Æthelred's crown than Thorkell himself. Northmen could be paid off. He'd done it before, as he hoped to do again. Unpredictable, charismatic English nobles with popular support, not to mention armies, were another matter. Men like that could make or break kings. They had to go.

Æthelred resumed his seat, his eyes drifting to the window. The night outside had changed, turning from an almost impenetrable blackness to a deep, enveloping blue. Dawn approached. He gestured towards the door, indicating he would be alone, his gaze returning again to the fire. Eadric moved to cross the room, the sound of footsteps light and easy-going on the stone slabs. Light footsteps on stone. Like his mother. In the chapel. From his dream.

An image filled his mind. Ælfric and his son, Ælfgar, staring at him with the others. But this night…a younger man with them. One he did not recognise. Dark hair. A full beard. Large, brown eyes. Broad, strong shoulders. His gaze was different. Not so accusatory. Just sadness. That was what he'd seen tonight. That was what was new. Who was he? What did this mean?

Nothing good. The dream always meant trouble. The fact that it had suddenly changed did not put Æthelred at ease. He turned his head just as Eadric reached the door, his hand reaching out to take the handle. Æthelred called out.

"How many sons does Ælfric have?!"

Eadric stepped back and turned, a hint of confusion on his face.

"I apologise, my king, can you repeat the question?"

"How many sons does Ælfric have?" Æthelred repeated, a tad calmer this time.

"As I recall, he has the one heir, Ælfgar, the one you had…" his voice faded. Æthelred knew what he meant, and he appreciated him not speaking of it now.

"Find out how many sons he has," Æthelred said evenly. "If a son younger than Ælfgar, perhaps with darker hair and broader shoulders, should make himself known, find out more about him. If he seems like a threat…treat him as his father deserves."

He understood. There was no need to spell things out with Eadric, Æthelred saw that. His obedience, intellect, and humble background were the reasons the king had ensured his star continued to rise at court. Æthelred knew he would do as he was commanded.

Eadric bowed again before he turned to leave. Æthelred went back to his window, becoming lost in thought as he stared out across the still-slumbering city, the first hints of morning birdsong drifting on the wind.

****

Eadric strode lightly down the hallway from the king's study, his mood uplifted, plans and possibilities unfurling in his mind. Those two guards outside didn't like him. He could read that well enough, the one who'd fetched him from his chambers having the manner of a man who expected to have to defend himself. Interesting that they could see it. Strange that some could not.

Everyone had their gifts, no? And Eadric, Ealdorman of Mierce and most trusted advisor to King Æthelred, certainly had his. He was pleased the king had responded well to his counsel, apparently believing his ultimate decision was entirely of his own mind. Suggestion was a powerful talent, Eadric knew. Now the die was cast.

"The king is well advised," Eadric muttered contentedly.

I

Days of hurried marching through rain. Mud encrusting boots so thickly it wasn't worth the effort to take them off. Precious moments of sleep snatched on cold, damp earth, the snoring of men and the shuffling footsteps of sentries an ever-present irritant. Stale bread, weak ale, and the threat of enemy attack, which, if their luck in this war proved consistent, would come when they were most vulnerable. All these things were a part of a warrior's life for as long as he could remember. A nightmare for some. A duty for all.

Today he couldn't get enough of it.

After over a week's worth of arduous travel, Alaric, son of the Ealdorman Ælfric of Hamptonscir, was within sight of his destination. The journey had not been easy, the incessant downpour at times turning the roads into a muddy ruin better suited to pigs than men. Now that was almost over. With just over two hundred of his best men, Alaric was traversing a last stretch of road just a half mile north of the town of Theodford, and with that, was within reach of a chance to rally against the heathen threat and strike a blow for the salvation of England. Any amount of hardship had been worth it. He'd come all this way again, five times and yet more, for half of such an opportunity.

He would not be alone. Marching forward at the head of his warriors, Alaric could see many others had already answered the call. Several thousand men were camped on a sodden expanse of heathland just a short distance northward, the lines of soaked and at times mud splattered tents offering welcome shelter to their likely march-weary occupants. Additional columns of soldiers could be seen moving into the camp from both the north and west, the men gradually dispersing into smaller, ad hoc groups intent on unpacking supplies and erecting shelter as quickly as humanly possible.

This was the mustering point for the new English army, one that, God willing, would put an end to the latest predations of the now infamous heathen warlord, Thorkell the Tall. The location was well chosen, for the area was partially enclosed by a man-made ring of heaped, solid earth intended to not only signify a rally point but provide a defensible position against attack. The village of Wretham to the north provided a convenient supply base, whilst a lake, now swollen by the downpour, was visible to the east. "Hringmere", the locals were said to call it. As good a name as any.

Alaric caught sight of a man on horseback heading in their direction from the camp. He called his men to a halt, the familiar scraping, shuffling ambience of two hundred pairs of marching feet easing off as the sound of heavy, ironshod hooves drew closer. His friend, Osmund, moved up alongside him, the man's cumbersome, crunching footsteps betraying his presence some seconds before his burly outline appeared in Alaric's peripheral vision.

"Ready to use those fancy manners of yours now, eh?" Osmund said cheerfully, flecks of rainwater showering off his saturated, rust-coloured beard. He was a larger man than most, Alaric no exception, and he struck a truly imposing image now, clad in a long coat of shimmering mail and a full helm that enclosed much of his face, save for those glittering blue eyes and red explosion of a beard.

"Fancy manners?" asked Alaric, confused.

"Aye, you have them," grinned Osmund. "A high and mighty thegn…a son of an ealdorman, no less, should have them, and you do. You charm the birds from the trees, so they say."

"They say?" asked Alaric, smiling. "Who says that?"

"Nobody," laughed Osmund. "I'm just trying to make you feel better. You have no charm to speak of, Alaric. In fact, I find you utterly repellent, especially after having been stuck with you for the entire march from Porteceaster. It's been harrowing, sir, harrowing! The smell of ye! I don't know how poor Æva stands it! Lord have mercy!"

Osmund again fell to laughter, Alaric joining him. The banter between the two men was often fierce, and some might make the mistake of thinking they despised one another. The wise would suspect otherwise, however. Men as close as brothers often expressed fellowship in less than flattering ways, complimenting each other with what could sound like the harshest of insults. This latest exchange of nonsense between the pair was entirely good-natured, and Alaric would be happy to let it continue if they didn't have important business to attend to.

The rider from the camp had by now eased his horse to a clattering halt about a dozen paces ahead. The face of the man sitting atop the rather fine black steed was largely obscured amidst a thick, beige woollen cloak, although a flash of metal from under his hood indicated he was likely fully armoured. He scrutinised Alaric for a moment, possibly trying to ascertain whether he was indeed the leader of these men based on the quality of his attire. The column of warriors at Alaric's back had now come to a complete stop, their number trailing down the road in a line of grey metal and towering spear tips. They were a fearsome sight, all mail hauberks, iron helmets, and stout linden shields, each man also carrying an axe upon his back or belt for use at close quarters.

Alaric stood at the head of them, his status as a man of noble birth conveyed by the fact he carried a sword as well as a spear, his helm standing out also via the decorative silver plate that hugged the contours of his visor. Although Alaric instinctively assumed he'd look as bedraggled as he felt, to the rider he still cut a fine figure, his helm shimmering slightly in the deluge, the deep green of his cloak parting to reveal expertly-wrought scale mail and the tell-tale sheathed sword of a man of good standing.

Satisfied he was more than likely addressing the right person, the rider finally spoke, his voice raised slightly to compensate for the sound of rainfall.

"Allow me to extend the greetings of my lord, the Ealdorman Ulfcytel of Eastengle."

"And allow me to extend greetings from my father, the Ealdorman Ælfric of Hamptonscir, and on my own behalf as his son, Alaric," came the response. Was that a fancy enough salutation? He didn't much care at this point. Osmund could get a laugh out of it later.

The rider inclined his head in respect, gazing back down the line of soldiers as if expecting Alaric's father to make himself known. "My father sent me and my men on ahead," said Alaric, aware that a question relating to the man's whereabouts was likely coming. "We were most eager to respond to your lord's request, so we have moved with extreme haste to meet you here."

"That's appreciated," the rider said, his face still inscrutable from the confines of his hood. "And the Ealdorman Ælfric himself? He is well?"

"He is in fine health, my friend," Alaric replied, deciding now might be the time to tell him what he really wanted to know. "He marches this way with a larger force of around two thousand men of the Hamptonscir fyrd. They should arrive within the week."

The rider nodded his head several times with some enthusiasm, clearly pleased by what he'd heard. Alaric could just about spy a smile of a sort cracking across the man's face, an image that lightened his heart. The chaos of the past year had been hard on the people of Hamptonscir, limiting the forces they could spare to venture beyond their borders. If the Ealdorman Ulfcytel was likely to be happy with what they could bring to his campaign, Alaric was glad.

In truth, Ælfric's decision to send his son on ahead was not entirely his own. Alaric had implored him, begged even, to be permitted to do a forced march, stressing the importance of joining Ulfcytel's army with all haste. A larger force with an ample supply train could not move with the kind of speed the situation required, so Alaric had hatched the idea of simply rushing northwards with some of their best men, thinking correctly that the veterans had the grit to endure such a harrowing journey.

His father had eventually agreed, despite some initial reservations. And it had worked. No matter what happened now, the Ealdorman Ulfcytel had a couple of hundred of Hamptonscir's finest at his disposal. The men could make a difference, and there was always a chance Thorkell could delay any move further north, allowing Ælfric to arrive with reinforcements. Alaric had made the right decision here. He knew it.

The rider had now dismounted and taken several steps towards him. Alaric sensed Osmund tense, the paw-like grip around his spear saying he feared he might pose some kind of threat. Alaric paid it no mind. Better to be too ready than not ready enough, and Osmund was hardly likely to attack this man for the pure sake of it. He wasn't a Dane.

At five paces distant, the rider halted and eased back the hood of his cloak, revealing a face that clearly did not belong to a man intent on violence. In fact, this one looked like he'd be more at home in a monastery library than a mustering field, his earnest expression and thin, light blond beard speaking of a still youthful naivety. Possibly the dourest part of his almost gentle countenance was the iron, open-faced helmet he wore, the severity of which failed to detract from a smile as genuine as it was infectious.

"I should add my name is Osbert," he said happily, again bowing his head as he addressed Alaric. "I am a steward of the Ealdorman Ulfcytel, tasked with helping to organise the mustering of this army."

"Then you'll know where the food is," Osmund interjected, matter-of-factly, although Alaric knew he took a certain pleasure in disrupting these formalities. Osbert didn't seem fazed, no doubt from being accustomed to men of Osmund's type.

"That I do," he replied jovially, "and you'll be glad to hear there's plenty of it. If you'll now follow me?"

With a single neat movement, Osbert pulled the hood of his cloak back into position. He then strode back over to his horse, gently taking it by the reins and easing the faithful beast around in the direction of the way he'd come. He set off at a brisk pace, tenderly leading his steed alongside him, a graceful gesture of his right arm signalling it would be correct to follow.

Alaric and Osmund fell into step behind him, the rest of the men doing likewise with an eagerness that said the news of food was likely spreading down the line. They followed Osbert for about a quarter mile up the road, the westernmost portion of earthworks now close at hand to their immediate right. Several groups of men were working on the "ring" encircling the muster field beyond, putting their backs into digging a long, shallow ditch that looked like it was intended to stretch across the entire southern facade. It was to defend against attack, Alaric mused, as anyone charging the earthworks would likely fall into the ditch and make themselves vulnerable trying to clamber out. They could then be shot with an arrow from the mud ramparts above, he thought, or smashed in the head with whatever happened to be available to throw.

It was good sense to prepare defences, but right now Alaric, Osmund, and the hundreds behind them were too fixated on the prospect of food and warmth to ponder such matters, and they filed past their labouring brethren without comment. Osbert continued to lead them north for several more minutes until he paused and turned right when the road joined a wider, more heavily trafficked intersection. The column of troops followed suit, arcing around and heading east, the previously heavy, scraping thunder of their footfalls soon replaced with a wetter, less pleasing cacophony as they became reacquainted with their old friend, mud.

They passed a score of forlorn-looking warriors tasked with watching the road, Alaric and Osmund both nodding in respect at the men standing vigil in the grey downpour. Lengths of raw timber had been heaved into position here to demarcate the boundaries of the camp, their presence intended to force an attacker into attempting to rush the relatively narrow passage Alaric's troops were now marching through. Any foe attempting to climb over the barricades would run the risk of being peppered with arrows or stabbed before he planted his boots on the ground, whilst a mass of men trying to storm the roadway itself would be forced into a narrow bottleneck and punished accordingly. Alaric thought it a wise measure, and he was again glad the Eastenglians were making such preparations. One never knew when they might come in useful.

They kept on marching, all following Osbert, and before long an increasingly dense thicket of rain-sodden tents hove into view along the left-hand side of the road. After several more minutes, Alaric again signalled for the column to halt, noting how Osbert had paused at another intersection. The road branched northward from here, heading towards Wretham, but not so far ahead and to their right lay an entrance to the ringed muster field. Osbert headed towards it, again gesturing for them to follow, leaving Alaric wondering why he'd stopped to begin with.

After another minute or so of marching, there was no doubt they were very much at the heart of the camp. There were tents everywhere, like a vast expanse of greying white, and armed and armoured men were bustling this way and that, turning the ground beneath them into a sea of mud. Rainwater swiftly filled the deep, messy imprints left by their footfalls, yet miraculously nobody slipped up, making Alaric suspect these men were already well accustomed to living here.

A small smithy also lay a short distance ahead, its workspace protected from the elements by a sheet of canvas hoisted overhead via wooden poles. A rather serious-looking man was sat within, his hands expertly working the head of a spear against a grindstone to turn blunted metal back into something usable. A few others were busy with something at a makeshift forge, each of them looking like they were the only men present who were currently warm.

Several onlookers began to cheer when they clapped eyes on Alaric's men. The sound increased in volume, spreading like a wave as others joined in until it was as if the entire camp was celebrating. The men of Hamptonscir returned the honour in their own way, the crash of hundreds of spear shafts drumming on shields thundering outward to be carried for miles upon the evening breeze.

"I can't remember the last time anyone was so pleased to see us!" Alaric shouted to Osmund, the racket only just starting to subside.

"Somebody was once pleased to see you?" came the predictable response, the barb rendered harmless by the size of the grin on Osmund's face. Alaric mouthed an obscenity back at him and turned to face Osbert, who was looking positively elated by the shield-hammering spectacle he'd witnessed. Osbert also seemed to have manifested himself a friend in the form of a grey-headed gent wrapped tight in a dark woollen cloak, the frown etched across his aged features suggesting he was quite uncomfortable in the rain.

"The mood is good here, is it not?" asked Osbert cheerfully, his hands placed on his hips.

"I'd say we're ready for a fight," Alaric responded, at the same time wondering if Osbert had ever been in one. "But not before we've eaten, I would hope?"

"Fear not," Osbert said, gesturing towards the stranger beside him. "This is Bertram, and he will get your men fed and set up for the night somewhere dry, although I expect the Ealdorman Ulfcytel will be wanting to speak with you. Will you follow me again?"

Alaric nodded at Bertram, who bowed his head in greeting. He then set off alongside Osbert, taking care with his footsteps whilst he attempted to traverse the abnormally muddy ground. He made it ten paces before he nearly lost his footing, managing to right himself at the last second and hoping beyond hope that Osmund hadn't seen him. He peered back over his shoulder, spying Osmund conferring with Bertram on the logistics of sheltering and feeding the new arrivals. He'd seen nothing.

"Don't let him near the ale!" Alaric called, pointing a finger at Osmund. His friend turned with a look of mock outrage, his hand rising to his chest in feigned shock. What was funny was the way Bertram gazed back and forth between them, unsure whether he really had just received orders to keep the man away from strong drink. Osmund would set him straight, no doubt.

Osbert led Alaric ahead and to the right, the pair passing through the opening in the ring wall they'd spied earlier. The space within seemed to have been turned into a storage area plus fort, with wide, sheltered berths housing barrels of supplies. A large number of severe-looking warriors were milling about, most of them trying to keep out of the rain whilst others stood vigil at the ramparts, staring out across the heathland in silent readiness.

Osbert headed straight for a grey pavilion; a place of importance, so it seemed, and one that apparently warranted its own path of narrow wooden planks leading up to its entrance. Alaric was grateful for something more solid to walk on, traversing the creaking yet stable pathway in pursuit.

They soon found themselves facing two particularly imposing guards standing watch outside the pavilion's entrance. The men here were likely from the personal retinue of the Ealdorman Ulfcytel, their equipment and demeanour suggesting they were more than capable of handling themselves in battle. Their shields were slung upwards and behind on their backs, their hands resting on the hafts of their war axes, their mailed hauberks heavy and long to the point they reached their knees. Like Alaric, they wore helms that covered the entire face, although theirs were lacking any decorative silver. These men were to defend their lord by smashing the enemy to pieces. Looking pretty didn't enter into it. Alaric approved.

Osbert nodded to the two giants when he came within a sword's reach. They stood aside from their path, allowing Osbert to pass within. Alaric followed, eagerly stepping out of the chill downpour and into some much-welcome shelter. He stood for a moment, taking in the change of environment, enjoying the slightly warmer air and the fact he could no longer hear the sound of raindrops bouncing off metal. It seemed like he'd been in the rain for so long he'd forgotten what it was like to not feel it. He placed his hands on either side of his helmet, pulling it free with a single effort and letting his arms rest in front of him. Out of the rain and bareheaded. Heavenly. Next thing, he'd be able to take off his boots.

He breathed out a long, deep exhalation, two parts relief and one part fatigue. Despite how Alaric felt, he still appeared somewhat presentable now his helm was absent, his dark brown eyes, thick wedge-like beard, and chestnut mane of hair serving to convey a certain presence.

He realised people were staring at him. Three, in fact. Osbert, and two powerful-looking individuals stood at a solid oak table strewn with candles, tankards, and one very large map. Osbert looked to the more senior of the two men, gesturing towards Alaric as he spoke.

"This is the Lord Alaric of Hamptonscir, son of the Ealdorman Ælfric, who has marched with great speed to aid us with two hundred well-equipped fighting men."

That was a good way of putting it. He had done just that.

"Was that your lot making that bloody massive racket just now?" came the gruff, demanding response from the man Osbert had addressed, his eyes fixed on Alaric and Alaric alone.

"I would say so. High spirits, you could call it," Alaric said lightly, returning the gaze steadily.

Their eyes remained locked for a few more moments, the man's expression inscrutable behind his vast silver beard and almost comically bushy eyebrows. His abundance of facial hair was at odds with his largely bald head, the scalp of which seemed to shine faintly in the flickering light cast from the candles. He was dressed in a similarly expertly-wrought coat of scale mail as Alaric's, an impressively thick cloak of rich, deep blue cascading back over a pair of broad, well-formed shoulders.

His paunch suggested he was partial to a tankard with a pie or two, yet the girth of his arms signified he was quite capable of putting a man down if required. His associate provided something of a contrast, possessing a thinner, more athletic figure, his shorter, neater beard and head of bountiful, light brown hair suggesting he were still in his youth, were it not for the smile lines across his face. His eyes flitted curiously between his rotund friend and Alaric, clearly wondering where this exchange might lead.

"Good, that was an impressive amount of hammering," silver beard finally said, his face cracking into a broad grin. "Do that again in a few days, and the Danes will soil themselves in fright when they hear it. I know I nearly did!"

"Thank heavens you didn't," the other man interjected, "we'd have had to abandon the camp in some haste." All four of them laughed, silver beard's mirth sounding like a cross between a pair of straining bellows and an enraged bear. It was good to hear.

"You'll know me as Ulfcytel," silver beard announced to Alaric, his voice straining slightly with the forming of words, his laughter slow to leave him. "Rumour has it I'm the Ealdorman of Eastengle, and I'm also told I'm in charge of gathering this army and holding off that Thorkell bastard until the king comes to finish him."

"Æthelred will be here," the other man stated, a certain familiarity to his tone.

"Let's hope so," Ulfcytel replied, a hint of dismay in his dark eyes. "Your brother-in-law hasn't exactly excelled himself when it comes to military matters, and I'm not confident of our numbers."

Brother-in-law? This man must be Æthelstan, and a man related to a king, even if only by law, deserved a certain respect…even if that king was as useless as Æthelred, Alaric thought bitterly.

"Æthelred will be looking to settle accounts with Thorkell ever since he forced him back from Lundenburg," Æthelstan said, although something about his tone gave the impression he didn't quite mean it. "A ruler doesn't like to be attacked in his home, and the army we are raising here presents him with a good opportunity to take the field and trap Thorkell between us and him."

Ulfcytel nodded to himself, seemingly willing to go along with the notion that Æthelred may have suddenly developed a backbone. Alaric was not so sure. Last year he and his father had raised the Hamptonscir fyrd to join the king at first word of him marching south. They were ready to depart with several thousand men when they'd heard the news that Æthelred had instead headed back to Lundenburg, apparently under the impression his southern thegns would not raise troops to support him.

This made absolutely no sense. They'd mobilised as many men as they had, yet the king had suddenly abandoned his campaign, leaving the south to fend for itself. Without the king's reinforcements, they'd had no chance of confronting the enemy directly. Retreat and humiliation had been their lot, and when Thorkell had grown tired of them and headed north, the surviving people of Hamptonscir had returned to their burned villages and ruined farmsteads, each wondering why the king had not come to defend his people. It was a bitter memory, and Alaric would speak of it.

"If I may ask, my lords…why would we assume the king would be willing to confront Thorkell here after he'd abandoned us in the south?"

It was a fair question, he felt. Ulfcytel did not respond immediately, instead leaning forward and resting his hands upon the table, a slight frown on his face as his eyes began to again pore over his map. Æthelstan spoke up, apparently irked by a question he felt he'd already answered.

"As I said, the king was attacked in Lundenburg. That's more than enough to force him to take the situation seriously. Up until then, Thorkell had contented himself with attacking settlements…"

"That were not as important as the capital?" Alaric interjected.

"I apologise if I sound insensitive, Alaric," Æthelstan replied. "I imagine you've had a hard time of it. But the fact is if your father had raised an army as the king commanded last year when he'd mar..."

"We did raise an army!" Alaric spluttered, his temper rising in the face of such falsehood. "He turned back before we could join him and left us at the mercy of the heathens!"

Æthelstan blinked a few times at the sudden escalation. Ulfcytel's frown deepened, not so much out of annoyance but concern. Osbert shifted from one foot to the other, uneasy at the prospect of witnessing a heated exchange. Let him watch, Alaric thought. It might do him good to see a clash of words before a clash of arms.

"Is that true?" Ulfcytel asked quietly, his eyes still on the map in front of him, his hands placed firmly on the table edge.

"It is true, my Lord Ulfcytel," Alaric said quickly. "The king commanded my father to raise his fyrd, and he did so. He then suddenly left us, abandoned us, without explanation, and retreated to Lundenburg."

Æthelstan responded with words more troubling than Alaric had heard in years. He didn't like consorting with so-called nobles precisely because of conversations like this, where cryptic remarks and snide retorts seemed the norm. All the same, what was said next caught him off guard.

"I'm afraid your father has a reputation for unreliability, Alaric. He's feigned illness twice now to avoid battle. Why would last year be any different? Can we really blame the king for being cautious?"

Alaric didn't know what he was talking about. He breathed in deeply, flexing his shoulders and drawing himself up to his full height. He had no idea what he was referring to, but to all but call his father a coward was a step too far.

"I'd ask my Lord Æthelstan to be mindful of how he speaks about my family, especially when it comes to spreading false rumours." Alaric mouthed each word a touch slower than necessary, hoping to make it clear he would not brook any dissension on this.

Silence fell, save for the ever-present sound of raindrops impacting on the pavilion. Æthelstan returned Alaric's gaze, an eyebrow raised slightly as if he didn't quite take him seriously enough to respond.

"Where is your father, Alaric?" asked Ulfcytel, sounding grave.

"He marches to join us here with about two thousand men."

"Why are you with us, and he is not?"

"He sent me on ahead. He understands time is of the essence and the journey long and difficult. And I wanted to be here."

Both Ulfcytel and Æthelstan exchanged looks. Alaric wasn't certain what that meant, but he was starting to feel more than a little uncomfortable. What did they know? What foul rumours had been spreading at a time when the kingdom was in peril? Who would waste energy with gossip when all effort should be put into fighting the enemy? Why should he stand here and be insulted after he and his men had just run themselves ragged to come and help these people?

"I'm sorry if we've offended you, Alaric," Ulfcytel said, apparently sincere. "Æthelstan simply speaks from what he has heard, and I'm afraid I share his concerns. But if you say your father is coming and you yourself will fight with us, then I know I speak for both of us in saying you are most welcome here."

"But what concerns…" Alaric was cut off by a sudden wave of Ulfcytel's hand.

"It doesn't matter now, my friend," Ulfcytel said sharply yet without malice. "What matters is that we have decent, God-fearing men joining us every day. With the king's help, our victory is assured."

"And if he doesn't help?" Alaric asked.

"Then we will pray all the more and fight all the harder," Ulfcytel said, the conviction in his voice soothing Alaric's temper. This man had a good heart, of that he was sure. He felt confident knowing he was in charge, and his reputation as the man who'd almost defeated Svienn Forkbeard was impressive in itself. There was a Christian in him, too, Alaric could see. A man of courage and faith.

Æthelstan was another matter. His words relating to his father had cut deep, and the fact he'd failed to explain himself when confronted didn't help matters. Ulfcytel seemed to appreciate his presence, though, and his status as brother-by-law to the king was no doubt useful when it came to giving their gathering army some legitimacy. Perhaps he was right. Perhaps the king really would march to aid them. Family ties mattered. Even a man such as Æthelred must see that, surely?

Ulfcytel continued staring at Alaric for a few seconds, his expression as difficult to read as ever due to the flickering candlelight and the vastness of his beard.

"You must be tired, Alaric," he murmured, a touch of sympathy in his voice.

"We have been on the move for some time, it's true."

"And it's getting dark," Ulfcytel said. "You should join your men and rest. I'm sure Osbert will see to their needs, right, Osbert?"

All eyes fell upon the dutiful Osbert, the man who Alaric had almost forgotten was there in the heat of his exchange with Æthelstan. A bite to eat and the company of Osmund seemed preferable to continuing any argument. Æthelstan could wait, for the moment. Alaric would discover what exactly he had against his father soon enough. He would have the truth from him. Honour demanded it.

"Bertram will have likely found your men a place to set up camp by now," Osbert said, turning to face Alaric. "I will take you to him, assuming my lords have finished all they would say?"

Both Ulfcytel and Æthelstan nodded, yet the latter's eyes lingered on Alaric with a coldness he didn't much care for. Alaric donned his helmet and inclined his head respectfully towards Ulfcytel before turning and exiting the pavilion, Osbert joining him a second later. They walked in silence back down the plank gangway and towards the exit in the ring wall, Alaric again struggling a little to keep up with Osbert's brisk pace amidst the continuing downpour.

The daylight was fading when they marched past the makeshift smithy, the men inside still busy with their work and very much blessed to have shelter and heat to aid them. Osbert led Alaric along a footpath that seemed to wind its way north east from the ring wall. A forest of tents greeted them on either side, many already occupied by fatigued yet fearsome-looking warriors in various states of undress.

They moved swiftly yet carefully for another five minutes or so, neither man saying a word whilst they focused on navigating their way ahead without slipping up in the encroaching twilight. Alaric got the impression Osbert was a little embarrassed. Chances were, he'd expected nothing but jubilation and comradeship when he'd presented Alaric to his commanders. Alaric resolved to remain silent out of consideration for the man's situation. Osbert would have little idea as to Æthelstan's apparent animosity towards his father. To question him over it would just add to his discomfort.

Eventually, the tents started to thin out into a stretch of open field hosting a significant number of men busy in the task of constructing themselves shelter. Alaric spied the considerable form of Osmund just up ahead, working with Bertram and a score of others to erect a canvas shelter that would ideally serve as a temporary eating area. Alaric joined them without a word, taking a wooden stake from a supply cart and holding it firmly in place for Osmund's hammer to hew it into the sodden earth. Osmund obliged, the sharpened wooden point disappearing into the turf under the weight of his blows.

Osbert also made himself useful, lending his arm to their endeavours with little hesitation. He comported himself admirably, even when he slipped and landed arse-first in the mud whilst helping attach the canvas to the now-completed wooden scaffold. Osmund heaved the smaller man to his feet with ease, a friendly chuckle upon his lips. Unfazed by his tumble, Osbert continued to assist them in setting up camp, working with the rest of them without complaint for the best part of an hour as the rain and darkness intensified.

By the time they were finished, Alaric was again soaked, and his armour felt like it had grown yet heavier, such was his fatigue. The three men sat inside the large shelter they had just constructed, their huddled forms gathered around a cauldron of stew just starting to bubble and froth atop a much-revered log fire. Alaric relished the warmth, and he soon relieved himself of his mail shirt and tunic in the hope of drying both next to the flickering flames.

About two dozen men shared the shelter with them, each looking to sate his appetite before retiring for the night. Alaric could see the exhaustion on their faces. He'd pushed them hard these last few days, he knew. They'd had to reach this place quickly, but now they were here, it was imperative they get some rest. He'd make sure of it before he himself succumbed to sleep.

Osbert left without eating, saying something about how he would dine with Ulfcytel. He parted company with minimal fuss, wishing them well and disappearing into the night with a weary Bertram. Alaric and Osmund ate in silence, the men around them doing likewise. The warmth of the food was almost heavenly, providing a stirring reminder that a man, if modest and reasoned, needed relatively little to be happy in this life. Osmund apparently felt the same, wolfing his share down as if he were just hours from starving to death. Given the size of him, perhaps that wasn't far from the truth.

"You like it here then?" Alaric asked Osmund, slightly amused at the speed at which he'd gotten through his meal.

"What's not to like?" Osmund replied, a few bits of stew still stuck in his beard. "It's got everything we need. I'd spend the rest of my days here, were it not for that huge horde of bastards heading this way."

Alaric wasn't sure if he was supposed to laugh, given his friend really hadn't said anything that wasn't exactly true. Neither man thought much of material comforts, and there was indeed a massive army of foreigners on the rampage who urgently needed killing.

"What do you think of the army so far?" Alaric asked quietly, hoping to get an honest answer on what he thought of their chances. Osmund stared into his empty bowl, almost as if wondering what had happened to his stew, before responding.

"It's good. It's well-equipped. Some hard nuts here, no doubt, and we're led by the man who almost defeated the Forkbeard. I'd say Thorkell is going to know he was in a fight, whatever happens."

Alaric nodded slightly. What Osmund had said was again true, but the reality was that not all of their army had arrived yet. The enemy host was considerable, and from what he'd seen of the camp thus far, the English were very much outnumbered. Victory would likely depend on reinforcements arriving in time. His father, essentially. And the king.

"How long do you think it will be before the rest of the fyrd joins us?" Alaric asked. Osmund gathered his thoughts, pawing casually at his beard and knocking loose a few pieces of barley he'd somehow failed to get into his mouth.

"No offence, Alaric, but I don't see your father being able to move like we just did. I'd say we give him a few days, but I don't think the enemy will allow us to just sit here and gather strength without them having a say in it. We may have to fight with what we have."

Alaric felt a little uneasy at his reply. It was indeed true that his father was getting on in years, and certainly not able to charge across country as they had done. That wasn't his fault, and after Alaric's little exchange with Æthelstan, he wanted to avoid any further talk of his father's apparent inadequacies. There was something in Osmund's tone, also, that he hoped he was just imagining. He held his tongue, reminding himself that his friend likely meant well.

He finished up and headed outside. It was dark, and the rain was incessant, but his men had done a sterling job of pitching every tent they'd been assigned. They took to them now, venturing inside to much-needed shelter, each and every one of them looking forward to a night's slumber without the weight of armour across their backs.

Alaric retreated to his own tent; a humble-looking thing no larger than any other. He managed to get inside without demolishing it, which was no small feat given it was getting increasingly difficult to see now they'd lost the daylight. Sleep, however, did not come easy, and it wasn't due to a lack of comfort or the trouble it took to finally remove his boots.

What did seem to be holding rest at bay was his earlier conversation with Ulfcytel and Æthelstan. What did they even mean about his father being unreliable? Why would the king have just abandoned the south, even if he didn't trust his father? Why was he still an ealdorman if he didn't have the confidence of the monarch? Why hadn't Alaric stayed in the pavilion longer and gotten real answers out of Æthelstan?

He knew the answer to that. He was here to fight the enemy, not brawl with a man he'd only just met. Ulfcytel at least seemed sympathetic towards him, and he was hopefully able to tell that he was genuine. Osbert had also impressed him, seeming like an honourable fellow eager to do what he thought was right. Alaric sincerely hoped the young man would survive the inevitable clash with the enemy. He made the sign of the Cross over himself as he lay amidst his sheepskins and offered up a brief prayer for his safety. The downpour continued to thunder outside whilst he finally drifted into sleep, words of piety repeating on his mind:

Lord Jesus Christ
Son of God

ALFRED READ

Have Mercy upon Me
A Sinner.

II

"We should attack and attack now! Damn the king! If he was even a man worthy of this land, let alone the bloodline of the great King Alfred, we wouldn't be in this mess!"

Oswy's furious words hung in the air, his audience taken aback by their sheer audacity. It was one thing to doubt the king. Many did, but to openly condemn him was another matter altogether.

Despite the tension, Alaric had to stifle a yawn. He was tired, and his mind was still foggy from being so suddenly roused from his unusually peaceable repose. He had no idea how long Osbert had been rustling outside his tent, half-whispering his name, until Osmund had simply bellowed for him to awake. The sound had shaken him from whatever dreams he'd been enduring, sure enough. It was then that Osbert had told him of their visitor. An envoy from Lundenburg had come. An envoy from the king.

The three of them had hurried southward through the camp, the first glimmers of dawn providing meagre light to guide their footsteps. When they'd passed through the ring wall and entered Ulfcytel's pavilion, Alaric had found himself in the middle of an argument, the king's "envoy" facing down a storm of harsh voices and demands for clarification. He had not brought good news. King Æthelred and his army were not coming.

Ulfcytel nodded towards Alaric when he entered. Æthelstan ignored him. Several others unknown to him glanced in his direction, whilst another remained fixated on the "envoy", a look of barely restrained fury on his face.

Osbert hurriedly whispered the man's name into Alaric's ear. Lord Oswy. The Lord Oswy. The legend. Or the inheritor of one. Oswy was son-in-law to the now martyred Ealdorman Byrhtnoð, the man who had so heroically died fighting Svienn Forkbeard at Malduna almost twenty years ago. Oswy had continued that legacy of defiance, frequently clashing with the king on how to handle the myriad threats from Scandinavia. With his bristling silver beard and towering, mail-clad figure, Oswy looked every inch a worthy inheritor to his father-in-law's legacy. Alaric was impressed.

The same could not be said for the man who'd just provoked his near-treasonous outburst. Æthelred's envoy was none other than Eadric, the Ealdorman of Mierċe, a little-known figure, to Alaric anyway, who had only been elevated to his lofty rank a few years ago.

Despite never having been in the same room until now, Alaric knew he had a reputation for cunning, yet whether that was in the service of the realm or for his own advancement remained to be seen. He was certainly doing well for himself, as he'd married one of the king's daughters shortly after becoming an ealdorman, effectively cementing his position as one of the most powerful men in England. Alaric did not know if the union was a happy one. Odds were the king was simply bestowing favours upon him, and Alaric somehow doubted either man cared much for the concept of love. Power and politics came first in their world.

In contrast to the towering Oswy, Eadric was just above average height and hardly outfitted for battle, dressed as he was in a dark green kirtle and deep crimson cloak. His lower half sported a similarly coloured set of breecs, complemented by some well-wrought, albeit mud-splattered, fur-lined boots. Typically for one of his standing, Eadric wore his thick blond coloured hair long enough so that the tips just passed his shoulders, although the slight curls gave him a touch of the feminine, something Alaric found hard to respect in a man.

Eadric's narrow shoulders also stated he'd not spent much time holding fast in a shield wall, and the soft contours of his face and pink, rose-tinted cheeks were only saved from boyishness by a neatly trimmed beard. Naturally, no English nobleman would be complete without a sword, and Eadric's dangled from a fine silver-studded leather belt, its red-jewelled pommel visible above the sheath.

Despite the evident quality of his weapon, Eadric still didn't look like much of a warrior. There was something in those grey eyes also, a hint of arrogance, or even worse, cruelty, that made Alaric feel a little uneasy. Overall, he felt it best to hold this man at arm's length, at least until he'd proven himself half-decent. Eadric, for his part, was still glowering towards Oswy, appearing shocked and angered both over what he'd said.

"Did you just damn your king, Oswy?" asked Eadric with more than a little ice in his voice, the menace unmistakable for an audience already uncomfortable with what had been said thus far.

"What would you have me say to that, Eadric?" Oswy seethed in reply, his face growing redder by the moment. "You march in here in the dead of night, amongst men who have turned out to defend this land, and tell us that our own king won't leave Lundenburg to face the enemy? What kind of king is that?"

Alaric found it hard to disagree. Ulfcytel even grunted in agreement. Æthelstan's expression was unreadable, but he'd made no effort to defend the king, perhaps feeling embarrassed at how his previous optimism had been proved wrong-headed. Eadric, at first, seemed unmoved by Oswy's emotional response, although what he said next had a more conciliatory tone.

"Think about the larger picture. A physical confrontation here isn't the wisest course of action. The king sees this, which is why he remains committed to safeguarding Lundenburg."

"And nowhere else?" Ulfcytel spoke now, moving alongside Oswy to address Eadric. Side by side, these two old heroes looked truly formidable. With men like these to lead his armies, Alaric was left wondering just why King Æthelred was so cautious.

"The king would have you lead this army south to unite with his forces at Lundenburg," Eadric replied, ignoring Ulfcytel's question. "Once this is done, Thorkell will no doubt be cowed by our numbers and be more willing to negotiate."

"Negotiate!" Ulfcytel thundered, this being his turn to lose his temper alongside the still bullish-looking Oswy. "We can't just abandon Eastengle! The enemy will burn and loot as they see fit and then likely lay waste to the north as an afterthought! What will we say in negotiations then? Please, Lord Thorkell the Murderous, do us the honour of leaving us the ashes of our own kingdom?!"

"The king believes Thorkell can be made to listen to reasoned argument," came Eadric's truly ludicrous response, something that he himself didn't appear to take all that seriously, given his sudden lack of eye contact with Ulfcytel. Alaric sensed a moment to interject. He took a step forward towards Eadric and spoke.

"Listen to what argument exactly, since the king let him burn the south already?"

Alaric heard Osmund mutter something in approval. Both Ulfcytel and Oswy rumbled to themselves in apparent support, with even Æthelstan appearing to acknowledge Alaric's words with a solemn nod. Eadric turned around slowly, looking Alaric up and down with those grey eyes of his.

"The situation last year was different," he said with a faint smile. "The king did not have the forces to defeat Thorkell's host after it landed. The Ealdorman Ælfric had failed to…"

"The Ealdorman Ælfric is my father," Alaric interrupted, "and we raised our fyrd to meet the king, just as it now marches to meet us here."

Eadric didn't appear disturbed by Alaric's claim. Whereas yesterday, Æthelstan and Ulfcytel had been almost surprised when he'd countered the false rumours about his father, Eadric reacted like he'd said precisely nothing. He instead just stood there, seeming to scrutinise Alaric's appearance as if trying to place him within a memory.

Ulfcytel spoke up again, his voice now conveying an air of calm authority rather than frustration. "As Ealdorman of Eastengle, the bulk of this army is mine," he said matter-of-factly. "I will not move my forces to Lundenburg and leave my people to be butchered. If Thorkell moves further into my lands, I will confront him. I will fight him. And I will kill him."

Good words, Alaric thought. Precisely what he needed to hear, and likely sentiments shared by most others present. He found himself wishing he'd been there with Ulfcytel when he'd confronted Svienn Forkbeard six years past. Perhaps if the king had then supported the Eastenglians with a proper army, the fearsome Ulfcytel would have given Svienn a forked skull to go with his beard. A pleasing image, at least to Alaric.

Unfortunately, King Æthelred had again failed in his duty, leaving the Forkbeard's army to escape to their ships, albeit severely diminished in number, thanks to Ulfcytel. History now looked to be repeating itself, for the king was yet again refusing to face down his enemies and was instead leaving his subjects to do the job for him. This would not stand, and Alaric would have his mind known.

"I will fight alongside the Ealdorman Ulfcytel," he announced, his words directed at everyone present. "If my father makes it here with reinforcements, God be praised, but if not, me and my men will fight with whatever resources we have at our disposal. We will not stand by and see what happened in the south happen here."

Ulfcytel and Oswy looked on in approval, Alaric feeling like he'd suddenly grown several feet in stature, such was the sensation from knowing these men respected him. Eadric took a step back from Alaric, turning to lean against Ulfcytel's generously sized map table. He gazed straight ahead at nobody in particular, his next words uttered with a quietness that contrasted with the boldness of what had been said thus far.

"Every one of you is set on doing battle with Thorkell, against the wishes of your king." It wasn't a question, they all knew that. Eadric was unhappy with their attitude; an attitude that would see them fight the enemy rather than retreat. Alaric couldn't understand him.

"It is not that we have turned against our king," Ulfcytel said, his voice again heavy with authority, "and let no man here claim that it was so. But I will not allow this land to be ravaged further. I will not give up an inch of English soil to this pagan, this heathen, this killer of men, women, and children alike."

The reminder that their enemy was indeed a Godless monster was a welcome one. Nobody in their right mind took the Northmen's apparent conversion to Christianity seriously. They'd made a show of it in the past, claiming they were as Christian as anyone else, but they'd never ceased their violent ways nor shown any real understanding of what the faith was about. They were also still in the habit of looting and burning English churches just as their pagan forebears had done; a fact that led Alaric to believe the modern Dane was about as Christian as any other murderous heathen savage.

And yet, from what he understood, various Scandinavian kings were still arrogant enough to claim otherwise. King Harald "Bluetooth", the father of Svienn Forkbeard, had been the first. Why he'd decided to adopt – or at least pretend to adopt – Christianity was a mystery, but, as expected, he'd spread his new "faith" via the sword rather than the Bible, effectively forcing the people of Denmark to convert or suffer the consequences.

Unsurprisingly, King Harald's rather unorthodox approach to evangelisation made him more than a few enemies, a point amply demonstrated when his own son ultimately rose up and deposed him. Svienn had not, however, undone his father's work, and to this day, the Danes persisted in calling themselves Christians, albeit whilst still often worshipping their old Gods and sometimes seeming to regard Christ as just another deity in their pantheon. It was idiotic, and impossible to take remotely seriously.

Neither had such antics failed to find an echo outside of Denmark. Olaf Tryggvason was another Norse king who, like the Bluetooth, had gotten strange ideas in his head, ideas that had led him to believe his fellow Norwegians should give up their old ways and adopt whatever it was he thought Christianity to be.

Alaric found it strange how he'd decided he was the man to institute such change, for he'd been no saint and never had been. Olaf had always lived a life of violence, attacking England and other lands as he saw fit, but he'd been brought to the negotiating table in 994 when King Ethelred had offered a sizeable sum of money to placate him. That wasn't surprising in itself, but what was unusual was that Olaf had agreed to be baptised, at the hands of the Archbishop of Canterburie, no less, with the king himself as his sponsor. Alaric didn't know why the man had agreed to that, but for whatever reason he had, and he'd soon left England in the company of English missionaries, apparently set on converting his people in Norway.

"Convert" was an odd word to use for what he did next. Olaf hadn't taken no for an answer, and he'd used extreme force to break the old religion and anything else he deemed to be in his way. He hadn't been shy about getting his hands dirty either, at one point even ramming a live snake down the throat of one of his rebellious jarls, killing him in the process.

How likely it was that Olaf had been able to pick up a venomous serpent and go on to insert it inside a likely armed Norwegian noble was a mystery, but the rumour, exaggerated or not, spoke to the brutal way the man had spread his new "faith". Alaric was not impressed, and he deeply resented the name of Christ being invoked to justify such blatant savagery.

Olaf's alleged conversion hadn't done him much good either. For reasons that Alaric was ignorant of, this supposedly Christian king had gone on to face some form of uprising, something that Denmark's Svienn Forkbeard had taken advantage of. In the ensuing conflict, Olaf was said to have been defeated in a naval clash with Forkbeard's fleet, apparently throwing himself into the sea rather than be captured.

This was one story. Others had heard it said Olaf had become a pilgrim and made his way to the Holy City of Jerusalem, where he endured to this day. Alaric was inclined to reject that rumour, finding it difficult to believe Olaf's conversion was ever genuine and that he'd more than likely met his end at the hands of Svienn. Greed, not faith, was the main motivator when it came to Norse behaviour. It was foolish to think otherwise.

Alaric was roused from his thoughts on recent history by the realisation that the pavilion had fallen silent. All eyes were again on Eadric, but if he was uncomfortable under such scrutiny, he showed no sign. What had he said?

"You mean to tell us that you yourself have spoken with the enemy before coming here?"

That was Æthelstan. He didn't look happy. No one did. Eadric, however, remained unruffled, not appearing to notice how close Æthelstan's hand now was to the hilt of his sword.

"You are correct, my Lord Æthelstan, as per the king's command, I sought Thorkell out before coming here."

"And what did the bastard have to say for himself?" growled Oswy. "And how did you even get near him? How does one walk up to a Dane and ask to talk?"

"Perhaps if you'd ever tried to talk to one rather than kill them, you might be surprised," Eadric said, a touch of humour in his tone. No one laughed. Æthelstan's hand was now resting on the pommel of his blade, Ulfcytel, Oswy, and the two men Alaric didn't know looking similarly guarded.

"Thorkell is open to discussions on the basis there's something in it for him," Eadric continued, this time without any attempt to provoke mirth. "He's a savage, yes, as you'd expect, but he's not entirely without intelligence. He knows that fighting a war for wealth is itself expensive. Why bother then if you can gain wealth by easier means?"

"And how long will the king do this?!" shouted a balding, irate-looking man Alaric had not met. "How does it make us look to simply pay off whoever comes here with ill intent? All it does is encourage every heathen bastard with a boat and an axe to grind! Can you not see that, Eadric? And where is Mierce in all this? Why have you not brought your fyrd to aid us? We sent requests across the realm."

"I can see it, Wulfric, with greater clarity than yourself," spat Eadric with some irritation. "And I received no such messenger with any request. I've only recently learned you were gathering here. But if you men are indeed committed to fighting Thorkell, it makes sense that I tell you where he is camped."

Silence again fell on the assorted company. Alaric hadn't expected this. He'd taken Eadric to be a mere plaything of the king; a man who would never act on initiative and remain an obedient thrall to the ever-ineffectual Æthelred. If he gave them the exact location of Thorkell...

"You'd have us attack Thorkell and kill him before he can rally his army to face us?" Ulfcytel had finished Alaric's train of thought for him. It did indeed seem Eadric was suggesting just that.

"Why not?" shrugged Eadric. "I cannot dissuade you in your thirst for confrontation. But if you do face Thorkell's army, many of you will die. You may lose. If you attack his camp whilst he's at rest…"

"Like a common brigand?! That's just not Christian!" came the immediate rebuttal from the man Eadric had called Wulfric. Fair sentiments, Alaric mused, since attacking in the dark whilst your enemy is flat on his back won't exactly put you on the path to sainthood. But did they have much of a choice?

"It's not, but if we don't win here, who knows how many more innocents will die," Oswy muttered, his shoulders slumped in resignation. "I will ask you, though, Eadric, how we are supposed to even get into his camp without simply having to fight a pitched battle once they see us coming?"

"That's a fair question, and it's here that a certain overconfidence may well be Thorkell's downfall," said Eadric, his hand reaching for one of the tankards scattered across the map table. Alaric wasn't even sure if the drink was his or if he was helping himself to Ulfcytel's. If he objected to having his ale pilfered, he made no mention of it, appearing eager to hear what might be said next.

"Thorkell's army isn't operating out of a single camp," Eadric explained after taking a swig, his hand then moving to wipe away a few flecks of ale from his irritatingly neat beard. "He seems to be under the impression we can't raise an army to do anything other than defend Lundenburg. Simply put, most of his men are still engaged in plundering after his sack of Gipeswic a few days ago. They are not expecting an organised force to sweep in and oppose them. They are scattered, dispersed…vulnerable."

"I find it very difficult to believe Thorkell doesn't know about us being here," Ulfcytel said sceptically. "We've been gathering men and supplies for some time now. Why would he be so careless?"

"Because he's used to victory?" Eadric hypothesised, looking nonplussed. "Let's be honest, the chaos and confusion sown last year when the Lord Wulfnoth betrayed the king would have left a real impression that England cannot organise a proper defence. Thorkell just doesn't take us seriously, I'd say. A mistake on his part."

Alaric found himself wondering what had happened with Wulfnoth. From what he understood, there was no indication he'd sympathised with the enemy or despised the king. The sudden accusation from Eadric's brother, Beorhtric, that he was guilty of treason was unexpected and hard to believe, although Wulfnoth's subsequent decision to go on the rampage with his own forces was downright bizarre. That storm, also, had seemed almost intended to cover his flight, and Alaric thought it really quite ominous how it had gone on to scatter the English fleet so that Thorkell might land. Was the heathen in league with dark, forbidden powers? Alaric didn't want to think of it.

"I find this a strange proposition, Eadric," said Oswy. "Even if we somehow get a force inside his camp, how do we know he won't just call in all his warriors? We'd be massively outnumbered, and there's no way to know his army is as scattered as you claim. Why don't we just march now and smash him to pieces with our full force?"

"Another fair question, my lord," Eadric answered. "I would say if you march with all the men here, Thorkell is liable to notice and fall back, gathering all of his men as he does so and gaining numerical superiority over us. Without the king moving up to support us, we'll be finished."

"Then return to the king and tell him to get himself out of Lundenburg!" That was Wulfric again. He wasn't wrong. Eadric didn't seem unsympathetic, either.

"King Æthelred will not leave the capital lest it fall into enemy hands," he said sadly. "I did try to tell him we had an opportunity to crush Thorkell here. He prefers to negotiate once more."

"So what happens to you if the king discovers somebody snuck into Thorkell's supposedly depopulated camp and murdered him?" Alaric asked this time. "Won't he be displeased that there'll be one less foreigner in the world to hand large sums of money to?"

"I'll take that chance, and I won't be implicated in what you do here," said Eadric, another slight smile creeping across his face as he again beheld Alaric. "Why would I be? I can simply tell the king that I informed you of his commands, as I have done…and shortly after, somebody attacked Thorkell's camp and killed him. He need not know much else, except that England will have become a safer place to live."

Alaric was now warming to Eadric. There was a certain something about him that hinted he may simply be a good man caught in a difficult situation. After all, he was just an ealdorman like any other and relatively new to the position as well. If the king would not listen to him, he could hardly disobey or shout him down. He had done as he'd been ordered, no doubt. But he'd also acted on his conscience in ensuring a threat to the realm might be eradicated. That was to be admired.

One of the men Alaric hadn't been introduced to suddenly spoke up. He'd remained silent thus far, his small, dark eyes flitting between the meeting's participants like he was attempting to imprint everything onto his memory. He looked capable for his middle years, dressed in a short mail shirt and leather breecs, a hefty iron cudgel hanging from his belt.

"A night attack on an unsuspecting enemy is feasible, my Lord Ulfcytel," he said, his voice gruff and unassuming. Alaric had taken him for a no-nonsense warrior when he'd first walked in, and he didn't seem wrong in that initial impression. Ulfcytel turned to him, a not-unfriendly look on his face.

"For those of you wondering," Ulfcytel began, "this here is Thurcytel, and he's captain of my Eastenglian forces here. He's as wise as he is ah… bald."

A ripple of laughter spread through the pavilion, in part due to the irony of Ulfcytel's impertinence. He himself had lost his own flowing locks some time ago, but he didn't seem bothered by it and probably didn't think anyone else should be, either. Likewise, Thurcytel wasn't irked by the reference to the barrenness of his scalp, instead speaking once more in his previously gruff fashion.

"Wars can be won with such sudden, bold moves, and something not dissimilar was attempted in our own nation's past," he continued, his eyes still moving from person to person as if trying to convince each of them in sequence. "Over a hundred years ago, the heathen warlord, Guthrum, surprised our King Alfred at his estate in Chipeham…had Guthrum succeeded in killing him, there would have been no Battle of Ethandun. There would have been no England. We could well have an opportunity right here to end this war before it spirals out of control."

Eadric nodded towards Thurcytel, a sincere smile creasing his boyish features. He seemed relieved to have something of a surprise ally here, and Alaric couldn't fault what had been said. Perhaps this really was their chance to do something that would echo throughout history. If that were so, he just hoped he was up to playing his part.

"I'm glad to see somebody appreciates the opportunity for what it is," Eadric said, still visibly pleased. "Like he says, a night attack is very workable. If successful, you'll have decapitated Thorkell's army. I don't need to explain what that will mean for the lives of all your men."

"Alright then, Eadric, but something else bothers me," said Ulfcytel, ambling over to his map table. "If we do try and sneak up on Thorkell the Tall-Bastard or whatever he calls himself…how do we know he won't have mustered his full strength by the time we get there? We could end up sending people to their deaths for no reason at all."

"Because I left him with the distinct impression you'd obey the king's instructions and move south to Lundenburg," Eadric stated. "Obviously, he doesn't know you've refused. He has no reason to think you'd disobey. He thinks we are weak, cowed, and compliant to the king. He will not be expecting you."

"So it's weakness to be obedient to the king now, is it?" Oswy murmured, a deep frown again marring his aged but energetic face. "I seem to recall you taking exception to me voicing my opinion of Æthelred just earlier, Eadric."

Eadric exhaled slowly, holding his hands up to his temples in exasperation. Oswy was spoiling for a fight with Eadric, and Alaric couldn't fathom why. If what he said was true, they'd soon be smashing in Thorkell's skull rather than facing a potentially unwinnable battle with no help from the king. Eadric had done them a favour, to say the least.

"What would you have me do, Oswy?" Eadric asked, more despairing than angry. "I have told you what the king desires of this army. You will not obey. So if I am not to see you all killed in battle, I must do what I can to salvage something from this chaos. You have an opportunity here to perhaps end this war now. Why not take it?"

"Why not indeed?" Alaric asked rhetorically. "I, for one, say we act on this. If what you say is true, Eadric, my men and I can get into Thorkell's camp and finish him before the rest of his troops are able to muster. We've done such grim work before. It's doable, I know."

"As have I," Ulfcytel said. "This is how I know these things are usually best handled with two groups. You attack a camp when you're outnumbered, and even if you catch them sleeping, most will just wake up and rush you. You need another lot to come in at the right moment when the enemy is all in a panic at being attacked from one direction. Hit 'em hard from another side, is what I mean. Use your scant numbers for maximum impact. It works."

Alaric knew what he meant. Both he and Osmund had done something similar last autumn, back when Thorkell was shadowing Canterburie. They'd never had a chance against his main force, but they'd raided a few camps being used to supply his rearguard, even freeing some captives in the process. They had learned the value of surprise in those skirmishes, that and the fact the enemy were capable of being killed just like any other men, regardless of their fearsome reputation.

"Alright then, so is it agreed?" Alaric asked, eager for the talking to finish and for the fighting to begin. "I will take a few score of my best and accompany Eadric to wherever it is Thorkell is camped. We'll attack at night, and the sound of our fighting will serve as a signal for a second group to storm the camp from the other side? Is that your thinking, my Lord Ulfcytel?"

"That does sound like a plan," he replied, running his fingers through his silver mane of a beard. "I can lead a batch of my personal retinue and…"

"Wait, my lord, if I may," interrupted Æthelstan, who had also moved closer as Alaric was speaking, the three men now encircling Eadric to the point he looked quite uneasy at their proximity. "As you have said, this army is yours to command. Most of the men are from Eastengle and will look to you first and foremost. I would suggest you stay with them. If all agree, I could assemble a force from my Norþanhymbrians to provide

Alaric with the support he requires."

Alaric felt a little indignant at the assumption he'd need help from a cold fish like Æthelstan, yet his offer was fair. He had no notion of the quality of the Norþanhymbrian troops he'd mentioned, but Alaric was feeling confident. Enough planning. More fighting.

"I would stress that the ealdorman himself should lead this assault," Eadric said, for some reason now placing an undue emphasis on the word "ealdorman". "With a task of such importance, we need a man who…"

"I don't think so, no," said Æthelstan, the sharpness of his voice cutting Eadric off in mid-sentence. "As I said, an Eastenglian army needs its Eastenglian leader. They know and respect him…and even if we kill Thorkell, we'll still need Ulfcytel and men like him to safeguard the realm against Svienn Forkbeard and his ilk. Alaric and I can handle the camp attack well enough."

Eadric paused, his thoughtful eyes suggesting he was thinking on a way to counter what had been said. Ulfcytel didn't speak up, looking like he'd been convinced by Æthelstan's words. Alaric didn't disagree either. Ulfcytel was needed here. He was too important, now and for the future.

"All right then," Eadric murmured, apparently resigned to Æthelstan's plan. "I will accompany you both with my escort. I suggest we stick to the woodland to mask our movements. Small force or not, I imagine there'll still be over a hundred of us, and that will draw attention."

"How long do you think this will take?" Ulfcytel asked, sounding almost exasperated now it seemed he wasn't going with them.

"Two days there, perhaps," Eadric replied. "If we're successful, you'll see us soon enough as we'll have Northmen looking for us. Without Thorkell, though, they'll be in disarray. They'll be finished as an effective force, God willing. They may even start fighting among themselves."

"Looks like it's settled then," Ulfcytel said cheerfully. "Let's drink on it, and with any luck, we'll soon be drinking again in victory!"

Ulfcytel strode past Eadric, the smaller man nimbly ducking aside, and filled several tankards at his table from a barrel of ale he'd somehow managed to keep hidden somewhere in the pavilion. Osbert moved to assist him, distributing drinks to all present, the lad appearing sincerely grateful when Ulfcytel insisted he take one for himself.

Ulfcytel raised his tankard in a toast, his company doing likewise and drinking in unison, the foamy, almost bitter fluid lifting their already high spirits. Dawn was finally breaking outside, its rays gradually penetrating the pavilion, and the oppressive rain was finally easing off to a slight drizzle. Anyone who walked in right now would no doubt think the men leading this army were unfit for service, given the hour at which they were indulging. They would be wrong.

The meeting had started with the promise of disaster. They'd been let down by their king, again, and the odds had looked to have turned decisively against them. Now in the morning light, there were new possibilities. Even without Æthelred's army, it felt like they had a chance of attaining something precious. Victory.

III

The sun had set several hours ago, the forest canopy blanketing them with a darkness undisturbed by either moon or starlight. An owl hooted some distance away, unworried by human activity and ignorant of the many concerns of men. A chill breeze drifted lazily through the thicket, its caress setting many thousands of leaves in gentle motion, the otherwise soothing sound doing little to relax already frayed nerves. Something else was out there. Something was coming. Something large.

Osmund emerged from a sea of ferns about twenty yards away, a look of bemusement on his face. He shrugged and shook his head. Alaric understood what he meant. This really must be the only entrance to Thorkell's camp, at least on the southern side. Æthelstan had departed with his men a while ago, heading for what Eadric had claimed was a second entrance on the eastern edge of the camp. This had been part of the agreed strategy, of course, but Alaric had still felt uneasy at splitting up, despite both men assuring him they would be ready to attack as long as he commenced his own assault here in one hour. They'd even left a candle clock behind so he could be precise.

Osmund joined him beneath the creaking, resplendent limbs of a vast and well-aged oak, the two of them crouching low to observe the enemy position about a hundred yards ahead. It was a Dane camp, no doubt about it, although whether it was the right one was uncertain, despite Eadric's assurances. The enemy had erected a ramshackle palisade that extended north and then east for some distance, yet the only entrance they'd been able to locate was situated just ahead in the form of a narrow gap manned by two bored-looking warriors.

These men had no idea how useful they were, given their torches were lighting up their position nicely, the pair of them clearly unaware they were being watched. Alaric's force had been doing precisely that for some time whilst they searched in vain for a way into the camp that bypassed the palisade. As it stood, the only way inside was simply to smash through the southern entrance, killing the guards currently idling there and taking whatever lay beyond by storm. Brave, but potentially disastrous. And it didn't help that the only man who really knew this terrain, that being Eadric, had now departed.

Alaric glanced behind him, spying the odd glint of dark iron amidst the trees and ferns that hugged the narrow trail they'd followed thus far. Alaric once again couldn't help but admire his men. He knew they were good at what they did, and they'd proved that to him over and over, but their efforts to conceal themselves were quite impressive considering the bulk of their arms and armour. There was nothing to be seen unless you knew already what to look for, and those flashes of metal and mail that were visible could easily be overlooked by any casual observers. These were men of subtlety as well as might. That's why he'd brought them.

Their numbers, of course, were thin. He'd taken about fifty of his original retinue with him, fearing more would only increase the odds of detection. He needn't have been so cautious. They'd not encountered any wandering foes at all, let alone an organised patrol. Was Thorkell really as overconfident as Eadric had made out? Did he really think the English were beaten? If what Eadric had said was indeed true, Thorkell's complacency might very well get him killed. Alaric would make sure of it, in fact.

When they'd left Hringmere, they'd been in high spirits. Every man had been made aware of what was expected of him, just as they were aware of how dangerous their mission really was. They'd initially made good time, doing the common sense thing and sticking to the woodland, Æthelstan's Norþanhymbrians moving almost as swiftly and competently as Alaric's southerners.

Their first night camped out was uneventful. Æthelstan seemed at ease in their company and unwilling to revisit previous tensions in regard to Alaric's father. Alaric had considered bringing the issue up with him, yet ultimately he'd decided against it, thinking it wise to keep Æthelstan sweet for the battle to come. They also couldn't risk an argument out in the wilds like this. Everything they did here depended on remaining quiet and unseen.

The next day had been different. As the afternoon came, they could see smoke on the southern horizon. Gipeswic was still burning. The enemy's decision to set the town alight was typical behaviour, and Eadric had claimed he'd seen the settlement aflame when he'd passed this way three nights previously in his efforts to reach Ulfcytel. What had become of its inhabitants, he did not know, and from the tone of his voice, he didn't much care either.

Alaric didn't understand how he could be so unmoved. The slow, steady destruction of his homeland under the ever-unready rule of King Æthelred was a source of constant heartache for him. Perhaps Eadric was just better at hiding his feelings, since he was a man accustomed to the role of diplomat rather than warrior. That would make sense, although his stoicism provided no comfort as they marched closer, the bitter smell of burning, charred wood soon reaching them on the wind.

Alaric knew every one of his men would be looking to settle scores. The stench of yet another torched settlement was bringing back memories, none of them good, and he was absolutely certain he wasn't the only one with his blood up. They couldn't reverse the damage done to the south last year, nor could they save Gipeswic now, but if all went as planned, they had a solid chance of getting up close to those responsible. Their swords and axes would then do the rest.

If they succeeded, Alaric hoped they'd still be able to get away and rejoin Ulfcytel, but even if they all died escaping, he'd be glad of what they'd achieved. These were dire times, yet history would remember them fondly as the men who'd dispensed some justice for the sake of a much-aggrieved land. That was a legacy he could be happy with. The man who had killed Thorkell the Tall.

"The candle thing has almost burned down," Osmund whispered hoarsely. "There is no other way in for us. We'll just have to rush them."

Osmund spoke the truth. There could be no subtlety to this, which almost seemed a shame given the stealth they had successfully employed up until now. The most viable course of action was to charge the camp entrance, kill the guards, and rush inside. If Æthelstan was in position, he'd no doubt hear the ensuing cacophony and make a move of his own. Thorkell would come rushing out of his doubtlessly large and opulent tent to find his people under attack from two directions. Alaric would then remove his head from his shoulders. Job done.

Things seemed as good as they were going to get. With any luck, most of those inside the camp would now be asleep or drinking themselves silly. Alaric stared at the candle clock Æthelstan had placed for him at the base of the oak tree. It was almost time. Almost. Now.

Alaric stood up. Osmund looked at him, slightly perplexed, wondering what he had planned. It was unlikely the enemy would be able to see him from this distance, the light cast by the torches of the guards at the camp entrance barely penetrating the surrounding undergrowth. Alaric motioned for Osmund to stand. He did so.

"I've an idea," Alaric said softly, "if we remove our helmets and do thus…"

Alaric took off his helm and tied his cloak tightly around his chest, concealing much of his armour. Osmund did likewise, looking nonplussed. He'd see soon enough why this was important, yet that still left the question as to where to put their helmets if not on their heads. He tucked his under his cloak, cradling it with his left arm. Osmund did something similar in imitation.

"Now hold on to me, like you're hammered," Alaric said.

Osmund didn't need to be told twice. He'd done this many a time in the past, although back then he'd actually been drunk, rather than just pretending as he was now, or would be. He allowed Alaric to grip him around the waist, in turn putting his own arm around his shoulder and stumbling forward as his friend started to move.

"Mutter to yourself, act like you've had a proper skinful or twelve," Alaric commanded.

As ordered, Osmund started to do precisely that, giggling idiotically and commencing a rambling monologue on "friends that stick around" and how "women don't get it". Alaric waved for the men behind them to stand down, mouthing something in their direction to make sure they understood. He'd call on them when needed.

They continued on like this for a few dozen paces before they were spotted by the two Danes on watch. Alaric kept up the charade, shuffling towards them with a burbling Osmund in his grip. Both sentries tensed visibly when they clapped eyes on them, only to then relax somewhat as they took in what at least looked like two of their own returning to camp, albeit worse for wear.

Alaric felt he'd been wise to have taken precautions with his appearance. If he'd left his helmet on, the silver-worked masterpiece would have advertised his status as an Englishman of some repute. Instead, they looked like two regular drunkards who were certainly not the advance guard of a force come to kill a certain foreign warlord. This ruse might actually work.

He chuckled to himself whilst Osmund droned on, his sober recitation of the kind of nonsense he talked when drunk proving too near the mark. One of the Danes started to laugh with him as they drew closer, finding Osmund's predicament fairly amusing. The second guard, being possibly more intelligent or perhaps just sober, remained silent, his hands resting on the grip of a particularly unpleasant-looking axe leaning back against his thigh. Alaric would have to kill him first.

They were now just a few feet from the Danes. The cheerful one grinned towards Osmund and nodded, mumbling something likely humorous. His more circumspect companion did what Alaric had half-expected him to, pointing to the bulge created by his attempt to hide his helmet under his cloak and barking what could only be a demand for an explanation. He'd also lifted his axe up, gripped in both hands with arms tensed like he intended to use it. Alaric wasn't going to wait around for that.

He released Osmund, who suddenly recovered from his drunken state and lunged at the still jovial Dane in front of him. He clamped a paw-like hand over his mouth, silencing him lest he try and cry out, and smashed a fist into his jugular. The Dane's knees buckled and gave way almost immediately, and he fell face-first like a toppled statue, his hands reaching up protectively towards his throat. Osmund resolved matters with a quick stamp of his right foot, leaving the unfortunate fellow twisted in the dirt, his neck snapped and bent at an unnatural angle.

His associate was not exactly thrilled with this turn of events, taking his eyes off Alaric and stepping forward to swing for Osmund. If he'd assumed it was preferable to kill the larger intruder first, he was mistaken, as he'd left his guard open in the face of an arguably more skilled opponent. Alaric drew his sword and swung left across his enemy's neck, opening his throat with it. He collapsed to the ground, spasming and choking in his own blood. Alaric impaled him through the chest, putting him out of his misery.

The victorious pair stood silently for a moment, listening out for any indication they'd been heard. The wind in the trees. The heaving of their own breath. A faint sound of harsh, mocking laughter and boisterous conversation from somewhere up ahead. Little else. They had not been detected. They could still do this.

Alaric crept forward, clearing the remaining few feet between himself and the palisade. He pressed himself up against the wooden edifice and peered around and to his left, looking through the entrance and into the camp proper. Nothing unusual. About ten feet of clear ground between himself and a mess of tents, worse than Hringmere, with several cookfires surrounded by clutches of drunken warriors.

They seemed to be enjoying their carousing and nonsensical conversations well enough, the racket they were making thankfully masking the sound of the recent scuffle. Alaric guessed that from the tents in view plus the number of men already visible, there were about a hundred fighters to deal with, although admittedly he could only see so far. Outnumbered two to one, at least, and that was just from what he could see here. Alaric wasn't worried. They had surprise with them. And scores to settle.

He and Osmund both retrieved their helms from the ground, having dropped them in the tussle. They then unfastened their shields from the harnesses on their backs, Alaric feeling reassured by the familiar weight in his hand.

He turned to where he knew his men were still watching from the trees. He sheathed his sword and reached down, picking up the still-burning torch of his fallen foe and holding it aloft. They understood the gesture. A dozen, two dozen, then all of his men came into view, their mail-clad forms of glinting helmets and menacing spear points emerging out of the darkness with a grim eagerness. Alaric smiled and let the torch drop. He then unsheathed his sword and slipped through the gap in the palisade, moving at a crouch. Osmund followed, likewise staying low, the larger man doing his best to imitate Alaric's attempt at stealth.

They'd made it about fifteen yards inside when more blood was drawn. A rather stout-looking Dane had emerged from his tent immediately in front of Alaric, yet he was so slowed by sleep he'd barely raised his weapon before he was cut down. Another, this one fully equipped, tried to tackle Osmund from the side, but the ginger giant threw him off with a twist of his shoulder and then reduced his head to a splintered ruin with one swing of his axe.

Too noisy. They'd been heard. And seen. Somebody cried out, a mix of anger and alarm, followed by another voice, similarly angry, and then more after that. That was it then. Alaric bellowed for his men, and the entire English force came screaming through the camp entrance, their furious battle cries reaching up into the heavens. They spread out, hacking and stabbing at the Norsemen just beginning to wake and stumble from their tents, showing no restraint whatsoever in the shedding of heathen blood.

The warriors Alaric had previously spied drinking and gibbering at their campfires had now spotted them, but a few were so drunk they were having trouble standing up. Those who were more alert looked confused and apprehensive, clearly wondering where their new visitors might have come from. It mattered little what they thought. They were dead men.

The English rushed forward, Alaric pounding the pommel of his sword off his shield, the warriors behind him screaming obscenities and challenges as they followed. About a score of them crashed headlong into the first group of drunken Norsemen surrounding a roaring log fire, overrunning their position in a frenzy of pent-up rage and brutality.

Alaric used the momentum of his charge to smash his first opponent to the ground with his shield. He brought his sword up overhead to hack downwards in a wide arc, the blade's edge splitting the Dane's skull as he struggled to sit up. Another warrior leapt in his direction, thrusting a jagged spear towards his undefended right shoulder. He shouldn't have bothered. Rather than impaling Alaric, he himself was pierced through the flank, the Saxon responsible continuing to run forward with such force that the Dane was carried on the end of his spear and deposited into his own campfire.

The man roared as the flames scorched his skin, the stench of burning flesh and singed hair mingling with the smell of wood smoke, sweat, and freshly shed blood. At some point, he managed to roll free of the fire and lie still, his left side a charred, raw ruin and his right drenched with blood. He would not last long.

Alaric lost sight of him when another Dane made an attempt on his life, this one leaping from the other side of the fire and through the flames in a bid to tackle him to the ground. Osmund caught him in mid-leap with a swing of his axe, the edge burying itself in his stomach with a sickening thud. The wounded warrior turned his head to scream something at Osmund, the sound harsh and high-pitched as he came to terms with the fact death was likely seconds away. He would be right. Osmund's second blow felled him like a tree, his now lifeless form toppling backwards into the fire.

A real brute then came bellowing out of the darkness to Alaric's left, fully armed and armoured in a crude mail coat, well-worn helm, and hefty war axe. He threw himself forward with a beast-like wildness, his base malevolence outshining any sense of self-preservation. He swung for Alaric, his axe heavy with purpose, but his aim was well off, his frenzied state ensuring his first blow fell short by several inches.

The second swing was no improvement, and Alaric only had to step back to avoid it, his sword unraised in a bid to provoke his opponent into overconfidence. The beast tried a third time, but again his efforts were predictable, and Alaric simply deflected the blow away with a well-practised twist of his shield. This wasn't an equal contest. This man may actually be a skilled warrior, but whatever force, supernatural or mundane, that had him addled this night wasn't doing him any favours, at least against a practised fighter of

Alaric's calibre. No amount of screaming and gibbering would change that.

Such pride was immediately punished when his assailant did the unexpected. Dissatisfied with his inability to lodge his axe in Alaric's skull, the Dane decided to simply throw his body weight forward, shoulder-first, crashing into Alaric's shield arm with a force that almost knocked him from his feet.

It wasn't all bad. Alaric's defensive instincts had kicked in from the sudden physical shock of having two hundred pounds of lunatic barrelling into him, a point well demonstrated by the fact the man was now slumped on his knees and clutching desperately at his throat. Alaric's right arm had automatically swung his sword upwards in a defensive arc as soon as he'd been hit, the tip of his blade carving a bloody line up and through the soft vulnerability of his opponent's jugular. The Dane's hands, chest, and stomach were now red with blood, his instinctual efforts to stem the flow doing little more than give the erroneous impression he was attempting to throttle himself.

Alaric would waste no more time. He took a step to the man's left and then forward so he came up alongside him. He then slammed his sword down, point first, inside and past the contours of his collarbone, sheathing the blade deep in his chest cavity. He gurgled and thrashed, but soon slid onto his side, still and silent. A cleaner death than the Dane would have given him, Alaric had no doubt.

He soon discovered why Osmund had not assisted him. Several yards away, a broken Dane lay sprawled at his friend's feet, the dead man's visage a grim, red ruin following a blow from Osmund's axe. Osmund himself had not been able to savour victory, however, and he was now struggling with two other Danes, one of which had made a grab for his right hand in an attempt to disarm him whilst the other hammered at his increasingly splintered shield.

Alaric stepped in and cut the first man down from behind, his sword parting flesh and leaving a deep, diagonal gash down his back. A now freed Osmund made a swing for the cur hacking his shield apart, causing him to stagger backwards and onto the spear thrust of an onrushing Saxon. He fell to the earth without comment, his ribcage splintered open by several feet of iron-tipped ash. Osmund grunted his approval.

They turned to evaluate the situation. The English force had managed to clear the entrance and carve a bloody salient straight into the enemy camp. Corpses and collapsed tents littered the ground, and by the looks of it, many a foe had been slain within seconds of being awoken by the ear-splitting roar from a half-hundred warriors eager for vengeance. The enemy should have really put more thought into their defence. Instead, they'd been caught out, either asleep or in their cups.

And they were still paying dearly for such laxity. Everywhere Alaric looked they were being cut down, his men a picture of grim determination whilst they went about their furious business. He saw a near-naked Dane being dragged from his tent not ten yards away, his cries pitiful as he was hauled through the mud by his remarkably long hair. If he placed value on his appearance he need no longer worry, for his head was soon parted from his shoulders, his Saxon assailant slamming him face-first into the dirt before decapitating him with one swing of his axe.

Another had decided to face his attackers, making a cacophonous show of roars and curses as he squared off against two Saxons. One of them feinted to the left, distracting the Dane and causing him to swing wildly at his shield. That was the only opening his compatriot needed. A second later and the Dane was on his knees, a torrent of blood pouring from a jagged wound across the side of his neck. He slumped forward and was still, his previous defiance unremarked, his lifeblood soaking the soil of the land he'd sought to harm.

From appearances, the English had the beginnings of a total victory. But Alaric had miscalculated. When he'd first surveyed the enemy position he knew his field of view was limited, as the camp was clearly of considerable dimensions if one considered the length of the palisade they'd scouted not twenty minutes ago. This was more evident now they were inside, for they could see the mass of tents here extending for some distance eastward, precisely where Æthelstan was supposed to be commencing his attack.

But there was no sign of him yet, and there was no way he could not know what was going on, given the sheer amount of noise they were making. Perhaps he'd encountered heavy resistance of his own. Whatever the case, it looked like Alaric would have to face considerably more than the initial one hundred or so opponents he'd previously estimated. That was not good.

As if to confirm his suspicions, about two dozen enemy warriors came howling out of the night. They were advancing at a rapid, enthusiastic speed towards Alaric's easily visible position near the fire, making a horrific, shrieking racket as they went.

Why these men had not been manning the entrance was a mystery to Alaric, as their presence in and around the palisade would have made it largely impossible for the English to have wrought the level of surprise devastation they'd just inflicted. Perhaps there was another entrance somewhere around here they had been watching, or some other location of importance that had not yet been revealed.

Whatever the reason, the English could not allow the enemy to seize the initiative. Alaric rushed forward to meet their charge, bellowing at the top of his lungs for his men to join him. They did so, a collective enthusiasm sweeping over them as they broke into another headlong rush, their cacophony of war cries echoing out into the night.

They'd covered a short distance before Alaric received a new opponent, this time a fully armoured warrior with the confidence to rush ahead of his brethren to intercept his advance. The Dane loped forward with a speed that said he was well-practised in moving and fighting, a skill he demonstrated beyond doubt when he used his momentum to leap slightly into the air and launch a downward swing of his axe toward Alaric's head.

Whilst gutsy, the attack was also predictable, his movements so deliberate Alaric knew as soon as his legs tensed to leave the ground that a strike towards his face was coming. Alaric continued his charge without slowing, raising his shield up and forward to allow it to take the full force of the incoming axe. The weapon's head buried itself in the shield, the strength of the blow enhanced by the momentum of Alaric's charge moving up to meet it.

He crashed into the Dane at speed, staggering him backwards under the weight of the contest. At some point, the Dane dropped his own shield to better grip his axe with both hands in a bid to pull it free. Ill-advised. Alaric thrust his sword towards his now exposed stomach, the blade's sharpened tip easily piercing the wrought iron scales and hardened leather of his armour.

Muscle and organs gave way to an onslaught of tempered metal, a torrent of blood soaking Alaric's lower half as the Dane was impaled. Alaric pushed with his shield arm as his legs continued to propel him forward, the now-expiring Dane giving up his desperate hold on the embedded axe and falling to his knees.

Alaric stormed past him, his eyes again fixed on the onrushing mob of heathens just a half dozen paces ahead. The now mortally wounded warrior used the few moments of life he had left to clutch at his stomach, his fingers tentatively probing the contours of his catastrophic gut wound. Whatever final thoughts he was having were cut short by the onrushing wall of Saxon shields, his kneeling form crumpling and disappearing under the weight of charging bodies.

The two forces finally met. The clash of shields was immense, the sound of dozens of men colliding at speed in a welter of hate and fury making Alaric's head ring. He was pushed forward by the man behind him, the two of them making the Dane immediately to their front stagger backwards. Whilst this was positive, it also meant Alaric's sword arm had been pushed forward against his own shield, making him unable to strike his foe, at least for as long as he was being carried along through sheer momentum.

His opponent didn't seem to have any such restrictions. His axe impacted off the edge of Alaric's shield twice, a third swing nicking the side of his helmet with a dull clang. If he'd not been wearing it, he'd by all chances have lost his left ear and a good portion of his face into the bargain. Alaric growled with effort and made another bid to free his arm, managing this time to pull it backwards as the man behind him shifted his weight. He found out why a moment later when the Dane in front of him suddenly toppled over, his face rent open by a spear thrusting over Alaric's shoulder.

He pushed forward into the breach, knowing well enough that the Danes' ad hoc shield wall would likely collapse if they got in behind them. The wounded man at his feet had other ideas, grabbing at Alaric's legs and tripping him up. They struggled in the dirt, Alaric losing his grip on both his sword and shield. Despite his injury, the warrior had some life left in him, and he snarled like an enraged wolf, his scuffed, bloodied fists raining down on Alaric's thankfully well-protected head.

There was only so much of that nonsense Alaric was willing to put up with. He knocked his hands aside and grabbed him around the throat, butting him in the forehead with the front of his helmet a second later. He then rolled the Dane over, using the reversal of positions to rain down punches of his own into his enemy's already bloodied face. He broke his nose with a wet crunch, knocking several rotten teeth free with a subsequent blow, the Dane's efforts to defend himself proving inadequate in his weakened state.

Large hands suddenly grabbed Alaric by the front of his shoulders and hauled him to his feet. His initial hunch that Osmund had appeared to assist him turned out to be ill-founded, as the man that now faced him was a mess of scar tissue and sharpened teeth, his breath also smelling like something had died in his mouth.

He didn't waste time introducing himself either, instead smashing the front of his helm into Alaric's with an ear-splitting clang. He then punched him in the solar plexus, the blow heavy and purposeful, and Alaric felt the breath leave his lungs with the doing of it. His knees threatened to give way, yet he somehow remained on his feet, bringing his guard up and deflecting several more punches in the process.

Alaric's helmet had been partially knocked out of position, revealing part of the right side of his face. The Dane noted this well and grabbed him with both hands around the throat, endeavouring to squeeze the life from him whilst sinking his teeth into his now exposed cheek. He bit deep, snarling as he did so, tearing through flesh with his bizarrely sharp canines.

This was intolerable. It was one thing to fight a man, but to behave as a total savage was another thing altogether. Unhappy with the prospect of losing his face, Alaric grabbed at the Dane's eye socket with his left hand, forcing his thumb down at a point onto the eyeball and pushing deeper. His opponent ignored him at first, but he soon realised the danger, releasing Alaric from his clenching jaws and grabbing at his wrist.

That was the opening Alaric needed. He swung his fist in a right hook to catch the fiend on the side of the head, knocking him off balance. Not enough. He stepped in with a classic uppercut, hammering the Dane on his chin with a dull thud and staggering him backwards. Better. Alaric used the moment to retrieve his sword from the ground, swinging it with both hands up and then down in a hammering arc connecting with the centre of the Dane's head. It didn't matter that he was wearing a helmet. Iron and then bone parted in a welter of blood. He dropped like a stone.

He wasn't the only one. The enemy shield wall had by now broken apart, and the better-equipped and well-motivated Saxons had pushed on through, stabbing and hacking at their now desperate and defeated enemy. More Danes fell, and the English rushed forward, stampeding over tents and corpses and putting down any stragglers brave enough to still face them. A few survivors could be seen fleeing into the night, likely heading to Thorkell himself to warn him of what was taking place. Let them do just that. Let Thorkell come charging out to face them, only to be attacked in the rear by Æthelstan. Alaric would then take his head.

But Æthelstan still wasn't here. The camp stretched out before them to the east, foreboding in the darkness and most certainly empty of any glorious charge from their Norþanhymbrian allies. Alaric retrieved his shield, taking the opportunity to also catch his breath and assess. They'd lost people in the last brawl. Alaric crossed himself when he saw them, broken and bloodied upon the ground, and offered up a quick prayer for their souls. They would mourn properly later.

"We're taking too long here," Osmund hissed, keeping his voice low to avoid spreading needless worry. He hesitated upon seeing the state of Alaric's face, the weeping, torn mess that had been his right cheek drawing the eye. He chose not to comment.

"This was supposed to be a quick raid; get in, kill Thorkell and leave," Osmund continued. "We're basically fighting everyone here. Don't get me wrong, I've been waiting for this, but the numbers are not on our side. We can't keep this up. As soon as the enemy wake up properly and realise…"

His voice trailed off. He was right. Time was of the essence. They had to push on, now, and finish what they'd started. There was also the chance that Æthelstan might need help. Time to move. And quickly.

"We can't turn back now, Osmund," Alaric said hoarsely, hoping his friend didn't think he was implying he was afraid. In all honesty, he was finding it a little hard to talk. The injury to his cheek was worse than he'd initially feared, and his mouth kept filling with blood. He spat some out before trying again, the crimson splatter going unnoticed on the otherwise gore-strewn battleground.

"What I mean is…we can still finish what we came to do," he said, struggling still to form words. "Æthelstan could also need our help. Something has gone wrong somewhere, and we can't just leave without him."

Osmund nodded a few times, accepting what he'd said without argument. The men again fell into some kind of order, and their now somewhat depleted number set off at a jog, Alaric and Osmund in the lead.

As they progressed, it became clearer still that Eadric had completely misled them on the size of this camp. It was large enough to shelter a small army, and it was more than suspicious that, so far, they'd encountered relatively few enemies. Where were the rest of them?

A minute passed before they found themselves approaching a large wood and canvas shelter, somewhat similar to the type they'd constructed a couple of days ago at Hringmere. A sizeable log fire was smouldering away in a shallow pit dug just off to the left, their path having taken them slightly uphill to the point, had it been daytime, they'd have been able to see over the palisade about fifty yards to their right.

The structure looked important and was decorated with a foreboding ram's skull placed directly over its single entrance. Alaric didn't know what that signified and he didn't care either, as he had no interest whatsoever in the dark and callous beliefs of foreigners. Judging from the murmuring behind him, some of the men were unsettled by the sight of it. He didn't blame them. He didn't like the look of it either, especially the way it seemed to glare over them in the shifting firelight.

Just as he was considering doing something about it, the skull suddenly split in half, a moment later falling to the ground and shattering into so many jagged fragments. One of his men had thrown a spear at it, destroying the cursed thing with remarkably precise aim. The spear itself had continued on its trajectory, tearing through the outer canvas of the structure and vanishing into the interior beyond. Somebody would have to retrieve it.

Alaric crept forward and up to the entrance, peering inside. There was nothing to fear. The place was deserted, yet curiously it looked to have been used as some kind of war room. Several long tables were arranged along the interior walls, displaying a plethora of crudely drawn maps detailing various regions of both England and what looked like Scotland. Alaric wrinkled his nose. He didn't think of the enemy as strategists, but from the evidence here they at least gave some attention to such matters. There must be a method in their madness he'd not seen before.

The centre of the chamber was dominated by a large wooden dais, its rough, slipshod construction indicating it had been built in a hurry from whatever timber was available. Alaric couldn't guess its purpose. Perhaps Thorkell was actually ridiculously short and needed an extra boost to give speeches to his men, the sobriquet "the Tall" serving as a means to mock him. That was a pleasing thought. Either way, the thrown spear was lodged in the dais. Alaric moved to retrieve it. He tore it free with one try, splinters scattering at his feet. Then the shouting started.

Several of his men hurried in, Osmund at the head of them. "A lot of blond bastards heading this way, it looks like they followed us from somewhere," he said breathlessly, alarm lighting up his normally placid eyes. Alaric hurried outside to get a look for himself. Osmund wasn't exaggerating. About two hundred yards back down the path they'd just traversed were several hundred Danes advancing towards them, their armour and weapons glittering in the light cast from their own torches.

They were approaching slowly, casually even, apparently confident of their numbers and unmoved by the fact the English had snuck into their camp and butchered scores of their brethren. That in itself was suspicious. None of this made sense. The lack of patrols around the camp. The presence of just two guards at the entrance. The disorganised resistance…and now the sudden appearance of serious reinforcements, albeit from the way they'd just come. Something was wrong, and Alaric's instincts told him it might yet get them all killed.

"Get inside, all of you!" Alaric commanded. His men didn't need to be told again, every one of them hurrying into the structure and out of sight, although Alaric made a point of returning the spear to the man it belonged to as he passed by. Once he was sure there were no stragglers, he slipped back inside, the Danes beyond continuing their advance with no real hurry.

Now what? There was only one entrance, and they'd just passed through it. For a moment, he considered making some kind of stand here, as the enemy would have to come through a relatively narrow space in order to get at them. He dismissed the idea, realising their foes could also just set the place on fire from the outside to roast all of them within. He didn't want to die like that.

A solution suddenly burst into his mind with crystal clarity. He rushed to the eastern end of the room, his sword at the ready. "We'll give them the slip and push on!" he shouted, making his first brutal incision in the canvas. Within mere seconds he'd slashed themselves a suitable exit, and Alaric went through first, feeling he should be the one to lead his men into parts unknown. Outside he could see something in the gloom up ahead, the faint hiss of wind in leaves greeting him on the night breeze. Trees. There were trees maybe just a few hundred paces away. This must be the eastern edge of the camp. They could escape.

The others exited the structure rapidly, one by one, and began moving swiftly to get some distance between themselves and those following them. They'd failed in what they'd originally set out to do, they all knew that now, but there was no sense in dying a pointless death. They were fortunate to have gotten as far as they had. The Northmen would not be forgetting this night in a hurry, that was certain. They'd received a bloody nose and no mistake.

They covered a good distance in record time, the men naturally motivated by the prospect of escaping into the forest. They soon reached what seemed like the edge of the camp, the long palisade to their right suddenly turning and giving way to a large, open maw of a gate before resuming its winding course to the north. And then they saw it. The ambush.

Æthelstan's men had made a good show of it, at least. They'd admittedly not made it far, looking like they'd only cleared the camp entrance before being attacked on both sides, if the pattern of bodies was anything to go by. There were roughly forty dead Norþanhymbrians, the entirety of his force, lying chaotically amidst the tangled forms of a comparable number of Danes. That was a good effort, considering the situation. The Norþanhymbrians were obviously not a people to take lightly.

They found Æthelstan himself curled up off to the side of the pathway, his eyes still open and beginning to dry out in the crisp night air. Somebody had hacked off one of his arms at the elbow. His banded mail coat was also split across his stomach, probably from taking something large and weighty, likely an axe, to his guts. His sword hung limply in his remaining hand. A dead Dane lay close by, part of his head looking like it had been bashed in by something sharp and heavy.

Alaric knelt down, removing what was likely a wedding ring from Æthelstan's hand.

He had a feeling somebody would want this returned. He then reached out and closed his eyes with his fingertips, making the sign of the cross a moment later. "Lord have mercy," Alaric muttered, hearing his words echoed back at him by Osmund and those within earshot. A brief moment of piety and calm. Alaric savoured it. It didn't last.

One of his men suddenly cried out in alarm. Alaric looked up, everyone now staring in the direction of the gate. A large force of Danes was emerging from the woods beyond and moving into position to bar their escape. What they'd been doing out there, he had no idea. What he was certain of was that the man leading them seemed unusual. Tall. Too tall.

He looked like a giant out of some kind of pagan myth. Heavily armoured in a coat of masterfully worked metal scales that reached his knees, he sported a long, rugged cloak of animal hide that billowed out behind his wide shoulders. Much of his face was obscured by a weighty, dark iron helmet, although there was no hiding the huge metallic grey beard that cascaded down from his anvil of a chin. He carried a large war axe, clasped in two gnarled, oversized hands, its edge encrusted with a dull, deep red crust. He stood for a moment, staring at the English force like he knew each of them. Like he'd been waiting.

It had to be him. Thorkell the Tall. He lived up to his name, after all. And he was to die, now, even though they were outnumbered. Even though the enemy had reinforcements in pursuit. Alaric was killing Thorkell tonight. He would then face his Maker, he knew, but not before he removed the head of the serpent that was this foreign army. Not before he killed Thorkell.

That might not be so easy. There was another warrior approaching who caught Alaric's eye, a brute of a man attired in furs and heavy, flint-coloured mail. He also sported a most striking helmet. It covered his entire face, like Thorkell's, and was similarly sturdy, but half of it had been painted red, although to signify what Alaric had no notion. He seemed loath to leave Thorkell's side, as if he were some kind of protector, and he was similarly equipped with a sizeable war axe alongside what looked like a brutally fashioned spear slung across his back. It mattered not. Thorkell would fall tonight. There was nothing this fool could do about that, red helmet or no.

"We know what we have to do," Alaric bellowed, standing up and away from Æthelstan's corpse to address his warriors. He intentionally deepened his voice so it carried further, again putting additional effort into his pronunciation to compensate for his face wound. The last thing he wanted to do here was slur his words.

"We came here tonight to make these bastards pay," he intoned, pointing his sword in the direction of the advancing enemy. "We can still do that. If we don't break them here, we die. I don't fancy dying, not whilst there's an England still out there to protect. Not whilst there's still a life to be had. Not whilst our noble brother, Æthelstan, lies here, unavenged and unburied."

A ripple of agreement spread through the men, and they hurriedly assembled into a line facing the enemy, shields and spears at the ready. Alaric wasn't a skilled orator, and he didn't have time to waffle on about "destiny" or "fate" or other such apparently inspiring things to get his lads fired up. They could see the situation for what it was. They were outnumbered at least three to one, probably more, and they knew there was another enemy force closing behind them. If they didn't prevail here, all was lost.

Others may have given into despair, resigning themselves to their fate and giving in, awaiting death and hoping it would be quick. These were no such men. Roaring in unison, the forty-five or so Englishmen left alive charged as one to crash into the enemy, their hearts overflowing with hate and defiance both. Then the bloodletting began again, shield clashing on shield, spears stabbing and axes hacking wildly. There was to be no holding back. Either they broke through, or they all died.

The melee was confusing, chaotic, and frenzied. The man next to Alaric dropped suddenly, a slashing blade from a particularly cruel-looking Dane tearing through his throat with ease. The brute responsible was no doubt skilled, but he'd left his arm extended and unguarded after delivering his strike. Alaric lashed out with a shout, slicing the Dane's hand off at the wrist. He collapsed to his knees, howling desperately with pain. Alaric heard him burble something in his lilting language, too quiet to be heard over the carnage, although from the streaks of fresh tears marring his face it was likely an appeal for mercy. Alaric kicked him in the jaw, the blow knocking him onto his back, apparently senseless.

A body smashed into him from his left. Alaric turned and saw it was the enemy, but this one was not long for this world, as he'd been impaled through the stomach. The Saxon responsible let go of his spear, thinking it irretrievably stuck in the Dane's gut, and drew his axe instead. He took a blow from somewhere on his shield, the impact making an audible crack and fraying part of the wooden surface. He lashed out with his weapon at whoever had struck him, being answered by a scream of pain from amidst the mass of brawling bodies.

Remarkably, the Dane with the spear in his stomach was still on his feet and staring like he didn't quite understand the severity of his injury. Alaric soon lost sight of him in the chaos, although the Saxon who'd wounded him reappeared a moment later and began staggering towards him, a thrown axe embedded in the side of his neck. He reached out for Alaric, his hands gentle and sincere, almost as if in his death throes he'd gotten the notion his commander could help him.

For a split second, there was nothing Alaric would have liked more than to know his name, to talk and pray with him, perhaps in a better time to have broken bread together and been as brothers. Each and every one of his men were fighting for their family as well as the kingdom. They'd trusted Alaric to lead them, and he'd led them to their deaths. The only way any of this would make sense would be if, by a miracle, they achieved what they'd set out to do.

The wounded man stumbled another step towards him, hands still outstretched. He then went down suddenly, struck from behind by the one who had presumably thrown the axe. Alaric charged forward, leaping over the man's body and barreling into his assailant. The fiend staggered backwards under the impact, losing the grip on his shield and struggling to maintain his footing. He was a wiry, weasel-like man, all flowing ring mail and blond hair, the cruel sneer on his face suggesting he found the situation vaguely amusing. He'd also pulled another one of those throwing axes from somewhere, this likely being some kind of speciality of his.

Perhaps he was special. Perhaps he was known in his home town for his skill with thrown weapons, and his friends liked to place bets on his accuracy. It didn't matter now. Alaric leapt at him, slamming the point of his sword into the bastard's midriff, sheathing fully half of the blade into his body cavity. The weasel cried out, or at least tried to, his sneer now an agonised grimace as his insides were reduced to a weeping, bloody ruin. Alaric kicked him in the stomach and off his sword, hacking at him again as he fell. He strode past the corpse, catching another Dane in the middle of some kind of war cry and cutting out his throat with a wild swing, silencing him permanently.

The enemy force was starting to crack under the fury of the English assault. Alaric couldn't tell how that was even possible, but he didn't dare stop to evaluate, nor would he question the desperate heroism of his men. They didn't have much time. There was still an enemy force pursuing from behind, and unless they'd all suddenly become deaf, they were likely aware of the situation and hurrying to close the trap.

Another Saxon warrior fell close by, his mail split open at the chest and his helm broken and crumpled inward. Osmund was roaring off to the right, seemingly in a frenzy, having picked up a second axe from somewhere and was using it to good effect. At least three Danes lay dead at his feet, and a wedge of several other Saxons had begun to form around him to press the advantage of having a huge, red-bearded lunatic with two axes on their side.

Osmund was in his element, fighting bravely as he always did, a true hero of the old Kingdom of Westseaxe. A man among men. Then he was dying, a thrown spear protruding from his chest, the point shattering the iron links of his armour and burying itself in his great heart. For a fraction of a second, his shining blue eyes fell upon Alaric, his mouth agape as if he wished to say something to his friend for one last time. Then his knees gave out. He fell backwards, coming to rest on the grass, his dead eyes fixed blankly on the stars above, the stampede of men and death continuing to whirl around him.

Alaric didn't have time to be shocked. Overwhelmed with hatred, he existed now to bring furious judgement down upon the foe, these accursed, miserable pagans, these harbingers of misery and desolation. The figure with the half-red helm had thrown that spear. He stood some distance away, just outside of the melee beyond the gate itself, guarding Thorkell whilst he watched the battle. Whether this was cowardice or prudence, Alaric knew not, but the events of this night all seemed to indicate Thorkell had been aware he was a target for assassination.

In any case, he was apparently content to just stand back from the fight and observe now that his man had dealt with the furious Osmund. Alaric saw his chance. He'd hack his way through this mob and finish this tonight, killing as many men as needed. He started with the Dane immediately in front of him, opening up his stomach with a savage side slash and head-butting him to the ground. He then spun to meet a threat to his left, bashing his shield into the face of another foe who was busy grappling with one of his men. The previously beleaguered Saxon regained his composure, taking advantage of his now dazed opponent to bring his axe down upon his head, cracking helm and skull alike. Alaric staggered onward over the corpse, pushing forward in his assault.

Somebody made a frenzied swing for his head, screaming furiously as they did so. Alaric swept his own blade out in an upwards arc, intercepting the Dane's blow in mid-air and severing much of his forearm. The fool's sword flew off into the grass about a meter from Thorkell's feet. Alaric ignored the Dane he'd just wounded, leaving him to crumple over onto his side and get busy with bleeding to death.

Alaric strode on, hacking and killing, his great fury ensuring he'd almost fought his way clear of the battle. Thorkell was just ahead, about a dozen paces away, and the beast looked to be alone, his guard elsewhere. Their eyes met amidst the clamour, the Northman calm and without emotion, the Englishman drenched in blood and sweat, overcome with grief and rage in equal measure. Alaric pointed his sword directly at him and screamed a wordless challenge. Thorkell just looked at him, content to stand there, his hands placed on the haft of his axe, the head of the weapon resting in the grass. He knew he had the advantage. He thought Alaric couldn't reach him.

As if in confirmation, a cascade of blood-curdling roars suddenly shook the night, the sound of yet more stampeding feet following a second later. Alaric turned and saw the force that had been pursuing them was joining the battle. It was over. They were all dead. They'd put up a heroic struggle, but this was the end.

The enemy reinforcements crashed into what was left of the Saxon force from the rear, cutting them down as they went. Astonishingly his men continued fighting, but they were seconds from death. Their fate was sealed. Alaric turned again to face Thorkell, tears of rage cascading down his cheeks, his teeth grinding with hatred. He took a deep breath and charged.

He made it at least three paces before the blow landed. He should have known, some might say, that the leaders of armies generally do not meet in battle, despite the stories claiming otherwise. The great King Alfred of Westseaxe never directly fought Guthrum at Ethandun, just as his grandson, the renowned King Æthelstan, never physically locked swords with the fiendish Olaf Guthfrithson at Brunanburh.

Alaric's last bid to complete his task and kill Thorkell was thus perhaps foolhardy to any casual observer, but the more charitable among them would understand it for the act of desperation it truly was. Alaric knew he was dead either way, so he'd concluded he'd do some good with the scant moments he had left rather than simply stand there and wait to die.

Regardless, the red-helmeted Dane charging in from his left was not about to let him succeed. Alaric hadn't seen where he'd gone or where he'd reappeared from, but he was on him now, striking suddenly and swiftly in defence of his lord. Alaric's prized helmet buckled inwards from the sheer force of the blow, the head of the two-handed axe biting deep into the silver and iron workmanship and ruining what had been a labour of love for the smith who'd made it.

Alaric couldn't remember who that was. In fact, he couldn't remember much of anything as he tumbled away under the impact, losing his footing and plunging headlong into what felt like a prolonged, uncontrolled descent. His vision whirled and whirled, his view alternating repetitiously between the wet, cool grass and the glorious star-filled sky above.

Some part of his mind told him he couldn't see out of one eye. The other part was just grateful when he came to a halt, although he had no idea where since all seemed like darkness. An ear-splitting cry of triumphant, unrestrained savagery then reverberated through the night, a hundred plus a hundred throats roaring in jubilation at the completion of some grim deed.

Alaric didn't know what that was about, but something told him it was the worst thing in the world. His head hurt and his hair was wet with something. He felt frightened that whoever was making that noise still seemed close. He just wanted it all to stop. He closed his one eye that could still be closed. And stopped.

IV

The calligraphy was beautiful, possessing a quality that made the letters appear as a natural, blossoming outgrowth of the paper itself. Æva had long been envious of the monastic life for several reasons, wondering just what exactly was involved when it came to transcribing with such elegance and devotion. An act of love, she thought, of both craft and God.

She ran her fingertips softly down the pages as she read aloud, feeling the need to have some kind of physical contact with the words themselves. She wanted to be connected to them, as closely as humanly and spiritually possible, seeing the text as a means to both knowledge and communion.

She was also doubly fortunate now, for she'd again been granted the opportunity to read to one who had long been denied such joys himself. There was real charity in the small things. Reading the Gospel alone, she was enlightening herself. Reading them to a man without sight was bringing them to life anew.

"Blessed are the poor in spirit, for theirs is the kingdom of heaven," she intoned, her voice light yet serious in recitation. "Blessed are the meek, for they shall possess the earth. Blessed are they that mourn, for they shall be comforted. Blessed are they that hunger and thirst after justice, for they shall have their fill."

The last verse always made a very special impression on her. She knew she was not alone in this since her husband was also fond of it, which was unsurprising considering his temperament. She looked over at Ælfgar, so different from his younger brother yet at times the same. They were both pious men, that she knew. That's what truly mattered.

Ælfgar was ensconced across from her in his favourite chair, ideally situated by the presently empty hearth, a long robe of simple grey wool his attire of choice on this otherwise unremarkable afternoon. He was in his middle years, five years older than her husband, his face having thinned out and his hair and beard again absent after his manservant had just that morning got to work with a razor.

Æva was quite the contrast to the ageing and almost sunken Ælfgar. She was in her mid-twenties, and very much in the prime of her life, so people said, although she didn't always feel it. She wore her red, straight hair long, tied and covered under a white linen veil, her blue eyes complementing a typically pale but otherwise healthy, fairly narrow face. She'd picked out a flowing, long-sleeved cyrtel of purple-dyed linen for the day, its high, gold embroidered neckline ensuring her modesty was maintained. It was here she also wore a silver crucifix on a metal chain; a perhaps extravagant display of piety that all the same was precious to her, second only to the gold-flecked wedding ring displayed prominently on her right hand.

They were once again seated in the library of Ælfgar's father, the Ealdorman Ælfric, itself sequestered away in the main tower of his seat of power at Porteceaster. It was a reasonably large room, well stocked with an assortment of texts in English, Irish,

Latin, and Greek, and contained several desks for transcription work that, to date, as far as she was aware, had rarely been used.

She would always sit in the same chair, on the north side of the chamber on the opposite side of the hearth from Ælfgar. It was not an opulent place, distinctly lacking in tapestries or rugs that may otherwise have added some vigour to the dour stone walls, but she favoured it, appreciating its modesty and veritable treasury of knowledge.

As always, the sea could be heard rumbling in the distance, the crashing of waves remaining within earshot regardless of where you went inside the stronghold. She continued to read, Ælfgar listening intently, taking the words to heart and attentive to every syllable. She'd at first found his expression hard to discern, his sightless eyes always obscured beneath a white or, at times, dark cloth bandaged around his head. Over time she'd learned to read his posture, becoming accustomed to the signs that he was either bored, indifferent, or indeed elated at her recitation. He was pleased, she could tell. She continued.

"Blessed are the merciful, for they shall obtain mercy. Blessed are the pure of heart, for they shall see God. Blessed are the peacemakers, for they shall be called the children of God."

"What do you think of that, Æva?" His voice was quiet and measured. He'd never asked her what she thought of her recitations before. She looked up at him from across the room, wondering how to respond.

"As it sounds," she said quietly, a shade of reticence in her voice. "That God lifts up those who seek peace, not men of war."

Ælfgar didn't respond immediately. He instead settled back into his chair, bringing his hand up to his eyes as if to scratch. He paused before lowering his arm, resuming his old posture and remaining motionless for a moment before he finally pitched her another question.

"And the pagans, then? How do you think God views our present difficulties with these…men of war…as you might say?"

"God has delivered England from such men before," she declared confidently, her self-assurance genuine, given what she knew of history. "He will do so again. Courage and faith, as Alaric says."

Ælfgar tapped his feet twice on the solid hardwood floor. He seemed a little displeased. Admittedly the room they were in was ever so slightly uncomfortable, the stones somehow retaining the chill from the winter that had thankfully now passed. Something told her, though, that wasn't what was bothering him.

"Do you always agree with whatever Alaric says?" Ælfgar asked coolly. Æva was starting to feel a little irked at his growing impertinence. She enjoyed reading to him, but she didn't like the implication she was somehow thoughtless or feeble-minded in believing her husband was generally right more often than he was wrong.

"My husband, your brother, is a very learned and capable man," she replied simply. "To go through life without courage or faith is to be blin…"

She hadn't intended to say that. She wondered how she could be so clumsy like this. It was a habit of hers, and Osmund had made a joke of it at times. That was truly something coming from him, given this was the man who'd once managed to demolish his own bed whilst attempting to find it whilst drunk in the dark. Either way, she had been insensitive. She owed an apology.

"I'm sorry, Ælfgar, I didn't mean to say that," she said, hoping he'd comprehend her sincerity. "My words were poorly chosen. I simply meant courage and faith were necessary."

He didn't seem too bothered about the accidental jibe. He stared ahead as he generally did, albeit now with a slight smirk on his face.

"No harm done, Æva. I've been without sight for a long time now. If I was disturbed every time somebody mentioned my condition exists or wasn't ideal, I'd be one very depressed man. Fortunately, that is not so."

She laughed, more out of relief than amusement. Ælfgar wasn't an intimidating man, physically speaking, but she wouldn't have his feelings hurt over a slip of the tongue. She knew in his heart of hearts that his blindness bothered him, and that he wasn't the only one. It was a difficult topic for his entire family and best left out of regular conversation.

Æva knew he hadn't been born this way, and she'd also gotten the distinct impression it wasn't from either accident or disease. She'd asked Alaric about this before, but he'd change the subject or fall silent. She'd given up inquiring, knowing better than to pry into things that might cause others pain.

She turned back to the Bible, grateful to be moving on. She went to begin the next verse when Ælfgar leaned forward in his seat, his hands on his knees and his brow furrowed with thought. When he finally spoke, he sounded indecisive, as if unsure how to pose a question he all the same felt he must.

"What…do you know of our king's predecessor, Edward?" He leaned back in his chair, his face at ease again. She wasn't sure how to immediately respond to this. She'd not even been alive when King Edward was martyred, although his death still weighed heavily upon the land. Kings ideally died of old age, their legacy secured and succession a matter of good judgement and character. For a monarch at such a young age to be murdered was a most horrific calamity, one England had not yet recovered from.

"I know only what is common knowledge," Æva said guardedly. "He was a boy king most cruelly snatched from us, God rest his soul."

Ælfgar exhaled awkwardly, his face now contorted into a half-smile, making her wonder if she'd said something stupid. She didn't like his attitude this afternoon. He was normally a picture of civility, wishing only to sit and listen to her recitations. Today something was off, and she couldn't shake the feeling it might be because Alaric was away in Eastengle.

"He was a reckless, arrogant child, just like our current king was in his day." Ælfgar now looked pleased with himself. He was trying to shock her. She wouldn't fall for it. Edward was young when he'd died, and arrogance coupled with intemperance were hardly uncommon accomplices to youth. The notion that King Æthelred was also capable of making poor decisions was hardly likely to raise any eyebrows. But he shouldn't talk so bluntly, least of all of the dead. It wasn't right.

"It's not for me to say," she replied neutrally, playing it safe and wishing she could either leave or get back to her Bible reading.

"It isn't, you are correct in that, my dear," Ælfgar replied, his reference to her as his "dear" something new and unwelcome. "What I'm interested in is how you might relate the murder of our poor King Edward to our current situation…is God punishing us for allowing such a supposedly good and holy young man to meet such a fate?"

"Why would God do that?" she said, still irritated at his over-familiarity. "Are you suggesting that God would unleash the Norsemen on all of England because somebody murdered a king?"

"Why not?" he said, his face irritatingly smug now. "Are there not precedents for this kind of thing? The Prophet Isaiah might say there were."

She understood his point. But it still wasn't the same. The idea that it was right and just to hold all of England to account for the sins of persons unknown was nonsensical. That wasn't the message of Isaiah, where an entire people had needed to be called back to faith and fidelity. The two situations were not comparable. She told him as such.

"I don't think Isaiah is of much help here, Ælfgar," she said evenly, hiding her continued annoyance well. "England still grieves for the loss of Edward, and the common man had nothing to do with his death. The Northmen have plagued our lands in the past also, long before King Edward's murder. I don't see how God is punishing us."

Ælfgar nodded several times in agreement, looking genuinely pleased with her reply. He seemed to be enjoying the conversation, yet Æva felt she'd do well to keep her guard up. She never felt truly safe when Alaric wasn't around, and Ælfgar had an odd temperament today.

"Right, good, yes," he said, a disconcerting grin breaking out across his face. "But you know of Archbishop Wulfstan? He is most certainly of the opinion that England's current troubles are punishment for our sins, particularly those committed against our martyred King Edward. You have heard him speak?"

Æva had indeed heard of the archbishop, and it was common knowledge that he believed the land's present woes were a direct result of the moral failings of its inhabitants. She'd also heard he was instrumental in influencing the king to issue an edict just last year commanding the populace to engage in a period of fasting, almsgiving, and repentance, even stipulating that his subjects should go barefoot on their way to church.

Both Æva and Alaric had committed themselves fully, delighted the king was taking spiritual matters so seriously. Yet as to Archbishop Wulfstan himself, she'd prefer not to gossip, and not only because it would be improper to do so. She had never even laid eyes on the man in person, so it wasn't wise to share an opinion. She also didn't want to give Ælfgar the satisfaction of using Wulfstan to prove whatever point he was trying to make.

"I'm afraid I do not know the archbishop personally," she admitted, shrugging her shoulders in resignation. "Yet I'm sure he's a very learned man and has his own reasons for saying whatever it is he says."

"Evasive," snapped Ælfgar. "But perhaps you are being truthful, since why would you know Wulfstan, being as you are?"

Another strange comment. This afternoon was really starting to prove wearisome. She couldn't just get up and leave either since Ælfgar was dependent on her to guide him. Her sudden absence might cause him to be trapped for hours in the library, banging his head off bookshelves and generally causing chaos in his search for the exit. Perhaps she should just get up and leave, then. She suppressed a chuckle at the thought.

Ælfgar was none the wiser as to her mirth, instead throwing another unwelcome question her way.

"...back to poor Edward...who indeed killed him? Some say our good King Æthelred had something to do with it. What would you say to that?"

That was vindictive hearsay, she thought. Æthelred was just a boy at the time. Siblings could fight, she knew that well enough, but for children to scheme, plot, and kill each other seemed a bit far-fetched. Ælfgar was also seriously pushing it in terms of what could or should be said about their current king.

"That sounds like a baseless rumour if ever I heard one," she replied. "Æthelred couldn't have done that. He was a child himself. Evil men killed Edward, that's all there is to it."

"Firstly, my dear, you don't know Æthelred, and I do," came Ælfgar's sudden rebuttal, his earlier affability leaving him in a hurry. "But you're correct in that he most likely did not kill Edward. An adult then, somebody in authority and able to command others, but also likely to benefit from Æthelred taking Edward's throne. How about...his mother? Queen Ælfthryth?"

The late queen of the lamentably late King Edgar was an interesting character, in part because of the role she'd played in both political and religious matters during her husband's most peaceable reign. This had not been without controversy, and Edgar's decision to have her consecrated alongside him at his coronation had provoked opposition within his own Witan. She had not been consecrated with powers equal to Edgar, far from it, but the king's decision was seen as unusual.

She'd also born Edgar two sons, first Edmund, who sadly passed away from illness before he made it to maturity, and Æthelred, their current king. Matters were made a little more complex by the fact Queen Ælfthryth was the third wife King Edgar had managed to obtain, his first, Æthelflæd, having passed away shortly after giving birth to Edward, the martyred king currently under discussion. Edgar had then married a woman named Wulfthryth, who had given Edgar a daughter named Eadgyth. Æva was unsure of what had happened following the birth, but she'd heard Wulfthryth had, for some reason, parted from Edgar, taking Eadgyth with her and somehow becoming an abbess at Wiltune Abbey.

There was a darker side to this story, however. Some said Edgar had actually abducted Wulfthryth, who at the time was already living a consecrated life which Edgar had interrupted by force. If that were true, then it was a disgraceful way for a king to behave and a black spot on the reputation of what Æva had understood to be an otherwise decent man. Whatever the facts of the matter, it seems Edgar had eventually seen sense and stopped his wild ways to marry Ælfthryth.

Had the boy, Edmund, lived, the succession would likely have been easy, given his status as eldest son to both the king and queen. Yet when Edgar died without having designated an heir, there were two claimants to the throne, the eldest being Edward, as son of Edgar and Æthelflæd, and the younger Æthelred, son of Edgar and Queen Ælfthryth. Æva thought it only natural that a mother would want her own son to win the throne for himself, but would Ælfthryth really have been so outraged when Edward became king?

In any case, Edward did indeed take to the throne in 975 at the tender age of fourteen. What kind of man he might have become no one could say, although Æva suspected Ælfgar no doubt considered himself an authority on this, given his earlier claim that the boy was "reckless" and "arrogant". How he would know, she had no idea. What she did know was that King Edward had died under the most suspicious of circumstances. Nobody knew with any real certainty who was responsible, but people talked, and some were of the opinion the young king had been killed by thegns loyal to his younger half-brother, Æthelred.

But who would give such an order? Not Æthelred himself. He wouldn't have even made twelve years of age at the time. That left Ælfthryth as a possible instigator. The fact that Edward had been pulled from his horse and killed by unknown assailants whilst attempting to visit Æthelred at Ælfthryth's estate at Corf strengthened that suspicion.

Æva had heard the story many times, and it never failed to make her melancholy. From what she'd been told, Edward had been busy with matters of state, long enough at least to have begun to miss his stepmother and brother quite keenly. At some point, he'd decided to travel to see them, possibly without the knowledge of his Witan or his court in general, deciding on a minimal escort to keep tongues from wagging as to his whereabouts.

He undoubtedly should have taken more warriors. According to the story, Edward was met outside of the queen's estate by a group of men, one of whom was alleged to be some kind of direct associate of the royal household. This man, whoever he was, had then taken Edward gently by the right arm as if to kiss his cheek, only for another to seize him by the left and stab him in the heart. The king was said to have uttered one single, solitary cry of grief before falling from his horse, his reign over before it had even really begun. The killers had then allegedly treated his body most disgracefully, affording it no proper honours and burying it without ceremony.

Æva liked what she'd heard next. An ealdorman, Ælfhere, she believed, had recovered Edward's body a year later only to find it was miraculously intact and free from decay. Ælfhere had then seen to a reburial at Sceftesberie Abbey, with both Æthelred and Ælfthryth in attendance. This public display of mourning had lifted some suspicion from the pair, and Æva had also heard it said that neither Æthelred nor his mother were actually at the estate when Edward was murdered, although she found that strange as it made Edward's entire journey there a fruitless endeavour. All in all, the queen remained a reasonable suspect, there was no doubt. Nobody had dared accuse her in her own lifetime, though, and with her son on the throne, nobody would presume to speak openly of it now.

Unless you were Ælfgar, of course. He was still staring at Æva – or as near as he could get to staring, given his sightless eyes were hidden from view – and apparently still expecting her to solve this mystery for him. She wouldn't dare say what she really thought, not because it was so unusual, but because she wouldn't be known as a gossip nor as a woman inclined to speak ill of others. Ælfgar would have to play his games elsewhere.

"I don't know anything about the late queen's intentions," Æva said flatly, an honest enough answer given that she really didn't. "Any woman would be proud to see her son become a king, but that doesn't mean they'd contemplate murder to see it done."

Ælfgar settled back in his chair, another slow exhalation escaping his lips. A sneer gradually grew across his face as he shook his head. Æva braced herself for a barbed comment. If his behaviour continued like this, she would leave him up here. It's not like he'd make an issue of it since Alaric would hopefully be returning soon. He wouldn't dare cause a scene then.

"My dear, you do disappoint," said Ælfgar, not bothering to hide the contempt in his voice. "I thought it unusual enough to encounter a woman as learned as yourself, but I should not have assumed your affinity for letters was any kind of guarantee that you could actually think."

"I would remind you that I am the wife of your brother," Æva immediately shot back, anger rising in her chest. Her whole afternoon was ruined now because of this strange change of character in him. She felt silly for having admired him previously. Just what could be wrong with him?

"Ah, of course, my dear younger brother, Alaric," replied Ælfgar, his sneer still very much on full display. "So learned, too, and pious, no doubt there, aside from all the mischief I heard he's gotten up to with that oaf of a man…what's his name…Osbert?"

"Osmund," she corrected. She didn't care for where any of this was going.

"That's the one. A real idiot, for sure. But he and Alaric were always inseparable for some reason. I always thought those two would die together in some ill-ventured scheme…which might come to pass, if all doesn't go well in Eastengle…"

Æva hastened to her feet. She'd had enough. She'd originally come here to perform an act of charity, not be badgered on affairs she knew nothing about. She'd give Ælfgar a piece of her mind, though, and no mista…

The door flew open with a crash, dispelling whatever fragile sense of civility yet remained. A guard stood there, all iron, mail, and leather, and out of breath from the climb up the stairs. His eyes fell on Æva. She froze. Had he seen her stand up? Did he think she was somehow about to attack Ælfgar?

"My Lord Ælfgar," he blurted breathlessly, his eyes thankfully shifting from Æva to address her brother-in-law. "The sentries have spotted a large force of men heading towards the stronghold. It looks like your father has returned from Eastengle."

Ælfgar got up without a word, moving past Æva and exiting the library on his own. He paused when he came to the steps beyond, waiting patiently for somebody to guide him. Æva was surprised at how adept he was at moving when he had to. In the past, he'd made a great show of requiring the assistance of others, particularly her. He'd been feigning helplessness, perhaps. But for what purpose? She didn't have time to think it over, instead gesturing for the guard to assist him.

The trio made their way down the long, winding stairs, Æva making the effort to keep an eye on her brother-in-law to ensure he didn't stumble. They reached the ground floor without incident, eventually exiting the base of the tower and moving into the main hall of the stronghold. They then ventured south towards the vestibule, their footsteps echoing across the bare stonework.

Æva always appreciated the effort that had gone into this part of the building. It was all cut and chiselled stone, which was impressive enough, but its walls hosted a plethora of tapestries and paintings, all tastefully neutral, even sombre, in colour, their finery gently illuminated by flickering torches ensconced at spaced intervals between them.

She got a real sense of history walking through here. One truly majestic image depicted King Alfred just after his victory at Ethandun, his sword raised aloft yet inverted and gripped just below the cross-guard, his right hand resting atop a rounded shield off to his side. He looked every inch a victorious king who, with God's help, had just delivered his people from the predations of the heathen. England had been born that day. It might have taken some time to finally come into its own, but its foundations had been laid at Ethandun and been made strong through the actions of brave and righteous men. It was a good beginning. One that had borne fruit.

Further on, she observed another piece, this one embroidered, of Edward the Elder, Alfred's son and successor. He was signing a charter at Tæeseford following his victory there, surrounded by his thegns and soldiers, all of them looking elatedly towards their king. Æva liked this one in particular as it included Edward's sister, Æthelflæd, Lady of the Miercians, atop her horse. The embroiderer had clearly gone to some effort to create the impression she was of some import in her own right, second in prestige to King Edward, undoubtedly, but still a figure of repute.

About ten paces ahead, they came to another painting, this one so complicated Æva at times struggled to make sense of it. Battles must be incredibly confusing, and whoever had made this piece had been trying to convey that impression, or so she hoped. She knew the figure in the centre was King Æthelstan, son of Edward and grandson to Alfred. He looked heroic, with his sword and shield raised up like he really meant it, yet his face was remarkably placid, like he was somehow untroubled by the sheer mayhem depicted around him.

This was supposed to be the Battle of Brunanburh, itself the culmination of the "great war" that had commenced when the Norsemen, Scots, and the Britons of Strathclyde had allied with one another to invade England. Whatever dastardly schemes they'd hatched had ultimately done them little good, for King Æthelstan and the English had defeated them handily at Brunanburh and smashed their ill-considered alliance to pieces. As confusing as this image was, Æva did like the subtle representation of Edmund, Æthelstan's younger brother and the future King of England, who was depicted alongside him and looking similarly serene.

Ælfgar strode on, unaware of her historical meditations, the guard staying close at his side in case he should require assistance. Another minute passed before they came to the vestibule and its pair of sizeable wooden doors, the guard heaving them open with the assistance of another who'd been on duty here. Daylight enveloped them, making Æva wince and briefly shield her eyes while adjusting to the sudden glare. Clouds filled the sky beyond, albeit without any evident threat of rain. That was positive, at least.

They passed through the echoing expanse that was the open doorway and moved quickly through the courtyard beyond. They then emerged into the open interior of the fortress itself; a place that had always proved a wonder to Æva in more ways than one. She'd been told it had originally been constructed by the Romans, although why they had abandoned it and these lands as a whole she was not too sure. She knew the hall and tower they had just come from were relatively recent additions, and that they'd been built by English hands perhaps a century or so earlier.

It was the fortifications themselves, however, that always drew the eye. The original Roman walls were like a vast square of towers and gates, enclosing in sheer stone what the Saxons had turned into a large, protected settlement. Buildings of wood and thatch had been constructed this way and that, providing homes and work spaces for those invested in the administration and upkeep of the Ealdorman Ælfric's holdings. Over time the place had become a veritable township in its own right, and smelled like one, too, what with the abundance of draft animals and all that went with a large amount of people living in one place.

Today their environs seemed even busier than usual. Æva, Ælfgar, and his faithful guide found themselves moving amidst a hive of activity, with many persons, residents and newcomers alike, bustling about, clearly animated by the news that Ælfric was returning. They moved through the hubbub, away from the great hall and into the main square at the centre of the stronghold, hoping their progress wouldn't be impeded so much they failed to meet the ealdorman as he entered the fortress.

They found little respite. The square was not only crowded but in a state of controlled chaos as an ad hoc marketplace was hurriedly dismantled. This was proceeding with some confusion, and the tradesmen were struggling with the effort of moving their produce and wares back into storage at such short notice. A clutch of irate soldiers were encouraging them to hurry, yet Æva noted they themselves were not helping. She frowned and tutted at them when she passed by. They knew who she was. They made themselves busy.

They had just turned left to head north towards the main gate when they saw it: a large column of troops, hundreds strong and many on horseback, pouring through the already opened gates and making their way towards them along the narrow, cobbled thoroughfare. But this was no triumphant procession or celebrated return for conquering heroes. As they edged closer, Æva could see what a sorry picture they painted. Mud splattered, exhausted, some sporting visible injuries, what was left of Ælfric's retinue had suffered great misfortune, their grim expressions conveying the notion their battered condition was not from some hard-fought victory.

The ealdorman rode at the head of his troops alongside Cenric, the fearsome commander of his hearthweru. They slowed to a halt before Ælfgar and Æva, both men marked by fatigue, Cenric, in particular, looking like he'd fought half the world and somehow survived to tell of it. Ælfric was hurt, favouring one arm over the other whilst he gripped the reins, his back twisted slightly like he was attempting to shift his weight away from a source of pain. His mail was crusted with mud up and across his stomach and chest, a green cloak draped across one shoulder looking similarly dishevelled.

Æva noticed his sword in its scabbard, the cross-guard of which showed signs of wear and flecks of what looked like red rust. She then noticed the spear points and blades of the men immediately around him were in a similar state. It wasn't rust. The Hamptonscir fyrd had not allowed whatever punishment they'd taken to go unanswered.

Ælfric made an attempt at a pained smile, giving Æva a sad nod before addressing his son. His voice, whilst hardly pleasing previously, was now like dry gravel, hard baked and jagged, whatever he'd just been through having drained him of all tenderness and warmth. Or so it sounded.

"Attend me in my chambers, Ælfgar, there are things we must discuss."

And that was it. He rode on, his pale grey war horse moving at a laboured trot in the direction of his hall. The column moved after him, each warrior that passed looking as grim as the one before, some of those on foot limping slightly or helping to carry others. A cart pulled by two burly workhorses trundled past, its cargo a bundle of wounded men too weak to walk. They gazed out at Æva with vacant looks, several of their compatriots lying motionless beside them, eyes closed, their skin sickly and pallid. She felt helpless.

Ælfgar had already moved off, the guard helping him to turn around and head after his father. Æva normally would have thought this was not done out of coldness, for the man had no sight and was thus unable to see the sorry condition of those around him. After today, though, she was not so sure as to Ælfgar's character, and the fact he'd just walked away without her was doubly irksome.

Panic began to rise in her chest when it became apparent that Alaric was not here. She'd assumed Ælfric's failure to mention him meant he'd be somewhere amongst the throng, believing her father-in-law would certainly tell her immediately if something had happened to him. He'd said nothing of the kind, but all the same, Alaric was absent from the column, or so it looked. She took to questioning a few passers-by, each time feeling guilty for harassing men who looked like they'd endured enough already. She couldn't see Osmund either.

The first three men she stopped claimed they didn't know anything. The fourth, a man of some means judging from the fine brooch that pinned his similarly fine cloak to his armour, had more to say, claiming Alaric and about two hundred others had left the fyrd when on the march about three weeks prior. He didn't know why and couldn't guess the reason. She'd have to find out.

Æva set out back the way she had come, passing through the main square as she went. The merchants had finished packing up, and the place looked like it was undergoing transformation into a kind of makeshift hospital and barracks for the returning troops. She wished she could help, regretting now more than ever she'd never learned any medicinal arts. Her regret eased a little when she saw the monks from the priory had been mobilised to assist. They might look a little imposing in their dark robes, but they knew their art. The wounded were in good hands.

She'd made it to the courtyard when she stopped to catch her breath. She felt dizzy, upset also at her earlier experience with her brother-in-law and the fact they'd just left her there, alone, to look for Alaric. She took a seat on one of the stone benches that lined the outer wall of the hall, hoping to calm her nerves. The sight of blood and injured men had brought certain memories to the surface, ones she did not care for.

She felt guilty too. She'd asked those soldiers where her husband was without once inquiring after them or who precisely had attacked them. She knew it was the Danes, that was a given, but she'd been so caught up in Alaric's absence she'd been unable to focus on much else. She didn't want to contemplate the possibility that he was dead. It would shatter her heart. And she'd have to raise Brandon alone. A child needed a mother and a father both. This couldn't be.

Several drops of water hit the paving stone at her feet. The sky, despite the clouds, had not shown much sign of rain, although at this time of year it wasn't exactly uncommon. She dabbed at her eyes with the sleeve of her dress when she realised she'd started to weep. She got control, a moment later rising to her feet and setting off towards the double doors of the hall. Now was not the time to fall apart. Alaric always had Osmund with him. Neither of those two would let anything happen to the other. That's the way it had always been. She had to hope.

Her strength returned when she strode back into the hall, the painted and embroidered images of great kings and great events stirring her heart once more. She hurried towards the tower staircase but turned right when she got there, remembering Ælfric had instructed Ælfgar to attend him in his own chambers. She knew the way. She'd get her answers soon enough.

The guard at the door didn't seem to mind her pushing past, knowing her by sight and not having received orders to prevent her entry. She closed the door behind her before turning to face her family-by-law, finding the pair of them sat at a rounded table, a freshly made fire crackling in the hearth behind them.

Ælfric made for a shocking sight. He'd been stripped down to his waist by one of the brothers from the priory, and the monk was now intently examining his wounds and applying some kind of tincture. She hoped it was potent. Ælfric's entire stomach and much of his chest had been discoloured, the sickly, red-speckled bruise having spread almost to his jugular.

Æva had little idea what kind of blunt force could have done such a thing. She herself had experienced bad falls from horseback before and yet not suffered that kind of trauma. If she had to guess, it looked like he could have been struck by an incoming rider and then toppled from his mount. And he'd survived that, at his age?

The old man turned away from Ælfgar, his eyes softening as he beheld Æva. He gestured for her to take a seat at the table, another sad, pained smile creasing his well-worn features. She did so, intentionally sitting some distance from her brother-in-law, who still seemed a little irritable and had scrunched up his face like he'd noticed a bad smell.

He wasn't wrong. Ælfric had not had the opportunity to bathe yet, but the familiar smell of a man who'd travelled far was, in this instance, accompanied by a strange, sugary reek coming from his bruised torso. Æva didn't know what that meant, but it was unlikely to be a good sign. Ælfric was old, too old to be out fighting. He'd lived a long life, full of war and excitement, so she'd heard, but was now very much worse for wear, even before his injuries. He'd kept his hair despite the passing of years; his long silver mane presently tied back and out of his eyes, a similarly coloured beard also tied into a narrow point that trailed just past his collarbones. His face showed his age, yet his deep, dark eyes still blazed with a certain spirit. They reminded her of her husband.

"Where is Alaric?" She cut to the chase, not wanting to wait around for any pleasantries or well wishes Ælfric may have had in mind. He didn't look like he was in the mood for small talk, anyway.

"The last time I saw my son, he was very much alive," Ælfric said, a little warmth returning to his voice. "He was eager to reach Ulfcytel's army quickly, thinking our larger force was moving at too slow a pace. He departed from our main column with a couple of hundred men just before we reached Reddinges."

"And what exactly did he hope to achieve with that?" Ælfgar butted in, apparently not bothered that nobody was talking to him. "Thorkell's army was considerable when it tore through us last year. What can Alaric and his usual company do against that alone?"

"I could tell he was eager, and time was of the essence," Ælfric continued, still looking at Æva. "Alaric has proven himself in the past, and my old bones were slowing things up. I knew that if he reached Ulfcytel, he'd make himself useful."

"So where is he now?!" Æva half-wailed, her composure starting to fray again as she took in the news that her husband was simply out there, somewhere, and certainly not at her side where he belonged. "Where is Ulfcytel? Did he defeat Thorkell? And what happened to you?!"

Ælfric's face suddenly twisted in pain, the monk's tender touch apparently not tender enough. The monk looked up, expecting to be rebuked, only for the ealdorman to sigh and shake his head, a moment later nodding for him to continue his ministrations. Æva couldn't help but wonder if the ealdorman should even be out of bed. That bruise was a serious matter for a man of any age, let alone one of such advanced years. If she hadn't wanted to speak to him so much, she'd have demanded he go get some rest and not worry about a thing until he was better. Unfortunately, she needed him awake. She needed answers.

"As I'm sure you've all worked out…the enemy had something to say about us attempting to join up with the Eastenglians," explained Ælfric, his voice smoother now that his pain seemed to have eased off a little. "We were about ten miles south of our agreed mustering point with Ulfcytel when one of my scouts rode in. He was a bit shaken, claiming what looked like Thorkell's main host was up ahead and laying waste to Theodford."

"Typical," Ælfgar muttered to himself.

"I sensed we might have an opportunity," Ælfric said, again ignoring his son. "We didn't know if Ulfcytel had yet moved to confront Thorkell, but we knew he must be in the area since Theodford was so close to his base at Hringmere. If Ulfcytel was rushing to confront the Danes, we could trap Thorkell between us, possibly flanking him and hitting him from different sides."

"Which did not happen," Ælfgar commented, like he had all the answers.

"It did not," his father said simply. "I still don't know where Ulfcytel was. All I know is that as we moved, the Danes turned and came charging up to meet us. Thousands of them. We made an initial stand at some hamlet a few miles north of Hametuna, I think, to slow them down."

"And did it?" Ælfgar asked, clearly knowing the answer to his own question.

"Somewhat," replied Ælfric, Æva sensing he was pleased to give his son an answer other than "no".

"They'd gotten themselves all twisted up and out of formation chasing us," he explained. "They came streaming in like they owned the place and smashed straight into our shield wall. For a couple of minutes, things were looking all right. Then I…"

"Fell from your horse, father?" Ælfgar was pushing his luck now with a snide tone like that.

"Fell after being struck, yes, Ælfgar, that is true, or do you seriously believe I look like a man who has only slipped from his mount?"

An awkward silence fell. Ælfgar, of course, could not see anything, but he'd warranted the rebuke, even if it didn't really make sense, given his condition. Æva decided to speak up.

"But you got away, with God's help, of course?"

"Yes, daughter, we did," replied the ealdorman, grateful to not have to respond to his obnoxious son again. "There was a lull in the fighting as some of the Danes got the message we were serious. They eased off, but then the rest of their host started to pour in and rush down the road at us…we fell back further south past the village, taking its few residents with us. I'd venture the Danes stopped chasing us when they got busy looting."

"How many men did you lose?" Æva asked, fearing the worst. The retinue she'd just seen trail through the gates couldn't have numbered more than five hundred, although it made sense that the rest of the fyrd would have disbanded earlier, the men returning to their homes as opportunity presented.

"Half," Ælfric said bluntly, another grimace creeping across his face.

"So we had almost two and a half thousand left over from Thorkell's earlier visit and now have just over a thousand?" Ælfgar asked, shaking his head with dismay.

"Something like that," Ælfric said, gritting his teeth as the monk began to bandage part of his shoulder. "There's the two hundred Alaric took with him. He would have moved fast with those. He's good at working the land, staying out of sight. I don't see why he wouldn't have made it to Ulfcytel."

He was trying to comfort her, Æva could see that. She appreciated the gesture, but it didn't help set her mind at ease. If Alaric had linked up with the Eastenglians, then they needed to know whether that army was still intact. Had Thorkell defeated them as well? She asked the natural question.

"So where is Ulfcytel? Do we know if he was attacked too?"

Ælfric took a deep breath, flexing his freshly bandaged shoulder. It clicked as he worked it, but if he experienced any more pain, he kept it hidden. He looked exhausted, more so than ever, and he most certainly needed a bed rather than being pestered with more questions. Æva again felt guilty. But she had to know what had happened.

"I don't think Thorkell had faced Ulfcytel yet," Ælfric mused. "Judging from the size and enthusiasm of the force that attacked us, it really didn't seem like they'd just fought another pitched battle. So that means the Eastenglians are still in the field, or at least were when we faced the Danes at Hametuna."

"Or Thorkell had inflicted such a heavy and one-sided defeat on Ulfcytel that the army you faced still looked reasonably intact."

Æva inhaled sharply at Ælfgar's cruel words. He was hoping to bait them both, for some reason trying his hardest to make a difficult situation even worse. She had no idea why. What she did know was that he'd made a mistake.

The slap echoed throughout the chamber, the monk still tending to Ælfric looking up in surprise at this sudden escalation. Ælfgar sat forlorn and suitably chastised, his head bent forward from the force of his father's hand impacting across the back of his skull.

"What the hell is the matter with you, boy?!" Ælfric spat. "We're talking about Ulfcytel here! You'll remember like everyone else what he did to Svienn Forkbeard!"

"But he still lost that battle," Ælfgar whined, sounding almost akin to a petulant child as he rubbed his bare scalp. "Everyone thinks he's a legend simply because he managed to at least make the Forkbeard know he was in a fight. How do we know he's still so formidable? How do we know he's even alive?"

Ælfric just stared at him, perhaps wondering on the true identity of this interloper who seemed to have stolen his son's appearance. Overnight, Ælfgar had gone from being a quiet and civilised man to a sneering bully eager to rub salt in the wounds of everyone present. Æva got up to leave, disgusted at the sight of him and unwilling to endure another one of his barbs. She'd think and pray on the situation. No one called after her as she slipped out into the hallway beyond.

She made her way back to her own chambers in the tower. She and Alaric had lived here for some years, occupying a generously sized pair of rooms close to the summit and adjacent to the library. His father had made it so, since he knew his son was a studious man and would enjoy the location. They'd been happy here, each of them eager to put the past behind them since they'd moved from…

It wouldn't do to think of such things now. She was barely holding herself together as it was. She stepped through into her quarters and closed the door. She saw then that Cenwynn was asleep in one of the chairs adjacent to the hearth. She wasn't angry. She knew the poor girl wasn't sleeping well. She'd had issues at home for some time now. Æva crossed the room quietly, her previously echoing footsteps now muted by the generously sized woollen rug that carpeted much of the floor. It wouldn't be right to wake her. She reached the door to her bedchamber and crept inside.

It was gloomy here, what with the window shuttered and the firelight from the hearth outside only reaching so far. Æva spied what she'd come to see, the small, huddled form on the bed lightening her heart. She moved closer, kneeling down and placing a tender hand on Brandon's shoulder. The child was fast asleep. Cenwynn had likely thought it safe for her to close her eyes now that Brandon wasn't likely to get into any trouble. Æva wasn't going to make an issue of it. She was grateful to the girl for volunteering so often to watch her son whilst she was otherwise occupied.

Brandon looked serene as he slumbered, having no doubt exhausted himself in some vitally important pursuit whilst Æva was away. Perhaps the king was due to visit, requiring Brandon to personally prepare the tower for his arrival, given no one else could possibly be up to the task. Maybe he'd decided Cenwynn had to help him search for would-be-assassins, requiring them to inspect the hall up and down and question anyone Brandon decided might be an intruder. Or the tower itself could be under siege, meaning he had to immediately lock swords with whoever happened to be near, the swords, of course, being sticks for firewood he'd snatched up that very moment.

That last game would require Alaric to actually be here. Brandon only ever wanted to do that when he was around, and he was always up for it. The boy had absolutely no idea what Alaric was capable of when it came to a real sword and a real fight. Æva hoped he would never have to see such things, but given the times they lived in, she thought it unlikely.

He'd also never noticed that Alaric looked nothing like him. Why would he? Children did not have suspicious minds, and Alaric was, in terms of his role in his life, very much a father. But when he saw his friends with their families, they tended to look alike. Brandon did not look like Alaric. He did not even look Saxon, and his blond hair, blue eyes, and angular face were far removed from the blunt visage and dark brown locks of his father. And it was starting to become an issue.

It had begun with some unkind comments from the other children. Light hair and eyes were not unknown among the English, especially from those living in the old Danelaw, but here in Westseaxe it was something of a rarity. Some of the other boys had noticed Brandon's looks and were aware on some child-like level that the people currently threatening the realm tended to be known for their blond hair and blue eyes. They'd teased him, calling him a Dane, sometimes even excluding him from games. Brandon hadn't taken it well, insisting he was as Saxon as they were and boasting of his father's skills as a warrior. The latter part was true. The former was not.

Æva didn't have the heart to tell him the truth. He was still too young to understand the terrible events prior to his birth, and too young to understand just how painful it had been for Alaric to accept him. One day they'd both tell him, when he was old enough. It was imperative that Alaric be here for that. He had to be here to make things better. He had to be here to help him understand.

But he wasn't here, and nobody knew where exactly he might be, other than that he was somewhere in Eastengle. She hoped beyond hope he'd made it to this Ulfcytel fellow. Wasn't he supposed to be some kind of great hero? And Alaric would have Osmund with him too. Wouldn't that be enough to keep him safe?

There would be no quietening her troubled mind. She could rationalise all she liked, but she knew in her chest something was wrong. It was like ice, pushing up from her stomach, the jagged edges pressing against her heart. She stifled a sob as tears again filled her eyes. She thought of prayer. Perhaps a visit to the chapel would provide some comfort. Not now. She felt exhausted. She was safe here. In the darkness, with her child. Nothing could get to them. All she had to do was wait. News would reach her sooner or later.

She got to her feet and crept over to her wardrobe, obtaining a light shawl from inside. She then eased herself back through the doorway into the main chamber, tenderly depositing the shawl over the still-slumbering Cenwynn. She'd take care of everyone she could. Brandon, Cenwynn, Ælfric, even Ælfgar once he got over whatever was bothering him and remembered the man he was supposed to be. She'd do what needed to be done.

Æva snuck back into her bedchamber, easing the door shut so that only a sliver of firelight intruded from beyond. She then quietly lay down on her bed, easing Brandon gently into her arms as she did. Her son mumbled incoherently, likely dreaming of something or other, the child then turning to return his mother's embrace. Æva could do this. She had the strength to hold out hope. Courage and faith would see her through. She closed her eyes, joining her Brandon in repose, words of piety repeating on her mind:

Lord Jesus Christ
Son of God
Have Mercy upon Me
A Sinner.

V

King Æthelred was jealous of his queen. She slept like an angel, if it could be said that angels slept, at peace with herself and very much undisturbed by the troubles of the age. As always, she was the very image of one too, her skin as pale and spotless as milk, her long auburn hair immaculate even at rest. Had she been awake, he'd have been able to behold those eyes, akin to faded emeralds, the sparkle of which rarely failed to captivate. Having Emma as his queen was one of the few instances in his life where Æthelred would dare to call himself blessed.

He otherwise felt almost as wretched as usual. He was slumped in a narrow wooden chair adjacent to his desk. He'd vacated his bed a short time previously and had been contemplating his slumbering queen ever since, hoping to imprint her likeness on his mind in a bid to calm his nerves. She'd been a rock in his life, a gentle touch or whispered word often able to soothe him in ways he didn't fully understand himself. Despite this, he still didn't want to wake her. It wouldn't be fair, and some things a king had to face alone.

The dream had come on again, as harrowing as always, those accusing eyes as terrible as last night and the night before that. Ælfric's currently nameless son was now appearing on a regular basis, always looking more grief-stricken than the other staring fools, like he ached for the realm itself. Whatever it was he wanted, Æthelred wished he'd obtain it and leave him be. Hopefully, Eadric's mission would resolve matters. He'd hear from him soon. Then he might finally get a full night's rest.

Emma was fortunate in that she never seemed to wake when he did. She slept through his disturbances and much else, her slumber so deep he'd begun to wonder as to the true depths of it. Æthelred felt like he could almost convene his Witan here, now, in his own bedchamber, and she wouldn't rise, instead continuing as she was, as still and peaceful as a child in the womb.

No such luck for Æthelred. No such luck for the King of England. Yet having her here did make things a little easier. He'd found this out from her absence, for the queen had been away this past month visiting her brother, Duke Richard, in her native Normandy. Æthelred had initially not been daunted at the prospect of enduring his nights alone, but it had only made things worse, his agitation becoming more intense and difficult to recover from whenever he slept without her. He was glad she was back. He hoped she was glad too.

Many might have seen their marriage as one of convenience. They would not be entirely wrong, for an alliance with Normandy was a much-desired state of affairs. The Danes had been in the habit of using Norman ports to resupply for attacks on England, so bringing Duke Richard onto Æthelred's side was a natural step to take. But after eight years of marriage, it had gone beyond politics. Emma had found a way into his heart, igniting something he'd previously thought dead. For that, he was grateful.

He tried to show it in a number of ways, firstly by continuing to call her by her original name, having learned some time ago how much she resented being referred to as Ælfgifu. He'd given her this English name upon their marriage, as was custom, and so he'd initially not understood her displeasure. His own saintly grandmother had borne that name, and he'd been saddened to hear how his new bride disliked it. He'd reverted to calling her Emma soon after, at least in private, his queen confessing her appreciation for his sensitivity. Perhaps she did have reason to dislike it. It had also been the name of his first wife, after all.

Æthelred got to his feet, not bothering to quieten his movements, knowing it would be almost unprecedented for Emma to be disturbed. He began to dress himself, undertaking the usual ritual of peeling the sweat-drenched undergarments from his body and depositing them somewhere Emma would be unlikely to slip on them.

He was just donning a thick woollen nightgown when he heard two muffled taps at the door. He had a feeling who that was. Why people refused to knock on his door like they meant it was beyond him. The entire purpose of knocking was to get the attention of someone, and those two feeble taps wouldn't have awoken anyone. Emma's slumbering form was testament to that, although perhaps she wasn't the best example, given she'd likely sleep through a siege.

Æthelred ambled over to his door, his feet uncomfortable upon the chill stones. He clutched at the heavy iron handle, the metal feeling unnaturally cold to the touch. He heaved the door open a crack, peering outwards into the gloom. As expected, a youthful face stared back at him, too young to have yet grown a complete beard, its expression apologetic. Cuthbert. Son of…whoever, Æthelred couldn't remember. But he was a faithful and hard-working steward. That's what mattered.

The young man spoke, his voice hushed to almost a whisper:

"Pardon me for disturbing you at this hour, my king, but the Ealdorman of Mierce has returned and is requesting entry to your great hall."

"Have him sent to my audience chamber," ordered Æthelred curtly. He shut the door, ignoring young Cuthbert as he bowed his head in acknowledgement. The king felt his heart hammering in his chest. Soon he would know. If Eadric had done his job well, Æthelred's reign was now a lot more secure, and he might soon be able to boast of obtaining the services of one Thorkell the Tall. If he had not…

He wouldn't worry about that now. There was no point in getting himself more stressed than he already was. The last thing he wanted to think about was the prospect of a victorious Ulfcytel, drunk on the adoration of his troops and lauded as a saviour of Engla…Æthelred caught himself, a scowl crossing his face. There was no point in resolving to not think about something if you then began thinking about it. He turned his attention to other matters. Like what to wear.

A good impression was important. All too often, he'd presented Eadric with a less-than-ideal image, spending hours conversing with him late at night when he'd again been awoken by his dreams. Æthelred was aware he'd looked less than regal then, appearing very much as a man overwhelmed by troubles.

He would be seen in a different likeness tonight. He dressed himself as the king he was, opting for a long-sleeved crimson tunic, dark leather boots with matching breecs, and a flowing purple cloak that reached almost to the back of his knees. He'd chosen this last item for a very specific reason, for he'd heard that purple was the colour of imperial authority among the Romans. This was still the case for the Greeks, who still considered themselves Romans, or so Æthelred understood. He wasn't entirely sure how much sense that made, but he liked the colour and the prestige it might convey.

Æthelred exited his bedchamber, his two personal guards falling into step behind him with well-practised ease. He'd doubled the watch outside his rooms since his wife had returned, desiring to make sure she always had adequate protection regardless of where he happened to be. It wouldn't do for him to simply wander off with his own guards at night and leave her undefended. Many might want Æthelred dead, he mused, and few of them would have any qualms about trying to get to him through Emma. That must not happen.

The trio thus left the queen's guards behind and marched down the hallway, the solid footfalls of the king's guardians contrasting with the soft, padded rhythm of his own steps. Æthelred strode straight past the door to his study, detecting the slightest moment of hesitation from his escorts when he did. The two men had no doubt gotten used to his preference for gathering his thoughts in the company of his books. It would not be so tonight.

The king carried on down the hall as far as it could go, eventually coming to a pair of imposing double doors. One of his men moved ahead of him and pushed, his great strength easing the creaking timbers open and outward into the space beyond. The king stepped through the gap made by his man's efforts, both warriors then hurrying to join him. There was little need to worry. The long, echoing expanse of the audience chamber was empty, as expected at this hour, occupied solely by motes of dust and what sounded like a few mice now hurriedly scurrying for cover.

Æthelred moved on ahead, his path illuminated by a host of slow-burning torches fixed into well-worn alcoves on both sides of the generously spaced chamber. He was making his way down the left side of a broad and impressively long banqueting table, its polished surface catching the light whenever he cared to look. It had been some considerable time since he'd used the thing for anything other than meetings and haranguing his ever-ineffectual ealdormen, but it pleased him to keep it around, knowing the scale of it served to awe visitors unaccustomed to such things.

About a half minute passed before he finished traversing its full length. He continued on, striding across a rather threadbare rug to then vault several stone steps before halting in the face of a solid yet ornately carved oak chair. His throne. He'd heard splendid tales of other kings sitting atop wrought metal inlaid with precious stones and other finery. Æthelred held that thought and sat down, wondering how his ungrateful subjects might view him if he were to obtain such an item. Would they be impressed? Would they take him more seriously then? Would any of them be more inclined to obey? Perhaps they might. But it would be an absurdly expensive project, and he couldn't shake the feeling he'd just end up looking immodest. He'd stick with what he had.

From his vantage point, that didn't seem like much. His audience chamber was gloomy, dishevelled even; a few faded banners displaying the old heraldry of Westseaxe, Mierċe, and Norþanhymbre alike doing little to provide lustre. He remembered this hall had been full of revelry and promise in earlier days. His loyal thegns had seemed to flock to him then, his ealdormen, too, all of them eager to bask in the presence of their young king.

Those times were long gone. Æthelred knew well enough he would not live forever, and the years of stress and calamity had taken an indisputable toll. A number of his heirs had died young, and it had been his sorry lot to be that of a father who'd buried several of his own children.

He could remember all of them, every single one, from the moment they'd first opened their eyes until the moment fate had closed them. Eadred had been the most recent, dying not so long ago of some sudden fever. He could not think on it for too long. The grief always threatened to overwhelm him if he dwelled. He was just glad he still had sons, and Emma had given him Alfred and Edward. They'd make fine rulers someday, he hoped, although as was typical in his life nothing was that simple. His older sons had a solid claim to the English throne, one they'd not relinquish without a struggle. Æthelred didn't want to see that. He loved his children, and the idea of seeing them fight over his kingdom was repellent.

A sudden noise sounded from up ahead to snap him from his thoughts. The double doors at the end of the chamber had begun to open, the hinges whining with stress as someone yet unseen struggled to make an entrance. Eventually, a gap was made large enough for a figure to slip through, and the doors quickly closed again under their own weight, the thunderous boom echoing out across the chamber.

The figure commenced the long walk down the length of the banqueting table towards him. Æthelred could tell who it was from the shadow it cast and the commotion it had made gaining entry. Eadric was not the most physically imposing of men, but he had a sharp mind and was loyal, and both attributes were valuable commodities. He soon emerged from the shadows and came into full view about twenty paces away, damp and certainly worse for wear, like he'd just run himself ragged through a thunderstorm. Perhaps he had at some point.

Eadric pulled back the hood of his cloak and halted before the first step leading up to the throne. He dropped to one knee, his wet, dishevelled blond hair tied back and away from his fatigued yet still piercing grey eyes. He steadied his breathing for a second or two, appearing as a man who was grateful for the opportunity to enjoy a moment of rest.

"My lord king, following your instruction, I have returned from the task you set me in Eastengle."

"And what do you have to say to me?" Æthelred asked, his heart starting to hammer in his chest again. These next few moments could make or break his reign.

Eadric looked up at him, then to the guards on either side of his throne. He raised an eyebrow. Æthelred should have remembered that what he had to say was likely not for anyone else to know but him.

"Wait outside," Æthelred commanded impatiently. His two protectors strode off without a word, eventually exiting the chamber and closing the doors behind them. Now they could talk.

"Go on, you may speak."

"It is with a heavy heart that I must inform you the Ealdorman Ulfcytel refused to heed your command to move his army south," began Eadric, his tone regretful, as if there was anything surprising about such a turn of events.

"Not only that," he continued, "but he was joined in his defiance by Æthelstan of Norþanhymbre, Oswy of Exsessa, Wulfric of Sūþsēaxe, and Alaric of Hamptonscir, who all rallied to him and his host in an attack on the forces of Thorkell the Tall."

Æthelred wasn't surprised by any of this. He'd not expected the boisterous Ulfcytel to obey him, and the fact that loud-mouthed clown, Oswy, had followed suit wasn't exactly startling. He'd hoped Æthelstan would have had more sense, though. Wulfric was an unknown quantity, and as for Alaric of Hamptonscir…

"Who is Alaric of Hamptonscir?" Æthelred asked, confused. He'd been told the Ealdorman Ælfric was leading the Hamptonscir fyrd to Eastengle, but he'd never heard of this Alaric. Unless…

"Alaric is the son of Ælfric, my king," said Eadric. "Tall, broad shoulders, dark hair, as you described…he'd moved ahead of his father's force in order to reach Ulfcytel well in time for any battle. An eager man, you could say."

Not as eager as Æthelred was to hear what exactly had taken place. Eadric was a man for drama and spectacle, things the king sometimes appreciated if he felt like being amused. Tonight he just wanted the facts, and quickly. He'd wonder why he was dreaming about a man he'd never met later.

"And the battle, Eadric? Tell me what happened! Did Ulfcytel defeat the Danes?"

"No, he did not," Eadric responded, finally rising from his knees. "Following your instructions, I made sure that any plan of his went awry without suspicion falling on you. Last I heard, he'd clashed with Thorkell as he advanced north. He put up a good fight, but his force was decimated. I do not know if he survived."

Æthelred breathed out slowly. Now that he finally knew, he did not feel much relief. It would be simpler to know that Ulfcytel had been killed rather than just be told he'd suffered a setback. The fact that Thorkell was still in the field and openly hostile was also hardly any kind of comfort. But it was something. Anything was better than not knowing.

"And the other men you mention? They fell in battle?"

"Alaric is dead, as is Æthelstan," said Eadric, sounding satisfied with himself. "I was nearly able to provoke Ulfcytel into attacking Thorkell prematurely in his camp outside of Gipeswic, but Æthelstan took his place. He and Alaric went in. They didn't come out."

Æthelred began to rub at his temples, finding the onslaught of information difficult to take in. "Just wait a moment," he asked, hoping to settle things in his mind. "Part of your mission, Eadric, was to open up negotiations with Thorkell to purchase his loyalty. Having him killed before that takes place is a little counterproductive, would you not agree?"

"Absolutely, my king," Eadric replied, folding his arms triumphantly. "That's why I met with Thorkell beforehand to bring him your proposal. I also made him aware of Ulfcytel and your displeasure with him. To expedite matters, I decided to formulate a plan to thin Ulfcytel's ranks, ideally by provoking him into overconfidence by giving him the location of Thorkell himself…with Thorkell's approval, of course."

"So, in other words, you told him to prepare a trap, as you'd be luring your fellow Englishmen right into it?"

"My king makes it all sound so sordid," Eadric muttered, all previous enthusiasm draining from his voice. "But had my plan worked as intended, Ulfcytel would have been killed before battle was joined, leaving you his army. I acted to save lives and to serve you, most of all."

It made good sense. Had Ulfcytel been caught up in whatever strange scheme Eadric had laid before him, it would have left an army that could be put to good use.

It didn't surprise him that Æthelstan had got in the way of things. He always had fancied himself the noble hero.

"So you led Æthelstan and Alaric to Thorkell's camp yourself?" Æthelred asked, wanting to get as accurate a picture of events as possible. "And they just attacked it without hesitation? This Alaric must have been a brave man."

"He was, and they did," confirmed Eadric. "They'd decided to only bring a small number of men with them, thinking they were acting sly by attacking at night. I didn't see what happened inside the camp, but I believe Thorkell caught Æthelstan quite quickly."

"And Alaric? How did the son of our least favourite traitor fare?"

"Judging from the noise, I think he made quite a lot of trouble," Eadric said lightly, as if men fighting for their lives against overwhelming odds was of minimal concern to him. "The sounds of battle carried on for some time. Seems like Alaric didn't understand he was dead. I imagine he's come to terms with it now."

Eadric was indeed a cold man, Æthelred decided, but his lack of scruples was of considerable utility. He'd hoped the death of this Alaric would ensure the fellow would vanish from his dream, and yet he had appeared to him this very night. Would he now have to put up with his staring indefinitely? He would hope not. Perhaps once the negotiations with Thorkell were properly resolved, things might change.

"So what are the Danes doing now?" Æthelred asked, his heart still fluttering in his chest. "Do you know what happened after they fought Ulfcytel? Where did they clash exactly?"

"A lake next to some old earthworks apparently built centuries ago or some such," Eadric replied disinterestedly. "Hringmere, it's called. I made sure to exploit some divisions in Ulfcytel's camp…one man, in particular, proved himself very useful…I can't tell precisely what happened, but it seems Ulfcytel might have gone into battle without his entire army."

"Right, and then what?" Æthelred prompted again, making a mental note of just how duplicitous Eadric really was. He'd have to keep an eye on that.

"The Danes burned the village immediately north of the battle site, Wretham, I think, and then headed south to attack Theodford. Then something surprising happened…"

"Oh? Did the brave citizens of Theodford fend them off?" Sarcasm aside, Æthelred wished they had. With Ulfcytel and his army out of the way, he needed to get Thorkell to sit down and take him seriously. That the man was content to listen to Eadric's scheming but then just revert back to ravaging the countryside didn't bode well.

"I don't believe they managed such a thing, no, my king," Eadric said, straight-faced and impassive, apparently under the impression he'd been serious. "I do know that the Ealdorman Ælfric made an appearance…I can only surmise he was unaware that Ulfcytel was already defeated. His force was overwhelmed by the Danes' numbers and beat a retreat back down south."

"So he's alive then?" Æthelred pressed impatiently. So far, he only had confirmed deaths of two people, one of them being his own brother-in-law, Æthelstan, and the other a man he'd never met but was all the same managing to stop him from sleeping. That wasn't good enough. He needed some surety in all this if he were to plan ahead.

His heart began to ache as thoughts of his first wife, Ælfgifu, suddenly filled his mind. What would she say now that he'd set in motion a chain of events that had killed her brother? Would she hate him for it? What of their children? How would they take it if they knew the truth; that their Uncle Æthelstan had fallen to the Danes as part of some black scheme triggered by their own father?

Æthelred lowered his eyes, hoping to hide the tears that now filled them. He tried to blink them away quickly, yet a single droplet was dislodged by his efforts and deposited itself on the hem of his cloak. He stared downwards, gazing through clouded vision at the teardrop soaking into the cloth. That was his kingdom, right there. The finest fabric, dyed with the colour of majesty, yet now stained by grief. That was his kingship. Legitimate, and at one time promising. Yet always marked by sorrow. King Æthelred the Sorrowful.

"Are you all right, my king?" Eadric's voice was soft, almost affectionate, his expression puzzled as to what he could be looking at. Æthelred gritted his teeth, wondering for a moment if the ealdorman really cared for him on some level. It was immaterial whether he did or not. He couldn't afford to show weakness now. Later, perhaps, when back with his queen. Not now. He rubbed his eyes clear with both palms, a sharp, shuddering breath filling his lungs.

"I'm fine, Eadric, just a moment's…indecision. Please, tell me if you know Ælfric survived?"

"I admit my information on that is a little patchy," Eadric said apologetically. "From what I can gather, at least some of his force managed to escape. If he's with them, they'll no doubt be looking to return to his seat of power at Porteceaster."

Of course. Ælfric had inherited a fine stronghold all to himself, its Roman walls as impressive as anything in Lundenburg. He'd enjoyed that for too long. Alive or not, it was about time Hamptonscir went to another. Somebody capable of loyalty. Somebody who didn't habitually retreat from battles. A good man. A king's man.

"In that case, I have a new assignment for you already," said Æthelred, regaining some composure following his previous bout of emotion. "I want you to take a few hundred men and head to Porteceaster. If Ælfric is there, arrest him. Arrest his entire family, for that matter, and bring them here."

Eadric nodded, deep in thought, his arms again crossed over his chest. The king was being decisive, he knew that, but in a time of extreme crisis it wouldn't be wise to leave a job half-finished. Hamptonscir was an important holding, even in its currently devastated state. With proper leadership, it would flourish. But where to find that leader?

"Who would you put in Ælfric's place?" asked Eadric, having the same question. "You'd need to assign a reeve to take over the administration of the county. Did you have anyone in mind?"

"What's wrong, Eadric?" Æthelred asked, the beginnings of a sneer forming across his lips. "Is being Ealdorman of Mierce not enough for you? I gave you my daughter also, if you don't recall?"

He had done just that. Eadric had been well rewarded for his loyalty to the crown. If he was implying he should get Hamptonscir also, he should think again. A man should only be so powerful.

"My king misunderstands my intent," Eadric said, a sliver of ice in his voice. "But there are things to consider, not just in Hamptonscir. Thorkell made it clear to me he'll only come over to your service if he receives a substantial sum of money. Until then, he says he'll continue to take what he refers to as "tribute" wherever he finds it."

"Just how much money is the ingrate asking for?"

Eadric named a sum. Ridiculous. He could afford to outfit a new army for that kind of money and beat Thorkell back to the sea. It would also require a new tax, one that would antagonise his already alienated subjects. Thorkell would have to be more reasonable.

"That's an impossible sum. I don't have it. We'll have to offer him something else."

"My king, if there was any other option, I wouldn't have dared bring this to your attention. Either we pay him and his army to come over to our side, or Svienn Forkbeard will notice our present troubles and come looking to add to them. We'd then be facing two foreign hordes instead of one, without the troops to deal with either. We have no choice."

"And why don't we have the troops to deal with either of them?" Æthelred demanded, his temper suddenly flaring as he rose unsteadily to his feet, his fists clenched at his sides. "It was on your advice that we interfere with Ulfcytel's efforts to defend Eastengle! Would his victory really have been so terrible?!"

His voice must have been considerably louder than he'd intended. The doors to the chamber suddenly flew open, his guards forcing their way through like they were the vanguard of an invading army taking the place by storm. Eadric spun around like that was actually happening, his hand reaching to his belt and the bejewelled hilt of the sword that hung there. Æthelred held his arms out towards his men in a placating gesture, eager to stop any further escalation.

"All is well!" he called, attempting to sound both calm and authoritative. "A misunderstanding! I commend you for your diligence. Now wait outside."

The twin armoured giants ceased their thunderous advance and came to a halt, their now silent and motionless forms truly imposing in the flickering torchlight. They then bowed, simultaneously, in acknowledgement of their king's command before turning and exiting the room, heaving the doors closed as they went.

They had not laid a hand on Eadric or even said a word, yet the effect they'd had on him was remarkable. He was breathing heavily, his chest heaving in and out with effort, his face pallid with fright. Æthelred motioned for him to take a seat at the banqueting table, preferring him to be sitting down rather than collapsed on the floor. Eadric did so, angling his chair to face his king, some colour now thankfully returning to his cheeks. Æthelred, too, sat down, once again nestling back into his throne.

"You surprise me, Eadric," he then said, his voice calm and measured this time. "I would have thought you'd be used to the sight of warriors by now. I know, for a fact, you know how to use that fine-looking sword of yours. What's gotten you so ruffled?"

"Apologies, my king," Eadric mumbled, his breathing still slightly laboured. "I am tired from my journey and have been exposed to some risk in the pursuit of my duties. Your displeasure and the appearance of your men was just… unexpected."

Æthelred would have to take his word for it. He knew Eadric could defend himself if he had to, but his life expectancy could likely be measured in mere seconds if he had crossed swords with his guards. Perhaps he was indeed just tired. His visit to Eastengle couldn't have been the most relaxing of affairs.

"I'll be sure to speak more quietly then to avoid any further interruptions," Æthelred quipped with a half-smile, although Eadric didn't look even slightly amused. "So tell me, as to what I said earlier…would Ulfcytel's victory over Thorkell really have been the calamity you say?"

"Yes, I believe it would have been. It is my opinion that such a turn of events would have seen his popularity peak, ensuring he'd be seen as the man to defend the realm against King Svienn. Since we know he was being joined by men known for their disloyalty to you, it is perfectly rational to conclude his victory would have boded ill for the future of your reign."

As always, Eadric had a way of explaining things that made sense, at least to Æthelred. The true calamity here was the decimation of Ulfcytel's army, a force which, had its leader simply obeyed his king, would now be heading south to join its strength to his. Eadric had done well to hatch a plan to remove Ulfcytel whilst leaving his army intact. It was just sheer bad luck that Æthelstan and this Alaric fellow had gotten in the way.

"I understand your position, and I thank you for explaining it to me again," Æthelred affirmed, sincere in his words. "It seems then we have little choice but to come up with the money required to pay Thorkell, lest we end up having to fight both him and Svienn at a later date…an impossible situation, I know you'll agree."

"I do agree, my king," said Eadric. "Svienn is certain to reappear as he has done in the past. Our only option is to have Thorkell fight him for us. Once Svienn is defeated and Thorkell is weakened from fighting him, we may be better positioned to…re-evaluate."

That was an interesting way of putting it, Æthelred thought. Once the immediate crisis was over and the invasions defeated, it seemed very possible he'd be able to deal with Thorkell as he pleased, at least as long as his forces were sufficiently depleted. The only question, for now, was how to pay him the amount required to bring him on side. He could then try to keep him in his service or dispose of him later, depending on the situation.

"I will levy a new tax paid directly to the crown," Æthelred stated. "I will need you to make a display of cooperation on this, to bring the other ealdormen in line. Mierċe will be obedient to its king, yes?"

"Mierċe will do whatever the King of England requires," Eadric said, inclining his head respectfully. "My troops will make sure of it. And speaking of such matters, I take it you still wish me to visit our friend Ælfric in Porteceaster?"

Æthelred had almost forgotten about that cowardly rat. He presented another problem in his own right, given it might be difficult to get him out of his stronghold should he decide to resist. A show of force would be in order, coupled with assurances that he and his family would not be harmed. That should be enough, at least until he had Ælfric close at hand and away from his base of power.

"Raise a force of your own Mierċians, people you can count on," Æthelred instructed. "Move fast for the sake of surprise, and don't harm anyone in Hamptonscir as you move, lest you harden Ælfric's resolve against you. Then surround his stronghold. Tell him he and his kin are to accompany you to Lundenburg. Make a good show of it. He's a coward, so he'll capitulate."

"And what if he doesn't?" Eadric asked.

"Lay to siege to his fortress. I doubt he'll have the men to resist you, even with his strong walls, not after his recent losses. Much of the south is in ruins anyway after their… troubles…last year. Nobody will be coming to aid him. So just get it done."

"And what about a reeve to replace him?" Eadric inquired a little too eagerly. If he thought he was getting the job, he was going to be disappointed. Æthelred had faith in him, but he wasn't about to let him overreach. He'd given him Mierċe and his daughter,

Eadgyth, bringing him into his family as a son. But a good father must guide his children. Eadric had a certain grasping quality to him, one that just didn't suit.

"Who would you suggest?" Æthelred asked, at least willing to listen to suggestions, just as long as Eadric didn't put himself forward for the position.

"I know a trustworthy man," Eadric announced, "one who has been loyal to me and put himself at great risk just recently to ensure Ulfcytel did not prevail at Hringmere."

"Who?"

"A certain thegn from Eastengle, but his loyalty to the crown did not allow him to continue in Ulfcytel's service once he openly defied you. Thurcytel is his name. He's a good man. A fighter."

"Alright then," Æthelred muttered dismissively. "Take him with you to Porteceaster. If he proves himself, leave him there with a couple of hundred men. If he doesn't manage to burn the place down or get himself deposed in an uprising, I'll consider making him a reeve."

"As you say, my king," Eadric replied, notably pleased that he'd agreed to his proposal. Æthelred made another mental note to have somebody he could trust accompany the troops left behind with Thurcytel. There was no sense in failing to keep an eye on this man, and Æthelred wasn't about to make him a reeve if he was just to be a pawn of Eadric. He'd only indulge him so far.

"So this concludes our business then, yes?" Æthelred asked, his knees cracking in protest as he rose from his throne a little too quickly.

"It does, my king," Eadric replied, imitating his lord by getting to his feet. "If it pleases you, I will rest for now and leave for Hamptonscir tomorrow morning. I'll also dispatch instructions to my thegns in Mierce for them to comply with any new taxes you deem necessary."

"I'm glad to hear it, Eadric. But we should keep it quiet as to the purpose behind such demands. It would be counterproductive to let it be known it's intended for the sake of mercenaries. Let's say it's for a new army. An army tax. A heregeld."

"That is a most excellent notion," Eadric concurred, bowing his head slightly in deference. "There is one other matter you might consider in this regard, if you'll hear me?"

"Speak, Eadric. You needn't ask permission."

"The Welsh. They owe you tribute as your loyal vassals, and they know what it is to suffer at the hands of the Norsemen. Why not ask them to make a contribution to this ...heregeld?"

"They may not be happy with that," Æthelred mused, "but it's worth inquiring and seeing what pressure might be applied should they prove uncooperative. You share a border with these people, Eadric. I'm assuming you have men who know the Welsh better than I?"

"I do," Eadric confirmed, "and I shall send word to have them open up negotiations on your authority. With any luck, we can convince our friendly neighbours to pay their fair share. Will that be all? Is my king finished with me?"

"I am."

Without further word, the Ealdorman of Mierce turned from the throne and strode towards the doors. Æthelred watched him go. These were critical times. He'd seen off the threat of the rebellious Ulfcytel and those foolish enough to join him. If all went well, he'd soon have the Ealdorman Ælfric in chains and a loyal man in power in Hamptonscir.

England remained a rich country, despite its ongoing troubles. It should not take long to raise at least some of the money required to bring Thorkell into compliance. The danger now was from his own ealdormen. He had to force their cooperation with the heregeld, and fast. Every moment lost was another moment that Thorkell was still active and no doubt looking to obtain "tribute" from whichever settlement took his fancy.

It wasn't all doom and gloom. Lundenburg was fortified and well-protected. The real centre of wealth and power in England was safe. He'd soon bring Thorkell to the negotiating table, and with any luck, he'd win him over for use against Denmark's Svienn Forkbeard should the accursed villain return. The Norsemen would fight anyone for money, even their own kind. All would be well.

Æthelred settled back into his throne and closed his eyes, content. Such a thing was a rare sensation in these difficult days, and it did not last. A wan face shimmered into view, grey and lifeless, its eyes sealed shut, rigid and stiff in the embrace of death. Æthelstan. Brother to his departed wife. Uncle to his children. Now robbed of life in yet another tragic episode of Æthelred's sorrowful reign.

He opened his eyes, a solitary tear slipping free and trailing down his cheek before falling into his lap. He looked down, once more scrutinising the purple of his cloak, the colour of authority again marred with his own grief. He spoke, his voice a cracked, quavering whisper, his previous confidence giving way once again to sorrow and regret.

"Forgive me."

****

Eadric finally made it through the doors, heaving one aside just far enough for him to slip through. It closed on its own, the echoing boom reverberating down the halls in all directions. Neither of the king's guards on duty had helped him. They'd frightened the daylights out of him earlier, for a moment giving him the impression they'd meant him harm. That wasn't right.

He approached one. The man just stood there, all metal and mail, helm hiding his face, a vast painted shield covering much of his upper body. Eadric stared into his eyes; one of the few parts of this giant of a warrior that was readily visible. He stared back, a pair of hard, dark orbs returning his gaze with something like…

"You don't like me, do you?"

The guard didn't respond to the question. He just continued to stare, eyes angled slightly down to compensate for Eadric's height. They carried on like this for a few more moments. Then he heard a squeezing, grinding sound as the man began to tighten his grip on the shaft of his spear. He was applying some real force, like he intended to crush it into greater compliance or snap it altogether. Eadric suddenly felt uneasy. There was something in his gaze. He wanted to use that spear on him. These men hated him.

He turned and walked away, hurrying to put as much distance as possible between himself and these royal killers. He felt the beginnings of panic seize his limbs as he thought he heard them begin to move after him, his relief almost intoxicating when they instead passed back into the audience chamber to rejoin their king. The doors slammed shut with the predictable crash. Eadric was alone again. Just how he liked it.

It didn't matter what they thought. Those men were irrelevant in the grand scheme of things, even if it was distressing to realise they perhaps saw him for what he was. Eadric would not spare another moment dwelling on it. He had a journey to plan and men to muster, and at the end of it all, perhaps a long siege.

He wondered if Ælfric had indeed survived his clash with the Danes, and if he had, would he be inclined to put up another fight? A siege of Porteceaster could last a long time, especially if the old man had time to prepare. Perhaps there were other means to force his submission should he feel like being brave. He would have to think on it.

Eadric was looking forward to it, though. He'd ensured Alaric was no longer among the living. Perhaps that was a weapon to be used, as it might sap Ælfric's resolve to learn his only…undamaged…heir had met a sudden and violent end. He'd have to evaluate once he got there. If he was of a mind to put up a fight, then telling him of Alaric's fate could only spur him toward continued resistance. He'd make a decision when the time came.

Some things were more certain. The king had agreed to his proposal to have Thurcytel placed in Hamptonscir as a possible reeve. That was positive, since he knew Thurcytel owed him and could thus be manipulated into continued obedience. It wasn't a huge win, and administrating the county was not the same as holding the kind of power that Ælfric enjoyed, but it was still the foothold Eadric had been looking for in extending his influence. Things were looking up.

Eadric reached the exit of the king's great hall. The two guards on watch unbarred and opened the solid oaken gates for him, allowing him to walk out into the night beyond. Eadric stepped through, wincing slightly as a damp chill washed over him. The stars were again on full display, the moon casting its gentle light over the slumbering city. He walked on briskly, hoping to dispel the cold, his footsteps continuing to echo, the paved courtyards and solid, stone buildings that made up Æthelred's seat of power ensuring sound carried far.

Lundenburg was seen as a place apart from the rest of the country, Eadric mused. Still protected and prosperous, Æthelred believed as long as he held it he would remain king, as if the land and people of England itself had little import if the capital yet stood. This was another error of his, one Eadric was happy to let him persist in. Indeed, the more the king became alienated from his own people, the more it aided Eadric in presenting himself as the single man he could trust.

This new tax, this heregeld, would exacerbate matters. The Welsh were unlikely to pay, but Eadric fully intended to have a force of his own cross the border and simply take what was owed by force. He'd be sure to see a share of the spoils remain in Mierce to pay the right people and line his own pockets. England, however, would require a more delicate touch. It was already taxed and resentful. Any additional burdens would be seen as yet another unjust imposition, but that in itself opened up new opportunities. Let Æthelred keep up the facade that the tax was to pay for a new army. It wouldn't work. Eadric would see to it that people heard a different story, one where the king was laying hands on the meagre fortunes of others to yet again pay off a foreign invader.

There would be outrage, that was certain. In raising the money to purchase the services of Thorkell, Æthelred would lose what little love remained in his much-maligned people. Aside from Eadric, of course. He would always be there as the king's obedient servant. And when Thorkell clashed with Svienn, out of the chaos would arise further opportunities. Æthelred would be a solitary king, alone without friends in a devastated land with mercenaries likely demanding more payment.

Yet Eadric's star would continue to rise. He had Mierċe. He had the king's daughter. He may soon have Hamptonscir, by proxy, at least.

What else might he eventually grasp?

VI

He couldn't tell night from day. Everything had faded and merged into a blur, his thoughts slipping in and out of consciousness seemingly at random. He had no idea how long he'd been here, trapped in this desolate limbo with nought but himself for company; a spirit without a body condemned to an existence of aimless drifting.

Sometimes he thought he heard things, muffled and distorted and impossible to place. Over time they became more distinct, the sounds echoing out of the grey nothingness of his surroundings into something recognisable. It was human speech. Words. Not his own, not his voice. A lighter tone, one at peace with itself, sometimes halting and exotic, spoken by somebody originally versed in an alien tongue from alien lands.

He felt like he should be able to do more, although why he could not say. In fact, he could not say much of anything. He knew. He'd tried, the results of his efforts thus far confined to a low, slurring rumble in his chest. That was something, at least, since he'd begun to forget he even had a body, believing himself to be nothing but a shade, cut off from anything as tangible as physical existence.

Yet the more he thought about such things, the more seemed to come back to him. He had a body, he was sure of that now. And it hurt. He wondered where the pain had even come from, thinking some mercy must have spared him from it when phasing in and out of the dark. The voice seemed to be becoming more insistent, too, as if whoever it was had a body of their own, outside of his, coming and going, with a regularity that seemed familiar.

The words were of significance. He'd said them himself many times, but the voice still sounded strange. Foreign. He heard it now, speaking softly yet with purpose:

"Our Father…in heaven,
Hallowed be thy…
Thy Kingdom…come.
…be done
On earth, as it is in heav…
Give us this day our daily bread. And forgive us our trespasses, as we forgive those that trespass against us. And lead us not into temptation, but deliver us from evil."

"Amen." He'd finished the prayer. He knew it was correct to say it. He'd said it before, often and on a regular basis. But why? More words now, still in that strange accent.

"Can you hear me, brother?"

He rumbled in his chest like before. He could do better than that.

"I hear…"

A sigh of relief. Then something visible; a hurried yet heartfelt gesture, a hand making a crossing motion across a chest and face. A kind face. Middling in years, short greying hair and concerned, gentle eyes. It spoke again, in that strange, awkward fashion, like it were unused to forming English words.

"Are you in pain?"

He was. His head was aching something fierce. He didn't know why he'd not felt it before, but he could now; the discomfort so severe he'd have thought nothing could numb it but death. Death. He remembered. He'd seen much of it. Somebody close to him, toppling backwards, despair and fear etched across their features, a spear protruding from the chest…an entire mass of men, screaming, roaring, and hacking at one another, bodies broken and falling, their last moments spent heaving and clawing at the unfeeling earth.

He sat up suddenly, a growl of pain emerging through gritted teeth. He fell backwards a second later, his head swimming and his vision blurring over. Then he slipped away again. Back into his disembodied state, or so it seemed. He saw somebody familiar there, the man he'd seen falling, now breathing his final, slow, rattling breath as he gazed upward, the life draining from his eyes.

This great ox of a man, beard and hair almost as red as the blood that poured from his wounds…he'd meant something. He'd mattered. They'd all mattered, these other men he saw fighting and falling with him, each one giving everything they had until their last was truly their last. A different kind of pain now made its presence known, deep and overpowering, aching through the heart. Horrific, smothering, impossible to bear.

The vision faded. The grey blur came back into view. Then a new sensation, something sharp and cold on his lips, trickling down his chin and then vanishing before it reached his neck. Then something soft, dabbing at his face. He could see again. The same strange man was there, a bowl in one hand and a cloth in the other.

"Are you thirsty?" the man asked, his voice still gentle.

"What happened?"

"I thought you might be able to help me with that," he responded. "But I don't want to tax you with questions. I think you've exerted yourself a great deal already."

He wasn't sure what that meant. But he could see far better now, and he could just about lift his chin and take in his surroundings. He'd been placed on some kind of ramshackle cot, a thick woollen blanket covering him up to his chest. The room was small and modest, with bare stone walls on all sides, save for a single wooden door several feet to his left and a narrow, arched window of stained glass facing his bed from about ten paces distant.

There was some kind of image worked into the glass, indistinct at this point, yet it comforted him to see it, despite the deep black backdrop of the night outside. The fellow tending to him was a source of calm also, seeming to radiate peace just with his presence. He would have his name from him.

"Who are you?"

"I am Father Dobron," came the reply.

"Where am I?"

"You are in our church."

"Porteceaster?" Why did he say that? Was that where he was from? He had a feeling it was.

"No, in the village of Offetuna…or what's left of it."

He didn't know where that was, but his words sounded ominous. Strangely enough, he had a feeling he knew what he was referring to, as if there was something terrible out there, something evil that needed to be fought. Is that how he'd ended up here? Was that how all those men had died?

"What's left of it? What happened? Where is Offetuna?"

"Eastengle," said the priest. "Our village is about ten miles from Gipeswic. Most people seem to remember us by how close we are to the town."

Eastengle. He was remembering now. An army he had to get to. He and the rest of his men. Gipeswic too. On fire, he could see it on the horizon, the smoke drifting over them on the breeze. The smell of ash, bitter and sickly as they advanced, him and Osmund, with Æthelstan and Eadric…

Eadric. He had to find that man. He had to find out what had happened. He'd told them to attack that camp. He'd left them in the woods and headed off with Æthelstan, saying they would attack from the east. Then Æthelstan and his men…all dead, like Thorkell had been expecting him. Like he'd been expecting them all.

"I need to change your bandage," said Father Dobron. He reached out and lifted his head slightly with one hand, moving with his other to prise something back from his face. He came away with what looked like a ragged piece of cloth, blemished in parts by a rust-coloured substance. He then leaned forward, filling his vision, as if to scrutinise the part of his face that was previously covered.

"Your wound is doing much better," he said happily. "The first few nights after I found you were difficult. You were feverish from the infection in your eye. I'm afraid I had to…"

What? What had he had to do?

"You should rest now," he insisted, changing the subject. "Are you able to tell me much on who you are?"

"I'm Alaric," he responded, the memories now flooding back in a veritable deluge. He didn't feel like telling him anything more. He was grateful to this man, if he had truly helped him, but he felt it was best to remain cautious until he found out where his real loyalties lay.

"It's good to finally meet you properly, Alaric." What did he mean by "finally"? Had he known of him before? How long had he been here?

"I've been with you for some time?"

"You have," replied Dobron. "I was out with Bill one night and…"

"Who?" interrupted Alaric.

"My horse," he clarified. "We were on the southern forest road. I thought there might be people heading to us to escape Gipeswic. Then I heard the fighting. It was too dangerous to approach, what with the heathens being as they are…but the next morning, everyone had left, and so I went into that camp. That's where I found you, in a ditch."

"How long ago?" Alaric asked with some urgency.

"You've been with me here for about a month."

A month! But the army! Ulfcytel! Young Osbert! What had become of them?! What had become of the rest of Eastengle?! He had to know. He had to get back to the army at Hringmere. If there was even an army to get back to.

He strained to sit up, his head swimming as he shifted position. Dobron placed a large yet gentle hand on his shoulder, steadying him whilst he struggled to stay upright. Alaric resisted falling backwards, fearing he'd be sent back to that dream-like blur to again contemplate his fallen brethren. His vision eventually cleared, coming back into focus with reassuring clarity.

That was good enough for him. He made a sudden move to exit his bed, kicking the blanket from his body and struggling to place his feet on the floor. He was all but naked aside from a roughly sewn nightshirt, the length of which extended just barely to the top of his knees. He felt a shock run up his legs when his feet hit the cold stone of the floor. It wasn't comfortable. But it confirmed again that he was alive. Now he'd see about standing up.

Dobron rushed to hold him upright as Alaric lumbered forward several paces, his trajectory only arrested by the priest's unusual strength. He stood motionless for a second, his left hand extended and resting on the door now facing him, Dobron supporting him around his right shoulder. His breathing was a mess, inhaling and exhaling in the manner of one who'd just run several miles rather than merely stood up from a bed. He would need to take things slower if he were to recover his full strength.

"You should get back in bed," Dobron said, his voice a little strained from the effort of holding him steady. Alaric continued to inhale and exhale forcefully, hoping the more air he got into his lungs, the more strength might eventually return to his muscles. It seemed to work, and before long the trembles in his legs had started to ease.

"Please, help me open this door?" Alaric asked, his voice hoarse from his exertions. Dobron aided him in shifting back a few steps before pulling the door inwards and open, a chill draft blowing in from beyond to replace the room's already frigid air. The two men hobbled unsteadily out into the nave of the church, Alaric's breathing still ragged. His vision again started to blur over, but Father Dobron somehow sensed his situation, manoeuvring him so he could rest up against a stone pillar.

Alaric slid to the floor, his strength failing him. He took the opportunity to again catch his breath, his sight gradually coming back into focus with each heaving gasp. He lifted his head, making the decision to review his surroundings. Imposing stone walls, interspersed every ten feet or so with smoothly arched windows filled with stained glass. Four pillars, strong and unadorned, rose up from the floor to meet a vaulted wooden ceiling, each one positioned close to the four corners of the nave and at right angles to each other. A worn stone step then led up to a simple altar, a pair of lit candles glowing warmly atop it.

But it was what lay just beyond that really caught the eye. The wall immediately behind the altar played host to not just a modest wooden cross but an assortment of holy icons painted directly onto the stone. Christ himself was depicted on the right, staring straight ahead, his right hand raised in blessing, his eyes deep and gentle. Just to his left was another image, this one of the Blessed Virgin Mary holding the Christ child to her chest; a simple yet profound display of holy maternity illuminated in gentle candlelight.

Another depicted Saint Joseph in his workshop, a boy Alaric assumed to be Jesus at his side. Joseph's gaze was cast downwards to look upon the young Christ, his arm extended so as to cradle the back of his head. Alaric had never seen such a perfect image of paternal protectiveness before. A dull ache emerged in his heart. If only his own son had lived.

"Are you all right, brother?" asked Dobron. He'd crouched down next to him out of concern. Alaric's face had indeed become flushed, his now sizeable beard and moustache failing to hide it entirely. He shook his head weakly, his voice again failing him under the weight of both physical and emotional turmoil. Father Dobron got up and headed swiftly away, passing through another door on the opposite side of the nave. He returned promptly, bearing a bowl of something alongside a large wooden cup.

"Please, have something to drink," he whispered, again squatting at his side. Alaric managed to take the cup in both hands, raising it to his lips. The water was cold, clear, and blissfully refreshing. He gulped it down, feeling some fortitude return to his limbs mere moments later.

Father Dobron seemed to be in his element here, having dutifully offered Alaric the bowl containing what looked and smelled like some kind of stew. He held that to his lips also, wolfing down the contents of what turned out to be a soupy mixture of barley, carrots, and torn chunks of bread. He let it settle, an impertinent belch, unfortunately, erupting from his stomach. He stared at Dobron in shame, expecting a rebuke for such a display, in church no less. The priest looked amused.

"I'm pleased to see you eat properly," he said. "For the first week of you being here, it was very difficult to get you to eat anything."

"What exactly happened to me?" Alaric asked, dabbing at his lips with the sleeve of his nightshirt. "I remember… falling after being struck…"

"Yes, I found you in a ditch just off the path inside the Dane camp," Dobron said. "Your head wound was…I didn't think you'd survive. But I had to try."

Alaric reached up towards the side of his head, his fingers probing tentatively. His skull felt rough and uneven, the hair on one side of his scalp cut short, presumably to allow Dobron to tend his injury. Something felt off and had done since he'd awoken, as if his limbs were always slightly outside his control and he was unable to judge the distance between himself and whatever was before him. He traced the jagged contours of his injury further towards his face, eventually bringing his hand around to touch his left eye.

And he saw nothing. His hand was hidden from view like it was not even there at all. He moved it further to the right until he could see it…then back left…nothing. He was blind in one eye. He swallowed, anxious and saddened. Dobron looked on, his expression remorseful.

"I am sorry," he said simply. "The injury was severe… you were unresponsive, and then a fever came on as the infection set in. I had to remove…"

"You cut out my eye?"

"It had withered and was rotting within you. You would have died if the infected flesh had not been removed. I was terrified of hurting you or causing more damage as I worked, but you never stirred. The damage was extensive, even without my doing. Even if the fever had somehow passed without my intervention…I don't think you'd have recovered your sight."

"Can I see it?" Alaric asked.

"Perhaps we should just get you back to be…"

"I would like to see, Father."

"Alright," Dobron submitted begrudgingly. He got to his feet and headed off, once again passing through the door to what Alaric assumed was some kind of storage room. He returned about two minutes later, bearing a crude hand mirror. Alaric took it from him as he again crouched next to him. The glass was dusty and blemished in places, like it had long been left in the damp.

It served its purpose regardless, conveying a reflection both familiar and unsettlingly different. The left side of his face was a mess, his hair cut away and his skull appearing almost dented inwards. The eye socket, whilst otherwise intact, was empty and sealed shut, the flesh looking like it had been somehow knitted together. It could be worse, but it looked horrific, and he'd have it covered up in the meantime lest he terrify everyone he came across.

His appearance was otherwise what he expected for a man who'd been incapacitated for some time. His hair and beard had grown long, although the latter did not fully cover the damage done to his right cheek, which was an ugly mass of jagged scar tissue, pock-marked and brutal. He ran his fingers gently across it, noting the contrast between the smoothness of his fingertips and the twisted, marred flesh.

He remembered now. That Dane in the camp. The one with the sharpened teeth. He'd tried to bite his face off, doing his best to strangle him as he went about it. Alaric had introduced him to his fists before splitting his skull with his blade. The memory pleased him. He'd delivered a little justice that night, at least.

Justice. That was something this land needed more of. And he was a just man, he knew that, or at least he aspired to be. And now, more than ever, it was the duty of just men to act. He raised himself up and off the ground, using the pillar to partially lift himself whilst Dobron supported him by his right shoulder. He stood. He felt stronger, his skin prickling slightly in the chill night air. He'd been out of action for too long. He had to do something.

"How far are we from the village of Wretham?" he asked. It was time to get moving. He had to find out what had happened to the army. He had an ill feeling on how things may have turned out. He needed to know for certain.

"I'm not sure," Dobron said after a thoughtful pause. "Perhaps two days travel…but please, at least stay the rest of the night. It's been days since you've been out of bed."

"Days?" asked Alaric, confused. "You mean I've been out of bed here before? I wasn't unconscious the entire time?"

Father Dobron shook his head. That worried Alaric. He had absolutely no memory of this place, let alone having been up and moving about here previously. Perhaps his injury was even more severe than the scarring and loss of an eye. But there was still no time to lose. He couldn't let fear deter him from finding out what had happened at Hringmere.

"Where are my clothes?" he asked, looking down bashfully at his white nightshirt, his bare, hardened knees and huge feet giving him an almost comedic appearance.

The priest hurried back across the nave and again passed through the doorway he'd been through previously. He came back momentarily, bearing two armloads of clothing with him. He gently handed his burden to Alaric, watching him carefully for any sign of sudden weakness that may indicate he was about to fall again. Alaric took the clothes from him eagerly. His scuffed, well-worn boots, woollen breecs, and most importantly his knee-length scaled mail shirt were all here, as was his green cloak, albeit looking a tad worse for wear.

No sword, though. Nor his prized helmet. If he remembered correctly, he'd felt it break when he'd been struck, the metal parting in two under the force of the dreadful impact. It had saved his life. He simply would not have much of a head left if he'd not been wearing it.

"Did you see a sword when you found me?"

"I'm sorry, I did not, brother," said Dobron, shaking his head sadly. "I did not stay long, I'll admit. I was concerned with whoever could yet be saved…it was just you and…"

"Somebody else?" Alaric interrupted, hope surging in his heart. Had one of his men made it? Perhaps Osmund, by some miracle? Could it somehow be his wounds hadn't been as severe as they'd looked?

"Yes, yes, there is somebody else here from the battle… we should go back to your roo…"

"No, Father, please," Alaric again interjected, his eagerness to find out the truth getting the better of his manners. "Who else is here? One of my men?"

The priest fell silent, a look of near-panic on his face. Alaric noticed his eyes drift nervously in the direction of the room he'd just come from. His man must be in there, resting, most likely. Alaric hurriedly set down the bundle he held and strode off towards the still-open door. He felt stronger now. Purpose had reinvigorated him.

He stumbled through the doorway into a room not dissimilar in dimensions to the one he'd awoken in earlier. This one appeared to be serving as an ad hoc storeroom, the far side to Alaric's left being filled with an assortment of kegs, barrels, boxes, and baskets that presumably allowed Father Dobron to live as he had been. The view to his right was far more interesting. Under another stained glass window lay a cot, again similar to the one Alaric had been given, this one still occupied by a sleeping human figure.

Alaric made his way over to him, placing a hand on his shoulder and rolling him onto his back. He beheld his face. A ragged, blond beard that reached to his chest. Shoulder-length hair of a similar colour. A jagged scar cutting across his visage at a diagonal from his chin to the edge of his right eye. Fine-looking eyes, brilliant blue, now staring upwards in fear.

Alaric recognised him. This was the Dane who had killed one of his men in the opening seconds of their charge on the gate. Alaric had sliced off his hand for that and then kicked him unconscious as he begged on his knees for mercy. His compatriots must have assumed he was dead and left him only for Father Dobron to find him. The priest had no idea how dangerous these people were. Alaric would have none of it.

He grabbed the man by the collar of his nightshirt, hauling him up and hurling him to the floor. Father Dobron was there, attempting to impose himself between Alaric and the fallen Dane, who had begun to gabble something in a panic at being so rudely awoken. Alaric eased Dobron aside, the priest attempting to take hold of his arm whilst imploring him to stop what he was doing. He ignored him, instead kicking the Dane in the back and heaving him to his feet.

The man put up a feeble struggle whilst Alaric dragged him from the room. Father Dobron was by now objecting strenuously, demanding Alaric cease with whatever it was he had planned. Alaric turned his head to speak to him when the Dane suddenly smashed his sole remaining fist into his jaw. He recovered quickly, manoeuvring around Father Dobron to again grab the Dane by his collar, a split second later butting him in the face with his forehead.

The Dane tumbled back, tripping upon the stone step and slumping awkwardly onto the floor just in front of the altar. Alaric was on him in a flash, smashing his right fist into his nose. It broke with an audible crunch, an eruption of blood and spittle saturating his beard. He continued to struggle, trying to shift Alaric's weight off his chest, both his fist and bandaged stump hammering at his sides. Alaric hit him again with his left, this time across the jaw, the impact yielding a rush of blood from the mouth as the Dane accidentally bit down on his own tongue.

Alaric unleashed a flurry of punches, pummelling his opponent in a frenzy of resurgent hate. He lost control, feeling on some instinctual level that he was back fighting with Osmund and the others to clear the gate and escape the camp. The Danes had to be defeated, even if it meant killing every last one, with any and all methods he had at his disposal. The priest had no idea who he'd brought back to his church. Alaric would set things right, ensuring his safety and taking some small revenge for his men in the process.

He delivered one, two, three, four more blows, his fists raining down mechanically as he set to work demolishing his foe's face upon the stone slabs of the church. He raised the bloodied, scuffed knuckles of his right fist to strike yet again, his teeth clenched and bared, only to find himself unable to move. Father Dobron had appeared from behind him and looped his arm up and around Alaric's right, the priest's left arm also now held tight across his neck in a bear-like embrace.

"Please, stop this, brother," he said softly, his manner astonishingly calm considering what was happening. "I do not know what has moved you to do this, but I cannot let you continue."

Alaric decided to make a contest of it, attempting to break free of Dobron's hold and finish what he'd started. He pulled his head up and back, trying to flex his shoulders in a way that would ideally weaken Dobron's grip around his neck. Then he saw them. The holy icons on the wall. The face of Jesus, looking down upon the struggling men in front of Him, their forms twisted in a heap of rage and hurt.

He didn't know if it was the way the candlelight was playing across the surface of the image or something else, yet Christ looked different than he had done earlier. He'd looked peaceful then, but his previously gentle, warm countenance had now changed to one of profound sadness. His gaze seemed to meet Alaric's, and his hand, although still raised in a blessing, now signified protest, as if commanding him to desist.

Alaric averted his eyes, catching sight of the Dane's battered face in the process. The man was a mess, Alaric's furious onslaught having reduced his visage to a bloody ruin of weeping bruises and blunt, brutal lacerations. Tears were pouring from swollen and bloodshot eyes, a faint sound, desperate and pleading, barely audible from his burst, split lips. Both his arms, intact or otherwise, were raised up to his face in a futile attempt to ward off further blows, his limbs weak and trembling as a frightened child.

Alaric exhaled slowly, his fist unclenching. He again looked up to behold the sorrowful face of Christ. Dobron sensed him relent, gently releasing him from his powerful grip. Alaric rose unsteadily, his strength again seeming to ebb from him as he took in the situation for what it was. He'd spared this man before for the sake of mercy. Now he'd brutalised him before the face of his Lord in the name of old scores.

Shame rose up from within, the sensation soon spreading to cover his entire body with regret. He looked on mournfully whilst Father Dobron attempted to tend to the Dane's wounds, the priest's hands working with a tenderness that defied the fury of Alaric's assault. He could stand no more, aghast at what he'd wrought in a house of God. He turned, striding towards the doors at the far end of the church. He heaved one aside just far enough for him to slip through and ventured into the night beyond.

The cold was a shock. He assumed he'd been indoors for his entire time here, enjoying the relative warmth of his room and blankets. Outside, the night air was almost unbearable, the damp chill reaching right into the marrow of his bones. He endured it well, shivering all the same as he took in his environs, a slight drizzle pattering off the stonework around him.

So this was Offetuna. Obscured by night and clouds that hid any moonlight, he couldn't see much of interest from his vantage point atop the short stone steps leading up to the church, although the village seemed untouched by the troubles that otherwise beset the rest of Eastengle.

From what he could see, there was a wide, muddy path leading away that carried on for some distance, its contours gradually vanishing into the gloom of what looked like some kind of market square. Houses of wood and thatch had been constructed around it, their unspectacular forms solidly reassuring in the dark of night. His view remained poor, for not a single light could be observed from the dwellings beyond, making him wonder if the entire settlement was either in repose or empty altogether.

Wide expanses of what were presumably fields for crops lay on either side of the village. Alaric couldn't see if anything was growing there, but he imagined they were unattended and gradually falling prey to weeds and brambles. What looked like woodland, dark and foreboding, lay beyond, the sound of the wind in the trees sharply audible despite the distance.

He slid to his knees, the cold, wet stone as uncomfortable as he could expect against his bare skin. He took to prayer, his hands clasped in front of him, imploring God to forgive his sins and give him the strength to face the trials ahead. He received little comfort. His thoughts proved difficult to gather, the prayers he knew by heart feeling empty and forced. All the same, he remained like this for some time, on his knees in the rain, enduring his own spiritual desert, his heart aching for a resolution that would not come.

He opened his eye, frustrated, and stared out and ahead at the path snaking its way to the centre of the village. He wondered where it might ultimately lead. Away from here, that was a given, to places he needed to be. His wife would be missing him. He missed her. He even missed little Brandon. That was a good sign, he thought. He'd softened to the boy. For a long time, he'd found it difficult, considering the manner of his…conception. He'd be sure to mention how he'd been in his thoughts to Æva. And Brandon, of course.

That was assuming he'd get to see them again. His wife almost certainly feared him dead. Æva would always worry, but now she had real reason to be concerned. He had to find a way to get word to her that he was alive. But first, he had to find out what had happened to Ulfcytel and his army. He felt a newfound sense of urgency, the chill raindrops and piercing damp awakening him from his despondency. He'd done wrong tonight, for which he must atone, but he wouldn't waste any more time. He'd been out of action for weeks. He had to get moving.

He rose and then turned, gently easing the church doors open and passing back inside. The place was again peaceful. Father Dobron was visible up ahead and knelt in prayer before the altar. He knew not where the Dane was, but he suspected the priest had put him to bed after tending to him, and the door to the storeroom now looked firmly shut.

Dobron rose upon hearing Alaric approach. He turned, his expression tranquil, like nothing had happened and all was well. He looked Alaric up and down as he stood before him, wet and shivering slightly from his time outside.

"Are you all right, brother?" he asked.

"I would like to apologise for my behaviour," Alaric began, his tone contrite and serious. "I lost control. I lost a lot of people not so long ago. That man who you have taken in was there. He must answer for his crimes. But that doesn't mean I'll do murder in a church."

Dobron didn't reply initially, his eyes becoming thoughtful. Alaric spied the painted face of Christ just over his shoulder, his expression once more one of gentleness and warmth. Alaric wondered if he'd been imagining things earlier, but he doubted it. Father Dobron finally spoke.

"You will be wanting to take him with you when you leave?"

"Yes," Alaric said sternly, "for he cannot remain here. He's dangerous; although you have my word, I will not harm him myself."

"Somebody else will harm him?" Dobron replied, an eyebrow raised quizzically.

"He's a Dane, Father. Part of an invading army. He killed one of my men in front of me. Justice must be done."

"By delivering him to those who will kill him?"

"It might not come to that," said Alaric, slightly exasperated now. "But I must get back to Hringmere to find out what happened to our army. I can't leave this man with you here. It wouldn't be safe."

"He has not harmed me," Dobron said bluntly. "He's been with me for as long as you have. His wound was less severe than yours, so he's helped me care for you. He's prayed with me. We manage to make ourselves understood to each other. He's talked about our faith. I don't doubt he came to this land as a warrior and did wrong. But the violent man you describe to me is not the one we have here with us tonight."

Alaric had no immediate reply. He didn't doubt the priest, believing it extremely unlikely he'd have any reason to lie. But why would the Dane do as he'd described? Why had he not just killed them both as soon as he'd recovered his strength, stolen what he could, and then fled to rejoin Thorkell? These were good questions, but he didn't have time to waste on them. He had to get going, and this man was coming with him.

"Father, I can't leave him here. He has to come with me."

"He is in no condition to travel after tonight," Dobron said firmly. "And I will not have him moved."

Alaric was at a loss. He couldn't compel the priest to do what he asked. That would be outrageous. But how could he leave him here with a man he knew could be murderously violent? What about justice for the Saxon he'd killed?

"Father, I beg you, this ca…"

"I will not let you take him," Dobron said, drawing himself up to his full height. "Do what you must. He stays here. You will have to physically remove me to get to him."

Alaric shook his head weakly. He had no time. The Dane only had one hand. He was unarmed. He'd now been severely beaten. He likely was no threat to anyone. But he had killed one of his men. That was a score Alaric would return to settle. For now, though, he wouldn't physically fight a man of God just to get to him. He'd leave it in the Lord's hands and return here when he could. He'd be sure to.

"All right, Father, I will not confront you on this. But I will come back here when I can. Forgive me, but...do you know if anyone in the village would be willing to loan me a horse so I can travel? I'm pressed for time and must make haste."

"Everyone is gone, brother," Dobron replied. "They fear the Danes. Word got to them that Gipeswic had fallen, and so they left. I remain."

"So you've always been here, all alone, since I and your other... guest..."

"Yes, for longer even," Dobron nodded. "I cannot abandon our church. I felt I might be of help here rather than on the road seeking safety. Had I left, I would never have found you."

Alaric appreciated his dedication. Any other man might have fled with everyone else, preferring to abandon his post than face danger. Father Dobron clearly took his calling very seriously. And it had paid off. Alaric owed him his life, a debt he intended to repay someday.

"That's commendable, Father," Alaric said sincerely. "In that case, I'm assuming there are at least some supplies around that could help me in my journey?"

"There are, but I wish you would rest a little longer," Dobron pleaded. "I need to cover your wound again, and you've shown signs of recovery before, only to slip back into unconsciousness. Travel is a risk."

He couldn't disagree there. It was for such a reason he allowed the priest to again bandage his head, Alaric sitting patiently on the step leading up to the altar as he worked. He noted he went to some effort to cover his now empty left eye socket; a wise move, given Alaric didn't want to horrify everyone he came across. He was emphatic that he would not stay another night, though. Dobron eventually relented, recognising his determination.

Alaric changed back into his old clothes and armour, his limbs aching and stiff after his long stay in bed. He missed his sword. It had been a precious gift from his father, made in the forges at Porteceaster for him and him alone. Dobron seemed to notice his loss and brought him a mid-length seax from his storeroom. He didn't know why the priest had such a thing, but he appreciated the gift. It wasn't a fit replacement for his sword, but it was far better than nothing at all.

Dobron led him past the altar and through another side door towards the rear of the church. They passed through several dark rooms, the priest eventually obtaining a torch from somewhere and lighting it to guide their steps. They moved on through another door - this one unadorned and easily missed - into the night air outside, emerging into a small cemetery carved out of the surrounding forest. The church here backed onto an expanse of woodland, the path he'd seen previously cutting past the cemetery before vanishing into the thicket. The sound of the wind in the trees again soothed his spirits, the faint light from Dobron's torch casting a gentle glow across the modest gravestones and verdant, overgrown grass of their surroundings.

Dobron strode out into the night, moving along the path towards the village proper, his arm held slightly aloft to better light the way. Alaric followed, pulling the hood of his cloak up lest the ambient drizzle soak his bandages. They moved past the length of the church and several cottages before coming to a makeshift stable, or what was in actuality more of a fenced and sheltered enclosure. There were two horses left here, and they each turned in curiosity at the approaching men, their dark eyes twinkling in the torchlight. Father Dobron led him to the second steed, this one a healthy, sturdy-looking beast, a pale grey in colour and likely used to heavy farm work. He began the process of tacking up the horse, asking Alaric what he intended to name him whilst he worked.

"I have no idea," Alaric replied, "I'm assuming his owner won't object to me taking him?"

"If he returns, I'll tell him it was an emergency and pay him," Dobron said, gently leading the steed out onto the pathway they'd come from. He seemed capable with animals, the other horse, a darker, brown version of this one, presumably being his own. "Bill" was his name, if Alaric recalled correctly. It suited him.

"In that case, I'll return him when I can, so you're not out of pocket," Alaric said, not wanting anyone to be in debt because of him. He already owed the priest his life. There was no sense in adding more to it.

"As you say," Dobron replied, all three of them now standing on the pathway in the rain. Dobron suddenly turned and headed off back towards the church, asking Alaric if he would wait a few minutes whilst he collected something. Alaric complied, staring at the horse's stoic face whilst he did and trying his best to think of a name for him. Nothing would come. The rain was intensifying, the darkness of night so enveloping his horse had become a dark, pointy-eared outline in his sole remaining eye. He'd have to get used to his diminished vision.

Alaric spied the light of Dobron's torch reappearing from the church entrance, the man hurrying to return to him with what looked like some kind of travelling satchel. He passed it to Alaric when he reached him, slightly out of breath from his exertions. Alaric looked inside before strapping it to his shoulder. A bounty of several stale loaves of bread and one very battered-looking waterskin lay within. It would serve him.

"I want to thank you sincerely, Father," Alaric said, offering him his hand to shake. Dobron took it and passed him the torch, shaking his hand gently in his sizeable grip.

"God be with you," he said in reply, his voice always so soft yet easily heard. Alaric remembered he'd never asked him where he was from. His accent was a mystery, but it was definitely neither English nor Danish. Dobron looked slightly perplexed when he inquired, shuffling his feet uneasily.

"I am from the East." A simple answer. He could have guessed that, though.

"Not Denmark, of course?" Alaric asked.

"No, I am not Danish."

"German?"

Father Dobron chuckled now, amused at the line of questioning.

"No, I am from further east. The Lord called. I answered. Wherever he commands, I go."

Alaric would have to be content with that. His geography wasn't the best. He knew the Greeks had a great empire to the east, but Dobron didn't look or sound Greek, at least as far as he could tell. Perhaps they'd talk on this if they met again and were out of the rain.

Alaric mounted his horse, gripping the reins with his right hand whilst holding his torch aloft in his left. Dobron told him his best bet was to ride straight through the village and onward once he reached the market square. He'd then come out onto the main road to Theodford, yet the priest was anxious he avoid it and stick to the woodland. The open countryside wasn't safe, he said. Alaric was inclined to agree.

"Thank you for saving my life, Father," Alaric said solemnly. "I'll be back. I give you my word."

Dobron smiled modestly and nodded, making the sign of the cross in blessing. A man of few words. Alaric turned his horse and headed towards the square at a slow gait, his expression forlorn beneath his hood. He looked back once. Dobron was nowhere in sight, the dark outline of the church only just visible in the distance.

"Wherever the Lord commands, he goes," Alaric muttered, riding on through the village and into the woods beyond.

VII

The journey was going as expected. He'd ridden through the night, his torch burning well enough and resisting the downpour, the hissing, fizzing sound of raindrops hitting the flames becoming part of the forest ambience. Dawn was just breaking when he put it out, the first rays of daylight rendering a torch unnecessary. It had been a risk using it to begin with. Anyone could have seen him through the trees and responded accordingly. But they hadn't. He was still alive, and he intended to remain so.

Alaric was now travelling at a robust speed along the mud and gravel route heading north from Offetuna. He had to make good time, and that meant keeping up the pace, even if it did mean taking the risk of using the roads. He fancied he could smell smoke on the wind, and this was confirmed around mid-morning when he chanced upon a burned-out hamlet. He'd not been able to see much as he approached, but when he crested an overlooking hill, the now destroyed settlement had finally come into view. It was nothing but a ruin, the stench of scorched timber and thatch making his nostrils sting. He couldn't see any movement, nor even any bodies. He went down to investigate.

He moved his horse at a slow walk, noting how silent the place was, as if even nature itself was numb in the wake of the undoubtedly violent scenes that had played out here. The Danes must have come perilously close to Offetuna as they headed north. Alaric wasn't sure how good their knowledge of England's geography was, but he was guessing they may not know the location of each and every village. They'd probably come across this nameless settlement by accident, setting it alight upon passing through. Alaric couldn't see anyone, dead or alive. He hoped the inhabitants had fled in time.

He paused and dismounted from his horse when he came upon the remains of a chapel. This had no doubt been the centre of life for those that lived here, but it was well and truly gutted now. The roof had collapsed inwards, leaving the rain to pour in unhindered, the interior otherwise scorched and empty aside from a blackened wooden crucifix still attached to the far wall.

Alaric went inside and prayed for a few moments, feeling the need to restore some sanctity to this forlorn place. He'd just finished and had turned to leave when he spied his horse nibbling on the turf outside; a reminder that he himself also needed sustenance. He took a swig from his waterskin, stuffing down a torn mouthful of bread for good measure. It tasted better than he'd feared. He genuflected before the crucifix and crossed himself before departing. Time to move on.

Several more hours passed on the road, his mount keeping up a good pace without complaint. He'd never been a good rider, but with one eye, it was even more difficult. There was something about distances that continued to confound him, making him feel like he was constantly misjudging objects as either too far or too close. He'd begun to worry on how this might affect his abilities as a warrior when he almost slid from the saddle, having become distracted by fearful daydreams of losing sword fights and perhaps his life.

He rebuked himself. He had to focus on the task at hand and the real risks rather than the ones created by his imagination. Such censure didn't help, only reminding him of how vulnerable he felt, especially now he was without his sword. For one foolish moment, he thought to turn around and again find Thorkell's camp and retrieve his blade. Osmund deserved a burial too. Then he realised the bodies of his men had been exposed to the elements for over a month, if Father Dobron's claim as to how long he'd been at the church was accurate. He shook his head, saddened by the thought. It was truly a mournful sight to imagine. They all deserved a proper Christian burial, but he had no time. He'd be sure to see to it once this conflict was resolved.

The evening was darkening the sky when he passed through another hamlet; this one also deserted and burned largely to ruin like the last. He didn't stop, riding straight through and continuing on well after night had fallen. This was ill-advised, he knew, and his horse was no doubt hungry and fatigued. He made a point of attempting to relight his torch, in doing so realising he had no means to make a spark and ignite much of anything. He discarded it and kept going, willing to risk the darkness a little longer.

He was just thinking about making camp when the ash smell returned. There was a solid chance another settlement was up ahead, destroyed like the others, more than likely, but still a place he might be able to find clues on the fate of Ulfcytel and his army. He upped the pace, spurring his horse into a gallop, eager to find out if anyone remained within what was most likely Theodford.

Harsh voices suddenly echoed from somewhere in the near distance. Alaric signalled urgently for his steed to stop, the beast's hooves clattering abruptly as it drew itself to a halt upon the road. They both listened intently, the horse's pointed ears fully erect, the pair of them staring ahead into the not-so-empty darkness. That sound again. Human voices, one calling to another in the night. Then another. And yet more. It wasn't English. And they were coming closer. That meant trouble.

He didn't waste time. He hurried his mount off-road and into some woodland to the north east, slowing to a walk so they might negotiate their way through the trees. None of this bode well. If Theodford really had been attacked, that would mean Ulfcytel had been unable to stop it. That could only mean he'd been defeated in the field, unless something truly unexpected had happened that had caused him to retreat without giving battle. He assumed Ulfcytel would have learned he and Æthelstan had failed to kill Thorkell fairly soon after the Danes started heading north. He would have had his own scouts, and the enemy weren't exactly subtle when they were on the move.

Alaric was trying hard to rationalise holding out at least some hope when he almost hit his head on a branch. They'd lost the daylight. It made no sense to be stumbling about on horseback in the forest like this. There was no sign of pursuit, and the foreign voices had faded with distance and then stopped. It was time to dismount and rest.

He was deep in whichever stretch of woodland he'd blundered into, the sound of the rain now muffled and remote as it drenched the forest canopy above. He settled down underneath the protective expanse of a large ash tree, drawing his cloak about himself to provide shelter from those raindrops that made it through the blanket of leaves on high.

His horse was snuffling at some undergrowth in the darkness, most likely both hungry and thirsty after their spirited ride through the desolate countryside. Alaric approached his newfound friend, sitting on his haunches and pouring out some water from his supply into the palm of his hand. The horse drank eagerly, a great rumbling of what Alaric could only describe as "happy horse noises" emerging from its throat.

He did this several more times, ensuring the beast received at least some relief from its thirst. He then resumed his place huddled under the ash tree, helping himself to another hunk of bread. Sleep came sooner than he'd thought, his repose occasionally disturbed by the cry of a fox or the rustling of creatures unknown. At one point, he almost killed his own horse, leaping up and drawing his seax at the thunderous sound of it lying down next to him. He chastised himself for his nerves, settling back down only to awaken perhaps an hour later, a scattered, gradual eruption of birdsong stirring him from his slumber. Dawn was coming. It was time to go.

He led his horse by the reins and moved ahead, thinking it wiser to navigate on his own feet rather than risk braining himself on another tree branch. After about another hour of walking, his situation had improved, the darkness of the forest receding in the face of dawn's early light. He remounted his horse, upping his previously cautious pace and again confident on his bearings now he could see the rising sun.

Another two hours or so passed, the morning light spreading out through the forest with a gentle yet stark majesty. This was indeed a wonderful place; the trees standing tall and uncompromising in their shifting, emerald beauty, a variety of tenacious wildflowers covering the earth in a veritable carpet of colour. Life was thriving here, as if all was right in the world and always would be, the delicate birdsong melding effortlessly with the soft sigh of the wind through the trees and the gentle patter of raindrops on leaves.

They plodded on, man and beast, eventually reaching a shallow, fast-flowing stream. Alaric dismounted, allowing his steed to drink its fill and graze on the dew-soaked vegetation that covered the banks. He finished off what water he had left, kneeling down a second later to refill his skin from the crisp, clear waters.

It was almost easy to forget his predicament, surrounded by such natural beauty. In any other situation, he'd be inclined to linger here, appreciating the company of his faithful beast and their newfound environs. Not today. Despite nature's view of things, not all was right with the world. He allowed his still-nameless companion to graze for another few minutes before he climbed back into the saddle, the pair of them again heading north west at some speed. Eventually, the forest started to thin out, the trees gradually giving way to a verdant, rain-drenched meadow extending as far as he could see.

He caught sight of a blemish on this otherwise pristine view in the form of a well-maintained stone and gravel road snaking its way north. Alaric recognised it in an instant. He'd travelled this very road just weeks ago on his way to Ulfcytel, he and his men marching purposefully to what they'd hoped would be battle and glory. He hurried onward, driving his horse into a galloping advance across the meadows.

They soon moved onto the road proper, the sound of hooves on stone sharp and echoing on the otherwise deserted thoroughfare. They charged on like this for some time, Alaric not wanting to slacken the pace now he was so close to discovering the army's fate. They cleared a slight rise in the terrain, the road arcing up past a copse of trees to reveal one of the saddest sights Alaric had ever seen.

Hringmere. The lake and the heathland expanded out before him as he remembered, although now it hosted a different spectacle. The camp was a wreck; its canvas structures collapsed and ruined, the once clear expanse immediately ahead of the old earthworks littered with thousands of corpses. The ruins of Wretham were just visible on the horizon, charred and broken, like the settlements he'd passed through on his way here. The Danes had been thorough.

He spurred his horse on, rushing down the roadway with all possible speed. He'd first met Osbert here, over there by the trees he'd only just hurtled past. The young man had been elated at the sight of his warriors marching to join his lord's army, and he'd done everything he could to make them feel welcome, despite certain awkward moments Alaric would rather forget. He prayed as he clung to his mount, hoping beyond hope that even if the situation was as dire as it looked, Osbert might have somehow survived.

He slowed his horse when they came close to the earthen "ring" that made up the camp's muster field. The entire area, road included, was thick with bodies, the ambient stench enough to turn the stomach in moments. Alaric dismounted, making his way over to the edge of the outer ditch that was originally intended to protect the earthworks from assault. The Danes had tried to take it by storm, that was evident, and the ditch itself was now home to a number of dead men, their broken bodies pierced with arrows or impaled on spears thrown from above.

The field immediately ahead of the ditch was absolutely choked, the dead lying so thickly they looked as if to claw at each other in a now silent struggle. Even in death, peace had eluded them; their rotted, decomposing faces twisted into snarling masks of pain and hatred. Alaric was having trouble telling Saxon from Dane, so intense had the fighting been, but he could see that at some point the English force had come undone, although whether it was from superior numbers or simple ferocity, he could not tell. Their losses had clearly been severe.

They'd not made it easy for the Danes, though. One huge, well-armoured Saxon warrior lay collapsed on his back, a broken spear protruding from his midriff. At least two Danes were dead at his feet, likely from his hand, the axe he'd been wielding now ruined and split from one bone-shattering impact after another.

A memory stirred. Judging from the look of his armour and the size of his war axe, this was one of Ulfcytel's own personal guards, of the calibre he'd encountered outside his pavilion prior to their first meeting. That meant Ulfcytel had committed himself to battle with his own retinue. But where was he?

Alaric stumbled back over to his horse, the smell from the morass of tangled corpses making his head swim. He climbed back into the saddle and headed north, eventually coming to the western road and turning right into the old camp. The rain was still coming down, almost as heavily as it had when he'd first come here, but unlike then the fortifications were now totally abandoned. More dead men lay here, scattered about the mess of timber barricades that was the western entrance, the ground beyond littered with refuse and demolished, waterlogged tents.

They continued on, the camp eerily quiet, the only sounds the pattering of the rain and the wet clop-clop of hooves heaving through mud. They soon reached the location of the old smithy, the once homely place providing no comfort since it had been torn down and the forge abandoned. To the north lay the ruins of Wretham, and immediately to his right was the entrance to the ringed muster field. Alaric remembered the welcome they'd received when he'd first come here. The cheering. The clashing of spears on shields.

It had stirred the heart. He wondered how many, if any, of those brave, jubilant souls were still among the living.

He dismounted, heading through the ring wall and into the muster field, hoping Ulfcytel's pavilion might still be intact and willing to yield evidence on his whereabouts. The place was devoid of human life, the barrels of supplies ransacked or moved elsewhere entirely. There were a few bodies present, all displaying the marks of callous violence, one fallen Dane missing his head entirely. Alaric smiled grimly at the sight of it.

Ulfcytel's pavilion was up ahead, looking a little worse for wear in the rain. Inside, everything was as it had been; the map table still present, the candles burnt out and extinguished. A plethora of plates and cups also littered the table, prompting memories of that last toast Alaric had shared with Ulfcytel, Osbert, Æthelstan…Osmund. As expected, he couldn't find the keg of what seemed to have been Ulfcytel's own personal supply. The Danes had probably drunk it all to celebrate their victory.

He was at a loss on how to proceed. The English had been soundly defeated here, and Ulfcytel was nowhere to be found. Theodford, Wretham, and what looked like all other nearby settlements had been destroyed. The Danes were also still present if the sounds he'd heard the evening before were anything to go by, and so he'd never be safe as long as he remained. He was alone, stranded in what was now enemy territory. He might as well be the last man alive in the world, such was the feeling of isolation.

There was only one option left to him, and that was to head back down south. He had a wife and child to take care of. It had also occurred to him that his father might be in danger. He'd seen little evidence that the main force of the Hamptonscir fyrd had fought here, but it was very possible his father and their army had been in the area at the time. He needed to find out for sure.

Alaric exited the muster field and remounted his horse. They turned around and headed back the way they'd come, both hanging their heads low in resignation. They left the sorry remains of the once thriving camp, following the road back towards the forest. He'd again avoid Theodford, not wanting to encounter enemy patrols. They continued swiftly, Alaric sneaking a look behind him as Hringmere receded into the distance. The sight made his heart ache. That stretch of rain-soaked heathland had represented the hope of a nation. Now it was just another place of butchery and defeat.

His morose thoughts almost cost him his life. When he turned back around to wisely face his direction of travel, he saw three riders on the road ahead. They'd spotted him, perhaps first seeing him earlier and following, and were heading towards him in some haste, yelling as they went. It wasn't English. And it wasn't friendly.

He decided in favour of reckless bravery. He spurred his steed into charging straight towards them, hoping they'd be surprised by such an aggressive move. They were, shouting in alarm, all three of them parting ranks to avoid the galloping horse and Saxon that rushed by. Alaric roared defiantly when he passed them, getting a good look at the closest man in the process. Dane. No doubt there.

Yet as startled as they'd been, they weren't in the mood for giving up. The trio came after him, pushing their mounts harder and harder, the horses whinnying in protest. Alaric did likewise, his steed needing little persuasion, such was the obviousness of the danger. They continued on like this, careering down the metalled road, the sound of hooves hammering stonework a sharp, rattling cacophony. Alaric laid eyes on the forest he'd emerged from just up ahead. It was his safest option. He could lose them in there, or confuse them enough so he might engineer a situation where he didn't have to fight them all at once.

He went for it, leaving the road and speeding across the meadows, the Danes giving chase. He reached the tree line soon after, charging through with lumbering haste, his pursuers attempting to follow. He could hear them cursing behind him, annoyed and flustered at his decision to enter the forest. He didn't waste time gloating, instead continuing his fast pace, knowing he had to get some serious distance between himself and the enemy before he could even think about slowing down.

Regrettably, Alaric had still not come to terms with the fact he only had one eye. He'd also failed to appreciate the complexities of riding at speed through a dense forest. More specifically, he'd entirely misjudged the distance between himself and the stout, overhanging branch of a flourishing oak, raising his arms in front of him at the last moment to protect his face from the impending collision. He fell, his forearms burning from the violent snap of the impact, landing flat on his back amidst a thankfully thick outgrowth of moss and the omnipresent wildflowers.

He lay there for several moments of agony, unable to move, the air knocked from his lungs. Panic rose in his chest. He felt like he was in danger of slipping into unconsciousness, once more descending into the dream-like state he'd been in for much of his time with Father Dobron. Then he was staggering to his feet, inhaling desperately and drawing his seax, the sound of approaching hooves demanding his attention.

The Danes burst into view all at once, their rumbling, snorting mounts crushing their way through the undergrowth. The riders laughed when they saw him, the sound mocking and cruel. They dismounted and drew their weapons, still gloating at his predicament, the heads of their axes having clearly seen some recent use.

Alaric planted his feet and assumed a high guard position, his seax raised in both hands. He silently rebuked himself, unable to fathom why it hadn't occurred to him to take a better weapon and perhaps a shield from Hringmere. The Danes continued guffawing and exchanging banter whilst they advanced, confident of an easy kill. Alaric thought to run or perhaps remount his horse, although where it was exactly he had no idea. It was too late now anyway.

The first Dane emitted a sudden shout and hurled himself forward, swinging his axe in a wild, sweeping arc towards Alaric's left shoulder. Alaric evaded the attack with a sudden leap of his own, bypassing the swing of his enemy and crashing into him at speed. He'd hoped to bring his seax down upon his opponent's head as he leapt, but he'd again misjudged the distance, instead finding himself pressed face to face with him and his arms entangled around his neck.

Alaric reacted quickly. He bit him, tearing at the man's nose whilst hammering his knee upwards to strike the groin. The Dane grunted and cursed, stumbling backwards and shaking his head. Alaric saw the opening he needed and lunged again. His aim was better, managing to curve his strike below the helmet, costing the Dane part of an ear and tearing a bloody chasm down the length of his face.

That was all the luck Alaric had. The second Dane was already on him, lashing out with a boot and kicking him in the side of his ribs. He stumbled, a third assailant then accosting him with a downward swing that he barely managed to parry. His blade embedded itself in the haft of the axe with a sharp crack, and so Alaric twisted his grip and pushed outward, hoping to tear the weapon from his foe's grip. He didn't see the end result as somebody smashed a shield into his side, knocking him completely off balance and staggering him into a nearby tree.

His left shoulder took the impact, the force of it sending a shock wave throughout his entire body. He managed to turn himself around, his back pressed against the tree, just in time to see the man he'd wounded earlier make a forward strike towards his face, his weapon extended straight and outwards to smash his jaw with the blunt head of his axe.

Alaric swung his seax up to parry, hoping to knock the incoming blow to one side. Again he misjudged the distance, unaccustomed still to fighting with one eye. He did, however, succeed in at least striking his opponent's weapon, although Alaric's defensive swing merely knocked the trajectory of the axe upward, the result being that he took the force of its head upon his bandaged and empty eye socket.

He collapsed in a heartbeat, slumping to the damp, grassy forest floor. His vision swum around him, unable to focus, the pain in the left side of his head overpowering. He felt himself roll over onto his side, clutching at his face and unable to do much else, such was his agony. More laughter. He couldn't see, but he could hear. The sound of heavy footsteps. Death was seconds away. He'd failed.

His thoughts drifted to his wife. He'd never see Æva again, never run his fingers through her red hair nor hold her close to his chest. He'd never get to be a proper father to Brandon, nor would he ever be able to find some resolution over the events surrounding his birth. He'd never give Æva another child either, as he'd not wanted to try again after the loss of their Alfred. There were so many things he'd wanted to do, yet all chances were now utterly spent. This was his end, and no amount of regret and remorse could change that. At least he'd gone out fighting. That was something.

The expected blow didn't land. Instead, a roar from multiple throats sounded from somewhere, which was soon followed by the sound of rushing footfalls and the snap-thud of weapons impacting on shields. Somebody cried out, pained and desperate, and a heavy thud came with it, like a body collapsing to the earth. A real tussle was afoot.

Alaric's vision cleared just enough for him to see a multitude of hazy forms moving and clashing around him. One fell suddenly, an outraged howl marking its departure from the fight. Another turned like it intended to flee, only to be struck from behind. It writhed on the ground, protesting, its voice piteous and fearful. A shape approached and appeared to strike it with a downward thrust of a spear, ending its lamentations permanently.

Alaric tried to sit up, the pain in his head intensifying with movement. Strong hands suddenly gripped him by the shoulders, heaving him upright and leaning him back against the tree. His hood was pulled back, something akin to water then splashing against his face, cool and refreshing. He felt the pain in his head ease by the smallest increments, his vision gradually sharpening back into focus.

Five figures, cloaked and hooded, stood around him, a sixth at his side and holding him steady with the pressing force of its arm. The three Danes lay dead around them, their wretched lives extinguished. Alaric felt uneasy, unable to see the faces of these men nor identify them by their armour. Were these people his saviours or something else?

"Are you alright, Alaric?"

The closest man had spoken. That voice. Speaking as if he knew him. He recognised it. Somebody he'd met before. Somebody he'd been worried about. They pulled their hood back, revealing a fatigued face, grim and hard yet youthful. Blue eyes, too, possessing some optimism, although faded, likely from having seen too much already. Unmistakable.

"Osbert!" Alaric gasped.

"It is," the young man replied, his old, infectious grin returning ever so slightly. "And we need to move. The Ealdorman Ulfcytel will want to speak with you."

VIII

Edmund made a feint to the left, shifting his feet and thrusting his spear so as to be able to recover and counter as needed. His opponent didn't fall for it, instead stepping out of the way and aiming a quick strike with his own spear towards Edmund's head. The young aetheling raised his shield just in time, the sudden, sharp impact sending a dull shock wave down his wrist and into his arm.

He sensed an opportunity, twisting the shaft of his spear up and across to intercept his opponent's weapon whilst it was still in contact with his shield. He successfully knocked it aside, a split second later pulling his arm back and stepping forward to jab his spear directly towards his enemy's now exposed shoulder.

It worked. Edmund's efforts were rewarded with a grunt of pain and surprise from his opponent, the man's disposition otherwise unreadable 'neath the iron and ring mail helm covering almost the entirety of his face. A cheer went up from his supporters in the crowd, his friend, Sigeferth, particularly vocal in his approval. Edmund grinned.

Such joy was not to last. His opponent drew his arm back and threw his spear straight towards Edmund's shield. It landed just off-centre, a few inches below the boss, sending yet another shock up his arm. He felt the added weight, the spear tip having embedded itself in the linden, the shaft visible as it extended outwards at an awkward angle.

His opponent hadn't missed. He was too good for that, instead opting to remove Edmund's shield from the fight by either shattering it or making it too heavy to use. The latter had taken place, for Edmund was now struggling to hold up his left arm, the added burden of the embedded spear threatening to pull his guard down and expose his neck and shoulder with it.

They both circled one another, his adversary now wielding an impressive-looking sword he'd drawn from his scabbard. Edmund still had the reach, even if his guard was compromised. He'd make use of it. He thrust once, aiming his spear for the head. Deflected with a casual sweep of the shield. He thrust again, this time towards the foe's sword hand, hoping to perhaps knock the weapon from his grasp. The cur simply brought his arm up and forward upon seeing the danger, bringing the flat of his sword down atop the shaft of Edmund's spear.

It wasn't a powerful blow by any means, but it bent Edmund's arm downwards, allowing his opponent to step forward in the brief second his weapon was effectively unusable. Edmund pulled his spear back and away, hoping to unleash a flurry of jabs to deter any more attempts to close the distance between them. The first almost hit home, but his adversary pivoted on his left foot and hopped away before the tip of the spear could catch him. A second aimed for his guts, but it was a clumsy strike that was easily swept aside with another flick of the shield.

Edmund was now in dire straits. He'd almost run out of room, and was unable to move backwards out of fear of disturbing the tables and chairs that played host to the braying, cheering, and increasingly drunken audience around them. His opponent sensed his uncertainty, sliding forward once more to the point he was now effectively inside the useable reach of his spear. Edmund opted to drop his weapon, moving his now empty right hand up to his waist to grasp the hilt of his sword.

It was the opportunity his enemy had been looking for. He stepped forward again, sliding the flat of his sword down and behind Edmund's shield. He then shifted his weight backwards, his blade levering the already encumbered shield from Edmund's fatigued grip. It clattered to the floor, the embedded spear still stuck fast. He was defenceless, almost. But at least he felt some relief in his arm.

That was all he was due. Edmund heaved his sword from his scabbard, swinging it aloft just in time to deflect a downward swipe towards his head. He parried another, this one a measured, calculated swing towards the left side of his face, and then another and another after that. Edmund was sweating now, a little anxious, too, on whether he'd be able to walk away from this with any measure of respect. He had to try something unconventional.

A fifth swing from his foe provided such a chance. Edmund decided on the unexpected, stepping forward to meet the incoming attack. He deflected it, barely, and then reached out and grasped the edge of his opponent's shield with his left hand, heaving him forward with all the strength his shoulder, back, and legs would grant.

He was unusually strong for his age, and it showed. Edmund twisted his body around to allow the now flailing man to stagger past him, extending his right foot as he went. As intended, the fellow tripped and lost his balance altogether, collapsing to the floor in an untidy sprawl. Edmund leapt towards his now prone form, striving to bring his boot down upon the wrist of his sword arm.

Edmund was quick, successfully pinning his hand to the floor with a downward stamp of his left foot. Another cheer erupted, and Edmund raised his head to take in the adoring crowd. A mistake. Something heavy smashed into him, sending him reeling to one side, a dull agony spreading across his knee. He recovered in time to see his opponent struggling to his feet, having bashed his shield into Edmund's extended leg in a successful bid to free himself.

The two men again circled each other, both very much aware of the capabilities of the other. The crowd was ecstatic, their interest redoubled in the face of Edmund's sudden and unconventional display. An exchange of sword blows followed, but Edmund could do little other than parry or leap aside, and his efforts towards a counterattack were repeatedly thwarted by the fact his opponent retained a shield.

Edmund's frustration started to boil over. He lunged, both hands on the hilt of his sword, edge facing up and forward, not as a means to pierce or slash but to lock his blade with that of the foe. Their weapons clinched together with a metallic crash, an agonising, high-pitched wail ensuing as the sharpened edges ground against the other. He drove his weight forward, pushing his opponent back with his greater strength, hoping to again send him crashing to the floor.

It was working. The bastard was forced to step back once, then twice, then a third time, the sounds of strained exertion very much audible from beneath his helm. Edmund had him. Then he didn't. He himself suddenly dropped to the floor, his still aching left knee giving out when it received a hefty kick to its already bruised side. He looked up just in time to see the iron boss of a shield smash into his face, his helmet coming loose and falling free whilst he collapsed onto his flank.

He struggled into a kneeling position, his head still ringing from the impact. He looked up and noticed the sharp point of a sword hovering menacingly just an inch from his throat, the towering, armoured form of his adversary poised to finish him should he resist. It was over. Applause and cheers filled the hall, the now victorious combatant having the good sense to keep his eyes on Edmund and not imitate his earlier mistake of looking towards their raucous audience.

He couldn't let it end like this. He flexed his left hand, its soft, pink flesh still well protected under the layers of hardened leather that made up his gauntlet. A brave move began to form in his mind. He went for it, grabbing his enemy's sword and heaving it up and away from his neck. Leather and linen gave way as the blade's edge bit into him, the skin of his palm stinging and weeping under the pressure. Surprise seemed to freeze his foe, and Edmund seized the moment, staggering to his feet and throwing his weight into a shattering right hook to the face.

The crash of his fist impacting on wrought, tempered iron was simply deafening, and no doubt doubly so for the poor fool wearing the helmet. The now surprised and indeed stunned man staggered backwards, almost dropping his weapon whilst he struggled to stay on his feet. The impact had also predictably numbed Edmund's right fist something fierce, his rapidly swelling knuckles and fingers initially refusing to cooperate when he bent down to retrieve his sword.

The two men seemed set to resume their contest when Sigeferth appeared between them, his hand reaching out to grasp Edmund by the shoulder. He raised his other hand to signal the crowd, the sounds of general clamouring and drunken uproar gradually giving way to silence.

"It's over," Sigeferth intoned, the depth of his voice carrying easily across the hall. "Despite Edmund's rather unorthodox fighting style, this was a contest of sword and spear, not wrestling. I hereby find his opponent, the Aetheling Æthelstan, the victor."

Almost riotous jubilation broke out, the sound growing in intensity when Edmund's elder brother removed his helm and raised his sword in triumph. He looked every inch a noble warrior, tall and handsome in his mail and leathers, his long blond hair and blue eyes giving him an air of innocence that belied his skill at arms. Edmund swallowed hard, his cheeks flushing with indignation. He'd not exactly followed protocol, that he could admit to himself, but it didn't make the sting of defeat any easier to bear.

Sigeferth noticed his consternation and leaned in closer, his hand still gripping his shoulder. "Don't beat yourself up, lad," he said smoothly, appearing to do his best to sound reassuring. "You did well to hold him off as long as you did. But the sword grab? Perhaps save that kind of thing for the battlefield next time."

Edmund nodded sullenly, knowing he was right yet unwilling to give voice to affirm it. Æthelstan had ceased to take in the crowd and had instead moved to grasp Edmund's hand in his. He allowed it, the two aethelings now turning to face their people together, hands clasped and held aloft in a display of mutual respect and affection. Edmund grinned, Æthelstan smiling back at him with his all-too-perfect face as the adoration of their audience washed over them. Life was good.

The two brothers cut quite impressive figures even without the added spectacle of their arms and armour. Æthelstan was the "handsome one", or so Edmund had heard, being taller than his younger brother by several inches. His blond hair, crystal-clear eyes, and muscular figure also made him appear akin to some hero of legend, his undeniable skill with all manner of weapons reinforcing that notion. He had a likeable character also, and was friendly and charitable to all he came across; a characteristic some fervently hoped would endure the burdens of eventual kingship.

Edmund was a little different. He was shorter and darker than his brother, his features simpler and coarser and possessing more of a brutish masculinity. He wore his dark hair long and tied back past his shoulders, a full beard also misleading some into thinking he was older than Æthelstan. He was stronger, too; a natural wrestler, some said, and had also been known to spend time studying history and statecraft whilst his brother trained with arms.

They were different but similar, as Edmund was also compassionate, if somewhat reserved at times to the point of aloofness. Despite superficial contrasts in physical appearance, the fierce sincerity of their characters and the deep bond between them left a distinct impression on those they met. They were brothers, no doubt there.

Sigeferth led them both through the crowd, seating the two aethelings at a broad oak table conveniently positioned furthest from the hall's draughty doors and close to the now raging hearth. Morcar smiled at them when they sat, Sigeferth's wife, Ealdgyth, looking as concerned as her husband resumed his place next to her. She wasn't one for conflict, even when it was just for display, preferring the peace and quiet of her household when it was notably less crowded. Edmund understood.

"Honestly, Edmund, the amount of punishment you can take," Æthelstan said jovially, his hand already clenched around a flagon of mead. "We should use you as a human shield of some sort. It's like you're made of iron!"

Edmund laughed, accepting the compliment for what it was. He drank deeply from his own tankard, the thing having wound its way into his grasp thanks to the speedy attention of a most diligent steward. It tasted sweet, like honey and berries in one, quenching his thirst whilst also numbing the various aches he'd been gifted from his dear brother.

Sigeferth watched them both, his expression like that of a proud father, his criticism of Edmund's "unorthodox" fighting style now forgotten. He was a good man, as was Morcar. They were brothers, these two, and easily the most influential thegns in the Five Boroughs. Both were now well into their middle years and a little out of shape, although Edmund had no cause to tell them that. Both were also of good temperament, comporting themselves as honest Christian men committed to their duties to both their king and those under their authority.

Sigeferth doted on his wife, and she on him, their dedication to the other making them exemplars of what Edmund imagined married life would or should look like. As if to illustrate that point, Sigeferth's hand found its way into Ealdgyth's gentle grip, the woman's previously worried expression giving way to something more akin to contentment.

"You boys did well," Sigeferth said, his voice raised slightly to make himself heard over the surrounding revelry. "Æthelstan's in excellent form as always, and Edmund…you've got the strength of an ox. Train hard and listen to your brother, and you'll be the equal of him in no time."

"It's true, Edmund," quipped Æthelstan, his face flushed from a combination of exertion, drink, and praise. "Train hard and listen to me, and stop throwing me around and punching me in the face when I don't expect it. It's disagreeable."

The whole table laughed at that, Edmund included. He knew he wasn't the fighter Æthelstan was and perhaps never would be, since his brother had a rare skill when it came to the sword and pretty much any other weapon. He wouldn't admit that to his face, naturally, although that was out of fear his head might grow even larger than its currently swollen dimensions. Yet he would learn. Æthelstan had a few years on him. Edmund would be sure to listen, train, and close the distance between them.

In the meantime, he was more interested in eating. One of Sigeferth's stewards had just deposited a platter of roast meats and vegetables right in front of him, doing the same also for Æthelstan. The two brothers ate, not bothering to wait for the rest of their companions, having worked up a ravenous appetite after their exertions.

Moments passed before the rest of the table was served, both Morcar and Sigeferth dining with considerably more restraint than the two aethelings. The lady Ealdgyth opted to merely pick at her repast, as if to keep up the appearance of eating without actually ingesting much of anything. Edmund couldn't understand her reticence, but it was possible she'd lost much of her appetite; the surrounding revelry likely off-putting for a woman of her refined sensibilities. He made an effort to tidy up his act, dabbing at his mouth with a cloth and endeavouring to chew his food rather than simply shovel it into his mouth.

Edmund was enjoying his time at Sigeferth's hall. The brothers had been here in Snotingeham for some weeks after travelling north to again clear their heads in light of their father's increasing eccentricity. It had made Edmund's heart ache to leave him like that since he'd initially wanted to stay with him and ride together at the head of an army to confront Thorkell. When the king had told them he would not be moving to assist Ulfcytel in Eastengle, the brothers had not been able to understand his reasoning. An argument had broken out, and hurtful words had been said, so Edmund had suggested to Æthelstan that they simply slip away to Snotingeham and the company of those who might appreciate them.

Sigeferth had been happy to accommodate them in the past, and this time was no different. He was a noble soul, and they'd developed a bond ever since he'd pulled Edmund from the river Trente some years back during a boating trip gone awry. He knew Sigeferth had no living sons of his own, his last male heir passing in his sleep at three months and Ealdgyth sadly birthing a stillborn before that. Her heart had given out after the death of their last child, preferring to spend long hours alone and refusing to entertain the prospect of another. Sigeferth seemed to understand, appearing more concerned with soothing his wife's grief than blustering over the need for a suitably strong and masculine heir. He had a good, gentle heart. A man's heart.

Tragedy or no, Ealdgyth had still been a gracious hostess when the two aethelings had come calling with talk of war and family squabbling. Weeks had then gone by, Sigeferth doing his best to entertain them, the brothers taking to training in a bid to try and forget their father's recent scolding. It hadn't always worked. Edmund found it hard to concentrate and was too often frustrated by his inability to match Æthelstan's skill. It also seemed foolhardy to be training for combat when there was a foreign army operating on English soil, and the only man brave enough to face them, Ulfcytel, had been abandoned by his own king.

He'd raised this with Sigeferth, but the old man had been reluctant to go against Æthelred. Their father was known as a vengeful king, and his actions on St Brice's Day almost eight years ago were still well remembered by many. Sigeferth cited this as an excuse for his inaction, arguing with some force that the Five Boroughs were once part of the old Danelaw territories and were thus liable to face Æthelred's wrath if they defied him.

It had made some sense, yet Edmund and Æthelstan were still of the opinion that the Boroughs should move to assist the Eastenglians regardless. Sadly, it was all academic now, anyway. About a week later, they'd received word that Ulfcytel had been defeated somewhere near Theodford, his army smashed and the ealdorman himself believed to be missing. There was no word of the fate of their uncle, Æthelstan, either.

Edmund had been despondent. Æthelstan had not taken it well either, for he'd suddenly left, departing on a long ride and not returning until the following morning. He'd apologised for his absence, admitting he'd not been thinking straight and had simply needed to be alone. They'd both loved their uncle very much. There would be no replacing him. It must be doubly difficult for his older brother, Edmund suspected. He was heir to the throne. Yet at this rate, he might not have a kingdom left to inherit.

Sigeferth had hatched an idea to raise their spirits. He'd suggested a gathering of his thegns to "test the waters", as he put it, something that might help them gauge the local mood on how to respond to the current crisis. He'd also admitted it was no doubt time for the Five Boroughs to start raising their fyrd in the event Thorkell headed north west after finishing his despoliation of Eastengle. It wouldn't do to be unprepared.

When Edmund had pointed out he'd have stood a better chance of defending his lands by joining with Ulfcytel when he'd had the chance, Sigeferth had agreed, admitting, also, that he'd half expected the Eastenglians to prevail. Edmund felt like he should have been angry over that remark, but he could somewhat understand what he'd meant. Ulfcytel had become something of a legend on the battlefield, but even legends could use reinforcements. Even legends could be killed.

The invited thegns had eventually come, the mood lifting considerably with the expectation of festivities. They'd piled into the ground floor of Sigeferth's hall, the place having been outfitted for a feast with a clustered assortment of long tables, chairs, and a hearth stocked with enough firewood to keep them going for weeks. The food and drink, too, were both sumptuous and abundant, but Edmund had a few reservations on that score, wondering if anyone would have the time or sensibility to talk politics after partaking in what was on offer.

At the last minute, Edmund and Æthelstan had pitched the idea of them entertaining the guests with a martial display. In truth, it was more Æthelstan's idea, and he'd argued convincingly that such a thing would put the thegns in the mood for valorous deeds. Sigeferth and Morcar initially advised against it for fear of either of them being hurt. Edmund didn't like that, suspecting they were concerned for his safety alone on the grounds they'd deemed it unlikely he'd be able to match Æthelstan. The two aethelings had argued their case well, however, assuring all present that they knew where to draw the line.

Edmund wasn't sure if that had been entirely truthful in light of what had happened, but it was all over now. The thegns had enjoyed the spectacle of seeing the brothers lock swords, and he liked to think they'd at least be of a mind to remember it and view them accordingly. Now all that remained was for Sigeferth to put his diplomatic skills to good use. They'd find out soon enough if anyone had the stomach for a real war.

He finished his plate, rebuking himself over a momentary urge to lick it clean. Ealdgyth had only just got some colour back in her cheeks, and he feared such a display would turn her stomach. He felt a great sorrow for her at times, the woman's dark eyes failing to hide the anguish they all knew she bore. He saw Sigeferth squeeze her hand, his fingers again interlaced with hers now that he'd finished his meal. Her face eased into a smile, her eyes gazing upon her husband's aged features with a sincere warmth.

Edmund took another swig of mead, stuffing a handful of freshly baked bread into his mouth a second later. He found himself wondering as to Sigeferth and Ealdgyth, thinking it remarkable that such an enduring love could flourish in an otherwise dark and brutal time. Sigeferth was about a decade older than his wife, yet his sparkling, even mischievous blue eyes gave him an air of vitality that contrasted with his silvered, shoulder-length locks and white torrent of a beard. He carried himself well, showing little sign of slowing from his more youthful days, although the way his gut hung over the belt that held up his already sizeable breecs suggested he was perhaps too fond of a good feast.

Ealdgyth was a vision, no doubt to both Edmund and Sigeferth, but in very different ways. She was a picture of dignity tonight, clothed as she was in a long, round-necked linen gown, dyed a deep blue in colour, her crown covered by a gold-embroidered white shawl. Being some years younger than her husband had ensured she was still blessed with youth, and her auburn hair showed little sign of thinning or fading to grey.

She valued the virtue of temperance also, her modest eating habits ensuring she'd retained a healthy figure despite being a mother to four daughters. Edmund admired her, finding himself perplexed and intrigued by the ways of women, albeit not in a way some might suspect.

He had no physical interest in Ealdgyth, viewing the prospect of hurting Sigeferth and becoming a party to adultery as absolutely horrifying. He was, however, fascinated by their relationship, and he often wondered if he might one day find a love as strong and enduring as theirs.

He could recall that his father had once valued such things. He'd loved Edmund's mother, Ælfgifu, after a fashion, and he'd seemed different then; more inclined to listen and certainly more willing to spend time with his children. Edmund would only admit to himself how hurt he'd been when his father had taken another wife so soon after his mother's death. Queen Emma was a strange one, always so cold and aloof, when his mother, Ælfgifu, had been the opposite. Yet his father was almost obsessed with her, showing her and their children a level of devotion Edmund couldn't recall observing in the past. It made him bitter.

Perhaps this was why he enjoyed the company of Sigeferth and Ealdgyth so much. They were not of his blood, but they cared for him and his brother in a way that had been lacking in their actual father. This in itself made his heart ache since he sometimes felt he was betraying his own family by thinking such things. And yet given the choice, he would still sooner be here, amid good cheer, rather than stuck in Lundenburg being either ignored or berated by Æthelred whenever he dared question his strange behaviour. He knew Æthelstan felt the same.

He noticed his brother appeared to be bleeding. Not a lot, but enough for a little to have soaked through his ring shirt, more or less where Edmund had struck him with his spear just earlier. Æthelstan had also noticed and begun peeking under his mail to get a closer look. He made eye contact with Edmund, shooting him a broad smile.

"It's not too bad, don't worry," he said, his speech a little addled. "It's a messy bruise more than anything. You're getting good with the spear, Edmund. Once we improve your accuracy when it comes to throwing them, you'll be able to decimate an entire heathen army before they can even charge!"

Edmund smiled at the thought. He enjoyed the spear, finding it to be of greater utility than the sword, which he tended to wield like a cudgel rather than the precise, refined weapon he'd been told it actually was. He was concerned for his brother, though, preferring he'd get his "bruise" treated rather than just laughing it off.

"Shouldn't you get it checked by somebody who knows what they are doing?" Edmund asked. "What if you spring a leak as you continue drinking? I don't want to clean that up."

Æthelstan chuckled, like he wanted to ignore that his brother was only half-joking. Sigeferth, fortunately, seemed to agree with Edmund, as the man had leaned in to sneak a look at the allegedly inconsequential wound. He shook his head, a slight frown on his face.

"It's nothing major, but I won't have the heir to the throne injured without me doing something about it," he said. "Morcar, will you finish stuffing your face and take our young friend here to see Father Wilfred?"

Morcar nodded, taking a final bite of barley bread before rising from his seat and ushering Æthelstan to join him. He went to object, his mouth agape as if he couldn't find the means. Sigeferth slapped him reassuringly on the back, mumbling some presumably comforting words that Edmund didn't catch. Æthelstan relented, rising with Morcar and ambling towards the doors, his face a touch resentful until he noticed others getting to their feet to regale him. His skill as a warrior had made a lasting impression.

Edmund wondered if he should follow. His left palm had been bloodied where the edge of Æthelstan's sword had cut through his gauntlet, and the knuckles on his right fist had swollen to the point he had to concentrate to grip his tankard. He poured some mead over his cut, the ensuing sting making his hand clench. Ealdgyth had observed his predicament and gracefully passed him a white linen handkerchief. He tied it around his left hand as a bandage, the fabric absorbing the mead and what little blood remained. It would suffice.

The hall was getting quite rowdy, the assembled notables either still eating or over-indulging in the mead and ale that had been provided. Somebody had started plucking at a harp, their discordant efforts unfortunately putting several others in the mood to sing. Edmund didn't know most of them, as the thegns had come from far and wide across the region. They knew him, though, or at least wanted to. It was nice to be liked, he supposed.

But he had concerns. They were here to address the present crisis, not drink themselves into a stupor. Edmund was unsure how they'd be able to discuss the political situation like this, thinking it preferable to simply feed these men and keep the drink in short supply so everyone remained sober and attentive. Sigeferth seemed to have sensed his concern, leaning forward across the table before speaking so he didn't have to raise his voice.

"Don't worry, this is how we do things in the Five Boroughs. I give these men their due in hospitality, and then we'll talk tomorrow once their headaches have eased off a little. It'll be fine."

Edmund wasn't so sure. The enemy was here, in England, laying waste to it as they sat drinking and feasting. He enjoyed a good feed as much as anyone else, but times of strife demanded action, not self-indulgence. England needed fighting men, and it wouldn't get them through swollen stomachs and bad hangovers.

"Hospitality is one thing, Sigeferth, but it's like we've almost forgotten we're at war," Edmund began, hoping his words wouldn't carry too much offence. "For all we know, Thorkell could be heading here right now whilst we sit about enjoying the good life. Why not get to business now?"

"You are entirely correct," Sigeferth said, his tone sincere, "but this is the way things are done here. As to your second point, we have received word Thorkell is still busy looting Eastengle. If he were already moving towards us, we'd know of it."

It was at times like this that Edmund wished he were king. Æthelstan was the first in line, and he was happy with that, but if Edmund were in charge he'd make some changes. He'd turn England into a land of fighters, ready to lock swords with whatever fresh horror might hurl itself upon their shores. The Northmen had plagued his people for generations now, and the brief reign of relative peace under his grandfather and great-grandfather was now nothing but bittersweet memory. Decisive action was required.

Defeating Thorkell would only be the first step. That degenerate savage, Svienn, who claimed to be King of Denmark, would have to be next. Edmund sometimes pondered the feasibility of invading Scandinavia at the head of a great fleet. The Danes were able to reach England that way. Why not do the same? Why not take the fight to them for once, hacking down their warriors on their own turf and introducing their people to some much-needed humility? He had the passion and drive to do this, and he thought it certain he couldn't be the only man who felt this way.

These were fantasies he'd long kept private, sometimes wondering if they were just boyish dreams. As he grew further into manhood, he was not so sure. He'd heard King Svienn had long struggled to expand his reign over Norway and perhaps the rest of Scandinavia, viewing England itself as just another conquest to be made in the establishment of his empire. It was only a matter of time before he returned, invading their lands yet again and perhaps making himself king over them. Edmund wouldn't allow that, but if a bloodthirsty heathen like him could attempt such things, why couldn't others? Why not establish a great empire of the North Sea, strong and just, civilized and Christian? England had the wealth. It just needed the will.

But would they ever gain it? Ultimately, Edmund would never sit on his father's throne. Worse still, he at times wondered if even Æthelstan would, since their father had grown so enamoured with Emma and their own children he seemed to have forgotten his grown sons. Edward and Alfred were good boys, as far as Edmund could tell, but it would be absurd to see them as heirs when a warrior like Æthelstan was still living. Edmund hoped his father was yet rational enough to see that, if he could see much of anything whilst under the spell of his green-eyed Norman queen.

Edmund was stirred from his thoughts by a sudden commotion at his table. What he assumed to be a messenger had entered the hall and headed straight towards Sigeferth to hand him a sealed letter. Sigeferth had opened it and begun reading, but from the look on his face, it was not good news. He then nodded and muttered something to the mud-splattered courier, gesturing for the clearly fatigued fellow to take a seat and await proper nourishment.

Sigeferth got to his feet and tucked the letter into his cloak. He called for a steward to tend to the messenger, motioning then for Ealdgyth and Edmund to follow him. They did so, making their way through the raucous multitude and out the double doors into the courtyard beyond. They turned left, following Sigeferth through the gravelled streets, the thatched buildings on either side casting growing shadows in the face of evening's encroachment. He refused to answer any appeal for explanation, instead stressing he would reveal all in the presence of Morcar and Æthelstan. They would have to wait.

They hurried on like this for some time, Ealdgyth clutching at her gown to prevent its edges from trailing along the worn, muddied stones of Snotingeham's byways. Edmund liked being here. The town had a particular charm to it, being of a sufficiently small size to lack the claustrophobia and detritus of Lundenburg. At this time of year, it was simply splendid; the vast, cloudless blue sky stretching on forever, the summer breeze conveying a certain energy that warmed the heart and stirred the mind.

The people, too, were quite a sight, strong and healthy and going about their business with a reassured ease. Most of them were farmers returning from work and looking to get back to their wives, although some were tradesmen, some of whom had set up a summer market close to the centre of town. Edmund tarried a moment when they passed through, purchasing a single apple from an overly enthusiastic vendor. It tasted as good as he'd expected. England's bounty was always a source of wonder to him. No wonder the heathens wanted this land for themselves.

They continued onto a broad thoroughfare lined with sturdy, majestic-looking trees, their boughs criss-crossing over them protectively as if to form a shelter with their resplendent limbs. Edmund knew where they were going. Saint Mary's Church was just up ahead. It was here they would find their friends.

They were soon climbing the weather-beaten steps leading up to the entrance. They passed within, striding through its wide open doors and into the high vaulted nave beyond. It was a touch too early for vespers, and the church was occupied only by a few pious souls lost in contemplation, their expressions hidden in shadow. There was no sign of Æthelstan and Morcar until the pair of them rose from kneeling a short distance from the altar, Edmund initially failing to spot them whilst they were huddled in prayer.

Æthelstan smiled when he caught sight of them, striding past his fellow worshippers to join his brother. He looked well, and the priest had found little wrong with him, his armour, as expected, taking the brunt of the spear tip to leave him with a mere flesh wound. Morcar, however, wasn't moved by the good news, and he looked as stoic as usual alongside Æthelstan, his long, jet-black hair and beard giving him an even darker appearance amidst the gloom.

"Everything is fine, as I suspected," Æthelstan reaffirmed, his tone hushed out of respect for his surroundings. "Father Wilfred simply washed it and applied a poultice, which I am told is to be removed tomorrow morning."

Sigeferth nodded, his attention on Morcar as he handed him the letter he'd received. He read it, his expression still neutral, either undisturbed by its contents or simply hiding his emotions better than Sigeferth. He handed the parchment back, a slight frown on his face, and spoke.

"This is an impossible situation for us to bear. What would you suggest we do?"

"We'll have to keep this to ourselves tonight," said Sigeferth, turning to amble back towards the church doors. They followed, eager to hear what he might say, Edmund struggling to mask his frustration at being kept out of the loop.

"In their current state, our fellow notables will react badly to this news, if they can even focus on the text," Sigeferth added, inadvertently vindicating Edmund's earlier opinion on the importance of sobriety. "I'll inform them tomorrow, assuming they don't hear of it before then. Let's hope clearer, cooler minds might prevail."

"What exactly is wrong?" Æthelstan asked, his voice returning to a normal volume upon passing back into the evening air. Their party halted atop the stone steps leading back the way they had come, the deep, elongated shadow of the church extending out and over them. It was a good view here, their elevated position allowing them a broad vista of the tree-studded avenue and the darkening mass of thatched roofs and stone chimneys that made up Snotingeham's modest skyline.

"Your father has imposed a new tax on us and the entire kingdom," Sigeferth said solemnly before passing him the letter. Æthelstan read it with interest, his eyes at times widening in surprise. He looked up at Edmund, dissatisfied, and pressed the letter into his younger brother's palm. Edmund received it eagerly, feasting his eyes on the familiar, flowing text of his father's hand.

At any other time of emergency, the demand might seem just. Their father had quite correctly described their present situation as one of "true calamity for Christian England," claiming Ulfcytel's defeat at Hringmere "would now require every sacrifice to ensure our continued defence." What he didn't mention was his refusal to help Ulfcytel, and this oversight was made worse by blaming the Ealdorman of Eastengle himself, claiming he'd "refused to obey the just commands of his king and instead wrought his own ruin in pursuit of glory for himself and himself alone."

That in itself was bizarre, as if their father thought Ulfcytel's mistake was in seeking to fight the enemy to begin with. What was truly ridiculous was his imposition of a new "army tax" on every hide of land a man might own. Edmund didn't care much for counting coins, but the amount demanded was absurd and likely to drive a small farmer to destitution. Only the wealthy could weather this storm, and even then, it would ruffle feathers.

What was also concerning was how he attempted to justify it. Stating that the monies raised would "train and equip a new force to decisively overawe and overpower our hated foe", Æthelred concluded his argument by claiming such a host would "go on to deter invaders for generations to come." That didn't feel right. No ruler would keep a professional army in the field "for generations" for self-explanatory reasons. Something was amiss.

"He's going to pay off Thorkell."

Nobody immediately responded to Edmund's words. He noticed poor Ealdgyth still standing there, confused and in the dark on what was being discussed. Edmund passed her the letter. He didn't know if she could read, but it made him feel bad to see her so excluded. She took it and began to scrutinise the parchment, Morcar answering Edmund in the meantime.

"You know the king's mind better than we do. But what makes you say that?"

"Because he's paid off Svienn before, and that Olaf whatever-his-problem-was before that. This isn't for a new army. Thorkell has demanded a huge sum after winning at Hringmere, and father is looking to pay up."

Æthelstan stared at his sibling, his eyes narrowed in concentration as if he were giving a lecture on the most complex attributes of statecraft. He was the elder brother, but he paid little attention to history or politics, spending most of his time training. Perhaps Edmund had a few things to teach him after all.

"That makes a lot of sense, I'd say," Sigeferth said, sounding pleased Edmund had shared his insights. "But in that case, the situation is even more calamitous. The king has pursued this policy of paying invaders to leave for some years now, and all that happens is they either come back or others appear looking to be paid off also. This tax will weaken the kingdom whilst inviting renewed aggression from overseas."

"Why can't we just march on Thorkell?!" Æthelstan spat, his eyes lighting up with anger. "All this talk of coin and politics just complicates matters. There's nothing here some strong backs and sword arms can't fix!"

He wasn't wrong. Edmund admired his brother for his passion and straight-talking attitude. Sometimes the best solutions were the simplest, and making Thorkell bleed was eminently desirable. But the best time for that would have been before the battle at Hringmere. If they'd thrown their efforts into facing him there, then thousands of warriors, not to mention one of England's best leaders, Ulfcytel, might have been saved. Instead, Edmund and Æthelstan had simply given up trying to change their father's mind and run off to Snotingeham. That had been a mistake. He could see that now.

"We should return," Edmund told Æthelstan, "and try to talk some sense into father. He has to listen to us now he thinks he's run out of options. It was one thing to ignore us before, but with this tax, he risks alienating his entire kingdom."

Æthelstan nodded slowly, taking in his words. Chances were he didn't want to go back to Lundenburg. He'd enjoyed his time in the Five Boroughs. They both had. But duty called them, and he was sure Æthelstan would rather inherit an actual kingdom with actual living people in it rather than just corpses and ashes.

"There's something else you might want to mention to the king," Sigeferth began, his face darkening noticeably. "If we pay this tax, we won't have any monies available to properly train and equip our fyrd. If Thorkell decides to head this way, our ability to fight him off…"

"We can't fight him off," Morcar interjected. "Let's be honest about that. Even without the tax, we'd be lucky to even thin out his numbers. With what the king is demanding of us…it's monstrous. We're being asked to give up everything we have for the greed of foreigners."

Morcar had a way with words, Edmund thought. He'd appreciate having a man like that with them when they faced his father. "Will you come with us?" he asked, sincerely hoping he'd agree. "It would make sense to have a representative of the Boroughs with us so it doesn't just look like a family squabble."

Morcar looked at Sigeferth, his face blank and devoid of emotion, as always. Edmund sensed he was looking for approval, for the two brothers rarely seemed to do much without the other. Sigeferth looked to be thinking it over, having just retrieved the letter from an increasingly worried-looking Ealdgyth. She was shivering. Evening had really crept up on them, and she wasn't dressed for hanging around outdoors.

"Let's go back to the hall," Sigeferth finally said, wrapping an arm and a portion of his cloak around his beloved. "It's getting dark, and I'd rather talk about such arrangements off the streets. We're foolish for saying what we have out in the open like this."

Edmund couldn't disagree there. He'd lost himself in the moment. If he were to be brutally honest, he also relished the opportunity to converse on a subject his older brother generally wasn't adept in. Æthelstan's solution to any problem was to fight rather than talk, which was generally a sound choice, but it wouldn't help them when it came to future conversations with their father. This was yet another reason why he wanted Morcar with them when the time came.

They began to make their way down the church steps and back to the tree-lined thoroughfare they'd followed previously. The daylight had receded faster than Edmund had expected, making Snotingeham's streets appear a little ominous in the deepening twilight.

By the time they made it to the hall, things seemed to have calmed down, the assorted thegns looking and acting as if they'd somewhat paced themselves when it came to drink. That didn't stop a raucous cheer erupting when they laid eyes on the two aethelings, each man present looking genuinely pleased they'd returned to sup with them. It was good to be loved, Edmund thought, and if these men were to put their adoration into action, he was sure the Five Boroughs could become a solid base of support in the event they had to defy the king. He hoped it wouldn't come to that. He loved his father, despite everything. He owed it to him to try and talk him around.

Sigeferth led them to the back of the hall and through the kitchens, all following when he turned to ascend a narrow flight of wooden stairs that led to his personal chambers. They passed through several doors before they entered Sigeferth's study, the upper level of his hall a warren of tight corridors and smaller chambers for both rest and contemplation. His study was a fairly large, austere place, suggesting Sigeferth preferred to do his reading with the minimum of distractions. It did, however, sport a more than adequately sized table for them to sit at.

Morcar closed the door behind them, both he and Sigeferth then taking the trouble to light an assortment of candles now that they'd lost the daylight. Ealdgyth made her excuses, claiming she was tired and required rest. Sigeferth stopped her when she turned to leave, handing her a freshly lit candle to take with her. They seemed to share a moment, his hand clasped in hers, their faces an image of mutual affection now captured in the flickering glow. She eventually turned and left, Sigeferth joining them at the now thankfully well-lit table.

"What else can we say?" asked Æthelstan, his manner implying he wanted to head back downstairs to rejoin the festivities. "Edmund and I will leave tomorrow and talk some sense into our father over this tax. Agreed?"

"And Morcar will come with us?" Edmund asked, feeling like he'd not had a definite answer from him.

Morcar nodded, his hands clasped in front of him. "I will do as you ask," he said slowly, seeming to think on every word before he uttered it. "And I agree with you that it would be advantageous for the king to see that the concerns over this tax are not merely those of his sons. I will endeavour to be of service in this matter."

"There is something else I would like to mention," Sigeferth said, apparently in agreement that Morcar should travel with them. "Have we considered the king may simply be…ill-advised of late? Word is he spends a great deal of time speaking with his new Ealdorman of Mierċe. What exactly do you know of this man?"

This was an awkward topic, and Edmund wasn't even sure how Sigeferth would know of it, considering his distance from the capital. It was true that his father had cut himself off from old friends and advisers over the years, believing few could be trusted. Edmund wasn't sure why exactly, but he'd heard his father had been led astray in the early years of his reign, having become caught up in myriad schemes involving either the seizure of Church lands or the appointment of favoured candidates to the clergy.

This was all before Edmund's time, admittedly, and he'd only asked his father about it once just to be told in no uncertain terms to never speak of it again. He'd also heard him repeatedly mention that "no one is truthful", which confused Edmund, although it did partly explain why he seemed to hold his own ealdormen in increasing contempt.

Except for one. The new Ealdorman of Mierċe, Eadric, was often given private audiences, sometimes in the dead of night. Edmund didn't know anything about what was discussed, and when he'd tried to talk to his father about it, he was told to mind his own business. Sigeferth was quite right in wondering exactly what Eadric was about, as the man had been a relative unknown prior to his appointment as ealdorman. Sadly, Edmund didn't really have all that much to tell him.

"He's a mystery, I'll say that," Æthelstan answered. "He seems to come and go as he wishes, often meeting with father on his own. I've asked them both what they talk about. Father wouldn't give me any details. Eadric gave me some yap about "serving the realm" or something. Not much to go on. I don't like him. There's something off about him."

"Mystery or not, the man casts a long shadow," Sigeferth muttered, his eyes troubled. "Have either of you heard the rumours surrounding the death of our kinsman, Ælfhelm?"

They both shook their heads, confused. They'd never met the man, at least as far as memory served. Morcar spoke up.

"My brother is referring to the Ælfhelm who was, until about four years ago, the Ealdorman of southern Norþanhymbre. You remember him?"

Edmund wasn't sure. Norþanhymbre, in its entirety, was now ruled by the Ealdorman Uhtred, who, as far as he could tell, was actually loyal to his father. And why would he not be? He'd been appointed to that position by Æthelred himself, yet it was strange the honour hadn't gone to their uncle, Æthelstan, who, as the son of the late Ealdorman Thored, should have been owed such a thing. Morcar continued speaking, taking the brothers' silence for what it was.

"Ælfhelm was murdered just prior to Uhtred being made Ealdorman of Norþanhymbre," he said, his next words sending a chill down Edmund's spine, "and we believe Eadric did it on your father's orders."

Edmund and Æthelstan remained quiet, unsure of how to respond. Edmund paid little attention to rumours, finding gossip infantile and downright annoying. But he knew and respected Morcar. He wasn't a man to make up stories and then spread them.

"I understand this is perhaps difficult for you lads to hear," Sigeferth said softly. "I wouldn't have liked to think of my father being in the company of a murderer either. But these are a sad sign of our times. Treachery and sin abound. No wonder God is punishing us."

"You sound like Archbishop Wulfstan!" Æthelstan half-joked, his face pale. Whether Sigeferth and Wulfstan were right about God's attitude towards England was a matter Edmund would ponder later. Right now, he had to hear more about what had happened to Ælfhelm.

"Why would Eadric do this?" he asked. "What does he get from it? And why would father order it so? And why even bother getting Eadric to do it?"

"Ælfhelm's family was a potential threat, as some would see it, to anyone wishing dominion over Mierce," responded Morcar. "He held great influence, in his own holdings and beyond. We believe the king saw an opportunity to remove somebody he saw as disloyal whilst allowing a potential ally to prove themselves. It's no surprise that Eadric was made Ealdorman of Mierce soon after."

"And I'm afraid your father was quite thorough," Sigeferth continued. "Once Ælfhelm was dead, the king summoned a meeting at his estate at Cocheham, inviting Ælfhelm's sons, Wulfheah and Ufegeat, to attend him. He then had the two young men blinded."

Both Edmund and Æthelstan inhaled sharply. "Why are you telling us this now?" Æthelstan asked, his voice hushed and low. "We've both known you for years, and you've never spoken of any blindings or plots. What exactly is the purpose behind telling us such things?"

"Because matters may be about to come to a head, if Eadric is really the kind of man we suspect he is," stressed Morcar. "We saw no reason to make waves unless we had to. We're loyal to the crown, despite the killing of our kin. And to answer another question that I'm sure is on your mind…Wulfheah and Ufegeat were not blinded purely on a whim. They had indeed made threats towards your father following Ælfhelm's demise. It was foolish talk from broken hearts. But the king acted on it, possibly on the advice of Eadric. Perhaps we should be grateful he didn't simply have them killed too."

"Where are they then?" Edmund asked, also wondering why he'd never heard of these men. "Surely they must require a great deal of care, being without sight?"

"It wouldn't do to have them here," Sigeferth said, shaking his head sadly. "If we took them into our household, the stigma of disloyalty would rub off on us. We can't put our own children at risk of what Æthelred may do if he thought we were some kind of threat."

"Or what Eadric might convince him to do," Morcar added.

"So where are they?" Æthelstan queried, a little exasperated now.

"Norþanhymbre," answered Morcar. "We still have some influence there. A good man, a local thegn, Thurbrand is his name…he cares for them in secret. They are safe, and they are harmless. They were in shock and grief when they spoke against the king. I would hope we can also keep this conversation between us. Please rest assured we mean no harm to your father. But we think, given all that's happening now, you should understand the situation for what it is."

"And what is the situation?" pressed Æthelstan sternly. "And what would you have us do with this information? We love our father, as difficult a man as he is. We'll never desert him, and I'll have words with any man who would suggest it."

"We would never ask you to!" Sigeferth exclaimed, his feelings clearly hurt.

"What we wish is for you to consider all the factions in play," Morcar interjected swiftly. "If Eadric does have sufficient influence over your father that he could convince him to kill without cause, then it isn't just a question of you changing his mind over tax reform. You could end up in a very complex and dangerous situation. Eadric is not a man to be crossed. You should know what he's capable of."

Edmund sighed deeply, taking a moment to gather his thoughts. Æthelstan continued to stare straight ahead at Morcar, his brow furrowed. Edmund would have liked to think they were exaggerating the situation, possibly due to the grief and bitterness they no doubt felt over the death of their kin. There could also be a darker side to all this. If anyone wanted to move against a king, bringing his sons over to your side would be a way to go about it.

But was that what Sigeferth and Morcar were doing? They'd never mentioned any of this before, and they'd had many opportunities in the past to manipulate them. Instead, they'd generally avoided discussing politics when they were present and seemed more concerned with them enjoying whatever time they had in Snotingeham. This was the first time they'd mentioned anything anywhere near as severe as what was being discussed now.

"I think we can agree that Eadric may be a problem for us all," said Æthelstan finally, "and I appreciate your efforts to warn us. I will keep this conversation in mind and conduct myself accordingly. Edmund, you agree?"

Edmund nodded, finding no fault with what his brother had said. He liked it when Æthelstan took the lead, as he had here. He was the eldest, and despite his headstrong nature and lack of book learning, he was no fool. They certainly needed to prepare for the possibility Eadric could try to move against them if he came to see them as a threat. If he was somehow behind their father's recent decisions, then attempting to convince him to change course could prove dangerous. They'd need support.

"Everything you've told us convinces me it's all the more important you accompany us to Lundenburg," Edmund said, his eyes on Morcar. "You don't know what our father is like of late. He ignores us, won't listen to advice…he only spends his time with Emma, their children…and Eadric. It will be easy for him to dismiss us, unless we have an ally."

"It could also present a new danger," Sigeferth cautioned. "He won't have forgotten the past. Morcar's presence could make him think there's a conspiracy against him, assuming he doesn't already. You did come to us after arguing with him…he will no doubt wonder why."

"I fear we either take that risk or we give up changing his mind at all," stated Æthelstan brusquely. "Nothing will come of this if it's just me and Edmund talking at him. A representative of the Five Boroughs would add weight to our words."

"I agree," said Morcar, turning to his brother to address him directly. "It is a risk, and I'll admit to some apprehension. But if we're to make the king listen to reason rather than be taxed into annihilation just so he can pay off Thorkell…we have to take some chances. This is one."

Now it was Sigeferth's turn to sigh, and his face remained troubled. He was worried about his brother and perhaps his own life. An angry Æthelred was a frightening sight and nothing to be taken lightly. Edmund knew that better than anyone. Yet still, they must try. He was glad Morcar saw that.

"All right then," muttered Sigeferth. "It seems we have little choice. Go with them, brother, and God be with you all. I have one more thing to say, though. A question for Æthelstan."

"Ask away," Æthelstan said, eager to dispense with any further drama. He wasn't one for theatrics, Edmund knew. All this cloak and dagger chatter wasn't to his tastes.

"Have you heard from your friend, Wulfnoth? We all heard what happened at sea. Do you know of his whereabouts?"

Æthelstan blinked, surprised at the sudden mention of his old associate. Edmund wasn't sure what to say either. Wulfnoth was a friend to both of them and a loyal man, at least they'd thought. He'd gone rogue a short time ago, causing chaos in their father's fleet and creating enough of a diversion, deliberately or no, to allow Thorkell to land unopposed. They'd not heard from him since, but the whole affair had a dark air to it, as if there was a great deal yet to be discovered.

"I have not heard from him," replied Æthelstan coolly, "and I wish it were otherwise. I don't understand what happened. As far as I'm aware, he was no traitor, yet suddenly the accusation was made, and he just flees with his men. It makes no sense."

"It doesn't, no, unless you consider the one who actually laid such accusations against him," said Morcar. "We've been told it was a certain Beorhtric, this man being none other than the brother of the Ealdorman Eadric."

Edmund saw where this was going. Morcar would be thinking Eadric and this Beorhtric were working together to ruin Wulfnoth. It wasn't an absurd notion when one considered what had been said already, yet it didn't assuage his hunger for facts and hard proof. Nobody present had been there when Wulfnoth had allegedly turned traitor. That was a problem, as far as Edmund was concerned.

"So you think Eadric has a hand in this too?" Æthelstan asked. "That's interesting, but why bother? He stood to gain from his move against Ælfhelm, sure enough. But who is Wulfnoth to him?"

"We're not sure," Sigeferth admitted. "And yet people talk. We hear things. Eadric may have an interest in keeping your father isolated whilst also working against your own interests as aethelings. With Wulfnoth disgraced and now missing…"

"We have one less ally," Edmund murmured. "It's true, he was close to us, like you two are. I miss him, and it's hard to believe the claims that were made against him. If Eadric is the power behind this latest intrigue, we'll need to be doubly careful. Until then…I could do with another drink."

Everyone voiced their agreement with that. They all rose from the table, Sigeferth ushering them out into the corridor beyond. They continued to the staircase, the senior thegn still leading the way, the light from the candle in his hands ensuring their forms cast dark, trembling shadows across the walls. Downstairs the festivities had become more sombre, almost as if those assembled had themselves been privy to the troubling revelations that now weighed on Edmund's mind.

They all sat at their table, no cheer greeting the aethelings this time, both Edmund and Æthelstan preferring to keep to themselves. The mead still tasted good, yet not as before, Edmund's darkened mood serving to temper some of its bite. He had little to say in the idle conversation that followed, and he retired early to once again make his way upstairs to one of the guest rooms he'd been allocated. Nothing felt right, and he had so much to think on. He hoped things would make more sense in the morning.

Sleep didn't come, at least not at first. He had to make do with just lying in bed and staring at the rafters above, hoping a ready answer to their problems might drift down from on high. All was reasonably quiet in the hall, at least. Many of their guests must have drunk themselves to sleep whilst a few die-hard revellers kept on. They didn't bother him. They sounded happy. He was glad somebody could manage that in these troubling times. They'd sober up and face the harsh reality soon enough.

He finally began to drift off, his mind settling on thoughts of his father. Convincing him of anything would be a difficult task. He didn't listen well, and was often irritated by his son's presence, even when he tried to remain silent. He'd been different ever since mother had died. He'd been even more so after he'd married Emma. And then Eadric had come, out of nowhere almost, a mystery to so many and yet taken into his father's confidence with alarming ease.

He'd tried to work all this out many times before. His father hadn't always been so difficult. When Edmund had been very young, he'd been almost loving, and he clung to those memories with great fondness even as the passage of time rendered them more and more remote. But that was then, and in Edmund's darker moments, he suspected his father no longer cared for him and Æthelstan, viewing his sons with Emma as his new heirs. That was a worst-case scenario, but part of him always drew his thoughts back to it, as if daring him to face the bitter truth. If it were indeed so, then it was a hard thing to come to terms with. It would break his heart, in fact. And it made him fear for himself and his siblings. It made him fear for everyone.

"Lord help us," he whispered as sleep finally claimed him.

IX

There had to be over a thousand men out there. They'd come with the dawn, assembling in ranks right in front of the western wall, now as motionless as they were menacing. She'd rarely seen such a mass of warriors, their faces unreadable at this distance, yet their weapons and armour were visible enough, the wall of shields and forest of spear tips giving clear indication of their intent.

Nothing had happened for some time. The new arrivals just stood there, staring up at the fort's sentries and ignoring all demands for explanation. They were almost like statues, grim and unyielding, the only evidence to the contrary the tangled mass of heavy footprints they'd left in their wake. Then he'd appeared from their ranks. Eadric of Mierċe, dressed for war, demanding the Ealdorman Ælfric present himself to "answer for his habitual failings and betrayals of his most aggrieved king". Pretty words wrapped around a bold demand. Or so Æva thought.

She'd been standing on the walls since she'd been summoned. Ælfric had hauled himself out of bed at first news of the approaching force, the dutiful Cenric giving him little choice. Surprisingly, the ealdorman had then called for her, requesting her presence whilst he exchanged heated words with his counterpart below. Nothing seemed to be progressing well. Eadric had presented a fresh demand on Ælfric as soon as he'd laid eyes on him: open your gates, surrender the fortress, and prepare to be taken into custody along with all family members. This wasn't diplomacy. It was an ultimatum.

Æva didn't want that man anywhere near her. She had precious little idea who he was, finding courtly personalities and the intrigue that often came with them tedious and depressing. This Eadric struck her as the kind of man who thrived in that environment, appearing to have a civil tongue that all the same spat the coldest of threats and the most insincere of promises. She was very, very glad the gates were secure. As long as they held their nerve, he couldn't do much to get at them.

She reached out for Ælfric, the poor fellow succumbing to a coughing fit in the midst of his latest exchange with the weasel outside. She slapped at his back, gently but with purpose, hoping to not further aggravate the plethora of bruises she knew still lurked beneath his robes. He wasn't dressed for battle, looking like he'd thrown on the bare minimum after the alarm had been sounded. He was shivering too. She worried for him.

He recovered swiftly, placing a gnarled hand on hers in appreciation. It had been some weeks since he'd returned from Eastengle to begin slowly recovering from his wounds, albeit not quickly enough. The news that had followed him was grim. Ulfcytel had been defeated and was now missing; his army smashed at a place called Hringmere. All of Eastengle was believed to be aflame, and the Danes were engaging in an orgy of looting and bloodshed, as they had so very many times before.

All wondered where the heathen host might strike next. Would it be another attack on Lundenburg? North into the Five Boroughs? Or south to finally take

Canterburie? All were fearful prospects, and no matter how many words were shared on the subject, the possibility of resistance seemed remote. England was again in crisis, unlike anything in generations.

That wasn't the worst part, at least for Æva. Alaric had still not returned. She'd kept the news from Brandon, telling him whenever he asked that his father was still off "being a soldier". The child was becoming restless, repeating the same question whenever he could. She wondered how long she could hold out. He'd have to be told the truth at some point.

She'd taken to grieving at night. It was easier that way, and she was able to maintain a facade of control during her daily duties as long as she vented her despair after sunset. This had not involved any trouble for others, since she'd found a spot beyond the walls where she could walk. She'd go alone, treading a solitary path through the trees and guided by little other than the moon, her heart now free to pour out its share of grief with each shuffling step.

She'd discovered a small pond to sit at, the waters dark and opaque, its tranquil surface in marked contrast to the state of her troubled soul. She'd pray here, desperate and unceasing, at times begrudging herself for demanding her Lord's attention so much. Sometimes it felt as if nothing and no one would answer her in her pain, and the one man who could heal her wounds was now lost to her. There would be no filling the space he'd left. There could be no replacing Alaric. She'd never love another. She'd remain alone until she saw him again in Heaven.

Æva had kept up this habit for some time, yet the guards at the gates were starting to mutter to themselves, even asking on a few occasions upon her return where she'd been and if she was all right. She had no words of any real meaning for them, intent as she was on crawling back into her bed, exhausted by emotion, until the sun rose again. Life would then resume as normal until the pressure just got too much, prompting another nocturnal wander. She realised it was dangerous, being out alone like that. She wondered how long she could keep it up before her father-in-law found out and instructed the guards to not let her leave. She hoped it wouldn't come to that.

Such concerns were now immaterial in light of their present situation. Eadric had spat some more words up at them, something about their "continued defiance" and "lack of cooperation with the king's most just instruction". He hadn't even explained why the king would want to take Porteceaster from them, let alone why they all had to come with him, yet he persisted, becoming more unlikeable with each passing moment. She didn't think much of him. But the massed men at his back were terrifying.

If Ælfric felt the same, she could not tell. He'd pulled himself up, chest and shoulders squared, reaching out also to take a spear from one of his warriors standing at his side. There was a whole line of them manning the crenellated wall; a fearsome sight for anyone looking up from below and a sterling reminder that the place would not fall without a fight. Ælfric stood there, soldier-like, weapon in hand, breathing deeply and slowly, in and out to settle his lungs. He coughed one last time, hawking up a mouthful of phlegm and spitting it over the battlement's edge. Æva grimaced. Then he resumed shouting.

"Eadric, I tell you now…unless you desist from this foolishness and pull your men back, I will have archers brought up to poke some holes into that smug face of yours!"

Æva wasn't sure how many archers they might have to make good on that threat. The fort was garrisoned by just a few hundred men after the rest of the fyrd, or what was left of it, had disbanded upon returning from Eastengle. Perhaps he was just trying to frighten Eadric. It was worth a try. Either way, the man's voice soon came echoing back at them over the walls, more indignant than ever.

"And I tell you, my noble Ælfric, arrows or no, if you resort to violence, I will respond in kind! You are outnumbered and in defiance of the king's instructions! Resist his will at your peril!"

They carried on like this for a few minutes more, Æva wondering how the two men were able to maintain their composure given the severity of the threats exchanged. She noticed Ælfgar was nowhere in sight, which struck her as unusual for a serious situation like this one. He'd sadly not improved on the bad behaviour she'd observed in him weeks prior, persisting in being as irritable, condescending, and downright unpleasant as she'd ever known him to be. She'd confronted him on it just days ago, again pointing out that she was the wife of Alaric, his brother, and was not to be disrespected. He'd laughed her out of the room, seemingly tickled by the fact she'd spoken of Alaric as if he were still alive. Ælfgar really was a cold man. She was glad he wasn't here now.

Eadric had now run out of patience, spitting something about "consequences" before retreating behind the wall of shields that made up the front line of his force. He reappeared a few minutes later, dragging an unidentified woman with him, his hand gripped tightly around the length of her hair. Æva had no idea who she was, and her simple white and beige apron dress said she was the wife or daughter of a common farmer. Given the level of contempt Eadric was displaying towards her, it was highly unlikely she was nobility, a suspicion reinforced when he hauled her out in front of him and held a blade to her throat.

"What say you now, Ælfric? Will you really sacrifice the lives of your own people just to keep me out of your hovel?"

Æva's father-in-law didn't respond to the jibe, presumably wondering who this woman was and how Eadric had procured her. Whatever the case, she was terrified, sobbing something unintelligible that otherwise failed to move Eadric's icy heart. He sliced open her throat a second later.

Æva held her hands up to her mouth in shock. The woman fell forwards onto her knees, a cascade of red pouring from the jagged gash across her neck. The image seared itself into Æva's mind; the woman's expression one of total panic, hands and chest wet with gore, fingers and palms desperately trying to stem the unceasing outpouring from her throat. She finally slumped onto her face, Eadric expediting matters by kicking her in the back, his mouth twisted in a cruel smile. She lay still, expiring in the grass, her killer staring up at them as if he'd just performed some impressive feat of arms.

"What of it, Ælfric?" he again called, sounding smugger than any person had any right to be. "Will she be the last, or will I have to depopulate all of Hamptonscir before you surrender to your king's will?"

"Who was that?" Ælfric asked, his tone neutral, unimpressed by his counterpart's callous display. "Was that supposed to frighten us in some way? You being a murderer? We know you're a killer and a snake. There is nothing new here!"

The Ealdorman of Mierċe didn't respond as he again vanished back behind his men. He soon reappeared, this time dragging what looked like a small boy. The lad was putting up a struggle, and he managed to kick Eadric in the legs several times, but the contest was unequal and could only go one way. Æva felt her heart hammering in her chest. She could not bear this.

"We have to do something!" she hissed towards her father-in-law. He looked at her out of the corner of his eyes, then stared ahead for a moment like he was thinking. He then whispered something to the man next to him, who promptly hurried off down the stone steps Æva had climbed earlier to gain access to the wall. She hoped Ælfric had a plan.

"What's it to be then, old man?" Eadric again called. "Surely you won't want to see any harm come to such a young fellow as this?"

With that last word, he'd again drawn his seax, its blade still red, and held it to the boy's throat. Æva started to grind her teeth, enraged at this stranger who demanded entry to her home upon the grimmest of deeds.

"If you think this is helping your case, you can think again," Ælfric spat, now visibly emotional at the sorry sight before him. "I would ask you to think on your soul. It isn't just men that gaze upon what you do today. God sees you, Eadric. God weeps for the blood you've shed here!"

"If it is as you say, Ælfric, then where is your God now? Will he not come and strike me down for my iniquities?"

"Your sins are your own, you little prick!" Æva screeched at him, her patience having run out. "You darken your own soul with what you've done here, and you will face judgement for it on the last day!"

She sensed Eadric's eyes upon her. She fancied she saw a moment's indecision upon his face, his sneer losing some of its certitude whilst he contemplated her words. Then the look returned. Arrogant and cruel. He pressed his dagger to the lad's throat, holding it there as if to wet its edge. The boy was trying to be brave, but she could see the tears on his cheeks well enough. Æva felt like she was close to panic. She couldn't imagine how it was for him.

"Open your gates, Ælfric," Eadric said menacingly. "Do it now, and I'll not only spare this youngster but that harpy up there with you."

Æva scowled at the insult and was considering a retort when heavy treads sounded behind her. She turned. The soldier her father-in-law had dispatched had returned from wherever it was he'd been ordered. He had a bow in his hands, already nocked with a single arrow. Ælfric took it from him eagerly, drawing the bow's string back as he took aim at Eadric.

"This has gone on long enough, snake!" Ælfric thundered. "Release the captive and any others you have there, and depart these lands. Tell the king to come himself if he would see me in chains, or at least send someone worthy of being called a man!"

Eadric peered up at the defiant ealdorman, the width of his grin suggesting he was genuinely amused by the spectacle. Without further comment, he slid his blade across the boy's jugular, slicing it clean open, Æva letting loose a sob just as Ælfric let loose his arrow. It arced through the air, a hit seemingly guaranteed given the height advantage of the bowman and Eadric's relatively close proximity.

A dull thud echoed out and across the fortress walls. Eadric stood unharmed, the arrow buried in the shield of a man who had appeared from the mass of soldiers at his back. He'd moved fast, almost unnaturally so, and was now content to stand there, staring up at them and entirely unconcerned with the dying boy at his feet. Eadric laughed to himself, as sickening a sound as Æva could ever imagine.

"Is that it, old man?" he mocked. "Do you have anything else you'd perhaps like to shoot or throw at us? My friend here, Thurcytel, can't possibly catch it all on his shield."

Ælfric turned and began barking orders. More men appeared on the walls, each bearing a bow of their own. Somebody passed Ælfric a more ample supply of arrows, and the old man nocked another and took aim, commanding his troops to do the same. They stepped into position, poised and deadly, those warriors without bows heaving their spears up and back, ready to cast them down into the enemy's ranks.

The men below erupted into a frenzy of movement, and Eadric promptly vanished within a mass of interlocking shields arrayed outward in expectation of the impending bombardment. Ælfric roared an order and let loose, his men atop the wall answering his command by unleashing a shower of arrows and hurled spears.

Æva had never seen anything quite like it. A deluge of projectiles smashed into the enemy's front line. Shields trembled and shook under the deadly downpour, a few fracturing and coming apart, the men behind crying out as spear tips and arrowheads tore deep into their flesh. Gaps in their ranks began to appear, and Æva's heart leapt when the survivors started to fall back, slowly and orderly, their shields still raised in the face of the continuing onslaught.

The men of Hamptonscir refused to let up, pouring arrow after arrow into the enemy force, but the foe eventually slipped from the effective range of their bows, and so Ælfric called for his men to cease fire. It had been enough. The once lush, grassy expanse below was now marred with arrows, broken spears, and shattered shields, the moans of dying men rising up to meet them. Despite it all, Æva felt sorrow for them, noting with some distress that the real villain behind all this, Eadric himself, did not appear to be among the casualties.

He soon made his presence known, screaming something at them from far off, his face a tiny red, enraged spec in the distance. The warriors along the wall found that amusing, and his protestations were met with a huge mocking cheer. Despite the high spirits, it had to be said that relatively few of Eadric's men had fallen, and the sadistic Ealdorman of Mierċe was still in possession of hundreds upon hundreds of men, outnumbering those in the fort more than three times over. But they'd driven them off, and they had the high walls. Eadric had nothing but grass. Æva was astounded. She'd never seen Ælfric look so alive.

Æva returned to her rooms in the tower, relieved to experience some quiet after the terrible events she'd witnessed. Ælfric had assured her the immediate danger had passed and that he'd no longer need her, although she had no idea why he'd thought she'd be of use to start with. Something told her they'd not seen the last of Eadric, and she also had a feeling Ælfric would again want her present for when he returned. She wasn't looking forward to it. But she'd do as she was asked.

She'd spent some time with Brandon, instructing him in the alphabet, when a guard had again knocked on her door. She'd answered, unsurprised to then be invited to a meeting at the ealdorman's request. It was easy to guess what he'd want to discuss, and her heart sank a little to be told that Ælfgar would also be present. This would be a trying time.

It wasn't all bad news. Cenric would apparently be there. He was easily the best fighter they had and not the kind of man to succumb to panic in any form. He'd always been here in one role or another, always attached to the family and always loyal and diligent in his duties. He was older than both her and Alaric, closer, in fact, to Ælfric's age without yet succumbing to any of the usual burdens of seniority. She liked him. He was a friend to Alaric, and he'd taught him much over the years on combat and campaigning, his green eyes lighting up whenever it came to a sparring match or imparting some rare snippet of refined wisdom on how to knock another man down.

He was tall, broad also, yet not excessively, his shoulders, chest, and arms thick from years of wielding a variety of weapons in training or actual warfare. His face bore the signs of the latter; one half of it marred from some old wound that he'd taken years back from one of Svienn Forkbeard's raiders. The blow had broken both his cheekbones and jaw, leaving Cenric somewhat dented, if that was the word, and his skin rough and pockmarked despite the partial concealment provided by his long, silver and charcoal beard.

Despite his simplicity, there was a mystery to him. He sometimes gave the impression he knew more about Ælfric than he was comfortable speaking on, making Æva suspect there was some kind of secret between them that weighed on his conscience. He'd also apparently had a family once, comprised of a wife, three girls, and two boys, only for them to all be absent one day and ever since with no explanation offered, at least to Æva. She'd never dared ask Cenric himself. She had too much of an ill feeling about it.

She'd made her way to the meeting, once again descending the steps of the tower to join the ealdorman, his son, and Cenric in his quarters. She was immediately presented with grim news. Ælfric had read out a letter apparently penned by Eadric and delivered by a messenger on horseback, claiming he would be taking one family from the nearby villages, per day, and executing them until they surrendered. He'd also included some colourful insults directed at Ælfric and herself as the "red harpy" that she didn't care to repeat to anyone. Eadric was clearly a mad dog that needed putting down.

Their resulting discussions decided little. She tried to be of use, yet Æva felt awkward and out of sorts considering it was her first-ever meeting of such a nature. She also wondered if her father-in-law had concluded she should somehow take Alaric's place, since, in the past, he'd usually decided matters concerning his holdings with just the help of his two sons. That would be highly unusual, but eminently possible if he hoped for his line to continue through her and Brandon, given he and everyone else believed the boy to be his natural grandson. She didn't have the heart to tell him it wasn't so. She had enough upset and strife to deal with as it was.

Ælfgar's verdict was both simple and heartless. He wasn't disturbed by the innocent lives that had been cruelly ended beneath their walls, claiming it was just a "scare tactic" that would only "intimidate the frail of heart". His father rebuked him for that, rightly informing his son that the people who'd died were not pawns to be brutalised and sacrificed in some sadistic power game. Æva had concurred, prompting Ælfgar to state she was "womanish" and had no understanding of such matters. She'd admitted he was correct. She was new to strategy, and she was indeed a woman. She congratulated him for having noticed. Cenric had laughed. Ælfgar had scowled. Ælfric had then tried to change the subject, suggesting they attempt to bring more of the local population within the fortress walls for their own safety. A noble proposal, she thought.

Cenric dissented. He pointed out they had only a few hundred men; a relatively small number for a stronghold of this size, and that sending them outside piecemeal to gather up unarmed and likely frightened villagers would leave them vulnerable to Eadric's superior force. He also opposed allowing any newcomers inside their walls, claiming Eadric would have spies operating in the area who may attempt to sabotage their defence. Æva wasn't sure how that would work, but Cenric knew his craft. His words carried weight. Alaric had always thought so.

The ealdorman's mind had been made up regardless. Nobody would enter or leave these walls, he'd said, and with any luck, their guests would get tired of waiting outside and head back to Mierċe. Æva wasn't so sure, remaining fearful that Eadric would follow up on his threat to cause further harm to defenceless people. Ælfgar ignored her. Cenric was sympathetic but adamant they had to secure the fortress before taking further action. Ælfric agreed with him.

She again returned to her chambers, spending the rest of the afternoon with her son and the ever-helpful Cenwynn. The girl had once more stepped up to watch Brandon whilst Æva was away, always somehow knowing when she was most needed. Æva felt relieved at their company. Brandon was entirely innocent of the day's events, and Cenwynn had only mentioned it in passing, wondering aloud as to what all the shouting had been about.

Æva took her to one side and out of earshot of Brandon, informing her there was a hostile force active in the countryside and that the fortress may come under direct assault. Cenwynn took the news well, stating there couldn't be much out there that could take their walls by storm. Æva agreed, admiring her fortitude but stressing she was to keep this a secret from Brandon. Cenwynn understood. She was a good sort. It was then they heard another knock at the door. Æva answered, a gruff soldier informing her that Ælfric was again requesting she attend him at the western gate.

Eadric and his men had returned with the evening. They were easily spotted, lit up against the horizon by their own torchlight, yet they were staying far enough away so that they could not be shot at with any real accuracy. Æva couldn't believe it. They'd gathered what looked like about a dozen villagers, snatched from who knows where, and placed them on their knees in a row ahead of them. A figure she assumed to be Eadric himself then executed them, one by one, sliding his blade across their throats with disturbing ease. Some attempted to rise, desperately endeavouring to resist, only to be cut down, Eadric's men tolerating no survivors.

She felt sick, the murmurs, gasps, and expletives from the soldiers on the walls indicating she was not alone in her revulsion. Something like smoke could also be smelt on the wind. She couldn't tell what direction it was coming from, but something had been set alight somewhere. Eadric and his force then moved off into the encroaching darkness, no doubt intent on further barbarism. This was intolerable. Something had to be done.

"I have a notion that could help our situation," Ælfric said quietly, having approached her as soon as he'd seen her climbing the steps up to the battlements. He was dressed for war this time, his upper body clad in a long shirt of ring mail, an impressive-looking blade also hanging from his belt. His face was otherwise largely hidden beneath his helm, this one equipped with a fine-looking curtain of mail that hung down from the helmet itself to cover his jaw and throat. She'd not have known it was him unless he'd spoken, so well protected did he appear tonight. She was glad he was taking the situation so seriously.

"What is this notion of yours?" she asked as they navigated their way back down to ground level, their footsteps echoing up across the sheer stone walls. She hoped it would involve some measure to prevent Eadric from continuing to harass the local farmers. They were vulnerable out there, and she wasn't sure how many more grisly sights she could stand to take in.

"Eadric wants me and my family," the ealdorman began, removing his helm once they'd reached the ground to commence their walk back to the main hall. "I do not intend to fall into his hands just to prevent further loss of life, especially if that means putting you and my sole remaining son at risk."

Æva felt tears come to her eyes. He'd all but admitted he thought Alaric dead. She'd hoped it somehow wasn't the case, thinking her husband might still be alive as long as his father held out hope. Now she knew otherwise. She could contain her grief no longer. She had to say something.

"Your sole son? So your mind is made up on Alaric? You think him dead?"

Ælfric didn't reply at once, instead walking alongside her in silence whilst they approached the market square. His boots sounded heavy and ponderous on the cobbled road, like he'd become suddenly fatigued after the otherwise heroic display he'd put on earlier. When he finally spoke, his voice was strained with sadness, confessing to fears he'd no doubt carried for some time. It hurt her more to see him like this.

"I don't want to think of it, Æva, but it's been weeks now without word. We know what happened at Hringmere. If Ulfcytel had survived, we'd have heard. If a man like that can't withstand the storm that came upon them…"

She knew what he meant. If a hero like Ulfcytel was gone, then Alaric couldn't have survived either. There was a grim logic there, but she didn't want to hear it. They had no idea what had really happened. For all they knew, Alaric could still be breathing, lost in the countryside or perhaps a captive, even. That wasn't a savoury thought. But it was better than being dead.

"I won't believe it until I see a body," she said, tears trailing down her cheeks unbidden. "I won't accept it until I know for sure. I won't. I can't."

Ælfric just carried on walking, silent in the face of her resolve. She had no idea what he might be thinking or whether he thought her foolish or even mad. And yet she knew men were obliged to control their emotions, especially those in positions of authority. He couldn't just fall apart in front of everyone, let alone at a time like this. The few words he'd spoken on his son were no doubt tearing him apart inside. Perhaps she was favoured after all, for she was freer to display her feelings than any man could be. A curious thought.

They reached Ælfric's hall, passing through its exterior courtyards and proceeding inside towards his chambers. Ælfgar was there already, sitting at his father's table and polishing off a bowl of some kind of stew. He appeared at ease with himself, like all was well in the world and he was entirely undisturbed by recent events and not likely to take note of them. A steward Æva didn't know was waiting on him, the bored-looking chap glancing up at them as he refilled Ælfgar's cup. She didn't envy him. Waiting on what had become an insolent snake of a man could not be easy.

She sat down, her back to the door, Ælfric taking a seat between them. The steward brought him a cup of wine, offering her one in turn. She declined, preferring to keep her wits about her, also afraid that in her grief-stricken state the taste of alcohol could push her into habits she'd rather not think on. She had so many worries. She did not intend to add to them.

Ælfgar continued eating, having already half-drained his cup of its contents. The ealdorman settled himself into his chair, looking very much in charge now he was attired in his armour. They all sat there in silence, save for the irritating sound of Ælfgar smacking his lips. Æva almost leapt upright when somebody else suddenly sat beside her. It was only Cenric. She was safe, although she had no idea how a man of his size could move so silently. Perhaps she'd just been lost in thought.

"I've again called you all here to discuss the situation with our new friends from Mierce," announced Ælfric, satisfied that his intended audience was now present. "As you will have seen, Eadric hopes to brutalise my people and thus shame me into surrendering the fortress. I will not do so. But I won't leave Eadric free to maim and slaughter as he pleases either."

"What will you do then?" interrupted Ælfgar, finishing off the last of his wine. "We don't have the numbers to confront him in the open, and we can't raise reinforcements as long as we're trapped here. We're besieged."

"You are partially right," conceded his father. "But Eadric's force is entirely on land, and his stated goal is to have me and my kin here surrender to him. I will inconvenience him by spiriting us away by sea. Tonight."

"So we're fleeing?" asked Æva, aghast. "What will become of our home? What will become of the people in it? Eadric is bound to take it out on them once he realises we've fled."

"He may do, which is why the garrison will continue to hold the walls," Ælfric explained. "Only Cenric will accompany us. His subordinate, Cuthbert, will take over the organisation of the fort's defences. He's up to it, Cenric?"

"I would say so, my lord," responded the man himself, "but may I ask where you intend for us to go? If I'm right in assuming I am to be your bodyguard, I would like to know what dangers we might face."

"A good question," said the ealdorman, "and I will answer. We'll go to Suthhamtunam, where I will rally the local garrison and march back here, gathering fighting men to me as I go. Once I arrive, Cuthbert will sally forth through the gates to join me. We'll then chase Eadric all the way to Mierce. Should he decide to fight, I will kill him."

Cenric grunted in approval, a grim smile breaking out across his face at the prospect of retribution. Ælfgar carried on eating like nothing had been said, either unimpressed or totally accepting of his fate. It was left to Æva to pose a question.

"And my son? Will I be permitted to bring him with me? I can't just leave him alone here with those men on the loose outside. It's too much."

"Of course you can bring Brandon," chuckled Ælfric, shaking his head slightly in mock dismay. "I would not have my grandson left here alone without his mother."

Æva tried to suppress a twinge of guilt. She knew he didn't know that Brandon was not of his blood. Alaric had never told him, nor displayed any willingness to do so. Yet there was something about hearing Ælfric give voice to a lie, as if it were the simplest and most wholesome thing in the world. There was nothing to be done about it presently. She wouldn't take the risk of randomly blurting out the boy's true ancestry. Not now.

"There are several vessels currently docked out on the wharf," Ælfgar commented abruptly, finally finishing his stew to begin making his way through another cup of wine. "All of them will be perfectly suitable for such a short trip. When will we be leaving?"

"As soon as possible," his father said. "Gather only what you can't do without. I've already had words with one of the captains, and payment has been promised. We'll slip away into the night and be in Suthhamtunam before dawn. Then Eadric will regret the day he ever came to Hamptonscir."

Æva appreciated his resolve. And it was a good plan, almost foolproof as far as she could tell. She departed back to her chambers, intent on preparing Brandon for the journey. Cenwynn had been waiting for her, yet her earnest, welcoming smile vanished rapidly when Æva tried to explain that she was leaving.

The poor girl took some time to calm down. She'd gotten the wrong impression and begun to panic, thinking Æva had meant the fortress was about to fall and she'd be left to the mercies of those who took it. Æva felt terrible, and so made the proper effort to explain the walls would still be manned and she would be returning soon with reinforcements. Cenwynn eventually relented, asking only that they hurry back and save her from boredom. Æva smiled. Her first in a while.

She quickly dressed for the journey, donning a thick grey hooded cloak in case the weather turned once they were on the water. She made sure Brandon was similarly attired, informing him they were simply "going on a journey by boat" for the fun of it. The child had no idea what had taken place outside the fortress just that evening. She intended to keep it that way.

Æva met Ælfric and the rest of his party over by the eastern gate. The old man had thrown on a thick cloak of his own, yet his sword and mail were still visible from the front, his helm again concealing much of his face. She hoped the waters remained calm. He'd be in trouble if he fell overboard with all that extra weight.

Ælfgar had managed to procure himself another warrior from the garrison to help guide him, this one a surly-looking fellow with a jet-black beard protruding from his helmet. She felt a brief pang of sorrow for her brother-in-law. The poor fool was always so dependent on others, and the severity of their situation was almost certainly making him feel more vulnerable than usual. She thought to offer him a reassuring word, only to decide against it. She wasn't in the mood for his forked tongue. Perhaps the sea air might return him to his senses and remind him of the man he used to be. But she doubted it.

The sight of Cenric helped put her mind at ease. He looked like an absolute monster of a man when in full battle dress, his armour bulking out his already sizeable frame. He'd come more than prepared, sporting a hefty spear clutched in one hand, a sheathed sword and what looked like some kind of cudgel tucked at his belt. With Cenric around, she could almost feel pity for anyone foolish enough to challenge them tonight.

They hurried on through the gate, the guards on duty heaving the huge oaken doors back and open with some considerable effort. The party moved out into the night beyond, Ælfric carrying a single torch to light their way. They proceeded down a wide, gravel and stone avenue built to allow the transit of heavy goods and materials from the wharf up ahead to the fortress behind. Æva kept Brandon close, the night air feeling strangely uncomfortable despite the freshness of the sea-borne breeze. She hoped this wouldn't take too long.

The worst-case scenario didn't happen. She'd feared Eadric might have somehow sequestered some of his men along the route they now travelled, hoping to perhaps apprehend them as they hurried down to the wharf. Fortunately, nothing of the kind took place, and before long she could see how foolish such fears were, since any assailants would be certain to be spotted by the soldiers on the fortress walls and shot full of arrows before they could do much of anything. All the same, she was glad to have almost reached what she assumed to be their ship, the vessel being moored just up ahead and ready to transport them away to safety.

They stepped off the wharf and onto the deck, Ælfric moving to exchange some hushed words with what Æva assumed to be the captain. She initially felt like she might struggle to keep her balance, as the ship seemed to repeatedly shift beneath her feet whilst it bobbed gently in the admittedly calm waters of the harbour. It was an impressive vessel, appearing as a sleek, wooden hulk of some considerable length, its single mast sporting a presently furled red and white sail. It was largely empty tonight, giving Æva the impression the crew had unloaded whatever they'd been transporting prior to agreeing to the journey to Suthhamtunam.

The crew themselves were few and far between, consisting mainly of about two dozen oarsmen sitting at their oarlocks in lines down each side of the deck. Æva was surprised at this, thinking a ship this size would require more people. They otherwise paid the newcomers little attention, their hairy, weather-beaten faces largely expressionless whilst they huddled at their stations. Ælfric had probably ordered the captain to keep their identities a secret from his people. A wise decision.

She made her way close to the front of the ship, wanting to look out across the water. She'd regained some of her sense of balance by the time she reached the prow, making her think her decision to take cautious steps until she got used to being off solid ground had been a wise one. She couldn't see much ahead; just darkness and the shifting of the sea, neither of which filled her with confidence. She set Brandon down, huddling next to him on the deck. The boy closed his eyes and fell asleep on the spot. She wished she could rest so easily.

Æva lay him across her lap and wrapped her arms and cloak around him. She then leaned back against the hull, the shifting of the deck providing a strange comfort. This continued even when the oars hit the water and they cast off, the ship now gliding through the surf at an impressive rate. The men knew what they were doing, each one putting his back into the rowing with stoic determination.

Ælfric wandered over in her direction, his footsteps heavy and sullen. He reached the foremost part of the prow and stopped, staring out into the blackness as they made their way south west and away from the harbour. He still held his flaming torch, the light shining out across the water, the smell of charring wood proving to be quite pleasant. The wind remained manageable, the breeze merely tugging at the edges of his cloak, although she was unsure whether it would stay that way.

She sensed she might have an opportunity here. She eased the sleeping Brandon from her embrace and rose to make her way over to Ælfric. She paused, removing her cloak and placing it around her son, partially folding it to function as a pillow. It would have to do. Brandon carried on slumbering regardless, as content as if he were in his own bed.

Ælfric heard Æva approach, turning his head slightly before resuming his gaze out to sea. She moved up alongside him, staring out into the dark, unsure of what he could be looking at, if anything. The sea air washed over her, sharp and clean, the dark waters surging and parting around them as they ploughed ever onward. She'd never been out on the sea before, thinking it cold, unpleasant, and frightening, but she could now understand the allure some spoke of. There was something captivating about it, like the deepening expanse stretching out before her was privy to some great mystery no human mind could hope to grasp. She took to simply staring for a moment or two, gazing upon its shifting surface, the starlight at times reflecting off the water in a way she found really quite beautiful.

"You wished to speak to me?" Ælfric half-mumbled, the sound of his voice snapping her out of her reverie. She did indeed, and yet she wasn't sure where to begin. The events of the past day were unlike anything she'd experienced in years. Safety had to be a priority, she supposed, especially with Brandon in tow. She'd start with that.

"Can you trust your people in Suthhamtunam?"

"I do trust them," replied Ælfric, still staring straight ahead. "Eadwulf and his boys have done the place proud since its reconstruction. He's loyal to me and the king."

"That's what I mean," said Æva, "he's loyal to the king. And the king wants us in chains and deprived of our home. What if your Eadwulf puts that above any affection he may have for you as his ealdorman?"

"I can understand your fears, Æva. But as it stands, I'm not even sure Eadric has the king's blessing to be here. He's been an acquisitive little rat for a long time now, and I wouldn't put it past him to simply lie to try and justify whatever it is he thinks he's doing."

"And what if it isn't just words?" Æva asked. "What if he really has been ordered by the king to take us away and seize our home? Does Æthelred have cause to be displeased with us?"

Ælfric exhaled slowly, the action sounding metallic and peculiar from beneath his mailed helm. She'd heard it said that King Æthelred was not easily pleased and had even become unstable in recent years as crisis after crisis afflicted his realm. Perhaps he had indeed sent Eadric to apprehend them, although if he'd given the order to be so brutal, she failed to see how he could ever claim to be just in his rule. Kings had authority. But it was how they exercised that authority that counted.

"I have failed him in the past," Ælfric admitted, turning his head slightly towards her. "It's often hard to gauge his mood, now more than ever. I was not always as I am now…I have…sinned. And dragged others into sin with me. Our family has suffered for this greatly, and Æthelred does struggle when it comes to forgiveness. I'd hoped he might one day manage it. I fear I was wrong."

"What do you mean?" asked Æva, now perturbed. "Are you saying you have done him wrong? And he's punished you before?"

"It's a long and complex affair, my dear," came the response, the man clearly not wanting to give too many details. "Events long past got out of hand, and Æthelred thought to make an example of certain persons."

With that last word, Ælfric turned to briefly glance back down the length of the ship. Æva looked where she thought he had, wondering who or what he'd meant. She saw her son, asleep close by, doubly insulated against the night and still as peaceful as anyone could be. Further back was the crew, still positioned in lines running down either side of the deck and rowing like it was the easiest and most natural thing to be doing at this hour. She spied Ælfgar behind them, seated with his bodyguard close to where they'd embarked, looking to be in conversation with both the ship's captain and Cenric.

A knot of suspicion formed in her stomach. Ælfric had clearly just looked in the direction of his irksome and very blind son. Nobody had ever told her how exactly he'd come to find himself burdened with such a handicap. Not the man himself, not her father-in-law, not even Alaric. Had the king…

"Æthelred took Ælfgar's sight." She wasn't asking. She'd merely given voice to her own realisation. She'd heard of barbarous rulers inflicting all manner of punishments on their enemies, but to blind a man for the wrongdoings of his father sounded monumentally unjust. There had to be more to this.

Ælfric had turned to face her. He looked quite intimidating now, the torch in his hand lighting up his full figure against the prevailing night sky. She still couldn't see his face, but she sensed he was displeased, her words perhaps coming too close to some truth he'd rather she did not approach.

"There is no need to bother yourself with these matters, daughter," said the ealdorman, his voice authoritative yet without malice. "Politics is a difficult thing to be involved in, and one should not leap to conclusions, especially when it comes to kings. Do you understand?"

Æva nodded, feeling uneasy. She'd always known Ælfric as just another old soldier, full of stories and memories, yet well past his prime. Now she wasn't so sure, for his actions today at the walls had demonstrated he was not without strength. He'd also survived two separate campaigns against the armies of Thorkell; last year when the Danes had attacked Hamptonscir directly and again more recently when fighting in Eastengle. He wasn't a man to cross.

And yet she wanted to ask more. His lack of denial as to her statement that the king was indeed responsible for Ælfgar's blinding had piqued her curiosity. She then realised that to act on that curiosity would be a fool's move. Ælfric was unlikely to tolerate the subject being broached further, and attempting to press him on it would do considerably more harm than good. She relented. She'd find out the truth somehow. Right now, she had other concerns.

"I need to know my son will be safe," she said. "If your Eadwulf believes the king wants us apprehended, we could have fled Porteceaster for nothing."

"Put your mind at ease," said Ælfric, turning again to gaze across the waters. "Odds are Eadwulf hasn't even heard of our situation. Why would he? And if he has and is so eager to do the king's supposed will, why did he not march against us with Eadric? Eadwulf is loyal to me and will be doubly so when he sees me getting off this ship with Cenric in tow."

That made sense. Æva couldn't imagine why this Eadwulf would have heard that the king was after them, assuming that was even true and Eadric wasn't just lying. Having the Ealdorman of Hamptonscir turn up in person would help remind the man of where his loyalty should lie, especially when backed by a giant like Cenric. Then it would be just a case of raising a force and confronting Eadric. Hopefully, they'd then learn the truth of what the king was up to. Perhaps then they'd be able to find her husband. She decided to inquire as to precisely that.

"Have you had any thoughts on Alaric?"

Ælfric's shoulders seemed to sag, as if his recent martial vigour had partially left him at the mention of his son. She felt sorrow at the sight of it, but she needed answers from him. They couldn't defeat their enemies here only to ignore unfinished business. And she wouldn't just give up on the man she'd promised before God to love, honour, and obey. What Ælfric said next was thus one of the sweetest things she'd heard in a while.

"Once this irritant otherwise known as Eadric of Mierce has been dealt with, I'll send Cenric and some men to Eastengle to search for Alaric."

"That sounds dangerous," a voice from behind said, both Æva and Ælfric turning to face it with some haste. She had no idea how a man as huge as Cenric had been able to get behind them without being heard. Yet there he was, illuminated in Ælfric's torchlight like nothing was out of the ordinary. A master of stealth as well as arms. Ælfric gave voice to her thoughts, a chuckle escaping his lips.

"How do you move like that, Cenric? I don't even know how it's possible, given your...dimensions."

"I get where I have to go, my lord," Cenric replied, his voice light and cheerful. "And I notice young Brandon is slumbering. He doesn't need me making a racket up and down the deck when he needs his rest."

"That's very decent of you," Æva said, sincere in her appreciation. He nodded in acknowledgement, turning to Ælfric before speaking again.

"And as to your dangerous proposal, my lord...that was a hard fight the Danes gave us in Eastengle. And yet you and I know these heathens die like anyone else if you hit them hard enough. If you send me back there, I'll find your son and bring him home to his good lady here."

Æva didn't know if she'd ever felt such relief. She'd been lost in grief until now, hoping beyond hope that Alaric would just walk on through her door one morning and gather her up in his arms. Nothing of the kind had happened, and her sadness had only intensified as the notion that her husband wasn't coming home became more pronounced by the day.

"You have my thanks also, Cenric," said Ælfric, appearing similarly grateful for the man's noble words. "I'll admit we should have done this sooner. With all that's happened and the wound I sustained...I'm afraid my emotions got the better of me. I'd lost hope of anyone coming back from Eastengle alive. The thought of my son..."

Ælfric suddenly passed his torch to Cenric. The old man then bowed forward slightly, holding his gauntleted hands up to his helm and lifting it from his head. He removed it entirely, holding it in his hands and bringing them down to rest in front of him. His aged features were marked with sadness, and tears had welled around his dark eyes to almost spill down his silvered cheeks. His breathing was faint but laboured, and he appeared as one who was only now dealing with a sadness he'd had to suppress for far too long.

"It's not easy to be a man," he said, his voice quiet and pained, Cenric having already grunted in acknowledgement of what he'd said. "I would never show my grief like this to just anyone. But I didn't want you, Æva, to mistake my inaction for indifference. When I heard that Ulfcytel had been defeated...with no word from

Alaric…I despaired. And I'm sorry for that."

Æva was astonished. She'd felt like she'd been suffering in isolation, condemned to maintaining a facade of normality during the day whilst weeping bitterly alone at night. It had never occurred to her that Ælfric had been suffering with her, albeit with the added burdens of both his position as ealdorman and the wound he'd taken in battle. She didn't know what to say. She instead reached out, placing her hand gently upon his shoulder. He smiled at her sadly, blinking his tears away with some effort.

"I'll find whoever you want me to find," Cenric said firmly. "It'll be a mess up there. It certainly looked that way when the Danes went after us at that village near Theodford. But if I can bring Alaric back, I will, even if…"

Even if he was dead. Cenric had caught himself before he could finish his sentence, his expression suggesting he thought himself the most foolish man in the world. Æva wasn't upset. She'd been struggling with that possibility for night after agonising night for some time now. She'd be glad to have her husband home, even if it was just to say goodbye properly. She'd have an answer then as to what had befallen him. That was preferable to not knowing entirely. The uncertainty would drive her mad.

"Don't feel embarrassed, Cenric," she said, feeling sorry for him since he clearly meant well. "Anything you can do, anything you can find out, will be appreciated. God bless and keep you, truly."

She realised then that she'd forgotten about her husband's best friend, Osmund. If Alaric was actually dead, then Osmund would have certainly perished at his side, for the two of them were simply inseparable. As far as she knew, Osmund had no family, and his first and only wife had taken her own life after their child had died in infancy. The poor fellow had gone on to suffer so terribly, and Alaric's efforts to share his burdens had seen them become as brothers. She would like to discover what had happened to the man. He was a noble soul.

"Do you remember Osmund?" she asked, looking to Cenric still.

"Aye, lady," he answered, stifling a sliver of laughter at the mention of him. "He was a funny one, and a better fighter I've rarely met. I think it's fair to say he remained at your husband's right hand no matter what happened. And I can think of easier things to do than fight him and Alaric both. Chances are any Dane who tried it didn't live long enough to regret it too much."

That was a comforting thought. Æva decided she would continue to allow herself the luxury of hope. Hope was always preferable to despair, and if Osmund had stayed close to Alaric, as was his wont, that improved their chances of survival considerably. With Cenric soon to come to the rescue…she caught herself. Hope was good, but getting carried away and assuming absolutely everything was going to turn out perfectly would set her up for disappointment. There had to be some realism here.

"If Osmund is not with my husband," she said cautiously, "then please at least try to find out what happened to him. I'd like to know."

"I understand, my lady," answered Cenric. "He was a decent man as far as I could tell. I'll discover his fate, be sure of that."

There didn't seem to be much else to say. She thanked them both, Cenric for his comforting words and Ælfric for having trusted her enough to share his pain. She returned to her son, lying down next to him on the deck and partially covering herself with the cloak she'd draped over him earlier. A little cold and uncomfortable, but she wouldn't risk waking him. She closed her eyes.

Mere moments seemed to have passed when she thought she heard Ælfric calling for her. She sat up, noticing how the previously brilliant night sky had retreated in the face of the now emergent dawn. She looked around, taking in her surroundings, the stark, grey light of the approaching morning lighting up the horizon.

All seemed peaceful. The crew remained at their stations, ploughing their oars rhythmically and tirelessly through the yielding surf. The sea had gotten slightly rougher, its waves impacting on the hull with a repetitious slapping sound, although it as yet showed no sign of disturbing their progress. Brandon was still asleep beside her and looked to have barely moved during the night. She wondered just how long it would be until the child awoke and requested something to eat. Knowing him, it wouldn't be too long.

Æva joined her father-in-law at the prow, unsure if he'd even slept, the sight before them drawing her attention. She could see the coastline off to her right, the land seeming to rise out of the waves like some great, moss-coloured beast, the familiar forests and gentle hills of old Westseaxe receding into the distance. There were signs of human activity up ahead, and before long the curve of the shoreline gave way to what looked like the stone and timber contours of a significant port.

As they came closer, Æva spied the outline of several other ships moored along a sequence of jetties, the wooden structures protruding out into the waves like blunted spears. She could see people moving atop them towards the shore, some heaving chests and crates likely filled with precious cargo destined for sale elsewhere.

Beyond the docks arose a mass of buildings, mainly yellowing thatch and dark stone brick, that poured out and across the shore to spread inland like a carpet. A sturdy-looking stone wall encircled much of it, something Æva presumed had been constructed some time ago to fend off attackers. The town looked like it had certainly grown since then to spill out beyond its protective boundaries and host a population she'd guess to be in the range of several thousand. This had to be their destination.

"What do you think?" Ælfric asked, sounding enthused despite apparently having not slept.

"It looks…am I right in thinking this is where our journey ends?"

"For now, but we won't tarry long. Give me enough time to talk with Eadwulf, and we'll be marching home with an army at our back."

She hoped that was true. Fleeing Portceaster had been the right decision. There had been absolutely no sense in remaining trapped within the fortress for the sake of safety alone. But there was something about large towns that unsettled her, this one in particular. She couldn't quite put her finger on it, but as they drew ever closer, her unease seemed to grow.

The crew expertly manoeuvred their vessel alongside one of the emptier jetties, their efforts soon assisted by several rough-looking men throwing them a sequence of ropes to haul and then tether them in place. Brandon awoke with a start when the far side of their hull bumped against the wooden jetty, his eyes wide and forehead furrowed with dismay. Æva calmed him with the promise of a good breakfast, and the boy eagerly followed when they disembarked, their ship bobbing up and down erratically as if in protest at their leaving.

She followed Ælfric down the length of the jetty, the waves swelling and frothing below them. Cenric and Ælfgar came up behind her, the latter supported by the guard he'd arranged to accompany him from Porteceaster. He looked unsure of himself, and he'd required a great deal of help to disembark and amble after them in pursuit. She stifled a laugh when she imagined him blithely wandering off the edge and tumbling into the sea. She shouldn't think like that. It wasn't charitable. But it was funny.

A flock of seagulls flew overhead, their piercing cries cutting through the crisp morning air. When she finally stepped onto dry land, Æva felt strangely relieved. They'd only been at sea for some hours, but the journey had been a novel yet uncertain experience for her, and the surety of solid ground was very much her preferred environment. Ælfric strode on without remark, clearly in no doubt as to where he was and where he was going. They all followed, the ealdorman leading them through the surprisingly open streets, their footsteps hard and sharp upon the stony ground.

There were few people about, and the town looked oddly depopulated, although that was almost certainly due to the time of day. Yet the place still felt strangely lifeless, the thatched houses and occasional glimpse of a steeple or tower appearing almost ominous in the light of what was otherwise a pleasant morning.

Cenric moved up alongside her, his tense manner suggesting he felt as uneasy as she was. Ælfric had by now stopped at the entrance to what looked like some kind of walled enclave. He was exchanging words with two armed men standing guard, the pair of them looking unusually vigilant for the hour. Whatever he'd said to them had the desired effect, the two men turning to push open the doors behind them and allow Ælfric to pass within. They all followed, Brandon driving the guards to laughter when he suddenly asked whether they'd had their breakfast yet. Æva smiled, assuring him they'd have something to eat soon.

They were now moving through a modest courtyard, a short cobbled path leading them towards what could only be the heavily thatched hall of somebody important. Ælfric halted again, hammering on a pair of sturdy-looking doors until they were opened from within. He stepped through, the rest of them again following.

Inside, it was fairly empty, the interior consisting of a flat, wide ground floor, its walls decorated with an assortment of shields, weapons, and tapestries that spoke to the presence of a man of high standing. Two warriors stood on either side of the entrance they'd come through, having just opened up in the face of Ælfric's knocking. Æva also spotted two other armed men guarding a single figure now standing at a table on the far side of the chamber.

This had to be Eadwulf. Aged, with grey hair and beard, and perhaps also a little overweight, the man was otherwise unremarkable save for the brutal-looking axe he had tethered at his side. He looked to Ælfric, his face unemotional as the ealdorman approached and leaned over to embrace him. Æva hurried to keep up, Cenric matching her pace. She felt anxious. This place bore an ill feeling.

"Eadwulf!" Ælfric exclaimed, removing his helm and placing it on the table before him. "I bet you didn't expect to see an ealdorman gracing your home at this time in the morning!"

Eadwulf simply stared at him. Æva stared back, wondering what he could be thinking. She then heard the sound of heavy footsteps, turning in time to see several more warriors emerging from side rooms on both their left and right. Cenric tensed. So did she. Ælfric's hand drifted towards his sword. Then Eadwulf spoke, his voice cold and bereft of feeling.

"You would normally be right in that, Ælfric. But I'm afraid your days as an ealdorman are soon to end."

He went for his axe. Ælfric drew his sword with a shout. Cenric raised his spear, Ælfgar's bodyguard baring his teeth as he did the same.

Eadwulf's men charged.

X

He'd thought in the past he could kill whenever necessary and not have it bother him. Now he'd killed a man in his sleep he wasn't so sure. There was something about it that sickened his stomach, as if he'd tarnished a part of himself that should have always remained undefiled. It was easy enough to say it was war, or that such actions were taken when you had no other choice. These were just words people used to lie to themselves about the grim deeds they'd sooner forget. It wasn't good enough. Alaric would face what he had done.

They'd slaughtered the eight or so Danes they'd found in the forest clearing. The first two had been on watch when Alaric, Osbert, and the rest of the men had attacked them. Osbert had killed the first, accosting him from behind and sliding his seax across his throat before he could so much as gurgle. A large man going by the name of Eadwald had grabbed the other from the side, wrestling him to the ground and strangling the life from him, Alaric placing his boot on his arm to prevent him from drawing his weapon.

They'd then dispatched their slumbering companions, butchering them whilst they lay flat or curled up in what they'd no doubt all assumed would be just another night's sleep. One awoke just as Alaric placed his left hand over his mouth and stabbed him through the throat, his eyes wide with panic as the blood flowed from his body.

Alaric held his gaze, noting how the light in his eyes flickered and faded to nothing within the space of a few seconds. Somebody behind him had then awoken and tried to cry out, only to fall silent when one of Osbert's men put an axe through his head. The noise he'd made was irrelevant anyway. There was nobody left alive to help him.

It wasn't certain what they'd been doing here. Thorkell's main force was believed to be some distance off towards the west, continuing its campaign of plunder and predation. Osbert suggested some Danes may be looking to separate from his army and double back, hoping to prey on refugees attempting to return to their homes. A strange notion. Yet Alaric thought there could be some truth to it.

In any case, this had been the second party of Danes they'd come across, excluding the three men who'd pursued Alaric on the road from Hringmere. They'd killed all of them, in this instance by sneaking up on them in the night, or by day when they'd ambushed a similar group after lying in wait in the ruins of a burnt-out farmhouse. Alaric had preferred that encounter. At least the man he'd killed there had been awake and on his feet, axe in hand.

He'd realised then there was something off about Osbert. Alaric hadn't expected him to be the same young man he'd met over a month ago. Back then, he'd had an air of endearing optimism that Alaric knew would likely vanish with his first taste of battle. He'd seen it happen before, and he suspected he'd gone through the same process many years ago. But this was different. It wasn't just that he smiled less and avoided conversation. Osbert was now a little too good at what he did, taking lives as if they were of no consequence at all. Perhaps Alaric had just grown soft. He had spent a long time recovering from the wound he'd taken at Gipeswic. Maybe he was the one who'd changed.

Their group had spent the rest of the night heading north, remaining ever-alert for traces of the enemy. The forests of Eastengle were dense and provided a welcome refuge, but Alaric had been caught by surprise here before and refused to let his guard down. They got to talking, making the effort to speak softly as they traversed the woods. According to Osbert, Ulfcytel had indeed survived the battle at Hringmere and retreated with a skeleton force to the forests north west of Wadetuna. Alaric wasn't sure where that was, but Osbert said it was close and that he'd been sent out from there only days before to scavenge for supplies.

Osbert had not expected to find Alaric, thinking him dead or captured following the attack on Thorkell's camp. Alaric was at least comforted in that Osbert seemed genuinely pleased to see him. The lad hadn't completely changed for the worse. But he wouldn't talk about what had happened at Hringmere, and his face darkened whenever it was brought up. Alaric decided to leave him be for the moment. Not all wounds were of the flesh. He'd find out what had happened once they reached Ulfcytel.

They'd hurried on, Osbert stressing they did not have far to go until they reached relative safety. They were currently making their way through yet more woodland, traversing a low, forested slope that wound its way down towards a narrow roadway snaking off to the south and east. Alaric crouched just behind a tree, his left hand using it for support as he caught his breath, his ears straining intently. There was something up ahead, moving along the road below. He lay down on his stomach, his palms spread out on the hard, cool ground, Osbert and his men doing likewise. They could hear hooves. Horses then. More than one. Definitely more than one.

The first rider hove into view, the rest of his company a moment or two later. There were about twenty of them, all armed with an assortment of spears and a few blades, several of them also attired in truly spectacular coats of mail that contrasted sharply with the more regular, village-forged armour of their escorts. Their helms, too, were works of art, covering almost the entirety of their faces, possessing what looked like silver and gold plate worked into their surfaces. It reminded Alaric of his own helmet, before it had been destroyed. There was a good reason why. These weren't Danes. They were Englishmen.

He saw Osbert had come to the same realisation. He was staring at Alaric, unsure of how to proceed. Were these men reinforcements from the north? Whoever they were, they could hear them now, several of the riders chattering to each other in restrained, serious tones. It was English, for certain. Alaric decided to find out what was going on.

He got to his feet, his arms held up and over his head, palms facing outwards in a gesture of placation. He took a few steps forward. Then the yelling started. He'd been spotted almost immediately, and the entire column wheeled to face him, erupting in a flurry of raised voices and brandished weapons. Alaric continued making his way down the slope, his arms still raised, hoping to look as non-threatening as possible. He couldn't tell if Osbert was behind him. Had this actually been a bad idea?

Somebody bellowed for him to stop moving and identify himself. He responded eagerly, giving them his name and also mentioning his father. That didn't seem to mollify them, as another demand followed, instructing him to come out into the open. He obeyed, making his way down to them with nimble steps. He stood on the road's edge, the riders moving out to surround him, their spears pointed towards his chest. Somebody barked a question as to whether he was alone.

"I have told you who I am," Alaric scolded, "so at least do me the honour of letting me know who you are."

"I would say that's a reasonable request," came a civil yet authoritative voice, possibly from one of those in the ornate armour. Alaric saw he was correct when one rider removed his silver-inlaid helm, revealing a visage that could only be compared to a sledgehammer. It wasn't a brutal or unpleasant face by any means, but it was robustly built, the young man's long dark hair, beard, and eyes giving him an overly serious look, akin to one who had the weight of the world upon his shoulders and yet fancied himself strong enough to take it. His snorting, jet-black beast of a mount only added to that impression, both rider and horse looking to be of a similar temperament. He spoke again, his words almost causing Alaric's jaw to drop in surprise.

"I am Edmund, son of King Æthelred."

Alaric lowered himself on one knee. Of all the people to meet in this ravaged place, he'd stumbled upon an aetheling. He was about to ask what he was doing in Eastengle when more shouting started. Osbert and his men had emerged from the tree line and were advancing towards them. Alaric quickly explained who they were before Edmund and his escort thought they were in an ambush. It seemed to work, the men calming down and allowing Osbert and company to approach.

"You are survivors of the battle at Hringmere?" Edmund asked, his thick-set, gauntleted hand still gripping the hilt of a fine-looking sword.

"We'd been told it was a disaster," said the rider next to him, this one also attired in similarly elaborate armour, a deep crimson cloak draped around his shoulders. Before Alaric could answer him, he'd removed his own helm, his blue eyes, blond hair, and almost clean-shaven face contrasting sharply with Edmund's fiercer look.

"My name is Æthelstan, and I am yet another son of King Æthelred," he said, his expression surprisingly amiable. "You have, of course, just met my younger brother, Edmund. Don't anger him. He doesn't fall over when you hit him like other men."

Alaric smiled awkwardly, dumbstruck at the fact he was in a conversation with not one but two aethelings in full battle dress. Æthelstan was heir to the throne and, from what Alaric had heard, an incredibly skilled warrior. To meet them here was quite astonishing, and he very much desired to know what exactly they were doing, once he managed to overcome his nerves. Osbert was looking similarly taken aback, he and the rest of his party also dropping to one knee out of respect.

"Don't worry, my friends," came a softer voice from a still-helmeted rider. "We mean you no harm. This is dangerous countryside, is all. We had to know who you were, for I don't think I could have it on my conscience if I let these two die in an ambush."

"I appreciate that, Morcar," Æthelstan said jovially, "but I have no intention of dying just yet. Besides, it was obvious these men were not Danes. They don't stink of excrement, for one."

Everyone laughed, Alaric too. Æthelstan gestured for them to rise from their knees, the party complying with some relief given the hardness of the road. Osbert found both his courage and his voice, confirming they were indeed survivors of Hringmere on their way to the Ealdorman Ulfcytel. That got a reaction, the aethelings appearing to simultaneously sigh in relief and then nod towards the other in affirmation. These two were definitely brothers, there was no doubt about that.

"That is excellent news," Edmund said, sounding genuinely glad. "We'd heard Ulfcytel was missing, and so feared the worst. Where is he now? And do you know if our uncle, Æthelstan, is also among the living?"

Alaric went to speak, his words instead catching in his throat. He'd known that Æthelstan was the brother of the king's late wife, Ælfgifu, but he'd never expected to just blunder into his nephews, nor have to break news to them that could give them cause for heartache. And yet he must do precisely that, right now.

"I'm afraid he fell in battle," said Alaric, his eye downcast. "He fought well, that I can assure you. But despite his bravery, he was overcome. I'm so sorry."

The brothers looked to each other, both visibly saddened. "And Ulfcytel?" asked Edmund again. "Since he lives, where is he?"

"Some distance away," Osbert answered, "and hiding out with the other survivors. We've been snapping at the enemy's heels for weeks now, hitting them whenever we think we can get away with it, but Thorkell has moved from reach."

"He has indeed," said the rider Æthelstan had referred to as Morcar. "He's sacked Cantebrigie already and laid waste to all around it. It's now too dangerous to take the direct route to Lundenburg from the Five Boroughs, so we decided to head east and then hasten south, hoping to discover what had become of the brave Ulfcytel as we travelled."

The Five Boroughs. Alaric knew who this man was now. Morcar was a man of considerable standing there, and his father had spoken of him in the past. Alongside the noble Sigeferth, the pair of them effectively ruled the Five Boroughs together, or at least that was what Alaric had been led to believe. They were good men. That's all he needed to know.

"Will you come with us then?" Alaric inquired, knowing Ulfcytel would be pleased to have the two aethelings with them. He didn't give voice to some of his other thoughts, thinking it very possible they'd be angered if he outright asked them why they'd not travelled to Hringmere to support them when they'd needed it. The king had likely forbidden it. He was surprised when their next words confirmed it.

"I'm afraid we must speak with our father," said Edmund. "He forbade us from giving aid to Ulfcytel, despite failing to provide any good reason as to why. Unfortunately, his latest decision compels us to act. We must change his mind, with all haste."

"What exactly has happened?" Alaric asked, confused. He felt awkward to pester them like this, but they seemed to be quite respectful towards him, perhaps because he'd been careful to mention he was the son of the Ealdorman Ælfric when they'd first demanded he identify himself. It was good to have connections. But Alaric had a feeling these two would be gracious even if he were a common farmhand.

The two aethelings again looked at each other, their expressions unsure, as if they were reticent to answer his question. They then looked to Morcar, who simply nodded towards them, apparently content to leave the decision in their hands. Æthelstan broke the silence.

"I'm afraid our father has imposed a new tax on the kingdom. It is quite considerable. Too considerable. We fear he is attempting to pay Thorkell to leave England in peace, crippling his kingdom just to pay off another murderous foreigner. We wish to reason with him."

Alaric wasn't surprised. Æthelred had done this before, lavishing gifts on those who came to his shores with bloodshed and theft on their minds. It was foolish, for his actions simply encouraged return visits of yet more heathens demanding payment. A display of strength was what was always needed. He couldn't fathom why the king was unable to see that. He kept his opinion to himself. He didn't want to antagonise the aethelings by insulting their father. He had a feeling they'd heard it all before, anyway.

They were otherwise satisfied to let them be on their way. Both of them requested Alaric convey their good wishes to Ulfcytel, saying if he wished to return to Lundenburg, they'd be honoured to be blessed with his company. Alaric wasn't sure how that might turn out, but he promised to tell him in any case. Æthelstan gazed down at Alaric as he turned to leave, scrutinising his rather sorry appearance.

"Recent events have not been good to you, have they, my noble friend?"

"I'm afraid not," Alaric replied, uncomfortable. He hoped unkind words were not about to follow. He couldn't just tell him to shut his face or else.

"What happened to your sword?" Æthelstan queried, placing his helm back on his head. "I imagine a son of Ælfric had one at some point?"

"I did," Alaric mumbled, looking down at the seax tucked into his breecs. "I'm afraid I lost mine in battle. Things went badly, in more ways than one."

Æthelstan suddenly unsheathed his sword, Alaric and Osbert flinching at the rapid and unexpected movement. He flipped it around with expert ease, extending it hilt-first towards Alaric, his expression now hidden beneath his helmet. Alaric wondered what exactly he was up to.

"Take it," Æthelstan commanded. "I have a spare and then plenty more after that. I won't have a good man like you wandering around here without a proper weapon."

Alaric reached out, astonished. He gripped the blade, feeling the weight when Æthelstan released his hold on it. It was a work of art; its pommel and cross-guard all quality iron with what looked like silver plate. It was heavy, too, like a sword should be, its killing power more than evident as he held it up to the sunlight. Alaric went to sheath it within the long-empty scabbard that still hung from his belt. It didn't fit. The blade was broader than his previous weapon. Æthelstan saw his conundrum, removing his silver-studded belt and sheath and tossing it to him. Alaric caught them in his left hand, again astonished at his generosity.

"Don't thank me," he said casually, "like I said, I have plenty more."

Without a further word, he turned his horse and began to proceed down the road, his mounted escort stirring into motion with him. Edmund smiled and nodded at Alaric and Osbert both before placing his helm back upon his head. He then turned to ride after his brother, yet Alaric saw how Edmund made a point of nodding towards each and every one of Osbert's men as he passed. A fine gesture, he thought. He watched them go, and the aethelings and their entourage soon disappeared from view, leaving them alone on the road.

They quickly got over their chance encounter, and Alaric and company scurried back up the slope and into the trees to resume their previous course. They'd travelled several more miles through scrub and forest when night eventually came upon them, their party deciding to continue on rather than waste time with sleep. It would have been impossible to see much in the dark if it were not for the fact Osbert had fashioned himself a torch and made a spark, although how he'd managed to do that in the blackness, Alaric had little idea. They hurried along, Osbert's torchlight casting long shadows through the forest, the hooting of owls and scurrying of tiny beasts thankfully the only things to make themselves known.

Dawn came. Alaric wasn't sure how far they'd travelled, but Osbert was insistent that Ulfcytel's hideout was just a few miles off and ensconced somewhere in even denser woodland. Alaric had been in the lead for the past hour, Osbert and the rest of his men following just behind him, the light of dawn bathing the forest in its familiar glow. Normally this would be a pleasant time, for the summer mornings had been as gentle and temperate as anyone could remember. It was a shame he didn't have the opportunity to enjoy it for what it was. Alaric leaned against a tree anyway, taking a moment to catch his breath, the sound of morning birdsong soothing his tired mind.

Osbert moved past him, signalling for the rest of them to follow. They hurried after him, Alaric included, feeling at least grateful for the opportunity to exercise after spending so long languishing in Offetuna. He owed Father Dobron his life, but it was good to be moving again. He was just sad the horse he'd given him had never come back. Hopefully, he'd find his own way home.

Alaric could tell they were really getting into the wilds here. The forest canopy had thickened considerably, the blanket of leaves and entangled branches serving to obscure the daylight to the point much below was now wreathed in shadow. If they were being pursued, he'd have been grateful for that, yet in this instance it made him feel uneasy, and the woods had taken on a smothering quality he didn't appreciate.

They'd made it another mile when they began to hear the faint sound of running water. It was at first almost indistinguishable from the rustle of leaves, but it grew louder with time, eventually turning out to be what Alaric had suspected, the stream flowing fast and clear as it ran from somewhere to the north west. They moved alongside it in that direction, Osbert again leading the way, claiming they didn't have far to go.

He wasn't wrong. Ulfcytel had hidden what little was left of his army in possibly the densest stretch of forest Alaric had ever been in. The encampment was almost impossible to spot in the gloom, and it was huddled beneath a sandstone cliff that hid it from any wandering eyes looking in from either the south or east. Alaric's party had approached from the west, following the stream, although even from this direction it was easily missed unless one knew exactly what to look out for.

It was, perhaps, a little misleading to refer to this as an encampment. It was more of a man-made clearing, appearing as if Ulfcytel's people had just layered the forest floor at the base of the cliff with bracken and heaved some fallen branches into position to further conceal their whereabouts. They'd lived like this, over two hundred men, for weeks, hitting the Danes when they could and scavenging from ruined villages before returning, the summer warmth and thick canopy of leaves above ensuring their hideout was relatively comfortable.

Osbert led him in, nodding towards a man on watch that Alaric had not actually spotted lurking behind a tree, spear in hand. About thirty men were up and awake, the rest still lying or sitting amidst their beds of leaves, a few murmuring in recognition when Alaric came into view.

Two men approached him, their movements rapid and eager, each of them dressed in well-used ring mail shirts, iron helms, and tattered cloaks. Alaric recognised them. They were part of the contingent of veterans that had accompanied him when he'd separated from the rest of the Hamptonscir fyrd to march at speed into Eastengle. They stopped and exchanged a few words, the men pleased to see him and their smiles bright and genuine upon their otherwise unkempt and abundantly bearded faces. Alaric enquired as to how many of the men of Hamptonscir were here. His heart sank when they informed him they were the only survivors. The rest had died at Hringmere.

Osbert ordered his men to go and get something to eat. He then strode on through the clearing, beckoning for Alaric to follow. He did, and before long the pair of them were moving along the base of the cliff. They carried on like this for a few minutes, following a narrow trail that took a sudden turn when the cliff curved inward, each man vanishing from view within a tangle of rocks and oversized boulders. It seemed like a maze in here, the walls all pale stone and crumbling shale, and just as Alaric was about to ask Osbert if he were lost their path suddenly sloped downwards, leading them out into a shady, sandy defile marked by clutches of hardy vegetation and gnarled trees. Then he saw him.

Ulfcytel had lost weight, his paunch looking like it had disappeared almost entirely. He was still broad, his arms retaining their killing power, no doubt, but recent events had certainly trimmed him down. He'd turned this narrow, rocky bastion into some kind of planning area akin to his old pavilion, carving what looked like a crude map into the sandy floor. He spun around when he heard the newcomers approach, breaking off his conversation with several other burly, bearded warriors Alaric didn't recognise. Their eyes met.

Ulfcytel took him in, his mouth seeming to open and close slightly, his vast beard failing to hide his expression of surprise. He stepped forward, approaching slowly, both his hands outstretched. He reached Alaric, putting his palms on his shoulders and patting at him like he was testing to see if he were real. Alaric pulled his hood back, revealing more of his bandaged face, the scarring on one side easily visible. Ulfcytel breathed out slowly at the sight, still holding Alaric by the shoulders as if he might slip from his grasp.

"How did we come to this point, lad?" Ulfcytel whispered, his voice soft and laden with emotion. "What happened to you? What took you from us only to bless us with your return?"

"The attack on the camp," Alaric began, trying to gather his thoughts. "Thorkell was there…it was like he'd been expecting us, luring us in to spring a trap. Æthelstan and all his men were killed. As were mine. I got close to Thorkell…I tried…"

Alaric's voice faded as he remembered his frenzied efforts to hack his way through the melee and face Thorkell in combat. It had all come to nothing, struck from the side as he had been in what should have been his moment of glory. He almost felt like he could remember the sight of the man who had done it. There was something distinctive about him that he hadn't recalled previously. He focused his mind. Ulfcytel would require a deeper explanation than that.

"My eye is gone," Alaric admitted, gesturing towards his bandage. "I was hit in the head as I rushed Thorkell. We'd fought our way through the camp, but it was half-deserted. Then they suddenly seemed to get reinforcements, and Thorkell himself appeared to block our escape. I passed out after being wounded and woke up in a church in Offetuna. A priest had found me and tended to me."

"And then what?" Ulfcytel asked, gesturing towards Osbert, "the lad here found you?"

"No," Osbert corrected, "we found him in the forest north of Theodford."

"He and those with him saved my life," Alaric stated appreciatively. "I'd travelled from Offetuna to see if anyone was left at Hringmere. There was nothing but corpses. I was at a loss about what to do or where to go. Then I was attacked on the road. I fled into the woods, but…I can't…"

He gestured towards his face, Ulfcytel looking nonplussed. He then removed his bandage, exposing what lay beneath. Ulfcytel nodded sympathetically, his gaze lingering on Alaric's crushed and ruined eye socket. He understood. Or at least he seemed to. Fighting with one eye was incredibly difficult.

"Well, bloody well done to Osbert for saving you then!" Ulfcytel boomed, his face breaking into a broad, bristling grin. Osbert said nothing, merely nodding his head in acknowledgement. Humility was a strength, and one Alaric approved of. He was about to voice such sentiments when Ulfcytel spoke again, his brow now furrowed with concern.

"You were the only survivor from the attack, though? What of our friend who led you there, Eadric?"

"I never saw what happened to him. He led me and mine to one side of the camp and then headed off with Æthelstan's force, saying he would lead them to the ideal spot for a flanking assault. I found Æthelstan, but…"

Alaric reached into the pocket of his breecs, remembering something. He still had Æthelstan's wedding ring from when he'd removed it from his hand in the hope of returning it to his beloved. Ulfcytel stared at it when Alaric held it up to the light, his expression curious.

"What is that? Your ring?"

"No…I took it from Æthelstan's body. I suspect his wife would like to have it."

"You'd best hold on to that," Ulfcytel advised. "I know she'll be glad to have it returned, when we get the chance. Yet I must ask you…you never saw Eadric after that night?"

"I did not, alive or dead," replied Alaric, pocketing the ring once more.

Ulfcytel exchanged a look with Osbert, a deeper frown now etched on his face. He cleared his throat, holding a closed fist to his lips, lost in thought.

"You've no doubt guessed our battle did not go well," he eventually said, stating something of the obvious. "What you may not know is that we were betrayed. Given what you've told me about your attack on Thorkell's camp, I'm of a mind to think there may be something afoot with our own Ealdorman Eadric."

"What exactly took place?" Alaric inquired, eager to finally hear the details of the battle. Ulfcytel paused a moment and took a deep breath, like a man steadying himself before undertaking some arduous task.

"They came screaming up from the south almost a week after your departure. We saw them coming. We assumed you'd been killed, so we decided to come out and meet them. I led one-half of the army, hoping to provoke the Danes into charging us outside the earthworks. When the time was right, the rest of the army would sweep in around the lake and then down, hitting Thorkell in the flank whilst he was still occupied with us."

"And that didn't work?" Alaric asked, already knowing the answer in his heart.

"It did not," Ulfcytel confirmed, "and not because it was a bad plan but because I put Thurcytel in charge of the flank attack."

Alaric remembered who he meant. He'd met the man when they'd all gathered to discuss the situation after Eadric had arrived to inform them the king would not be coming to assist them. If he recalled correctly, he'd been a fellow of some standing in the Eastenglian forces and had spoken well on how they had a chance to end this war in one battle just as King Alfred had won at Ethandun. Alaric had appreciated what he'd said. So what had happened?

"He failed to attack on time?" Alaric suggested, a little confused.

"He failed to attack at all, Alaric! He moved his force into position all right, only to retreat at the moment he was supposed to charge in and help us. The battle then became one massive brawl in the open field. The Danes' numbers started to grind us down. Some of the lads knew something had gone wrong and started to break, falling back into the camp and…"

Alaric had seen what he meant. The heathland was absolutely littered with bodies, and he'd been able to tell many had attempted to retreat only to be cut down whilst they fled. Some seemed to have made some kind of a stand inside the camp, but the fact they were now dead was evidence enough they'd been unsuccessful. He wasn't sure the news that they'd ultimately lost due to treachery rather than simply being outfought made things any easier.

"Why would Thurcytel betray you?"

"I'm not sure," Ulfcytel murmured. "What I do find interesting is that it was both him and Eadric who were adamant we should attack Thorkell at his camp. I didn't think anything of it at the time, but after what you just told me, coupled with what Thurcytel did during the battle…"

"Why would the men you gave him obey his command to abandon you?" Alaric wondered, wanting to cover all possibilities. "I mean, is it that easy to believe thousands of Englishmen would comply with that kind of order when their own brothers were fighting for their lives? And what happened to those men? Where are they now?"

"These are good questions, Alaric, and I wish I had easy answers. It's possible Thurcytel simply lied to them, telling them I'd ordered him to withdraw for whatever reason. As to where they are now…Thorkell moved north and then west after ransacking our camp, torching Wretham and then Noruic. If he caught up with those men, I'd say he would have killed them."

"And Thurcytel? Are we sure he didn't flee out of cowardice?"

"No," Ulfcytel answered emphatically. "I know him. He's no coward. I'd wager he escaped to safety. I don't know for sure if there's a connection between him and Eadric, but my instincts are telling me there is. You didn't wander into a trap and we weren't betrayed out of sheer bad luck. There is something going on between these men."

"Why would they do any of this, though?" Osbert now asked, dismayed. "What do they gain from our defeat?"

"That is something we will need to find out," said Ulfcytel, his voice darkening. "But first things first…whilst you two were away, we found out something very interesting about Thorkell's intentions. Let me show you."

Ulfcytel turned and began to walk towards what looked like another collection of rocks towards the back of the defile. Alaric and Osbert followed him, taking care not to disturb the map of Eastengle that had been carved into the sand. Ulfcytel soon vanished behind one particularly large boulder, Alaric stepping after him eagerly as Osbert followed.

The defile was larger than he'd initially thought, the rocks and this boulder appearing to have masked its true dimensions. About a dozen paces away were two warriors standing vigil beneath a rather grim-looking willow tree, the thing having grown tall and strong despite the apparent unsuitability of its environs. At its base sat what looked like a man, his wrists and ankles bound with rope, his face hidden from view and his head hung low in resignation. Alaric noted he was also tied to the tree by a cord around the waist. Whoever he was, the Eastenglians didn't want him leaving.

They approached him, Ulfcytel halting at the tree, his eyes fixed on the man at his feet. Alaric could see the fellow had been stripped down to his undergarments and severely beaten, his long, blond hair ragged and dirtied with dried earth and blood. Ulfcytel suddenly lashed out with his boot, kicking him in his left shoulder and knocking him onto his side. He barely grunted, seeming content enough to now lie there until one of his guards hauled him back into a sitting position.

"Our friend here came to us soon after we'd retreated from Hringmere," announced Ulfcytel, still looking down at the man he'd struck. "His friends were a bit overconfident… they separated themselves from Thorkell's main force and pursued us, night and day, without rest. Of course, he didn't know the terrain like we do, which helped when it came to luring him and his inbred followers into a nice ambush. He gave himself up once I'd broken his wrist and slaughtered the rest of his men. He's been quite chatty ever since."

"Chatty?" inquired Alaric, unsure of what he could be getting at.

"Yes, talkative, provided he's given sufficient motivation. Otherwise, he just sits there. We've found ways to make him more lively."

Alaric understood. He didn't like it, viewing torture as the method of a coward and a sadist. Ulfcytel certainly was not a coward, nor had he previously displayed any appetite for cruelty, but perhaps he felt he had no choice now. Information was always a valuable commodity. Its value increased exponentially in times of war, and they needed every possible advantage if they were going to turn this situation around. And yet it was a slippery slope, and the ruin of many a man had been wrought by compromising on moral matters for the sake of expediency. Would it profit them to win this war if they lost their souls in the process?

"What has he told you?" Alaric asked, opting to leave any discussion on the rightness or wrongness of what Ulfcytel had done to a later date. "Is he a nobleman? Somebody of high standing in Scandinavia?"

"We think so. He was certainly attired as such when he still fancied his chances against us. He's told us all manner of things about Thorkell. That his brother is here with him…as are a force of Norwegians led by a youngster named Olaf. He's also told us what Thorkell plans to do next."

"Which is what?" asked Alaric again, feeling a little awkward that he seemed to be the one always asking the questions.

"He intends to attack Canterburie this time. He believes our King Æthelred will look to pay him off or bring him over as a hired mercenary. In the meantime, he's all about burning and pillaging. Once he gets done ravaging the west, he's heading south to plunder what he can before marching east. It's then just a short journey and he'll be in a position to take the Holy City."

"How long have you known this, Ulfcytel?" Alaric breathed, his mind filling with nightmarish images of Canterburie falling to the heathen. It made him sick. It must not come to pass.

"About Canterburie? Not long. But it's good you're here. You'll prove yourself useful, I'm sure. We're going to take the initiative, lad. If the Danes' ships are still moored at Gipeswic, then I say we head down there, cause as much chaos as we can and steal a bunch of them to get ourselves to Canterburie before Thorkell even knows what we've done."

It was an audacious plan. Risky, too, but what wasn't in their current situation? Besides, having Ulfcytel in Canterburie would provide a major morale boost for the city's defenders. When word got out that he'd survived the despoliation of Eastengle and had returned to lead the defence of one of England's most prominent and holy of cities, there would be uproar. The people would flock to them. It would be like something of legend. Achieving it by stealing some of Thorkell's own ships made it all the sweeter. Alaric smiled as he imagined the look on his face. He still intended to kill the Norse bastard for the sake of Osmund. Perhaps he'd soon get that chance.

"If we reach Canterburie in time, the people will no doubt rally to you," Alaric began, thinking aloud as he struggled to contain his excitement. "You and Oswy are both famou…"

"I'm sorry, Alaric," Ulfcytel interrupted, his eyes now downcast. "I should have told you earlier. Oswy fell at Hringmere alongside his son. Wulfric too."

Alaric shouldn't have been so surprised. After all, if Oswy were here, he'd have made himself known by now, since the man had been about as quiet and subtle as a hammer from what Alaric had seen of him. Yet to hear that England had lost another great man still saddened his heart. Oswy was dead. The last living reminder of the legendary Byrhtnoð, hero of Malduna, had passed on. God rest their souls.

"Let's not think on the past too much," Ulfcytel declared, placing a huge yet reassuring hand on Alaric's shoulder. "There was defeat at Hringmere, but valour too. The men from Cantebrigie fought well. Your own Hamptonscir lads were like a rock, refusing to let the Danes dislodge them until…"

"Until all but two of them were slain," Alaric murmured. "I know. They saw me when I was coming to speak with you. They told me they were the last ones left."

Ulfcytel hung his head, his hand still gripping Alaric's shoulder. He exhaled a deep, long sigh before he began to move forward, leading Alaric and Osbert away from the prisoner and back the way they'd come.

"It must have been hard for you to find that out so suddenly," Ulfcytel continued as they walked, his voice low and gentle. "I grieve for all of my men. But we must hold their memories in our hearts and do what they would want us to do. They'd want us to make their deaths worthwhile. We owe it to them. To Oswy, Æthelstan…that big bloke you had with you when we met to discuss…"

"Osmund," Alaric clarified. "He died fighting. Two axes, one per hand, hacking the bastards down. Then he took a thrown spear in the chest."

"I thought something like that must have happened," said Ulfcytel, nodding his head sadly. "That's a good death for a man…he went down defending his people, his country. Family, faith, and country…if you die for anything, make it one of those. Two is better. To die for all three…that's a hero, right there."

Alaric didn't know how to respond. He didn't disagree, but his grief was still too fresh. He'd speak on Osmund sometime in the future when he felt ready, but for the moment he was just shocked he no longer had a best friend. Some might tell him he'd get used to it, but he didn't want to. He'd always miss Osmund, and life without him just wouldn't be the same.

"Did my father ever arrive with reinforcements in the end?" Alaric asked, changing the subject, although he had a feeling he knew the answer already.

"We never laid eyes on him," Ulfcytel said, confirming his suspicions. "But interestingly, we know there was another battle around Hametuna. From what my people tell me, it looks like your father came close to reaching us, only to be overwhelmed and retreat back down south. If it helps put your mind at ease…nobody attired as an ealdorman was found among the dead."

That was something, at least. The chances were his father was alive and recovering from his ordeal within the safety of their stronghold at Porteceaster. He could imagine the place now, precisely as he'd left it, his and Æva's rooms sequestered away in the tower overlooking the great hall, the whole settlement protected by sturdy Roman walls. The thought brought him some reassurance. His family would be secure there until his return.

The three men strolled out of Ulfcytel's rocky hideaway and back down the trail that swerved around the base of the cliff. Osbert lingered behind them, his silence a tad conspicuous, making Alaric again wonder what exactly had happened to the lad during the battle. It still felt like something was wrong, like something wholesome had left the young man and a certain coldness had taken up residence in its place. He'd endeavour to speak to him again the next time they were alone. He had a feeling he needed a little help.

Alaric and Ulfcytel continued to talk as they walked. The ealdorman was surprised to hear of his encounter with Edmund and Æthelstan, but he was dismissive of their offer for him to return to Lundenburg, stressing he'd run out of both trust and confidence in the king and, as such, would be in danger there. When Osbert pointed out that Ulfcytel's wife, Wulfhild, remained in Lundenburg and would surely vouch for him, he fell silent, a worried frown on his face. Alaric knew Wulfhild was a daughter of the king. That would surely work in Ulfcytel's favour, or so one would think. There was bound to be more to the situation, if his expression was anything to go by. Alaric decided to leave well enough alone for now.

They soon finished traversing the trail and had begun to move into the centre of the forest clearing, the men gathered there parting like water upon noticing just who walked among them. Ulfcytel came to a stop, drawing himself up to his full height and placing his hands on his hips, looking very much like the man in charge. All his warriors were now on their feet, many of them swiftly abandoning their efforts to cook themselves some breakfast. Alaric noted the way they seemed to naturally cleave to him, his authority conveyed without even a single word. Ulfcytel was a true leader of men.

"Apologies for interrupting your leisurely morning," Ulfcytel began, causing a ripple of laughter to spread through those assembled. "But I felt you should know our long lost friend, Alaric, has returned to us."

That prompted some more murmuring, some of those gathered probably wondering who he even was. Alaric noticed the two veterans from Hamptonscir in the crowd, pointing him out as they whispered to those closest to them. Their explanations seemed to fall on glad ears, and those who heard them nodded and smiled in acknowledgement. It was good to be appreciated.

"What I must now tell you may seem dour," Ulfcytel continued, his voice carrying effortlessly around the clearing. "You all know what happened at Hringmere. You all know we were betrayed by our very own…Alaric here was part of a group that bravely attempted to kill Thorkell several nights before we faced him in battle. We'd been told this was a possibility by Eadric, the Ealdorman of Mierce. But it was a trap. Only Alaric survived. We were betrayed then, and we were again betrayed on the battlefield."

His audience remained silent, each man present likely suspecting it was no random fluke that Thurcytel had abandoned them when they'd needed him most. Alaric felt Ulfcytel again place a hand on his shoulder, having also drawn his sword from his scabbard to hold it aloft. The men stared, captivated by the sight and eager to hear more.

"Our own king may not have come to aid us, and our own brothers may have turned against us," he declared, "but I tell you, we have a chance to strike back. Thorkell is in the west, murdering as murderers do. But the fool has left his fleet moored down in Gipeswic. Exposed. Vulnerable. We may not be able to face him in battle, few as we are…but we can make life as hard for him as possible. We'll start by attacking his prized vessels."

That got a response. The men began nodding emphatically, some further signifying their agreement with an enthusiastic "aye!"

"There's more we'll then do," Ulfcytel boomed, his sword still brandished above his head. "We've been made aware that Thorkell plans to again threaten Canterburie, perhaps even raze it to the ground. We won't allow that. After retaking Gipeswic, we'll kill all the Danes we can find…and then use their own ships to get us to Canterburie, where we'll rally all of England to its defence, in God's name!"

That really did it. The men erupted into cheers, many pounding their fists in the air with jubilation. Others hammered the shafts of their spears upon their shields, the drumming cacophony spreading out and through the trees to startle bird and beast alike. All despondency faded away, the sting of defeat now replaced with a most vigorous determination. They might only be the battered survivors of a once sizeable host, but they still had a war to fight. With a clear direction and goal, they had a purpose again.

The camp soon became abuzz with activity, each and every man dedicating himself to preparing for a long journey through potentially dangerous territory. They were still dependent on stealth, and Ulfcytel was insistent that they avoid the roads and stick to the forests. This would slow them down, it was true, but it only took one Dane to spot them and flee into the west to alert Thorkell, and in open country his superior numbers would be the end of them.

They waited out the rest of the day, Alaric making a point to talk to the two men from Hamptonscir. They were named Bana and Eamon, and both of them had not previously known each other well, their friendship only taking root after they'd realised they were the last survivors from down south. Their account of the battle at Hringmere was as Ulfcytel had described, and they spoke with pride on how the men of Hamptonscir had held fast even when others were fleeing. They too had nearly fallen, so they said, and were quite content to die with their brothers until Ulfcytel had staged a fighting retreat with his own personal retinue that had cut a swath through the enemy vanguard, saving their lives in the process. Alaric believed every word. These two were men of quality.

Alaric made sure to get something to eat, enjoying the company of Eamon, Bana, Osbert, and a clutch of others whilst they gathered around a campfire to share a meal. The other men were interested in the attack on Thorkell's camp, and Alaric ended up having to tell the same story several times over when he was asked by multiple people.

They all shared Ulfcytel's suspicions, believing the ease with which they'd fought their way into the camp was no doubt due to Thorkell having been alerted to their presence so he could spring a trap. It would be foolish, Eamon claimed, for Thorkell to have simply fortified his camp to keep Alaric and Æthelstan out. If he'd been told that men of note were coming for him, he'd have wanted to lure them in so he could either capture them or confirm the kill, perhaps hoping it would lead to a leadership crisis in the English resistance.

Alaric silently wondered if that were true. He wasn't a hugely important man, but Thorkell had certainly been up to something that night. Perhaps he'd been told he had a chance to trap and kill Ulfcytel himself. That would make more sense. Thorkell was no fool. He'd likely heard of Ulfcytel and his exploits and jumped at the chance to eliminate him, thinking his victory in Eastengle would then be assured. Instead, he'd had to fight his way through thousands of furious Englishmen at Hringmere, and whilst he'd won, he'd certainly taken losses. It was only logical he'd have wanted to avoid that if other options were available.

Alaric soon found himself dozing off, the warmth of the fire and his unusually full belly making him drowsy. He rested for a while, removing and folding his cloak to use it as a pillow, the hubbub of good-natured conversation easing him to sleep. Osbert woke him with a start, reaching out to shake him awake with one hand. He opened his eye, noting that night had descended on the forest with what seemed like an unusual rapidity. It was time to move.

They set off, the two hundred survivors of the Battle of Hringmere moving out into the woods, their way lit by a smattering of blazing torches held by roughly every tenth man. They didn't bother to try to conceal the noise they made, and Osbert claimed their remote location and the thickness of the forest would ensure sound travelled only a short distance. Alaric was glad. He'd been nervous about the ruckus that had followed Ulfcytel's speech. It would be embarrassing to be killed by the Danes because they'd given their location away by cheering a lot.

The night progressed without incident, although Alaric felt considerable relief when the trees began to thin out and fresher air started to flow through his lungs. They still kept to the woodlands, moving south and east, Ulfcytel deciding they'd move closer to the coast to keep the distance between themselves and Thorkell's reputed whereabouts as lengthy as possible. The night remained oppressively dark, and the sky had become a veritable blanket of clouds that concealed the land from both moon and star. That would work to their advantage.

Dawn came, and much of the next day was spent shuffling through another nameless stretch of forest. They'd encountered no living souls the night before, and from the looks of it Eastengle was now a place of emptiness and unease, its people either dead or gone.

The second night was a little different. Their forward scouts had briefly urged the main column to pause in their advance, claiming they'd seen evidence of activity up ahead. Ulfcytel decided to move up in force, the men fanning out in a wide, encircling formation intended to trap any foe before they could retreat. They instead found themselves surrounding just another burnt-out hamlet, the people the scouts had detected turning out to be several families attempting to rebuild their homes.

Osbert had been right. People were coming back to the region already, which added substance to the notion that the small groups of Danes they'd fought previously were indeed deserters from Thorkell's army looking to rob returning refugees. Alaric would have thought any self-respecting Dane would want to stick with their leader, earning themselves both renown and loot from his victories. It occurred to him it was no doubt easier and safer to rob unarmed and frightened people than fight actual battles. Cowardice and opportunism in equal measure. Contemptible.

Ulfcytel spoke to the families himself, telling them the war was far from over and the area was not yet safe. They were reluctant to leave, yet they knew him well enough as the Ealdorman of Eastengle and were not willing to defy him. They eventually agreed to come with them, and Ulfcytel then told them of their plan to reach Canterburie, where he would ensure they were provided for. Alaric admired his compassion. They continued on.

Within an hour, they'd come to agree their attempts to mask their movements were counterproductive. Any tracker worth his salt would be able to follow them, considering the impossibility of concealing the trail left by two hundred armed and armoured men, and so their efforts at avoiding detection were merely slowing them down. Besides, the refugees they'd picked up were hardly inconspicuous, and their number contained at least one newborn child that insisted on howling into the night at distressingly regular intervals. They couldn't just leave these people now. But stealth was no longer much of an option.

They threw caution aside and began moving rapidly along the route south, hoping to ultimately surprise the Danes at Gipeswic and be at sea before any word could spread. Another day came and went, the night passing soon after, their force making better time than ever as they rushed along the sun-baked road towards their destination.

Eventually, they came within sight of the ruins of Gipeswic. Alaric and Ulfcytel had joined their scouts atop a sparsely wooded hill commanding a half-decent view of the town. The rest of the column had stopped about a quarter mile to the north, lying low amid the ferns and long grasses that blanketed the area. The situation was precarious. But at least they'd made it.

It was about mid-morning, and the sky was bright and clear, the night's thick cloud cover dispersing with the sunrise into an assortment of white wisps and trails draped upon a backdrop of soft blue. The golden light of the sun blazed down upon them, its rays playing softly across Alaric's skin. Nature revelled in its touch, the abundance of butterflies and the buzzing of several comically fat bees gorging themselves on wildflowers reminding him of better times down south.

These were not better times, though. There was fighting to be done, and Gipeswic would not retake itself. Alaric could see that well enough. The enemy was occupying the ruins in some force, looking like they were using the remains of the town as a supply base from which to guard Thorkell's ships. The vessels themselves were partially visible and moored in haphazard rows along the banks of the wide-flowing river Arewan to the south and west. There looked to be hundreds of them, sleek and menacing, each capable of conveying a decent number of warriors whilst still maintaining their customary speed and agility. They would serve them well for the crossing to Canterburie.

That all depended on whether they could even get near them. The Danes had left a garrison of what looked like several hundred men within Gipeswic itself, and the odd patrol was also visible moving up and down the banks of the river. They may not need to defeat all of them in open battle to get up and aboard the ships, but a partial approach just wouldn't work, since the English were bound to have difficulty securing their prizes, let alone escaping downriver, with the Danes pursuing them.

"It appears there are hundreds of total bastards in our way," Ulfcytel muttered. Alaric looked to where he was concealed not three feet away, settled down in several flowering bushes. Alaric had trouble taking him seriously, his normally grizzled visage and vast silver beard looking faintly absurd when surrounded by delicate flowers.

"We can lure them out," Alaric whispered. "Give me about thirty men, enough to look serious, and I'll lead them to the river bank like we're going to make a move for the ships. I bet the Danes will respond with twice that number of men to chase us off. Then you swing in with the rest of the force and cut off their retreat. We'll crush them."

"That will still leave Danes inside the town...but I like it," Ulfcytel replied quietly, his head bobbing to avoid a circling bee. "They've gotten used to seeing us on the defensive. They won't be expecting this. I'll wager the heathen dogs down there have not seen a real fight in a while. We'll be more than a match for them, man to man. There's a lot of tree cover down by the river, too...they won't see us coming."

The pair of them nodded to one other, satisfied with their semblance of a plan. They then turned and slunk back down the hill, their scouts following behind. It didn't take them long to cover the distance back to their main force, the men doing well to conceal themselves as effectively as they had. Neither Alaric nor Ulfcytel wanted to wait, fearing any moment squandered would increase the odds of discovery. They briefed those who needed to know of the plan, Alaric selecting Osbert, Eamon, Bana, and a host of others they recommended to accompany him to the river bank.

It must have been around midday when they came within a hundred yards of the water. Alaric and his party of thirty were just north west of Gipeswic and easily within spotting distance, if it were not for the blessedly thick vegetation. They'd crawled much of the way here, navigating through the long grasses face-first, the men leaving their shields, helmets, and spears behind so as to reduce the chances of being seen. About eight Danes were now wandering in their direction in what looked like a standard patrol, their casual manner suggesting they had absolutely no idea what was presently lurking in the undergrowth.

They waited, the Northmen ambling further along the riverside. At about a dozen yards out, one of them suddenly stopped and began staring towards them, his body tense and his expression perturbed. He took a step forward, then another. Alaric wasn't sure which one of his people wasn't properly concealed, but he wasn't going to sit around for them to sound the alarm on their own terms. He decided to escalate matters. He stood up and charged.

All of his men leapt to their feet and followed him, their cries shattering the previously peaceful ambience. Alaric drew the sword the Aetheling Æthelstan had given him, rejoicing at its weight and the knowledge that he was about to use it. It proved itself well enough, its edge splitting the skull of the first Dane stupid enough to get in his way. The man tumbled to the earth, his face a mask of surprise and shock, the top of his head a broken ruin.

His compatriots fared no better, for they were startled by the sudden charge and barely able to ready themselves before they found themselves overrun. Alaric saw Bana cut down one unprepared Dane with a savage slash to the throat, the poor fool collapsing with a pained gurgle just as another leapt over his body to avenge him. Bana exchanged a few blows with his new adversary, this one unwilling to give up just because he was massively outnumbered. His heroism was cut short when Osbert appeared behind him and planted his axe between his shoulder blades. The Northman staggered forward a step or two, then fell forwards onto his face.

Another Dane attempted to flee, his courage breaking after seeing his brothers so quickly defeated. He started back towards Gipeswic, making a piteous wailing sound, his legs working frantically. Eamon intercepted him, leaping upon him from the side and tackling him to the ground. He got to his feet, kicking the Dane whilst he lay prone before bringing the full weight of his axe down upon his exposed neck. Blood sprayed up and out across Eamon's boots, soaking the previously delicate green grass a sickly crimson. At least the wailing had stopped.

They made a dash towards the river bank, hoping to get a good look at the ships and give the Gipeswic garrison the very real impression they meant to damage or steal them. The grass beneath them started to thin and grow sparse, the earth then giving way to a muddy expanse that ran another twenty paces or so before vanishing beneath the water. They moved carefully here lest they should slip, Alaric knowing well enough that such terrain could be treacherous to those burdened by armour and weapons.

The enemy vessels looked even more impressive up close. They were sleek yet solid, many of them daubed with an assortment of vibrant, even jarring, colours painted in long and peculiar patterns across their hulls. A great number had been decorated to represent various mythical creatures, their prows intended to appear as the gaping mouths of dragons or serpents. Alaric wondered if the Norsemen really expected people to fear them on account of that, finding some of the images almost ridiculous. He made his way down to the nearest ship, the water coming up to his stomach, and stabbed his sword point into the glaring eye of the supposedly terrifying beast before him. It didn't react. He wasn't excessively surprised.

Alaric commanded his men to begin hewing their axes into the hulls of those vessels within reach. They intentionally made a truly tremendous racket, shouting furiously as they hacked away. They did little damage, but that wasn't why they were doing it, since their true purpose was to make the Danes rush out of Gipeswic and pursue them. Their display of vandalism did the trick, for a veritable flood of Danes soon began pouring out from the ruined settlement and advancing towards them. They really didn't want them near those ships. Good for them.

Alaric gave the order to fall back, his warriors following him out of the water and up along a narrow trail that ran the length of the river bank and away from the town. The Danes were closing fast and in some numbers, Alaric guessing there were about a hundred or so bearing down on them. He had his people run quickly enough to keep their distance, but not so speedily that they outpaced the Danes entirely or made them think they'd been frightened off. They had to make them chase them. They had a trap to spring.

He soon lost track of how long he'd been running. He thought he'd know when Ulfcytel sprung into action, expecting with good reason for the Danes to shout in alarm at seeing another force suddenly appear between them and the town. He'd heard nothing of the kind, and the men chasing them continued to howl and cackle to themselves, apparently relishing the prospect of slaughtering their outnumbered foes.

Somebody cried out just behind him. Osbert had lost his footing whilst trying to leap over a slick of mud that had emerged from the river bank and up across the trail. Eamon grabbed him by the cloak, trying to haul him up and onto his feet. It wasn't enough. Alaric turned back, dragging Osbert along between himself and Eamon, the lad eventually managing to regain his balance and resume running. They'd lost precious seconds, the shouts and roars behind them becoming louder and louder. Alaric looked back over his shoulder. The Danes were close. Too close. Something was wrong. They were in trouble. Alaric ran a prayer through his mind.

He'd never known his prayers to be answered so quickly. A shattering roar suddenly ripped through the dappled trees overlooking the trail. The Danes slowed and then halted their pursuit, each man glancing about in trepidation. Ulfcytel himself then barrelled into view and launched himself into them, his sword rising and falling as it hacked into mail and flesh. He was followed a split second later by what looked like the entirety of his force, over one hundred and seventy warriors, the men sweeping over the now outnumbered Danes in a screaming, thundering wave of metal and sinew.

Alaric spun on his feet and drew his sword, Osbert and company joining him in a spirited charge back the way they'd come. They threw themselves into the melee, tearing into the Danish flank as it swiftly unravelled in the face of the combined assault. The enemy had been taken completely unaware, and Ulfcytel's decision to ambush them directly rather than just trap them between himself and Alaric was paying off. They'd never seen him coming. Alaric was impressed.

He put his first man down, impaling him through the side whilst he tried to fend off the blows of another Saxon who'd just charged from the bushes. The Dane started to topple over only to be impaled a second time, the spear from his first opponent smashing aside his shield to cut deep into his torso. Alaric pulled his blade back and out, a brief spray of blood from the now expiring foe saturating his otherwise mud-splattered breecs. The rest of his men stormed past him, tearing into the enemy force with a terrible enthusiasm, their cries confident and assured.

Alaric felt a brief flash of anxiety as the familiar cacophony of battle swirled up around him. For a moment, he thought himself back in Thorkell's camp, fighting for his life, his men dying around him, Osmund too falling to that thrown spear. He shook himself out of it. He might not be in as dire a situation as he was, but he still needed to have his wits about him. He couldn't avenge Osmund if he fell here.

He cut another man down, hacking the hand and then the arm from his body before he could so much as raise his shield. His skills seemed to be returning, his body compensating a little for his handicap, but the sounds of battle were overwhelming, the assorted screams, roars, and bellowing curses making his head ache in a way he'd not known before.

He then laid eyes on what could only be a Dane of some authority. He'd strode into view amidst the turmoil, the metallic bands rising up his arms indicating he was a man of means, his beard and hair suitably long and the markings upon his face highlighting his seniority. The other Danes appeared to be inspired by his presence, fighting all the harder despite the evident difficulty of their situation. He himself was giving it his all, wielding a long, heavy axe that sliced or outright crushed any man unfortunate enough to fall under its weight.

Skilled or no, he was just another foreign invader to Alaric, and his pretty jewellery and flowing tattoos wouldn't save him from a most deserved fate. He had an opportunity here, too, since the fancy Dane was presently set on killing whoever had just slain the man next to him, which for the moment meant he was busy raining blows down on one of Ulfcytel's men. The Dane had the advantage, and the Saxon he'd targeted was only alive as he'd been able to bring his shield up at the last moment to block that axe. It had partly splintered under the impact and wouldn't last much longer. Alaric had to act.

He lurched forward and stabbed his sword downwards towards the Dane's left knee. He hit his mark, and was immediately rewarded with an agonised grunt and a stumble as the foe's leg buckled and gave way. Alaric reached out with his left hand, seizing him by his flaxen hair and pulling him towards him. He then bashed him in the face repeatedly with the grip of his sword, cracking his visage like a spoiled egg. The Dane flailed at him desperately, trying to bring the haft of his axe up to shield himself. It was a wasted effort. Long, large weapons like the one he wielded were well and good for shock value, but they had disadvantages, especially when fighting in such close proximity. He was learning that lesson now.

Alaric finally released his hold on the Dane's hair before gripping his sword with both hands, allowing his arms to drop down so his blade now pointed upwards from the waist. He then worked the tip forwards and up, brutally eviscerating his opponent from the navel onwards, the fool's furs and ornate leather armour doing absolutely nothing to protect him from the tempered iron now tearing through his innards. There were cleaner ways to kill a man, if a murderous heathen bastard like this could be considered as such. Alaric's boots would really need a scrub after this.

Somebody else made a swing for him, Alaric pulling his head back sharply so that the axe's edge merely nicked the tip of his nose. He barrelled into the one responsible, shoulder-charging him with his sword pointed outwards like some kind of spiked battering ram. He felt the tip run up against the grey metal of the man's armour, the taut, interlinked rings parting and disintegrating. The Dane fell backwards with an enraged choking sound, Alaric falling atop of him, his hands wet with gore and his sword fully enmeshed in the Dane's body cavity.

He got to his feet and retrieved his blade, wincing slightly at the sound of metal scraping upon bone. The enemy were broken, and those Danes still among the living were falling to panic and fleeing back towards the river. Some tumbled over whilst scrambling off the grassy trail and into the slick mud of the bank. The English bolted after them, any Dane who had slipped or was just slow soon disappearing beneath thundering footfalls and flailing axes.

Some of the Northmen attempted to wade out and board several of their vessels, assuming their best chance of escape was to simply row out of reach of their tormentors. It was a desperate move, and Alaric and the rest of the men were not of a mind to let them do it, instead storming after them with all the energy they could muster. The battle kept on, the river's previously peaceful, pristine waters flowing red as the fighting spread out across the shallows, the Danes' increasingly hopeless efforts to resist or escape driving them into a terror-stricken frenzy.

Alaric found himself struggling with a new opponent, each of them now waist-deep in water. They flailed wildly at the other, Alaric feeling his lip split open as he took a fist to the face. He tried to bring his sword up for a downward swing, but the Dane anticipated the move, striking him again in the chest and following up with a side swipe of his axe. Alaric fell, his weight dragging him beneath the surface, his vision all clouded light and swirling shadows.

The Dane fell after him, the weight of his body pushing Alaric down until he came to rest on the riverbed. Alaric couldn't see much at all, his descent causing the silt and mud below to billow upwards in great clouds to obscure his vision. What he could see was that his opponent was dead, his vacant eyes and the clouds of reddish fluid emerging from the back of his head suggesting he'd been struck from behind.

Despite that, he was still a threat since his weight was serving to push Alaric down further into the riverbed. He gritted his teeth, bubbles pouring out from between them, and tried to haul the Dane to one side. He eventually managed to free his left arm and claw desperately upwards, but he was still unable to shift the corpse or slide himself out from underneath it. His chest was burning, his eye bulging also. Panic seized his heart. He couldn't hold on much longer.

Somebody grabbed him by the wrist to lift him up and out of the Dane's morbid embrace. Alaric broke the surface, his mouth agape, and desperately refilled his lungs. Ulfcytel released him from his vice-like grip, the man's entire face and upper body drenched in blood. Alaric wasn't sure what was more disturbing, that or the fact he was smiling through it, his expression downright manic as the whiteness of his teeth shone through the gore.

"Sorry about that, lad. I saw you go down and decided I'd best split that bastard's head. I didn't think he'd be rude enough to try and drown you after that."

Alaric tried to return Ulfcytel's smile, his lacklustre grin more of a pained wince. He then checked the tenderness in his side. His mail had taken the brunt of the blow from the Dane's axe, but he'd have a troublesome bruise soon enough. He'd be fine. But he'd prefer to stay away from water for a while.

Wounded or not, the battle was now largely over. One group of Danes had actually made it aboard a ship, thinking they might escape their pursuers and live to fight another day. The English, however, had flowed up after them in pursuit, shouting and raging like men who knew their vengeance was close at hand. The fighting had then spread across the deck, and the Danes were all killed before they could even put a single oar into the water. Most were now lying face down in the river, their bodies hauled overboard by the dozen or so jubilant Saxons presently roaring in triumph from on high.

Ulfcytel strode back towards the shoreline, the water lapping at his waist and thighs as he emerged, grim-faced and victorious, into the sight of his men. Alaric followed at his side, the pair raising their swords in salute. Their twin blades shimmered when they caught the sunlight, and their warriors let rip with a great screaming cry, the savage cacophony of victorious men carrying far and wide across the otherwise depopulated landscape. Their win here had been sudden and total. The Danes had been caught unprepared, out of position, and entirely surprised, and they'd paid a heavy price, their bloodied corpses lying in a great trail from the sight of the initial ambush to the muddied river bank and beyond.

But that wasn't all of them. They could hear shouting from somewhere distant, possibly inside Gipeswic itself. What was left of the enemy garrison had not emerged yet, but it was fair to surmise they'd watched the slaughter on the river trail with trepidation. Alaric imagined them wondering where this English force had come from, thinking they'd probably assumed their task guarding the ships would be an easy one following the battle at Hringmere. He was glad to prove them wrong.

Yet time was still of the essence. There was no telling who or what else might be in the area, and without such knowledge their ragtag force was still vulnerable to attack. They'd won here because they'd tricked the Danes into fighting on their terms, but there was no way to ensure that success could be repeated now they'd made their presence known. As if to reinforce that point, several men on horseback suddenly bolted out of Gipeswic and headed north, the clattering of hooves and the cries of the riders carrying on the wind. They'd gone for help. It was time to hurry.

Ulfcytel was of a similar mind. He ordered the men to begin gathering up their wounded and secure them for transport in the ship they'd stormed just earlier. The ealdorman also sent a score of his people to fetch the refugees they'd picked up nights before. The three dozen or so adults and children had been sequestered in a ditch a few hundred yards to the north west, but there was always the risk the Danes might somehow spot them now they were on alert. Alaric wouldn't put it past those riders they'd just seen to attack them out of spite.

Those remaining applied themselves to boarding three more of the enemy ships, the men having to wade out up to their waists and even shoulders to scramble up onto their decks. They worked quickly, unfurling sails and manning oar locks, and before long a grand total of four ships were fully crewed and making their way out into deeper waters. Alaric just hoped their wounded would last the journey.

Ulfcytel ordered Alaric and the fifty warriors still on dry land to begin boarding as many of the other vessels as they could to do as much damage as was humanly possible. They secured one more so as to be able to load the refugees when they arrived, boarding yet another to be used to make their own escape when the time came. The rest were fair game, and they set upon them with enthusiasm, hacking into them with their axes to topple masts, shred sails, and shatter oars. It wouldn't render them entirely inoperable, but it would delay and inconvenience the Danes when they attempted to use them in future. Alaric was disappointed their efforts to set them alight came to little, as the flames from the few torches they had proved ineffective. That was a real shame. He'd have liked to have seen Thorkell's fleet burning in the river. It would have made for a good memory.

He'd just finished throwing a batch of oars overboard when he heard a sound on the wind. The surviving Danes holed up in Gipeswic had begun to emerge from the town and advance towards them, fully armed and up for a fight. It wasn't an army, as the battle they'd just fought had wiped out over half of the original garrison, but it was a formidable sight, especially now most of the English force was embarked and had already managed to row some distance downriver. They were turning around, having seen the danger, but it wouldn't be enough. They'd have to think fast.

Alaric looked to Ulfcytel, hoping for instructions. He seemed troubled, perhaps thinking of cutting his losses and escaping from harm even with the refugees still en route. Fortunately for them, the men he'd sent to fetch them appeared along the river trail seconds later, the non-combatants they'd rescued clustered around them for the sake of safety. They were a little out of breath, but they'd all made it through the trees in excellent time. Now all they had to do was embark and make their escape.

They started to bundle the refugees onto the ship they'd set aside for them. The Danes had by now broken into a run, their frenzied war cries growing louder with each passing moment. Alaric decided to expedite matters, leaping into the water and rushing ashore. He began bellowing at those left to hurry aboard, but they were slow and panicked, the sight of the enemy charging towards them unhindered appearing to have shocked them to the core. One anxious old man was particularly hesitant to wade out into the river, looking like he'd suddenly frozen in fear. Alaric simply grabbed him and hauled him along, the man going limp whilst Alaric half-swam, half-dragged him towards the waiting ship.

The survivors already aboard reached down off the deck, gripping their ageing companion by the shoulders as Alaric helped lift him to safety. Alaric scrambled up the hull after him, his efforts aided when persons unknown seized him by the wrists and heaved him upwards. He soon found himself face down on the deck, his limbs burning with effort. He ignored the pain and struggled to his feet, hoping to review the situation.

All of the refugees had made it, those strong enough joining the few warriors on board in rowing their vessel away from danger. They were already putting some distance between themselves and the enemy, and yet Ulfcytel was still up to his waist in the water, as was Bana and about ten others. Alaric screamed at them to hurry, for the howling Danes were mere moments away, their faces lit up with delight at the prospect of avenging their recently slaughtered brethren.

Ulfcytel looked at Alaric and then back towards the Danes like he was thinking of fighting them. Bana seemed to see it, too, grabbing the ealdorman with a shout and hauling him further into the water. The pair of them started to swim, the other men following suit, Bana making sure he stayed behind Ulfcytel in case he should have any more strange, suicidal ideas. He gestured as if to call out to Alaric when he took a spear in the back, his body crumpling in on itself and vanishing beneath the surface. The man following him died also, the thrown spear actually impaling him through the neck. The Danes had good aim.

Alaric shouted for the oarsmen to slow, the distance between them and Ulfcytel having continued to increase. Nobody had given them the order to commence rowing, but the men were anxious to get underway and escape. Alaric didn't blame them. But they were now in trouble, and they'd left their own people in danger.

He grabbed a spare oar and reached out with it, extending it past the stern and into the water in the hope of somebody taking hold of it so he could pull them in. He did so with one warrior, heaving him through the shallows and towards safety. Alaric was trying to steady his nerves when a spear suddenly slammed into the deck beside him. He hauled his man aboard and passed him the oar so he could do the same for others before wrenching the spear free and casting it back towards the river bank. He was rewarded with a high-pitched scream and the sight of a Dane collapsing into his comrades. Alaric too had good aim. He must be finally getting used to his reduced vision.

Ulfcytel was in peril, the waters around him now clouded red. Alaric didn't waste any time, tearing off his belt and mail shirt and leaping overboard, the ear-splitting splash he made further drenching those nearby. He surfaced momentarily, his buoyancy improved with his reduced weight, and began swimming frantically towards Ulfcytel, the ealdorman struggling to stay afloat.

Alaric soon saw why. A thrown spear had nicked his left leg, leaving a serious gash down the back of his thigh. He'd already lost a lot of blood, and additional spears were raining down around them, their throwers laughing from onshore. Alaric saw only one way out of this. He took a deep breath, gesturing for Ulfcytel to do the same. He then gripped him by the shoulders and launched himself beneath the surface, dragging Ulfcytel with him.

He looked around, his vision again all blue haze and bubbles, and managed to spot the dark, blurred mass of their ship's hull, the tips of its oars rising and falling as it powered through the water. He then swam like he'd never swam in his life, trying to pull the weakened Ulfcytel along with him, his chest burning as he used up what oxygen he had in his lungs.

Ulfcytel seemed to understand what he was hoping to accomplish, and he began kicking his legs with gusto to speed them on their way. It was a good effort, but Alaric could tell he was weakening, the blood from his wound leaving an alarmingly large red trail in their wake. Several spears surged past them, the Danes intent on peppering the area. Alaric carried on as long as he could, struggling and flailing towards their escaping vessel, Ulfcytel doing his best not to be too much of a hindrance.

It didn't last. Alaric couldn't fight his desire to breathe nor suddenly grow a pair of gills, and his burning lungs eventually forced him to breach the surface. He was now floundering about ten feet from the ship's stern, his breath frantic and forced as he hauled Ulfcytel up and around in a bid to shield him from any more projectiles. In truth, they had not gone far, for Alaric's desperate ploy was just that, desperate, and not something he could have realistically expected to pull off. Swimming underwater whilst fully clothed would be hard enough, but dragging a man like Ulfcytel along with you for any real distance just wasn't feasible.

What motivated Alaric was his belief that he himself was expendable. If he died, it would be a personal tragedy for his wife and family, but England may otherwise be unaffected. If Ulfcytel died, it would be much worse. As far as Alaric was concerned, he was the one to lead them to victory against Thorkell. It was for this reason he'd half-drowned them both attempting to save him, and it was for this same reason he now used himself as a shield, hoping to take any incoming spears in the back rather than see Ulfcytel slain.

If Ulfcytel himself appreciated such dedication, he showed no sign. His eyes had closed, his beard hanging limp and sodden in a great dripping trail from his jaw. The tip of an oar suddenly splashed the surface close by, one of the men Alaric had helped earlier now wielding it as a means to rescue him in return. He lunged for it, keeping his right arm around Ulfcytel whilst he grabbed at the oar with his left. He made it, his grip strong and true, their saviour on deck shouting with relief as he began hauling them in. Alaric didn't have the strength to climb aboard himself, let alone lift Ulfcytel onto the deck, but a veritable forest of arms reached down to assist, pulling them both from the water and to safety.

Alaric must have passed out briefly, awakening to find himself flat on his back, his rescuers gathering around him to heave him up into a sitting position. His limbs were shaking from the ordeal he'd put himself through, their strength almost entirely expended from his do-or-die attempt to rescue Ulfcytel. Alaric turned to see the man himself lying on the deck, motionless, only to then suddenly come to, his body convulsing as he hacked up a deluge of river water from his lungs.

The old man Alaric had helped earlier rushed to attend him, pushing past the others to ease the ealdorman onto his stomach. He then began hammering at his back, his blows methodical and almost rhythmic as Ulfcytel continued to retch and splutter. It seemed to work, although Ulfcytel didn't get up, instead rolling onto his side and groaning, his eyes closed. The old man then began to see to his leg wound, the practised movement of his hands suggesting some proficiency with the healing arts. Alaric was now doubly glad he'd saved him.

The other ships they'd appropriated had begun to close around them, forming a protective line whilst they moved away from Gipeswic and downriver towards the waiting sea. Alaric smiled upon seeing the commotion along the shore. The enemy had looked to pursue them by boarding one of the ships that had only recently been rendered inoperable. It would profit them little, for Alaric had personally helped throw its oars overboard, having also hacked away at its sails to the point they were effectively useless. The Northmen howled in outrage and frustration upon realising the extent of the damage. It was a sweet sound to English ears.

The Danes still had hundreds of other vessels lining the river for them to choose from, yet they seemed to be giving up, likely because they could see the English force was again united and already speeding away. It had to be said the bastards had displayed some cunning in their counterattack, waiting as they had for the English to divide their forces so they'd not have to fight their full strength all at once. It had nearly worked, and they'd nearly killed Ulfcytel, an honour that would have certainly catapulted them to fame.

But they hadn't. They'd failed. Thorkell should really have left a bigger garrison here. His arrogance would hopefully be his downfall. Failing that, Alaric could always have another go at removing his head from his shoulders.

Eamon and Osbert waved to them from one of the vessels now off their port side. They looked concerned, probably also feeling guilty for embarking and rowing away before the evacuation was complete. It wasn't their fault. The situation had been confusing. These things happened in the heat of the moment, especially when they'd been facing one danger after another for weeks now. He wondered, though, if Eamon had seen Bana die. He'd talk to him when he could.

Losses and mishaps aside, they'd secured victory here, there was no doubt about that. Battered and bruised as they were, they'd been successful in hitting the enemy and securing their escape. He doubted Thorkell would be overly slowed by what they'd done to his ships, but it was the thought that counted. Anything they could do to hurt him, they'd do it.

Alaric wandered along the deck, checking on Ulfcytel as he went. He was alive, breathing, and clearly in good hands, his elderly caregiver confirming he was indeed well-versed in tending to the sick and wounded. Alaric thanked him, being thanked in return for having saved him when his own courage had failed. He nodded and continued on, making his way up to the prow to behold what lay ahead.

They were almost to the mouth of the river, the sea stretching out before them in a shimmering, sun-drenched expanse of blues and greens. He'd never been one for the water, preferring the solid, assured feeling of dry land beneath his boots. Today he was glad, though. They had a purpose once more. A destination. The Holy City. Canterburie.

XI

"I don't want you two upsetting your father like you so often do. He's already troubled enough without his disobedient sons returning to make his life miserable."

Emma's words cut deep, not in that they'd hurt Edmund's feelings, but because he couldn't fathom why she thought she could speak to him like that. Who was she again? A foreigner, married to his father for political purposes. Yet she thought she was a queen, able to prevent the heirs to the throne of the Kingdom of England from speaking to their own father. Intolerable.

There was something about the way she carried herself too. She was stood out in the hall, hands on her hips, her gold-threaded, cream-coloured dress flowing down and out across the stone slabs as if to demand attention purely on merit of its unnecessary flamboyance. Her face also was irritating, all scrunched up, pale aside from her jarringly rose-tinted cheeks, her green eyes glowering at them from beneath a cascade of plaited, reddish hair. Even the shawl she wore atop her head seemed designed to provoke, its purple and gold colouring contrasting with the cream of her dress to give her the appearance of some kind of poisonous mushroom.

Edmund stifled a laugh at the thought, the queen's scowl deepening at the sight of his barely restrained mirth. He didn't actually want to offend her any more than he had to, but the lady was testing his patience. He had to make that clear.

"Let us through, Emma. We have urgent business to discuss with our father. I promise we won't take up too much of his precious time."

Emma's nose wrinkled with additional irritation, likely over his failure to refer to her as queen. He wouldn't ever address her as such. She was nothing of the kind and never would be, no matter how much she might want it to be so. A Queen of England had to be worthy of the title. Emma wasn't worthy or particularly adept at much of anything, aside from gossiping and placing demands on others.

Morcar moved to position himself between them. His movements were subtle, his manner temperate, his very presence introducing an element of calm into an otherwise tense atmosphere. He bowed before speaking, looking very much the noble thegn at court now he'd changed out of his armour and into something more suitable, his dark, silver-embroidered tunic and matching breecs complementing his flowing black hair and beard perfectly.

"Apologies, my queen, but the aethelings are merely fatigued from the trials of the road. It was a long and dangerous journey for us, things being as they are, and we are tired. If you would be so gracious to let us pass, I promise we will be mindful of the many stresses the king is no doubt enduring."

Morcar's words seemed to have an impact, for Emma's expression changed, ever so slightly, from rank displeasure to mere irritation. The two guards stationed on either side of the doors to the king's audience chamber also relaxed, their postures easing from simmering agitation to generic discomfort. Edmund didn't envy them. Theirs was a difficult position, and when a queen argued with the heirs to the throne, there were no easy choices on who held authority over the other.

"I appreciate somebody displaying a degree of civility here," Emma said, flicking an accusative glance at Edmund and Æthelstan. "But even so, the king is not to be disturbed. He is discussing urgent business relating to the fate of the traitorous Ealdorman Ælfric."

"What's Ælfric supposed to have done now?" Æthelstan snapped, his impatience getting the better of him. It was a fine testament to how irritating Emma could be that she regularly tested the normally placid and likeable Æthelstan. The man generally had the patience of a saint.

"I believe he was involved in a recent plot against the king. Fortunately, the good and loyal Ealdorman Eadric has put a stop to it."

All three men, Edmund, Æthelstan, and even Morcar, tensed at the mention of Eadric. Ælfric may have a reputation tarnished by cowardice and intrigue, but it was nothing compared to Eadric's grim deeds. Regardless, Æthelstan's patience had run out. He made a move for the doors, stepping forward to barge past Emma. She refused to yield, placing a pair of dove-white hands on his chest, her face twisting in outrage. Æthelstan would have none of that.

"Get out of my way, Ælfgifu. Move, or I will move you. Make your choice."

Edmund had rarely heard his brother speak with such menace. His voice was otherwise quiet, his eyes locked with Emma's, yet the ice in his tone left nothing to ambiguity. Emma looked to the guards behind her, an expression of embittered helplessness on her face. They'd stepped forward to meet Æthelstan's advance, but Edmund could tell they were undecided about what to do, their gazes flitting nervously between the aethelings to Morcar and back to Emma again.

To her credit, Emma read the situation well. She didn't have the authority to stop them from seeing their father, and she was certain to be aware she couldn't order the guards to manhandle or even attack them purely because she might wish it. She stepped aside, her head lowered in resignation, those fierce emerald eyes sneaking a resentful look towards them as they passed. Æthelstan certainly knew how to get under her skin by calling her Ælfgifu. It was a badly kept secret that Emma hated the English name the king had given her upon their marriage. Edmund didn't blame her. It was the name of their mother, after all.

The aethelings pushed open the heavy double doors, Morcar slipping between them whilst the two brothers applied their impressive strength. The doors folded inward as they proceeded, the echoing thud of their closing reverberating down the length of the chamber. They began the long walk past their father's banqueting table, Edmund catching sight of the king himself perched atop his throne some distance away.

He had company. Edmund spied the Ealdorman Eadric standing off to the side, his harsh gaze fixed on the three cowed figures hunched before their father. Another man stood behind them, his back towards Edmund, and had the look of somebody of authority, given the three spear-armed warriors standing vigil around him. The king, as usual, was flanked by his heavily armoured bodyguards, these two almost always at his side and ready to give their lives for him at a moment's notice. Edmund admired their dedication.

Their father's appearance had improved since they'd last laid eyes on him. When they'd left, he'd been his typical, hollow-eyed self, his face marked with worry as it generally had been for as long as they could remember. Now he seemed to have gotten at least some life back in him, and he looked fairly regal atop his throne, his flowing purple robes and the circlet of gold-studded silver upon his head giving him an air of genuine majesty. There was a king in him, Edmund knew that, and in more peaceful times he might have been an effective ruler. Peace, unfortunately, had always been so very elusive.

And yet Edmund wasn't sure if he cared for the look upon his face as he beheld those huddled at his feet. Triumphant, smug, gloating…all such words could be used to describe Æthelred's expression now. There was a cruelty there, jagged and cold, and he was obviously enjoying himself at the expense of others. That wasn't right.

He looked over at his sons when they came closer, Eadric and the others doing the same. Edmund thought he recognised one of those directly facing his father's throne, but the abundance of bruising across his face made his identity uncertain. Whoever this man was, he'd been subject to some violence, a notion further reinforced by the evidently frightened woman at his side. Edmund didn't recognise her either, but he noted her flowing red hair put Emma's to shame. The lady had a look of defiance to her, too, despite her anxiety.

There was another man with her who was also a mystery. He'd been the only one in the chamber not to have turned to look at him and his brother, and Edmund soon saw why, for he wore some kind of cloth around his head to obscure his eyes. Edmund assumed this must be because he was blind, although his body language implied he was at least aware and very uncomfortable with his present company. Their father's voice soon cut across the room, the menacing sarcasm of his words suggesting it probably hadn't been the best time to disturb him after all.

"God has returned my wayward sons to me! Dear Æthelstan, pray tell your old father why you and Edmund have decided to grace me with your presence now…in the company of the good Morcar, no less!"

Edmund didn't care for his tone as it was, but the manner in which he'd mentioned Morcar was truly venomous. They'd made a mistake coming back so soon. Perhaps they'd made a mistake leaving to begin with. Without his loyal sons to protect him, their father had been vulnerable to yet more bad advice from who knows who. If that were true, there was nothing they could do about it now. They'd weather this storm and see what good could come of it.

Æthelstan, Edmund, and Morcar all bowed low before speaking. They were unable to stand directly before the throne, as would otherwise be proper, owing to the strangers present, but formality mattered here, and Edmund, at any rate, would give his father the respect he was due. Æthelstan spoke first, his flowing mail shirt, crimson cloak, and belt of weapons reminding all he was very much the warrior aetheling who had every right to be here. He'd attired himself as such on purpose, Edmund knew. They'd expected Eadric to be present, and Æthelstan intended to make it clear he wouldn't shirk from confrontation should it prove necessary.

"We have important matters to discuss, father. This tax you have imposed on the realm…it…"

"What of it?" Æthelred interjected, his previous smugness giving way to a more measured demeanour. "I am the King of England. England needs a new army. I have issued a tax on England to get us this new army. Is this presenting some kind of difficulty for you, my boy?"

Æthelstan bristled at being talked down to in front of others, his face flushing an interesting shade of pink. Morcar stepped forward, his persona as always the epitome of calm. He then unfurled the original letter they'd received announcing additional taxes on the Five Boroughs.

"My good king, what you command of us is not feasible," he said, flicking the fingers of his right hand across the parchment to emphasise his point. "We are already paying substantial taxes to the crown as it is. What you call for here will cripple whatever trade we are still able to cultivate. We also won't be able to properly pay for our own fyrd. Should the enemy turn their att…"

"This is really quite a ridiculous scenario," Æthelred interrupted again, his hands now extended, palms facing up, in mock exasperation. "Eastengle is in ruins," he went on, "and the entire south is devastated. Cantebrigie is on fire. And here I am, dealing with two ingrate sons and a petty thegn from the five whatevers complaining that I'm expecting too much of them when it comes to the defence of the realm."

"It is not that we won't pay our fair share, my king," Morcar continued, unperturbed by the interruption and insult, "but not all will react to this as patiently as we have. Some thegns may not look to respectfully petition you for redress as we do now. They may simply rebel."

"Do you seek to threaten your king, Morcar?" said Eadric from his position leaning against the stone wall to the left of the throne. His face was partially masked in shadow, but his manner was relaxed, comfortable even, in a way that set Edmund on edge.

"I would never presume to do such a thing," replied Morcar evenly. "And yet I will tell you now that this tax will impoverish the realm to the point no man will be able to defend his lands. That man will then look to the crown as to why. Not all will be as polite or restrained as I am."

"How they decide to express their opinion is of little consequence," Eadric shot back. "What matters is that they obey, rather than pestering their king with petty objections."

"Respectfully, my objections are not petty," said Morcar, turning from Eadric to again face Æthelred. "You risk alienating your own people, my king. May I sugge…"

"No, you may not," Æthelred answered bluntly. "I have grown weary of disobedience. Take Ælfric here. He defied me last year when I commanded him to raise his fyrd to support my efforts to contain Thorkell in the south. Yet he suddenly found himself a backbone when Ulfcytel asked him for aid. He defies his king and only takes action to support his own interests. I will not have it."

"That is not true!" the bruised man before the throne suddenly declared, Edmund assuming this must actually be Ælfric, Ealdorman of Hamptonscir. They'd only recently met a man claiming to be his son, Alaric, on the road down from the Five Boroughs, but he'd never mentioned that the king might be displeased with his father. Edmund could tell that both Æthelstan and Morcar were likely thinking similar thoughts, their expressions doubly serious in the face of Ælfric's distress.

"It is NOT true, I tell you," he said again, his voice cracking in desperation. "I have told you this, Æthelred, time and again. We DID raise the Hamptonscir fyrd, and yet you retreated to Lundenburg without warning, leaving us at the mercy of Thorkell. Had you decided to fight wi…"

"Shut up, man!" the king thundered, his hands clenching into fists. "I will not have it from you! Not after all this time! Not after what you did with my fleet! Not after Wiltune! And did you think I'd be forgetting Abbendone either?! Surely your boy, Ælfgar, is a living reminder of the consequences of your actions there?!"

Ælfric fell silent, Edmund's eyes now drifting to the blind fellow hunched several paces across from him. Edmund assumed this must be the Ælfgar his father was referring to, yet if he were, he made no effort to confirm it, although his posture indicated he was now doubly uncomfortable at what had been said. Edmund was in the dark. Whatever scores were being settled here seemed to be from before his time.

Others appeared to understand more than he did. The red-haired woman beside Ælfric looked like all the colour had suddenly drained from her cheeks. She mouthed a word once, then again, making a third effort to summon the strength to give herself voice.

"Wiltune? W-what about Wiltune?"

"Pay it no mind, my dear," Æthelred answered casually, his anger now strangely absent. "The destruction of Wiltune was just yet another time your father-in-law has failed me."

Father-in-law. That would mean this woman was married to one of Ælfric's sons, perhaps this Alaric they'd met on the road. Edmund wasn't sure if that could be the case, but she looked absolutely shattered, like she'd been bearing a burden for some time that had finally gotten the better of her. Being separated from a husband could do that, in addition to all the present drama. He'd be sure to speak to her in private if he got the opportunity. News of her husband might relieve her of some of her very evident troubles.

His father showed no such concern, gesturing instead for the unfortunate woman and her two male companions to be taken away. Ælfric again went to object when one of the three guards behind him laid their hands on him, his voice trailing after them as he was dragged back towards the doors. The woman remained silent, as did the younger man, seemingly resigned to their fate, whatever that might be. Edmund hoped his father had not decided on bloodshed. Ælfric may be a fool and much more, but he didn't deserve death.

"I think it's time we all sat and talked, as a family," the king announced, his face now unnervingly cheerful. Emma had slipped back into the room whilst Ælfric and company were dragged out, making her way towards them with all her usual pomp and self-importance. She ignored the two brothers and Morcar, instead climbing the steps to the throne to take Æthelred's hand. He allowed it, the pair of them then gazing upon the other as if they'd only just been married.

"What do you say, my sons?" inquired Æthelred, managing to tear his attention away from Emma's eyes. "Shall we not break bread together?"

"Are we going to discuss the tax you've…"

"No, Æthelstan, that can wait," their father said, yet again interrupting his eldest. "There are times for politics, and I've had more than my fill of them. For this afternoon, let us speak on easier matters. Alone."

The king's glare fell on Morcar, insinuating his presence was no longer welcome. Morcar performed a simple bow before turning and leaving, giving Edmund and Æthelstan a reassuring nod as he went. Eadric followed after him, his face unreadable, his blond curls appearing strangely feminine when viewed from behind. Edmund watched him go. He'd have serious words with that man, soon enough.

Their father wasn't joking when he'd said he wanted to talk as a family. He seated them all at the banqueting table, sending for their dour, taciturn brother, Eadwig, as well as the children he'd had with Emma. Eadwig was an enigma to both Edmund and Æthelstan. He was third in line to the throne but distant and hard to read when it came to his other brothers. He wasn't as capable a warrior either, preferring his books to the exclusion of much else, his deep eyes and large forehead giving him a scholarly appearance that suited his habits.

Despite his aloofness, Edmund was fond of him. He'd long wanted a real friendship with him, yet his cold personality was hard to get around, and most of their interactions had felt forced, leaving Edmund frustrated and saddened. The most recent example of this was when Eadwig had declined to accompany them to the Five Boroughs following the argument over their father's refusal to aid Ulfcytel. Edmund assumed Eadwig had his reasons. He just didn't know what they were. He didn't seem overly pleased to see them now either, and he only nodded and smiled passively when taking a seat across from them. Edmund made a point of reaching over and warmly shaking his hand in his. It was important that somebody make the effort.

Emma left and then reappeared, bringing her three children with her. Edward was the eldest and was a confident sort, strutting on ahead of his mother to take a seat next to his father. Both Alfred and Godgifu were more reserved, the latter clinging nervously to Emma's ridiculous gown. Godgifu and Alfred were still of an age where they were having trouble understanding there were other people in the world besides them and their mother, so gatherings like this were a little overwhelming. Edmund gave Edward an exaggerated, comedic scowl from across the table. The boy responded by baring his teeth at him and then sticking his tongue out. Edmund and Æthelstan laughed. He was a good lad.

A flock of stewards made their presence known, bringing platters of roast meats, vegetables, and a basket of freshly baked barley bread. Edmund hadn't been expecting a feast, but he made sure to obtain a tankard of ale, feeling the need to steady his nerves. He tried to bring up the issue of the new tax yet again, but his father dismissed him with a wave of his hand. The king was more interested in the food, laughing and smiling with Emma as if he were a far younger man in far better times. Edmund was pleased to see him so happy. He just wished he'd address the present crisis first.

Æthelstan seemed to be adapting himself to their situation, as he was presently demolishing a platter of fresh greens, parsnips, and pork like it were nothing but air. Edmund merely picked away at the side of beef that had been placed before him, unable to relax. Emma was carrying on like nothing was wrong, acting as a fount of good cheer as long as it concerned either the king or her children. It was different when she looked over at the two brothers. Then those eyes grew hard again, freezing over to the point you'd be right to wonder if this was the same joyful mother you'd beheld just a moment prior.

Everyone knew what she was about. You didn't marry a king just to have his children from a previous marriage upstage your own. She wanted Edward on the throne. She could dream on. Æthelstan was the heir, and he didn't look like he was going to be dying anytime soon if his appetite was anything to go by. The real danger was that she might convince the king to designate their own children as sole heirs, overlooking his grown sons altogether. Edmund and Æthelstan had long suspected that was her intent, yet they were in the dark on whether their father would ever agree to it. Neither of them would allow a boy king to take the throne, even one as good-natured as Edward. They would not be denied their birthright by the schemings of a foreigner like Emma. That was all there was to it.

Edmund tried to make conversation with Eadwig. It was heavy going, and he was a man of very few words. Edmund often thought Eadwig knew more than he let on, suspecting his quiet and unapproachable persona was a deliberate facade intended to hide his true feelings and intentions. Edmund got that feeling from him now, but sometimes the mask slipped a little, the odd fleeting glance suggesting he was as uncomfortable as Edmund over their father's preference for festivities over action. Perhaps they could talk later in private. There was a lot of knowledge in that large head of his. Some of it would no doubt come in useful.

His father was similarly unresponsive, despite his otherwise hospitable demeanour. He largely ignored Edmund when he mentioned Wulfnoth - their friend who Morcar and Sigeferth believed had been framed by Eadric and his brother - simply stating that the man was a "traitor" who was "best forgotten." Likewise, he wouldn't be caught out on the subject of Eadric and what advice he was still in the habit of offering, at one point telling Æthelstan to "focus on swordcraft, not politics, lest you get confused." No matter how hard they tried, their father would not budge. Matters of import would have to wait, apparently.

Edmund downed what was left in his tankard and rose from his chair. He made his excuses to his father, claiming he was tired from his journey, giving Æthelstan a knowing look and reassuring pat on the shoulder as he turned to leave. There was one particular relative of his whom he knew to be in Lundenburg and yet had not been summoned to their little feast. Edmund had a feeling it might prove fruitful to pay her a visit. His father didn't call after him as he walked away from the table. He was more interested in his queen and their children. Edmund had expected nothing more from him.

He passed through the double doors into the corridor beyond, turning immediately left and heading down the long, draughty stone hallway towards his father's chambers. He then took another left when he was just outside, proceeding down another corridor and passing through several more doors until he came to a narrow archway. He stepped through, emerging into a sun-drenched inner courtyard, the familiar sights and scents of flowering plants and bountiful fruit trees greeting him like old friends.

Edmund had always liked it here. He'd had the luxury of spending many an afternoon amid the trees when he was but a boy, and he'd missed it. He still was young, it had to be said, and the place hadn't lost too much of its magic with the passage of years, remaining a veritable treasury of beauty, colour, and fruits the likes of which he'd rarely found the equal of elsewhere. It was always well maintained, for his father had gone to great efforts to secure the services of the best gardener he could find to keep his little slice of Eden in pristine condition. Edmund couldn't see old Osbern now. He must be attending to something else. Then he saw the view to the south east. The one that never failed to captivate.

He could see out and over his father's halls from here, his elevated position permitting him a clear panorama extending over the city. The Temes cut across his field of vision from the east, wide and strong, the river skirting around the southern walls to continue its long course towards the western horizon.

Lundenburg always seemed so alive to him, the crowded streets and heaving marketplaces conveying a certain power and flavour that was quite unique. There was also a strange energy to the place, something he at times found hard to describe. The population enjoyed the most secure habitation in all of England, and yet they were oddly restless, like they somehow resented their confinement and yearned to expand beyond. It showed in their temperament, and Edmund had a feeling that the longer this war went on, the worse it would get.

He turned his attention back to the Temes. He'd always enjoyed watching the ships, and on most days it was easy to spot some heading upriver to offload their cargoes along the docks and wharves of what was still one of the most lucrative markets in all of Europe. The docks themselves lay outside the fortified walls and had been damaged in Thorkell's recent siege, but they were still operating, and their speedy repair was a priority since they supplied the city with much of its trade. There was a certain power in wealth, and whilst Edmund suspected true kingship was better sustained in faith and virtue, it was undeniable that England's prosperity was in part due to economics. Lundenburg's position as a haven for maritime commerce was a large factor in that.

Yet things were changing. The number of ships out on the water had gradually diminished as the years of strife continued. England had acquired a reputation for instability and risk rather than sound investment, which was deterring a lot of foreign merchants and the money they brought with them. There were still several vessels out there today, their oars heaving their sleek wooden forms through the sun-kissed waters, but it was different from when he was a boy. Back then, the bustle of the Temes had truly been something to behold; the river turning thick with strange beasts of oak and sail, their holds brimming with even stranger wonders from far-off lands. It was no longer so. Instead, an ill feeling held sway over the city, as if it were waiting for something terrible to occur that had been a long time in coming.

Edmund shook himself free of such thoughts. He wasn't here to linger, instead turning to make his way directly between the trees, across the grass, and through another stone archway. He might return later if he could. The gardens were dear to him for a number of reasons, and there were far worse places to spend a summer evening.

He strode down another corridor and vaulted up several flights of echoing stairs until he came to what may have been mistaken for just another wooden door leading into just another spacious bedchamber. He knocked and waited, hearing some consternation inside, the door eventually opening just far enough for a rather pallid, dark-haired woman to peer out, her eyes narrowed in the gloom.

She was a bit older than Edmund, and was dressed in an unassuming dark robe and shawl, giving him the impression she'd not been expecting a visitor. She recognised him instantly, throwing the door open and launching herself into his arms with a squeak of excitement. Wulfhild was always rather free with her emotions, and whilst she could be very stubborn, Edmund would be the first to admit this was a common enough quality in their family. It was also a characteristic she shared with her husband, Ulfcytel.

Edmund managed to prise his sister from his shoulders and pass within, promising to tell her in full of his trip north. The air in her chambers was more than a little musty, the plethora of plates, bowls, and cups scattered across her table indicating she'd been more or less alone here for some time. Edmund took a seat, pushing what looked like the remains of this morning's breakfast out of his way. She sat across from him, still excited to have company and entirely unconcerned with the clutter.

"Did you receive an invitation from father today?" Edmund asked, wondering why she'd not been at the feast he'd left earlier.

"Invitation?" she queried, sounding surprised. "To what? To stare at him on his throne and not talk to me?"

"Father gathered everyone in his audience chamber. They are no doubt still there, eating and drinking. All the family. Except for you."

Wulfhild's face seemed to crumple downwards, her expression now a combination of bitterness and genuine sadness. She shook her head weakly, folding her hands neatly on the table, her shoulders slumped like they'd taken on some sudden burden. When she spoke again, all happiness had drained from her voice, and she sounded as pained as he'd ever known her to be.

"He never spends time with me, Edmund. Nobody does. Since Ulfcytel sent me back here…it's like I'm a stranger. You'd not have thought he was my father, the way he looks at me. I'm not surprised he wanted everyone there but me."

"I want you there!" Edmund exclaimed, his heart aching at the sight of her so troubled. "As does Æthelstan, I'm sure. I bet Eadwig has noticed your absence, too, but he'd have to check in some book before he believed it for sure."

She laughed. Their studious brother had long been a source of good-humoured amusement between them, something Eadwig himself was most likely aware of. Jokes aside, Edmund had a feeling why their father had grown so cold towards her, and it wasn't because of anything she might have done. Her husband. He was the real issue here.

"How was father, you think, when he saw you here after Ulfcytel had sent you away from Noruic?"

"He wasn't the same," she answered. "It was like he was one man when I left Lundenburg and then a completely different person when I came back. I don't know what I've done to offend him or why he's content to leave me here, but I make do."

Edmund found it strange that she hadn't mentioned her husband or inquired as to his whereabouts. He had no idea how she really felt about him, but Ulfcytel had always seemed a decent enough man, at least to Edmund, and it was odd that she hadn't asked after him. Had nobody told her what had happened at Hringmere?

"You do know that Ulfcytel faced Thorkell in battle? That he was defeated?"

If it were possible for his sister to look even more unhappy, she managed it. She turned pale, even more so than before, and dark circles appeared under her eyes as if by magic, her mouth opening slightly in apprehension. Nobody had told her. That was cruel.

"…is he dead?" she breathed, her chestnut eyes wide and glistening with tears. Edmund was glad he'd been the one to break the news to her. Thanks to Alaric and that Osbert fellow, he knew her husband was very much alive.

"No, not at all," Edmund said, reaching out to take her hand in his. "We met some survivors from his army on the road down from Snotingeham. He's in Eastengle still, hiding out in the forest."

"What's he doing there?" she asked, incredulous. "Why doesn't he come here and get me?"

Edmund didn't have a ready answer to her question. If he had to guess, there were two issues to consider, the first one being that Ulfcytel was loath to abandon Eastengle and was looking to get revenge on Thorkell. The second was that there was now some bad blood between himself and the king. His father had not mentioned such a thing to him directly, but he shared relatively little with him these days anyway. It was possible he'd decided Ulfcytel was some kind of enemy, and the ealdorman himself was aware of it and wished to avoid the king as a result. How that had come to pass, though, was a mystery.

"I don't know," admitted Edmund, squeezing her hand reassuringly, "but we can find out. Tell me…how did Ulfcytel seem before he sent you here? Was he troubled? Were you getting on well?"

"He is good to me…but he was always busy. He kept saying he was going to stop Thorkell. But he said it might not be safe for me, and when Thorkell attacked Gipeswic, he sent me here. He hasn't…he hasn't been close with me since…"

Edmund caught the gist. He'd heard about her losing the child, regretting still that he'd been unable to visit her when he'd first received the news. It wasn't his business, and he'd never gone through such an ordeal, but he still sympathised with them both. Ulfcytel probably had not visited her bed since. He didn't know the man well enough to guess why, but he'd heard these things could place a significant burden on any marriage. He sincerely hoped he didn't blame his sister for what had happened. It was not her fault, and he'd take issue with any man who claimed otherwise, even one as ferocious as Ulfcytel.

"Has father said much about him?" Edmund asked, changing the subject. "Do you know if they still get on?"

"He doesn't talk to me," Wulfhild answered weakly. "He only ever spends time with Emma or Eadric. But what would I really know? I'm always here. Alone."

Edmund had started to put two and two together, and he didn't like it. Their father was ostracising his own daughter due to some kind of disagreement with her husband. Edmund would have none of it. Neither would Æthelstan when he found out. He'd do something about this right now. He got to his feet, leading Wulfhild up and likewise as her hand remained clasped in his.

"We're going to the feast," Edmund announced, his tone brooking no dissension. "You're a part of this family, and you won't be excluded anymore."

Wulfhild reacted to his words like they were the sweetest thing she'd heard since her wedding day. She followed him with a half-skip but paused at her door, imploring Edmund to wait. She then vanished into a side room that abutted her main chamber. Edmund waited. And waited some more. He had an inkling she was changing her clothes, yet he couldn't fathom why it might possibly take so long. Just as he was about to check on her, she reappeared. She'd donned a deep purple dress and headscarf, her raven hair also brushed and tied back into something far more presentable. Edmund smiled and nodded. He wasn't good at compliments and had no interest in dresses or the various things women did to preen themselves. If Wulfhild was happy, then he was happy. She smiled back at him. That was enough.

They proceeded out from the chamber and down the stairs, soon coming to the inner courtyard and its gardens and the scent of flowers in bloom. Osbern was there this time, pruning an already well-maintained apple tree. Edmund clapped him on the shoulder as he passed, the two exchanging pleasantries whilst Wulfhild plucked an apple from a low-hanging branch. She bit into it with some force, and it must have tasted good, for she looked perfectly happy now, appearing as an almost entirely different woman from the one who'd peered from her door not half an hour ago.

They continued on, passing through the archway towards their father's rooms, the pair still walking hand in hand. Edmund decided to regale her with stories of his visit to the Five Boroughs. There wasn't really much to tell once he'd left out the politics and his troubled conversations with Morcar and Sigeferth, but she was enthused to hear of the duel he'd had with Æthelstan, expressing regret she'd not seen it. They should have just taken her with them. Anything was better than being stuck in that room, alone. Then he wondered why exactly she might have liked to see him getting a beating from their older brother. Perhaps Ulfcytel's martial spirit had rubbed off on her.

Before long, they'd reached the sizeable double doors leading to their father's audience hall, the two guards stationed on either side pushing them back and open so they could pass within. Their family was as Edmund had left them. Æthelstan was predictably still eating and drinking and trying to make conversation with Eadwig. Their father seemed to be ignoring them both, and Emma scowled upon seeing Edmund and Wulfhild, yet her children smiled when they saw their elder half-brother had returned. Edmund resumed his seat next to his brother, placing his now increasingly nervous-looking sister on his left.

Æthelred glared across the table, displeased that Edmund had dared presume his sister could join them. One of the stewards passed her a platter of what looked like some kind of pie, and Wulfhild did her best to appear relaxed whilst she nibbled at it from under her father's gaze. Edmund got himself another tankard of ale and stared back at him, eventually catching his eye. The king seemed to soften slightly, deciding perhaps to withhold any objection to Wulfhild's presence now he could see Edmund would make an issue of it. All seemed well. Then Wulfhild made the mistake of speaking.

"Tell me, father, do you intend to send anyone to rescue my husband from Eastengle?"

Æthelred's jaw tensed, his eyes hardening. Edmund felt unease take hold of his stomach, robbing him of what appetite he still had. He'd not told his father of his encounter with Alaric. Nor had Æthelstan, as far as he was aware. Judging from his reaction, this was news to him and far from welcome. Edmund again wondered what exactly Ulfcytel could have done to displease him.

"What, daughter? What did you say to me?"

She repeated her question, a slight quaver creeping into her voice. He downed the rest of his wine and then wiped his mouth on his sleeve, his manner akin to one who'd needed to steady themselves after receiving harsh words. Edmund didn't understand what the problem was.

"Your husband's army was destroyed," their father stated. "He's missing, probably dead. I would not waste lives looking for him after a defeat on that scale."

Wulfhild looked to Edmund, her eyes desperate and hurt, making him fear she suspected him of having lied about Ulfcytel's fate. He wasn't a liar, and he couldn't have her thinking otherwise. He had no choice now. He had to tell his father of what he and Æthelstan had learned.

"I'm afraid I have news to the contrary," Edmund said slowly and carefully. "We had to take a detour when travelling here since the countryside is so dangerous now. We passed close to Theodford and encountered a party of warriors on the road. Survivors of Hringmere. They confirmed Ulfcytel yet lives."

Edmund was genuinely grieved by what happened next. The king's face appeared to transform, his eyes flashing with a sudden and unprovoked malice. Both Æthelstan and Wulfhild shifted uncomfortably in their chairs, perturbed at how their father now beheld his own son.

"Who were these men? Did they say how he had survived, what his plans were?"

"Not exactly," answered Edmund. "One went by the name of Alaric, claiming to be a son of the Ealdorman Ælfri..."

Edmund ducked his head down and to the left, managing to just avoid the cup as it sailed past him to shatter on the stone wall beyond. Its fragments clattered to the floor, the entire room falling silent with them, all eyes now on the king and his sudden act of violence.

"YOU are a LIAR, my boy!" he screeched, leaping up from his seat, his teeth bared. "You do not know what you speak of! You heard me say that name in my sleep, didn't you? And now you hope to mock me in front of my queen!"

Æthelstan stood up, eager to defend his younger brother. Wulfhild stared down at her food, her eyes clenched shut, Edmund wondering if she'd ever been witness to this kind of behaviour before. Edmund didn't respond immediately, instead contemplating his father's visage, wondering what had turned him from the man he once knew to the bestial creature that now raged before him.

"I have heard nothing said as to your sleep, father," replied Edmund shakily, "and I do not understand why you would try to harm me so. I tell you nothing but the truth. The man claimed to be called Alaric, he was a son of Ælfric, and he was on his way to Ulfcytel."

"What did this man look like?" his father demanded. Edmund described him as he remembered. His recollection clearly wasn't what the king wanted to hear.

"What exactly is the matter?" asked Æthelstan forcefully, his voice slurring slightly under the influence of all the mead he'd been putting away. "You attack my brother, your son, for the crime of bringing you news? I will not stand for this, father!"

"He said Alaric was dead," Æthelred blurted at nobody in particular. "He said it was done...Ulfcytel..."

Emma was on her feet and beside the king, whispering what sounded like soothing words into his ear. He seemed to relent at her touch, his eyes closing and his hands moving to rest tenderly on her hips. Edmund appreciated what Emma could do for his father, and it was obvious she had an influence over him that was as unique as it was powerful. He just didn't trust her to always use it for good.

It didn't seem to last long, either. Æthelred suddenly snapped his eyes open, snarling a single word before turning and storming towards the exit.

"Eadric."

His guards followed him, all three of them vanishing from view, the doors opening and then closing with their usual echoing boom. Emma gathered her children up to follow, gifting both Edmund and Æthelstan with a hateful scowl. The brothers glared back at her, unyielding, Eadwig and Wulfhild staring ahead in stunned silence. Edmund watched Emma saunter away, observing how she had to knock on the doors and get the guards beyond to assist her with their weight. She soon disappeared, no doubt chasing after his irate father. He felt his older brother's reassuring grip on his shoulder, his breath sweet with the stench of mead as he leaned in to speak.

"I can't say what any of that was about, but I think we'd better find out who this Alaric fellow is. Deservedly or not, our father clearly thinks he should not be among the living."

Edmund nodded and took another swig of ale. Æthelstan was right. He often was. They had best find out what Alaric was really about. And who better to ask than his father, the Ealdorman Ælfric? Edmund had a feeling a great deal now depended on it.

XII

He had nowhere to go. He'd failed on all counts, losing his home and falling short in the duties assigned to him. Perhaps this was a punishment well-deserved, his own sins and those of all England warranting such hardships. He didn't know the truth of it. The horrors they'd been subjected to couldn't have anything to do with the righteous and merciful God he prayed to. Yet there were plenty who might say otherwise, and in his darker, despairing moments, he was inclined to almost believe them.

He sat up, brushing off the thin woollen blanket that had lain across his chest. There was a moist chill in the air, the abandoned farmhouse somehow managing to feel colder inside than it was outside. He wondered who had lived here previously. This had been a home for someone once, as it was of a size to adequately house a young family with room to grow. The now empty, soot-covered hearth could have been a place for them to gather, the children huddling before the warm glow of the flames to hear their hard-working father regale them with tales from myth or Scripture. The now partially collapsed kitchen may have witnessed similarly wholesome scenes; a mother lovingly preparing food in expectation of her husband's return, the children pestering her as children do for yet another taste and then another after that.

Whoever they were, they'd never come back, or if they had they'd decided to move on to better prospects elsewhere. He wasn't sure where that might be. Chances were, whoever lived here was simply dead, their corpses mouldering in a field somewhere, forgotten and passed off as just yet more victims of England's unceasing scouring. Most of southern and now eastern England had felt Thorkell's gentle touch, making sorrowful scenes such as this one commonplace for anyone still around to look. Nobody seemed to have much hope of things getting better, and confidence in the king's ability to protect them had sunk to yet another low after news of the defeat at Hringmere. These were times to endure, even if the burden seemed impossible to bear any longer.

These were grim thoughts, so he shook himself free of them, trying to focus on his predicament in the here and now. He didn't want to think about the family that may once have lived here, knowing that to dwell on such things would only bring painful memories bubbling to the surface. He had to head further north. His charges had been taken either to Mierċe or Lundenburg; the capital by far the more likely destination. If they were still alive, there would be interrogations and accusations of all kinds of nonsense before being thrown in a cell. That was the more optimistic scenario. They could just end up being executed. He had to hurry.

He'd slept in his armour again, largely from not feeling secure enough to disrobe before sleep. His pursuers had not let up, the hunt continuing for hours and hours. He'd lost precious time evading them, spending several days hiding out in ruined buildings like this one. He did his best work at night, making good progress across the countryside, the darkness a valued ally in his efforts to avoid detection. He'd eventually come to this abandoned cottage, peering inside cautiously so as to not startle any potential inhabitants.

Seeing it was empty, he'd taken the opportunity for what it was, snatching a few hours of sleep upon the hard ground.

It was still cold, so he pulled his cloak about himself and raised the hood past his ears before venturing outside. Dawn had arrived, the sun's first few rays lighting up the eastern horizon in an eruption of glowing, bronzed clouds. He set off along the road, his journey ever northward, his empty stomach no deterrent when it came to fulfilling his duty. He would save his lord or die in the attempt.

He moved swiftly, and within a matter of hours he'd drawn close to the village of Aultone, or so it seemed if his memory still served. His stomach wound was healing nicely, his initial fear that it was deeper than it looked easing with time. He'd taken no chances, all the same, making sure to clean it thoroughly in a stream he'd stumbled across two nights back, his efforts aided in no small part by the clear moonlight cascading from the cloudless sky.

The abandoned cottage had also contained an assortment of linen sheets stashed in a cupboard across from the kitchen. He'd torn several of them into strips and tied them around his midriff to serve as bandages. From what he could tell, he'd almost stopped bleeding, the sharp, pincer-like pain of his wound having faded to a dull ache. He'd remained clear-headed, too, and focused on the task at hand; itself a good indication he was not about to succumb to either blood loss or infection. If he could just find something to eat, he'd be almost content.

Aultone didn't look particularly impressive when he came upon its outskirts. It was a small place, not more than a dozen households, some of them partially scorched black and undergoing repair after Thorkell's army had swept through here last year on their way to threaten Wincestre. Thankfully, an inn was still operational just off from the village green, the generously-sized wattle and daub structure proving a welcome sight to one so fatigued and famished.

He entered through a pair of open doors, the dimly lit interior hosting several tables already occupied by a group of farmhands who'd snuck off early for lunch. They looked up briefly as he approached the bar, perhaps curious about who this hooded stranger was and where he'd come from. They'd have to keep on wondering. There was no chance of him removing his cloak. A fully armed and armoured man would draw unwanted scrutiny.

The innkeeper didn't seem to much care who he was, instead appearing reasonably pleased to see another customer on what was undeniably a fine morning. He purchased what he could with the few coins he had left, settling for a large bowl of porridge, several thick slices of bread, and a hunk of cheese. Ale, whilst normally obligatory, was in this instance replaced with a cup of water. The last thing he needed was a fuzzy head.

He deposited himself on a stool at the bar, breaking off pieces of crumbling cheese to flavour his otherwise unadorned bread. He tried to eat with temperance, thinking his instinct to wolf down everything before him would only attract attention. He polished off his porridge in short order, dabbing at his mouth and beard with his sole remaining slice of bread. It was then he heard footsteps behind him. Heavy footsteps. Men in armour.

A glance over his shoulder revealed the situation. Three men in ring mail, rounded linden shields, and open-faced iron helmets, each also with a hand axe tucked at the waist. They'd entered the way he'd come. He'd been foolish to eat with his back to the door like that. Had they actually been looking for him, he'd have been in trouble.

Instead, they were intent on questioning the other guests, asking them… no…they WERE looking for him, inquiring if anyone had seen a man with his look and his name. It was time to leave.

He stood up and made a casual move for the doors, patting at his belly like he were just another farmer satisfied after a good feed. He'd almost made it when a gauntleted hand gripped him by the right shoulder. He paused, fighting hard against every instinct screaming for him to spin around and launch the man into the nearest table. He heard a voice now, demanding, inquiring, tired from the road.

"Not so fast there. We have some questions for you before you get back to work."

He didn't reply, instead turning around to get the measure of whoever had addressed him. He was young, this one. Too young to die. If he could talk his way free, it wouldn't turn to bloodshed. He wouldn't have the life of a young Englishman on his conscience.

"We're looking for a man about your size, answering to the name of Cenric. He attacked our Lord Eadwu…"

He saw where this was going, and he could tell by the way the young man was peering at him that it was only a matter of time before he'd demand he remove his hood so they could get a look at his face. Then the charade would be over. He'd have to fight his way out of here. He decided to act first.

Cenric slammed his fist into his stomach, the poor lad's breath leaving him in a strangled gasp. He saw an opportunity, reaching out to tear the helm from the youth's head and bring it down with some force upon his now exposed crown. He dropped like a rock in water, collapsing to the mud and straw floor of the inn in an untidy tangle.

His two companions reacted swiftly, drawing their axes and roaring at him to give himself up. Cenric pulled his hood back and opened his cloak, exposing his burnished mail shirt as he drew his sword and readied himself for the contest. This would hopefully be over quickly.

The first man flew at him, his axe sweeping in towards Cenric's unprotected head. He dodged it easily, stepping to his right and allowing his attacker to be carried forward by his own momentum. Cenric bashed him around the head with the flat of his sword when he passed, the sound of metal on metal reverberating around the room like a church bell. His opponent grunted in discomfort, dazed and yet still on his feet. That would soon change.

Cenric stepped in from the side and slammed his boot into his knee. He buckled, unbalanced and in pain, allowing Cenric to grab him by the front and hurl him backwards into a nearby table. It collapsed under his weight, the patrons sitting there joining the other locals in fleeing the inn, their voices raised in alarm. He decided to worry about them later, for the last warrior was still standing and demanding his attention. This chap was brave, letting loose a roar and charging towards him, axe in hand. He had courage, but he was clumsy, and Cenric only had to kick a nearby stool into his path to knock him off balance.

He was on him a second later, his left hand grabbing his wrist and twisting it with a vice-like grip. He tried to resist, but he was no match for Cenric when it came to the grapple, and he soon released his weapon, an agonised squeal escaping his lips. Cenric then slammed his knee upwards into his groin and butted him in the face with his forehead, the open nature of his helm doing little to soften the impact. The man went limp. Cenric let him drop to the ground, his mouth split and bleeding. He'd have a lot of trouble walking for the next few days, but at least he was alive.

The warrior he'd knocked into the table was getting up, murder still very much on his mind. Cenric pointed his sword towards him and made a gesture with his left arm at the two men now lying haphazardly around them. He hoped he'd see he was outmatched. He bellowed for him to give up and leave just to make sure. It seemed to work, the man finally deciding discretion and flight were better options as he bolted for the door.

"I am indeed the one you seek," Cenric said, unsure if the two battered men at his feet could hear or even cared anymore. "But I did not attack your Lord Eadwulf until he drew a weapon on the Ealdorman Ælfric, who, if you recall, is owed your allegiance."

Neither replied, although the young chap he'd knocked out with his own helmet let out a low moan. "Sorry about that, youngster," Cenric said gently, tapping at his side with his boot. "I didn't have much of a choice there. You'll be fine, you and your friend here."

Cenric turned to apologise to the innkeeper only to see that he'd already fled. There was nothing else for him to do here. He stepped outside into the open air, half-expecting to be met with more foes intent on bloodshed. Nobody was about, but he could hear some shouts of alarm receding into the distance. He'd outstayed his welcome.

He headed north, running for what seemed like miles, his stomach aching in protest at such exertions so soon after eating. Nobody seemed to be following him, and the only sounds he could presently hear were the wind in the trees and the singing of birds. He'd run into some thick woodland, thinking it would mask his movements in his bid to avoid the main roads from Wincestre. From his perspective, that had been a wise choice, since word would certainly be spreading of his actions back at the inn. If only he hadn't stopped to eat. All that fuss and bother could have been avoided.

A sudden cramping of the stomach nearly caused him to fall. He stumbled and reached out, arresting his descent by grabbing hold of a nearby tree. His fingers dug into the bark, and for a moment he thought he might fall anyway, so lightheaded had he become. His guts were protesting without pause, forcing him to mobilise all of his iron will so as to not vomit. He lay down on the bracken floor, flat on his back, holding his belly, trying to slow down his breathing. It eventually seemed to work, the pain subsiding and his breath becoming easier, his lunch still safe within the confines of his stomach. He needed to keep it. He'd need the nourishment, and wandering back to Wincestre for some fine dining wasn't the best idea. He couldn't afford it anyway.

He instead headed north west, traversing the woodlands as best he could and creeping ever closer to the capital. If there was one blessing to be thankful for, it was the weather. It was quite glorious, the sunlight playing off the leaves and greenery around him, the almost uninterrupted blue of the sky peeking in from above the treetops. It would have truly been a miserable task to attempt this journey in winter. Spring and summer were always best for going on the run, he decided.

He got to thinking on how he'd come to be in this predicament. When Eadric had appeared with his army before their walls at Porteceaster, he'd been at first confused, wondering why he'd decided to come with such force and spout such outlandish claims. When the bastard had actually started killing people, he'd been up for the fight, hoping Eadric would be foolish enough to attack the fortress directly so he could hack his bastard arms off before hurling him from the battlements.

Eadric had proven himself far from foolish. He'd prepared well, presumably buying off the local thegns so Ælfric would have nowhere to go if he abandoned his stronghold. Lamentably, Ælfric had gone ahead and done just that, and Cenric had agreed to it, much to his regret now. He should have thought longer and harder on what to do. Instead, they'd been outwitted to the point Eadric had achieved his mission without even having to get his hands dirty, aside from all the innocent throats he'd cut. Cenric would make him pay for that.

Yet it was Eadwulf's betrayal that had come as the real shock. Something had felt wrong when they'd arrived in Suthhamtunam. Cenric had a sense for these things, but he'd foolishly said nothing at the time, although he'd noticed the lady Æva seemed to have felt it too. Ælfric, however, had just stridden onward, confident that Suthhamtunam was safe and loyal until Eadwulf had pulled an axe on him. He wasn't to know, of course. Nobody could have known just how far the treachery went.

All had descended into chaos as soon as Eadwulf and his men had drawn weapons. Cenric had floored the first man who'd tried to lay hands on him, turning then to see Ælfric exchanging blows with Eadwulf. The ealdorman looked like he had the better of him until he was grabbed from behind by one of the attacking guards. Cenric had killed them, but Eadwulf had taken advantage of the distraction, using the opportunity to smash the haft of his axe into Ælfric's head. The old man had gone down without a whimper, and Cenric, enraged, had responded by attempting to ram his spear through Eadwulf's chest.

He couldn't exactly recall what had happened next, but he remembered being tackled from the side before he could draw blood. He'd managed to fling them into Eadwulf's own table, but then another had made a grab for the lady Æva. He'd decided to forget Eadwulf for the moment, instead dropping his spear and drawing his sword to fight better at close quarters. He'd severed the hand that had been placed upon Æva's shoulder, the warrior it belonged to falling back and away from her with a cry, his bloody stump a fountain of crimson.

Æva had remained remarkably in control even though she was drenched in blood, and she was quite cooperative when Cenric had begun to back her away towards the door, the plan being that he'd shield their retreat whilst fighting off any further assailants. She was still carrying the young Brandon, the boy mute and frozen with fear. Cenric's heart ached for him. Eadwulf would pay dearly for all this.

Poor blind Ælfgar had been surrounded, his bodyguard crumpled at his feet after taking a spear through the guts. He'd done well, killing one of Eadwulf's men and cutting up another, but they were massively outnumbered, and there were still perhaps a dozen hostile warriors, not to mention Eadwulf himself, intent on apprehending them. Æva had cried out when two men grabbed at her, the pair of guards from outside now bursting in to join the fray. Cenric had turned to deal with them only to take a wound himself, the spear thrust from the flank splitting open his mail and slicing a bloody gorge across his stomach.

He'd lashed out furiously, finding his aggression rewarded with a shout of pain as the man who'd struck him fell back, his hands clutching at his now bloodied face. Cenric had then gone into a frenzy, believing his situation impossible and death to be imminent. In his desperate rage, he'd somehow managed to fight his way back outside, his chest, hands, and stomach wet with gore, the vast majority of it not his own. He could taste blood, again not of his own body, making him think he'd bitten somebody in his fury and blanked it out. He couldn't see Æva, but there were men pouring from the hall entrance, their hard eyes a clear indication of their intent. Cenric had done the only thing he could. He ran.

It wasn't his proudest moment, by far. In battle, he'd prefer to die with his lord, and his actions in the recent past proved this. All had seen how the Ealdorman Ælfric had been knocked from his horse in Eastengle when Thorkell's army had attacked them, just as they'd seen how Cenric had led the hearthweru in his defence, smashing the enemy vanguard apart in a fighting wedge of muscle and iron that had ultimately retrieved the wounded Ælfric and dragged him from harm's way. No man that day could have called him a coward. But this situation was different. Eadwulf clearly wanted Ælfric and his family alive to deliver them to Eadric. Cenric was expendable. He could die here for no real purpose or escape to effect the rescue of his lord and punish the guilty for their treachery. He'd chosen the latter.

It had not been easy. He was a large man as it was and not given to running at speed. His wound also slowed him down, his pursuers always seeming to be just a few paces behind him. No matter what he did, he couldn't lose them, and he didn't dare attempt to escape down any winding alleys, thinking it common sense to assume his enemies knew the town far better than he did. He was running out of options. There must have been about eight men chasing him. Eight men against one wounded man, even one as capable as Cenric, were not good odds. He had to do something to improve them.

He turned a corner and raced on, the men continuing to chase after him with undiminished vigour. The street started to broaden and open up, the formerly dense, confining byways easing out onto the waterfront vista that was Suthhamtunam's docks. The weather had turned rougher, the spray of the sea hurling itself up and over the wooden wharves and smoothed stone of the harbour. Cenric fancied he had a chance at escape. The ship they'd used to travel from Porteceaster might still be here. His heart sank as he ran closer and saw it was not so. The vessel was nowhere in sight. His options had diminished yet further.

Cenric didn't slow, instead charging down the length of the jetty that had previously hosted his ship. He never stopped, leaping right off the end and into the heaving waters with a deafening splash. He let himself sink, eventually feeling solid sand beneath his feet, his descent marked by a chaotic mass of bubbles and a slight trail of red from his open wound.

He'd at first suspected he may have simply killed himself by drowning rather than fighting. He was heavy, and his lungs had already begun to twitch and ache in protest at his ongoing breath-hold. He swam backwards underneath the jetty he'd leapt off, its dark, fuzzy silhouette now directly above him. He couldn't risk making a break for the surface. His pursuers would still be up there and looking into the waters for signs of life. He instead swam forward to the next jetty on his left and the one after that, his lungs burning with outrage. He made an effort to head to the surface, noting with some dismay how hard it was, his armour and weapons weighing him down to the extent he again feared all was lost.

This wasn't how he'd ever thought he'd die, and so he clawed at one of the jetty's wooden support struts in desperation, eventually managing to heave himself up through the water. He surfaced, gasping in lungfuls of air, the waves lifting him up and down in rhythm. Nobody seemed to have spotted him, but he couldn't tell who was directly above him either, the stout wooden planks of the wharf's construction concealing them from view.

He stayed like this for about a minute more, hidden in shadow, his hands gripped around the sea-soaked timber that had saved him. No alarm had been raised, and nobody jumped into the water after him. For the time being, he appeared safe and relatively hidden. Yet he couldn't afford to be complacent. He was too heavy for a protracted stay in the water, and his armour and stomach wound would likely get him killed if he remained like this. He'd have to make some emergency changes to his attire.

The boots were the first to go. He kicked them off with some effort, then tore off his cloak, mail shirt, and leggings, relieved at how buoyant and at ease he now felt in the water. He then took another deep breath and again allowed himself to be pulled beneath the surface, moving as he descended to the next jetty and then the one next to that. He surfaced again to get his breath back and then repeated what he'd done, eventually finding himself directly underneath the very last jetty on the eastern side of the harbour.

Cenric had then simply waited until he was sure nobody was above him before swimming out and away from the town. When he was about twenty meters distant, he thought he heard somebody calling after him, the frequency and intensity of their cries seeming to grow when he failed to respond. He put all his strength into the swim, hoping to get some space between himself and whoever it was making all that noise. He kept on going, his limbs burning with effort, and yet before long he was again in trouble, the strength of the current pulling him out deeper into the grey waters.

He passed out, the taste and smell of salt and water thick in his mouth and nostrils. He wasn't sure what happened after that, and he considered it a minor miracle when he awoke, face down, upon a narrow beach, the crash of waves upon shingle filling his ears. Nobody was around, and the view back west was hidden by a jutting, jagged cliff face extending out into the surging waters. Cenric pushed himself up onto his feet and began to stagger inland, hoping to work some strength back into his legs. He'd done it. He'd escaped, although his wound was still bleeding, a faint red trail having followed him across the stones as he moved towards a copse of trees.

He'd rested there for perhaps ten minutes, rising to then follow what looked like a narrow, sandy path leading away from the beach and into a forested ravine. The cliff edges on either side looked climbable, but they were doing a wonderful job of masking his movements, their sheer sides wreathing his entire route in shadow.

All seemed peaceful. There were no shouts of alarm or stampeding search parties. He'd made it, or at least he'd escaped the immediate danger in Suthhamtunam, which was a good beginning in his book. Perhaps his lack of importance had worked in his favour, since it wasn't impossible that Eadwulf's men had assumed he'd drowned and wasn't worth bothering with any further. It wasn't an unreasonable conclusion to come to. He had nearly done just that.

He exited the ravine, his trail turning eastward through a widening thicket of swaying, golden-hued beech trees. If he could just get to Porteceaster, he'd be safe. Cuthbert and the garrison would have been able to hold the walls, and Cenric could get his wound treated before planning his next move. It was his only realistic option. He decided in its favour.

The journey back had been uncomfortable, albeit uneventful. It had been cold, and his first night in the wilds had involved a lot of shivering by a campfire he'd constructed for the sake of drying the few clothes he had left.

Sleep had also proven elusive, and Cenric was more than aware he was taking a risk lighting a fire when there was still a chance Eadwulf's people could be searching for him. The mud and bracken of the forest floor were also uncomfortable enough to ensure his rest was shallow and frequently interrupted, causing him to sit upright in alarm at every rustle from the undergrowth.

When morning had come, his clothes were found to be merely slightly damp rather than soaked. He'd dressed quickly, making sure to then cover the embers of his fire with earth before heading eastward. He felt better now he wasn't quite so uncomfortable, and the deep chill he'd picked up from his time in the water had eased off in the face of the summer air. His newfound optimism hadn't lasted long. By around midday, he could smell and see smoke on the wind, the bitter scent bringing a renewed sense of foreboding.

He soon saw why. He'd just emerged from another thicket when he laid eyes on Porteceaster itself. Somebody had set the town outside the walls on fire; its once solid stone and thatch buildings now blackened and collapsed in smouldering ignominy. A fair amount of smoke was still billowing up from somewhere, the wind carrying much of it westward back towards Suthhamtunam. The fortress looked otherwise unmolested, but something still felt off, there being a heaviness in the air that spoke of grim deeds undiscovered.

His instincts had been vindicated when he'd crept closer. On the road immediately outside the western gate were several dozen dead men, their lifeless forms hanging from a line of hastily constructed gibbets. Cenric recognised them. These were his soldiers. Cuthbert was among them, swaying in the breeze, his dead, glassy eyes gazing out across the fields. A red stain was visible on the left side of his stomach, several of the others also bearing similar injuries. They'd not gone without a fight. But something terrible had happened here.

A harsh voice had then shouted in alarm from the walls. Cenric hadn't stuck around to find out who it belonged to, since it was obvious he'd been spotted by someone with less than friendly intent. He made a dash for the town, several arrows slamming into the dry earth as he ran. Whoever was now on the walls wasn't inclined to let him escape, but he was thankful their accuracy left a lot to be desired, allowing him to make it out of bow shot in relative safety.

There wasn't a lot left. Porteceaster had been made up of three primary points of interest: the Roman fortress, the town itself, and the harbour and wharf they'd used just nights ago to get to Suthhamtunam. The settlement outside had never been properly rebuilt since Svienn Forkbeard and his Danes had burnt it down years ago. It was too dangerous, and so most of the original inhabitants had opted to move inside the fortress and join the population living within its confines. A few brave, or perhaps just stubborn, souls had remained, maintaining an inn, stables, and a small smithy. It was to the smithy that Cenric had headed.

It didn't look like much and never really had, but being set on fire hadn't done it any favours. Cenric hurried inside; if one could call it an "inside", given the thatched roof had collapsed and several of the walls had toppled inward. He couldn't as yet hear anyone approaching in pursuit, but he was of a mind to make himself ready for that eventuality and draw blood if he had to. Fortunately, some luck was still with him in the form of several racks of weapons and armour that had survived the fire relatively unscathed. He'd been hoping for something like this, but he'd not expected to be blessed with such abundance. God really was good.

He'd helped himself to a new shirt of ring mail, even finding some padded breecs, boots, and a cloak that had somehow withstood the heat. He felt better already, the added weight reassuringly heavy, although he noticed he made a lot more noise now when he moved, which was doubly unfortunate in his situation.

It was time to leave, regardless. He made another dash outside and entered what was left of the inn. Predictably, nobody was home, but the kitchen was almost entirely intact, the solid stones of its construction ensuring it had endured the flames much better than the rest of the structure.

Cenric drank and ate, the ale and bread he'd managed to find tasting heavenly to his deprived lips. His repast was interrupted by somebody making noises outside, the shuffling of boots and low, harsh grumbling now unmistakable. It was time to go. He slipped out by the kitchen entrance and continued east, scuttling across a stretch of dry grass that lay just ahead of yet more woodland.

He dared sneak a look behind him when he reached the tree line, thinking himself safe from view. There were men looking for him, attired as those who had come before with Eadric, demanding they surrender. They'd taken the fortress. Cenric had no idea how, and he wasn't inclined to stick around and ask. He'd return, though. They'd killed his men. That was something he couldn't ignore.

All that had been several nights ago. Cenric had headed north on the assumption Eadwulf would seek to hand over the captive Ealdorman Ælfric and his family to Eadric, who would then return to the king in Lundenburg. He'd made it past Wincestre the next day, but his pursuers never seemed far behind. It was a shame. He'd been pleased with how he'd escaped from Eadwulf, thinking his men had assumed him drowned. Perhaps whoever had shouted to him as he swam away had informed the authorities.

He'd been fortunate in that he'd not had to fight again until those three men had surprised him at the inn in Aultone. He was also lucky to have been able to subdue them as he had, since he'd not wanted to kill fellow Englishmen who were only attempting to do as they'd been ordered. Even so, they were bound to tell others about what had happened. Cenric would be lucky to make it to Lundenburg without further violence.

He continued north west through the woods around Aultone. Night soon crept up on him, but he decided to keep going, the moon's light proving strong and illuminating as he progressed through the forest clearings. All seemed peaceful, the almost total silence disturbed only by the crunching of twigs and the occasional hoot of an owl. Cenric knew how to navigate by the stars. Barring human intervention, he could keep going like this and be in Lundenburg in a matter of days.

The weather, unfortunately, had other ideas. A thick layer of cloud swept in some time past midnight, unleashing a thunderous downpour upon him and all the creatures of the forest. Cenric didn't like storms, finding the sound of thunder to be unsettling for reasons he wasn't entirely sure of, but he kept going, trying to brace himself against the deluge. Things got worse when what was left of the once abundant moonlight faded out to be replaced by an almost impenetrable blackness, reducing his world to a sightless hell of booming thunder and icy, pounding rain. Trees creaked and groaned around him, straining against the wind, prompting him to spend the rest of the night lurking within a sea of ferns, his cloak pulled up and tightly around his body to protect himself. Anxiety kept sleep at bay, and by the time the storm had begun to pass, the first rays of dawn were already filtering through the forest. That was all he needed. He got up and hurried on.

He'd cleared another few hundred yards when he came across a muddy, nettle-infested trail clumsily cut through the forest to the north east. He followed, intrigued by the sequence of tracks, thinking himself lucky he'd found such a thing in light of the recent weather. Storm or no, a number of men had passed this way very recently and been weighed down by armour and weapons if the depths of their bootprints were anything to go by. There'd been horses, too, and something else, some kind of heavy, wheeled construction, most likely a cart carrying cargo or something else.

Riders. Armoured men. A cart. All heading in the direction of Lundenburg. Cenric felt a surge of optimism. Eadric and his captives could have passed through here. Cenric may be on the right path. There was hope, after all. He hurried along with a spring in his step, his eyes and ears ever alert for further signs of his quarry.

By midday, the surrounding forest had started to give way to more open ground, a larger road to the west becoming visible through the diminishing thicket. There was some activity going on just beyond; a few cottages and the golden expanse of barley fields reminding him that not all parts of the country had been entirely devastated. This area had done a remarkable job of rebuilding, the whole region appearing as if Thorkell had never harmed a soul when he'd smashed through here last year on his way to Lundenburg. It was a testament to English fortitude that the people had returned so soon, eager to save what they could and recommence their lives.

Not all had come back with noble intentions. Three men, in particular, were now staring in Cenric's direction from just up ahead, their manner and dishevelled appearance suggesting they were outlaws. He continued walking towards them, hoping he was perhaps mistaken, unfortunately finding as he got closer that he was likely correct in his original assumptions. They were all armed and menacing with it, each bearing a light spear clutched in filthy, mud-caked hands. They grinned at him, their expressions of the predatory kind, like they thought they'd caught somebody in a trap and precious little could go wrong for them. He'd teach them otherwise if he had to.

The largest of the trio stepped out onto the trail to bar his path. He brought his spear up to point in his direction, the weapon looking like it had seen better days, what with all the chips and splinters running down its shaft. Cenric halted several paces from its reach, intending for the man to come to him if he fancied some bloody business. If he took him down, the others would turn tail and flee. He was the biggest, after all.

"That's far enough now," the man with the spear said, his voice thick and sickly, like he had too much phlegm in his throat. "We'll be taking whatever you've got on you and sending you on your way."

"Did you see anyone come by here recently?" Cenric asked, unwilling to take his threats seriously. "Men on horseback and such? Perhaps with some captives?"

The man looked back at his associates, each of them shaking their heads as they moved out to join him in confronting Cenric. They were all absurdly over-confident, and they'd made a serious error if they thought he was just a common traveller. This could be the end for them if they pushed it.

"We did, sir, we did," sneered the head brute. "It looked like too much for us humble folk to handle…looked like some fancy types falling afoul of other fancy types. Not our concern, 'specially with all those big blokes on horseback. You, on the other hand, look a lot more… manageable. You'll be giving us what coin you have on you now. You can then go on your way, no problems."

Cenric was at least grateful they'd all but confirmed the tracks he was following had indeed been left by Eadric and his escort. It was just a shame they'd chosen this course in life. In his experience, the path of a bandit rarely paid off, proving to be a short and troubled one for those desperate or foolish enough to take it. But Cenric could play along with them. He opened up his cloak, intentionally acting nervous like he was going to cooperate by reaching for his coin purse. He took some small satisfaction in seeing their eyes widen in alarm when he drew his sword instead.

"You have a choice now, friends," Cenric said, holding his blade up to the light. "You can let me pass in peace, albeit after handing over your weapons and stolen money, or we can escalate matters. Decide."

He could tell he'd caught them off guard. None of them would have expected to encounter a man with a sword wandering the woods on his own. Chances were they now thought he was some kind of thegn and, as such, a recipient of substantial training and experience in actual combat. He was just wondering if he should tell them who he really was when the larger one let out a ragged scream and thrust his spear towards his head. He'd found his courage. It would do him no good.

Cenric stepped aside, the incoming spear tip just slipping past his left ear. His attacker had seen he'd overreached, but it was too late. Cenric swung his sword across the shaft of his spear, splintering the sorry thing in half. He then swung again, slicing off the first few fingers of the man's hands whilst they gripped the now useless stick of a weapon. He shrieked and dropped what he'd been holding, his fellow bandits looking on in horror at the severed fingers lying in the mud.

One recovered from his shock, his dark, determined eyes locking with Cenric's. He saw the man had decided to kill before he'd even begun to thrust his spear, so Cenric acted on instinct, splitting open his throat with a savage forward thrust of his sword. He severed the hamstrings of the now fingerless bandit as an afterthought, ensuring he wouldn't be getting any notions about suddenly attempting to grapple him from the side. Only one bandit remained standing, his knees trembling in the face of the bloody work that had been wrought in the space of mere seconds. Cenric grinned at him.

"Give it up, there's no need for you to die here. Just leave your weapon, leave whatever coin you have…and find yourself another profession."

He didn't need to be told twice. The would-be-robber dropped his spear, his shaking hands then tossing a small purse in Cenric's direction before he dashed off into the woods. Cenric picked up the purse and added its contents to his own, doing likewise with the man he'd killed. The larger bandit was still alive, but he was having trouble standing up with the choice wound Cenric had given him, instead flopping around in the mud as he tried and repeatedly failed to get to his feet. Cenric informed him he was losing blood and that continued physical exertions would be unwise. The man responded by saying something uncharitable about his mother. Cenric's boot caught him in the lower jaw. He lay still.

Things proceeded well from that point on. He camped out in the woods again that night, making a small fire to keep himself company. The forest was unusually dark, the trees doing their best to ensure little to no moonlight ever got through their rustling canopy of leaves. He'd already counted out the money he'd acquired from the thieves he'd defeated, noting he had more than enough to get himself a good breakfast if he could find an inn along the road.

It then occurred to him that the money he'd obtained had likely been taken from others. The bandits had probably plagued this area for a while, making life a misery for less fortunate souls guilty of nothing but attempting to survive in these troubled times. He felt a twinge of guilt until he rationalised that his cause was a noble one, and the money he'd acquired would be put to far better use in pursuit of his goals than if it had remained with the bandits. He held on to that thought until it occurred to him there were probably more of them in this wood than the few men he'd encountered earlier. He got up and kicked some earth and leaves over his fire, allowing the pitch darkness to close in around him. He had permitted one of them to flee, after all, and he didn't fancy being murdered in his sleep. Better safe than sorry.

He was up and moving before dawn fully arrived. The clouds had begun to part a little before he'd awoken, and so by the time he was back on the trail, the sky was clear enough to allow some starlight to become visible from the forest floor. This eased his passage considerably, and by mid-morning, Cenric felt like he was enjoying an almost leisurely summer stroll, the path he was on soon emerging out of the woods to pass through several sun-drenched fields as it snaked its way towards Reddinges. He could see the town up ahead on the horizon, apparently undisturbed by Thorkell's previous marauding and remaining very much a bustling gateway to the final approach to Lundenburg.

He decided to risk heading into town in pursuit of something to eat. He'd approached the outskirts around midday, wandering through the western gate of its solid wooden palisade without incident. The people he passed on the way in had a certain air to them, possessing a quiet, hopeful determination as they tended the fields, their beasts of burden applying themselves to their tasks without complaint or trepidation. The men guarding the gates had a similar demeanour, the townsfolk within appearing almost optimistic whilst they went about their business. Cenric felt a burden lift from his shoulders as he proceeded eastward through the bright, bustling streets, the stress and tension from his troubled journey easing from his body. Whatever shadow he'd been in since he'd fled Suthhamtunam had now vanished.

Despite his lifting mood, he still had a duty to perform. There was no way to tell if Eadric and his escort had passed through here. He'd lost their tracks a while back, all traces vanishing within the avalanche of foot and hoof prints that marked the main approach to the town. He needed more information, so Cenric decided to try his luck in picking up the local gossip by heading for the inn just off the main road from the gate. It couldn't hurt to listen to the locals and ask a few questions of his own. An armed convoy with captives would certainly have gotten some attention.

It was a decent establishment, appropriately named "The Jug of Ale". Inside, it was all solid timber and high rafters, the many patrons looking amiable enough whilst they sat enjoying their lunch and ale. It was well furnished, and decked out with an assortment of rugs, tables, chairs, and a stone hearth that gave it a homely yet august feel, as if one had walked into the hall of a local thegn. A wide wooden staircase lay towards the rear of the building, presumably allowing guests to retire to the upper levels for the night, should they wish. Cenric tried to imagine the luxury of sleeping in a proper bed. He pushed the thought aside. He couldn't stay long.

He approached the fellow he assumed to be the owner. He was a particularly stocky-looking man who was remarkably pleased to see another paying guest, although his enthusiasm seemed genuine rather than a product of simple greed. Cenric ordered some lunch, and he was glad to find a seat watching the entrance and yet close enough to a window to allow the warmth of the noon sun to cascade over him whilst he ate.

The owner was pleasantly talkative, responding well to Cenric's casual "anything unusual happen here lately?" by effectively confirming Eadric and company had indeed passed through Reddinges about a day ago. He wasn't able to put a name to him, but the description was close enough. His recollection of seeing a "bound woman with red hair and an angry look" was also useful. There was only one person that could be, and it pleased Cenric to know Æva remained defiant. It was turning out to be a productive day.

He paid up and left, relieved that he'd successfully resisted the temptation to rent a room so he might get some quality rest. He continued east through the town, the sun still very much on full display, its reassuring warmth perhaps one of the main reasons why everyone seemed so free of worries, at least on the surface. There was nothing quite like an English summer, Cenric thought, but then again, he'd never actually been anywhere else, so perhaps he couldn't say. In any case, he eventually left Reddinges behind him, thinking his visit a pleasant one as he made his way towards Lundenburg.

He camped out again that night, holing up in some undergrowth off the beaten path. He felt a little exposed here, for much of the forest had been cut back for the sake of farmland. Thankfully the night passed without incident, and Cenric rose again just before dawn to continue on. He kept up a rapid pace despite his lack of breakfast, and by early afternoon he found himself gazing upon his final destination. It never failed to impress. He paused, taking in the high stone walls, the broad, winding river the only obstacle between him and their wide, imposing gates. He'd made it. Lundenburg awaited him.

The capital looked more or less as it had the last time he'd been here. It was huge, spreading out across the northern banks of the mighty Temes, its indomitable fortifications enclosing it on all sides. A sequence of docks and jetties erupted along its southern facade, extending into the water to accommodate river-borne traffic and the trade that made England rich.

In better times, the population had naturally grown, the city's importance making it a destination for travellers and traders near and far alike. That had come to an end with Svienn Forkbeard's first invasion, and his armies had ravaged the buildings outside of the walls to the point the vast majority of the population had given up attempting to construct anything new. Despite such trials, it remained an impressive city and the greatest in England, providing a home to thousands in what was still the economic and military centrepiece for the entire country.

Cenric wasn't the only one to slow and consider the city arrayed before them. The number of travellers on the roads had started to increase after he'd passed through Reddinges, and the main route towards the Temes was full of people, some accompanied by horses and donkeys laden with goods and belongings. Cenric made sure he blended in, glad of the crowd's anonymity as he plodded towards one of the river crossings and the ferry boats that lay moored there. Most others were heading east along the road, eager to make the bridge some distance away, but Cenric didn't want to waste any more time slogging on foot, preferring to avoid the bridge and the prying eyes that might come with it.

He thus joined a half dozen others in boarding a reasonably small vessel, noting as they got underway how the waters looked oddly empty, the ships heading in towards the city seeming to be fewer in number than was usual. War was bad for business, no doubt, and despite Lundenburg remaining secure, the devastation wrought elsewhere would only deter foreign visitors and the commerce they brought with them.

Cenric had time to think on this whilst his vessel ploughed its way through the waters, the waves slapping against the narrow hull in time to the splash of oars. Lundenburg was prosperous precisely because it had become a hub for trade. If that dried up, where would that leave the city? Surely the king could see the reduction in shipping from his own window? Did he have a plan to set things right? Or did he care more about settling old scores with his subjects? Cenric thought the latter was more likely.

The ferry captain proved successful in guiding his ship to the opposite bank, the oarsmen slackening their efforts as the current dragged them in. They berthed at a solitary jetty extending out past the muddied shallows, and Cenric disembarked with the others after paying what turned out to be a pleasantly modest fare. He made his way from the bank and onto firmer ground, eventually rejoining the ambling crowds along the well-trod road approaching one of the western gates.

The city walls were even more impressive when viewed from up close. They were vast, almost unlike anything he'd seen before, their huge shadows swallowing him and his fellow travellers up. The Romans had built them to withstand just about anything, and the English had done their best to maintain them ever since. Many an invader had learned the hard way that Lundenburg could not be taken by brute force, and Thorkell and his mob were merely the latest to receive such a deserved lesson. If only he'd try again now. Cenric liked the thought of battling him here, facing off against his horde whilst they hurled themselves against the walls. It was a foolish fantasy. Thorkell wouldn't fall for it, not again, and Cenric had others to lock swords with.

The crowds ahead were now passing through a wide stone and timber gate, the warriors on duty appearing fortuitously disinterested when inspecting new arrivals. In all fairness to them, searching absolutely everyone passing through would have been time-consuming and largely unnecessary, since the vast majority of those moving up to the gates looked to be commoners, merchants, and those returning home from errands and labours elsewhere. Cenric was relieved nobody bothered him, and his sword remained safely unseen in its scabbard beneath his cloak. He didn't want to have to answer questions about his right to have such a fine weapon in his possession.

He was soon struck by how congested the city had become. Since King Svienn and now Thorkell had made it dangerous to live beyond the walls, the city had effectively run out of room to grow. This part of town, Westceape, he'd heard it called, was just downright depressing, the noisy, crowded streets feeling more than a little claustrophobic with their packed, dilapidated buildings and the vast stone edifices of the walls behind them. The smell also was at times overpowering, the byways and alleys hosting mounds of refuse that only a few hardy souls had been tasked with removing. Cenric didn't envy them or anyone else unlucky enough to live here. Yet squalor or no, it was preferable to being dead, and in that sense, the advantages of living within the walls were undeniable.

The air cleared a little when he made it into what he assumed to be the city centre, his path taking him across a narrow bridge close to an impressive stone church before continuing east and then north. The crowds were unceasing, hemming him in and slowing him down to a frustrated crawl he yearned to break from. He'd lived in Hamptonscir most of his life, enjoying its verdant forests and scattered villages, all of which seemed like a world apart from the bustling hive he now occupied.

The narrow streets began to widen a little as he wandered into what he suspected was the main approach to King Æthelred's hall. He could see it now, the place looking even more imposing than he recalled, the "hall" as such actually being an entire sequence of buildings, towers, and an encircling stone wall. If Ælfric, Æva, and Ælfgar had been taken anywhere, it would be here.

This part of the city looked as crowded as the rest, although the buildings appeared better maintained, likely due to the greater wealth the local denizens undoubtedly possessed. Cenric made a brief circuit of the walls surrounding the king's royal halls, unfortunately remaining at a loss about how he might gain entry. Every entrance was gated and guarded, the walls themselves without blemish or handhold that might otherwise facilitate attempts at climbing. As it stood, the place looked impregnable. Æthelred certainly valued his security.

The afternoon was swiftly turning to evening, the shadows cast by the surrounding buildings growing longer and darker with the sun's descent. Cenric noticed his stomach grumbling, remembering he'd again not had anything to eat all day. He'd never be able to figure out a way to rescue his lord if he were befuddled from malnourishment. He found another inn ideally situated across from the eastern gateway to the king's apparently unbreachable residence. He'd eat, rest in a proper bed and then think on what to do.

He managed to get the first two done easily. The inn was well-built and well-kept, but the outside sign was a little unnerving, depicting a human figure suspended on a gallows alongside the text "The Hanged Man", which presumably served as a name for the establishment. Inside, it was pleasantly spacious after the prolonged claustrophobia of the city streets, but some of the patrons appeared a little eccentric, having somehow devised a way to race cockroaches across a long table. They were quite pleased with their efforts, some even placing wagers on which cockroach would come out ahead of the others. Cenric didn't partake. He wouldn't lower himself to gambling, even if he had the cash to spare. He didn't like cockroaches either.

But he'd become distracted, which was enough to make him trip slightly on his way past, ensuring he bashed his head against the surface of the bar, quite forcefully. Everyone turned to look, Cenric rubbing at his forehead and flushing with embarrassment. The owner appeared from out back, asking if he was all right. Cenric nodded, still a little flustered, and took him in, thinking him an unusual fellow to look upon.

The man was even taller than Cenric, and the years had not been easy on him, his face so weather-beaten it was as though he'd been employed as a scarecrow for the past several decades. Haggard or not, he was a friendly sort, and Cenric enjoyed speaking with him whilst he dined on an evening repast of roasted beef and boiled vegetables. Sadly, he knew nothing of any unusual goings on or visitors to the king's halls. It was the same for the patrons, and as expected, most of them were more concerned with gossip about Thorkell's movements to the north. He couldn't blame them. He left them to their ale and ventured upstairs to the room he'd rented. Solitude might be helpful for clearing his head.

His room was absolutely splendid for one who'd just spent days sleeping rough. It was small but snug and cosy with it, the window and shutters overlooking the street beyond ensuring he got a steady supply of fresh air. He could also see over the walls of the king's compound from here, and whilst it was interesting to watch the comings and goings of his underlings, he still couldn't see any way to get inside. He sat down on his bed and took off his boots, the straw mattress and fresh woollen blankets providing a level of comfort he'd almost forgotten existed. He removed the rest of his clothes and armour and got under the covers, resolving to never take the sensation of having a pillow beneath his head for granted ever again. He slipped into a deep, dreamless slumber within seconds.

Morning came too soon, the light from the shutters and the singing of birds stirring him from rest. He got dressed and headed downstairs, the alarmingly tall owner greeting him with a broad smile. Cenric took the trouble to ask him his name as he demolished a breakfast of boiled eggs and toasted bread. Godwin, he was called, and apparently the inn had been owned by his family since its construction back when Lundenburg was a part of the old Kingdom of Mierce. He was proud to have it, and he hoped his family would keep it as such for years after he was gone. Cenric envied him. He had little real knowledge of his ancestors. He'd been raised alone by his father after the sudden death of his mother when he was merely a babe in arms. It was a short and sad story, but it was the only one he had.

The morning dragged on, the daylight failing to provide Cenric with any fresh answers on what he should do. He'd taken to patrolling the area outside, fancying if he looked hard enough, he might just discover some hidden portal through the walls that would allow him to sneak in and scout the place for traces of his lord. There was no such thing, of course, and he didn't want to be seen taking too much of an interest lest the guards attempt to apprehend him. There was no point in having come all this way and survived so much just to end up a prisoner himself.

The day soon turned to night, the streets emptying themselves of people. Cenric headed back to the "Hanged Man", informing Godwin he'd need his room for an additional night. Godwin agreed, sounding pleased at the prospect of having him around for longer. Cenric was grateful for the hospitality, and he dined that evening upon a truly huge bowl of vegetable stew. He even allowed himself to partake in a cup of mead before retiring upstairs, and he again slept well, despite the revelry of several drunken rascals below. At least somebody in the kingdom wasn't beset by worries.

The next day brought nothing but frustration. There was no way into the king's halls, and if he were honest with himself, Cenric didn't know for sure if Ælfric was even in there. Æthelred might have executed him or sent him into exile, or at the very least stripped him of his title and thrown him into prison elsewhere. Nobody at the inn had anything to say on anyone unusual passing through, let alone a column of armed riders with captives in tow. It seemed he'd reached a dead end.

He took to wandering by the river, putting himself to use earning a few coins loading bales of wool onto several vessels bound for Normandy. It was honest work, and Cenric had little else to do, and he soon developed a rapport with his fellow labourers. They were good men, if a little rough, yet they too had not heard anything of interest outside of the usual talk about their Scandinavian visitors. One man he befriended held a particularly glum outlook on the situation, joking that the day would come soon when the king himself would be boarding one of these ships to go into exile with his "Norman queen". He laughed when Cenric suggested the king might die in battle instead, saying that would require Æthelred to actually lead an army. He had a point. Æthelred was not a warrior king like his forebears. If he were, things might be different.

Night once again crept up on them, the stars emerging stark and resplendent across the heavens. He was returning to his lodgings when a sharp, refreshing wind started to roll in from the sea, but it did little to lift his mood. He was trying to stay hopeful, yet he couldn't deny he was starting to feel a tad useless. He'd been filled with optimism after passing through Reddinges, believing himself to be close behind Eadric and perhaps able to enact some kind of dashing rescue. It hadn't occurred to him that his journey might end with high walls, guarded gates, and no idea what to do next.

He'd been attempting to relax and enjoy a supper of mutton stew when several newcomers had entered the inn. They looked like sailors, having certainly come from what could be any number of ships currently moored along the river, and were predictably interested in the local ale. What piqued Cenric's curiosity was their claim they'd come from further north, saying something about undertaking a dangerous cargo run from Scotland. That meant they would have sailed past the coast of Eastengle on the way here. Cenric had to ask what they'd seen. They knew more than he'd expected.

They claimed Ulfcytel was alive. Not only that, but they'd seen him in the flesh, saying the lunatic had carried out some kind of surprise attack on the Danes up in Gipeswic. Cenric's eyes widened as they told him more, the men insisting Ulfcytel had somehow stolen several of Thorkell's own ships and was using them to reach Canterburie with what was left of his army. They didn't know why he wanted to get there, but they did tell him he'd been wounded in the recent fighting and ended up pulling his vessel alongside theirs to purchase medicinal herbs. What they said next thrilled Cenric's heart. Alaric was with him.

They hadn't been able to recall his name precisely. What they did say is that Ulfcytel had been accompanied by a man claiming to be a "son of the Ealdorman Ælfric" and that he was "broad and dark-haired", albeit with a bandage covering his left eye. Cenric assumed he must have been injured at some point, as the rest of the description fitted him perfectly.

What was also interesting was how the sailors were under the impression he was Ulfcytel's right-hand man. Cenric wasn't sure how that could have happened. Ulfcytel was an ealdorman and would have captains and thegns of his own...unless most of those had already fallen in battle. If that were the case, and it seemed very possible, then Ulfcytel would have had to make do with entrusting authority to those few capable men he had left. Could Alaric be one of them? If so, it was a wise decision. The lad was a formidable fighter and knew how to inspire others. It was good he was making himself useful.

Cenric was elated, thanking the sailors for their time and buying them a round of drinks. He didn't join them, instead returning to his seat to ponder what he'd learned. He still remembered how he'd pledged to the lady Æva to bring Alaric home to her. He'd meant those words, although, in all honesty, he'd thought at the time Alaric was most likely dead. Now he'd been told he was alive and in the company of the legendary

Ulfcytel. If he could reach Canterburie, he could find them both and tell them what had happened at Porteceaster. Ulfcytel remained a man of repute as well as an ealdorman. If he now held Alaric in high esteem, then it stood to reason it might be possible to get him to assist his imprisoned family.

Cenric finished off his stew and wandered over to Godwin, thanking him for his hospitality and informing him he would be leaving in the morning. The man seemed sorry to see him go, taking his hand in his and stressing he would be welcome back if he ever chose to return. Cenric thanked him again, inquiring about whether he could purchase some bread and water for a journey of some distance. Godwin proved to be very accommodating, providing him with what he'd asked for and even throwing in a small travelling satchel free of charge.

All seemed prepared. Cenric retired to his room again, sleeping as well as could be expected given those below insisted on drinking themselves into a furore. When he rose the next morning, he dined on a more than adequate breakfast of eggs and yet more eggs, making sure to shake Godwin's hand one final time before heading for the door. He stepped out onto the road beyond, the air still crisp from the night's chill, and headed for the north eastern gates of the city. If Alaric and Ulfcytel were in Canterburie, his place was at their side. With any luck, he'd be returning with them soon to reunite Æva with her husband whilst freeing her and her family from a most unjust imprisonment.

His steps felt lighter as he proceeded through the winding streets. They were quiet and largely empty, the earliness of the hour ensuring most of the city's inhabitants had not yet risen from their breakfasts. Cenric paid it no mind, thinking instead on what lay ahead. He had a feeling the next few weeks would require much of him, perhaps even more than he'd already given in his escape from Suthhamtunam. Whatever was asked, he'd offer it gladly. He had a clear objective now. He would prevail, and when he did, he'd be sure to see that justice fell heavily upon Eadric of Mierċe.

XIII

Æva had never thought she'd have to entertain an aetheling. She'd been around men of standing for most of her life, but none had ranked as high as an actual heir to the throne. She didn't know what to say to him. This wasn't because she was in awe of him, suspecting any son of King Æthelred to be as foul and unjust as he was. This one looked like a thug also, possessing a brutish visage she'd expect to see on a common brawler rather than a man of royalty. Why he'd come to visit her in her plight, she wasn't sure. It wasn't like she could just tell him to leave, either.

She sat staring at him from across the table. She'd been confined to what was, to all intents and purposes, a cell for days now, or what seemed like days. She knew they'd taken Ælfric and Ælfgar elsewhere, but where exactly was uncertain. She supposed that was a small mercy. She didn't think she could stand being locked up with Ælfgar.

Her "cell" wasn't large, sporting a single cot in one corner and a narrow table with two chairs further towards the door. She also had the luxury of a barred opening in the southern wall that commanded a view of the city beyond. She'd taken to peering through it, sometimes feeling as if somebody out there was looking back, pondering her plight. She dismissed the notion. Nobody was coming to help her.

Her attitude towards the visiting aetheling soon changed. She'd initially taken him to be just another viper in the nest, here to gloat or brag about some self-serving scheme he was looking to set in motion. He'd instead told her something that had lifted a heavy, unbearable burden from her heart. Alaric was alive.

She'd pressed him for more information, her cheeks wet with relief. His previously blank expression changed at the sight of her so moved, his wide, dark eyes filling with an unmistakable compassion. Edmund, he said his name was. She'd of course heard of him. One of Æthelred's boys from his first marriage. Perhaps not everything sired from the king was as hateful as he was.

Edmund, all the same, had little else to tell her. Her husband was alive and in Eastengle, or so it was the case when he'd come across him on the road. He admitted he appeared to have sustained some kind of head injury, Æva feeling a flash of concern and frustration at the thought of it. Osmund hadn't been with him, or at least Edmund didn't know the name, nor had a man of such dimensions made himself known to him. That wasn't good. Alaric without Osmund was almost unheard of.

She wasn't surprised, however, to learn that Alaric had been moving to meet up with the Ealdorman Ulfcytel and the other survivors of Hringmere. She wasn't angry. She just knew Alaric would always put duty before everything else. He wasn't about to just slink off home after one defeat. Sometimes she wished he would. She might have some peace of mind then. But was it fair to wish her husband to be something he was not?

"Now that I have brought you this news, perhaps you can tell me why my father is so enraged with you and your family?"

She didn't know how to respond to Edmund's request. For a brief second, she feared she may have misjudged him, suspecting he was feeding her false hope about Alaric for the sake of some ulterior motive. If that were the case, he was very good at hiding it. He looked and sounded as sincere as anyone could be. Was it really so hard to believe that he, too, was confounded by the king's behaviour?

"I can't say why he believes we've done him wrong," she said, brushing a strand of red hair away from her face.

"No idea at all? You'll recall my father spat quite a list of alleged wrongdoings at Ælfric. Something about his command of a fleet? Something about Wiltune? Do you know anything about these matters?"

"If you want to know, why don't you ask him yourself?" She hoped he would. She didn't want to talk about Wiltune. It was a shock to her that the king had even brought it up. What could her father-in-law have to do with it? Surely the burning of Wiltune was just one of many such incidents in their long war with Svienn Forkbeard? What was so special about it compared to all the other villages and towns he'd put to the torch?

"I do intend to speak with the ealdorman, be sure of that," Edmund replied. "Yet I tell you now, lady, that my father has developed some kind of fascination with your husband. For reasons unknown to me, he was under the impression he was dead, and did not take kindly to being told otherwise."

"Who is Alaric to a king?" Æva asked, genuinely confused. "They've never met, as far as I know. And even if he had been killed, why would your father ever hear of it?"

"These were my thoughts, also," murmured Edmund, a large hand reaching up to rub the contours of his sizeable forehead. "I'll admit, I told my father of my encounter with Alaric upon the road. To say he reacted violently to the news…well, that's exactly what he did. To make matters more confusing…he gave me the distinct impression the Ealdorman of Mierċe had told him Alaric had been killed. Who is Eadric to Alaric? A friend?"

"No," Æva said flatly. "Eadric is no friend to us. He's a bastard killer. He laid siege to our home and brutalised our people in the hope of forcing Ælfric into surrendering."

Edmund sat back in his chair, his long, slow exhalation giving her the impression he was troubled and yet unsurprised at the news of Eadric's savagery. She had no real idea as to the comings and goings of King Æthelred's court, but she had a feeling Eadric was not a popular man, and was perhaps only protected thanks to the favour of the king himself.

"And Ælfric would not submit?" Edmund queried, his eyes narrowing.

"No, he would not. He had his men hurl spears and arrows at Eadric's army until it backed away from our walls. We then slipped away to Suthhamtunam in the night…we thought we'd be safe, but we were betrayed and handed over to Eadric by Eadwulf."

She quickly explained to Edmund what had happened once they'd reached Eadwulf's hall. She was at a loss as to what had caused the man to turn on them, thinking it probable Eadric had bribed him to ensure Ælfric had nowhere to go should he abandon his fortress. Edmund nodded in agreement with that notion.

"So your man Cenric got away?"

"I think so," Æva affirmed. "He tried to get me and my son out. He killed several of Eadwulf's men, but there were too many. Last I saw, he was still fighting in the doorway. I don't know what happened after as somebody grabbed me and slipped a bag over my head and…"

"They separated you from your son?"

"Yes, but he was with us on the journey here. They separated us again before they brought us before the king."

Edmund was frowning, a deep, angry cleft appearing between his eyebrows. He looked like a man who frowned a lot, the repeated action leaving a mark on him despite his otherwise youthful countenance. He asked her for her child's name. Æva told him. What he said next brought her yet more relief.

"I will see Brandon returned to you before the day is out."

Æva resisted the urge to again succumb to her emotions, her every instinct demanding she shower this man in gratitude after he'd delivered both news of her husband and offered to return her son. She wasn't a fool, though. Edmund might be the good man he appeared to be, but she was far from home and in the belly of a very particular, very deadly beast. She'd keep her wits sharp and her emotions in check. She thanked him all the same, the sentiments sincere despite the brevity of her words.

Edmund rose steadily to his feet and turned to leave. She could see now there was a certain strangeness to him, as if he bore a profound burden that had restricted his height yet caused his shoulders to grow out to accommodate it. There was little about him that struck her as "royal" or "princely"; his anvil-like face, dark hair, and thick wedge of a beard looking common enough among any number of warriors or farmhands across the realm.

Yet it could be said that this was something that made him unique here. Edmund didn't just look like any other honest Englishman tilling the fields or manning a shield wall. He acted like one. Nobody else had come to visit her. No well-spoken envoy, no lady in fancy attire, certainly not the king himself, had bothered to bestow so much as a kind word on her. Yet Edmund, one of the most powerful men in the kingdom, had done that and more, his actions and words relieving her of a grief that for weeks she'd feared might ultimately end her.

Edmund looked, acted, and was a man of integrity. Even if he were surrounded by snakes - having been born into such environs by accident of birth - he remained more akin to the thousands of brave Englishmen who'd died fighting for the realm at Ethandun, Brunanburh, and Malduna than his cruel father and any of his courtly intriguers. Maybe in that sense, he was exactly what England needed.

He took his leave, unaware of her musings. She sat alone with her thoughts, the echoing slam of the door gradually subsiding into silence. She'd begun to tire, so she went over to her cot and sat down, taking the single, worn woollen blanket and draping it over her knees. She wasn't entirely sure where she was, assuming from the lofty view from the window and the many stairs she'd been hauled up that she'd been confined to some kind of prison tower. All of it was solid stone, and all of it was frigid to the touch, the cold seeming to seep up from around her feet and into her very marrow. She lifted her legs onto the cot and lay down, shivering slightly as she pulled the blanket up and over her. She hoped she wouldn't be here long. She didn't think she could handle a winter here.

Sleep proved elusive, the light from the window indicating it was still relatively early in the afternoon. Her thoughts also wouldn't slow down, her mind switching from one anxious scenario to the next without pause. She had a tendency to worry, so she'd been told, but recent events had exacerbated that unfortunate habit to the point she wondered if she could do anything else.

Her thoughts turned to Cenric. The chances he'd been able to escape Suthhamtunam were slim, but even if he had, where would he have gone? Eadwulf and Eadric would have people keeping watch on the roads, and Cenric had sadly never given her the impression he had a lot going on upstairs. He was a fighter, yes, and a very good one, but intelligence didn't seem to be his forte. She hoped she was wrong, but the harsh reality was that he was probably dead somewhere. Eadwulf wouldn't even know his name. Same for Eadric. He wouldn't be important in their self-serving world, so his life was easily disposed of. It would be up to her to remember the sacrifice he'd made attempting to save her.

She then got to thinking about the king's recent exchange with Ælfric. She didn't understand much of what had been said, but it was clear Æthelred believed Ælfric was somehow responsible for the destruction of Wiltune. She'd not wanted to ever think on those events again in her life. The burning of her home town was easily the most painful thing she'd ever had to bear, and the people she'd lost that day could never be replaced. She'd previously put it down to bad luck, thinking any number of settlements could have suffered such a fate in these times of trouble and strife. From the way Æthelred had spoken of Wiltune, though, it seemed there was more to it. This hadn't been just another raid. Something had gone awry, and Ælfric had ended up taking the blame.

It was seven years ago, yet she could still remember it all so vividly. She always would. The stench of burning timber, the unearthly howling of the invaders, the icy fear reaching up to grip her heart…they were all carved into her memory, never to diminish with the passage of time. One thing, in particular, would always stay with her. The sight of her child, Alfred, lifeless on the floor, his tiny crown split and bloody. Then the look on Alaric's face when he beheld his son, his hands cradling the boy's broken body as he shuddered and shook under the crushing weight of his grief. She'd never seen her husband like that before or since. Something had died in him that day, his soul withering and hardening with the pain of it all. She could relate. They'd never been the same since.

It had all started so promisingly. Alaric had moved in with her after their wedding, admitting he could do with getting out of his father's shadow and staking a claim for himself in Wiltunscir. They were a long way from his father's seat of power, but it had meant a great deal to Æva to be permitted to stay close to her parents. Alaric had seen that and been more than accommodating, purchasing a sizeable property within the town and assuring her he'd never force her to move anywhere she did not wish.

She could still remember the day they'd taken up residence in their new home. It was a beautiful place, built from pale stone and partially thatched, the main hall sporting a flint roof whose solid, wooden rafters seemed to extend up and up to a dizzying height when viewed from the inside. It had been homely despite its impressive size, possessing a quality and atmosphere that made her feel like she belonged. Æva hadn't wanted any servants, preferring the solitude and space of being left alone with her doting husband. It had felt like perfection.

Then Alfred had been born. If she'd been happy before, then every day now felt like a dream, for she'd been gifted by God with a perfect, almost indescribable joy to complete her life in ways she'd never thought lacking. His birth had been a little difficult, it was true, since Alfred had been a rather large baby and was apparently unwilling to decide precisely when he was to be introduced to the world. She'd pulled through, eventually, and as she dwelled on the memory of holding him for the first time, she again felt tears return to her eyes. He'd had a perfectly pink, scrunched-up face, his tiny hands all wrinkled and pawing at her cheeks in what she liked to think was recognition. She could remember Alaric's arm around her shoulders, his voice hushed and breathless after he'd burst back into their bedchamber the moment the midwives had told him the news. There'd been a special something to his manner that morning, a curious cross between reverence and happiness. It had suited him.

Æva had never felt so close to her husband as they got used to sharing their home with the ever-demanding Alfred. Alaric had insisted they employ some help, and Æva had, in time, relented to the idea of handing over her kitchen to a stranger. It had not been easy, and Alaric, bless his heart, had tried to cook for both of them in the final stages of her pregnancy, but the results had been fairly mixed, if not outright awful. She'd kept that to herself, of course. He'd meant well, and to a warrior like him, a good meal was whatever he managed to hold over a campfire after a day's march. They had different tastes, that's all.

They'd got on well with the woman they'd hired. She'd also been a source of some assistance when it came to Alfred, since she'd had a grand total of nine children herself over the years. Alfred was a "healthy boy", she'd always insisted, although in hindsight that may have been due to how Æva worried over him, fearing every cough, cry, or splutter might be the onset of something terrible. Leofgifu had always set her straight, stressing she had nothing to worry about and that babies always let you know if something wasn't right. Æva had grown to appreciate her in the months that followed. Her cooking wasn't bad either.

Then war had reared its head again. Word reached them that Svienn Forkbeard had landed in the far west and overrun Execestre in a sudden assault. He'd even been joined by some of the Norse mercenaries the king had taken into his employ, the traitorous dogs abandoning the English cause in a single heartbeat. Æthelred had taken stern measures, ordering the death of all his remaining foreign hirelings, without exceptions. His purge, however, had soon spread, and a great many merchants and visitors from Scandinavia had been caught up in it, paying with their lives for something they'd not done.

Opinions were mixed as to the how and the why of it. Some had said the mercenaries had been plotting to assassinate the king himself, and that they'd only joined the English ranks as part of a ruse to help facilitate that goal. Æva couldn't know the full truth, but she'd felt at the time the king had been a little overzealous. Killing mercenaries was one thing, as some of them had indeed defected, but too many innocents had died with them, and the fact it had all taken place on Saint Brice's Day was just distasteful.

Right or wrong, the bloodletting hadn't done much to slow Svienn's advance. Execestre's fall had come as a shock to Æthelred's new Norman queen, Emma, who had reputedly entrusted one of her own countrymen to oversee its administration. Æva didn't understand why Normans would ever have been brought into affairs of state like that, but the word was that Execestre had been given to her, symbolically at least, as some kind of wedding gift. Æva didn't quite understand that either, but Alaric had heard that Execestre had been targeted precisely because of the Norman presence within the city and what it had apparently meant to Queen Emma. Svienn was sending a message, so went the logic, informing the English their new alliance with Duke Richard II would do them no good. If that was intended, he proved it well enough, advancing like lightning from the ruined city to threaten the heartland of all England.

King Æthelred, to his credit, had acted swiftly, issuing prompt commands for the combined fyrds of both Wiltunscir and Hamptonscir to come together and repulse the invaders. Alaric had left Wiltune soon after with one hundred retainers, intending to muster with the rest of the fyrd in expectation of receiving reinforcements from Hamptonscir.

At the time, Æva had thought the goal was to confront Svienn and his host some miles to the west, effectively blocking his path before he could do any further damage. She would be safe, Alaric had assured her, claiming that even if the Forkbeard got past them, which he wouldn't, he'd be more interested in pushing toward Wincestre than attacking a place like Wiltune. She'd believed him. He hadn't been lying. He'd just been wrong.

She remembered his departure vividly. He'd looked so ferocious atop his huge, dark brown steed, his face hidden beneath the iron plate of his helmet and his hand gripping a formidable red-tasselled spear. His shield had been slung over his back so he could clutch the reins, but he was well protected even without it, his torso, arms, and thighs all covered by a shimmering, granite-grey coat of expertly wrought ring mail. His sword, his most prized possession, rested in the iron-studded scabbard at his waist, a jet-black cloak of some length billowing out behind him. If her husband had ever wanted to make himself look truly terrifying, he'd managed it.

His horse appeared as eager as he was to face the enemy, the beast stamping its hooves and snorting with impatience at the delay. The men behind him were similarly mounted and attired, their brutal, ironclad forms contrasting sharply with the delicate cherry blossom cascading down around them. Spring in all its glory had come early this year, and the trees lining the main avenue toward the northern gate were in full bloom. Even without them, the town was a more than pleasing sight, every cottage, hut, and hall looking truly picturesque beneath the cloudless, deep blue sky stretching majestically from horizon to horizon. An almost perfect, peaceful image, were it not for these fearsome men of war.

Alaric had removed his helm and leant down in the saddle to kiss her. The company behind him were also saying goodbye to their sweethearts and family members, the whole affair swiftly becoming a tearful one as loved ones struggled with the fearful notion they might never see each other again. Æva lifted Alfred up to behold his father, the little fellow making an assortment of gurgling sounds in apparent greeting. Alaric reached out to gently pat his son's head, his gauntleted hand looking oversized and faintly menacing as it caressed Alfred's scalp.

They said one final goodbye, and Alaric winked at her before placing his helm upon his head and riding on. His companions followed, the entire column departing at a spirited trot, their helms and spear tips sparkling in the sunlight. They looked like heroes from some epic poem, riding out to do battle with anything and anyone that might dare threaten them. Æva couldn't imagine what it must be like to be on the wrong side of such men. King Svienn would now surely be made to answer for his many crimes.

Nearly a week went by with no word from them. Life seemed to go on as before, the mood in Wiltune suggesting the war was very far away and would always remain so. How wrong they were. The worst day of her life was about to come to pass. There was no sign of its coming, and it had begun like any other, Æva rising to feed Alfred at her usual time just after dawn. He was putting on weight and getting greedy with it, too, and Æva had found herself looking forward to the day he'd be eating solid food rather than feeding so demandingly at her breast.

Despite that, all seemed well, the morning looking like it would again be pleasant as she sat nursing her son in the main hall, the light from the windows conveying a delicate warmth upon the cool flagstones. She'd then heard a shout from outside, assuming it to be nothing but a fleeting argument. Then another yell came. Then another. A sudden crash. Something that sounded like metal impacting on metal. Then a scream. An entire uproar now, like everyone in the town but her was both outraged and afraid.

Leofgifu had rushed in, hammering the front door shut as she moved. She was deathly pale, her hands trembling and eyes wide with fright. Æva had gotten to her feet, her dress now pulled up for dignity's sake, but she'd kept Alfred pinned to her chest, her heart racing in apprehension. There was another noise coming from outside, like the howling of savage men who'd long ceased to care for words such as honour or mercy. The sound shook her to the core, imprinting itself upon her memory. Worse was yet to come.

The front door came crashing inward like it was made of paper. A true brute stood in the entryway, his body encased in flowing yet crudely forged mail, his eyes so hard you'd have thought they were made of ice. His flaxen beard and hair were marked with grey streaks, his seniority apparently failing to cool the hateful passions radiating out from him in a baleful aura. He held a strange helmet at his side, one half painted red with the other left as burnished metal, and Æva was just wondering what this might signify when he stepped forward and planted his axe in Leofgifu's skull.

Æva didn't scream as the old woman's head came apart. She just stared, clutching her baby tightly in her arms, unable and unwilling to bring her eyes up to face the nightmare now loping towards her. Whoever this murderous cur was, he'd brought friends, for several other similarly belligerent Danes were following at his heels, their demeanour almost as unpleasant. Some were breathing heavily like they'd recently been fighting, the red fluid splattered across their arms and armour lending strength to that notion.

The lead fiend reached out to try and prise Alfred from Æva's grasp. She hissed at him through bared teeth, kicking at his shins and throwing a punch towards his chest. He laughed, the sound soulless and cruel, his revolting breath washing over her to the point she felt violated just from breathing it in. He struck her, slamming his fist into the side of her head, and she let go of Alfred, so forceful was the blow. She looked up from the floor to see the Dane holding her baby up to stare into his eyes, the child perfectly silent in the face of his ancestral enemy. Æva struggled to her feet just in time to see him suddenly grip Alfred by the legs and dash his head upon the floor, the boy's skull cracking with a sharp snap.

She didn't fully comprehend what had just happened. It was too much, the magnitude of the horror she'd witnessed proving impossible for her mind to immediately process. She did remember how the Danes had laughed at the sight of her son's body, as if what they had done was akin to some good-natured jape played on an unsuspecting friend. The blood of innocents was nothing to them, and the fact they'd just murdered a child made absolutely no impression upon their consciences at all, assuming they could even be said to possess such things.

They'd then beaten her, their blows reducing her to a state of semi-coherence. She was actually grateful for that, since the ordeal ensured she had relatively little memory of the lead Dane forcing himself upon her, his disgusting breath again seeping up invasively into her nostrils. She'd eventually passed out, thankfully, but she could remember thinking that her death must be close, and in her beaten, miserable state, she'd welcomed it, deciding eternity in heaven with Alfred was preferable to continued existence in this merciless, fallen world.

She hadn't died, though. She could recall coming round, the pain rising from between her thighs shocking her back into a state of alertness. The house had been ransacked, and she could smell smoke pouring in from the windows, a loud crackling sound following with it. She'd crawled over to Alfred, his crumpled body still wrapped in the tiny white shawl she'd given him. She'd sat there for some time, her face a bruised mess, rocking her son in her arms, refusing to focus on his shattered, bloodied crown or the tiny, dead eyes staring up at her.

Somebody had eventually pulled her up and out of the now burning house. She could remember the streets and how they were awash with chaos; the buildings on fire, the cherry trees that had so recently been filled with white blossom hacked down out of sheer spite. She couldn't see the Danes, but one only had to look to Wiltune's inhabitants for evidence of their passing. Many of them had been slain in the street or dismembered and hung up as if for amusement, the sheer brutality of the spectacle a redoubled shock to her senses. She'd wondered where her parents were. Then she'd wondered about Alaric. If the Danes were here, that meant he must have been defeated and perhaps killed. If so, her life was over as far as she was concerned. She might physically survive this day, but that was just flesh, all of which would perish sooner or later.

She saw then that at least some of the townspeople had survived. Most of them were like her, disorientated and in shock, some openly wailing out their lamentations whilst their homes crackled and burned. Ash and heat had replaced the blossom and butterflies of days gone by, and both were working to snatch the breath from her lungs. Her still nameless rescuer, however, wouldn't let up, and he hurried her along towards the town gate and the safety they all hoped might lie beyond. She could see this was where the Danes had broken through to commence their slaughter. It had been easy for them. Wiltune had been completely unprepared for an attack, its best fighting men leaving with Alaric in the pursuit of death or glory. She'd been almost certain there and then that they'd found only the former.

The survivors had fled to some kind of sanctuary out in the forest, Æva included. She'd sat down away from the others, huddled and wretched and peering back at Wiltune from between the trees, the billowing smoke from its fires rising up and over them like some predatory spirit. She still had Alfred in her arms, refusing to let him go. She could taste blood in her mouth, and several of her teeth were loose, the treatment meted out to her having left relatively little of her body unblemished.

Night had come on rapidly. Æva refused all offers of nourishment and bared her blood-stained teeth at anyone who tried to reach for Alfred. They'd gotten the message, the other survivors deciding it best to leave her well enough alone. She'd not slept, remembering the snapping, hissing roar from beyond as the town was consumed, the harsh light of the flames penetrating the tree cover to cast eerie, unsettling shadows. She'd stayed awake that whole night, motionless and brooding, her dead child cradled in her arms. Dawn had eventually come, and with it a familiar voice, the only living voice she presently cared to hear.

She'd let Alaric hold Alfred. She'd not seen him cry before, but he did now, his tears flowing without restraint. He didn't relent, pouring out a lifetime of sadness within the space of a few minutes, his son's body clutched gently at his chest. She could recall Osmund standing there, his head hung low in grief, like he was feeling his friend's despair with an acuteness that could only come from genuine brotherhood.

Æva clung tightly to her husband, her heart filled with relief that he was still among the living. She hadn't yet come to terms with what had happened to Alfred, nor indeed what had been inflicted on her after. Alaric was alive, and she thus had a lifeline, something she could cling to in the face of the despair she knew would soon reach up to claim her.

By that point, Wiltune had become a smouldering ruin, and word soon reached them that Æva's parents had been butchered attempting to reach her home. She'd been told that her father, rest his soul, had tried to fight, and that the Danes had cut his arm from his body before finishing him. It could have been worse. They'd at least left her mother undefiled.

The Danes had disgraced themselves in other ways. They'd attacked Wiltune's church, breaking through the doors and murdering Father Wilfred. They'd then desecrated the place, so threatened as they always were by the Christian God and his message of repentance and salvation. It had always been so. The darkness hated the light, and would seek any opportunity to snuff it from existence. The death of Father Wilfred, however, meant they were without the means to give Alfred a proper burial. Alaric had needed to take matters into his own hands.

He'd dug a small grave further into the forest, his surviving men standing witness whilst he laid his son to rest. They'd formed a circle around their commander, each of them dour and soldierly, their armour battered and dishevelled from some recent clash she'd yet to hear of. Alaric had broken down after depositing Alfred into the grave, and so Osmund had intervened, allowing his grieving friend to take a step back so that he might finish the job. Æva had said little, as had Alaric, the pair of them instead standing hand in hand whilst Osmund gently eased the earth over Alfred's shrouded form.

They'd marked the spot with a makeshift cross atop a mound of stones piled over the grave itself, ensuring Alfred would be safe from any roaming beasts intent on disturbing him. Osmund had prayed aloud, his "Our Father" rising up past the treetops and into the soot-filled sky. Æva liked to think of Alfred's soul rising with his words, his essence parting from this troubled world and ascending into the gentle embrace of his Lord and Saviour. Osmund had lingered with her and Alaric for some time after, sat apart from them and yet always near, his huge, reassuring presence enough to remind them they need never be alone.

Alaric had then gathered the survivors together, informing them of what had happened after he'd departed from them. Svienn Forkbeard had proven to be a more cunning beast than they'd imagined. He'd split his main host into several smaller warbands to make himself harder to pin down in a single engagement. One of these had attacked Alaric and his men when they'd attempted to link up with reinforcements from Hamptonscir, preventing the English from forming a single cohesive army. Another had headed south to attack Wiltune before moving on to the fortifications at Sarum. Typically for their kind, the Danes had not attempted a siege, probably out of fear of Sarum's walls and the resolute men behind them. They were pitiful. They'd fight when they felt certain to win, but recoil when faced with those capable of defending themselves.

As to where exactly the Ealdorman Ælfric and his men were, Alaric had not said. He'd never told her, but she'd sensed at times in the years that followed he harboured some resentment towards his father, making her wonder if Alaric either blamed him or suspected him of failing them somehow. Was this what King Æthelred had meant when he'd condemned Ælfric just recently? She had no way of knowing for sure, but she owed it to herself to find out. She owed it to Alfred.

Word had then reached them that Svienn had retreated to his ships, content with the misery he'd caused and burdened with loot and slaves aplenty. Alaric and Æva returned to Hamptonscir, since there was little reason to stay with her parents and child dead and Wiltune a charred ruin. They'd aided the survivors as best they could before leaving, Alaric and his warriors helping to bury and pray over those that needed it. Æva could barely remember her mother and father's funeral, so numb had she become, but it was a blessing a priest had by then come to assist them from elsewhere, Alaric insisting he also pray over and bless the grave of his son. She'd felt like a husk at that stage. Empty and worn out, all hope and emotion long drained from her shattered heart.

Ælfric had been pleased to see them. He'd arranged for them to live in the impressive tower adjacent to his hall at Porteceaster, believing the stone walls of his fortress would be a better place for his son to raise a family with the realm still so imperilled. She'd sadly not gotten much of an opportunity to spend time with her husband, instead enduring many an hour grieving alone whilst he remained occupied with military matters. It was not his fault, but it just made things harder. Solitude was a poor accompaniment to bereavement.

When her belly began to swell, things had gotten even worse. Alaric had not been intimate with her since Alfred's conception, and his grief had then stalled his passion to the extent she feared he might never yearn for her again. That left only one explanation as to what was happening. Heartbreak over her son's death wasn't enough. Æva would now have to contend with the horror of being with child from the seed of the man who'd murdered him.

Alaric hadn't said a word when she'd told him. He'd instead sat with her on their bed, her hand swallowed up in his, staring straight ahead like he were sifting through any number of possible responses. He'd then leapt to his feet and drawn his sword, his furious roar echoing violently across the walls of their chamber. He'd laid into the table - a modest thing they'd sometimes used to eat supper whilst taking in the view from their window - and reduced it to splinters, his rage destroying it in the space of a few seconds.

She'd shrunk back from him, alarmed at the sudden violence. He'd seen her apprehension, and the sight of her so cowed had cooled his fury to the point he'd again broken down in tears. He'd tried to hide it with his hands, scrunching his face into his palms like he could disappear into them and be safe from either rebuke or ridicule. She had gone over to him, easing his hands from his face and placing them on her hips as she held him.

He'd calmed down, her comforting touch restoring him to his senses. She'd stared into his dark, tearful eyes, knowing in her heart he wouldn't hurt her. She'd told him there were things they could do to set everything right. She didn't have to bear this child. She'd heard of a concoction that could be made for just such a scenario. With any luck, they could obtain it and, with a few sips, let the past remain the past.

Æva had never forgotten what he'd said in reply. What she'd suggested was wrong, she understood that, but heartache and desperation had pushed her to the brink. Her husband was no doubt suffering like she was, but he'd been spared the spectacle of his son's murder and the horrific ordeal that had followed. Perhaps that had allowed him to maintain a certain strength when it came to his own Christian convictions. Either way, she remembered his words perfectly, his tone soft yet firm as he gazed down at her, his hands still resting on her hips.

"There may come a time when the people of England abandon God…abandon all that's good and holy and gentle…but today is not that day. This child growing inside you knows nothing of brutality. It knows nothing of cruelty or predation. It is innocent, totally innocent. It is a part of you, and I love it as such. Dire wounds from cruel deeds will not be healed with yet more cruelty."

She'd been surprised. In her hopelessness, she'd thought he'd be glad to be rid of it, thinking the anguish and rage he'd just displayed was a sure sign he'd not play father to a foreign child conceived by force. Æva realised as she now contemplated these memories from her cold cell that she'd then still not truly known Alaric and the depth of his heart, nor the level of hardship he'd endure for the sake of what he considered right. The fact he was still out there, somewhere, surviving against all odds to continue fighting the enemies of England was testament to that resolve.

His words had soothed her troubled soul, but she'd still felt considerable regret at what she had proposed. The child could never learn of what had been discussed here. They'd put it all behind them, dispensing with the bad memories the way they'd shake off an unwelcome dream or unsettling thought. Faith, hope, and love would see them through. It was either that or allow their brokenness to triumph over them. They had too much yet to live for to allow that.

She'd carried the child for those remaining months in the tower, Alaric initially trying to prevent his father from discovering her situation. There soon came a time, though, when Æva was of such a size there was no hiding it, and yet they need not have worried, for Ælfric was beside himself with joy at the prospect of "again becoming a grandfather." Neither of them had the heart to tell him the full truth. She knew the old man had been devastated by Alfred's death, lamenting over and over on how he should never have let them leave his fortress. It wasn't his fault. But they didn't need the situation to become even more difficult. Ælfric would be spared the burdens they endured. It was a kindness, if anything.

When Brandon was finally born, Æva had felt like it were the end of her troubles. She cared not for the child's real father, fancying him dead somewhere and unable to harm others. Brandon was not his son. He would never be his. Brandon was HER child, an English boy with an English name, to be raised to love the Lord his God with all his heart and all his strength and love his neighbour as himself. That was to be his path. They would bring the good out of this situation and be all the more blessed for it.

These were not just hopeful predictions. She'd known as soon as she'd been handed her new baby that it would always be thus. He'd gazed up at her, his huge blue eyes drinking her in, and she saw then there was not a scrap of malice in him. He was perfect, entirely innocent of any evil, great or small, an unblemished soul enjoying his first moments of a long and gentle life. There was no way anyone would take him from her arms or from her heart. Æva would die first.

The next few years, however, had presented a few obstacles she'd failed to consider. Alaric had trouble being a father. It wasn't that he was unkind, but he was often remote, and he became more so when the boy's Danish heritage began to manifest in his distinctly foreign features and shining blond hair. Æva found herself wondering if Ælfric suspected anything, fearing his reaction if he somehow learned the child was not of his blood. If he'd had any such inkling, he'd kept it quiet, proving himself as generous and kind a grandfather as any child could hope for.

Alaric, though, remained troubled. He'd drifted from Æva, getting lost in drink and comradeship with the ever-boisterous Osmund. Æva sometimes worried Alaric might tell Osmund of Brandon's true ancestry, or that the big man might work it out himself from the boy's appearance. If he had been told, then nothing came of it, and to be honest, she doubted she'd even know if he had, for Osmund was not the type to judge or make unnecessary trouble. She was glad he was such a good friend to her husband. She knew he needed it. She wondered how Alaric might cope with the trials of life if he were gone.

Æva stretched out on her cot, trying to work the aches from her legs. She could picture the day Alaric had left for Eastengle. He'd looked formidable as always, his armour exaggerating the width of his already broad shoulders. With Osmund next to him, they'd look truly imposing, and Æva had felt gladdened by the sight of it, knowing these great warriors would fight to defend the other until their last breath. Brandon hadn't felt the same. He'd feared for them, and he'd run to Alaric just when he'd been about to join the men marching from the main square to the eastern gate, attaching himself to his leg and imploring him to stay.

Æva could tell her husband had felt awkward, but then he'd knelt down and whispered something in Brandon's ear, a gauntleted hand placed delicately upon his scrawny shoulder. Whatever Alaric had said had done the trick. The boy stopped crying, and a faint smile had crept across his previously troubled features, his expression turning from one of anguish to quiet contentment.

That was until Osmund had ruffled his hair, his huge mailed paw seeming to almost swallow up his head. Brandon had feigned outrage, informing him in no uncertain terms that he was a warrior too and wouldn't have his hair dirtied by a "giant smelly oaf" like him. Alaric had laughed, claiming it was the best description of Osmund he'd ever heard. Osmund had pretended to cry, sticking his bottom lip out and making weeping motions over his scrunched-up eyes. Brandon, bless his soul, had actually looked concerned for him. Then Osmund grinned. Brandon smiled back. All was well.

That was the last time she'd seen either of them. They'd marched off through the fortress gates, Alaric embracing and kissing her one last time before joining the flood of men and spears pouring ever onward. Sorrow started to rise in her chest again. A lot could happen in the space of weeks. Edmund might have seen Alaric alive, but that didn't mean he was guaranteed to stay that way. For all she knew, he could be dead now, his life crushed from his bones in some desperate clash in the ruins of Eastengle. She might be alone after all. With Alaric dead and Ælfric imprisoned or executed, what chance did she have in this world? Had she allowed herself to wallow in false hope as a prelude to a final despair?

She sat up and held her head in her hands. She'd lost track of time, the light from the window having dwindled considerably. Night couldn't be far off. An even chiller breeze was seeping through the bars, and Æva stifled a shiver, wondering how many hours had gone by with her enmeshed in her troubled past. This ill feeling could not be allowed to get the better of her. There was still hope. There had to be.

She looked up when the door to her cell started to scrape open. Edmund wandered in, his eyes twinkling like he was pleased. She saw why a half second later. Brandon was with him, alert and at his side, his eyes wide with emotion upon seeing his mother. He made a sudden dash towards her, Æva reaching out to gather him up in her arms. She lost herself in the embrace, all previous anxiety dispelled in a single instant. Æva opened her eyes, gazing through tears of relief towards the most noble aetheling.

"Thank you, Edmund."

XIV

He'd been waiting for this. He'd worked up a real thirst, of the kind that couldn't be quenched by mere earthly waters. Now he was moments away from relief, his very soul yearning in anticipation. He dropped to his knees, the stones beneath him reassuringly solid, the hundreds of voices behind him lifted in worship and adoration. The sound of them filled his surroundings, thickening the air with reverence. Somebody else spoke, this time in front of him, a figure in robes of purest white, uttering words he'd long ached to hear.

"The body of Christ."

He paused before responding, the features of the one who'd just spoken now partly obscured by smoke. The air inside the cathedral was heavy with incense, the grey, scented trails curling up towards the ceiling like prayers to Heaven. He cleared his throat and uttered a single word, one no less profound for all its brevity.

"Amen."

The robed figure extended his hands towards him, something small yet deceptively precious resting upon a spoon gripped between the fingers. He opened his mouth, taking the body of Christ upon his tongue, a few seconds later drinking his fill from the chalice that was offered. He rose with purpose, heading back the way he'd come to resume his place among the congregation, the taste of wine fresh upon his lips. He knelt amongst them, a renewing strength filling his limbs, the Blessed Sacrament restoring and healing his soul in ways that defied easy description. Words of holiness filled his mind, his hands clasped close to his chest, the murmurings of a Christian warrior at prayer rising upward alongside the praise and petitions of the hundreds of others around him.

"Lord Jesus Christ
Son of God
Have Mercy upon Me
A Sinner."

He'd lost track of how long he'd stayed like that, his thoughts focused intently on the holy name of his Lord. He often felt as if his heart were being filled with light from this prayer, the repetition of the words and the emptying of his mind serving to strengthen him in a fashion that, like the Eucharist, he struggled to put into words. Time passed regardless, and when he eventually opened his eye, much of the cathedral had emptied, leaving him almost alone in the silent expanse of its majestic interior. Only one remained. The priest who'd blessed him with Holy Communion stood behind the altar, his person gently illuminated in the light of a dozen candles. His eyes were closed, his head bowed slightly. Prayer had claimed him too. He should not be disturbed.

Alaric stood up, a dull ache in his knees from his time humbled upon the stones. He gazed at the figure still standing quietly at the altar, the clouds of incense finally clearing enough for him to see his face. He seemed like the type who took his vocation seriously, looking slender yet energetic from habitual fasting, the smile lines that creased his well-aged visage alluding to a gentle spirit. He wore a full beard that reached to his collarbones, his almost entirely white hair cascading out past his wiry shoulders. Alaric thought to speak with him, hoping perhaps to gain spiritual insight on his recent trials. He decided against it. He might be late if he did. Ulfcytel and the archbishop would be expecting him.

Something akin to regret pulled at his heart. He didn't want to leave. There was a real sense of peace here, similar to that which he'd experienced at the church in Offetuna, although there were obvious differences, as Father Dobron's chapel was a very humble place likely used to holding not more than three dozen worshipers. Canterburie's cathedral was something else, its towering stone walls, shimmering stained glass windows, and majestic eastern apse serving to overawe to the point of breathlessness. Alaric wasn't sure if he could ever get tired of being here, walking as he was in the footsteps of Saint Augustine. This was holy ground, no doubt.

He turned to make his way towards the entrance, his echoing, solitary footsteps cutting through the weighted silence. He passed through the sturdy, square block of the cathedral's narthex, collecting his belt, cloak, scabbard, and sword before venturing towards the doors that led into the world beyond.

A refreshing breeze washed over him upon making his exit, the wind seeming to tug at his freshly trimmed beard and hair almost playfully. Canterburie stretched out before him, the encroaching night just beginning to shroud its skyline. Alaric could see well enough, since the towering doors he'd just emerged from were flanked by a pair of flickering braziers that served to light up the entire western entrance of the cathedral. The light was strong enough for him to see much of the imposing central tower just behind him, its grey form soaring upwards towards the stars just beginning to appear around its summit. He'd never been up there, at times wondering what could be contained within. He'd not admit this to anyone, but he was a little nervous of it, sometimes fearing during services that the entire structure might somehow collapse, crushing them flat.

He shivered at the thought, his hands instinctively clutching at his cloak to pull it tighter about him. Autumn had crept up on them, and the streets were blanketed with leaves, a cooler, damper atmosphere gradually replacing the gentle summer evenings of days gone by. The weeks he'd spent here felt like an odd dream compared to the harrowing reality he'd endured in the ruins of Eastengle, and he'd at first struggled to get used to it, finding simple luxuries like sleeping in a bed to be out of place and peculiar. He'd acclimated in time, but then a new set of worries had replaced the old. This was a place of refuge, he'd tell himself. A refuge that must be defended. He'd forget that at his peril. It wouldn't do to let himself turn soft.

In all honesty, there was little chance of that happening. Every time he saw his reflection, he could see his ruined eye staring back at him; the image so disturbing he'd contemplated hiding it forever behind a patch or some kind of cloth headband. He wasn't a vain man, but he had at times thought himself handsome, and this injury had sadly ensured relatively few would ever presume to describe him as such, apart from his wife, he hoped. He'd eventually decided to leave his eye as it was, knowing he had nothing to be ashamed of and that it would ideally serve to unnerve those he met in battle. Given their future plans involved a huge amount of fighting, he hoped this would be the case. He quite liked the thought, actually.

He began the long trek towards his home, or what at least would be for as long as Ulfcytel required him to be here. He missed Porteceaster dearly, and yearned to return to his wife and family so long as duty and war did not call him elsewhere. He'd sent a messenger to them when he'd first arrived here, hoping to let them know he'd survived. That was weeks ago now, and there had been no word whatsoever, the messenger himself also failing to return. There had been no news of the enemy heading that far south again, so Alaric couldn't see what the problem was. After his business tonight was concluded, he'd see about sending someone out to investigate.

He strolled onward, the evening air filling his lungs, the sensation cool and revitalising in contrast to the heated, dry incense he'd inhaled beforehand. The cathedral he'd come from had been constructed on a gentle rise that presently gave him a commanding view of the city, the faint lights from its many buildings flickering invitingly as he made his way south and west along a broad, flat stone thoroughfare.

It was easy to like this place. It was bereft of anything akin to Lundenburg's smothering atmosphere, yet it was still a veritable haven of activity, spiritual and otherwise. He had little notion of its exact population, but he knew the total headcount had surged in recent months as refugees from Eastengle flocked to their sheer stone walls. The monks at the abbey had sprung into action, throwing themselves into a still continuing campaign of charitable works that had successfully housed the newcomers either here or within one of the nearby villages to the south. Alaric approved. Doing God's will sometimes began with the simplest of acts. Love of thy neighbour, whoever he was, was fundamental.

He hurried through the narrowing streets, the city becoming more cluttered and confined the further he moved from the cathedral. He was now in the western quarter and fairly close to the curtain wall that encircled the entire settlement. The garrison had their main barracks here, the adjacent buildings also housing a sequence of storage areas, stables, and smithies to keep the men equipped. It had been a natural decision for the man in charge of pretty much everything within the city, Ælfweard, to house the new arrivals in such a place. Both Ulfcytel and Alaric couldn't complain. They were grateful for the hospitality, and sleeping under a roof was an extravagant luxury compared to what they'd gotten used to in Eastengle. Their hosts had been most gracious.

It was just starting to rain when Alaric spied his destination. The hall's front doors were easy to spot, for they were lit up by a cloaked and hooded figure bearing a torch amidst the deepening shadows. Alaric clapped him gently on the shoulder when he passed, a gesture of support and affection as much as anything. Eamon hadn't taken the death of Bana well. He was now the only survivor from Hamptonscir who had faced Thorkell at Hringmere. Alaric recognised the burden of grief whenever he caught his eye, and so he'd resolved to stay as close to him as possible in the struggles ahead. Whatever he was presently feeling, Eamon still looked confident and imposing enough as he stood guard, and all knew he was committed to carrying out his duties to the best of his ability. Alaric would always respect that. He'd share a couple of ales with him later if he could.

The inside of the hall was as Alaric had left it, occupants included. The place was spartan, comprised of a single, elongated chamber with a number of side rooms branching off halfway. He could see Ulfcytel's solid frame about twenty paces ahead, the old warrior sitting contentedly near the head of the table and conveniently close to the fire smouldering within the confines of a generously sized stone hearth. His features looked somewhat haggard in the flickering light, making Alaric again suspect his brush with death at Gipeswic had affected him more than he'd care to admit. Ulfcytel was a skilled combatant with courage in abundance, but that was as long as he had a weapon in hand and a foe in front of him. Being forced to retreat into water to almost drown whilst having spears lobbed at him was a different situation altogether.

Alaric knew he was grateful for the rescue, but there was a lot he wasn't telling him. He could read the signs. He'd nearly died recently too. It wasn't something you just shrugged off with a grunt and a prayer. Those moments when a man seriously considered his death as imminent would always linger in the mind, seeping their way inside to permeate the very soul. Alaric had still not come to terms with his own experience, and he imagined it was the same for the ealdorman. He was just thankful they'd encountered those merchant ships once they were at sea. The herbs and supplies they'd sold them had been instrumental in Ulfcytel's swift recovery.

Osbert sat with him, the lad a reassuring presence that rarely left his side. Alaric had taken the opportunity to speak with him once they'd spent a day or two in Canterburie, hoping to discover how he'd fared once they'd been parted on that fateful morning for the attack on Thorkell's camp. He could tell Osbert was disturbed by his first taste of large-scale combat, suspecting his experience at Hringmere might have broken and then hardened his heart. After a few drinks, Osbert had finally admitted what had happened.

He'd panicked, losing his courage when the Danes broke through the English lines, and the shame of it afflicted him still. Old Bertram had died in front of him, so he'd said, fighting to defend Osbert whilst he'd been rooted to the spot in fright. He could tell that weighed heavily upon his conscience, but admitting his own fears was a brave thing to do. Alaric had not known Bertram, only meeting him once, but Osbert had, and Alaric had no reason to disbelieve him when he said he owed him his life and could and should have saved him in return. Alaric didn't judge him. Osbert hadn't wallowed in his fear. He might have frozen, trembled, vomited, and everything else, but he'd snapped out of it and kept on fighting and survived. There was a warrior in him and a skilled one too. He'd seen him fight enough times now to know that.

But that hardness had lingered on, and whatever soft edges Osbert had possessed when Alaric had first met him on the road from Theodford had more or less vanished. He'd at first feared he'd become unbalanced and cold, like a man who was either too fond of killing or was just generally indifferent to the suffering of others. He hoped things wouldn't go that far. There was no point in becoming a great warrior if one lost one's God-given humanity in the process. He looked content enough now as he sat in his mail and leathers, although there remained something in his eyes. An emptiness. Something important had left him and wouldn't be coming back.

They had company. Osbert and Ulfcytel were sitting across from two others, one a sleek, angular-looking man dressed in a fine green tunic and matching breecs, a sapphire-blue cloak draped across his shoulders. Alaric recognised him, his thick yet neat auburn hair and beard in marked contrast to Ulfcytel's bald scalp and silver face rug. Ælfweard was his name, and he was a capable and intelligent man, qualities to be expected given he was a reeve of the king himself.

Alaric had at first been dismayed to learn such an individual held power in the city, believing him liable to make life difficult for them on the king's orders. Nothing of the kind had transpired. Ælfweard had turned out to be an accommodating and polite host, but his good manners hadn't prevented him from posing a deluge of questions as to why Ulfcytel had suddenly appeared on his doorstep with several hundred soldiers in tow.

There had been no room nor will for subterfuge. They all knew who Ulfcytel was, just as word had already spread about his defeat at Hringmere, although the details of the battle and the treachery of Thurcytel was news to Ælfweard. His face had grown a little paler when Ulfcytel had told him he had reason to believe Thorkell eventually intended to make his way back to Canterburie. He'd allowed them inside the walls then, settling them and their warriors up here in the western quarter.

Alaric had recently learned what had happened to the Scandinavian noble who'd originally informed Ulfcytel of Thorkell's plans. He'd not seen him on the march to Gipeswic, and Ulfcytel had since told him he'd released him back at his forest camp. He'd taken some rather brutal precautions, removing the man's tongue and both his thumbs before sending him on his way. It was a harsh fate, and Alaric couldn't shake the notion that it might have been fairer to have simply killed him. What was certain was that he'd not be telling anyone of Ulfcytel's intentions, nor would he ever be able to take up arms again. That was some relief, Alaric supposed. The bastard had come here to make England bleed. He'd now been taught the full magnitude of his mistake.

The man seated next to Ælfweard was a relative unknown to Alaric. He understood he went by the name of Leofwine, yet he'd not had the opportunity to speak with him at any real length. All he knew of him was that he was in charge of Ælfweard's garrison forces inside the city and that he was a good man. He seemed decent, looking like the capable fighter he was reputed to be, and was also a man of faith if his regular appearances at the cathedral were anything to go by. There was something about him that reminded Alaric of the Aetheling Edmund. Dark-haired, for sure, and bearded like most men, but also restrained in his temperament, akin to one who'd had the burdens of vanity and self-interest stripped away from him to the point he thought only of duty. The mark of a good soldier, that was. A leader too.

Alaric took a seat next to Ulfcytel, removing his cloak beforehand to drape it over the back of his chair to soak up some heat from the hearth. Ulfcytel passed him a cup of something without a word, Alaric appreciating the sweet warmth of the mead after his trek through the now increasingly rain swept streets. The bad weather had intensified, and the sound of raindrops pattering off the roof was clearly audible over the crackling fire. He didn't envy Eamon having to stand watch in that.

Ælfweard beheld Alaric with a not-unfriendly gaze from his crystal-clear blue eyes. The reeve had gotten used to his presence in meetings with Ulfcytel, since he was now effectively his second in command. Alaric was still getting accustomed to that. He'd prefer the position had been earned rather than thrust upon him out of necessity following the death of almost every other man of rank at Hringmere. He'd make the best of his situation. Honour demanded it.

"Ælfweard was just congratulating us, Alaric," said Ulfcytel, a hint of mirth in his voice. "He's impressed that our men have been able to finish the ditch around the walls so quickly."

"It was most certainly a noteworthy feat," Ælfweard responded, his words directed at Alaric and Ulfcytel together. "Yet I am a bit concerned it will slow traffic into the city. We now have only one road open, and the ditch will fill up with water soon enough and present a hazard to anyone att…"

"Attempting to storm the walls by force, yes," quipped Ulfcytel, a half smile on his face. "And trade has slowed to a crawl because of the war. One road and one gate are enough for the kind of traffic we're seeing heading into the city. And they'll become a choke point when the Danes arrive…they can either cross the ditch and fall about getting shot at, or storm the road…whilst getting shot at. It's a headache for them no matter what they try."

"And you are so very good at giving Danes a headache, Ulfcytel," chuckled Ælfweard, amused now. "What would you do without the joy of inconveniencing them? You'd be bored silly, I'd venture."

"There's always some bastard spoiling for a fight, Ælfweard," he replied, his smile fading. "If it wasn't the Danes again at our door, it would be somebody else. The Scots, the Welsh…Normans, perhaps, someday, and then somebody else after that. Everyone wants a piece of England, and everyone thinks they can have it. That's where me and the lad come in."

Ulfcytel had inclined his head towards Alaric with that last comment. There would have been a time when he'd have felt elated that the famous ealdorman had singled him out for approval like this. Now things were different. Alaric had gone through too much to feel buoyant at the fact Ulfcytel respected him. They'd fought together and saved each other from harm and likely death in their escape from Eastengle. Ulfcytel's inference that he and Alaric were serious about fighting this campaign was merely a statement of fact. Both of them knew all of England was at stake, and both of them would die fighting to defend her. That's all there was to it.

Alaric settled back in his chair, enjoying the newfound warmth of the hall. Despite his pragmatic attitude, he did still appreciate Ulfcytel in many ways. He'd taken the time to spar with him these past weeks to the point Alaric was far more confident of his fighting abilities now he had only one eye. He'd become a good friend also, showing himself to be patient and kind as well as generous with his loyalty. Alaric would never tell him that, of course. It wasn't his way, nor the way of any other man he knew. Real friendship was based on ties deeper than idle flattery or mutual affirmations. Men did not need to be coddled by other men. Respect was enough. It had been that way with Osmund. It would be that way forever.

"Am I to understand the archbishop is coming here to discuss the situation with us?" asked Alaric, wanting to get down to business rather than engage in small talk. He'd so far been frustrated in his hopes of meeting such a renowned figure as Ælfheah. His piety and humility were well known, and these were both traits Alaric admired intensely. Too often, Christians of any rank made a big show of their faith, as if to stress to others that they believed and thus gain prestige from the repeated mention of it. At its worst, he sometimes felt Christianity was in danger of becoming a cult of sycophancy, comprised of people whose sole act of faith was to repeat to one another that they loved Christ as a flimsy cover for the fact they didn't really care about much of anything.

Alaric felt isolated and alone in the face of such behaviour. He was a faithful man, desiring to come closer to God because it was both the natural and rational thing to do. But he felt that striving for the good and holy should not be limited to the mere formal observance of worship. Faith did not end with the physical boundaries of a church, nor the rising and falling of the sun on the last day of the week. Faith was a steady process that required the deepest commitment to the security and flourishing of one's neighbour, land, and country. Words of piety had to be an expression of that commitment, not something to merely repeat and then forget about when nobody was within earshot.

From what Alaric had heard, Archbishop Ælfheah was of like mind. He cared intensely about others, putting great effort into their spiritual and physical well-being. Yet he reputedly wasn't a soft man, and had no issue with calling a sin exactly what it was rather than seeking to validate people in their frailties or pride. He'd heard he didn't care for earthly trappings or prestige either, and had in the past rebuked the rich and lordly alike whenever their wealth and egos caused them to forget the common good. Alaric wondered if he'd ever clashed with the king. He probably had, but an Archbishop of Canterburie would be difficult to move against. Position and popularity could protect him, even from a man like Æthelred.

Two others strolled into the hall before anyone could answer Alaric's question, their cloaks heavy and sodden from the downpour outside. Osbert rose and helped them, hanging their cloaks off the back of several empty chairs adjacent to the hearth. Alaric took a good look at the newcomers, recognising the form and likeness of the priest who had just administered the sacraments back at the cathedral. He smiled at Alaric and took a seat next to Ælfweard, his gait slow and measured, although if that was from age he could not tell.

Another man accompanied him, dressed in a simple yet darker habit that signified his membership of a holy order. This one's face had a harsh edge to it, his eyes sharp and sparkling as he took in his present company with an excessively hard gaze. He was younger than the priest, his hair and beard still blessed with colour, a fact that unfortunately failed to detract from his otherwise jagged countenance. Alaric felt unsettled just from looking at him, feeling like he was scrutinising and judging them over their mere existence. He didn't like it. He hoped he had a good reason for being here tonight.

"You walk fast, young man," said the priest to Alaric. "I had noticed your prayers and had hoped to catch up with you on the way here. Sadly, I'm not as light on my feet as I once was."

"You wanted to discuss something with me?" Alaric asked, curious on why he'd followed him here, if indeed he had.

"Nothing in particular, although it's always nice to see newcomers in the cathedral. I know the ealdorman wished me to attend this meeting partly to make your acquaintance, so here I am. I'm glad to meet you, Alaric. My name is Ælfheah."

So this was the archbishop. There was no other reason for him to be here, since this meeting had been called partly for his benefit. Alaric was even more impressed now. A man of Ælfheah's standing could clothe himself in as many precious jewels and fine robes as he might fancy. Instead, he wore the simple attire of a priest, giving away nothing that would announce his rank and station as he went about his duties.

"I-I must apologise," Alaric stuttered, suddenly nervous. "I had no idea. I took you for a…"

"For a regular, standard, common-as-anything priest?" Ælfheah inquired, a mischievous twinkle playing across his faded green eyes. "That was the idea. When one partakes of the body and blood of Christ, all focus should be on Him and His bountiful mercy. My own apparent magnificence shouldn't enter into it."

"He's not wrong," Ulfcytel interrupted. "I once knew a priest who was so full of himself I could barely stand to hear his sermons. Empty talk it was, of no substance or passion, just a lot of waffle that seemed more about making people feel warm and fuzzy rather than actually doing or being anything. And that's all he cared about. That and how amazing he apparently was."

"And did you pray for this man?" Ælfheah asked quietly, his head nodding slightly at Ulfcytel's recollection. Perhaps he knew this priest he'd spoken of, or one like him. Clergymen who fit the description were not exactly uncommon, sadly.

"I admit I did not." Alaric fancied he saw Ulfcytel's cheeks flush a little redder with that confession. That was something. He imagined there were very few people in the world who could make him do that.

"Something to think about, perhaps," the archbishop mused, his manner remaining warm and sincere. His proposal was gentle yet entirely correct. It was always so very easy to criticise others, especially in their absence. Perhaps the criticism was well-founded. But it didn't excuse you from failing to wish them well and pray for a change of heart.

"Shall we get started?" Ælfweard asked, his eagerness suggesting he wanted this meeting to begin on topic rather than stray off into a discussion on theology.

"By all means," the archbishop conceded. "I know our friends here have endured much in bringing us news that our city may soon come under attack. Let us talk about how we might prevail in such circumstances."

"Firstly, I have additional information on the enemy's whereabouts," Ælfweard began. "The Danes didn't stop once they overran Cantebrigie but carried on west, burning as they went. Last word is that Northantone is now surrounded. We don't know how long they can hold out, but the reported size of the enemy force suggests they have little hope without reinforcements."

"What can we do?" asked Ælfheah, "and dare I presume it foolish to ask if the king will be leading an army to confront them?"

Both Alaric and Ulfcytel stirred in their seats, the ealdorman looking like he'd had to stifle a laugh he otherwise would have had no shame in releasing had the archbishop not been present. There was no point in going over Æthelred's recent conduct. All of England was now aware he'd done absolutely nothing to defend Eastengle. All of England was also aware of his latest tax proposal. Ælfweard had shown them the letter he'd received from Lundenburg. An absurd amount of coin had been demanded, likely to bankrupt much of the country, assuming similar amounts had been requested elsewhere. Alaric wished he could be sure it really was to pay for a new army. Something didn't add up.

"My Lord Ulfcytel and the dutiful Alaric are of the opinion the king will likely not march to Northantone's aid," said Ælfweard diplomatically. "I'm afraid to say that I, too, doubt we'll be seeing any decisive action against Thorkell. The king has made his position clear enough. We are to pay the amount demanded so he can raise another army. Unfortunately…"

"Unfortunately, you can't afford it." Alaric didn't consider it good form to interrupt others. He appreciated Ælfweard, but the man placed too much emphasis on fine words when a straight answer was enough.

"No, we can't afford it," he confirmed, looking a little flustered at Alaric's interjection. "I told the archbishop of the king's demands as soon as I received his letter. That was several weeks before you and the ealdorman here came to be with us. What I wanted to mention to you all is that I received a response from Lundenburg just yesterday to my request for clarification on how to provide the king with the revenues he requires."

"Oh?" Ulfcytel murmured, his huge grey eyebrows arching up towards his bald scalp in curiosity. "You told the king you couldn't pay and he's…what? Gone and told you to think of a way so he doesn't have to?"

"Somewhat, but this letter is a little odd. I don't think it's been dictated by Æthelred, or if it has, there's a change in him I've not seen previously. He sounds… menacing."

"What exactly did he say?" Ulfcytel asked again. "Do you have it with you? May I see it?"

Ælfweard fumbled about in his cloak for a few moments, his face troubled. He eventually retrieved a single sheet of folded parchment from somewhere, passing it gingerly across the table into Ulfcytel's trembling paw. Alaric hadn't noticed him shake like that before. That was not a good sign.

Ulfcytel steadied himself well enough and commenced reading, his brow creased in concentration. Whatever he'd read had not impressed him, yet he had no immediate comment, instead passing the letter on to the archbishop. Ælfheah read it swiftly and handed it to Alaric, his expression largely neutral were it not for the hint of worry in his expressive eyes.

Alaric glanced over the parchment, impressed by the precision of the flowing text he presumed had been written by one of Æthelred's scribes. Alaric didn't know the king personally and so could not judge his state of mind, but the message was frankly bizarre, threatening to arrest and "suitably chastise" Ælfweard if he didn't "enact measures to ensure Canterburie pays its share towards the heregeld."

"Has he threatened you before?" Alaric asked, raising a quizzical eyebrow over his single remaining eye.

"Not like that, no," Ælfweard answered. "There was a time when I thought I had his confidence. I must have, otherwise I would not hold the position I do now. But I didn't expect him to react like this. I didn't actually refuse to pay. I explained we can't, unless we tax the general population so much what little trade we receive dries up altogether. Nobody is going to want to sell their produce here if they know our purses are all empty."

"Winter is also something we must think on," Ælfheah said quietly, his hands clasped in front of him to rest neatly on the table. "We've got a lot of desperate people here from Eastengle. Seeing the city come together to provide for them has been heartening, but if we hand over the kind of money the king demands, we'll have nothing left to cater for emergencies. A food shortage is very possible, especially if we come under siege."

"Then don't pay him," stated Ulfcytel, having suddenly taken to scratching his beard as if an ant or some such had snuck into the thicket of hair to call it home. "There's no indication this army tax is for an actual army anyway," he added. "We know he's fond of paying invaders to leave us alone, not that it works, and we also know from the captive we took in Eastengle that the Danes expect him to eventually hand over God knows how much coin to them. And even if he does raise a force, he'll just hand it over to one of his incompetents rather than lead it himself. This tax isn't what it claims to be, mark my words well."

"Why wouldn't he have you lead it, Ulfcytel?" asked Archbishop Ælfheah. "You seem good at that sort of thing, judging from your past endeavours. I'm assuming there's a reason why you never received reinforcements from Lundenburg before you met Thorkell in battle?"

"If there was, I'm afraid I can't say for certain what it could be," admitted Ulfcytel sadly. "Like Ælfweard here, the king once thought well of me. We were friends. He gave me his daughter as wife. I thought we had good days ahead. But he's always been erratic. Insecure. This is what happens when a boy doesn't have a strong father figure in his life and instead has a domineering bitch for a mother. It's an open secret that Queen Ælfthryth dealt with her husband's death by smothering and controlling Æthelred so that he didn't know which way was up and which was down. We're paying for it now."

This was fascinating to Alaric. He'd heard the stories that the queen had plotted to murder Æthelred's older half-brother, Edward, so that Æthelred himself could ascend to the throne. Alaric didn't know if she was actually responsible for Edward's demise, but she seemed a reasonable suspect. He knew also that Ælfthryth had gone on to wield a tremendous amount of power after the dark deed was done, forcing the young Æthelred to endure his mother as a kind of regent. Alaric wasn't sure how that could have shaped his personality, but he would think it likely he'd had a troubled childhood. Lonely, perhaps, without a father or brothers, and also frightening, if what he'd heard about Queen Ælfthryth had any truth to it. She wouldn't have killed one boy just to see her own escape from grasp. She'd have been hard on him. Too hard.

Fear coupled with isolation. Alaric could see how that might make a man erratic, indecisive, paranoid even. There could be anger also, if his mother had sought to control and perhaps mistreat him. He knew the king could get angry. Everyone did. Perhaps with good and virtuous men around him, he might be different. It was something to think about. Maybe Æthelred's real problem was that he simply needed a friend. Past trauma coupled with the pressures of power and responsibility could crush a man.

"I'll admit, I'm old enough to suspect the king may not have had the upbringing every child deserves," said the archbishop, his tone heavy with regret. "I don't think it's unwarranted to suspect he may bear a great many wounds on his heart, wounds that have never fully closed. Given that his reign has proven…troubled, shall we say…the pressure could be getting to him more than ever. That might account for any sudden changes in his behaviour."

"I don't disagree, but what do we do in the here and now?" Ælfweard asked. "What if he does come to Canterburie to arrest me? I'm caught between a rock and a hard place. Either I ruin the city by paying the taxes he demands, or we face his wrath coming down upon us. What do I do?"

Ælfweard looked genuinely troubled. He was in a difficult situation, Alaric could see that, one that wouldn't be helped by any brazen displays of defiance. Alaric also wondered if he'd bothered to inform the king that Ulfcytel was now with him in Canterburie. It would be interesting to gauge his reaction then. Surely he would be pleased to hear his son-in-law had survived? Perhaps not. They needed a solution, though. Alaric thought he might have one.

"Tell the king what we know," he proposed, "and write to him again to tell him you have it on good authority that Thorkell plans to attack the city and that we need all of our present resources. Tell him Ulfcytel is alive, and that he obtained information on Thorkell's intentions from a captured Scandinavian noble. He'll be compelled to act. This isn't just some village under threat here. This is Canterburie. How would it look for him to continue pestering us over a tax dispute when the home of Saint Augustine is under threat?"

"That's not a bad idea, Alaric," Ulfcytel concurred, having just sat down again after rising to pour himself another cup of mead from the keg he'd stashed next to the hearth. "I am worried, though, how he may react to the news that I yet live. For some time now, even before Hringmere, I've felt like the king has grown more and more distant from me. I think we can all agree there was at least some reason he wouldn't lift a finger to help me in Eastengle. I'd venture he's convinced I'm best removed from whatever game he thinks he's playing."

"But what can he do, assuming he does actually mean you harm?" Alaric asked before draining what little was left in his own cup. "If the Danes are now besieging Northantone, he'll need every man ready to defend Lundenburg should Thorkell head south. He can't afford to send a force to Canterburie. It would require thousands of men to fight their way through the walls. He can't spare that. And can we be sure he despises you enough to even try?"

Ulfcytel again rose from his chair, taking Alaric's cup from him and refilling it from his keg. He had a slight limp now, the wound he'd taken at Gipeswic ensuring he'd never be quite the same in perhaps more ways than one. Whilst his torn flesh had been knitted shut, he didn't seem as sure on his feet anymore, his already sizeable weight proving difficult to bear. All were silent in thought as Ulfcytel wandered back over to gift Alaric with a full cup, the old man patting him affectionately on the shoulder when he reached out to take it.

"You are correct," he said softly. "So by all means, let's do as you say. Inform the king that I am alive and what we know of Thorkell's plans. But remain guarded. It's true that Æthelred won't have the men to take Canterburie by force, either to get to me or obtain his much-desired heregeld. But just remember how he dispatched the Ealdorman Eadric to us. Remember how he misled us all, only to vanish once the damage was done. Æthelred will have other means of settling scores that don't require him to send an army to do it for him."

"Are you suggesting the king might attempt to have you killed?" Ælfhcah had learned something from Alaric. He'd gotten straight to the point. "That sounds like quite a proposal," he continued grimly, "even for one as troubled as Æthelred. You're his son-in-law, remember? The man must have some lines he won't cross."

"I am," Ulfcytel said, ambling from Alaric's side to resume his seat. "Yet sometimes I wonder if he's the same man he was when he allowed me to marry my Wulfhild. I cannot get over the fact he left us to fight and die unaided… my guts tell me he views me as some kind of threat now…and that his wish was to have Thorkell kill me so he wouldn't have to."

"But you gave Svienn Forkbeard the fight of his life not so many years ago!" Ælfweard objected, still finding the notion that the king would seek to kill a man like Ulfcytel difficult to swallow. "There was talk that even the Danes admitted it had been the hardest battle they'd fought in England in decades. Why would the king want you dead after such a service?"

"I have my suspicions as to why, Ælfweard, and I'll tell you now I do not believe it any coincidence that Æthelred's attitude towards me started to change soon after a certain Eadric became Ealdorman of Mierċe. He's had the king's ear ever since…and has used every opportunity to pour poison right into it."

Both Ælfweard and the archbishop made no attempt at reply. Everyone knew that the reign of King Æthelred had been both long and difficult. What was less well known was how Eadric had managed to bring himself into the king's inner circle after such a relatively short time in power in Mierċe. Alaric was at a loss to explain it. But he respected Ulfcytel enough to take him seriously when he voiced his suspicions.

Of course, Alaric had met Eadric back at Hringmere, but he still didn't know much about him. Nobody did. And that could be a real problem. The man was a mystery, and for one of such prominence to remain an enigma to most others usually meant he was intentionally trying to cover his tracks. That meant trouble. Alaric would make sure their paths crossed again. He had some explaining to do about what exactly had happened that night they'd attacked Thorkell's camp. He needed answers. For the sake of his men. For the sake of Osmund.

"So we're agreed?" Ulfcytel asked, his voice breaking the heavy silence. "Ælfweard will respond to the king's demands by informing him of the threat now facing Canterburie, and how we learned of it?"

"Yes, I will do as you say," Ælfweard confirmed. "Yet I will stress that the possibility of the king using some kind of subterfuge against you worries me. This is a big city. We receive a lot of visitors, even now, and word of your presence here is spreading. Just yesterday morning, we had about a dozen warriors arrive at the gate, declaring their allegiance to you and what's left of your army. An assassin could easily infiltrate such a group of men to get close to you."

"That is a good point," agreed Alaric, turning to address Ulfcytel directly. "We had wanted to spread the news of your arrival here to rally people to the city's defence. But if we actively send word to the king that you're here…when I spoke before, I felt it unlikely he'd risk taking action overtly. But he doesn't have to be overt. He could send anyone, claiming to be anyone, in order to do something terrible. The possibility of infiltration is all too real."

"It is, but to hell with him!" Ulfcytel declared, both the archbishop and Ælfweard flinching in discomfort. "The situation is too severe for half-measures. I may die tonight, choking on this mead, or slip and fall when rising from bed to empty my bladder. But that will be just one man dead. If Thorkell takes this city, he'll not only brutalise its people, he'll desecrate one of the holiest sites in all of England. That is what should be our main focus. Send the letter to the king, Ælfweard. If he still has half a mind intact, he'll see the danger we face and come to our aid. If he does not…we'll deal with whatever happens as it happens."

Alaric could tell Ulfcytel had grown tired of talking. He was initially willing to raise concerns himself on the wisdom of sending word to the capital, but his patience for discussion had limits, especially when so much else was already at stake. Alaric agreed they should focus on the bigger picture, that being the defence of the Holy City, but Ulfcytel's last outburst was a little reckless. The threat of an assassin's blade was a severe one. It should be treated as such.

"I concur with what you have said," Alaric began, his voice deliberately measured and controlled. "But it would help put my mind at ease if you allowed me to organise and lead a new personal guard for you. You need to know you are more than just a single man, Ulfcytel. With Oswy dead, you are one of the few remaining living symbols this land has of past glories. Your presence here has already begun to galvanise the people into thinking that we might not just endure, but perhaps win. We can't afford to lose that. You understand this, I think."

The ealdorman nodded slowly, his expression thoughtful. A strange calm descended on the room, the gentle crackling of the fire putting Alaric more in the mood for silent introspection than grand strategy. The rain continued to pour down outside, its muffled hammering giving him a sense of warmth and safety as he sat protected within the confines of the hall. Ælfweard, Osbert, and Ælfheah must have felt the same, the three of them looking relaxed and almost content in the flickering firelight. The sound of Ulfcytel's next words was similarly temperate, despite the severity of the subject.

"In truth, it's likely that even if the king believes that Canterburie is threatened, he won't send us much help. But we have to try. I won't let whatever ill will he harbours towards me get in the way of fighting this war, and I also won't deny him the opportunity to at least learn of our situation so he can perhaps make the right decision. Think about it. At Hringmere, it was my army and my lands that were at stake. Canterburie is different. And even if he refuses us or takes action against us…word will continue to spread of our noble task and the terrible outcome we'll face if we fail. Good men will continue to flock to our banners. That's what we need now. Good men with noble hearts and sharp iron."

Ælfheah was now smiling gently at Ulfcytel, apparently placated by his admittedly sober and clear-minded evaluation. Ælfweard still looked a touch uncertain, but Alaric had a feeling that was probably more to do with the decision to avoid the tax issue in favour of focusing on the politics of how to handle an angry Æthelred. Numbers were his forte, he suspected, hence why he'd been appointed reeve to such a place of import. He also seemed like a gentle and honest man. War and intrigue would be way outside of his comfort zone.

"Which reminds me," said Alaric, "just how many men do we have? We arrived here with just over two hundred equipped fighting men. Combine that with the city's garrison and those at least capable of bearing arms…what kind of an army will we have when Thorkell arrives?"

"I can answer that," Leofwine announced confidently, the man having been silent until now in the face of their weighty deliberations. "Combining the men who came with you and those we already had in service, I'd say we have just under five hundred warriors, all of them equipped with the usual assortment of mail, helms, spears, and axes…if we muster those men that can be mustered and properly equipped that number will triple, but it goes without saying these won't be the best quality soldiers. Of course, with our predicament, we have no choice."

"That's a good number," Ulfcytel mused. "We'll keep most of the levies in reserve. The square outside the cathedral will make for a good staging area. The men you have presently, we'll space out along the walls. I'll lead half of my veterans; Alaric will command the remainder. We'll ensure we're placed at critical points and able to move as needed. That way, we'll have two highly experienced bodies of men, mobile and able to charge into the thick of it where the fighting is fiercest. Make no mistake. When the attack comes, we'll be outnumbered, and Thorkell won't be deterred by our walls. This battle will be decided by stout hearts first and strong arms second. Which is where you come in, archbishop."

"Me?" Ælfheah asked, surprised. "The last time I took up arms was when I shooed a mouse away from my pantry, and I felt bad about that after. You're not expecting me to deck myself out in those metal scales you wear and fight atop the wall?"

Ulfcytel laughed, the sound booming from his heaving chest. Alaric was glad to hear it. He'd been so troubled since his recent brush with death. He and the archbishop should spend more time together. They'd all need spiritual direction for what lay ahead. The fact Ælfheah had a sense of humour was a delightful bonus.

"No, my friend," Ulfcytel said through a broad grin, his mirth subsiding so the table had thankfully ceased shaking. "I would never intentionally put you in harm's way. What I mean is I'd like you to pay attention to your sermons. Make sure everyone knows what's at stake. But not in a mournful way. Remind the people that there is room for fury in righteousness. Remind them of the place they fight for. Remind them they have an opportunity here to take up arms against a people who would see us wiped from God's own earth."

"In all seriousness, I had a feeling you'd say something like that," Ælfheah admitted, his smile almost as broad as Ulfcytel's. "I can do as you ask. I would have done it anyway, even if you'd never mentioned it. The Church is a hospital, in a way, and so I will endeavour to help heal our people of any doubts and fears. When the time comes, they'll know what they are fighting for."

The intense-looking man who had up until now kept silent at the archbishop's side suddenly spoke up. Alaric had wondered why he was so quiet, surmising he was here to aid the archbishop if he required refreshment or some such. Alaric wished he'd remained silent for the duration of their meeting. He hadn't heard such demoralising bilge in some time.

"We should be calling upon them to repent," he declared, his voice painfully sharp, raw even, in contrast to the more personable Ælfheah. "Thorkell is an instrument of God, sent here to punish England for its sinfulness. We would be better served by telling the pe…"

"What is the meaning of this?!" Ulfcytel cut in, surprised and outraged at the sudden interjection. "Whoever you are, you are to refrain from uttering such deluded gibberish in my presence, or indeed anywhere else!"

Ulfcytel's tone left no room for ambiguity. He was on his feet now, his hands placed palms down on the table, his ferocious gaze falling upon the unfortunate doomsayer. Just as Alaric thought the archbishop would attempt to defuse the tension, the man dared speak again, unperturbed by the prospect of angering Ulfcytel further. Alaric was speechless. It was bad enough to talk this kind of nonsense, but to display such brazen disrespect was another thing entirely.

"You have no authority over me, Ulfcytel. You may be a master of war, but I am a man of God, and I'm telling you that God is deservedly scourging England for its many sins. We deserve this beca…"

"Leave this room," ordered Ulfcytel, his voice a low, menacing growl. "I don't care who you think you are, or what madness you've convinced yourself of. Get out of my hall. Now."

"I fear that is for the best, abbot," Ælfheah urged, placing a hand on the man's forearm to emphasise the point. "I should not have asked you to accompany me after the difficult day you've had. Go and rest now, and we shall speak of this again tomorrow."

For a moment, Alaric thought he might defy both of them. Fortunately, whatever recklessness had taken hold seemed to gradually ebb, and the deluded fool instead rose from his seat. Alaric watched him go, noting the flash of defiance on his face upon breaking eye contact with Ulfcytel. He parted company from them without a word, departing from the otherwise comfortable hall like nothing had taken place, the sound of the rain outside intensifying briefly as the outer doors opened and then closed behind him.

"I must apologise for Abbot Ælfmær," Ælfheah announced with a sorrowful shake of his head. "He does not see the situation as you or I might. The Church is divided on how to view the current crisis. Ælfmær shares the opinion of our Archbishop Wulfstan in that we are being punished for our great sins."

"And how can anyone possibly know that?" Osbert suddenly demanded, his flushed cheeks suggesting he'd been very much disturbed by Ælfmær's outburst. "Is God in the habit of announcing he intends to punish men, good and evil alike, by unleashing misery and bloodshed upon them? How is that just?"

"A point well taken, young man," Ælfheah conceded, "and yet you could say the Bible alludes to this kind of problem…a faithless people may find much taken from them."

"This is all very fascinating," Ulfcytel smouldered, his temper still hot, "but I won't submit to the idea that God has willed the merciless savagery we now contend with. God sent His only begotten Son to save mankind, not condemn it. It's staggering that some could think He'd just forget all that and decide to unleash thousands of bloodthirsty bastards on us just to watch us suffer."

"I understand, and I don't disagree," said Ælfheah, "and yet I will say we would do well to pay attention to our faults. We are not a nation of saints. Heathen practices still continue in this land. Men betray one another just as they readily lie whenever it suits them. We turn against our brother and put him in chains to make him work for our own enrichment, with neither his consent nor welfare in mind. Injustice and sin are very much a fact of life for us, even in more peaceful times. We all need to repent and take a different path. Thorkell's bloodletting has just made that more obvious."

"But why even claim God is somehow directing the will of a beast like Thorkell?" Alaric asked, still a little numb in the wake of Ælfmær's ill-chosen words. He found it hard to believe he was an abbot, and of a monastery as esteemed as the one they had here in Canterburie, no less! He'd not visited the abbey yet, but after what he'd witnessed tonight, he had no intention of doing so. He had better things to do than argue with a lunatic, and there was no doubting that Ælfmær was one of those.

"It's one thing to accept we are all sinners," Alaric continued, thinking it might do to explain himself further. "Yet it's something else entirely to claim God is actively directing foreigners to murder and brutalise us as punishment. What do we learn from that? That we're to obey God out of abject terror? Was that the message of Christ?"

"You are correct, my friend," admitted the archbishop, a gentle smile again on his face as he beheld Alaric. "Abbot Ælfmær is just voicing the opinions of a certain element in the Church and within the city that, in my view, are taking things too far. Neither Thorkell nor King Svienn are instruments of God. They are murderers who will ultimately be judged by God for that very reason. But I will say our fortunes in this conflict would be very different if we started acting more like the Christians we claim to be. I'm sure you'll agree England has long suffered from treacherous, self-serving men who have repeatedly sold their people out for personal gain…even in the face of foreign invasion."

Everyone could agree with Ælfheah on that score. It was indeed entirely true that England's supposed "nobles" were often a truly venomous bunch, forgetting their obligations to their fellow countrymen as they looked for ways to serve only themselves. Many, many times now, it had seemed like their efforts to resist the Northmen were being hampered by their own leadership, a problem which extended far beyond the personal shortcomings of King Æthelred.

Perhaps the two problems were intertwined. Perhaps the unreliability and treachery of Æthelred's court was serving to further destabilise the king as he staggered from crisis after crisis. Maybe what the king needed was to be removed from bad company and those who sought to manipulate him for their own ends. Alaric once again couldn't shake the notion that he might not be the real villain in all this. The root cause of their problems lay deeper, far beyond the misfortunes and personal demons of their ill-advised king. He would give this some thought.

The rest of their meeting passed without incident, the subject of God's will and England's many shortcomings finally put to one side. Much of their deliberations were now fixed on the issue of feeding the city's inhabitants, especially since the flow of refugees was unlikely to slow with the enemy still devastating the countryside. After some discussion, they all finally agreed on the feasibility of importing food from France. This had been done before, so Ælfweard said, and the word was the sea route remained relatively clear and funds very much available since they'd already agreed to defy the king's heregeld. If all went well, they'd be able to stockpile enough food to resist a siege for months, even with the added burden of feeding an enlarged population. That would require acting now, though. Nobody could know when the passage to France might be closed, either by poor weather or Norse predation at sea.

The military situation was also optimistic. Whilst Ælfweard was at times sceptical of Ulfcytel's notion of rallying "all of England" to defend the city, the archbishop was more supportive, arguing it made sense to publicise their situation as much as they could to force Thorkell into one single, unwinnable battle at his expense. Ælfweard was a man of numbers, Alaric thought, and didn't seem particularly gifted when it came to either military or political matters. Fortunately, Ulfcytel was, and with Ælfheah's support, they were able to win the reeve over.

They eventually agreed to send out another general summons to every scir still intact, calling all men who were capable of fighting to rally to the city's defence. They had admittedly done this several weeks ago, yet the returns had been modest, with just a small trickle of fighting men travelling to join them. Perhaps time was all that was needed. Once word spread and Thorkell actually started bearing down on the city, Alaric imagined more people would see the severity of the situation and respond. He'd pray on it.

They'd finally run out of things to discuss, Ælfheah and Ulfcytel together confessing a desire to get some rest and await further news. Alaric offered to accompany Ælfheah on his way back to the cathedral, fearing some mishap if the archbishop was left to wander the streets on his own. Ælfheah agreed, and they said their goodbyes before exiting the hall into the rain-swept night.

Eamon remained on watch by the entrance. He cut a sorrowful figure as he gazed out into the darkness, his torch somehow still lit despite the deluge thundering down around him. Alaric paused to assure him he'd return soon to have him relieved. He felt guilty. They'd all sat inside discussing in comfort and warmth whilst Eamon had endured out here, silent and alone in the blackness. Alaric would really have to get him an ale at some point.

They hurried through the streets, Alaric and Ælfheah, both men pulling the hoods up from their cloaks for the sake of protection against the chill downpour. Alaric regretted it was too noisy to talk, the sound of raindrops hammering on stone and earth proving an impediment to any conversation he might otherwise have liked to have. They were about halfway back to the cathedral when Alaric sensed something was wrong, as if some presence had suddenly drawn closer yet dared not show itself. He wasn't a superstitious man, but any warrior worth their salt took their instincts seriously, especially when sensing danger. It had saved his life before. It would save his life tonight.

Something suddenly lunged at him from the mouth of an alley. He jerked his head back and to the right, the edge of the long seax sailing past so closely Alaric could reach out to grab his unknown assailant by the wrist. He did so, hauling him out into the street, the archbishop staggering forward in an effort to escape the unexpected tussle.

Alaric kicked at his opponent's legs and twisted his arm, causing him to drop his weapon and slump to one knee. He felt a sting of pain as he was struck in the groin, his attacker responding fast by smashing his left fist up and between his legs. He fell forwards, gasping for breath, and landed on top of this mystery fighter, their features still hidden by a dark, rain-sodden cowl that clung tightly to their face.

Time was of the essence in any fight, and this was no exception. When suddenly attacked, you didn't have the luxury of knowing how many opponents you may be facing, especially when fighting in conditions where visibility was less than optimal. Canterburie at night certainly fit that description, even without this unrelenting downpour.

It was for that reason Alaric knew he had to act quickly. This man he now struggled with was almost certainly not operating alone. If he had accomplices, and it was incredibly unlikely he didn't, they'd be moving to assist him with all haste. It was thus imperative Alaric deal with him now and get back to his feet, sword in hand. He'd then be in his element. Outnumbered or no, few could match his skill with a blade, especially when using the masterpiece the Aetheling Æthelstan had gifted him.

In that spirit, Alaric ignored several more punches to his ribs, instead bringing himself up to straddle his opponent and unleash several savage blows down towards his face. He then gripped him around the temples and began forcefully lifting his skull up and then down so it impacted, hard, upon the wet stones beneath them. It made an awful sound, the fluid "crack" of skull on rock sending a shiver up his spine, but he persisted, his now dazed foe proving too disorientated to resist. He repeated the action several more times, only relenting when his opponent went limp. Whether he was dead or yet living, he could not tell.

He was just standing up when something hit him from behind. He tumbled forward, trying to use the momentum of the impact in a controlled way to create some space between himself and whoever had struck him. He was only partly successful, fearing for a moment he might barrel into Ælfheah whilst he struggled to regain his balance. When Alaric finally managed to right himself, he could see him up ahead, the old clergyman looking like he'd run away from the fighting to get help. Another figure was moving down towards him from further up the street, this one also cloaked and hooded in the face of the night's rain. It was moving rapidly, evidently intent on closing the distance with the archbishop as quickly as possible. That didn't bode well.

Alaric spun around, aware that whoever had struck him previously was no doubt hoping to follow through with another attack. His fears were well justified. There were now four men before him, all attired in similarly dark cowls and robes as the man he'd just incapacitated, each also bearing a wicked-looking seax. The closest one predictably made another move towards Alaric, stepping forward to deliver a piercing jab at his left shoulder. Alaric had to finish this quickly. If these were assassins, it was more than probable the archbishop was their target. He had to get back to him before the approaching figure could accost him.

His attacker was quite skilled, and almost able to compensate for Alaric's sudden feint to the right. Had he been a little quicker or carrying a shield, things may have been different. Instead, he was caught out on his unprotected side, his seax sailing safely over Alaric's left shoulder whilst Alaric pivoted to deliver a brutal two-handed swipe to his lower ribs. They gave way, the sharp cracking sound audible even over the thundering deluge. The assassin staggered and fell, the deep, sloshing puddles around him surging red as he bled out upon the stones.

The others tensed, unsure how to overcome this man who'd already dispatched two of their brethren. Alaric put their hesitation to good use. He spun around and began running towards the archbishop, his hood falling back from his head and the rain stinging his face. He could see Ælfheah up ahead, his form hunched and feeble and the unknown figure towering over him. Alaric had rarely seen anyone of such size, their stature and attire giving the impression they were some kind of vengeful spirit come to punish the archbishop for some long-overlooked crime. He saw the blade in its hand. A good sword. He didn't have a moment to waste.

He let out a roar whilst he pounded down the street, bringing his own blade up and around in a looping arc to connect with the figure's head. It stepped back and away with remarkable agility, the precision of its movements suggesting whoever this was had been well-trained in combat and avoidance. Alaric righted himself to duck and slide under any counterblow, positioning himself between the figure and Ælfheah. For some reason, it made no attempt to attack him, but Alaric could hear approaching footsteps. The figure's surviving three companions had come to finish the job. Alaric gritted his teeth and prepared himself. He'd kill the more skilled opponent first before finishing his friends. There was no time like the present. He stepped forward to attack.

"Alaric!"

That voice. Familiar. Very familiar. Confusion and indecision seeped into his mind, tempering his bloodlust. The figure had spoken. It knew who he was, but there was no time to talk, for their original three attackers had almost reached them. Alaric turned to face them, raising his sword up into a high guard. He then began moving backwards. The archbishop grunted when they collided, but he soon got the message, recognising that Alaric wanted him to fall back whilst he shielded him from harm. The cathedral was not too far off. If he could get Ælfheah inside, he'd be safe.

Then the unexpected happened. The tall figure raised its sword and launched itself at Alaric's foes. Its form was perfect, severing an arm and then the jugular of the first man to approach. The other two circled around, moving quickly to take up positions on either side of it, hoping for some opening they might exploit. Alaric rushed into the contest, catching one of them off-guard with a quick thrust towards his chest. He deflected it with his own weapon, yet wasn't prepared for Alaric's forward momentum, instead toppling over backwards when Alaric twisted his weight to allow his shoulder to careen into his jaw.

Alaric hadn't seen what happened to the last man, occupied as he was with finishing his own opponent with a downward swipe to the head. When he turned, he saw a body lying motionless at the mystery figure's feet, the neck twisted at a peculiar angle. The figure then looked straight at him, causing Alaric to instinctively raise his blade into a defensive posture. It seemed to gaze at him for a moment from beneath its cloak, its hands then rising to tear at its hood and reveal a face he'd not thou...

"Cenric?!"

"Yes, young master, it is I," Cenric half-shouted, struggling to make himself heard over the rain. He'd removed his hood entirely now to show off his sodden locks and bedraggled beard, the rest of his face leaving Alaric with the distinct impression he'd been without proper sleep for some time. He'd done well for one so exhausted. Alaric had never been able to best him in training. He could see why tonight.

"I heard you were here," Cenric added, stepping closer to both Alaric and the bemused archbishop. His eyes betrayed him. He was troubled, emotional, a rare sight for a man such as he. Whatever he was about to say, Alaric had a feeling he wasn't going to like it. He wasn't wrong in his premonitions.

"It's your family, Alaric, it's your father and brother... it's Æva and young Brandon...Eadric of Mierce came with an army. He took them. He took them away. He took them to the king."

XV

The horde was vast beyond counting, stretching out and across his view atop the hill like a human tide. A great scar now marred the landscape, the valley beyond appearing as if some terrible force of nature had swept through it to blight the very earth as it went. If only that were the case. Storms and floods were one thing. What he faced here was far worse. If there was a more fearsome spectacle to lay eyes on than this host, he didn't want to know of it.

Truth be told, he'd seen some of them last year when they'd besieged Lundenburg. But it had been different then. He'd had the capital's high walls to protect him; a boon that had ensured the resulting battle had been won for the English. It was another matter now. There was nothing between his people and the enemy. They were right there, standing in their multitudes, as grim and silent as the dead and yet more than capable of being stirred into shocking violence at a moment's notice. He knew this. The state of his country was evidence of that.

The Northmen had drawn themselves up into ranks facing outwards from the wide, sloping mouth of the valley, the strange, fearsome beasts depicted on their banners appearing almost as unsettling as the battle-hardened marauders bearing them. Every man here was an experienced killer, drawn from the ranks of numerous vicious warbands from across Scandinavia. All had braved the dangers of the sea to reach this country for one singular purpose: to seize its wealth. Taking life was just a means to that end, and he had no doubt they would continue to reduce his lands to absolute ruin if they thought a single coin remained unplundered.

He'd initially thought there were easier ways to prevent this than the physical exertions of battle. The enemy's greed could work in his favour as a means to stop the bloodletting so that more civilised options might be considered. If they wanted wealth, he could give them wealth. It had worked in the past. Yet things had not been so simple with this lot, and he was starting to doubt whether they ever would be. Looking at them now left him wondering if there was anything that could truly sate their appetite for plunder. He suspected many in their ranks relished the prospect of violence for its own sake, holding renown as a warrior to be as valuable a commodity as silver or gold. From their perspective, they could probably take whatever they wanted, regardless of what was discussed here. He wasn't sure if they were mistaken in that belief.

He'd first spotted them an hour ago, his stomach twisting with dread at the thunderous sound of their marching well before they'd come into view. It had taken some time for their entire force to become visible, so vast was its size, and he'd at first feared they might attack, for the Northmen had let out a chilling howl as they clapped eyes on his men. Just as he'd been convinced they were about to charge, they'd settled down, instead forming themselves into a broad, defensive position commanding much of the flat plain they now stood on. He'd never been so relieved in his life.

It hadn't lasted. Although not immediately hostile, the Norse presence was grinding on his nerves, making him agitated and uncertain on how to proceed. He'd seen many a warrior or assembled host in his time, but these men were a world apart, possessing a certain animal ferocity that unsettled the nerves. There was an emptiness there, making him wonder if the frozen harshness of their native land had gradually leached the souls from their bodies, leaving them barren and vacant when it came to anything other than avarice and violence.

If his own men felt the same, they gave no sign. That made him feel better, at least, and yet he couldn't shake the possibility they were secretly as nervous as he was. The sooner they could finish their task here and head home, the better. He'd been away from his wife and children for too long. He suspected he wasn't alone in harbouring such sentiments. What each man did here, they did for those waiting at home. It would always be thus when it came to a noble cause.

The infamous Thorkell had finally decided to respond to his summons. He'd sent out a rider as soon as it had become clear the enemy force was not looking to attack, re-stating his offer for the fearsome warlord to come parley. He'd agreed, sending his man back to him with the news he would be coming to discuss matters and that his brother, of all people, would be with him. He wondered if he should feel honoured. There were not many men who could get Thorkell's attention, let alone have him come treat with them in the company of his own kin. Good things could come of this.

He thought he could see him now, or somebody who might be him, moving through the ranks, their fellow Northmen parting around them with bowed heads and solemn nods. They'd be heading towards them soon, up the slope to the summit of the hill they were ensconced on. It was here they'd decide the future of England. He hoped and prayed he would be up to the task. He hoped and prayed history would think well of him and judge him in accordance with the difficulties he'd faced. He didn't want to be remembered as just another ruler who'd lost his throne.

King Æthelred looked back the way he'd come. He'd had a dozen of his elite hearthweru accompany him up here, including his two royal protectors who, as usual, stood on either side of him. They all looked magnificent in the otherwise grey, sombre light, an armoured vigil of blade and spear assembled 'neath the fluttering, white dragon banner of Saint Edmund.

Eadric was also with him, looking strangely potent in his armour as he gazed out and down towards the enemy force. Ecgberht, the commander of Æthelred's troops, stood next to him, appearing as serious as any man of his station should in such a situation as this. Æthelred was glad to have him. He was a dependable man, a great warrior, and a close friend of his sons, Æthelstan and Edmund. Their characters were similar in more ways than one. They all despised Eadric too.

Æthelred hoped that he cut a similarly impressive figure as his companions. He didn't feel it. His legs still ached following his ascent up the hill, and his crown also rested uneasily upon his head, uncomfortable and peculiarly heavy whilst he stood already burdened in full battle dress. He knew it was necessary, for a king had to look the part in any negotiation, but it bothered him how his body was failing him. He wasn't a young man at all, but it was yet another worry to contend with. The sword at his hip was at least some comfort. Aching limbs or no, he was sure he remembered how to use it well enough.

His blade wasn't the only leverage he had. Back down at the base of the hill was his army, or what passed for an army in his sorry circumstances. It wasn't much; a few thousand or so soldiers arranged in solid, disciplined lines, the men peering out towards the enemy from behind thick wooden shields. Æthelred knew the Northmen could overpower their position if they wished, but they would still lose men doing it. He'd hoped they'd at least see there was more to be gained from talking. He was glad it now seemed to be the case.

Eadric had long assured him that Thorkell was receptive to negotiation. He'd been right on this before, speaking directly with the man himself to ensure a possible cessation of hostilities once sufficient payment was delivered. Æthelred had done all he could to implement the necessary taxes to attain such a sum, but the amount was vast, and there was no certainty his subjects truly believed his claim that he intended to outfit a new army. Eadric had, of course, convinced him this was the only way, arguing quite rightly that making an ally of Thorkell was vital when it came to dealing with the inevitable return of Denmark's much-loathed Svienn Forkbeard. There could be no arguing with that. Svienn was always the main threat, or at least as comparable a threat as Thorkell. They'd forget that at their peril.

As wise as he was, it had been hard to learn how Eadric had been wrong about the fate of Alaric. He'd assured him the man was dead, cut down in a fool's attack on Thorkell's camp originally intended to remove the unreliable Ealdorman Ulfcytel from play. Æthelred had been furious when Edmund had told him otherwise, and Eadric had been unable to calm him with a credible explanation. Alaric was alive, and Eadric had failed him, and that was unacceptable to Æthelred. He couldn't put it into words, but he knew instinctually that Alaric's repeated appearance in his dreams bode ill for both him and his rule. He'd sleep better knowing he was no more. They couldn't afford loose ends.

The immediate danger posed by the foreign invasion was easier to understand. Thorkell had carried on doing what he did best following his ravaging of Eastengle. He'd pressed north without rest, he and his men storming and then sacking Northantone just weeks ago on St Andrew's Day. He'd then set himself on a course southward, burning as he went, seemingly looking to again enter Westseaxe and lay waste to it as he had so much else. That would not stand. Eadric may have assured him Thorkell was open to switching sides if he could be paid enough, but he'd already gone too far. They'd have no country left to defend if things carried on like this. He had to listen to reason. Æthelred couldn't pay him if he had no subjects left to tax.

He'd been a hard man to pin down. Thorkell knew how to avoid being engaged if he didn't wish it, a talent that defied comprehension considering the sheer size of his force. It was as if whenever Æthelred was in the east, suddenly Thorkell was in the west, and if he rode to face him there, he'd appear somewhere else, turning up in the south when the English were northbound and so on. No matter what happened, they couldn't make him stay put, giving one the fretful impression he was toying with them before moving in for the kill. Æthelred did not approve.

His Witan had predictably been of little use. He'd summoned all of them, minus Ælfric and Ulfcytel, of course, once Thorkell had commenced ravaging Buccingahammscir, hoping they might have fresh ideas. He'd naturally kept it a secret that he ultimately intended to pay Thorkell off, instead thinking his ealdormen might have at least some suggestions on potentially holding the enemy in place and preventing them from doing any further damage. Nobody had said anything of much worth, and most of the contributions from those assembled had consisted of whining and sniping at the severity of the new heregeld.

They were scared; he could see it on their faces, yet also predictably narrow in their outlook. They only cared for their own lands, and the concept of uniting against a common foe seemed difficult for them to grasp. Eadric had spoken in the heregeld's defence, putting on a big and massively dishonest show on how it was necessary to outfit a new army. Nobody else had seemed too impressed, and they had no ideas of their own, leaving Æthelred no option but to dismiss them, his time again wasted. It wasn't just that they wouldn't help their king. They wouldn't even help their neighbours. They looked out for themselves and themselves alone, and that was truly sickening. Æthelred was glad to see the back of them.

Some had proven more irksome than others. Morcar had headed off to Snotingeham along with Edmund and Æthelstan. Æthelred had wanted to speak to Edmund, since he felt guilty for almost harming him the day he'd learned Alaric was still alive. Æthelred had not put on an impressive display, there was no denying that, and his anger had frightened both his queen and their poor children. It had also been unfair on Edmund. He was not to know of the situation, and it had been unjust and unsightly for him to have assumed otherwise.

Sadly, his outburst had provoked others into fleeing with them. Eadwig, his youngest living son from his first wife, was one of them. His daughter, Wulfhild, had also gone, perhaps still resenting his cool welcome ever since her husband, Ulfcytel, had sent her from Noruic. Æthelred felt he had much to regret, even more than usual, as his children were deserting him when he needed them most. Was he such an awful father? Had he really seemed so terrible that day he'd lost control at their banquet? Why could they not forgive him?

Eadric naturally had ideas as to their reasons. He'd argued in private that Morcar was attempting to drive a wedge between him and his family, even encouraging Æthelstan to plot against him in an early bid for the throne. Æthelred wasn't so sure about that. Æthelstan was a brave and capable young man, but he had no head for politics, and plotting harm against others really wasn't his style. Eadric hadn't given up, claiming Morcar might use Æthelstan and Edmund to stir up discontent over the heregeld, using the brothers to advance his and Sigeferth's ambition of controlling the throne by proxy. It was no coincidence that he'd appeared in Lundenburg with the two aethelings precisely for the sake of confronting him.

The thought had chilled Æthelred's blood. He'd retreated to his study, pacing frantically and trying to settle his disturbed mind. No matter how he looked at it, Eadric's suggestion had a certain weight. It made no sense for Morcar to just appear in Lundenburg with two of Æthelred's own sons if there wasn't something deeper afoot. Was he being mocked? Was Morcar wanting to show him how influential he and Sigeferth remained despite their family's decline ever since Uhtred had become Ealdorman of Norþanhymbre? The more he thought on it, the more it seemed like truth. They were trying to use his sons to get to him in payment for past slights. They wanted him toppled from his throne.

If that were the case, he would have to act fast. He had many means to protect himself. Declaring his eldest child by Emma, Edward, as his immediate heir was one of them. That would see off any potential threats from the Five Boroughs, but it would also irritate his grown sons beyond measure. It might just be worth it, in the final balance of things, for he would brook no challengers to his rule. He certainly wouldn't tolerate Morcar attempting to manipulate his family for the sake of settling old scores. He'd be sure to make that known once the immediate crisis was resolved.

That left him with just one other problem: the longevity of the Ealdorman Ulfcytel. Whilst it was believable that he'd survived the Battle of Hringmere, information on his whereabouts was still hard to come by. Eadric's spies had heard rumours he'd been involved in some kind of skirmish with the Danes further south, but they'd not uncovered anything concrete. Without an army, Ulfcytel was considerably less dangerous to his rule, and so Æthelred was content to await further information and now focus exclusively on the threat posed by Thorkell.

As if on cue, a clutch of warriors led by several powerful figures emerged from the front ranks of the enemy host and commenced striding up the eastern side of the hill towards them. The lead figure was large, unusually so, making Æthelred think this was more than likely to be the appropriately named "Thorkell the Tall". As he came closer, Æthelred could see it must be him. His beard was vast and grey, which suggested seniority, and his armour and helmet were solid but fairly ornate, which indicated he was a man of means. His battle axe, still strung across his back, thankfully, was exceptionally broad, giving the impression he was a warrior of considerable strength and ferocity. All in all, Æthelred felt it safe to surmise this was indeed Thorkell, and the way the others followed his lead seemed to confirm it was true.

There was another noteworthy fellow moving up alongside him, this one in possession of a curious dual-coloured helmet that hid the entirety of his face. One half was dull iron whilst the other had been painted over a brilliant crimson, although whether that depicted rank or was done out of idle fancy, he could not tell. He was naturally shorter than Thorkell, yet there was a familiarity between them, the two men appearing to exchange words as they ascended towards them.

Æthelred pulled himself up tall, or at least as tall as he could get, when the Norse party finally reached the summit. They came to a halt a half dozen paces away, Thorkell towering over the score of ferocious-looking warriors he'd brought with him. Æthelred's men tensed on either side of him, both parties eyeing the other with considerable unease.

Ecgberht, in particular, glowered towards Thorkell with a look that could wither crops. He was a fighter, was Ecgberht, and he hated the Danes as any good man should, but Æthelred needed him to keep that under control for the time being. Thorkell didn't look troubled by any of it, yet the silence between the two sides persisted, and Æthelred, for his part, couldn't find the words to break it. Fortunately, Eadric finally stepped forward, his confidence no doubt buoyed through his past encounters with Thorkell, and spoke.

"It is a pleasure to see you again, noble leader," he said with a low bow. "May I present the King of En…"

"King Æthelred, yes," intoned Thorkell, his voice rumbling up from his vast chest like some great primaeval force. "King Æthelred of England, yes. We see your banner."

The dragon of Saint Edmund. Your presence here and the offer I assume you've come to make is the only reason your army below is still intact."

Æthelred opened and then closed his mouth. That was direct. He actually appreciated that. He'd been expecting an unrestrained savage with no knowledge of himself or his country. He should have known better. Æthelred decided to be similarly direct.

"I'm glad to finally make your acquaintance, Lord Thorkell. Let me assure you I come here in good faith and that my offer to take you and your men into my service still stands. I would have it so. Let there be no further dissension between us. Cease your harrying of my lands and people, and you will be paid well."

Thorkell made a quick yet dismissive gesture towards Eadric. "I named my price when your man here first came to us with your offer. Have you the monies I requested? Pay us, and you will have us as your own."

"The amount requested is considerable...I have had to announce a new tax, but we need time. Your continued violence against my people is complicating matters. I can't tax them if you lay waste to their property and take what is theirs. You understand this, yes?"

"I understand King Æthelred has many troubles and many enemies," Thorkell replied, taking a single step forward. Æthelred fancied he saw his two royal guards tense even further, each lowering their spears by a half inch in anticipation of violence. If Thorkell saw it he was unconcerned, the towering brute instead continuing to speak in his rumbling, hard timbre.

"I also know England is a place of great wealth. We have enjoyed much of it. Your people are generous. I know you can obtain the sufficient monies to take us into your employ. Until then, my men will continue to collect tribute. They would not have it any other way."

"Your efforts to obtain "tribute" are destroying this country and those within it," Ecgberht suddenly spat, the man apparently unable to control his temper. "This is no mere transfer of wealth you've set yourself to. This is murder and pre..."

"My man here simply wishes to raise a point," Æthelred said, irritated that Ecgberht would dare interrupt like that. He was a good soldier and commander, it was true, but that was the sole reason he was needed here. He had no business speaking on his king's behalf. To assume he did was the height of impertinence and would not stand.

"Which is what?" Thorkell asked. "That my warriors behave as warriors? Would you seek our services if we became fishermen?"

"If it were up to me, I would kill you and drive your inbred hirelings back into the sea..."

"That's enough now, Ecgberht!" Æthelred bellowed, his patience exhausted. "Step back and rejoin your men below. I would not have you disrupting these negotiations any further!"

Ecgberht paused, his venomous gaze still boring outward to meet with Thorkell's. He then looked upon his king, his face defiant. Foolish. He had no idea of the true complexities at hand. It was easy to think everything could be solved with a strong arm and sharp sword. He would think that, being the warrior he was. A ruler had to see a broader picture. He'd ensure he understood this when opportunity arose.

Thorkell didn't seem to be offended. He watched Ecgberht as he strode back through the hearthweru to rejoin his troops, content for a time to ignore all others in favour of scrutinising this man who'd spoken to him so abruptly. Whether this was out of malice or admiration, nobody could tell, since his helmet obscured most of his features. As if reading their thoughts, Thorkell suddenly lifted his hands up to his head, removing his helm and allowing them to stare upon the face that, aside from Eadric, perhaps, was unknown to all of them.

Æthelred was surprised. He'd been half-expecting a hideous monster under there, or at least the visage of one who never ceased to sneer, snarl, or otherwise scowl at all who dared stand before him. Instead, Thorkell looked remarkably human. Unnaturally large, yes, but still just a man, his flowing grey locks and long beard looking like they'd belong on any number of elders in any number of villages. His jaw was huge, true, and his nose appeared to have been broken several times, but he had a determined look, his eyebrows both bushy and prominent to the extent they seemed to almost partly conceal his eyes within the narrow pits of their sockets.

Those eyes, though! Æthelred hadn't really been able to discern them before, but if there was something unsettling to Thorkell's countenance, it was there. They were a faded blue, common enough for his kind, but also empty of spirit, as if there was nobody home and all that lay beneath was rigid ice. They were cold. Cold eyes, no doubt, but beyond cold, like Thorkell wasn't quite right in himself or had been born apart from the warmth of others. Æthelred found it hard to describe, yet he felt a shiver begin to creep up his spine the longer he stared into them. And yet he couldn't look away. He must not seem weak.

The two men next to Thorkell had also removed their helms. One of these was the man he'd seen earlier wearing the helmet that had been daubed red across one-half of its surface. He looked somewhat similar to Thorkell, although he was shorter, and his eyes possessed a more natural blue without any ominous undertones. He was younger but still seasoned in his own right, and his blond hair and beard were rent with great streaks of silver, his face also conveying a restrained ferocity that said he'd rather be fighting than talking.

"This here is my brother, Hemingr," Thorkell announced, gesturing towards the shorter man. Æthelred could see it now. There was quite a resemblance between the two men, but also a pronounced difference that he couldn't quite put into words. It must be a good and wholesome thing to have a brother like that, Æthelred imagined. Perhaps if he'd had such a man at his side, his reign might have taken a different course. That was idle conjecture, naturally, and he shouldn't be distracted from the task at hand. Things had to go well today. His reign, troubled as it was, depended on it.

Æthelred nodded respectfully towards Hemingr, the man returning the gesture with a curt nod of his own. Thorkell clearly thought very highly of his brother to allow him to present himself here. There was no doubt a real closeness between them, something that might be open to manipulation or exploitation if needed. He'd have to think on it when he had time.

Thorkell then gestured to the other warrior who'd also removed his helm; this "man" looking so young Æthelred suspected he might be Thorkell's son. He was otherwise unremarkable, his blue eyes and wavy blond hair so typical of his people. He had a way of staring, though, not in a rude or aggressive way, that implied he might have a greater part to play in the unfurling drama than his young years might otherwise suggest.

"This here is Olaf Haraldsson," said Thorkell, "and he is the leader of our

Norwegians."

"I know of you, English king," announced Olaf, apparently unwilling to wait for Æthelred to address him first. "I know you lavished wealth upon my countryman, Olaf Tryggvason, to turn him against Svienn Forkbeard. We hope you'll be as generous towards us."

"I would be," Æthelred began, his attention turning back to Thorkell, "but at the risk of repeating myself, I will say that I cannot afford to pay you the amount you require if you insist upon ravaging my country further. Your campaign is self-defeating. I would suggest a truce."

"We have a truce between us," Thorkell replied blankly. "We are talking. We will not kill you."

"A longer truce," Æthelred corrected, "so I have a semblance of a kingdom left from which to collect taxes. This makes sense for both of us. You know this."

"No, English king, it does not," Thorkell responded, his arms lifting up to fold themselves across his barrel of a chest. "You have no other option. I know what awaits you. King Svienn is already planning the final conquest of your people and intends to sail with an invasion fleet within a year. You cannot resist him. You need me to do that for you. I think you will quickly come up with the coin I require now you know this."

Æthelred could feel his heart beat a little faster at the mention of yet more enemies arriving on his shores. Eadric had advised him previously that Svienn would indeed look to take advantage of his current troubles, but to have it confirmed, from Thorkell, no less, was beyond unsettling. There was no way England could survive fighting them both. One had to be turned against the other.

"Why are you so willing to fight against Denmark?" Eadric asked, his voice steady as he put the question to Thorkell. The towering Norseman turned his head to look upon him, his face betraying no hint of recognition or warmth. Whatever rapport Eadric claimed to have developed with him was apparently fictional.

"We have different goals. My Jomsvikings fight for wealth and renown…but once we've taken what's owed, we leave those who are left to their own affairs. Svienn would be ruler of all Scandinavia and England, too. His way is a new way. Me and mine are an obstacle to that way, as he sees it. King Æthelred is also in his way. So we fight him, yes?"

Æthelred couldn't fault his reasoning here. He'd known for some considerable time that Svienn had great ambitions when it came to both Denmark and Scandinavia in general. Æthelred had successfully undermined those ambitions when he'd turned Norway's Olaf Tryggvason to his side, and it was just bad luck that Svienn had ultimately crushed him some years later. What was clear was that not all Scandinavians desired to live under a single ruler, whether that was Svienn or anyone else. He could use that. The question was how.

"What else do you know about King Svienn's intentions?" Eadric inquired, eager as always for any additional information. "Just how long do we have before he's likely to again attack us?"

"As I said, perhaps a year," Thorkell responded. "He believes you to be weaker than ever and ripe for conquest. I do not disagree with him in this. Yet there is bad blood between us. He is not a man I would see rule. His son…"

"Son?" Æthelred interrupted, his curiosity piqued. "He has a son come of age?"

"Not old enough to rule, as you would do things here, yet he shows great promise, or so that's the talk. He acts like a man beyond his few years; ruthless and ambitious, like his father, but perhaps wiser. Time will tell if he is stronger."

"Does this young man have a name?" Eadric asked.

"Cnut. His name is Cnut. Svienn holds him in high regard already. He will likely be with his father when he again sets foot on English soil. Svienn will want to instruct him…in conquest and kingship."

This was interesting news. If Svienn was bringing this young Cnut with him, that meant he intended for him to learn by his example. This wasn't just another raiding expedition like they'd seen in the past. King Svienn was coming here to make England his own and leave it as an inheritance for Cnut. Let him try, Æthelred thought. Let him make this final bid for the throne, only to be cut down in front of his own brat. That would be a fitting and deserved end for a man of such hubris.

"I would agree we have a common enemy, and I'm relieved you see it that way," Æthelred announced. "You are certainly correct that your assistance against any invasion from King Svienn would be most welcome. But I stress again, you can only be paid for that assistance if you allow me to collect the required monies. Your reaving and pillaging is an impediment to our entire enterprise."

Thorkell let out a great sigh, like he was simultaneously angered but fatigued by the circular discussion. When he spoke again, he'd softened a little, suggesting something had finally clicked in that hard head of his.

"How long does King Æthelred need? Be warned, we will not be deceived."

"Not long," Æthelred said eagerly, "and I can assure you your men will be provided with food and ale for the coming winter. There will be no further need for violence between us, and come spring, I'll…"

He paused. Something was audible on the horizon, akin to the faint rumblings of distant thunder. This was getting louder, though, and if his ears didn't deceive him, it appeared to be coming from the valley immediately behind Thorkell's vast army. Æthelred could see from his vantage point atop the hill that they themselves were aware of it, the rear ranks turning in confusion to identify the disturbance.

He could see it now. Something was emerging from the valley, moving fast, trying to catch them all unaware. Men on horseback, hundreds of them, fanning out into a wide formation, their objective the rear of the Norse host. He strained his eyes, hoping to catch some detail on who they were. They were good riders, the hooves of their mounts kicking up streams of mud and water as they thundered down upon their quarry. Then he saw the banner they carried. The Five Boroughs. These men were Englishmen. His subjects. And they were about to ruin his already delicate negotiations.

Thorkell turned to look behind him, his eyes then flicking back to Æthelred in confusion. The advancing horsemen let out a shattering roar that echoed out from the valley and across the plain, their front line then smashing into the rear of Thorkell's army. The Northmen parted and disintegrated before them, many a man smashed flat under flailing hooves or impaled on thrusting spears. A bloody swathe was soon cut through their ranks, yet the rest of the horde was slow to react, those Danes furthest from the fighting looking like they were unsure of what was even happening. Æthelred wasn't the only one taken aback here, then. This entire situation said that Thorkell, too, had been caught completely by surprise.

His fortunes were not about to improve. Yet another force, several thousand strong and also flying the colours of the Boroughs, had appeared and was charging in on foot. They were eager for it, displaying no fear as they rushed into the carnage, their massed, fearsome cries likewise thundering out of the valley and into the ears of men for miles around. What was taking place was now clear enough. This was a full attack upon Thorkell's host, likely hatched from the duplicitous minds of Morcar and Sigeferth to ensure all of Æthelred's efforts here came to ruin. He couldn't say why they would do this. But if he escaped this debacle, he'd make sure they paid for it.

It occurred to him then that escape might prove difficult. Thorkell snapped his head back towards Æthelred, his expression one of absolute, unrestrained fury. Æthelred hadn't known it was possible for a face to flush such a startling shade of red, but Thorkell had somehow managed it, such was his rage. His eyes also had suddenly come to life, burning with an inner fire sparked by the spectacle of violence. Æthelred feared him, now more than ever.

Thorkell heaved his axe from his back, gripping the heavy, brutal thing tightly and securely in his equally coarse, rough hands. He took a step forward, and Æthelred's guards rose up to meet him, their spears and shields raised. Thorkell's men did the same, forming around their leader with a grim enthusiasm. Æthelred had to do something. They couldn't win this battle. Surprise or no, the men attacking the enemy below were still vastly outnumbered. Æthelred had to stop this before they all died here.

"This is not my doing! These men act without my consent! None of this was supposed to happen! We were supposed to make a deal!"

"King Æthelred complains too much!" simmered Thorkell, his voice thunderous and sharp to the point it seemed to split the air. "We will not be deceived, and we will not be denied what's owed!"

What exactly he believed he was somehow owed Æthelred wasn't sure. What he did know was that Thorkell had turned around and was hurrying back down the hill towards the battle, his escorts struggling to keep up with his long, loping strides. Why he'd not made an attempt on his life was a mystery. Perhaps Thorkell didn't take him that seriously, or he actually believed him on some level when he'd said this attack was not taking place on his order.

Æthelred continued to stare after him, his bellowing voice still audible as he roared for his men to form up and join him in a counterattack. His men roused themselves upon seeing him stride through the ranks and towards the fighting, the presence of their towering, murderous leader stirring them into action. Æthelred felt a pang of sorrow for those who would soon have to face him. If there were many fates to avoid in his world, exchanging blows with Thorkell the Tall was one of them.

The king lifted his eyes up and over to the battle itself, a single Saxon warrior on horseback drawing his attention. His armour was splendid, the silvered metal scales glittering in the afternoon's pale light, his skill also exemplary as he thrust and stabbed into the broiling mass of savage men beneath him. His own troops looked to be energised by his presence, his prowess inspiring them to press on and emulate his valorous deeds as best they could.

"Æthelstan," he breathed, a dread feeling clutching his heart as recognition dawned. "What mischief have you fallen prey to? What have you and your brother wrought now?"

His firstborn son gave no answer to that, focused as he was on cutting his way through the enemy. It was a fool's endeavour. Despite his skill and as surprised as his foes had been, he and his men were massively outnumbered. Defeat was merely a matter of time.

His spear suddenly snapped as if to illustrate that point, the shaft breaking halfway as he drove it through the mailed torso of an attacker attempting to unhorse him. He drew his sword in a flash, the motion fluid and well-practised, his blade arcing down upon the enemy in a glittering, red storm of blows. Some Danes attempted to part around him, preferring to find themselves easier opponents, whilst others continued to hurl themselves forward, eager to take down this formidable warrior. Æthelstan hacked the arm from one of them before twisting in his saddle to cleave at the head of another, his precise, lethal strikes ensuring a carpet of bodies now lay around the stamping, ironshod hooves of his steed.

Despite the chaos around him, he seemed to lift his head, his gaze falling on the hill and the great fluttering banner of Saint Edmund. Their eyes then met. It was him. He knew it was him now, the single look they shared confirming in Æthelred's mind that this was indeed his son. Impulsive. Arrogant. Impressively skilled with all manner of weapons yet ill-suited for the throne, even if he were still first in line. He wouldn't be for much longer. This stunt of his was the final straw. England would not be ruled by such a man.

Æthelred would come to blame himself for what happened next. It was as if God, if he were to be so cruel, had heard his thoughts and acted, a blow from somewhere cutting Æthelstan's horse from under him and sending him tumbling from the saddle. The Danes seemed to sense what had happened and began attacking with renewed vigour, the entire horde moving to contain and entrap the smaller English force now struggling to continue its dwindling momentum. Æthelred strained his eyes to look for his son, unable to see what exactly was taking place. He couldn't see him. He'd not got up. The fighting was intensifying. Æthelred started to panic, fearing him likely crushed under the hooves, boots, and bodies of the deathly melee. He wasn't gone. He couldn't be. Not just like that. Not now.

"We should go, my king," Eadric said sternly, appearing at Æthelred's side to snap him out of his fearful monologue.

"That's my boy down there!" Æthelred cried, his voice high-pitched. He couldn't lose Æthelstan. He might be a disobedient fool unsuited to authority, but he couldn't lose him today. Not after all he had already suffered in his life. He'd lost so many of his children. He could not lose another.

"Thorkell's numbers will win him this battle no matter what we do here," said Eadric, content to ignore the question of the aetheling's safety. "If you attack him, all our work will have been…"

"Thorkell will not have my son!" Æthelred screeched, his teeth flashing. If the ealdorman had anything else to say, he decided it best to keep it to himself, instead following meekly whilst Æthelred began hurrying back down the hill towards his waiting army, the hearthweru also matching his frantic pace. The force he'd mustered to accompany him had as yet not joined the battle, having not received any orders to move to assist their fellow Englishmen in their ill-considered gambit. That was about to change.

Æthelred howled at the top of his lungs for Ecgberht to form the men up for an immediate advance. His commander looked over at him from his position in the front ranks, apparently either confused or unable to properly hear him due to the distance between them. Æthelred broke into a run, his voice straining as he continued screaming orders to commence the attack. Thousands looked to their king, alarmed and elated to see him possessed of such vigour. Ecgberht finally heard him, and his face lit up with a savage grin, a ripple of enthusiasm then spreading throughout the entirety of the English force. They were outnumbered, it was true, but they'd all had enough of holding back. Today would be a day to remember.

Several horn blasts erupted from somewhere, the signal clear enough to all who heard it. Ecgberht's warriors began their advance, their strides long and powerful and their shields and spears at the ready. The Northmen were now largely coiled back towards the entrance to the valley and surrounding what was left of the men of the Five Boroughs, and so Æthelred would have to act fast if he hoped to save his son. Several thousand furious Englishmen smashing into Thorkell's rear would have to suffice.

King Æthelred mounted his horse, his warriors speeding past him, the air thick with war cries. Eadric had found his voice again and was yammering on, protesting his decision and claiming Thorkell still had the advantage of numbers, regardless of how many men he'd lost from surprise. Æthelred barked at him in reply, telling him to find his horse and join him with the rest of the hearthweru. Eadric went pale. The prospect of battle frightened him. Æthelred understood how he felt well enough. He'd never been a strong man. But now he had no choice.

He drew his sword. His personal guard had found their mounts, Eadric included, the men forming around him in a protective wall of mail and spear tips. Æthelred snapped at his horse, startling it into motion so they might take up position just behind the front lines of the infantry. They were advancing as a wall of shields, the men in front presenting like a rolling wave of solid wood and tempered iron. Spears bristled from the line as it swept onward, the men struggling to keep their formation secure, such was their haste. Ecgberht could be heard bellowing from somewhere, telling them to keep things orderly, but it didn't matter too much. What mattered was that these men were good and strong and brave. With these qualities, they might just stand a chance of winning.

Æthelred glanced behind him, hoping to gauge the disposition of the rest of his army. There were several thousand others following them, his comparatively meagre force now looking fearsome indeed as it thundered forward in anticipation of battle and bloodshed. The king had positioned himself and his guards as a mounted unit on the centre right of the army, intending to observe and bark orders if not directly take part in the fighting. Æthelred was more than aware he was an elderly man and thus disinclined to lock swords with any of Thorkell's savages. Some might call that cowardly, and there was some truth to that, but it was also true that it wouldn't work wonders for the men to see him dragged from his horse and hacked apart. He'd inspire them better by remaining alive.

It was having the desired effect. The men took heart at his presence, gladdened perhaps that their king had come to join them against their much-hated foe. They churned onwards with furious enthusiasm, their front line of shields a flat wedge of brute force aimed directly at Thorkell's distracted host. Horns and drums blared and pounded, imploring the men to press on, the warriors themselves responding with frenzied roars and the hammering of shields.

In any other time, the king might have found it discordant, chaotic even, the sights and sounds of so many men intent on violence perhaps overwhelming the senses. Not today. Today it was one of the most magnificent experiences he'd had in his life. He felt elated but enjoyed clarity, feeling as if all the troublesome complexities of the past had finally given way to a crystal-clear certainty. Æthelred looked to his left and spied his banner, the white dragon of Saint Edmund, in the hands of one of his guards. It looked magnificent in the fading grey light, the dragon appearing almost as ferocious as the men rushing onward before it. They were inspired by it, he could tell. He hoped the Saint would pray for them today. If anyone had reason to wish to see the Norsemen defeated, it was him.

The English force finally smashed into the enemy with a sound akin to crashing, grinding metal. The Northmen had made some effort to prepare for it, so furious had the sound of the Saxon advance been, but they were hard-pressed, as their admittedly huge army was now attacked from two separate sides. Despite this, they were fighting back fiercely, refusing to be intimidated, their shields ready and raised to take the worst that could be hurled at them.

Æthelred felt up to the challenge, knowing they had to break through them if they were to have any hope of saving his son. He screamed encouragements to the warriors surging past him, waving his sword upright in the air to signify that he was with them. His men responded well, throwing themselves forward with an almost frenzied vigour, their front ranks pushing outwards like a rising tide that threatened to spill into the enemy's centre.

He'd not seen such sights in years. The scene immediately before him was utterly frenetic, the wedge that was the vanguard of his army locking fast with a similarly stubborn mass of Danes. Spears thrust and jabbed from over and between shields, tearing at metal and flesh whenever their tips found their mark. Men fell amidst the contest, the terrible, grinding clamour of shield wall on shield wall drowning out the cries of the wounded. No mercy would be asked for today, as everyone already knew the Norsemen had none to give. It had always been so.

He thought he saw Ecgberht fall. He looked like he'd taken a downward blow to his leg, causing him to stumble forward out of the front line and into the clutches of the enemy. He caught himself at the last moment, lurching upright and deflecting the swing of an axe descending towards his head. He then lashed outwards in retaliation, teeth bared and eyes alight with hate, his sword opening the throat of the man who'd sought to slay him. Æthelred spurred his horse closer to the fighting, his mounted hearthweru following at a trot. The king's battle lust was up, something that had not happened in an age. He would have the scent of blood in his nostrils. He would save his son.

A thrown spear sailed past his head and impacted on the shield of one of the warriors behind him. Æthelred grimaced and hewed his sword in the air in the direction it had flown from, a guttural snarl erupting from his throat. One of his men hurled a spear, the projectile arcing up and down to disappear into the enemy ranks, several others following a second later to finish off whichever Dane had just tried to kill him. Æthelred liked to think he heard a scream from somewhere, although the intensity of the ambient noise made pinning it down impossible. Men were dying, that much was obvious, but thousands of others were still very much alive, their furious roars echoing out across the landscape as they fought on.

The English advance was grinding to a halt. It wasn't just the stout defence they'd met, but the enemy numbers were a problem in their own right. There were just so many of them, and they kept pressing forward, flowing up like a wave to spread over and around their flanks to entrap them. Thorkell's host may not have been quick to react, but it was fully awake now, like some great and terrible beast that was slow to anger but equally slow to placate. Æthelred's men were fighting well, and they had smashed a gore-splattered crater into Thorkell's centre line, but he had a feeling their fortunes were about to change.

A sudden, redoubled cacophony of roars and curses to his right added strength to that notion. The English lines were being bent inwards, the enemy looking like they'd successfully flowed around their vanguard to fall upon them all along their flank. Æthelred spurred his horse into motion, his men hurrying with him towards the point of crisis, the banner of Saint Edmund still held aloft and resplendent in the wind.

Æthelred soon saw the danger. His men here were starting to buckle, the weight of bodies pressing in on them too much for their already reduced numbers to contain. If that wasn't bad enough, a number of exceptionally savage-looking Northmen had begun tearing into them, their long axes hacking through wood, metal, and flesh alike. One berserker was impaled when a particularly brave Englishman ducked and then pivoted before he could be struck, his spear splitting his assailant's torso as it entered and exited his body. He himself collapsed an instant later, his skull cleaved in two, the twin-headed axe of his screaming, filth-splattered killer making short work of him. Blood soaked into the earth, dark and heavy in the dimming light, the frenzied howling of the attacking Danes rising in volume. They could sense their advantage.

Æthelred looked around anxiously, unsure of what to do. He had no idea what was happening on the other side of the battle, and the banners of the Five Boroughs were entirely obscured from his vision, if they were still present at all. His centre line was also in trouble, and Ecgberht and company were struggling to retain control in the face of Thorkell's counterattack. As bad as that was, things were far worse here. They were being slaughtered, and if this kept up, the enemy would overwhelm their right flank entirely and begin rolling up the English shield wall. Defeat would then be a foregone conclusion.

He had to act. His grip felt weak, his palms moist and clammy as he held his sword. Anxiety welled up from his stomach and into his chest. A cold sweat beaded his brow, the smooth metal of his crown as uncomfortable as ever upon his increasingly hairless head. The enemy was so fierce, their multitudes so vast, and their leader like something out of a nightmare. What could men do against such blind malevolence? What could he do, in the autumn years of his life, to stem such a force, to retain his kingdom and pass it down to his children? What could any of them do?

Æthelred was more surprised than anyone when he found himself charging towards the fighting, his horse galloping forward to plug the breach in their flank and have him save the day single-handed. His hearthweru stormed after him, the hooves shaking the very ground, their spears levelled and blades raised in anticipation of the coming clash.

They made contact, the Danes parting or knocked aside by the armoured, horse-borne warriors barrelling into them. The king found the courage to lash out, his blade impacting upon raised shields and iron helms in an echoing, hollow staccato. The edge found its mark, tearing open the face of one stinking heathen who'd laid hands on Æthelred's mount in a botched effort to drag him from the saddle. His personal guards were alongside him, cutting the enemy down with brutal, sweeping strikes, the Danes struggling to contain this avalanche of horses and men that had come upon them.

Eadric had remained close, looking like he'd recovered from his earlier doubts as he hacked at the enemy, his skill with a sword surprisingly impressive for a man of such slight stature. He fought with a certain precision born of study and practice, a blow here slicing across the throat of one man, the next removing the hand and then the head of another before he could bring his shield up to defend himself. Æthelred admired his resolve.

The feeling didn't last long. One of his royal guards suddenly fell from his horse, although who had struck him Æthelred could not tell. His own steed reared up a moment later, forcing him to cling on in terror, his mind racing with fearful thoughts on what might happen should he fall into the baying, brawling mass of men below. His panic escalated as he slid down onto the cold earth, his horse falling over onto its side and trapping his right leg beneath it. The creature rumbled to itself, its eyes wide and desperate, a splintered spear visible from a torn, jagged wound to its chest. The poor beast would not last the battle.

Æthelred couldn't move. He was trapped, and his only immediate option was to pull at his leg with both hands in a futile effort to free himself. His head ached terribly, yet whether that was from the fall or the horrifying clamour of battle, he did not know. He'd made a mistake here. He shouldn't have attacked, knowing full well he did not have the numbers. There never had been any real hope. Their actions were those of desperate men willing to entertain any sliver of optimism if it might stave off despair a little longer. He'd gambled and lost, and now he was paying what was due. This was the end. And it was all his doing.

"You're a stupid boy! A stupid, ungrateful child! To think I did so much for you, just to see you always make a mess of things!"

Æthelred shook his head furiously, trying to dispel his mother's voice from his mind. It wasn't his fault. He tried to do good, he'd always tried, but everything always went wrong, like everyone and everything was against him. They thought he'd killed his brother, they thought he'd killed Edward when he hadn't, they all thought he'd gained his throne by killing his own kin. They thought…

"Now King Æthelred, we will take what's owed!"

Thorkell stood over him, his towering, ungodly form blotting out what remained of the daylight. He was drenched in a combination of mud, sweat, and blood, looking like he'd cut through an entire forest of men with that axe of his, such was the pungent, metallic stench of viscera billowing out from him. He'd lost his helmet somehow, but that made the situation worse, for his face was thus entirely exposed, his lips curled upward in a predatory sneer. The giant stepped forward, a single hand reaching out like he intended to snatch the crown from Æthelred's head. It fell upon his throat instead, the pressure building as Thorkell tightened his grip. Æthelred clawed desperately, trying to tear the hand away so he might breathe, his eyes widening in horror as he lost himself in Thorkell's dead gaze.

So this was how it all ended, he thought. His own life throttled from him, his last sight on this earth the face of a merciless killer who cared for nothing but loot and slaughter. His vision swam in and out of focus, both throat and lungs burning hot with agony as Thorkell continued his crushing death hold. All of it was for nothing. All the intrigue, all the hatred, all the pain he'd borne and all the betrayals he'd suffered were for no real purpose. In the end, King Æthelred had died in battle trying to save his son; itself a pleasingly heroic final episode in what had otherwise been a lifetime of frustration. He wondered if Emma might be proud of him. Ælfgifu too. She had so loved her baby Æthelstan.

Thorkell's face seemed to suddenly collapse inward from one side. He didn't know what had happened, but Æthelred fancied he saw a single spurt of blood fly out of his mouth, the unseen blow looking like it had shaken his very jaw. Another followed, this one catching him on the temple, the gauntleted fist not letting up as a third and then a fourth punch crashed into the fiend's increasingly bloodied visage.

Æthelred breathed in sharply as he was released, his vision swirling back into clarity to reveal an image of his own royal guard who'd just earlier been toppled from his horse. He'd survived, albeit minus a weapon, and he was now demolishing Thorkell's face, the towering brute dazed and staggering under the surprise onslaught.

Æthelred felt himself being pulled up and away, the immense strength of whoever it was that now held him releasing his leg from the weight of his dying horse. Somebody spoke in his ear, their voice dull and metallic from within the confines of their helmet. "My king! My king!..." they said, urgently and persistently, babbling something also about loss and retreat. He wasn't surprised. That always seemed to be his lot, but for the moment he couldn't do anything but stare at the contest ahead, Thorkell and Æthelred's saviour appearing as titans clashing amidst the surrounding storm of battle.

His man had Thorkell by the throat, the villain's marred and broken face truly terrible to behold. He seized his attacker's hands, tearing them from his neck and attempting to bend them back, a bestial snarl emerging from a grimacing mouth of reddened, slab-like teeth.

They struggled and slipped upon the muddy ground, unwilling to relent before the other. Æthelred could hear a tremendous rumbling from his man's helmet, suggesting he was pouring every ounce of rage and hatred into the contest. Both men, Saxon and Dane, were shaking with effort, such was their strength, but neither was making much headway, their hands still clasped together as each tried to push the other back.

Thorkell buckled when the Saxon stepped forward to slam his boot down upon his foot and deliver a savage, armoured head-butt to the jaw. He'd had to leap upwards a little for that, such was the size difference between them, but it worked well, and Thorkell almost fell as he staggered backwards. Was that fear now visible in those blue eyes?

If it were, it was momentary. Thorkell was canny and not easily defeated, even if taken by surprise. Æthelred's loyal servant slumped to his knees, his hands reaching upwards towards the spear impaled through his neck. Thorkell had simply snatched a discarded spear from the ground after righting himself and hurled it with such force and precision his victory could only be denied by a miracle. He let out a single, savage bark of triumph upon seeing his aim prove true, and the dying Englishman slumped over onto his side a few moments later, his spasming limbs gradually easing into stillness.

Æthelred looked away, his head still ringing and his limbs leaden. Whoever had pulled him free of the fighting had bundled him atop a horse, his mystery saviour then sitting in front of him to take the reins and usher them away. All three of them, men and beast, then galloped at speed as the English flank finally collapsed, the king's spirited charge into the breach doing little in the end to deter an enemy of such ferocity.

He could hear their screaming, undulating howls of victory whilst he fled, and he knew the defeat of the entire English force was now inevitable. He heard Ecgberht and Eadric bellowing orders, imploring the men to retreat, the blast of horns that had not so long ago seemed so magnificent turning dour and ominous as the day was lost.

They rode past what had been the English centre. It was now like a vision from some nightmare, depicting a flood of dirtied, bloodied men falling back in a state of barely controlled chaos. The Danes surged after them, hacking down stragglers and the wounded, the English shield wall coming apart entirely under the weight of their terrible wrath. A few brave souls held fast, fighting to the death so their countrymen might escape, one man even pulling a spear from his own body to defend the wounded friend at his feet. Both of them were dead, they each knew that, and the pair vanished from view as Æthelred was sped onward and away. He looked back one last time, hoping against hope to see any sign of his son.

There was nothing. The shattered remnants of his army were in full flight. The Danes were pursuing, their numbers still by far the larger, but the desperate heroism of some was preventing a total rout, allowing a trickle of survivors to get away.

It wasn't enough. Defeat and dishonour were again Æthelred's; a bitter repast he'd rarely been spared in all his long years. His heart swelled with sorrow as a vision came to mind. His boy, Æthelstan, dead amidst the battlefield detritus, his body beaten and cut and stripped of life, a ruined, sorrowful shell left to rot and wither. Æthelred should have been able to save him. He should have kept him close, where he would always be safe. He'd failed as a king. Now he'd failed as a father.

****

Hereward rode on, his gallant steed spiriting them away from the fight. His king was like a dead weight behind him, but it was manageable, for Æthelred had become so emaciated and frail in his advanced years it was little bother for the horse. Hereward had felt compelled to do what he'd done. He was his king's thegn, sworn to his majesty, and so when he'd seen him fall he'd had to act. He thanked God he'd been able to pull him away thanks to the heroic actions of his bodyguard. Thorkell had almost met his match with that man. It was just damnably bad luck that the bastard had eventually prevailed.

And so the day had been lost. They'd made a good show of it, and that first heady phase of the battle had gone well in their favour, but the numbers were always against them. There was nothing else for it now. The foe would hold the place of slaughter.

He thought he heard something over the sound of hooves, faint and fleeting. Another moment passed until he heard it again, this time clearly enough. Grief-stricken, desperate, the sound a man makes in those first agonising moments of heartbreak, knowing he might never recover from the shock of what assailed him. He knew that sound. He'd been there too. He remained quiet whilst Æthelred wept his bitter tears, knowing that silence might be just what he needed. He'd let him have his dignity. It might be all he had left.

XVI

Edmund winced as his bruise was revealed, his entire left side looking like the flesh had been pummelled until fit to burst. That wasn't too far from the truth, the blow he'd taken from that axe winding him so severely he'd nearly passed out. He hadn't, though. His brother had been right about him. It was like he were made of iron.

It was just a shame Æthelstan couldn't say the same about himself. Edmund peered over at him from where he sat, hoping he'd be showing some sign of life. He was breathing, but that was it, and the two monks working on him were becoming increasingly frantic in their efforts to prevent his wound reopening for the third time. They'd laid him out on the table of their dining hall, Edmund and Morcar feeling almost guilty after dragging the bloodied and battered aetheling through the pristine halls of their monastery. They'd made an awful mess of things, filthy and dishevelled from battle as they all were, but there had been no other option. If these monks couldn't save him, no one could.

Edmund winced again when a third monk began dabbing at his bruises, the wet cloth he was using feeling painfully rough upon his already tender flesh. Morcar stood anxiously over the monks working on Æthelstan, his face a mask of concern. Edmund reached out to take his brother's hand, edging his chair a little closer to the table. A sharp, throbbing pain surged through his torso, his body protesting at his continued insistence on movement. He didn't care. He needed to have his brother's hand in his. He needed Æthelstan to know he would not leave him.

He was cold. He didn't return his grip either, his fingers otherwise limp and sticky with his own sweat and blood. Edmund held on to him, the burning in his side intensifying as he maintained the posture. If there was even the slightest chance that Æthelstan was aware of him, then he'd stay like this for as long as he had to. It would help him to know he was at his side. He deserved that much.

It had all started out so well. They'd raised their army in record time, the men of the Five Boroughs proving eager to answer their summons despite the encroaching winter. Edmund had been surprised they'd even managed to get an army together at all, fearing the thegns, Sigeferth included, would reject their plans for a campaign.

They had taken some convincing. Nobody wanted to die, and confronting Thorkell's army was seen as a sure way to go about that. They had listened to their proposal with patience and respect, eventually coming around to Edmund and Æthelstan's logic. The military option was the only option, and if the king wouldn't listen to reason, then his people had little choice. Thorkell was destroying the country, and delivering yet more wealth into his hands in the hope he might relent was no solution. He had to be stopped, now. They had to fight. And so they would.

They'd set out for Northantone at the head of their host, knowing Thorkell to be there. They'd hit him in the flank and pin him against the walls of the town, making him bleed to the point he'd have little choice but to lift the siege and head elsewhere. It was a dangerous plan, but attacking the enemy by surprise whilst they were occupied with a siege was as good as it was going to get in terms of available strategies. They'd work with what they had.

Unfortunately, Thorkell did things faster than most men might expect. When they'd finally reached Northantone, there was little left but corpses and cinders, the entire settlement looking like it had been ransacked of all valuables before being put to the torch. The men had been demoralised by the sight, and before long some thegns had spoken of heading home, thinking their campaign no longer had a purpose with Northantone in ruins.

Morcar had argued otherwise. There were still opportunities for victory, he'd said, especially if an over-confident Thorkell were to head south to attack Lundenburg. They could smash him there, between their spear tips and the king's high walls, winning glory and the gratitude of a monarch in a single day. This couldn't be just about securing their own lands. All of England was at stake, and so it was up to all true Englishmen to act.

That had done it. Thorkell himself had helped. Reports from their scouts had said he was heading south at such a rate the capital was more than likely his next target. The fyrd had then chased him for over a week, his movements turning erratic as he headed this way and that, almost like he was playing games with them. Wherever he went, he left nothing but desolation; his army seeming to crush the very life from the earth itself. Edmund had rarely felt so empty as he had upon witnessing village after village so utterly ruined, their inhabitants either dead or missing.

They'd then gotten word that the king himself was actively leading a host of his own to confront him. That was remarkable news to all who heard it. Edmund had thought him almost lost, resigning himself to doing nothing whilst he waited for his reeves to collect him a suitably massive sum to give to Thorkell. To know he was now marching to battle at the head of an army was a welcome, albeit astonishing, development. If they could link up with him, they'd be all the stronger.

Things had not gone so smoothly. Æthelred had apparently made camp several miles south of Bernecestre, deciding to rest and water his army close to the entrance of a shallow valley. They didn't know if there was anything more to it, but the enemy was said to be heading straight for him, making them think Thorkell knew he was there. The king had to be aware of the danger, so he'd either decided to give battle against a superior force or attempt a parley. They found their answer as to which a day later.

The men of the Five Boroughs were good fighters, Edmund knew, and their scouts were clearly no exception. They'd surprised and annihilated an enemy foraging party with the break of dawn, even bringing a prisoner in for questioning. Morcar had been less than gentle with the man, it must be said, and the Dane's fiery defiance had soon turned as wet and fluid as his bowels. They hadn't kept him alive after that, beheading him once he'd told them all he knew. It was grim, dishonourable work, but they'd had no time for half-measures. The future of the entire kingdom was at risk.

Æthelred was indeed looking to negotiate with Thorkell, so the prisoner had said, hoping to dissuade him from his murderous course and come over to his employ. Apparently, Eadric of Mierċe had already proposed this to Thorkell just prior to his attack on the forces of the Ealdorman Ulfcytel at Hringmere. Æthelstan's and Edmund's suspicions had been correct all along. This heregeld their father had inflicted on the realm was nothing of the kind. It was all a lie; the promise of funding a new army merely a means to ensure the cooperation of the Witan. The true purpose of the tax was to provide the revenues necessary to pay Thorkell and his men to fight for Æthelred.

It didn't seem possible he'd been able to acquire such a sum already. The Norsemen were guaranteed to demand a hefty price to even cease their attacks, let alone actually come over to fight for the crown. As far as Edmund was aware, the treasury held nowhere near such a fortune, and so it seemed feasible this meeting was some kind of delaying action to placate Thorkell and bid for more time. It made a certain cowardly sense, Edmund had ventured, but what their father was doing was still a mistake. Æthelred could not be permitted to tax England to ruin just to shower foreigners with gold. It would be a foolish move even if Norse mercenaries could be trusted, but they most certainly could not. He thought he'd learned that lesson already.

Sigeferth had been the first to give voice to the plan they'd eventually embarked on. They should continue to pursue Thorkell's forces and engage his rearguard once they confirmed he was negotiating with the king. The terrain Æthelred had chosen for this meeting would suit their purposes, he'd argued, since the valley would shield their advance until they were in a position to strike. Thorkell would be both surprised and possibly cut off from his own men, should he indeed have committed to meeting Æthelred at an agreed location between their respective armies.

It had all sounded workable, aside from a few nagging details. The first was that they were massively outnumbered. Judging by the ruinous evidence of their passing, the enemy host undoubtedly dwarfed their own, and there'd be no engaging it without substantial risks, no matter how favourable the terrain. The second concern was that their only chance of victory depended on Æthelred breaking his truce with Thorkell and charging in to assist them. As huge as Thorkell's army was, a surprise attack from two separate directions would unnerve them, possibly resulting in a general rout. Stranger things had happened in war.

Æthelstan and Morcar had been hesitant. There were no guarantees Æthelred would respond to their intervention by attacking Thorkell, especially if the king really did wish to acquire his army for himself. They could end up ploughing into the enemy, only for Æthelred to just sit there and watch them be slaughtered. That was a valid concern. Edmund had needed to think fast to find a way to convince them. Fortunately, the almost obvious then occurred to him.

Thorkell was a stranger in these lands. He wouldn't be able to tell one Englishman from another, and he certainly wouldn't be able to identify the men of the Five Boroughs. Englishmen were just Englishmen to him, and for them to attack him whilst he met with Æthelred in good faith would smack of treachery. He'd think Æthelred had lured him into a trap. And why not? He was the King of England, and they were still his subjects. Why would they seek to undermine him so, if it were not part of a broader plan he himself had set in motion? Thorkell would have to respond immediately. He'd have to attack Æthelred's army.

All of them had expressed some anxiety at that notion. None of them wanted to see Æthelred hurt, and if they attacked just as he was speaking with Thorkell, there was every chance the bastard would try and murder him. But as they'd all agreed, this was no time for half-measures. Years of war had devastated England's once rich and prosperous lands. Æthelred's efforts to pay off the enemy were now crippling what little trade and commerce they had left. He could not be permitted to squander whatever riches yet remained just for the sake of hiring an army that was likely to turn on him anyway. Physical force was the only option they had. The heathens must be defeated.

For a while, Edmund had dared to hope they might be. Their mounted charge through the valley had been perfect, the thundering of hooves and the howling of war cries penetrating to his very bones. Morcar and Sigeferth had followed at a jog with the infantry, intending to smash into the enemy whilst they were still dazed from getting hit by the cavalry. It was a brave move. And for a time, it seemed to pay off.

The Danes had been lax, believing England to be all but broken. They were most certainly not expecting to be attacked from the rear. They'd cut a merciless swathe through their ranks, the English force a tsunami of pounding hooves and jagged metal cascading onward without pause. Edmund thought the enemy likely to break, yet despite their shock, they were not beaten. They'd found their courage, the fiends broiling up at them like a swarm of angry insects. A charge from horseback could be magnificent, but cavalry needed freedom of movement, and the massed infantry of Thorkell's host soon hemmed them in, threatening to pin them in place for a slaughter that would then be inevitable.

They'd tried their best. Edmund had speared at least three Danes whilst he whirled and pivoted in his saddle, his steed doing its share of kicking and biting at the foe now rushing to contain them. Æthelstan had looked unstoppable, his crimson cloak billowing out as he charged, his spear a terrible, bloody lance reaping its own grim harvest. They'd all raced after him, the ground still shaking with the pounding of hooves, the men screaming their hatred and defiance right into the faces of the enemy.

Edmund's spear had broken off inside the chest of a Dane, the unfortunate man then collapsing under the weight of his steed. The rest of their horsemen were pressed in around them and fighting for their lives, the heathen's numbers threatening to overrun them in the narrowing, corpse-strewn salient they'd created. Sigeferth and Morcar had caught up and charged in, the roars of several thousand Saxons rending the air. It was magnificent, as if England were a beast that had suddenly come to life to throw off its tormentor, but it was still desperate. If their father, the king, didn't come to their aid, this would all be for nothing.

It was then that he'd seen his brother fall. He'd lost sight of him in the bedlam, but he'd then spotted him a way off, looking up towards the hill in the near distance and the fluttering banner of Saint Edmund. Their father must be there. That was his banner of choice, displayed to signal his presence so that he and Thorkell might talk on when and how to hand English gold into his murdering clutches. Æthelstan paused to gaze upon it, his berserk fury seemingly spent, his armour dented and bloody from over a dozen successful contests. Edmund still wondered what exactly he'd been thinking.

Whatever it was, it had distracted him from his next opponent. He'd been a wise one, deciding to hack away at the legs of Æthelstan's horse to cause the beast to come toppling down to the earth. Æthelstan had fallen from the saddle, his helmet rolling from his head as he landed upon the hard, desolate ground with an audible crash. It had been an awkward fall. He'd not been remotely prepared for it.

Edmund had charged towards him at a gallop, in his haste almost knocking over several onrushing Englishmen. Morcar's warriors were pushing in, seeking to drive the enemy back, the sound of axes and spears clashing off wood and iron ringing in the ears. The fighting was furious everywhere you looked, but it was most intense where Æthelstan had fallen. The Northmen wanted to get to him, hurling themselves forward with eager shouts and brandished axes. Edmund knew what this was about. They wanted the glory, the honour, that would come from taking his head. They would not have him. Edmund would die first.

He cut a man down with a side slash to the neck, his sword cleaving through flesh and bone. Another flew at him, his axe scything through the air towards Edmund's legs. Blood flowed, the heavy, rusted axe head battering away at his mail to pummel flesh and shake bones. Edmund cried out, his horse rearing up to kick at his bold attacker with its bloodied hooves. The man screamed, the sound cutting short with a sickening thud as something hit home. He'd been kicked in the face, his helm crumpling inwards under the impact. Edmund's horse stampeded over him, snapping him like a twig and snorting and bellowing in a fury of its very own. It was a good horse. Morcar had chosen it for him, and chosen wisely.

Edmund snarled as somebody else tried to rush him. They didn't try to kill him immediately, instead deciding to clutch at his injured leg whilst howling ferociously in an attempt to tear him from his mount. The Dane fell before he could complete his dastardly task, a Saxon warrior on foot accosting him from behind and splitting his head into bloody fragments. Edmund nodded in thanks and looked to his right, seeing his brother's dying horse before him, Æthelstan himself struggling to sit up amidst the thrashing, swirling melee. A particularly burly Dane was cutting his way closer, his sword red with gore and his eyes alight with malice. Æthelstan was in serious danger.

Edmund tried to steer his horse to intercept him, but his efforts were repeatedly frustrated by the fighting. People kept getting in the way, and he couldn't just ride over any of his compatriots, so he slid from the saddle, knowing he was better off on his feet. He lost sight of his brother again whilst he fought his way closer, his vision becoming partially obscured when he was sprayed with blood from persons unknown. He rubbed feverishly at the faceplate of his helmet, his clumsy gauntlets initially doing little to snatch the fluid from his eyes. He looked up, blinking and squinting and yet still moving forward, his vision clearing just in time to see Æthelstan take a sword to the guts.

To his credit, he'd managed to get up. He'd staggered on, dazed and without a helmet, his normally immaculate mane of hair caked with dirt and blood. The Dane who'd gone to such efforts to reach him in this state must have thought luck was with him, since the aetheling appeared so enfeebled and confused that victory could only be a certainty. He'd then impaled him through the stomach, the length of his sword vanishing into his already bruised and battered flesh. He held him on his blade, grinning into Æthelstan's face with broken, rotten teeth. He wanted to savour the moment, Edmund thought; sealing it into memory to regale others with stories for years to come, his reputation secured as the one who'd killed England's heir.

Whatever his intentions, they mattered little. Edmund stormed upon him, his face a red mask of righteous fury. He hewed his sword down across his exposed wrist, and the Northman shrieked in agony and surprise, Æthelstan sliding off his blade and again falling to the earth, the Dane's weapon and severed hand joining him a split second later. Edmund finished the job, hacking once, twice, three times in a descending figure-eight motion, his foe's face, head and neck coming apart under the punishing assault.

Edmund let him fall, the heathen's body slamming into the ground in a welter of blood and tearing, disintegrating flesh. He then rushed to his brother, kneeling down beside him. He was bleeding profusely, the sword looking like it had pierced right through his stomach to leave a brutal, jagged exit in the small of his back. Æthelstan must have been seriously concussed to begin with for that man to have gotten the better of him like this. His physical strength must have been something too. It was no easy task to penetrate a full coat of mail with one single strike, and his brother's armour wasn't exactly average when it came to quality and craftsmanship.

He rolled him onto his back, hoping to apply pressure to his stomach wound. Æthelstan fluttered his eyes, appearing to slip in and out of consciousness, his head lolling backwards and a trickle of blood emerging from his mouth. Edmund could see now that he'd sustained an injury to the side of his head, although precisely how remained a mystery. A fall from a horse could be a serious affair, but with a helmet on it shouldn't have proved so catastrophic. Perhaps he'd been struck when Edmund had been occupied elsewhere.

Another blood-curdling roar swept over them. Edmund looked up to see a fresh mob of foreign bastards rushing towards him, cutting down Englishmen as they came. They had to get out of here. He lifted his brother up off the ground, Edmund's unusual strength depositing him across his left shoulder so he could still grip his sword.

He was staggering away from the fighting when he heard something behind him, very much akin to the sound of a man running to attack. He turned. It was as he'd suspected. The Dane launched himself straight at him, his expression manic and his axe clutched above his head. Edmund barely avoided the initial strike, almost falling over backwards as he stepped aside with the unconscious Æthelstan. They exchanged a few more blows, yet Edmund was unable to score a clean hit in his burdened state. Then he was hit himself, right in his side, the axe head parting the metal scales of his hauberk to dig into his ribs. He nearly fell again. But he didn't. He couldn't.

He launched a downward swing towards his opponent's knees, cutting at his left leg and causing him to pitch forward. It was a fairly standard technique, generally used to disrupt an enemy shield wall, the point being to hack at an enemy's legs so he fell forward where he could be grabbed or dispatched accordingly. It worked here, and Edmund snarled with satisfaction as he swung his sword upwards and then down. The Dane fell, his severed head rolling away with a surprised look on its face.

It wasn't over. More foes were breaking through, their numbers and ferocity pushing the English back further. Edmund was again almost bowled over when yet more of Morcar's men stormed past him to hack into the advancing enemy, the whole place further degenerating into a savage brawl of flailing axes and shattering shields. Morcar himself suddenly appeared beside him, his armour dirtied and dented as if he'd fallen off a cliff into a huge puddle of mud. Edmund didn't ask what had happened, but he was grateful for the assistance, the pair of them carrying Æthelstan between them whilst they hurried away.

Edmund's horse reappeared from out of the chaos and approached, as though it had been seeking Edmund out ever since he'd dismounted. Edmund was temporarily taken aback, thinking the beast would have done the sensible thing and fled. He wasn't about to question their good fortune, however, and so he and Morcar lifted the wounded Æthelstan up into the saddle. He slumped forward immediately, and they both had to reach up and physically hold him in place lest he fall off another horse for a second time in a day.

Edmund went to mount up, intending to speed his brother away from the fighting and return once he was in good hands. Morcar stopped him and took him to one side, gesturing for one of his men to come over and take the reins. A burly-looking fellow Edmund didn't recognise answered the call, Morcar instructing him to ride with the aetheling and deliver him to their people back at their encampment.

"I should go with him," Edmund said in protest, straining to keep the grief from his voice. "He's my brother. He needs me at his side."

"Think of what that would look like," Morcar said, his voice hoarse from shouting over the surrounding din. "You both led us into this assault. Everyone saw your brother fall. If they see you both retreat, they'll think we're all lost! They must see you're still on your feet and won't leave them!"

Morcar was a wise man, and his advice here was sound. Edmund wanted desperately to go with his brother, yet if he did, it would indeed look like the battle was over. He had to stay. He had to let the men know there was still an aetheling among them. He had to let the enemy know their actions here would not go unpunished.

Morcar's man rode away from the fighting, Edmund's dutiful steed bearing him and the unconscious Æthelstan back into the valley and the safety it harboured. Edmund's memory of the battle was a little patchy from that point on, in part due to the injury he'd taken to his side. He remembered Sigeferth fighting alongside them as they were pushed further and further back, the ground they'd gained from their initial charge now almost entirely lost. Horns and drums had then been heard in the distance, signalling somebody, somewhere, to advance, the raucous cries of what seemed like thousands rising up in answer. That could mean only one thing. Their father was coming to help them.

He couldn't see much, but they could all sense something had happened, each man in their diminishing army fighting with a renewed confidence even as the Danes continued to hammer into them. They could at least hear some kind of conflagration taking place on the other side of the plain, but in their situation it didn't seem to be making any difference, and the enemy's numbers were still sufficient to continue pushing them back. Hours seemed to pass, the daylight fading with the passage of time, Edmund's sword becoming almost unbearably heavy as the fighting ground on and on. Hardly any of their warriors were still on horseback, and their infantry looked to have lost a third or more of their number. This would be a hard-fought victory, if it came at all.

They then heard yet more drums, the sound mournful when compared to their earlier exuberance. Edmund knew what that meant. Retreat. The king was falling back. They'd failed. Not because their plan hadn't gone into operation but because they'd simply been outfought. The enemy host was a vast, fearsome beast, one that would not be undone by force of arms. Perhaps their father had been right all along. Perhaps words rather than swords were the solution here. Were they, Edmund and Æthelstan, the real fools in all this?

It certainly seemed like that from where Edmund was now sitting. The monks had finished tending to his brother, and they'd done the same for Edmund, bandaging him so his entire torso seemed to have been wrapped tight with linen. They'd all left the dining hall to tend to others, Morcar and Sigeferth staying put, both men maintaining a silent vigil whilst Edmund sat, his brother's hand still clasped in his.

They'd been lost in their thoughts for what felt like hours, their only source of illumination a sliver of moonlight pouring in from the narrow, arched windows at the head of the chamber. There was a stillness here that Edmund appreciated, the gentle silence in marked contrast to the hammering uproar of what he'd just been through. They'd lost the battle, but they'd done well to retreat as they had, the men falling back through the valley in some semblance of order. The Danes had attempted to pursue them, but they were as tired as they were and soon gave up the chase when night came upon them.

Those men still on their feet had slogged through the darkness, many carrying or dragging their wounded friends with them. They'd found the still unresponsive Æthelstan back at their makeshift camp just north of the ruins of Bernecestre, Edmund thanking Morcar's man, whose name was Godric, for having taken him this far. There was no rest to be had, though. The enemy might resume their pursuit of them come morning, and Æthelstan needed the attention of those skilled in the healing arts.

God must have been with them that night. There was precious little explanation for how they'd come across the monastery other than divine guidance, dark as it was. And yet they had found it, off the beaten path, the flickering light from the brazier at its front gate serving to guide them. The monks had been fearful at first, only unbarring their doors when they'd confirmed they were indeed Englishmen in need of aid. They'd then swarmed out to greet them, every one eager to aid the many wounded and bring some final, comforting words to those they could not.

Sigeferth had ordered the rest to continue back to Snotingeham. It was too much of a risk, he'd said, to have the army just stop, for their numbers would make them too visible and be liable to put the monks in danger. It was a miracle in itself, he'd also said, that the monastery hadn't been burnt along with everything else as Thorkell had swept by, and so they were to do everything they could to ensure they remained safe.

Edmund had agreed, but he'd also wondered precisely how the monks had avoided detection when so many others had not. He thought to ask but didn't want to risk appearing rude, knowing for certain they had to keep these monks on side if they were to be of any use with his brother. His situation was indeed dire. He'd not stirred the entire time. He just lay there, his eyes closed and sunken, chest rising and falling rhythmically, defying death.

There was no telling how long he could survive, and the monks had been more than gracious in allowing them to carry him inside and lay him out as he was now. They'd not said much about his condition, preferring to work in silence, but they had admitted he was "severely wounded" and that the next few hours would tell "how things go from here". Edmund suspected the truth was much harsher, thinking the monks inclined to try and soften the blow and spare him any additional grief. He could read the situation well enough. If his brother survived the night, it would be another miracle for them. He would stay with him throughout, sitting just as he was, his hand in his, the pair of them as close as could be, awaiting the morning.

He must have fallen asleep, his prayers lulling him into a dreamless repose that persisted until disturbed by the coming of dawn. The chamber was cold, the emergent morning outside bringing a sharp, biting chill. Æthelstan hadn't stirred, but his breath was still coming, slow and shallow, his face as pale as the light creeping in from the windows. Morcar and Sigeferth were slumbering close to the hearth, their cloaks wrapped tightly about them.

Edmund struggled to get up, his pain returning as he fetched his own cloak. He draped it over his brother from the neck down, hoping to insulate him lest he catch some ailment that might spell his final end. He resumed his seat, once more taking Æthelstan's hand in his, noting with concern how frigid he seemed to the touch. They sat like this for a while longer, Edmund's head hanging low in silent prayer until he heard doors opening from behind him.

One of the monks he'd met last night entered the chamber, a flask of something held out in his calloused hands. He pressed it close to Æthelstan's lips, wetting them with what looked like clear water. His eyes then fell upon Edmund, his aged, grey-bearded face marked with concern.

"How do you feel?" he asked quietly to avoid disturbing the others.

"Like I've been hit with an axe," Edmund replied ruefully, the monk's face slowly cracking into a modest smile at the simple honesty of his answer.

"I'm glad to see you at least are doing well, but I'm sad to say two of your men passed in the night. The rest seem to be doing better."

"I would see them," Morcar said suddenly from over his shoulder, Edmund almost falling from his seat in surprise at his sudden appearance. He'd not heard him wake nor noticed his approach, making him wonder for one panicked moment if he'd sustained some kind of injury to his ears. He put the thought to rest. He was just distracted. He had many worries, yet his ears were not one of them.

The monk nodded at Morcar's request, the pair of them then leaving the chamber and heading for wherever it was in the monastery the monks had laid out the recently dead. The sound of their departure appeared to stir Sigeferth from his slumber, the man rising and depositing himself upon another chair adjacent to Edmund's.

"How is he?"

"No change," replied Edmund. "He's cold. His hand is like ice. I've tried to keep him warm, but…"

"You must be cold, too, Edmund. You look like one huge, bandaged bruise. I'd say let me help you put your tunic back on, but I doubt you want me acting like your mother."

"My mother is dead, she doesn't act like much of anything."

Sigeferth fell silent, awkward after Edmund's sullen reply. He hadn't been fair to him. He was only trying to help, and his description of him as a "huge, bandaged bruise" wasn't inaccurate. He'd do well to get some clothes back on, but he'd need help to do it. The monks had bandaged him so tightly it was a struggle to even move.

"I'm sorry," Edmund said. "I don't want to seem ungrateful. If you could fetch my tunic and help me…just don't mention this to…"

"I won't," Sigeferth said as he slipped Edmund's tunic over his head and chest. "It's not ideal to need help getting dressed, but I think you have an excuse. I also think it's fair to assume the man who did this to you is feeling worse this morning."

"I don't think he's feeling anything," Edmund mumbled, his movements awkward and painful as he struggled to adjust his arms so they'd slide down into the sleeves. "I cut his head off if I recall correctly. I don't think he was up for telling me how he felt after that. I don't expect he'll write to me either."

"I'll take your word for it," replied Sigeferth, resuming his seat, Edmund finally managing to get himself covered and settled. "Cutting a man's head off isn't something you just imagine or easily forget. I'll wager his head isn't the only one missing its body after yesterday."

"I'll wager," Edmund agreed, mirroring Sigeferth's words. He again took his brother's hand. Silence returned to the room, the two men content to let their thoughts wander awhile. The monk who had dropped in earlier soon reappeared, and Morcar with him, looking as happy as they could be given their circumstances. Sigeferth inquired about their wounded, Morcar informing him that some of their warriors were too badly hurt to be moved. Edmund grit his teeth. They had to leave. The danger wasn't over, and if the enemy tracked them here, they and all the monks would die. Hard decisions loomed, and Edmund really didn't want to have to be the one to make them.

"What do you think of your father's behaviour, Edmund?" Sigeferth asked, changing the topic, much to Edmund's relief. "I don't think I'm alone in saying I'd feared he wouldn't actually attack Thorkell and might instead leave us to fend for ourselves."

"I'm not sure," he replied. "I'm not sure about a lot of things. I can't make sense of his actions. I never did learn why he was so enraged to hear this Alaric fellow had survived the trials of Eastengle, either."

"Alaric?" asked Morcar, taking a seat alongside him, the monk again checking on the still motionless Æthelstan. "This is the man your father was dreaming about, or some such? A hard thing to want somebody dead because of a dream."

"Hard and strange, that's my father," said Edmund, "although I'm still flummoxed about the situation. The fact he had Alaric's wife, father, and brother in captivity, too, was odd. None of them really understood why when I went to question them."

"The father is an ealdorman, though?" inquired Sigeferth. Edmund had told them of his conversation with Alaric's wife, Æva, some weeks ago following his return to Snotingeham, also informing them of the Ealdorman Ælfric's predicament in general. He had gone to see Ælfric just after he'd reunited Æva with her son, yet the old man had been reluctant to speak with him, instead protesting his innocence and refusing to engage further. His blind son, Ælfgar, also hadn't been much help, looking irritatingly smug in the face of Edmund's inquiries. Whatever knowledge the man had on his situation, he took some pleasure in hiding it.

"He is indeed an ealdorman," Edmund confirmed, wondering if Sigeferth had somehow forgotten who he was or was merely inquiring just to take his mind off his brother's plight. "The Ealdorman Ælfric of Hamptonscir…one of the most powerful men in the kingdom, as if you'd really forgotten, Sigeferth."

Sigeferth didn't reply. He was looking up at the monk, who was, in turn, staring straight at Edmund as if he'd said something truly astonishing.

"The Ealdorman Ælfric has been imprisoned by the king?"

"He has," Edmund replied, wondering why the monk might be so interested. "Along with his daughter-in-law and his son."

"Ælfgar?"

"Yes, Ælfgar," Edmund confirmed. "Forgive me though, brother, but why the interest? You seemed shocked to hear the name Ælfric."

"You must forgive me also then," replied the monk, "but perhaps Ælfric's crimes against us are not so well known outside of the Church. I'd imagine the king had good reason to imprison him. If only he'd seen fit to do it sooner."

"Why would you say that?" Morcar asked, his eyes lighting up a little at the prospect of acquiring new information.

"Perhaps it's not for me to say, but if you are interested, we do have a brother here who hails from Abbendone. He's a curious fellow. A thegn before he came to us. Wulfgeat is his name, but I will ask you to be tactful. He's left that world of intrigue and deceit behind him."

"Wait, Abbendone? Wulfgeat?" Edmund asked, confused. "I'm sorry, brother, but what does such a place and such a person have to do with Ælfric falling afoul of the king?"

"A lot. The Ealdorman Ælfric was one of those who tried to take advantage of our king's youth and loneliness following the death of his mother. He manipulated him into seizing certain lands that rightfully belonged to the Church. Abbendone was such a place, and it was here Ælfric used his influence over Æthelred to see his brother and son receive a share of the spoils. Wulfgeat objected to the whole sordid business. Things didn't go well for him after that. And so he came to live with us."

"Which son of Ælfric was involved?" Morcar pressed.

"Ælfgar, as I recall. The king later recanted of his misjudgement, realising how he'd been misled. He then punished Ælfric by having Ælfgar blinded."

All eyes fell on Edmund. He knew what they were thinking, surmising he must have known of these events given he was, after all, a son of Æthelred. He had never heard of any of this, though. He'd only so much as seen Ælfric a few times in his life, always when he was visiting Lundenburg for the sake of a Witan. He'd never met this Ælfgar until he'd tried to speak with him in his cell, and as unpleasant as he seemed, he thought it overly harsh to have had him blinded for the alleged schemes of his father.

As fascinating as it all was, this wasn't the time or the place for such a discussion. Æthelstan was lying right here and still close to death by the looks of him. He didn't know if he could hear them, but Edmund just wasn't in the mood for discussing treachery and yet more treachery as if somehow there could ever be an end to it in this sin-addled world. He'd inquire about this Wulfgeat later, but in the meantime, he simply wasn't interested in the troubled past of an imprisoned ealdorman, nor why his own eccentric father was having nightmares about his son. His brother was all he cared about now.

Æthelstan suddenly squeezed his hand, a feeble grip, but a marked change from the previous limpness. Edmund stood up in a heartbeat, his wounds protesting at his sudden movement. He gazed down at his brother, Æthelstan's eyes now fluttering like he was struggling to open them. Morcar, Sigeferth, and the still unnamed monk gathered around him, each looking on with renewed hope.

Æthelstan opened his eyes and looked up at Edmund, a weak smile upon his face. He drank from the monk's offered flask, emptying it almost entirely before he shook his head to signal his satisfaction. He tried to speak, sounding more like he was about to engage in a coughing fit, a weak, rasping voice eventually emerging from between his lips.

"I'm sorry…brother…but…I think you'll have to go ahead and be king without me."

Something looked to be fading from Æthelstan's eyes. Edmund had heard people call the eyes the "windows to the soul", and he'd dismissed the notion as foolish sentiment at the time, but it looked very much the case here, and not in a good way. His brother was dying, and the truth was in the eyes, as if his soul was drifting from his body even as he spoke. Edmund gripped his hand tighter, his own eyes filling with tears as he gave voice to a denial.

"Don't say that! You'll be king! Don't leave us now, Æthelstan! Please, don't leave me to face all this alone!"

If his brother had the strength to comply, perhaps he would have done. Yet he'd given his all, and the wounds he'd sustained were severe to the point he should really be dead already. His gaze wandered to Edmund's side, noting how his hastily-donned tunic had fallen open to expose some of his increasingly blood-stained bandages. Æthelstan seemed to take in his injuries, his slight smile growing more pronounced when he again locked eyes with Edmund.

"I told you," he whispered. "You have sides of iron. You'll be our warrior king. Edmund…Ironside."

Æthelstan's gaze again shifted, like he was staring at something just over Edmund's shoulder. His breath weakened, eventually giving out altogether, a long, slow rattle emitting from his lungs. Then he was still, his eyes fading with his breath. Edmund protested, demanded, implored his older brother to remain, to stay as he was, to be at his side in the trials ahead, to be their king. He received no reply, the only sound now heard the unashamed weeping of his own grief-stricken heart.

XVII

They'd lain the bodies out, all three of them, within the confines of the yard. They were in a terrible state, each one cut, pierced, or otherwise mauled, their clothes stiff with their own fluids. Eamon rubbed his palms on his breecs, his hands still slick and sticky with the blood of the man he'd killed not twenty minutes prior. It didn't help. He'd need a proper wash after this.

Filthy or not, his exertions had saved Alaric's life. The first of the intruders had made a right hash of it, thinking that by launching himself into some kind of berserk fury he'd get the better of him. None of that had gone his way. Alaric had moved fast, knocking him off his feet with a pommel strike to the face. He'd fallen hard, too hard, hitting his head on the cobbled stones outside Ulfcytel's hall, his skull fracturing with an audible crack.

But he'd not been alone. Another attacker had emerged from the shadows, catching Alaric entirely off guard. Eamon had then appeared from somewhere, ambushing the sneak with some stealth of his own, his axe parting the man's forearm from his elbow with a brutal swing. A third assassin had tried to rush them, this one similarly skilled in avoiding detection and again attempted to remove Alaric's head from his shoulders. It was always directed at him. Nobody else.

He'd been killed, of course. The indomitable Cenric had proved himself more than useful, storming in with a strong thrust that had stopped the attacker in his tracks, the jagged iron tip of a spear buried deep in his chest. They'd then dragged the corpses into the secluded yard adjacent to the hall. The people of Canterburie were troubled enough as it was without witnessing blood and bodies on their streets. It was some small mercy that evening was upon them. Casual onlookers would see little in the deepening twilight.

"They want you, Alaric, not me."

There was no measure of blame in Ulfcytel's voice. The assassins did always seem to come for him and nobody else. There was no indication as to why, and they'd not yet taken any of them alive. It was all a mystery, and Alaric didn't like it.

"Something tells me I was supposed to die that night at Thorkell's camp," said Alaric. "It's like fate is trying to balance itself out. Complete what should have been done."

"That's miserable talk, Alaric," Cenric muttered. "You survived because the Danes thought you dead with everyone else. These men were sent by other men for worldly reasons, nothing more."

"You're right, Cenric…but I was supposed to die there. Eadric set us up that night, and he's found out I walked away from it…not in one piece, sadly…but he knows I walked away."

The four men stood in silence, their expressions grim as they continued to stare down at those they'd killed. Ulfcytel had that look when he was deep in thought, Alaric always thinking he appeared stuck between deciding to go on a murderous rampage or simply sit down and enjoy another horn of mead. Nobody questioned that Eadric, and perhaps the king, were the ones sending these troublemakers into the city. The curious thing was why Alaric was being targeted rather than anyone else.

They'd originally thought they were going after Archbishop Ælfheah. When the first batch of bastards had made their presence known, it had been to attack Alaric as he escorted the archbishop through the streets on their way to the cathedral. Alaric had immediately assumed he had to defend Ælfheah to the death, thinking the mystery figure that had ultimately turned out to be Cenric was just another assassin. Cenric had waded into the brawl on his side, proving himself yet again to be the monster he'd always been when it came to a fight.

But that hadn't been the end of it. Three days later, another two men had attacked Alaric outside the smithy, the pair of them almost taking his head off whilst he sat chewing on his lunch. The old blacksmith himself had come storming out to face them, swinging his hammer like he meant it and cracking the ribs of one of them before he could even turn to face him. Alaric had recovered swiftly, killing both him and his accomplice within the space of a few seconds. It had been the height of bad manners to interrupt his lunch like that. He'd dropped his bread and cheese too.

There'd then been another incident about a week later, this time involving four attackers that had waylaid both Alaric and Ulfcytel as they returned from inspecting some new recruits. Alaric had suspected they were after the ealdorman and had thus bundled the protesting Ulfcytel into an alley so they'd only have to face two opponents at a time. That had worked, and they'd dispatched three in quick order, but the sole survivor had tried to flee, prompting Alaric to embark on a chase in an effort to capture him alive.

That was a forlorn hope. Eamon had heard the commotion and come charging into the street, his axe cutting the assassin's legs out from under him as he sped past. Alaric had closed in, hoping to question the bastard and get some information about what precisely was going on. It was not to be. The injured man hadn't been one for giving up, instead producing a blade from his boot that he'd then attempted to ram through Alaric's remaining eye socket. Eamon had reacted fast, his axe caving his skull in with a single downward swipe. Alaric had been grateful for the speedy response.

Another attack followed several days later, just as Alaric was leaving the cathedral after attending vespers. He'd had to run back into the narthex that time, surprise and then fear making him realise it would be foolhardy to try and face his five attackers on his own. They'd moved after him through the panicking crowd with menacing ease, their eyes fixed on Alaric. Chaos had ensued, the townsfolk reacting to the presence of drawn blades with predictable alarm. Fortunately, several watchmen had overheard the commotion and come running to investigate, causing the troublemakers to give up and vanish into the night.

Alaric hadn't known what to say. The reeve, Ælfweard, didn't know either, and sadly had no answers on who these men were or what they were doing in his city. He'd then suggested they perhaps close the gates, cutting off the threat and trapping the hoodlums so they could be apprehended later. Alaric had disagreed. They needed Canterburie open. Warriors were still coming almost every day, responding to Ulfcytel's noble summons to defend the sacred bastion of Saint Augustine against the encroaching heathen host of Thorkell the Tall. Sealing the gates entirely would send the wrong message.

Then the most recent attempt on his life had been made, resulting in the three dead men now laid out at his feet. As usual, his attackers seemed fairly ordinary in equipment and attire, wearing little armour and fighting with easily concealed weapons. Alaric wondered if he should beware any of the recruits that had arrived. They'd all come armed and armoured. They could make his life difficult if they so chose.

"I'd say Eadric is behind this, mark my words," said Cenric. "If you think he wanted you dead in Eastengle, then it stands to reason he still desires it. He wasn't messing around when he came to Porteceaster. I reckon you're the last piece of whatever puzzle he wants to finish off."

"I think it's time we had a talk about your father," said Ulfcytel quietly. Alaric turned to look at him, his eyebrows raised. Cenric was also looking over at the ealdorman, a hint of confusion playing across his otherwise soldierly countenance.

"What do you mean? What do you know about him?"

"You'll recall we nearly had this conversation when we first met in my pavilion at Hringmere? You were confused on why Æthelstan and I were a little…unsurprised that your father had not arrived with the rest of the men from Hamptonscir. We should discuss this. It may shed light on our current ordeals."

Alaric simply nodded, gesturing for Cenric to accompany him as he followed Ulfcytel's lumbering form out of the yard and back into his hall. Alaric remembered that initial conversation well. Osbert had led him into the pavilion to meet with Ulfcytel, mercifully granting him an opportunity to get out of the incessant rain. Alaric had then taken an almost immediate dislike to the now deceased Æthelstan, who was acting like he was goading him into defending his father's honour. Ulfcytel had defused the tensions, but he hadn't corrected Æthelstan in the slightest. Alaric had endured sore feelings over it at the time.

He hadn't had much of a chance to inquire further about why they'd seemed to hold his father in such low regard. Events had moved so swiftly from that point on, Osmund's death and Alaric's own injury incapacitating him when he should have been fighting with the rest of Ulfcytel's army. His journey from Offetuna, the battle at Gipeswic, and their ultimate escape from Eastengle had also left little time for revisiting past conversations. Perhaps now was indeed an opportunity to shed some light on unfinished business.

They entered the hall through the rear entrance, moving past two surly-looking guards to slip through the narrow door into the interior. Alaric and Cenric followed as Ulfcytel moved on into the main chamber where they'd held their meeting with the archbishop, Eamon apparently deciding to remain outside and guard the bodies of the men he'd help slay.

They found Osbert sat within and close to the hearth, poring over several parchments spread out on the table before him. He'd originally come running when he'd heard the fighting outside, looking disappointed with himself when he realised it was all over by the time he'd drawn his weapon. Alaric was glad. He'd become increasingly protective of the young man as time had gone on, insisting he accompany him to regular services at the cathedral. Osbert had been willing, yet something was also holding him back when it came to prayer. Alaric knew the signs. He'd been there himself. Osbert felt guilty over what had happened to Bertram and did not feel worthy to stand in the presence of his Lord. A spiritual sickness. It needed healing.

Osbert looked up when Ulfcytel approached, the larger, older man taking a seat next to him. Alaric's unease increased when he noticed Ulfcytel make a gesture towards Osbert. The lad seemed to understand, rising to his feet and making his way to the front entrance and the streets beyond. He nodded towards Alaric when he passed by, his departure leaving just him and Cenric alone as they stood before Ulfcytel.

"Will you both sit?"

"I have a feeling I'd rather be on my feet for this," Alaric said coolly.

"Are you happy for your man Cenric to hear this? This is a very private matter. I would not want to cause you further embarrassment."

"Cenric is loyal to me and my family. Always has been. He should know everything he can know on what is happening here."

"I understand," Ulfcytel nodded, looking almost distraught behind that vast beard. He took a deep breath, steadying himself for whatever he thought was about to happen. He'd been wise to. His next words were simply astonishing.

"Your father once attempted to betray the king for the sake of Svienn Forkbeard."

Alaric's remaining eye widened in shock, his hand instinctively dropping to his sword. Cenric inhaled sharply, apparently as surprised as he was.

"I appreciate that neither of you have attempted to kill me," Ulfcytel continued, his face deadly serious. "Allow me to explain. Just a year after the Battle of Malduna, our king summoned a great fleet to depart from Lundenburg to hopefully catch Svienn in the open sea and defeat him. Your father, Alaric, is believed to have alerted Svienn to the impending attack, ensuring our defeat was a foregone conclusion."

"Why?!" Alaric thundered, his voice afflicted by dismay and anger in equal measure. "Why do this?! What could he have possibly gained from such a thing?!"

"That's the big question, and I don't have all the answers. What I do know is that the king ordered your brother…Ælfgar, is it?"

Alaric nodded.

"Well," continued Ulfcytel, "he ordered him blinded after the…"

"I know!" Alaric interrupted again, his indignation difficult to restrain. "I know it was on Æthelred's orders that my brother lost his sight! But this level of treachery? From my own father? To betray us all for the sake of Svienn?!"

"I understand this is hard for you to hear, Alaric," said Ulfcytel patiently. "For whatever reason, your father did inform Svienn of the disposition of our fleet. He then claimed illness as a means to abandon his own ship before we met the enemy in battle. The king took his revenge on your brother soon after."

Alaric turned to Cenric, hoping to gain some kind of answer from the man. He was calm, appearing more or less resigned to what he was hearing. There was, however, a troubled look in his eyes, the kind one might have when reliving some distant memory that one would prefer to leave undisturbed.

"I know of the battle you speak of," Cenric said quietly. "I was there. I had not been brought into Ælfric's personal service then, but I was with the ships and crews he'd brought up from Suthhamtunam. He did leave us the night before battle was joined…we never knew why, and many of us never came home. Svienn was well prepared for us."

"None of that means my father told Svienn you were coming!"

Cenric didn't say anything to that, preferring to ignore Alaric's harsh tone in favour of silence. Alaric considered it a point well-made that nobody had any real knowledge of his father's intentions, even if it were true that he'd abandoned the fleet for whatever reason. Ulfcytel seemed to sense what he was thinking, although Alaric had, at this point, wished he would simply stop speaking.

"I understand your position," he said sympathetically, "and I don't know for sure what was going through your father's mind. But the king told me what exactly had transpired just days later. Æthelred was different then. More stable. Coherent. He was quite convinced your father had turned on him, and given his whereabouts during the battle…"

"No disrespect, Ulfcytel, but why would my father retain his rank if he was a traitor? Surely the king would have his head?"

"He believed punishment had been enacted with the blinding of your brother. There was reputedly some other business your brother was mixed up in, something about the acquisition of Church lands. I paid it little heed at the time. Æthelred, though, was very much aware his position as king was vulnerable. Your father could have given him more of a headache had he been removed and free to lead a possible uprising of southern thegns. That is why he was permitted to keep his title."

"And how do you know he was not simply unwell? Does my father have to be assumed a liar?"

"No, but he employed this excuse a second time. Seven years ago, in fact. For reasons unknown, he refused to engage Svienn's forces as they pressed towards Wiltune, claiming illness was…"

"Say that again," Alaric demanded, his voice cracking slightly with emotion. "Say that again, about Wiltune. Please."

Ulfcytel paused a moment, a look of concern passing across his face. There was no reason to assume Ulfcytel was intentionally speaking falsehood. They'd been through too much together to just start lying to one another for the sake of some courtly intrigue, and Ulfcytel was not the type of man to engage in such low pursuits. He was a man of honour, and as much as Alaric wanted to disbelieve him, part of him knew he was likely telling the truth.

"Your father feigned illness to avoid attacking Svienn's forces as they closed in on Wiltune. The entire settlement was ravaged and bu…"

"I know," Alaric breathed. He felt weak, so he reached out to steady himself on one of the chairs immediately in front of him. He sensed Cenric step closer, his burly hand gently clasping his right shoulder. He struggled to steady his breathing, the memories of his troubled past rising up to overwhelm him.

"We waited for him, my men and I," Alaric began, his voice frail. "The plan was to link up with both Ælfric and the Hamptonscir fyrd and go on to hit Svienn before he could move further east. I don't know what happened. My father never came. Then the Danes attacked my men. We barely got out only to return to find Wiltune…"

"Gone."

Cenric had finished his sentence for him. He knew what Alaric and Æva had been through there. He knew what had happened to their baby Alfred, although, like everyone, he was in the dark as to Brandon's true heritage. Alaric took a deep, shuddering breath and pulled himself up straight. Ulfcytel should know of his loss.

"My son, Alfred, was killed there."

Ulfcytel rose unsteadily from his chair. He leant forward over the table, hands upon the surface, fixing Alaric with his deep, concerned eyes.

"I had no idea, lad. I almost regret bringing all this up now. Did your father tell you why he'd not had his forces join with yours?"

"No," said Alaric with a slight shrug, his voice still barely above that of a whisper. "He never told me. He said Svienn had been a wily foe, outmanoeuvring us, confusing us as to his real intent. I don't know what to think. But my father wasn't there. He never even saw battle. I did. My wife did. That's all I have to say."

Ulfcytel leaned back on his heels, his right hand raised to paw at his beard thoughtfully. A chill silence descended, the only sound audible the soft crackling of firewood smouldering away in the hearth. All outside seemed quiet also, the recent clash of iron on iron now far from everyone's thoughts. Cenric's voice suddenly cut through the silence, posing a question towards Ulfcytel.

"Is it correct to say you believe King Æthelred has kept these past…slights…in mind and has now finally decided to deal with my Lord Ælfric?"

Ulfcytel nodded, still thoughtful. "Those are my suspicions, yes. The south has been devastated, so there's no chance of a rising in defence of Ælfric. It's also possible that Æthelred is working to settle some scores to put himself in a better position to face Thorkell. He did, of course, command Ælfric to raise an army last year after Thorkell had landed, only to be again de…"

"No!" Alaric interjected forcefully. "That is not what happened! I told you and Æthelstan this before, during our very first meeting. My father DID raise our fyrd only for the king to head back to Lundenburg. We could have stopped Thorkell there and then, had we the men."

"Then I fear we're back to discussing a previous problem," Ulfcytel said. "Somebody is misdirecting our king, feeding him bad advice…manipulating him even."

"Eadric."

Cenric and Alaric had spoken in unison. There could be little doubt the Ealdorman of Mierce was heavily involved in all of this. Even if the king had every reason to hate Ælfric, it was more than evident Eadric was directing that animosity towards his own ends. Cenric had told him in some detail of Eadric's brief but brutal siege of Porteceaster. Alaric found it hard to imagine the man would take so much satisfaction in his callous work if he didn't stand to gain from it.

"No doubt," Ulfcytel concurred, "although, as you told us, Cenric, Eadric was claiming to be acting on the king's orders when he apprehended Alaric's family. So Alaric probably is the last loose end in this sordid affair that he wants tied up. Hence the assassins."

Panic suddenly swelled in Alaric's chest. If the king did indeed want him dead because of his allegedly traitorous father, then that could mean he'd already executed him. His father may not be simply languishing in a cell somewhere. He could be dead. Along with his brother and his wife. Perhaps even Brandon.

"Then if Æthelred is that serious about my death, it stands to reason he's murdered my family already. My father…my Æva…"

Alaric almost doubled over, such was the weight of his despair. He only had the one eye capable of weeping, yet he placed his hands upon his visage as if he had two, both grief and shame overwhelming him. He felt Cenric's steely embrace across his shoulders, the man's voice speaking softly yet firmly into his ear.

"Have faith! Had the king wanted them dead, he would have just had them killed when we were set upon in Suthhamtunam! And people told me they'd seen them all on the road to Lundenburg, held captive, yes, but alive. We don't know the full story yet, but we must stay strong, Alaric. For Æva. For Brandon."

"Do they even know I'm alive?!" Alaric exclaimed, turning to face Cenric, his tears now on full display. "There's no way for them to know I even made it out of Eastengle. They could have died thinking I was another tangled corpse at Hringmere!"

"I told Æva I would find you and bring you home!" said Cenric, holding Alaric by the shoulders, his voice a low, determined rumble. "She'd been despairing, yes, but she had hope. And I did find you! Against all odds, I escaped Suthhamtunam and found you! And now all that remains is one final struggle…one last ordeal to see that this city stands tall and its people remain safe. And then, Alaric, we will find your family. I swear it, with God as my witness, I will be at your side in this."

"As will I," Ulfcytel announced, his tone heavy with intent. "I know how much you wanted to go to your family when Cenric first told you of their plight. You chose the noble part in staying here to help us defend this place. You sacrificed your own personal interests to serve many. For that and more, I will always be grateful to call you a friend. And because of that, once this battle with Thorkell is over, I will do everything in my power to see your family returned to you."

"Even if my father is a traitor?" Alaric asked, his voice still weak with distress.

"Even if that is so. I'll be honest with you, Alaric, there was a time I'd have wanted to have Ælfric's head for what he'd done. Good men died because of him. I was confused when I was told he was marching to aid us in Eastengle. But he did. You did. And he can't be all bad if he raised a man like you. If he has done what the king believes him to have done… well…come what may, we will discover the truth of all this together."

Alaric steadied himself, both Cenric's and Ulfcytel's words sinking deep into his heart. It wouldn't be rational to think his family were dead simply because assassins were attempting to kill him. A man could drive himself insane fretting over matters that he had no way of knowing and were outside of his control. His task presently was as it had always been. Canterburie must be defended.

Yet what he'd learned here had shaken him. If Ulfcytel was correct, his father wasn't just a traitor but had actively played a role in his son's death. Alaric couldn't believe, or perhaps just didn't want to believe, that such a thing could somehow be true. Ælfric had grieved for his grandson. He remembered it well. There had to be some explanation. He had a strong feeling the only way he'd get to hear it was from his father's own mouth.

Alaric took a seat, hoping to settle himself after such harrowing revelations. Ulfcytel passed him a mug of something from across the table, Alaric eagerly sipping at what predictably turned out to be mead. Cenric sat next to him, the three of them drinking together as they sat huddled amidst the dancing firelight. Night was creeping in, the hall becoming host to the ever-lengthening shadows he'd grown accustomed to in his many evenings here with Ulfcytel. The fire kept them at bay, yet they always persisted, the darkness clinging to the corners and alcoves in defiance of the light.

Osbert made his way back into the hall, the young man appearing through the main entrance after making himself scarce on Ulfcytel's orders. He looked well, sitting at their table and gratefully accepting a mug when it was offered. Eamon came in a minute or two later, his expression serious, informing them he'd already arranged for the night watch to take up their duties around the hall. Alaric motioned for him to join them, knowing he most likely needed it. He'd spent a lot of time on guard duty himself of late. It was time for him to rest those feet of his.

"Have our two missing friends made themselves known?" Alaric asked. The three men they'd killed earlier had more than likely been from the party that had tried to attack him outside the cathedral several nights past. That meant at least two other assailants were still loose in the city, perhaps planning a further attempt on his life.

Eamon shook his head and took a deep sip of mead. "There's no sign of them," he said, his dark moustache now flecked with foam. "It was foolish for them to try to attack you here, regardless. If there are survivors still active in the city, I'd wager they will wait again to catch you on your own. My advice is you don't give them the opportunity."

"Wise words," said Cenric. "I'd add we can't afford to let our guard down, even when surrounded by our own people. These idiots have probably worked out that random attacks in the street are not working. It seems to me that the next attempt on your life will be from some of the warriors flocking into the city from elsewhere. I'd suggest, Alaric, that you don't get too close to any of the new arrivals whenever they assemble for training or outfitting. I have a feeling we'd come to regret it."

"How am I supposed to lead these men in battle if we can't trust any of them?" Alaric asked, a more rhetorical question than anything else. "Will I really have to watch my back as well as my front once the fighting begins?"

"That's troubling, yes," Ulfcytel admitted, his eyes again thoughtful. "I'd suggest we command together then. Stick close to me, and have Cenric with you too. Few people are going to be foolish enough to go after you if they think Cenric is going to be on hand to give them a slapping, right Cenric?"

"That's right!" Cenric answered triumphantly. "I will do more than slap them, though, should anyone be so bold as to make a move like that. Dismember would be a better word to choose."

Alaric laughed, surprising himself with the sound of it. Everyone joined in, even the usually grim-looking Eamon. It was a harsh thing to find amusing, but in all fairness, that wasn't why they were laughing. Cenric's attitude was precisely what they needed, and his blunt humour had served as the shock they'd required to lift them from their low spirits. Being indoors, by the fire, and with plenty to drink was also a great comfort. They might be about to be attacked by thousands of ferocious madmen looking to burn their city, but for the moment, they had good company and good drink. That counted for a lot.

A distraction soon came. The front doors of the hall again creaked inwards and open, the night air doing its best to temporarily push back the warmth before they could close. Two visitors had come. Both Ælfweard and Leofwine looked like they could do with some rest. The reeve was well attired as usual, appearing to have taken great care in deliberately choosing an outfit of blacks and greys to blend with the dark mail tunic that covered his torso. Leofwine looked like the warrior he was, his grey, undecorated cloak parting to reveal a sturdy shirt of ringed metal extending down past his knees. He was armed, a robust-looking spear clasped in his right hand, his left gripping a rounded shield close to his side. He never seemed to be apart from Ælfweard of late, always looking prepared, an impressive sword also visible in a scabbard at his hip. Given the security situation, Alaric was not surprised.

They had a severe look to them tonight, one that perhaps was not entirely a product of fatigue. Ælfweard took in the room, his eyes darting between those sitting at the table before finally settling on Ulfcytel's burly form. He raised his hand up to his short, well-groomed beard and cleared his throat, pausing again as if pondering his words carefully before speaking.

"I'll get right to the point. I received word not an hour ago that King Æthelred has attacked the armies of Thorkell the Tall as the latter made his way back south through what's left of Oxenefordscir. There were losses on both sides. The king's eldest son, the Aetheling Æthelstan, is dead."

"Dead?!" Alaric exclaimed, his eye widening with alarm. "What happened? He fought alongside the king? Why would Æthelred face Thorkell now? And who retained the field?"

"I'm afraid the heathens were victorious," Ælfweard answered sadly, "but they didn't emerge unscathed. Word is Æthelstan led a surprise attack alongside his brother, the Aetheling Edmund, and Sigeferth and Morcar with all the fighting men of the Five Boroughs. The king is reputed to have then attacked Thorkell's host as it turned to deal with his sons. Fighting carried on for the rest of the day until the king withdrew back to Lundenburg."

"But young Æthelstan actually fell?" inquired Ulfcytel with some urgency. "People saw this with their own eyes?"

"They did. He is dead…and Edmund, Sigeferth, and Morcar have retreated with what was left of their force to Snotingeham. The king is believed to be unhurt, although he's…more unstable, shall we say. He is said to have entered a period of mourning and refuses to engage further with matters of state."

Alaric's mind began to race. If he remembered correctly, both Edmund and Æthelstan had admitted when he'd met them on the road that they disagreed with their father's decision to levy an additional tax on the realm. It was logical to surmise they'd been unable to convince him to relent and had thus decided to take matters into their own hands by attacking Thorkell's army. But why would Æthelred have then followed them in such a bold course of action? It was out of character for him, to say the least. Perhaps the aethelings had acted alone, hoping their bravery on the field would shame their father into joining them.

"Do we know if Æthelred intended for any of this to happen?" Alaric asked, giving voice to his thoughts. "I mean, what was he even doing with an army outside of Lundenburg's walls? That's unusually aggressive behaviour for him, at least as far as this war is concerned."

"We simply don't know," Ælfweard admitted with a resigned shrug. "But there was a sizeable battle, and it seems Æthelstan and company were the instigators. It's a shame. He was a great fighter. I knew him."

Alaric rose from his seat and drew his sword in one smooth movement. He held it out in front of him, staring down at the flat of the blade now shimmering in the gentle firelight. The silver plate along the hilt and cross-guard sparkled majestically, as if rejoicing at being beheld by so many. It was a fine and worthy gift, one that had served him well already. Alaric had the feeling it would be with him for a long, long time. A life companion. In the short term, he'd honour the fallen aetheling by beheading Thorkell with it.

"Æthelstan gifted me with this when we met by chance last summer," announced Alaric, Osbert nodding solemnly at the memory. "He acted like he wasn't making a sacrifice, telling me he had plenty more. I don't know how true that was, but in my mind, he didn't have to do that. He chose to honour me when he saw I was in need. I've not forgotten it and never will, and I tell all of you here that I intend to see our lost King Æthelstan avenged. Thorkell has already taken so much from us. I look forward to settling the balance with this very blade."

All those seated began hammering their cups upon the table in approval of Alaric's words. Mead sloshed and spilled as the cacophony continued, Osbert looking particularly enthusiastic given he'd had the honour of meeting Æthelstan and Edmund with him. They'd not really spoken of it since, but Alaric suspected the chance encounter had affected him quite deeply. It was a shock to both of them that recent events had taken them to such a sorry conclusion. At least Æthelstan had won a good death, defending his realm in the face of overwhelming odds. He'd be remembered.

"What else can you tell us?" Alaric asked Ælfweard, the clattering of cups now subsiding. "Is there word on Thorkell's present movements?"

"That is perhaps the most important piece of information I've come to give you," answered Ælfweard. "After the battle, he carried on as he did, laying waste to the south west, as expected. But he's moving east with a new purpose now, burning all he finds, of course, but marching east. He has his eye set on a larger prize, I'd say."

"He's coming for us then," said Ulfcytel. "There's not a lot left for him to ravage, unless he's stupid enough to attack Lundenburg again, which he isn't. He'll smash his way past the capital and then…"

His voice drifted off. It didn't matter. Everyone knew what he meant. Canterburie was the choice target. There was little in the English south, east, or west that Thorkell hadn't attacked yet, and the city had only been spared last year because Ælfweard had paid him off at the last minute. They were next. Thorkell was coming for them, to finish what he'd started. They had to prevail. There was no other choice.

"There will be no attempt to pay Thorkell to leave us alone," Ulfcytel rumbled, like he was sensing the apprehension around him. "Those days are over. There will be no negotiations. No compromises. We face him here. Nothing else will do."

That provoked another round of clattering cups from those seated, yet Ælfweard looked a little hurt, thinking perhaps that some barb had been directed at him. He thought wrong if that were the case. Nobody blamed him for his actions when he'd faced Thorkell the last time. Canterburie had been without the means to resist him then. They'd had too few men, and Thorkell's host had been both fresh and vast in number. Ælfweard had taken the only course left open to him. The fact the city was still standing was testament to the rightness of his decision.

Their ad hoc meeting soon broke up, Ælfweard heading back to his tower in the southern quarter under the protection of the ever-watchful Leofwine. Alaric retired to his lodgings inside the hall, his bed in one of the side rooms just off from the main chamber. Cenric always insisted on remaining with him, stressing he wouldn't be able to sleep if he were out of his sight and unguarded. The hall was well protected as it was, but Alaric had decided to humour Cenric, secretly thinking the man was just trying to make himself useful. He'd always been so very loyal to his father, and with assassins on the loose, his natural instincts had come into play. He let him sleep in his chamber, arranging for several furs and blankets to be placed on the otherwise hard floor to grant him at least some comfort. Cenric needed rest as much as anyone else. He'd be of little use in a fight if he were exhausted.

The night passed without incident, the watchmen stationed outside proving enough to deter any troublemakers. Alaric and Cenric then ate breakfast together, their repast of honeyed porridge and warm milk proving more than enough to satisfy their appetites. Ulfcytel himself had, for some reason, taken to trying to toast bread over the embers of last night's fire, insisting also that they share the finished product with him as he munched away and sprayed crumbs out and into his beard. Alaric chanced a nibble of the blackened slice he'd been given. It was better than he'd feared.

The day's drama soon began. The man Alaric had hired weeks ago to get a message to his wife finally returned from Porteceaster, informing him of what Cenric had already told him regarding the town being sacked and the fortress itself taken into the possession of Eadric's soldiers. Alaric went to pay him for his efforts, thanking him for at least having attempted to get word to his family. Then the messenger dropped a name. Alaric recognised it. So did Ulfcytel, although his reaction was a tad more dramatic. Alaric had rarely seen a man so visibly flushed with anger in such a short space of time.

"Say that again, my man! Who now reigns in Porteceaster?!"

The messenger looked taken aback, evidently unused to such esteemed company and most certainly unused to seeing them so animated. He hesitated before responding, thinking on what had been asked of him and most likely wondering why it even mattered. He then dropped that hateful name again, his tone hesitant as if fearing Ulfcytel's reaction.

"Thurcytel. Thurcytel is the name I heard. The locals say he's been given stewardship of Porteceaster for his services to the king. What services those might be, I know not."

Ulfcytel remained silent, his hands closing in on themselves to form trembling fists. Alaric remembered this Thurcytel well. He'd been one of the ealdorman's Eastenglian notables back at Hringmere when they'd all met before their attack on Thorkell's camp. When he'd finally seen Ulfcytel again following his and Osbert's journey through the forests, he'd learned Thurcytel was not of such noble character. In fact, he'd cost them the Battle of Hringmere by retreating with his men just as he was supposed to hit Thorkell's host in the flank. Ulfcytel's instinct was that there was a connection between this betrayal and Eadric's own sinister antics. This messenger had all but confirmed it.

Unfortunately, the man knew nothing else of import. There was always the slim chance this was another Thurcytel he'd heard spoken of, but Alaric doubted it. The fiend must have been known to Eadric before he'd even appeared in Ulfcytel's camp. They'd hatched this plan, the pair of them, intending to lose the battle for Eastengle for the sake of some petty intrigue that was yet to be fully revealed. It was repulsive. Perhaps England really had become as mired in sin as the likes of Abbot Ælfmær insisted.

The abbot himself was also a strange one. After Ulfcytel had shouted him down that night they'd all met with the archbishop, he'd made himself scarce, but not for long. He'd been heard preaching in the streets, calling for the population to repent of their sins lest they be punished by the Northmen God himself had unleashed on them. Alaric was fine with repentance, but these sermons were demoralising with their repeated insistence that God was somehow an instigator behind Thorkell's murderous invasion. Ulfcytel had ordered him to desist, even getting the archbishop to threaten him with appropriate censure. That had worked, yet Alaric still had an ill feeling about that man. They'd be hearing from him again before all this was over.

"So now we know where Thurcytel bolted to after he betrayed us," Ulfcytel seethed, his fists still clenched at his side. "We'll get to him later. Too many good men have died because of that hell-bound swine."

"Did you hear of anyone by that name when Eadric besieged you in Porteceaster, Cenric?" Alaric asked.

"I don't recall," Cenric answered flatly. "Eadric had a lot of men with him. There was a man standing near him like he was some kind of bodyguard. I don't know who he was, but it could be this man you speak of now."

Alaric finally dismissed the messenger, the poor man looking grateful to be able to escape a conversation he clearly had no comprehension of. Ulfcytel sat down again and resumed pawing at the remains of his toast, his expression pained as he pondered what he'd learned. Alaric considered the situation clear enough, and spoke words to that effect, stating that Thurcytel had been rewarded by Eadric for his role in betraying them at Hringmere. It stood to reason, also, that Eadric was seeking to place an ally in a position of power now that Alaric's father no longer held sway in Hamptonscir. It was all probably part of some broader plan that only Eadric knew the true dimensions of.

"This also suggests Eadric's hold over the king is greater than we might have thought," Alaric continued, his mind working quickly as he speculated on recent events. "If he can get his own people appointed to positions as valuable as the one Thurcytel now occupies…"

"I hear you, Alaric," Ulfcytel answered, an impressive feat given he'd had to speak around the mouthful of toast he was chewing. "Eadric is no doubt working to have allies placed where it would suit him most. Our problem is we know so little about this rat of a man other than that he's identified us as an obstacle to whatever plans he has in motion. Another problem is we can't do anything about it just yet, what with that massive army heading straight for us."

"I would say we focus on what's in front of us first," Cenric suggested. "Everything hinges around the battle to come. If we win, the Ealdorman Ulfcytel will attain a level of renown that will see his name spoken with respect in the courts of kings across the continent. Your word will carry so much weight you'll no doubt be able to play a greater role in convincing our own King Æthelred to…relent."

"Relent?" Ulfcytel asked, his eyebrows rising slightly. "Or abdicate? You can speak freely, Cenric. You've no doubt noticed Æthelred and I no longer hold each other in high regard, even if he did somehow manage to grow some testicles recently when he attacked Thorkell."

"I wouldn't want to talk treason, my lord," Cenric admitted, his face now doubly serious. "I don't have a head for this sort of thing. I just want what is best for England. The family I'm sworn to is imprisoned, unjustly. I would prefer to reason with the king on this so he might see them freed. I think you'd be the man to do that, no? As I said…your words carry weight."

"You say you have no head for this, my friend," Ulfcytel said darkly, "but I fear you've stumbled upon the heart of the matter. My reputation speaks for me. I take no false pride in that; it is what it is. I've always fought the enemies of this land, and had I defeated Thorkell at Hringmere, my reputation would have soared yet higher. That, I think, explains a few things. The king knows what people say about him. He also knows what people say about me. I'm a threat. And I bloody well will be even more so once we're done with Thorkell here!"

"You believe Æthelred has wanted you out of the way for some time?" Alaric asked. "Even before Hringmere? He wanted you defeated to prevent you from becoming even more of a rival?"

"Aye, but I never wanted to be his rival. I just wanted to do my duty. Can I help it if me and my men fought well when we stood up to Svienn Forkbeard years back? Can I help it that they rallied to me again when Thorkell came calling? I won't apologise for that, but in these times, that's enough to get a man marked. I wasn't sure before, but now we know that Eadric and Thurcytel were working together…"

"Could they have acted alone?" Cenric ventured. "You say the king can be erratic and prone to bad decisions…could this Eadric just be doing as he pleases now?"

"Again, there's truth to what you suggest," Ulfcytel affirmed. "Æthelred is indeed troubled to the point Eadric is getting away with a lot without his knowledge…and yet I think Eadric worked on his fears about me…convinced him that I intended to use a victorious army against him. That would have gotten him the approval he needed to set in motion his and Thurcytel's plan to cost us the battle."

"And kill Osmund, Æthelstan, and all of my men," Alaric added.

"I thought Æthelstan died just recently?" queried Cenric confusedly. Alaric explained that the Æthelstan he'd referred to was the king's brother-in-law, the sibling of the king's late wife, Ælfgifu. He also explained how they'd journeyed together to attack Thorkell in his own camp after being so deceived by Eadric. Cenric was visibly grieved. He'd never met Æthelstan, but it was a sad thing to hear of yet another good man falling to treachery.

"Which reminds me," Alaric said as he retrieved Æthelstan's wedding ring from his pocket. "I still have this. I wonder if I'll ever get to give it back to his beloved."

"That's the same ring you took from Æthelstan's body? The one you showed me before?" asked Ulfcytel.

"It is," answered Alaric.

"You've carried that far now," Ulfcytel nodded approvingly. "You should hold on to it. Once we're finished here…"

"Once we defeat Thorkell, save Canterburie, save my family, save the kingdom, and everything else?" Alaric was smiling now. They had many things to attend to, all of tremendous import. But such was life. And they were very much alive.

"Yes!" Ulfcytel laughed, Cenric also emitting a chuckle. "Once we've done all that and seen off any other sudden invasions or terrible catastrophes, then we'll travel to Norþanhymbre and return Æthelstan's ring to his wife."

"You know her?" asked Alaric.

"I do not, no," Ulfcytel admitted. "So we'll have to do some investigating. But it's important we do this. It's important to do justice to all under our care, great or small.

As you have done unto the least of these, my brethren…"

"You did it to me."

Both Alaric and Cenric had finished Ulfcytel's paraphrasing of Holy Scripture for him. He was right, of course, and these were always words to keep in mind. They'd faced many trials now, suffering misfortune and betrayal. There were many other ordeals on the horizon and no safe course that would see them secure either victory or honour without yet more hardship.

But they remained men of faith. They were Christians, and Alaric, for one, would sooner go screaming to his grave than compromise on his obligations to his Lord Jesus Christ. It was one thing to fight great battles and win lasting renown, but to focus purely on that was the way of pride rather than virtue. Æthelstan's wife was somewhere out there, broken-hearted over the loss of her husband and wondering how he'd been taken from her. He'd see that she was given some comfort with the return of this ring. It was a hard path they were on, and so little was certain. But he'd make sure this was done.

XVIII

They'd come out of the night, the combined radiance from a thousand torches lighting up the horizon as if the land itself were aflame. That wasn't so far from the truth. They'd seen Reddinges burning just the night before, the dull red glow expanding to cover the western approaches until dawn. Now it was Estreham and what looked like a half dozen other settlements were on fire. There'd be more soon enough. Thorkell's horde had shown no mercy in the past. It wouldn't be any different now.

King Æthelred pulled his robes tighter, his altitude atop the curtain wall ensuring he was woefully exposed to the winter's cold. His teeth rattled as he continued to gaze out over the worn stone parapet, unable to tear his eyes from the terrible conflagration taking place just a few miles across the river. He supposed he should be grateful they were keeping their distance. If they came about and headed north towards the city itself, he wasn't sure what he'd do. The losses he'd taken at Bernecestre had been significant. Lundenburg had never been more vulnerable.

Ecgberht stood to his left, surveying the burning horizon with a look that gave away nothing of his true emotions, if he even had any. Æthelred envied him. He'd been unable to quiet his nerves since Bernecestre, the dreams and that damnable Alaric returning each night to haunt him like never before. Not even his queen had been able to calm him. There would be no consoling him now. He'd lost his firstborn son. Æthelstan was gone, his body smashed and ruined alongside his army. He'd not seen a corpse nor received indisputable proof of his demise, but he knew it was so. A father could feel these things.

Æthelred turned his head to both his left and then his right. The battlements as far as he could see were lined with warriors, the men assembling on Ecgberht's boisterous command to flock to the walls and prepare to repel an assault. Their helmets and spear tips caught the starlight as they stood motionless in the night's breeze, each one of them staring out into the dark in shared horror at the sight that assailed them.

Not all of them were true fighters. Desperate times had called for desperate measures, and so Ecgberht had set about packing the walls with common folk to hopefully fool the enemy into thinking a garrison of thousands was waiting for them. It was a clever ruse, and it might work if Thorkell's men didn't come too close. Æthelred, however, could see a different picture. The men were afraid, and many would struggle to hold their own if it came to a fight.

Æthelred's teeth again began rattling audibly in his mouth, the noise prompting Ecgberht to gaze in his direction with his typically hard expression. Both he and the king were dressed as if battle might come upon them at any moment, yet that was where the similarities ended. Æthelred was aware he made for a sorry sight, sensing he looked old and fatigued even as Ecgberht appeared as potent and menacing as ever. He wanted nothing more than to return to his hall and his thoughts, savouring his isolation whilst wallowing further in grief. Yet he dared not leave the wall. If Thorkell were to actually turn and attack them here, he'd be expected to remain as he was.

"Can I assist the king?" Ecgberht asked, his tone suggesting he was putting some effort into hiding his disgust at Æthelred's frailty. He knew Ecgberht despised him, now more than ever. They'd all loved him so very much when he'd given the order to attack Thorkell just weeks ago, but defeat had changed all that. None of them truly cared for him. It made no difference. Obedience was all that mattered.

"You may not," answered Æthelred, his eyes still focused on the distant flames of yet another burning village. They were like a line of glowing dots now, running from left to right, the ones furthest to the west dimming as they burnt themselves out whilst others sprung to life 'neath Thorkell's brutal touch. It was quite a sight, if you could somehow forget what it all signified.

"The king looks tired," Ecgberht insisted. "Thorkell is continuing west into Cantwara. Our ruse has worked. He'll remember the beating he took here last year when he attacked our walls. He'll be moving on to easier targets."

"Is that supposed to make me feel better?"

"No," Ecgberht answered, "but it means the greatest city you have is safe for a time. You should attend to your family. Your children will…"

"Will what? Want to comfort their beloved father after the death of their brother, Æthelstan? Shall I regale them with tales of how he was stupid enough to attack our foreign visitors and how I was too weak to save him?"

Ecgberht scowled, the look unmistakable despite the concealment granted from his thick dark beard and sturdy iron helmet. He didn't maintain eye contact for long, turning instead to continue staring out over the walls with the rest of his men, his attempt at comforting his king a wasted effort. Perhaps Æthelred had been too hard on the man.

"Ecgberht…" Æthelred began, his voice unsure, timid even. His commander turned to face him, his expression again neutral.

"I'm sorry for my harshness. You've always served me well. I see that. And you're right. I am tired. I think I should rest."

"I will let you know if the situation escalates," said Ecgberht, his persona once more very much that of the dutiful soldier. Æthelred nodded, the gesture slow and hesitant, fatigue and sadness making even the simplest movements difficult to carry out. Ecgberht gave a short bow in response, the king then turning and moving back through the men and towards the nearest stairwell. His two personal guards followed, only one particularly well-known to him. The other had given his life to save him at Bernecestre. Æthelred would remember him.

That was if he could make his way down these stairs first. He'd not wanted to ask for help, thinking it vital the men see their king was at least strong enough to climb these steps under his own power. He'd needed the help of his guards to get up here to begin with, and his descent was no different, the entire experience turning out to be one of protracted embarrassment. He was just glad everyone's attention was still focused on the horizon.

When he'd finally made his way down to street level, his side was again aching, the fall he'd sustained in the recent battle continuing to bother him in the form of a recurring cramp. This wasn't the only injury he'd taken. Thorkell had tried his best to strangle the life from him, and so his throat, too, was still visibly marked, his flesh appearing as if it had withered at the heathen's terrible touch.

Perhaps it had. Who knew what dark powers that man was aligned with? He certainly had something protecting him. He'd survived the hammering his bodyguard had given him, seemingly on a fluke. Perhaps Thorkell really was allied with forces too terrible to mention. After all the devastation he'd caused, was that so implausible?

Æthelred didn't care to dwell on such matters, finding them more than unsettling whilst making his way through these already dark and ominous streets. Everything was so hushed, the pervasive silence disturbed only by his own slow, echoing footsteps and those of his guards. He doubted everyone was asleep. This was fear, and his people had every right to be afraid tonight. They were expecting the worst, like prey animals frozen in fright at the approach of some wild beast. He understood exactly how they felt. He'd seen that beast. He'd faced him. It was a miracle he'd survived it. So many others had not.

By the time Æthelred had made it back through the double doors of his hall, his side was aching without relent, the pain so debilitating he'd needed to reach out and place his hand upon the stone walls to catch his breath. Young Cuthbert was waiting for him within, the dutiful lad eagerly passing him a cup of warm milk with what tasted like a generous splash of honey. Æthelred took it eagerly, his hands basking in the warmth of the cup. The drink wasn't bad, either.

He gestured for Cuthbert to follow him and headed for his chambers. He decided on another destination upon reaching his door, opting to take a left down another stone passageway and through several more doors and archways until he came to his garden.

Æthelred paused to take in his surroundings. All of his children had loved it here, the carefully tended flowers and shrubberies proving a delight to them alongside the admittedly splendid view of the city beyond. Things were a little different tonight, for the place had a forlorn sense to it, as if the faint echoes of past times were peering in with regret on the undeniably terrible present. Even the plants themselves seemed sombre in their seasonal bareness, the trees creaking gently in the wintery breeze, their rigid, skeletal forms conveying the impression that they, also, were now resigned to some tragic and inescapable fate.

"Bring me wine," Æthelred said quietly. "One flask. Two cups. And the prisoner. Æva. I would speak with her."

Cuthbert vanished back the way they had come, his echoing footsteps gradually subsiding into silence. Æthelred looked out across the dark, snaking expanse of the Temes, the light of the stars above reflecting off its subdued waters. No ships were out there tonight, not that he could see anyway. The morning wouldn't bring much more activity, he knew that much. Lundenburg wasn't safe. Nowhere was. To all intents and purposes, he wasn't even King of England anymore. This was his last bastion. How long he'd have it, he did not know.

He turned as footsteps approached, three sets this time, his guards shuffling uneasily on either side of him to behold whoever was coming. Cuthbert reappeared soon enough, bearing a wooden tray festooned with two cups, a wineskin, and what looked like a platter of cheese. A defiant-looking woman dressed in a tattered grey robe came after him, her side flanked by what Æthelred assumed to be one of the guards from the prison tower. A frown creased her forehead, her lips pursed in a way that might suggest she'd eaten something sharply disagreeable, her red hair also jutting out at odd angles as if she'd slept on it over and again. Of course she had. She'd no doubt looked like this for weeks now.

Æthelred took the cup of wine offered to him by Cuthbert, the boy then leaving the tray and its contents balanced upon the short stone wall that separated the garden from the sheer drop down into the rest of the walled compound. The king ordered both him and the prison guard to leave, each retreating back into his halls without a word. The woman just stood there, her arms wrapped around her midriff, shivering in the cold, her eyes averted. He had no real idea who she was, and he didn't much care. Her husband, though, was another matter.

"What manner of a man is Alaric?"

That got her attention. She looked directly at him, her frown deeper, her lips twisting faintly into what he approximated to signify some level of disgust. She'd probably painted a pretty picture in her head by now as to what he was like, perhaps thinking him an incompetent and cruel king who'd presided over disaster after disaster only to then imprison her and her family. It wasn't inaccurate. But her opinion was irrelevant. He repeated the question, sharper now, and she answered, her voice like ice as it cut through the air.

"He's a Christian man. You would do well to ponder such matters."

Both his guards shifted slightly on their feet, her barb unexpected, at least to them. Æthelred ignored it. His mother had possessed a sharp tongue that would put hers to shame, and nobody had ever been able to make him feel as worthless and utterly powerless as his mother. This Æva was a rank amateur by comparison. Æthelred decided to take the sting out of her. He extended his arm, offering her his wine. She took it, glaring at him whilst he filled the second cup and took a sip, her own cup untasted. It was good stuff. Sharp but not bitter. The warm glow in his stomach was more than welcome too.

"So he's a good and holy man, is he, your husband? Prayers? Church? Loving his neighbour as he loves himself?"

"As you say," Æva replied, her frown still pronounced.

"But not his king?"

"He has never intended you harm. None of my family have."

Æthelred laughed at that, the sound frigid like the surrounding night. Could she really not know what kind of man Ælfric was? And his firstborn son, the now blind and bumbling Ælfgar? Surely a grasping little rat like that would give her ideas on the character of the family she'd married into? Or was this Alaric something different? He doubted it, but love did cloud the senses. She was likely just ignorant of the situation. A woman such as her wouldn't be included in the schemings and intrigue of her snake of a father-in-law.

"Why did he move to join with Ulfcytel in Eastengle?" asked Æthelred. "Hamptonscir is far away from there. Why did Ælfric not do what he usually does and look out for himself?"

"My husband implored him to assist the Ealdorman Ulfcytel," came her answer. "He's like that. He didn't want Eastengle to suffer the fate that Hamptonscir had endured. He wanted to fight."

That didn't make any sense. Both Alaric and Ælfric had been presented with several opportunities to fight Thorkell after he'd landed. Neither of them had moved to join with Æthelred's army when he'd come south to defend his loyal thegns. Their inaction and refusal to raise troops had cost the kingdom greatly. How many people would be alive today if Ælfric had simply done as he'd been told? Æthelred could be dead, even, had Eadric's spies not alerted them to the reality of Ælfric's treachery. Æva should know this.

"Your father-in-law had a fine chance, as did your husband, to fight the enemy when I told them to raise the fyrd last year. But they didn't. I could have smashed Thorkell there and then, with their help. But they failed me. What say you? Was that particularly Christian of them?"

"What are you even talking about?" Æva hissed, her eyes visibly flaring despite the darkness. "The fyrd was raised. We had men and arms ready aplenty. Then we got word you'd run back to Lundenburg and left us to it."

"Nonsense," Æthelred spat, indignant in the face of her falsehoods. "I know what happened. And do not think to lie to me again, girl. I may be in the autumn of my life, but I remain king."

"I'm not lying!" she protested, her eyes having lost none of their intensity. "What I say is true! What do you even want from me? To bring me here just to talk about my husband and threaten me if I don't give the right answers?"

"Something like that," he admitted, making no effort to disguise his callousness. "I would ask you again, though; what manner of a man is Alaric? Does he have certain ambitions, yes? He blames me for our current woes, I'd venture?"

"Ambitions?" she asked, still refusing to take so much as a sip from the cup she still held. "To be a king? To threaten you somehow?"

Her laugh wasn't entirely unpleasant. It was two parts bitterness and one part actual mirth, and for that part, Æthelred was glad to hear it, even if it was at his expense. It had been too long since he'd heard such a sound in these gardens. It had been common once, long ago, when his sons, Æthelstan, Edmund, Eadwig, and Ecgberht, with Eadred, too, had played here. He missed it, but he had no time for entertaining fond memories now, so he pushed them from his mind. It wouldn't do him any good to become emotional in front of his "guest".

"I'm glad I amuse you," he said without resentment, "but I would have you know there are many who despise me. Many who would like to see me gone. I believe your husband is one of them. What does he have planned?"

"Nothing! For heaven's sake, he's never even met you! All he knows of you is what anyone else knows; that you are King Æthelred, son to King Edgar, brother to our martyred King Ed…"

"Yes, yes, that's better!" he snapped, interrupting her before she could even finish his half-brother's name. "Now, tell me about Edward. Was he the rightful king for you both? Would you have preferred him to rule rather than me? Did Alaric speak of this?"

"How can I answer that?" she sighed, exasperated. "I didn't know Edward. Neither of us did. All we know of him is that he was murdered, and you then took the thr…"

"You think I killed him, is that it?!" snarled Æthelred, his previous resolve disintegrating with a suddenness that surprised even himself. "You think I killed Edward?! You think I murdered him so I might be king rather than him?"

His skin prickled, the hairs on the back of his neck standing erect. All eyes were on him, even his guards turning their heads to look upon his loss of control. Æva stared at him, aghast, unsure of what to say, her already pale face now looking positively wan in the delicate starlight.

"I never said that," she whispered, afraid. "I didn't know the situation…everyone said that…"

"Said what?!" Æthelred bellowed, suddenly lurching forward to ensnare Æva by the wrist. She struggled, trying to pull her hand back and away, his steely, skeletal grip enough to frustrate any such efforts. He could see the panic well up in her eyes, her fear intensifying with each passing moment. He would have his answers before morning.

"Speak to me!" he shrieked again, his hold tightening further across her straining wrist. "Alaric thinks I killed Edward?! Is that why he stares at me with the others? Is that why he appears in my dreams? But why doesn't he look like the rest of them? Why does he stare like that, like he's sorrowful or mourning or who knows what?! Tell me!"

"I don't know what you're talking about!" Æva howled. "How should I know who killed your brother? How is Alaric responsible for your dreams? We just wanted to live our lives in peace! But you always had to be so bloody useless!"

A sharp slap echoed across the garden, followed by the dull thump of something heavy impacting on grass. Æthelred hadn't actually decided to strike her, but he had on instinct, his left hand forming a fist and smashing into the side of her head with remarkable precision. He looked down at her form, motionless now, her face obscured by the tangled chaos that was her hair. He gestured for his guards. They hurried over, each man taking an arm and hauling her to her feet.

She was still breathing, and conscious also, her eyes narrowed and beholding him with a mixture of apprehension and hatred. He felt something in his chest. Guilt. He'd not intended to do that. She hadn't been wrong on all counts. If he were a good ruler, things would never have reached the crisis point they had now. He'd have been able to save his realm. He'd have been able to save his son. She had no idea of all the difficulties he had to contend with, but in the final analysis, he suspected Æva's opinion would carry the day when it came to how history was written. That hurt him even more.

He had one of his men aid the prison guard in carrying her back to her cell. He downed the rest of his wine, making sure to refill his cup before quaffing that also. This garden was too full of memories, the image of the child, Æthelstan, playing here with his brothers and sisters straining his already aching heart. Æthelred's own brother, their martyred King Edward, had also favoured this place. He remembered him here, like an age ago now, always so happy but so full of himself, like nobody else in the world mattered. What might their late father think? Who knew. King Edgar "the Peaceful" wasn't one to share his thoughts with anyone, let alone them. He'd remained aloof from the affairs of his children, as remote as the stars that now lay scattered across the sky.

What about their mothers? Which one? Æthelred's mother, Queen Ælfthryth, had hated Edward, knowing he was next in line for the throne. She would glare at him, her expression as venomous as could be, but only when she thought nobody was looking. Æthelred always saw it, though. She hated it when he saw. There would always be trouble later for that. He'd always be in the wrong. He was always at fault. Nothing he ever did was good enough, nothing he ever did was ever fruitful, nothing ever worked out, nothing worked out, nothing worked out, nothing worked out, nothing worked…

"My king?"

"What?!"

His remaining bodyguard stood perturbed, unsure of what to do. It was the new one, the replacement, and the poor fool was unused to his mood swings and very much alarmed at what he now beheld. Æthelred caught himself. What had he been doing? He'd gotten lost in his thoughts, panic and sadness seizing him in a bid to overpower him. He'd started muttering, raving almost. Embarrassing. It was just as well there'd been only one man here to witness that. He sighed anyway, his teeth again chattering as if to add to his humiliation. He should leave this place. It was late. Rest might settle his nerves. There was always the small chance the dream wouldn't come.

His slim hopes were dashed soon enough. The dream returned, awakening the troubled king with a suddenness that saw him sit bolt upright, fearing for his sanity. It was as before, Alaric and the others, with Ulfcytel and even Edmund, all staring at him whilst his brother, Edward, lay dead in the chapel. Alaric still bothered him the most, and not only for his relatively recent appearance. He always looked so…regretful. What was the real cause of that profound grief he saw in those wide, dark eyes? Was that pity there too? For whom? Was there something to all this that Æthelred simply wasn't grasping yet?

Emma, his Norman queen, slumbered as usual, undisturbed by her husband's plight. He considered waking her, wondering if her sweet words and gentle touch might assuage his turbulent mind. He couldn't. He knew what he looked like, gazing down into his washbasin, his eyes wide with fright and his bedraggled, haggard face more marked with age than seemed natural for even his admittedly long years. He let Emma sleep on, sparing her from his unceasing troubles.

He began his nightly ritual, stripping himself out of his sweat-drenched gown and searching for something more suitable for his nocturnal wanderings. He even tried brushing his beard and hair, sweeping his lank, grey locks back and away from his balding scalp. It made little difference. Æthelred looked as well as he felt. Nothing would change that. He donned a simple gown of charcoal grey, the sombre colour suiting his mood. He didn't care to wear anything on his feet. The sting of the cold stone upon his skin reminded him he was at least alive.

Æthelred crept out of his bedchamber, closing the door gently behind him. His guards took up position around him as was their wont, both men following him whilst he shuffled delicately down the hall on his usual route towards his study. Inside, it wasn't much to look at. Whereas previously it had housed an impressive assortment of tomes, the place now looked like a madman had been let loose, the shelves having been kicked apart and their precious books scattered across the floor. He cared not. He was past such concerns now.

He opened the shutters on his window and took in the expanse beyond. This view had always stirred him, even in his darkest moments, the sight of his city reminding him of what he both possessed and what might yet be possible. Lundenburg seemed different now. Fear was in the air, cloying and smothering, its terrified populace huddled in their homes and praying for God's intervention. Æthelred thought of praying with them. Should he call upon his Lord, asking him to remove his heavy burdens before he was crushed to ruin? Should he call upon him to comfort his breaking heart now his firstborn was no longer among the living?

He turned around to face the room, the painfully sharp winter wind snapping at his back. He again drank in the sorrowful sight of his ruined study. He wished he could say he did not know what had possessed him to act in such a way, but that would have been a lie. It was grief that had done it. When he'd returned from the battle, he'd been mad with remorse, unable and unwilling to hide his pain. His queen had tried to help him, assuring him everything would be all right as long as they remained together. Æthelred had sent her away, retreating instead to his study to weep alone. Then Eadric had been foolish enough to disturb him.

That had gone as well as could be expected. Eadric never knew when to leave well enough alone, instead blathering at him about how the battle had been a mistake and how they should have just retreated immediately and not alienated Thorkell from future negotiations. He never once mentioned Æthelstan. He never once mentioned any of the men who'd just died. All he could think on was politics, strategy, what they should be doing, what they shouldn't have done, what might come next, and so on. Æthelred couldn't stand it.

He'd let Eadric know that, sure enough. He couldn't remember striking him, but he'd been told he had, and Eadric had been spotted fleeing his study in some haste, his hands held up to his face to conceal his bloody nose. Æthelred's temper hadn't been satisfied with that single act, and so he'd apparently demolished his own bookshelves, his fists and feet lashing out to send their contents flying across the room. His guards had come running, weapons ready and shields raised, thinking some unknown assailant had accosted him through the window. They'd found only their king, sitting amidst the ruins of his sanctuary, his face hidden as he sobbed into hands wet with blood and tears.

The next morning he'd received yet more unwelcome news. A letter from Canterburie, something about his reeve, Ælfweard, making what sounded like an inane excuse for not paying his share of the heregeld. As annoying as it all was, Ælfweard's words had revealed something unexpected. Ulfcytel was with him, and this Alaric, too, the dastardly rogues coming to him after fighting their way out of Eastengle with what was left of their forces from Hringmere. The letter ended with yet another surprise, stating that Canterburie was likely to come under attack from Thorkell's armies, or so they thought, thanks to information provided by a "captured foreign notable".

Æthelred hadn't cared to think on it at the time, so overwhelmed was he by his recent misfortunes. Then he'd been seized with panic, realising their recent losses had left the capital vulnerable to attack. If Lundenburg fell, then Ælfweard's blatherings would be of no consequence. England would have had its heart torn from its body. The rest of the country would then inevitably collapse, and Æthelred's troubled reign would finally end in tragedy and ruin. His children also, Edward and Alfred, his sweet daughter, Godgifu, his queen too…they were all at risk now. He had to protect them. He had to be a king one last time, if that's what it came to. He'd not surrender what little was left to him without a fight.

It had not come to that, at least not yet. Thorkell's movements had been easily visible for the past several nights, the flames of his passing a painful reminder of his brute savagery and total contempt for human life. If he were heading east, then perhaps Canterburie was indeed his real target. Ælfweard was right then. The Holy City may face attack, and soon.

He moved to sit on the edge of his window, his eyes still lingering on the clutter and carnage before him. He held his head in his hands, trying to settle his mind and think on at least the beginnings of some kind of strategy. An immediate military solution wasn't tenable. Recent events had proven it was impossible to fight Thorkell and his "Jomsvikings", as he himself called them, with anything but overwhelming force. He couldn't obtain any kind of force, overwhelming or otherwise, without money, and the widespread foot-dragging and back-biting over his new tax meant he wouldn't be able to march to relieve Canterburie anytime soon. They'd have to fight alone.

Eadric had been right all along. Everything had depended on bringing Thorkell into his service. The heregeld had been a lie at first, intended to mislead his ealdormen into paying Thorkell to fight for them against King Svienn. It wasn't so much a lie presently. He did need a new army now the possibility of even talking to Thorkell had evaporated. From his perspective, Æthelred had led him into a trap, attacking him by surprise whilst he dangled the prospect of gold and riches in front of his face. There was no chance of convincing him that Æthelstan had acted alone whilst under the influence of the treacherous Sigeferth and Morcar. Not after Æthelred himself had led thousands of men in a frontal assault into the midst of his own host. The opportunity for peace had now well and truly gone.

There was only one path left open to him, barring immediate flight overseas. The north of the country was relatively unscathed, as were the Five Boroughs and also Dæfenascir under the leadership of the reclusive Ealdorman Æthelmaer. He'd ensure they paid their due in both men and gold. The Ealdorman Uhtred in Norþanhymbre was more than likely to cooperate, given Æthelred's leverage over him. Sigeferth and Morcar would have to be punished for their disloyalty and for their manipulation of his sons, although that would have to wait since their popularity could be an issue for him. He'd have to bide his time until he was better prepared. Then he'd deal with them properly. He'd already dispatched a rider to Snotingeham with a message informing Sigeferth to return his surviving children and warning him of reprisals. Let him stew in that awhile, wondering what might come next. He'd strike at his pleasure.

If all went well, Æthelred would still have a significant portion of the country within his grasp and ready to serve him. Norþanhymbrians were hardy folk, if Uhtred's victories over the Scots were anything to go by, and the men of the Five Boroughs combined with Eadric's Miercians would make for a fearsome host. The resources of Dæfenascir were also relatively untapped, and if he could rouse the local ealdorman, Æthelmaer, into activity, he saw no reason why he wouldn't rally to his king's side. Even if Canterburie were lost, and it looked like it would be, a prolonged siege would see Thorkell distracted. With a little luck, this might allow Æthelred to raise a force that could impede him, especially if he took additional losses in Cantwara.

These were the most optimistic scenarios Æthelred could currently think of, and considering how disunited his country had become, he wasn't sure if he would see them come to pass. They also didn't account for the problem of Svienn Forkbeard. If Thorkell were not simply lying, the Danish king would soon be launching yet another invasion of his lands. The revelation that he had a son, Cnut, was currently immaterial, yet it did tell Æthelred that Svienn had a designated heir and was bringing him to England for a definite purpose. Time would perhaps open up further possibilities, one where Thorkell and Svienn's animosity for one another could still be turned to Æthelred's advantage. He'd have to wait and see.

That left one single matter – his adult sons. There was a chance Edmund was still alive, assuming he had indeed fought alongside Æthelstan. He'd need to speak with him to find out what had happened and also break bread. He knew he'd neglected him and his brothers and sisters for some years now. That must change. He couldn't lose Edmund, nor Eadwig, or Wulfhild. He had to keep them safe.

Edmund was also potentially dangerous. He wasn't the fighter Æthelstan had been, nor had he the charisma, but he was good and brave and pious. Men respected that and would follow him. Technically, the bookish Eadwig may also be a contender for the throne, but Æthelred knew his scholarly son would have a hard time staking a claim without Edmund's support. That wasn't likely to be forthcoming if he knew his son as well as he thought. Edmund would be the one people would look to call king, perhaps even whilst Æthelred was still among the living. He had a feeling Sigeferth and Morcar might be doing that already, for their own dark purposes, of course. He had to get word to his children and bring them back home.

His mind settled on his daughter, Wulfhild. He'd been unkind to her ever since her husband, Ulfcytel, had sent her back to Lundenburg from Noruic, and it had not been fair. He'd let his animosity towards her husband cloud his judgement, withdrawing from her as if she were somehow tainted. He'd been wrong about so much, in recent years and beyond. Perhaps Ulfcytel really didn't mean harm. Maybe this was all just a misunderstanding. Could he still somehow be the man he'd once been glad to call a friend?

He was being foolish. Ulfcytel's popularity was always too great for Æthelred to be entirely comfortable. What's more, his own defeat at Bernecestre would have further damaged his reputation as king. It was thus very probable that Ulfcytel would soon be seen as the man to save England from the widening jaws of total defeat. Æthelred wouldn't have it. The best thing the brave Ealdorman of Eastengle could do now was defend Canterburie and give his life for it, ideally taking this Alaric character with him. He'd then declare him another lost hero of England, like he had with the great Byrhtnoð of Malduna. Ulfcytel would be honoured across the land, and Æthelred would rest easy, knowing his prowess and renown would never threaten him again.

He turned around, once more looking out upon his city. Dawn was many hours away, and the wind was picking up over the skyline, its icy fingers reaching out to tug and tear at his robes.

He didn't care. He might be an old man, miserable and alone, but he was still a King of England. He would face his trials, as he'd done many times before. No matter what happened, a son of King Æthelred would take the throne someday, even if he had to fight his way through rivers of blood and tears to see it done. It would happen. His line would continue. As would England.

XIX

"You'd have thought they'd have gotten the message by now that we're not in the mood for company."

There was no real humour in Ulfcytel's statement. Christmas had come and gone, both he and Alaric attending the services at Canterburie's cathedral with all due reverence, the month of January following soon after with a deluge of snow that had as yet failed to clear. Then they'd come. The Danes, emerging in their thousands out of the swirling darkness to the west. This was what they'd been expecting. This was what they'd been preparing for. In truth, Alaric didn't think he'd felt any braver for it.

They'd made a tremendous racket, surrounding the city on three sides and screaming up at the defenders in a cacophony of threats and dire promises. It was a horrifying sound, the Norsemen raging and snarling with a hatred that defied reason, and to Alaric's shame he'd felt fear, this spectacle of such total and overwhelming malevolence chilling him to the bones. Then he'd looked to the others that manned the walls with him. They were warriors all, and more than that, they were Christians and Englishmen. Each man present was willing to give his life for the love he bore his family, his homeland, and his God. That there was the difference between them and the enemy. The Northman fought out of greed and the thrill of spilling blood, whereas the Englishman defied his violence for the sake of protecting that which he held dear. Alaric took courage from that. Let the heathens scream and hate. Canterburie would face them undaunted.

The first assault had come on swiftly. They'd rushed the walls in one great mass and predictably floundered upon reaching the trench works the defenders had dug months back. They'd absorbed an absolute storm of arrows in the process, and many a Dane had died in the ditch, bleeding their last and denied the glory they'd no doubt expected to win. The rest had eventually reached the walls, but their flimsy ladders were not up to much, and almost every man who'd made it up to the battlements had been cut down before he could put up much of a fight. Alaric would know. He'd killed several, slicing them to pieces and hurling their remains back into the slathering horde below.

The Northmen had then retreated, chastised by their defeat and instead opting to surround the city like they hoped to starve them into submission. An entire week had then passed, the snow refusing to let up, Alaric thinking how the weather was most likely a curse for those shivering outside under the foolish notion Canterburie might run out of supplies. There was no chance of that. They'd prepared well, spending much of the money they had on purchasing food from abroad. They could last like this for months. He doubted Thorkell could.

A second assault was more determined. They'd again thrown themselves at the walls and bloody fighting had followed, the Danes surging up at the defenders like men possessed. They'd even breached one of the gates, and hundreds of bloodthirsty bastards had then come charging through to try and hack their way past a forest of Saxon spears.

They were brave, but it was not to be, and the enemy was again flung from Canterburie's walls and cleared from their streets like discarded timber. If Ulfcytel had wished for a great battle to finally settle accounts with their foreign visitors, he'd gotten it. Both sides had taken serious losses. It remained to be seen who would ultimately prevail.

The foe had assembled tonight like they had previously, Thorkell's army glittering in its own torchlight as it spread out to face the city's southern wall. The snow was still falling in the icy blackness of night, the movements of the enemy host leaving a churned-up mess of slush and footprints that served to mar the otherwise pristine winter landscape. They seemed weary, the cold getting to them after their long siege and so far fruitless efforts to break into the city. Alaric was glad of it. Every man they'd put down so far had done grim and terrible deeds in Thorkell's ravaging of England, and each one of them had been deserving of his miserable fate. All that was left was to deal with those that yet remained among the living. Then honour would be well satisfied.

Alaric glanced about from his vantage point atop the wall. Canterburie was well protected. Their fortifications may not be as impressive as Lundenburg's, but they were solid and manned by brave warriors looking to again prove themselves. Men from the countryside had been pouring in for weeks prior to Thorkell's appearance, eager to respond to the summons to defend the city. This had ensured the formation of a sizeable garrison, one that was still numerous even after their recent losses. With any luck and God's abundant grace, this upcoming battle would again go in their favour.

The city otherwise appeared dark and almost abandoned once you looked out from the fortified walls. Alaric knew Ælfweard had ordered anyone incapable of bearing arms to stay indoors, although Archbishop Ælfheah had opened up the cathedral so the inhabitants could join him in praying for deliverance. He could see the cathedral now, behind him and to the east, imposing and yet beautiful in the snow-swept night, its windows lit up from the service within. Canterburie's other, more modest wood and thatch buildings seemed to huddle around it as if seeking protection, this house of God appearing very much the heart and soul of the city, now more than ever.

Alaric turned back around in time to see a rider emerge from the thicket of men that was the Norse horde. He was moving towards them, a single hand raised in the air, hoping perhaps this would deter any attempt to riddle him with arrows. The brave man was soon joined by several other horsemen, each also raising a hand as they fell into line beside the other. They had some difficulty fording the ditch the defenders had dug previously, only appearing to see it at the last minute, so covered it was by fresh snow. Ulfcytel barked something for the men surrounding them to hold off, aware that their people would be eager to hurl their spears at any Dane stupid enough to come within reach. Alaric realised what was happening. Thorkell had sent these men to talk.

He spied the man himself soon enough, sat atop a horse at the head of his many thousands of men. Thorkell still cut an unnaturally huge figure, his dark grey steed appearing larger than normal to accommodate his weight. His great axe was slung across his back, his dark ring mail armour and black wolf hide cloak giving him a shadowy appearance even as his form was illuminated by a nearby torchbearer.

There was another alongside him that Alaric recognised, this one having that distinctive red and black helm that couldn't fail to jog his memory. There was no chance Alaric could ever forget such a man. He'd been there the night they'd attacked Thorkell's camp in Eastengle. He'd killed Osmund. He'd nearly killed Alaric. He owed him for that. Scores would be settled before the breaking of dawn. Alaric would see it done.

The first rider had now made it within shouting distance of the walls. He looked up at them, gabbling something in that strange accent. Alaric could tell Ulfcytel was at least listening to what they had to say, but none of it sounded like it was worth responding to. They hadn't bothered speaking to them before, and this just sounded like demanding nonsense, none of which was likely to be honoured even if anyone was still foolish enough to trust a Dane.

Thorkell apparently wanted them to pay him double the amount he'd extorted from Canterburie when he'd last been here, a "gracious" offer, so they said, that they'd do well to accept lest their "city burn here tonight". Alaric looked to the reeve, Ælfweard, standing a short distance away atop the battlements and marked out from the other warriors with his distinctive sapphire blue cloak. He caught Alaric's eye, his expression bewildered beneath his light iron helm.

Ulfcytel looked to him also, like he was asking for confirmation on whether he felt inclined to accept this latest offer and pay the Danes whatever they wanted. Ælfweard shook his head firmly. It was as Alaric thought. The city couldn't afford such a ridiculous sum. Thorkell was playing games with them, going through the motions of dialogue and acting like he were a man of restraint and reason before he again swept over them.

The ealdorman reacted swiftly, snatching the spear from the man next to him and hurling it into the Norse envoy to smash him from the saddle. He was killed instantly, and a collective snarl of gleeful rage erupted from the Englishmen upon the wall, several following Ulfcytel's example by hurling their own spears at the remaining Danes below. They fell soon enough, their bodies twisted and broken upon the reddening snow, the whinnying of their fleeing, panic-stricken horses carrying on the breeze.

That was all the answer Thorkell apparently needed. He let slip a single, pointed gesture with one hand, and the night erupted, the massed cries of his warriors pouring outward to wash over the terrified city and its still defiant defenders. The horde then surged towards the walls, gibbering and snarling, the burnished metal of their armour stark and ugly against the frigid whiteness of their surroundings. Alaric gritted his teeth, an involuntary growl escaping from between them, his heart upping its pace in expectation of bloodshed.

The enemy again reached the ditch, but it did little to impede them, this human tidal wave merely slowing as individual Danes either leapt across or slid downward to climb up onto the opposite side. Their situation was helped by the fact it was full of snow and corpses, the enemy at some points stepping on the bodies of the recently dead to use them as a kind of bridge. It was a macabre sight. The defenders would have to be more forceful if they hoped to stop them.

Ulfcytel had the same thought. He roared for the men to commence firing, his voice a thunderous, bellowing racket that carried out across the snowy plain and into the ears of Thorkell himself, or so seemed likely. His warriors responded immediately, an absolute deluge of thrown spears and piercing arrows erupting from the wall to pepper the maniacs beyond with some much-deserved torment.

It was as Alaric had hoped. The ditch again became choked with yet more bodies, the Danes falling to both spear and arrow as they struggled to clamber out of it. The horde, however, would not desist, and those behind pushed on and across, raising their shields up and over their heads to form a solid wall of wood and iron. The odd man was still caught out, falling back into the snow with a cry, but their numbers were too great to be thinned by mere arrows. Axe and sword would decide the balance of things tonight.

Something else would be needed, too, at least from the enemy's perspective. They'd become fixated on the southern wall, specifically the fortified gate not twenty yards from where Alaric stood. Why they had chosen this spot for the point of attack was a mystery, since the Danes immediately below them had no means to reach the Saxons on the wall and no method for breaching the gate. To all intents and purposes, they were now stuck, hiding behind their shields with no means to push forward and no will to fall back. Alaric was not impressed.

Then he saw something moving within their ranks. It was hard to spot at first, given the darkness, but he could definitely see men dragging something across the ditch, the warriors closest appearing particularly eager to conceal its movements with their shields.

"It's another ram," Ulfcytel growled. "They'll be hoping to force the gate inward whilst we're occupied with all these idiots milling about below. I don't know why they keep trying it. It doesn't end well for them."

Alaric could see he was right, although the "idiots" below were not just milling about but were hurling spears up towards the walls in the hope of returning some punishment to the defenders. Canterburie's fortifications were solid stone, but they didn't tower over the enemy like those at Lundenburg or Porteceaster. It thus wasn't too hard to throw a spear that height. As if to demonstrate the fact, several Saxons fell nearby, one toppling backwards into the streets behind them. Alaric looked down to where he'd fallen. He lay twisted at an odd angle, a spear still in his chest. He wouldn't be getting up.

"Can I trust you?" Ulfcytel suddenly asked, unperturbed by the exchange going on around them. Alaric looked at him in confusion. He hoped that was a rhetorical question. He found it hard to believe the ealdorman would suddenly doubt him now.

"Of course you can," he replied, trying to hide his confusion. Ulfcytel stared at him a moment longer, as if sizing him up. He then nodded, apparently satisfied.

"I know," he said, "but prove it once more. Get down into the street and help Osbert defend the gate when they come crashing through."

Alaric didn't need to hear any more. He moved swiftly away from the wall's edge, vaulting down the stairwell and into the street, Cenric and Eamon hurrying after him. He could see Osbert and a few hundred others up ahead and to the right, presenting a wall of shields and sharpened iron to any enemy foolish enough to try and make a breach here. This was a very defensible spot, and the gate itself was solid and largely undamaged, having been relatively unmolested up until now. Bales of hay and some lengths of timber had also been hauled into position here, confining any enemy who might make it through so they'd be funnelled into the waiting thicket of spears.

Even if the English found themselves being forced back, and they perhaps would, reinforcements from elsewhere along the walls could be brought down, attacking the enemy in the flanks as they tried to capitalise on whatever ground they'd seized. Holding this gate, even if Thorkell tried to pour his entire host through it, was very possible with a hope and a prayer. Killing every bastard who dared test them would also help.

Osbert bowed respectfully upon seeing Alaric take position close to him in the shield wall. Somebody passed him a spear from over his shoulder, although whichever of the hundreds of men behind him had done so, he wasn't sure. Everyone looked more or less the same now, all decked out in iron helms and ringed mail, the only real difference between Alaric and the rest of them being the precious sword in his scabbard. Æthelstan's blade. He'd reach for it soon enough.

Several more warriors crumpled off the walls, pierced by spears hurled by the besieging hordes outside. There was no time to help them, for the wooden gates abruptly buckled inward with a crash. They weren't breached, but they'd been hit hard, and they continued to be, again and again, as something unseen repeatedly pounded away from the opposite side. There was only one explanation for that. The enemy had got their ram into position. It was now only a matter of time.

Alaric looked up and to his right, hoping to glimpse Ulfcytel and learn more on what was happening out there. He couldn't see him presently, but the wall itself was still thick with defenders hurling whatever makeshift projectiles were available out into the night. He hoped each one found its mark.

The Danes were not deterred by such antics, for the gate suddenly burst open to reveal the Norsemen's ram, itself really a felled tree carved into a point, and the howling thousands that awaited them. The Danes stormed forward without hesitation, scrambling up and at them, their axes and blades thrashing at the defenders' pointed spear tips in a frenzied attempt to deflect them. A futile effort.

Alaric roared and thrust his right arm forward, ramming his spear through the gullet of the first Dane within reach. Osbert killed a man, too, impaling him through the guts as he was pushed forward by the weight of bodies behind him. Dozens of others met a similar fate running into the mass of spear points, but the Danes didn't let up, instead hurling themselves onward with all the manic courage their kind were known for. Many died on the spot, pierced or outright impaled, their cries pained and panicked, the frozen ground running red with blood.

Despite this, the heathens continued flooding into the gate, making Alaric wonder if Thorkell had committed his entire offensive into this one particular point. The press of bodies was immense, and the fighting only became closer and more chaotic when the Danes began to successfully edge forward, their baying multitudes cutting into the defenders with scant regard for their own losses.

Alaric's spear shattered into halves as somebody split it with the swing of an axe; that same man then making another swing to try and bury said axe in his head. Alaric drew his prized sword, pummeling the tip forward and taking the edge of his opponent's axe upon his shield. The Dane grimaced and shrieked when the heavy, thickened blade cut him open, a splash of entrails and fluids splattering down and outwards. Alaric pulled his arm back for another strike.

There was no need. The foe was out of the fight. He'd fallen, arse-first, and was now trying with trembling hands to push the steaming, fleshy ropes that were his guts back inside himself. Alaric stepped forward and kicked him in the face before bringing his boot down upon his neck, noting the dull snap that sounded over the braying melee. His men kept on with their own bloody work, cutting into this thrashing tide of killers still trying to sweep over them. The air felt heavy, that thick, metallic stench of blood rising up and into his nostrils. The smell of battle. He'd grown quite accustomed to it.

Time seemed to slow, or at least he lost any appreciation for its passage. His whole reality was now focused on death, his every move geared towards hacking and stabbing at this legion of fiends that, despite their casualties, were gradually pushing them back. He'd lost count of how many of them he'd cut down, and every one slain seemed to be immediately replaced with yet more. Saxons were dying, too, slaughtered by Danes pushing in among them after smashing gaps in their shield wall through sheer weight of numbers. It was a brutal, crude tactic that cared little for the loss of life on either side. But it was working.

Cenric was bellowing something, his shield bashed, dented, or otherwise chipped beyond recognition, his great voice thundering out his hatred for every Dane that dared come within reach of his deadly arm. He looked terrifying, his entire front drenched in crimson, from his boots to his lank, blood-sodden beard. His eyes were agleam with a furious vigour, each life he took seeming to spur him on to even greater feats of martial prowess. Alaric felt further emboldened by the sight of him and the example he set. There was no room for softness here. These men they fought had come to rape and kill a city. Each of them now cut open upon the ground had gotten what was owed; a bloody end at the hands of righteous men.

Then the shouting started. That was an understatement, since the roar of war was inescapable. This was a different kind of shouting, of the kind men make when taken unawares or alarmed to the degree they were at risk of falling into despair. Alaric couldn't see what was happening, the press of bodies around him proving too great. He could barely get his breath, so extreme were his exertions, his shield also now rent and ruined to the extent it no longer served a purpose. He let it go, looking around frantically towards the city streets behind. Something was there, moving up. Reinforcements? But then why the outcry?

He soon understood. They were reinforcements, but not for them. Danes were emerging from the streets immediately behind the gate, as if they'd somehow gotten into the city from some other entry point and moved swiftly to attack them from the rear. This couldn't be. No gate into the city was unguarded. Something must have happened, some trick, deception, or even betrayal. But how? Whatever the truth of it, his men were about to become trapped between the thousands pushing through the gate and those hundreds looking to cut into them from behind. He had to think fast.

Ulfcytel did it for him. The old man must have seen what was happening from atop the wall, doing the only thing he could before the entire battle went against him. He'd abandoned the walls altogether, leading the hundreds of men with him in a flailing, furious counter-charge at the enemy now rushing in from the streets. It was a brave move, but he wasn't fast enough, and the Danes attacking from the rear still smashed into Alaric's men as feared.

Everything turned to total chaos. The English shield wall broke apart in confusion, each man now fighting his own battle as the conflict spread out beyond the breach and into the city proper. Osbert fell, his mail rent asunder and blood flowing from his shoulder and neck. Alaric rushed to him with a shout, tearing into his attacker with shattering, sweeping blows that knocked him from his feet, his life extinguished and his head parted from his shoulders. Cenric barreled in from somewhere, using his momentum and sheer mass to hurl another Dane to the ground before impaling him through the chest.

Alaric knelt at Osbert's side, trying to quickly evaluate his wound. It didn't look good. The bastard who'd done this had been going for his throat, but Osbert's quick reactions had seen his aim go awry and his axe land just above the collarbone instead. The bone itself looked broken, and the head of the axe had been large enough to leave a bloody cleft of torn flesh extending from his right pectoral to just past his neck and shoulder. Osbert's eyes remained open, but they were wet with fear, his blinks rapid and his breathing panicked. Alaric had to get him out of here.

He picked him up, his legs trembling with effort, and heaved the young yet still sturdy man atop his left shoulder. He staggered back through the brawling mass, the blood and fury seeming to swirl and spread outward with its own terrible energy. He couldn't see Ulfcytel, yet he could hear him roaring and bellowing orders from somewhere up ahead. Something then hit Alaric in the back, whatever it was prompting a surge of icy pain to flow outwards from between his shoulder blades. He staggered forward and skidded to his knees, Osbert tumbling from his shoulder. Alaric turned around from where he knelt, half-expecting to take an axe in the face.

He'd angled his head to the left just at the right moment, the axe's edge instead clipping the side of his helmet rather than burying itself in his skull. He still slumped forward under the impact, almost falling atop the wounded Osbert. He somehow managed to roll over him, clattering onto his side and spinning around onto his now bloodied back before hauling himself up off the ground. The Norseman who'd hit him didn't let up, screaming like the madman he was as he unleashed more blows in his direction, his heavy, deadly axe scything through the air.

Alaric was steadily driven backwards by the sheer fury of this raging berserker, the tenacity and damnable malevolence of his assault leaving precious few openings for his blade to exploit. He'd lost sight of Cenric and was seemingly alone amidst the thundering chaos, his every effort now dedicated to protecting the possibly expiring Osbert from this savage maniac before him.

And yet Osbert wasn't as helpless as he looked. Alaric's attacker suddenly stumbled forward, a look of agonised surprise etched upon his face. Osbert hadn't let go of his axe as Alaric had thought, appearing to play dead only to suddenly lash out at the Dane's ankles once he came within reach. The foreign bastard staggered into Alaric, clawing at his face, the two men then toppling over together to begin the long, brutal process of attempting to beat the other to death.

He was strong, very strong, and his fists hit like a smith's hammer, his burly hands splitting both lips and nose in an avalanche of desperate violence. Alaric soaked up the damage and returned the favour, smashing his forehead into his repeatedly in a great clanging, thundering crescendo of metal helm upon metal helm. They carried on like this for some time, punching and clawing and snarling, neither man able to fully overpower the other. Then Alaric spied an opportunity.

He twisted his weight around, bringing his knee up in a hammering arc to connect with his assailant's groin. That got a result. The man went almost limp with agony, appearing to bite down on his lip, his jaw clenching shut and a muffled yet furious whine escaping his throat.

Alaric struggled upright, inhaling frantically and looking around for his sword. He saw it to his left and bent down to retrieve it, intending to finish the contest quickly and with some hope of cleanliness. The Dane recovered faster than he thought possible, kicking at his legs and again knocking him over onto his back. He managed to grip his sword all the same, bringing the edge up and across his neck to defend himself from any potential blows heading towards his face. That settled matters.

The Dane's own enthusiasm was his undoing. He'd thrown himself forward to land atop Alaric, face-first, looking like he was hoping to bite him in the throat or strangle the life from him. Whatever he'd intended, he'd merely given Alaric an opportunity. He reached out and behind with his left hand to pull the Dane closer, like a loving wife might caress the back of her husband's head to ease him in for a kiss.

This was admittedly different, Alaric instead using his grip to force the Dane's exposed neck down towards him so that his soft jugular met the raised edge of his sword. He then threw his right arm outward, the motion ensuring his blade opened up the entirety of the foe's neck as it cleaved its way across it. A shuddering fountain of gore erupted downwards to soak Alaric's face and chest in what was possibly one of the most revolting few seconds of his life to date. The Dane slumped and slid off him, jerking and spasming faintly, the life fleeing his body.

Alaric again stood, spitting and coughing in the hope of calming his sense of disgust lest he vomit up the contents of his stomach. He looked around, trying to evaluate the situation and not focus on his own hardships. Osbert had lost consciousness, and the gate itself was now in the hands of the enemy, the defenders falling back further in the face of the heathen's superior numbers. They were not overwhelmed, but the situation was looking more and more desperate. The gate, even when breached, had been a way of confining and thinning out the enemy until their losses might become intolerable. From the looks of it, that advantage was lost to them, and the Danes were pouring in as a torrent.

He finally caught sight of Ulfcytel and his men amidst the carnage, his screaming, hammering onslaught a marvel to behold. He was trying to contain the unexpected enemy force that had appeared from within the city itself, but there didn't seem to be any end to them, and the number of foes facing him was now almost as thick as those charging in through the gate. Just how had they gotten in?

Alaric pulled Osbert to his feet, once again using his now freed shield arm to lift the wounded man onto his shoulder. He continued to stumble through the bloodshed, trying to reach Ulfcytel's position. The battle had now turned to a level of savagery that Alaric had rarely witnessed before. Men were fighting like they no longer cared for their own safety, each hacking into the other with precious little regard for anything other than causing death and pain.

For the English, it was at least understandable. They were fighting for their homes, and their hatred of the enemy was grounded in generations of Scandinavian predation against their country and their people. The Northmen were fighting because they enjoyed it and the spoils that came after. That was it. They had no noble goals, and the very idea of doing good, to anyone, was likely anathema to them. Alaric despised every one of them. He'd get Osbert safe, and then he'd teach yet more of these barbarous vermin the full error of their ways.

Eamon appeared out of the fighting, his face fixed in a furious scowl and his armour rent and cleaved in a half dozen places. His eyes softened upon seeing Alaric, his mouth opening slightly in shock and concern when he beheld the wounded Osbert. An idea formed in Alaric's mind. Carting Osbert around like this was foolish when he'd been tasked with the defence of the gate. He wanted to see his friend helped, but he couldn't just forget his responsibilities or heave him all the way back to the sanctuary of the cathedral. He needed to be here.

He ordered Eamon to take Osbert, each of them as careful as they could be as they passed the injured man between themselves. The main fight was now happening both behind and in front of them, effectively sealing off the direct route to the cathedral. It might be possible to skirt around it, however, perhaps taking one of the side roads away from the gate and looping around the infiltrating enemy force to reach some kind of safety. How "safe" that safety actually was all depended on them defeating the enemy here, but it would at least get Osbert out of the fighting. He told Eamon as such. He headed off at a jog, carrying Osbert as if he were as light as a pillow before vanishing into an alley.

Alaric stormed back into it, hoping to hack his way through so he could receive input from Ulfcytel. By the time he reached him, the English position had become somewhat more organised, and Alaric rallied his men to him, their ranks reforming into a line in the hope of at least slowing the deluge of heathens flooding in from beyond the walls. It wouldn't hold for long, and they were a far cry from the force they'd been previously, but it was preferable to total anarchy. The men around him seemed more confident now he was again fighting at their side, their proximity to the raging Ulfcytel also no doubt putting them in the mood for bold deeds. Perhaps there was yet hope.

Ulfcytel was in his element, his charge into the midst of the Danish force having saved them from total disaster. He looked magnificent and yet also horrifying, wielding his sword and hefty shield both as offensive weapons, bashing Danes to the ground with his great bulk and hacking them to death before they could rise. He spun around upon hearing Alaric call out to him, his breathing laboured and skin wet with perspiration and blood, none of the latter seemingly his own.

"We can't stay like this!" Alaric shouted, struggling to make himself heard over the clamour. "The gate is lost! We have to find a more defensible position!"

"If we can't retake the gate, then Thorkell's entire army will just pour on in!"

"It IS pouring in!" Alaric lamented, his heart heavy with the realisation of it. "And we're getting smashed in two here! We need to regroup where we can keep them in front of us without any more surprises!"

Ulfcytel looked around, like he was evaluating the situation as it really was. Alaric knew he had a fine strategic mind as well as a talent for killing with his own hand. He hoped he could see what was happening and the futility of trying to make some kind of last stand here. It would cost them the city. It would cost them their lives.

"I'll hold here," Ulfcytel announced, "and you pull your men back eastward under the wall where it's clear. You then run to the cathedral to link up with our levies. I'll meet you there."

"But what will y…"

"Do as I say, Alaric. You said I could trust you. Now trust me."

Alaric didn't know how to argue with that. Ulfcytel had managed to pull himself out of some pretty horrific situations in the past. To him, this battle probably wasn't even that harrowing in light of the shock of betrayal and defeat he'd been through in Eastengle. It was also true that somebody needed to stay here and hold the enemy in place whilst the rest of the men fell back. If they all just ran at once, it would become a rout and they'd be cut down. Ulfcytel was right. Alaric knew what had to be done.

Calling attention to yourself in the middle of a pitched battle wasn't an easy thing. People were distracted enough as it was, and being attacked on two sides by several thousand frenzied lunatics only made things that much harder. Alaric had to resort to running into the midst of his men, bellowing at the top of his lungs for them to follow him. Some were hesitant, thinking him a coward who wanted to flee. Others were more trusting, these being the ones who knew him already from Eastengle. All the same, he soon managed to get a column of men to start disengaging from the fighting, leading them in a long, staggered line snaking its way east under the curtain wall.

More started to follow, Ulfcytel himself now using his booming, irresistible voice to implore them to fall back. The trickle then became a flood, although it was well-managed, Ulfcytel and his immediate company acting as a rearguard that prevented the Norsemen from simply overrunning their position. Alaric wanted to rush back over to him and fight at his side, his warrior's pride aggrieved at the very notion of turning his back to the enemy. Then he remembered Ulfcytel had commanded him clearly enough. Somebody had to organise the retreat. He'd never shirk from his duty.

They hurried back through the city, Alaric and hundreds of other battered and bloodied men jostling their way through the streets and alleys snaking towards the cathedral. The enemy was somehow everywhere, burning and braying in delusional triumph, and Alaric and company had to fight their way through several ad hoc ambushes as they retreated further. They did so gladly but took more losses, the flames from those buildings that had been set alight casting a baleful glow. There was no doubt in Alaric's mind now. Somebody had let the Danes in on purpose. Once again, they were betrayed.

By the time they arrived at the cathedral, somebody had pulled the rest of the city's garrison inward, abandoning the other walls and gates in a bid to defend what could still be defended. It was a good call, since it made no sense to try and man the walls now the enemy was within the city, and their position here limited the number of directions from which they could be attacked.

Alaric suspected the sober and soldierly Leofwine would be behind this, given he was still effectively the commander of the original garrison and would look to defend his city as best he could. True enough, he was here, rallying his troops in the wide, cobbled square outside the stone facade of the cathedral, an unusually belligerent-looking Ælfweard accompanying him. Alaric was relieved to see the reeve had made it. He'd been on the walls with them when this had all started, but he'd lost sight of him once the fighting had begun. Judging from the state of his sword arm, he hadn't been shy about getting involved. That was good. They'd all need that kind of courage if they were to defend this place to the last. The cathedral must not fall. Alaric couldn't bear to think of it.

"The enemy have outflanked us," Leofwine stated bluntly, like Alaric was somehow unaware of the situation and had been asleep for the duration of the battle until now.

"I know," said Alaric as tactfully as possible. "They appeared from behind us at the gate and…"

"Yes, I saw," interrupted Leofwine, "and it's worse than you think. Treachery has visited us this night."

"Treachery from whom?" demanded Ælfweard.

"A patrol of my watchmen came to me just after the fighting started, some of them wounded," Leofwine explained. "I'd assigned them to the western edge of the curtain wall once it was clear Thorkell would commit his forces to the southern gate. I knew we needed most of our men there, but I didn't want to leave all other entrances into the city unwatched."

"And?" Alaric asked, impatient now, although Leofwine's expression alluded to something truly terrible. If they had been betrayed, then they'd have to act fast. Justice would need to be served, and time wasn't something they currently had in vast amounts.

"Alaric, my men were set upon at one of the older, largely unused gates…but not by Danes. Englishmen did this."

Alaric understood. Somebody inside Canterburie must have waited for them to commit the bulk of their forces to countering Thorkell's main assault. Once that was done, they'd sought to secure and open up one of the less well-defended gates to the enemy, allowing them to infiltrate the city and take the defenders unawares. That would imply Thorkell had also prepared for this eventuality, as if he'd been in contact with a sympathiser willing to assist him.

"I don't know what to say," Alaric confessed darkly. "I think we all know there's no way Thorkell's beasts could have gotten within the walls without inside help. But who could have done this?"

Leofwine and Ælfweard exchanged a look. They then turned in unison to the cathedral entrance. Something stirred in Alaric's memory. A supposedly holy man, sat at Ulfcytel's table, daring to argue with the ealdorman himself about how Thorkell was God's instrument. There was something off about him, like his zeal had an intensity that gave him the quality of a fanatic. If he genuinely believed the Northmen were doing God's will in scourging England, then could he have been willing to lend his hand in aiding them?

"Abbot Ælfmær," stated Ælfweard, having come to the same conclusion as Alaric. "Abbot Ælfmær has done this. I should have been harsher with him. I should have had him incarcerated, but I didn't want to upset the archbishop. We were too tolerant of his nonsense about how England is suffering God's vengeance. Now I fear the abbot has played a part in our undoing."

"If he has, he's wasted his energy," Alaric growled, angered by Ælfweard's pessimism. "We're not defeated yet. Ælfmær's treachery may have cost us the gate, but we can still hold out here. We have hundreds of men and more still arriving. Ulfcytel will be here and…"

As if hearing his own name, the ealdorman came storming into the square, leading a line of brave, battle-worn survivors who'd opted to potentially fight to the last to ensure others could escape. Cenric was with him, jogging at his side like his situation was the most natural thing in the world and they didn't have a huge army biting at their arses. Alaric was glad. They'd been separated in the melee, and he'd feared the worst. He should have known better. Cenric just wasn't one for dying, as recent events continued to show.

"We held as long as we could, but the gate is lost, and Thorkell's inside the city," thundered Ulfcytel, his face as grim and ferocious as it was humanly possible to be. Alaric thought you could always tell a great deal about a man by how he comported himself in a fight, and Ulfcytel was no exception. When at ease, he was good-humoured, paternal even, but at times like this it was like he had almost unlimited energy to tap into, all directed towards butchering the enemy. No wonder Sviemn Forkbeard had learned to respect him. Perhaps Thorkell would endure the same lesson tonight.

"What would you have us do?" asked Alaric, gesturing towards the massed levies behind him. "It looks like we have over a thousand men here as it is. We'll need to defend the cathedral to the last. The Danes will want to loot and desecrate it. We can't allow that to happen."

"Then let's not," Ulfcytel agreed. "We may have lost the walls, but we can still make a stand here. Let's put these bastards down, tonight."

"Without control of the walls, we're at a disadvantage," Ælfweard said solemnly. "Thorkell's numbers…"

"I know," said Ulfcytel, "and I don't care. We either win here, or we die. I intend to win."

The reeve widened his eyes, unsure of what to say. He instead took a deep breath and looked back over Ulfcytel's sizeable shoulders, apparently evaluating the situation and what could be salvaged from it. Alaric followed his gaze, taking in their surroundings as he did so.

They were currently standing about a dozen paces from the western wall of the cathedral, the towering structure rising up into the cold, unfeeling night sky to loom over the snow-clad city.

Their immediate location consisted of a broad expanse of some kind of public square, the hard, clear ground appearing well-suited for what in better times would have been festivals and market days.

Tonight it was filled with warriors, those who had retreated from the walls forming defensive positions with the less experienced troops that had been held in reserve. From what they could see, the enemy was already advancing towards them down the broad thoroughfare that led to the southern gate, apparently intent on pursuing them now they'd established a foothold inside. They howled and shrieked as they came on, their cacophony of war cries hateful to the ear. They were confident. They thought they'd won. It was only fair they be dissuaded of that notion.

"I have a cathedral full of the aged and infirm here," Ælfweard said. "If we don't prevail, the Danes will kill them and everyone else in the city. We should have evacuated them all before it even came to this."

"I'll admit I thought it best we allow them to stay," Ulfcytel answered. "Men fight better when reminded of what they are fighting for. But this is another matter now. You may take a score of my men and get as many people to the northern gate as you can. Be quick about it, Ælfweard. I have a battle to fight."

The reeve didn't respond, instead striding away from Ulfcytel to immediately command a clutch of men from the many present to accompany him inside the cathedral. They vanished through its imposing entrance, the sound of panic and shouting now dimly heard from within. Ælfweard reappeared momentarily, he and his men hurrying on and away northward with what looked like a seemingly endless column of very scared, very vulnerable people. They'd be hard-pressed if the Danes found them, thought Alaric. All the more reason to fight hard here.

Both Ulfcytel and Alaric went to work, the two of them roaring, encouraging, and otherwise organising the square's defenders for the onslaught they all knew was coming. Within the space of a minute, they'd cohered them into a single block of muscle and metal, their shields interlocked and weapons pointed outwards, ready to face down whatever might be foolish enough to tackle them head-on. If the heathens were impressed or daunted by the sight, they showed absolutely no sign, instead rushing toward the square like they thought victory was already certain.

From the looks of it, the Danes had already gotten busy with one of their favourite pastimes: arson. Everything ahead from the square was now aflame, the multitude of buildings around the gate going up in smoke. Several groups of people, women mainly but some elderly men, then hove into view, having rightly gotten the notion that the safety of their homes was no real safety at all. Alaric couldn't understand where they had come from, since he'd assumed those hiding in the southern quarter would have fled earlier when it became obvious the Danes had breached the walls. They could have decided to remain indoors, he thought, hoping there was still a chance the defenders might prevail and they'd be secure. That would have changed as soon as the Danes started setting things on fire.

In any case, they were truly in a panic now and speeding towards the English front line with all haste, the enemy snapping at their heels. Many a man stood aside to let them pass, the fear-stricken mob moving through them in their efforts to escape.

Unfortunately, that meant the defensive formation that had only just been established was now compromised, and Alaric was just pondering what to do about this when the Danes charged them, the fiends piling into their now unprepared shield wall with a ferocity that bordered on the demonic.

The English were almost immediately in trouble, their men collapsing inwards under the weight of the sudden onslaught. They'd been charitable in letting the townspeople through, but they were paying for it now, the disruption to their once formidable defence costing them dear. Alaric stormed through the ranks, intent on getting into the thick of the fighting, Ulfcytel, Leofwine, and the ever-diligent Cenric at his side. The men needed to see their leaders were still with them. Alaric had a feeling they were moments away from a general rout. If that happened, it would all be over.

Ulfcytel rose to the occasion, bellowing for the men to take heart and stand firm. They did so, overcoming their initial shock and disarray to launch into a spirited counterattack. Alaric stepped into the fray, hacking and hewing as he went, determined to stay at Ulfcytel's side and lend his strength to his.

Cenric followed after him alongside Leofwine, the local men from Canterburie seeming particularly enthused to see their own commander fighting alongside them. Alaric didn't know much about Leofwine other than that he'd been charged with the city's protection for some time, but he could see he knew what he was doing and that his men trusted him. There was to be no disintegration and retreat like there had been at the gate, nor would there be any possibility of the Danes attacking them from the rear with their backs already against the walls of the cathedral. They would stand here and they would fight until either the Danes broke or every single Englishman lay dead. Nothing else would do.

Alaric hacked down with an overhead swing, splitting a Dane's helm and much of his skull. Another then flew at him from their front ranks, bashing his shield into his side and knocking him backwards. He winced, pained from the impact of the iron boss upon his ribs. His attacker saw him flinch, seeing the opening for what it was. He struck.

Ulfcytel may have been both larger and older than most warriors fighting here, but he was quicker than a man of his size had any right to be. The Dane's severed arm fell to the ground at Alaric's feet, its owner staring at his now detached limb in horror. Ulfcytel kept on at him, shattering his shield and overwhelming him with an absolute deluge of savage, unrestrained violence. His remaining hand came off, then his whole arm, leaving him alive yet helpless until Ulfcytel's blade splintered him in half from the peak of his skull to his solar plexus.

Alaric recovered quickly, throwing himself back into the fight, the men behind pushing onward with him. He could see a forest of spears now extending over his head and shoulders, the warriors at his back forming an offensive line to present a bristling array of stout ash and sharpened iron to anyone foolish enough to engage them. Many a charging maniac was impaled attempting to close the distance, and those that somehow managed to avoid such a fate soon fell to the scything blades of Alaric, Ulfcytel, and Cenric. For several glorious minutes, they seemed unstoppable, the English force rolling forward to almost eject the enemy from the square and send them packing back down the street they'd emerged from.

Yet battles are always unpredictable, and the certainty of victory can turn into the bitterness of defeat with remarkable rapidity. Neither Northman nor Saxon were known for favouring missile weapons, preferring to settle things at close range, but the Danes opted to use them now, perhaps feeling frustrated at the level of resistance they'd encountered so far. The arrows came on without warning, rising up over the burning buildings in the middle distance to pepper the entire square with jagged metal. Men screamed and fell as they were caught unawares, their shields otherwise at their sides or angled towards their front. The enemy must have a serious amount of men already inside the city to lay down that kind of barrage. This fight was not going to get any easier.

Ulfcytel let out an enraged howl upon taking an arrow in the leg, the damned thing hitting him a mere inch or so down from where the edges of his long mail shirt ended. As dastardly misfortune would have it, this was the same leg he'd taken a spear in during their battle at Gipeswic; an unpleasant quirk of chance that was no doubt not lost on the now red-faced and hopping mad ealdorman.

Both Cenric and Alaric rushed to his aid, the former extending his shield up to cover both of them so they might haul the old man to safety. The bombardment wasn't letting up, and the storm of arrows was now joined by thrown spears as the Danes they'd only just driven back did their best to add to their misfortunes.

The man immediately to Alaric's rear collapsed without so much as a whimper, the bent shaft of a spear protruding awkwardly from his mailed chest. Alaric said a silent prayer for him as he and Cenric hauled Ulfcytel over the corpse and further back through the ranks. They couldn't have him dying in full view. If everyone saw him fall right in front of them, the resistance had every chance of collapsing altogether.

Ulfcytel suddenly threw them off with a shout, his eyes sullen and resentful at whatever it was he thought they were doing. He reached down to his wounded leg and took the protruding arrow in his great paw of a hand. He tore it free, but did some real damage to himself in the process, his gritted teeth and additional beads of perspiration upon his face alluding to the pain he felt.

"You'll not stash me away with the rest of the wounded!" he snapped, Cenric still glued to his side with his shield raised to protect him from further harm. "I already had a limp, so I'll be limping a bit more after this. No harm done. We fight on!"

They didn't have time to argue. The heathens had decided they were softened up enough and were mounting yet another charge, their savage cries and thunderous footfalls echoing as they came on. Alaric could see they were putting some serious force into this one, for their front ranks were comprised of unusually large fellows all wielding what looked like heavy, two-handed axes. They looked exceptionally ferocious, this lot, and fired up with the kind of confidence that could only come from thinking their victory was a given. Alaric soon saw why.

Thorkell was with them. Alaric could see him, alongside that red-helmeted bastard, advancing just behind the outermost line of the assault. This would be it, then. If Thorkell the Tall had committed himself to this attack, then he intended to finish things here. Alaric was fine with that. It was about time the murderous bastard got his hands dirty.

He soon came to regret that thought. Thorkell hadn't obtained the reputation he had by being either a coward or inept when it came to a fight. He proved that when he and his warriors smashed into them, the English defence seeming to come apart and recoil in disarray within a few seconds of attempting to actually fight such monsters. Alaric barely managed to dodge the heavy, overhead swing of a seriously ugly-looking axe as one of Thorkell's elite rushed him, the head of the weapon burying itself into the ground and delaying the Dane by at least half a second whilst he pulled it free.

That was all Alaric required. He stepped in, swinging his sword up in a wide arc to connect with the Dane's neck. He dropped as expected, spluttering and choking on his own fluids, his life ending in an untidy, blood-drenched heap. Alaric raised his blade aloft, using the spectacle of his victory to add weight to his call for the men to stand their ground and fight on.

Many did, or at least tried, for the battle was an altogether different scenario now the Danes had deployed their very best. This was sheer savagery, even worse than the fight at the gate, and whilst the English were making a good show of it, what they were up against was beyond the experience of most of them. Thorkell's chosen elite were men of reputation, renown, and absolute malevolence, and to face them was a harrowing prospect, one that only authentically brave men would ever dare consider. Fortunately for England, it had no lack of brave men. Alaric liked to think he was one of them. He knew those fighting with him certainly were. That in itself gave him hope.

He'd somehow lost sight of Ulfcytel amidst the flailing press of bodies. He thought he saw Cenric over to the left, disembowelling a particularly vocal Norseman, the fiend sounding like he were both surprised and outraged that an Englishman had gotten the better of him. More arrows then came down among them, their gentle pattering accompanied by yet more screams and the heavy thud of falling bodies. Alaric thought it a risk for the enemy to shoot into the melee like that, but he could see their aim was directed more towards the rear of the English force pressed against the cathedral's walls. They were trapped here, with berserkers in front and death raining down from above. Only drastic action would ensure victory now.

Leofwine emerged from the chaos, his ring mail torn and shattered and his shield riddled with arrows. He'd lost his helmet and sustained a cut across his forehead, the blood seeping down into his eyes and saturating his beard to the extent he looked like he'd been tearing into the enemy with his own teeth. He leaned in closer to Alaric, wise enough to know it wouldn't be good for the men around them to hear his dire assessment of their situation.

"We're not going to be able to hold the square like this. Thorkell has had us at a disadvantage this entire time, and this is his final push. We have to delay him long enough so that the people who fled into the cathedral can escape."

Alaric stared at him, unsure of what to make of his words. The situation was desperate, that was undeniable, but they were not defeated yet. Getting as many people out of harm's way was a good idea, but he'd assumed Ælfweard had already seen to that. Had others sought refuge in there? Was the archbishop refusing to leave? If that were true, Leofwine was right to be concerned.

"Get inside and tell anyone left in there to make for the northern gate," said Alaric. "Make sure the archbishop goes with you. He's going to be a big target for Thorkell, probably for ransom money. We can't have him falling into their hands like that."

Leofwine nodded, his face twisting slightly in discomfort at his many wounds. He then hurried away from the main fight, his hobbling, fatigued form vanishing through the sturdy, wide doors of the cathedral. Alaric turned his attention back to the fighting, hoping to catch sight of the ailing Ulfcytel. He couldn't see him nor Cenric, but the battle was still going strong, the English unwilling to break before Thorkell's horde of braying killers. The toll for such defiance was a high one, and the square was now littered with corpses, bloodied and torn 'neath the falling snow. A terrible sight. But he could mourn the dead later.

He stepped back into it, joining his men as they stabbed, hacked, and otherwise gave it their all to withstand the dark tide pressing in upon them. Alaric caught one of Thorkell's men in the act of cutting a man down, the bastard's axe making short work of his victim's helm and coming close to splitting his skull in two. Alaric made sure justice came quickly, opening the Dane up with a stroke that sent his innards spewing across the ground, a second blow seeing his head roll away from his body to vanish into the surrounding stampede. Alaric plucked a discarded shield from the ground and began hammering the flat of his sword off its edge, his teeth bared in a snarl as he dared another of the heathen mob to come face him. He got his wish, just not as he'd initially envisaged.

Thorkell stepped into view, cutting a path straight for him in apparent acceptance of his challenge. Nobody could stand against him, and he killed with wild abandon, wielding his great axe with the skill and precision of a true master. He cut a horrifying figure storming forward, his vast, bloodied beard emerging from his dark, armoured head like the lolling tongue of some kind of demon. His eyes did nothing to dispel that notion, appearing aflame with a kind of other-worldly malevolence that rooted Alaric to the ground in apprehension. If there was any man upon the earth more fearsome than Thorkell the Tall, Alaric had never laid eyes on him. He hoped he never would.

Then Ulfcytel appeared. Everyone knew he was brave, but attacking Thorkell when already wounded was foolhardy, even for him. Nonetheless, he came on, charging out of what was left of the English ranks to tackle Thorkell from the side. The two of them rolled in the snow, each clawing at the other, Ulfcytel raining down blows with the pommel of his sword upon Thorkell's abnormally large helm. Alaric tried to get closer, making his way through the sea of bodies just in time to see Ulfcytel knocked backwards off Thorkell's front, the ealdorman struggling to get up and resume the contest.

Thorkell rose up onto his feet with a speed that seemed unnatural for a man of such size, his axe again in his hands as he advanced upon Ulfcytel. They exchanged several blows, their duel looking like it could go either way until Ulfcytel's wounded leg gave out, the intensity of his exertions too much for it to bear. Thorkell reacted swiftly, his axe sweeping out to cut across Ulfcytel's belly, the force serving to demolish the intricate rings of his armour and draw a not-inconsiderable amount of blood. Ulfcytel staggered backwards, a roar of pain and frustration upon his lips, the ever-ominous Thorkell moving to finish the job.

Alaric lashed out as he leapt, ducking under Thorkell's guard to deliver a sweeping slash to his midriff. Sparks flew off his armour as his blade made contact, the iron scales giving way under the deadly pressure. Thorkell made a sound akin to a grunt and a snarl both, forgetting Ulfcytel for the moment so that he might turn his attention to Alaric. The pair faced off amid the broiling carnage before launching themselves at the other, their furious blows scything the air, each knowing the victor here would be able to claim Canterburie as their prize.

It was like trying to fight some kind of evil spirit. Despite his huge size, Thorkell was in possession of a rare speed and agility that a man of his bulk simply shouldn't be capable of. There was an unnerving aura to him, too, giving the impression every single one of his sins had stuck to him; a lifetime of unconfessed, unlamented brutality pouring off his shoulders to befoul the very air itself.

Alaric mouthed the Jesus Prayer as he fought, knowing he needed every possible strength if he were to endure this encounter. Thorkell, for his part, simply kept on, wielding his axe like it was as light and agile as a practice sword. Alaric did well to avoid it, launching counterattacks when he could, but it was heavy going, and Thorkell was adept at evasion, his unusually thick armour also proving difficult to penetrate. The battle raged around them with unrelenting fury, the smoke from yet more burning buildings billowing upward into the night sky. It discoloured the snowflakes falling to the earth, half-melting them and turning them black, as if they were flakes of ash scattering upon some God-forsaken hellscape. The two men struggled on amidst it all, the world around them fading into irrelevance, each focusing all their strength and will upon doing harm to the other.

Fortunately for Alaric, the world had not, in fact, ceased to exist. Although it would pain him to admit it, Thorkell was the superior fighter, and Alaric had only survived as long as he had through sheer grit and the overpowering hatred that burned through his heart. His single eye also remained an issue, and it was a minor miracle and testament to the patience and training of Ulfcytel that he'd been able to overcome his handicap to the degree he had. It was in this sense a blessing that he found himself suddenly knocked down by the men surging up around him as they fought their own battles, his fall looking like it may actually have saved him from another arcing swing of Thorkell's axe.

He hit the ground hard, the pain from the wound he'd taken at the gate spreading across his shoulder blades and down to the base of his spine. He couldn't see, finding his view darkened and obscured in shadow by the forest of straining, desperate fighters around him. Thorkell's men were pushing forward yet again, forming a wedge around their towering leader to try and smash what was left of Canterburie's defenders. Those Saxons still fighting rose up to meet them, the two sides again tearing into each other in a last brutal dance to decide the fate of a city.

Alaric must have passed out, if only briefly. He came to his senses just a few feet away from the fighting, alive and unharmed. He wasn't sure how he'd gotten here, although his curiosity was sated upon being dragged upright, the very fatigued and battered form of Eamon helping him keep his balance. Alaric felt relief wash over him. He'd feared Eamon had died or otherwise fallen to misfortune after his escape from the fighting at the gate. He was more than glad to see that was not the case.

Eamon wasn't in the mood for exchanging pleasantries, instead hurrying Alaric over to the cathedral entrance and the sagging, resigned form of the wounded Ealdorman Ulfcytel. Cenric was standing next to him, his face marked with concern, the ground immediately before them playing host to several other wounded men in various states of unconsciousness. This was getting beyond desperate now. It was only a matter of time before their defeat was at hand. Something had to be done.

"Don't mind me, get back to fighting," Ulfcytel spat, his eyes flickering with irritation. "The bastard was just quicker than I thought he'd be. It's fine. Get back to fighting!"

Alaric ignored him, looking instead behind his own shoulder at the battle they'd come from. There were still hundreds of Englishmen resisting, and resisting well, but they were seriously outnumbered, and most of the square they'd previously fought on was now held by the teeming throng that was the enemy. The noise was intense and unrelenting, the sound of shattering shields and hammering metal splitting the air. He saw one Englishman staggering amidst the enemy, his shield thick with arrows, the axe in his trembling arm blunted and worn from killing blow after killing blow. He wouldn't relent, taking wound upon wound, and yet he fought on, going above and beyond what should be physically possible for any man to bear. Eventually, he went down, his head cracked and bleeding, the axe that had finally felled him as battered and bloodied from killing as his own.

Similar scenes were playing out elsewhere. He spied one man unlucky enough to have his spear break apart upon a Danish shield, so he'd resorted to fighting with his bare hands instead. He was slain in short order, but his comrades were beset with redoubled fury at the sight of it, killing the one responsible and flying into a despairing rage that saw multiple Danes hacked to pieces in mere seconds. More men fell, their blood soaking the earth as they shuddered and collapsed, but the enemy continued to press forward, their brute malevolence leaving them numb to their own losses.

Alaric stepped over to Cenric and took him to one side. They could all die here, but not Ulfcytel. This battle may be lost, but treachery had been their downfall, just like at Hringmere. If word got out that Ulfcytel had finally been killed, it would be a shattering blow to the country and its will to continue any resistance. He wasn't going to like it, but Alaric wasn't going to ask him for permission. Ulfcytel would survive this battle, one way or another.

"I need you to get the ealdorman out of here," Alaric told Cenric. "Carry him if you have to. I'm serious. Don't listen to anything he says. Get him out of here and through the northern gate. He has to survive. There's more at stake here than just one man."

"But what about the…"

"Don't, Cenric, please. If you remain loyal to my family, you'll obey me in this. Get Ulfcytel out of the city and far away from here. England depends on it."

Cenric nodded, his eyes lighting up with understanding. He turned, following Alaric's gaze to look upon the road to the north. A great many of the inhabitants were still on the move here in an effort to escape Canterburie before it fell altogether. They made for a sorrowful sight, hurrying and desperate, their faces white with fear. They were right to be afraid, and they'd made the correct decision in fleeing. None of them looked to be capable of fighting anyway. All such men had been conscripted weeks ago.

It then occurred to Alaric that if Cenric could somehow blend in with these refugees, he wouldn't be such an obvious target. He seemed to realise this himself, moving up alongside Ulfcytel without a word and hauling him up onto his shoulder. Ulfcytel protested, exclaiming something about how he "wasn't finished yet" and would "rather die than retreat". They ignored him, knowing he was fading from blood loss, the wounds to his leg and stomach still weeping profusely. They would need treatment, but there was no time at present. He'd have to hold on until Cenric could get him clear of the fighting.

Alaric didn't bother to watch Cenric dash off into the night, Ulfcytel's significant bulk atop his shoulder. He didn't want anyone to see him staring into the near distance, fearing they'd work out what he was looking at and think the battle was effectively over. All the same, about a score of men watched the wounded ealdorman being carried away, their expressions a mixture of curiosity and despair. Reassuring words were needed.

"He's injured. He has to get clear of the battle," he told them, his now hoarse and tender voice struggling to make itself heard over the fighting. "We have to hold the enemy in place so he and the rest of the populace can escape."

It wasn't the most inspirational thing he could have said to them. They didn't take it as such either, one inquiring whether all was now lost. Alaric didn't know what to say. He couldn't lie to them. When they'd first fallen back to the square, they'd had over a thousand men at their disposal. It was undeniable that most of them were now dead or wounded and that the enemy outnumbered them several times over. Alaric had no more words for them. He instead set off back towards the melee, beckoning for the men to join him. They followed, charging into the fight with all the ferocity they could muster. It wasn't much. They'd been fighting all night, and exhaustion had taken its toll. But they had to try.

Alaric could see up close just how dire their situation was. The English were being surrounded and pinned in place against the cathedral, their numbers thinning to the point Thorkell would undeniably have the victory if they persisted in fighting out in the open like this. Thorkell himself was still in the thick of it, no blade, axe, or spear able to touch him, his very presence inspiring his bastard kindred to even greater acts of frenzied aggression. His red-helmeted bodyguard was with him once more, cutting Christians down with scant regard for his own safety. He was arrogant. He didn't think anyone would be able to harm him. Alaric hoped to teach him the foolishness of that notion.

An idea then formed in his mind. Another retreat, for sure, but one that would at least narrow the confines of the battlefield and prevent the enemy's superior numbers from having much effect. Alaric began bellowing orders at the top of his lungs; a painful effort considering the amount of shouting he'd done already, instructing those left alive to fall back into the cathedral. Those immediately within earshot began withdrawing alongside him, the rest of the men noticing the movements of their brethren and following likewise. The Danes soon saw something was afoot, and they endeavoured to pursue, their fearsome cries echoing after them.

Alaric saw one of them leap upon an Englishman's back and drag him to the ground so that another could finish him. He wouldn't permit that. He grabbed the aggressor by the shoulder, heaving him upright and stabbing the length of his blade down into his neck and deep into his chest cavity. The Dane convulsed violently, blood fountaining from his mouth and cascading over his chin and chest. Alaric tore his sword from his body and let him fall, noticing the Saxon he'd so accosted was now on his feet and had speared the heathen who'd sought to kill him once he was incapacitated. They exchanged a look, Alaric and this unknown warrior, the latter's face saturated with a combination of fear and gratitude. They hurried on towards the cathedral entrance, the entirety of their force now following in the hope of finding sanctuary within.

It was a messy business, this fighting withdrawal, and couldn't have been otherwise. Many a man was hacked down, Saxon and Dane alike, yet the English again took the worst of it, since the enemy was loath to let them just break away and retreat without doing their best to finally overrun them. They failed in that, but by the time Alaric and his men had retreated into the cathedral, they'd lost a good number, and their force was now barely more than a hundred if his quick estimate was anything to go by. From over a thousand to one hundred, all in a matter of hours. It could be way worse, he supposed.

The fight soon became as Alaric had hoped. The enemy was adamant about pursuing them into the cathedral, but they were predictably having trouble getting through its double doors without being speared by the stalwart survivors waiting for them within. Alaric cut a man down trying to rush after him into the narthex, removing much of his head with one single blow. He then disembowelled another on the cold stones, eviscerating the screaming cur whilst those rushing in behind him were impaled or hacked apart in the narrow confines they now fought in. The sound was immense, the clamour and din of battle echoing off the walls, and despite the bodies falling thick and fast the enemy persisted, hoping to take this sacred place by storm. They'd pay for their irreverence with blood.

Alaric risked a look behind him, gazing further into the cathedral's interior and the vast nave that lay beyond. There were people there, arrayed before the altar, each one knelt in prayer like all was well and there was no herculean struggle going on just behind them. Alaric was incredulous when he saw both Ælfweard and Archbishop Ælfheah were among them. The old priest hadn't been taken out of the city to safety. He was still here, praying like he often did, albeit this time at imminent risk of capture or death.

Alaric broke from the fighting and rushed towards the altar. He dispensed with etiquette, grabbing Ælfweard from behind and lifting him off his knees before spinning him around to face him. The reeve didn't look surprised, instead appearing unusually calm, like he'd been expecting to have to explain himself to Alaric before the end.

"What is the meaning of this?!" Alaric seethed. "And where is Leofwine? He was supposed to take the archbishop out of here, Ælfweard! And I thought you had left with the other survivors? Why has the archbishop been permitted to remain? Did it not occur to you what Thorkell will do with him if he falls into his clutches?"

"I know," admitted the reeve, very much like he'd been preparing for this argument, "and the archbishop refused to come. Same for the rest of those you see here. I returned after ensuring the northern gate was clear so that more might escape, but Ælfheah won't leave this place, Alaric. I tried everything short of dragging him out, but he said if I did that, he'd regard it as if I'd assaulted him and hold it against me. As for Leofwine…"

Alaric followed Ælfweard's gaze to a darkened corner not far from the altar. Leofwine lay there with a number of other wounded, his injuries apparently worse than they'd thought, given he was very much unconscious and being tended to by a justifiably anxious-looking monk. That was at least a good enough excuse for failing in the task Alaric had set him. Ælfweard was hale and hearty, though. His tarrying here made no sense.

"You refused to evacuate the archbishop because you worried he might hold it against you?! Just get him up and…"

"There is nowhere we can go now, Alaric, you know that." Ælfheah's voice was soft but firm, and there was an unmistakable authority there now he felt the situation called for it. He'd not risen from prayer, and he was still knelt down and facing away from both the fighting and the argument.

"Even if I could escape, I would not," he continued. "This place is where I live and die. This place is where all of Canterburie lives and dies. I will not abandon my vocation here just because evil comes knocking."

"Don't you see, though?!" Alaric raged. "If Thorkell gets hold of you, he'll work out who you are quickly enough. You'll be brutalised, tortured even, before death comes, all for the sake of spite. Failing that, he'll use you to extract a huge ransom from the king. He'll know Æthelred won't be able to just let you die and retain any small measure of respect."

"No one will need pay any ransom."

"You don't understand, the king wi…"

"No. I will not have a ransom paid on my behalf. I refuse to accept it. I am not to be bartered. I will accept martyrdom. Thorkell will not use me to line his own pockets. The amount he'll ask for me will further bankrupt the kingdom. That will not happen."

"I'm not asking you to accept martyrdom!" Alaric fumed, his temper fraying further in light of the archbishop's intransigence. The old man had stood up to face him, dressed in the plain robes he always wore, his white hair unethered so it fell freely across his shoulders. His aged eyes glimmered with a certain defiance, yet they were not without their accustomary warmth. He likely understood Alaric's position and temperament. Alaric just wished he could understand his.

A great splintering sound erupted from the cathedral entrance, like something heavy and vital had been torn aside to collapse against the hard masonry. They all turned to look, seeing the previously stout, impressively tall doors of the narthex had fallen inwards, squashing several men flat amidst the timbers. Alaric looked at Ælfweard and the archbishop one last time before he hurried back over to his men. He hoped beyond hope God would be pleased with their refusal to abandon his house here. They could certainly use his aid now.

He arrived in time to witness Thorkell and his red-helmed accomplice fighting their way inside, both men having to almost clamber over the corpses of their dead to make headway. They were joined by yet more bellowing warriors pouring in through the now-destroyed entrance, the men opposing them seeming to dwindle in number with each passing moment. Alaric leapt into the fray once more, rallying his people to him for what would certainly be their last stand. They'd killed a lot of Danes, that could not be denied, and the narrow stone entryway leading into the cathedral was awash with gore and lifeless corpses. They fought on regardless, at times slipping and sliding on the remains of the fallen, their limbs trembling from fatigue and their voices hoarse with hatred.

He found himself face to face with "Red Helm", as he now thought of him, the brawling savage looking to have just dispatched one of Alaric's men via an unnecessarily messy dismemberment. Alaric stormed into him, utilising every last vestige of strength he had to hammer away at his defences until an opportunity came for a killing blow. He drew blood, cutting the bastard up along his left leg, a second strike landing across the fiend's right side to shatter metal scales and hardened leather until his blade met flesh. Red Helm stumbled, his guard dropping as he buckled under the weight of Alaric's furious assault. He could taste victory. He'd avenge Osmund if it were the last thing he did. Given the situation, it almost certainly would be.

Everything felt surreal now, the surrounding fighting muffled and slow as Christian and heathen brutalised and killed one another within the narrow, echoing hell they'd created for themselves. Alaric swung wildly, both his hands gripped upon the hilt of his sword, the blade sweeping outwards in a wide arc to connect with his opponent's head. The blow struck true, the man's helm flying off with a great clang to crash and bounce against the stone walls. He was dazed, a rush of blood flowing from the side of his head to stain his otherwise flaxen hair and beard.

Alaric blinked at the faint light now shining up ahead. The first rays of dawn were peering delicately through the ruined entryway, further illuminating this brutal scene in all its horror. The battle had lasted all night, the snow still falling thickly across the shattered city beyond, the flames of Thorkell's passing sending plumes of bitter, smothering smoke into the freezing air. There was nothing Alaric could do about these things now. The city was lost, but he could do one last thing, something that mattered to him and had done for some time. He drew his sword back in the face of his wounded, insensible opponent, uncaring as to who he was or where he'd come from. He'd killed Osmund. That was all that mattered. He'd die now as he deserved.

Unfortunately, the man wasn't as insensible as he looked, or he was simply better at fighting through the pain of his wounds than anyone Alaric had met previously. He lunged forward, slipping under Alaric's guard and tackling his legs out from under him. Alaric fell with a grunt, his outlook all stampeding feet, straining legs, and falling bodies. Red Helm was now atop him and pinning him in place, yet when Alaric went to sweep his blade across him, he found he couldn't move his arm. He soon saw why.

An unusually large boot was placed across his wrist, the pain growing in intensity as Thorkell bore his entire weight down upon him. Red Helm took advantage of the situation by straddling Alaric's chest to punch him repeatedly in the jaw, the vision in his single remaining eye blurring and spinning. Somebody lifted him into the air like it was a matter of some ease, and Alaric soon detected the scent of foul breath, blood, and sweat upon his nostrils. Thorkell's horrific visage loomed ahead, just inches from Alaric's bloodied face, a sadistic grin parting his otherwise inescapable beard.

Alaric could see the fight continuing just over his huge shoulder. The heathens were not giving up despite their losses, and they were hurling themselves upon Saxon shields with a kind of deranged enthusiasm born of bravery and bloodlust both. They were making progress but paying for it, and each step backwards on the part of the defenders was only purchased with yet more Norse dead. Canterburie's last stand was costing Thorkell dearly. It was on that subject that the giant now spoke.

"Get your men to give up. Your city is mine. I don't need to take your holy place here. I can burn it down with all of you in it if I have to."

Thorkell's voice was one of the more unpleasant ones Alaric had heard in his life. He'd heard many a deep, rumbling tone before, but this one was something else, sounding as though the sheer foulness within Thorkell's black heart was bubbling up within to vomit itself out through his throat. His threat to burn down the cathedral with all of them in it didn't make it any easier on the ears. Alaric wasn't here to parley, nor would he do anything for this revolting brute of a man who had all but admitted he was losing too many men trying to beat them. It was in such a spirit that Alaric opted to not bother with words, instead lunging forward to sink his teeth into Thorkell's face.

What happened next wasn't entirely clear. Thorkell had dropped him with a roar, Alaric noting he could taste fresh blood that certainly wasn't his. Somebody had then struck him from behind, possibly old Red Helm, which had sent him staggering and collapsing onto the sizeable flagstones just ahead. He crawled forwards, struggling to get up, feeling redoubled fear and panic as he realised his vulnerability amidst the tumult of brawling bodies.

Somebody somehow got a hold of his outstretched hand, pulling him through the carnage and further into the interior. Alaric managed to focus on the face of his rescuer. Osbert. Pallid, sickly, but it was Osbert. Alive. How long he'd been awake, Alaric had no idea. He thought him unconscious somewhere, wounded but otherwise safe. He wondered how he'd fared so far. A familiar sound, booming and hateful, suddenly filled their ears, the dreadful racket cutting short any opportunity to ask.

"I will spare your church here and everyone inside if you lay down your arms! Otherwise, I will desecrate and defile this place, keeping you alive to witness it before I tear out your entrails upon your own altars!"

That voice again. Thorkell had taken his ultimatum to a wider audience, the sheer wickedness of his proposition echoing out and through the entire building. Alaric stood up with a little help from Osbert. He could see his sword up ahead, discarded just behind where Thorkell now stood. He then saw the rather serious bite mark that marred Thorkell's left cheek. He must have sharper teeth than he thought.

"It is enough. Stop this fighting now, I command it. We'll agree to your terms, heathen."

Alaric turned around, the two score or so of his men still up and fighting doing likewise. The archbishop approached, his expression severe. He and Thorkell gazed upon the other, the towering foreign warlord looking beyond malevolent whilst he scrutinised the ageing, white-haired priest. Ælfheah comported himself well. There was a strength in him that went beyond brute force and physical power, something a monster like Thorkell would never fathom.

"We do not agree!" Alaric spluttered, bending down to retrieve a discarded axe from the ground. "If we deliver ourselves into your hands, you'll kill us all and destroy this place regardless! You'll only have Canterburie once we're all dead! Come, Thorkell, let us finish, you and I, that exchange we were having a moment ago!"

"I swear to you now, Englishman, that I will defile this place in ways you cannot imagine. If you put down your weapons, I give you my word upon the Gods that I will spare your lives and leave your holy things undisturbed."

"What good is your word?" Alaric spat. "Once we give up, you'll do whatever you fancy with us. Better to die fighting than go into captivity on the word of a disgusting animal!"

"You make a good point," rumbled Thorkell. "You can't know for sure if I'll keep my promise. But I have an army outside. If you keep fighting, you'll die sooner or later. And I tell you again; I will ruin this place so that people for generations will wonder how it could ever have been considered holy, such will be the degradation I will subject it to. Your Saint Augustine will be just a bitter memory. All of you will be just a bitter memory. Give up, and it will not come to pass. Decide now."

"We've decided," Ælfheah said. "Drop your weapons, all of you. Look to God alone now. Each of you has done all he could. We will pray this…man…honours his word and respects the house of our Lord."

The men all looked to the archbishop, unsure, their eyes then falling upon Alaric. They wanted him to decide. He saw Eamon amongst them, staring with the rest, hard-eyed and severe, but faithful to the end. Alaric didn't know what to say. He never thought he'd be in a conundrum such as this. Thorkell's offer was impossible to answer, but all the same he must choose, either finding certain death in an unwinnable battle or giving himself up to prevent the desecration of one of England's most holy places.

There was no real choice to be had here. Most of his men were dead, either outside amidst the burning city or in here. The battle was over. Now he just had one final ordeal to endure. The humiliation of surrender. His grip on the axe he'd picked up began to weaken, his fingers eventually going limp so that it fell to the floor.

"Do as the archbishop wishes," Alaric said bitterly. That was all he could bring himself to say. His words were followed by the sound of more weapons clattering upon the stones; the warriors who'd been prepared to resist to the end now cowed and subdued by the horror of Thorkell's terrible promise. The sound echoed across the nave and up into the rafters above, their shame repeating back at them until it finally faded to silence. All was lost now. They'd failed. Canterburie had fallen.

XX

One foot in front of the other. Focus on what's ahead. Fight through the pain. You've survived way worse than this. All you have to do is run. Just keep on going. You have a duty here. Forget your pride now. Orders are orders, and those orders are not going to change just because your legs hurt. Keep on.

Cenric was having trouble convincing himself. His thighs were burning, his shoulders, too, the weight of the unconscious ealdorman serving to push him down into the snow-covered road. Fatigue endeavoured to take hold of him, pulling at his feet to either trip or slow him to a shambling crawl. He wasn't sure when he'd last slept. He'd fought all night, that long, bloody darkness forever seared upon his memory. Mayhap his trials upon the road were light indeed compared to what he'd just been through.

Such rationalising didn't bring much relief. Dawn had broken, giving Cenric a better view of his surroundings as he trudged north, although to where or for what purpose, he had little idea. Canterburie was receding behind him, the smoke from the fires within its walls still billowing up into the snow-swept sky. The city looked terrible, the morning's austere light exposing the great wounds dealt in that terrible night of battle and bloodshed. Fully half of it looked to be aflame, and the remaining half was almost entirely shrouded in smoke and soot. The top of the cathedral was still visible, but barely, and Cenric felt it was only a matter of time until that, too, was obscured by ash. He turned away, deciding to fixate on the road ahead. The sight behind him was just too depressing.

Others joined him, panicked and hurrying. They were just regular people by the looks of them, the elderly and the infirm. They shuffled along, miserable and desperate, each aiding the other as best they could in their flight from the raging, bloody charnel house that had been their home. Cenric's heart went out to them.

It was with some considerable regret he decided he couldn't pause to help them. His charge was too valuable, his resources too meagre, and the hard truth was that the Ealdorman Ulfcytel's life was presently more valuable than that of anyone struggling along the road right now. If he succumbed to his injuries, there'd be little hope left for England, short of some radical transformation taking place within the personality of their ever-foolish King Æthelred. Since that was unlikely, it was up to Cenric to make sure Ulfcytel remained alive, escape the fighting, and recover to lead them once more. Alaric had wished it so. That was enough for Cenric.

And yet as important as he was, Ulfcytel was just too damn heavy. Cenric was stronger than many a man, and he'd always had stamina, but he could only run so far with a weight like this straining his back. He could tell he was slowing, his initially sprightly pace away from the battle becoming an agonising trudge the further he got from the city. The people fleeing were starting to overtake him, many of them sadly too preoccupied with their own troubles to even cast him a glance. Were they afraid of him?

If it were so, then not all of them felt that way. Cenric could hear hooves approaching, not the rapid beat of a rider upon the road but the slow, resigned clop of draft horses at work. A single cart hauled by two such beasts ambled past him, its driver slowing them to a halt as he spied Cenric and his significant burden. He looked like a good sort, long in years with a face that spoke of a life hard at work outdoors, his body otherwise well concealed in thick furs to keep out the biting cold. Someone Cenric assumed to be his wife sat up alongside him, as well-attired as he was. She lacked his stoic look, though. She was terrified, in fact. She likely wished they hadn't stopped.

"Are you alright there, sir?"

Cenric paused in his stride, the pain in his legs immediately lessening. There was no point in deceiving this man. If he meant harm, which was unlikely, Cenric was more than capable of taking care of it. Yet he couldn't carry on like this, hobbling through the snow with Ulfcytel bleeding atop him. He didn't know this area well, and if Ulfcytel carried on leaking, he'd die before they made it to safety. Considering their situation, it was also probable that safety was a long, long way off. If he'd ever needed a good Samaritan to come to his aid, it was now.

"No," Cenric replied, his breathing still laboured, "…but if you'll spare room for us in your cart, I'll make sure you're well compensated once we get to wherever you're going."

"No compensation is needed, but if you insist on paying me, I won't object too much." The man chuckled briefly, his face cracking like old leather, his smile a mouthful of ageing, broken teeth. "Best get you and your friend there on the cart," he then urged, "I have a feeling we'd all best get far away from what's happening back there."

Cenric smiled back, a pained, exhausted look that he hoped went some small way towards conveying just how grateful he was. He trudged over to the rear of the cart and heaved the dead weight that was the thankfully still breathing Ulfcytel up into its confines, Cenric's shoulders suddenly feeling joyfully light and free without that great bulk pressing down on them. He got up and into the cart alongside Ulfcytel, turning now to behold the two figures staring back at him from up front. The old woman still looked anxious. Cenric hoped she didn't think that he somehow might mean them harm.

The driver urged his horses into movement, the twin beasts setting off at the same well-measured pace they'd had before. Cenric turned his attention back to the still-slumbering Ulfcytel, making sure to lie him flat upon his back with his weight evenly spaced so as to not suddenly tip over or slide out of their ambling transport. The bleeding from his leg wound had eased, but his stomach was still a source of concern, the gash there appearing both wide and deep. He'd been a brave man to attack Thorkell whilst already injured. Nobody who'd witnessed it would be forgetting that in a hurry.

Cenric found himself speculating on how the contest may have ended had Ulfcytel been in better condition. He then wondered how he himself may have fared against the Norse warlord. Cenric knew he was good, especially with a sword, but Thorkell's fighting style was…odd. He moved strangely, too fast for a man of his size, his entire bearing having a certain feel to it that Cenric could only describe as unnatural.

His musings were interrupted by a faint voice from behind him. He snapped his head back to gaze in the direction of the sound, looking surprised to realise he shared the cart with two others he hadn't seen previously. They were children, a girl and a boy, both no older than ten by the look of them. Their presence up until now had been hidden by a large woollen blanket they were still intent on sheltering under. The lad had a look to him, like he fancied himself brave despite his obvious apprehension at

Cenric's presence. That reminded him of somebody. His own son, back when he'd been blessed with such a thing.

"They want to know your name," the driver said over his shoulder.

"I'm Cenric," he answered bluntly, his present state of fatigue robbing him of the capacity for any kind of enthusiasm when introducing himself.

"Were you in the battle?" the boy asked, overcoming his nerves.

"I was. Me and my friend here." He patted Ulfcytel on the shoulder, like they were indeed old associates, hoping the gesture might soothe the children's nerves. Ulfcytel grunted disagreeably, giving the impression he was protesting Cenric's claim that they were friends, a point not lost on the now giggling children.

"What's your friend's name?" the girl asked, her face half-hidden beneath the blanket.

"Ulfcytel."

The driver stared back at him, his eyes wide with surprise. "That's the ealdorman? Is he dead?"

"Yes, it is he," Cenric answered, "and no, he's not dead, although if you have anything available so that I might clean and treat his wounds, it would no doubt do some good."

The driver gestured towards something, his wife leaning over into the cart to point at several large sacks next to the children. Cenric ventured a look, opening one up to find several skins of both water and wine. Cenric was no physician, but he was out of options, for the ealdorman had turned almost as pale as the snow-covered landscape trundling past them. He reached inside, taking a skin of wine, in turn easing open the rent in Ulfcytel's armour to get at his wound.

It didn't look too bad, but he knew he couldn't judge since he was generally more skilled at creating wounds than healing them. The rather dramatic laceration across his stomach looked somewhat clean, and so he opened the wine and poured it over the aggrieved flesh. He'd seen this done before as a means to prevent infection, and it had seemed to work then. He prayed it would at least do something beneficial now. It would be embarrassing to have fought so hard and run so far just to accidentally kill Ulfcytel through his own carelessness.

"Let me help," said the driver's wife, clambering into the cart proper to rummage through yet another stash of belongings. She'd overcome her nervousness, but Cenric could tell she still wasn't entirely comfortable having him here. It then occurred to him what he must look like. He'd been up all night, fighting and killing, and the blood and gore of countless men was still splashed across his armour and gauntlets. It was a marvel the children hadn't outright panicked at the sight of him.

The old wife retrieved something before turning to ask Cenric to help her remove Ulfcytel's mail shirt. He managed it with some effort, the cart being of a size that, whilst they could all fit inside with relative ease, was all the same too confined for comfortable movement. Ulfcytel was a big man also, looking like a bear in human form when stripped of his garments, his huge arms and chest covered with thick silver hair similar to his overspilling beard.

His stomach, which was presently their main concern, still made for a sorry sight, what with the red chasm Thorkell's axe had left across it. Ulfcytel grumbled to himself when the wife set to work bandaging his gut, the poor man shivering as the winter air caressed his exposed skin. Cenric was glad when she finished and draped several blankets across him. It was imperative he retain as much body heat as he could.

They trundled on like this for some time, Ulfcytel snoring and muttering whilst wrapped in the soft woollen cocoon of his bed. Cenric wet the ealdorman's lips with water from another skin, lifting his head slightly to allow him to drink. He did so, taking in a good amount of fluid, Cenric half-expecting him to start talking and barking orders, such was his enthusiasm for what was offered. That was as animated as he got, and he soon lolled his head back once more to resume his slumber. Cenric wondered if he was dreaming, perhaps replaying his frenzied encounter with Thorkell in his mind. He had a feeling that would be something that would always stick with him, should they survive all this.

Canterburie had by now long vanished from view, the only evidence of its location being the faint trails of smoke that still drifted lazily across the horizon. The snow continued falling, making the road increasingly hard to spot as all ahead of them merged into one single expanse of bleak, desolate white dotted by the occasional stand of haggard, leafless trees. They were heading north, that was clear, but his newfound friends had not offered any information on their destination. That should change.

"Where are we going to?" Cenric asked, hoping he didn't sound ungrateful. They had saved him a great deal of stress and bother. Demanding they take him to wherever he wished simply wouldn't be right. That being said, his task here was of vital importance. He couldn't be hindered in that, even by people as generous as this.

"My brother's farm," came the response from the driver. "He lives up near Witenestaple. 'Course, he had to run to us in Canterburie when Thorkell burned him out a year past, but he returned and helped rebuild. Seems only fair he help us out now, right?"

"Does he have anything to help a wounded man?" Cenric asked, fearing it quite unlikely a simple farmer would know anything about healing an axe wound to the guts.

"No, but he has a comfortable enough home. Nothing like bed rest and a good feed to set a main straight, I'd say."

Cenric wasn't so sure. Ulfcytel wasn't dead, and his wounds were not yet showing any signs of infection, but he was still worryingly pale. He also couldn't tell how severe the injury to his leg was, nor if there were still fragments of arrow embedded in his flesh from where he'd so brutally torn it out. He poured some wine over it to be on the safe side.

His musings on the health of his commander were interrupted by something more urgent. Screams sounded from further down the road behind them. Three riders hove into view, moving at some speed, each lashing out with sadistic fury at anyone within reach. The refugees tried to scatter, many hurling themselves off the road altogether whilst others succumbed to panic and froze in place. They become easy targets for the riders, their blood soon mingling with the thickening snow as the murderous trio rode on, undeterred by the callous wrongs they'd just committed.

They must be Danes, outriders from Thorkell's army, sent now to harass those escaping Canterburie. Cenric couldn't see how much death and misery they'd wrought already, but they were rapidly closing the distance between themselves and his cart. They may have been sent out just to kill and rob, but there was always the slim chance they were somehow aware the Ealdorman Ulfcytel had escaped. Cenric had no way of knowing that, but he wasn't about to let them just murder as they pleased. If they'd attacked these people thinking they were in for an easy fight, they were dead wrong. Their cowardice was sickening. It was time they faced a real opponent.

One of the Danes galloped directly for them, spurring his unfortunate horse onward until it began to gape in protest. He hurled a spear at them with a shout, the thing slamming into the wood just an inch or so from the still unresponsive Ulfcytel. Cenric tore it free and slipped off the cart, his boots sinking several inches into the snow and slush below. He braced, his right hand clutching the spear as he readied for the throw, his practised eye tracing the movement and speed of the charging rider rushing ever closer. He waited for his moment. Then it came. He let fly.

Cenric's aim wasn't as good as he'd hoped. The spear arced through the air well enough, yet instead of hitting the rider, it embedded itself in the neck of his still protesting horse. The poor beast's legs gave out from under it, Cenric feeling a pang of remorse as it was cast over by its own momentum before crashing to a halt in a heap of heaving flesh and flailing legs. The rider was thrown clear, landing with a soft thump amidst a bed of snow just off the roadside. He was floundering, struggling to get up. Cenric would use that.

He dispatched the Dane quickly, slicing open his throat with casual precision, the fool still straining to sit up. His two compatriots had noticed what Cenric had done and turned their mounts away from the scattering crowd of refugees to ride directly for him. He imagined they fancied themselves fearsome as they rode closer, their faces lit with pent-up rage, assuming this Saxon who had got the better of their friend would fear them now he was outnumbered. They had no idea who they were dealing with.

Cenric dashed onto the road and tore the spear from the neck of the dying horse. The poor thing let out a heart-rending shriek as he pulled the shaft free of its body. He always felt sorry for these noble creatures, thinking it a cruel accident that God had made them so strong and biddable only for a fallen humanity to exploit them as weapons of war. He put the beast out of its misery, impaling it a second time through the neck, his work precise and clean. It lay still now, its death rattle deep and bass as it slipped away.

One of the Danes was coming right at him, slowing his horse to a trot whilst stabbing downwards with a spear from the saddle. Cenric was already prepared, his legs braced and spear held aloft, a quick sequence of thrusts sending his attacker falling backwards into the snow, his hands and chest slick with blood. Few horsemen could realistically expect to take out a man on foot and armed with a long-reaching weapon. It was foolish to try, unless one had the advantage of surprise and was already charging at full speed to simply ride the enemy down. This Dane must have been seriously overconfident to think him such easy prey.

And yet the bastard wasn't finished. He'd got up from his fall, his guts a mess from where Cenric's spear had punctured through his mail. He then stumbled onward, still up for the fight, his face contorted with rage and pain. Cenric was impressed. This one was certainly a better foot soldier than a rider, what with his ability to withstand physical punishment and keep going. He put him down in any case, impaling him through the stomach with a solid jab that split open his snow-flecked mail shirt in a shower of fine metal ringlets. He should have hired a better smith before coming to England.

The third and final horseman had reached him. This rider was skilled and angry with it, letting rip with a sequence of thunderous roars and snarls whilst he jabbed at

Cenric from on high. Cenric moved around him, trying to widen the distance between them both. He stumbled slightly and sank further into the snow, his route back along the edge of the road leading him into a slight defile that had otherwise been hidden. The rider wouldn't ease off, coming after him without pause, his great dark horse clearly unperturbed by either the thick snowfall or the body of its slain brother.

Cenric stumbled again, this time falling over onto his side and half vanishing beneath the snowy carpet rising up to greet him. He fumbled about, trying to regain control of his legs, his weight seeming to shift and then shift again as he struggled to right himself. He could hear the mounted Dane getting closer, the sound of hooves crashing through snow loud in his ears. He managed to sit up, flipping over now to try and push himself upright into some kind of fighting stance. He made it, but he'd taken too long. The Dane was on him.

Or he would have been if he were still in the saddle. Cenric turned to see the horse standing there, its head bowing up and down anxiously. At its feet was its former rider, howling ferociously and clutching at the left side of his groin with both hands. Blood was flowing in abundance, saturating his clothes and armour and staining the snow around him a brilliant red. The old man, the driver of the cart who'd picked him and Ulfcytel up, stood just a couple of feet away, his shaking hands clutching a bloodied axe better suited for chopping wood than felling a warrior. He had done just that, though. He'd worked with what he had. Cenric was grateful.

He made his way over to him, nodding in appreciation. The old man looked pale, upset, like he was unaccustomed to fighting or had not done so in years. The Dane was squealing and howling, the axe looking like it had damaged something particular and specific. Cenric almost felt sorry for him. He finished him quickly, spearing him through the throat and then leaving him, the weapon still embedded in his neck. He didn't want to keep it. His sword was good enough, and he didn't like using the tools of the enemy. There was no telling what grim deeds they'd been used for.

They hurried back to the cart, the old man still dazed at what he'd wrought with his own hands. A clutch of onlookers had formed on and off the road, stopping to marvel at the brief yet bloody clash between Cenric and their Danish tormentors. None of them approached, likely wondering who this warrior was and why he wasn't in Canterburie with the rest of those still fighting. Cenric ignored them and resumed his place at the back of the cart, the driver also taking up his spot at the head of his draught horses as he whipped them back into motion. Ulfcytel slept on, unmoved by the drama, the cart's motion rocking him slightly like a child in the crib.

They remained silent for some time, the wife and two children again appearing afraid of Cenric after seeing what he could do. That bothered him. He was a man of violence, anyone who knew him understood that, but it was always directed, always in defence of his country, faith, and those who needed it most. It wasn't right or just that these people should see him as a possible threat. Then another thought occurred to him. Did they think him a deserter? Did they think he'd abandoned Canterburie, hoping to sneak away with the refugees and save his own life whilst others fought on? He couldn't have anyone thinking that. The shame would be too much to bear.

"I didn't flee the city," he announced suddenly, loud enough for everyone to hear clearly. "I'm not a deserter. I was ordered by the second son of the family I serve to get the Ealdorman Ulfcytel away from the fighting and somewhere safe."

The driver looked back at him, as did his wife and the two children. None of them knew what to say, their horses the only ones to continue as they were, one huge hoof in front of the other. When the old man spoke, he sounded frail, like the shock of the recent combat had pushed him way outside of his comfort zone.

"I thought you were just old soldiers trying to get away. Doing my Christian duty in helping you, so I thought."

"You are doing your Christian duty. Ulfcytel was wounded, facing Thorkell himself. The battle wasn't going our way. The enemy…"

"Is the city lost? Is my father dead?" That was one of the children now, the girl, her eyes filling with tears.

"Who is your father?" Cenric asked, not wanting to just admit that Canterburie was more than likely in the hands of Thorkell the Tall. He hoped he was wrong, but things had not looked good when he'd made his escape.

"Edwin, he's called, and he's a warrior!" The boy sounded enthused, like his father bearing arms was the most heroic thing in the world. Given the circumstances, it probably was.

"Edwin is my son," said the old man. "My name is Oscar, and this here is my wife, Sweterun, or just Swet for short. These are my grandchildren, Cwen and…"

"Stefn!" That was the boy again. A proud lad and proud of his father by the sound of it. Cenric shot him a grin in acknowledgement. He hoped for his and his sister's sake that this Edwin was somehow still alive. He wondered also if Edwin had a wife to mother these two children, and if so, where was she? He decided not to ask. He had a feeling there would only be sadness waiting for him if he did.

"So what do we do?" Oscar inquired, sounding more sure of himself. "Since there's the great Ulfcytel in my cart, I can't just take you to my brother's holding in Witenestaple. I mean, would that be alright?"

"Of course it will," Cenric said reassuringly. "Ulfcytel isn't a man for luxury and comfort. Chances are, as soon as he wakes up he'll want to get straight back to fighting. We need to just keep him safe until he heals up and calms down."

"So everything really must be over then, if even the likes of Ulfcytel can be brought low?" Oscar sounded faint now, as if any hope he yet had of his son remaining alive was rapidly diminishing. Edwin had most likely sequestered the children here with their grandparents whilst he attended to his duties defending the walls. Cenric had never even heard of the man until now, but he felt increasingly pained that Oscar would likely never see him again.

"I don't have any answers," Cenric said sadly. "The fight in the main square was confusing. The whole battle was confusing. You probably worked out quickly the bastards had broken into the city without us knowing?"

"Yes," said Oscar, "and I was hoping you'd know how. One moment the streets were empty, and then suddenly there's people running everywhere in a panic, saying Thorkell was inside. I made a decision then to get my horses and get out."

"And that was the right choice," Cenric assured him. "I never saw how they'd got in, but there they were, attacking us from behind whilst we tried to hold the gates. It was a mess. All of it. We fell back, but the fight got even worse. Then Ulfcytel was wounded, twice over. Alaric told me to get him out."

"Who?" asked Oscar.

"My Lord Alaric. Son of Ælfric, the Ealdorman of Hamptonscir."

Oscar again looked back over his shoulder, his expression quizzical. "You do mix in some important circles, don't you?"

Cenric chuckled at that. He wasn't much of anyone, born on a cold floor in a half-burnt hut just north of Mideltune. His life story wasn't particularly interesting, and he didn't care to share it now, but he did sometimes marvel at how far he'd climbed just from his capacity to break heads.

"You could say that," answered Cenric. "Sometimes I think I've been unlucky in life. Other times I think God has put me right where I need to be."

"And where is that?" asked Oscar.

"Here. Not to brag, my friend, but those Danes on the road were not messing around. I think we can all agree it was a good thing we came across one another."

"Aye, I won't argue there. We'd have been in real trouble if it were…"

"I'd have fought them off!" That was the boy, Stefn. He was deadly serious, even as Cenric, Oscar, and Sweterun erupted with laughter. His cheeks soon flushed with embarrassment, a frown creasing his features upon realising he was the object of mirth. Cenric didn't want to hurt his feelings. He'd speak on his behalf.

"And I believe you, young Stefn. One day you'll be a warrior like your father. For now, though, I think you should look after your sister first and let me worry about the Danes. If all goes well, you'll be big enough soon."

"It's true," Oscar said, also aware the boy had taken their laughter for derision. "I need you to keep your sister safe. It's been too many years since I wielded a proper weapon, and I'll need your help, Stefn."

"You hit the man with your axe, though," Stefn corrected, noting his grandfather had indeed felled one of the Danes on horseback.

"I did," Oscar acknowledged with a nod. "But that old axe is for wood. I just saw our friend fall and thought he might need some help."

"I appreciated that," said Cenric. "I should have thanked you there and then, but you looked…"

"Troubled?" asked Oscar. "I was. And am. I've not had to fight anyone in years. Not since Malduna."

"You fought at Malduna?" Cenric was surprised. The Battle of Malduna was one of the pivotal events of the early days of King Æthelred's reign. Cenric was a young man at the time, but he remembered how everyone had talked of it. It was yet another heroic defeat for the English, and a heavy one, but legends had been born there, and the accursed Svienn Forkbeard had not walked away unscathed.

"I was there, yes," Oscar said with a sigh. "It was as you've no doubt heard. I didn't feel too heroic when it was all happening. Too many dead friends. The poets usually leave stuff like that out."

Cenric grunted in agreement, unwilling to pressure the old man into speaking on what were likely to be painful memories. He understood how he felt. He'd been in enough battles to know they were frequently messy, terrifying, and downright horrific affairs, facts that were almost always absent from the songs composed well after the event by people who'd not even been there. He didn't blame people for wanting to focus on glory and heroism rather than blood and tears, but he didn't think it unreasonable to hope for a more balanced approach in recalling the past. It was just a more honest way of looking at things, in his view.

Indeed, too many youngsters continued to rush into battle thinking it would all be romance and valour rather than heartache and loss. He'd been such a naive youth once, in a hurry for the fight, only to find himself struggling and failing to hold back tears as he said goodbye to a brother on the battlefield. It saddened him that his experience was far from unique. He hoped the young Stefn here wouldn't have to go through anything like that. Something told him, though, that the boy almost certainly would. He had a warrior's temperament already. If his father had fallen at Canterburie, he'd want to get even. It was understandable, but he'd need to be reminded there was more to life than vengeance. Such passions could consume a man, eating him up from the inside so that, in the end, there was not a lot left. Cenric could attest to that.

Nobody spoke for a while, a bleak quietude settling over them as they continued along the bumpy route to Witenestaple. The children fell asleep, the excitement and fear of their hurried flight from the city having worn them out. Oscar and Swet remained up front, hunched and forlorn amidst the persistent snowfall, the warmth of their furs apparently doing little to keep them from melancholy. They were probably thinking about this Edwin of theirs. Cenric really felt for them. It would be hard enough to lose a son, but to then have to contemplate raising grandchildren in the winter years of life was daunting indeed. But what other choice did they have? They were good people, he could tell, and they'd do what had to be done. Perhaps Ulfcytel could help them somehow. He was a man of means, after all.

The ealdorman suddenly coughed, a hollow, rattling sound that was as alarming as it was abrupt. His eyes opened briefly, his hands also clenching into fists like he was panicking. Cenric reached out to him, putting a gentle hand over one of his fists, hoping he might realise he was safe. Their eyes met. He saw fear there. That was a hard thing to see in a hero like Ulfcytel, but there it was. He had every right to be afraid, Cenric supposed. No man could be expected to bear all the burdens of the world, even one such as he.

"Are you alright?" Cenric asked, his hand squeezing slightly upon the still-knotted fist. Ulfcytel continued to stare up at him, like he couldn't remember who he was. They'd not known each other long, only meeting for the first time after Cenric had helped Alaric fight off the first of the mystery assassins outside Canterburie's cathedral. That seemed like an age ago now. Perhaps he really should re-introduce himself.

"You remember me?" he asked pleadingly. "I'm Cenric. I commanded the hearthweru of the Ealdorman Ælfric. I came to Canterburie to find his son, Alaric, if you remember?"

"Of course I bloody well remember you! But why is it so damn cold?! I'm freezing my beard off here!"

Cenric let out a long exhalation, feeling both relieved and also tickled by Ulfcytel's customary bluntness. Old Swet passed them another blanket she'd found somewhere, Cenric thanking her before draping it over Ulfcytel like he were a child being tucked into bed for the night. Its thickness added to the woollen layers already present, the prospective warmth hopefully assuaging any fears of his beard freezing off, if such a thing were possible. He drank some water when it was offered, partaking with some enthusiasm despite his weakened condition.

Swet again produced something useful from wherever it was she was stashing these things, handing Cenric a hunk of bread she possibly thought he could feed to the ealdorman. Cenric considered it, realising then that the mighty Ulfcytel might not appreciate being hand-fed. Ulfcytel reached up to take it from him instead, the entire thing soon disappearing into the silvered avalanche that was his great bearded maw. He had an appetite. That was good.

"Where are we?" he asked, his voice still weak, or at least weak when compared to his usual rumblings.

"On the road," Cenric answered. "These good people picked us up outside Canterburie. We're heading to Witenestaple, where you can rest."

"Rest?! Heavens, man, what happened with the battle? Do we know how the slippery bastards got inside the walls like that?"

"I don't know, my lord. But when Alaric ordered me to carry you out of there, it didn't…"

Cenric paused as he beheld the children just a few feet away. They were awake, observing keenly the exchange between himself and Ulfcytel. The ealdorman continued staring at Cenric, expecting him to finish his sentence, his eyes then following his gaze until he saw the children too. He wasn't a stupid or insensitive man. He saw them for what they were and knew it wouldn't do to be talking about what they both already knew. Canterburie had fallen. There was no sense in announcing that in the company of these two innocent souls. They'd find out soon enough, anyway. Better that they hear it from their grandfather than two strangers on the road.

"And Alaric?" asked Ulfcytel, unwilling to drop the issue entirely. "How was he when you last saw him?"

"Very much himself. Alive and fighting. I can't say much more than that."

Silence enveloped them again. Ulfcytel appeared troubled under his blankets, feeling powerless, perhaps, that he couldn't control the situation as he was accustomed to. He eventually closed his eyes, slipping into a deep slumber that spared Cenric from further questions. Their journey carried on, the snow refusing to ease off as night began to fall across the frozen expanse of the horizon.

Oscar lit a torch and handed it to Swet, the cart itself being too heavily burdened to risk blundering off-road in the dark. Cenric could tell there were others out there, shuffling on their way in the dark, the sound of feet and hooves drifting in on the sharp evening air. They were all probably just looking for a safe haven in which to rest. He hoped they'd find it, but he kept his hand close to the hilt of his sword, just in case. There was no telling who or what else could be out there in the dark.

Swet climbed into the back of the cart, handing Cenric the torch and asking him to move up front with Oscar whilst she dozed with the children. Cenric obliged, sitting beside the old man to join him in staring out into the night, the two stout horses plodding on without complaint.

The surrounding woods had become denser, the bare, barren trees on either side of the road looming over them as they passed. There was always something unappealing about trees in winter, so Cenric thought, and it was worse at night, their unadorned trunks and branches appearing like ghostly, skeletal hands emerging from the earth to clutch malevolently at the sky. He chided himself. He was braver than many, although he'd never claim such a thing out loud. He didn't have any business getting rattled by some trees.

Oscar gradually eased the horses to a stop. There was a sound of running water upon stone close by, likely a stream or brook. Oscar dismounted from his position at the head of the cart and tended to the horses, unharnessing both and leading them away into the darkness.

He didn't ask Cenric to follow with the torch, instead seeming content to have him remain where he was and make do with the light of the moon and stars above. Cenric couldn't see what he was doing, but from where he was sat he could see some other kind of light reflected back at him. It was water all right, fast moving from the north west, a stream for certain. The horses must be needing to quench their thirst. They deserved it. They'd been worked hard this day.

Cenric remained vigilant, attentive to every sound and more than aware they were not out of danger, despite the distance they'd covered already. Thorkell's success in this war wasn't purely down to brute force or his ferocious capabilities as a fighter. Terror was a weapon of his, one Cenric suspected he enjoyed utilising. His men relished brutalising the local population wherever they went, and he didn't think their most recent visit to Cantwara would be any different. More riders could be out there right now, looking for easy targets, and should they find their little cart, they'd not be able to believe their luck. Killing Ulfcytel would be an honour worthy of song, even if they omitted any mention of the fact he'd been wounded when they'd done it. Cenric would, of course, die before he'd sit and listen to such a ballad.

Oscar returned with the horses, the two beasts licking at their lips appreciatively. He then re-harnessed them to the cart before joining Cenric up top. They moved back onto the road, continuing on their way at a brisk pace, the horses restored now they'd had a chance to drink and perhaps also feed. The forest around them continued to peer in at them, Cenric suppressing a shudder as his mind again began to see shadowy shapes and figures moving within the thicket. He inhaled slowly, exhaling afterwards in a like manner. He had to settle himself down. There were enough foes to fight without him dreaming up yet more.

"It's not just the Danes we need worry about," murmured Oscar, probably having noticed Cenric was ill at ease in the darkness. "There's a lot of desperate people out there with nowhere to go. We're a big target, and we have food and water. Wine too. People get silly when they are desperate. They do things they might not otherwise have ever considered."

Cenric knew what he meant, and it did absolutely nothing for his nerves. He'd rather they be attacked by Danes, fully armed and fearsome, than any number of despairing refugees just looking for something to eat. It was one thing to kill the heathen, foul as they were, but another altogether to fight regular people who had been driven to violence through the sheer misery of their condition. He'd do it if he had to, but he'd lament every life lost. Oscar seemed to sense his apprehension, changing the subject to something he suspected would be more to his taste.

"So you'll be wanting to hear about what it was like at Malduna?"

"Now?" Cenric asked, cautious as to whether speaking on such things and reliving old memories would be the best choice on a night like this.

"Why not? You have somewhere else to be? Everyone always wants to hear about it when they find out I was there. To see if the reality matches the legend, I suppose."

"So what happened?" Cenric was eager now, his troubled thoughts making way for images of heroism and great deeds.

"Some would say we made a mistake early on. You'll know Svienn and Olaf…that Norwegian bastard the king later bought off…well, they were initially stuck on an island when we turned up to fight them."

"Right," concurred Cenric, "but I'd heard they still had a fleet with them. It was either fight them there and then or just watch them return to their ships and attack somewhere else, no?"

"That's true," nodded Oscar, "you're a good student of history, I see. We wanted the fight, too. The men were baying for their blood, wanting payback for all the misery they'd already caused. So our Byrhtnoð gets this idea, you see, to go and…you've heard of Byrhtnoð, aye?"

"Yes," Cenric said blankly, wondering if Oscar was trying to be funny. Everyone knew of Byrhtnoð, the then Ealdorman of Exsessa. He was pretty much the main focus of all the poems and accounts that had been written of Malduna since his death there. Others had featured, too, but Byrhtnoð's heroism was more often than not the main subject poets chose to focus on. With good reason, in Cenric's opinion.

"Alright then," continued Oscar, a contented smile on his face. "So our first problem was that the bastards wouldn't move to come face us. They just dithered about across the causeway between us and them. They'd killed everyone who lived there, as in the island they were parked on, so they didn't have much to do apart from return to their ships and pop up somewhere else. Byrhtnoð could see that, so he decides to go and talk to them."

That wasn't anything unusual, Cenric thought. Verbal interactions between the English and their Scandinavian tormentors were fairly common, almost always so the latter could demand payment on the promise they'd then depart without causing further harm. It rarely worked, and at this point, he was surprised anyone could ever have bothered trying. The Norsemen simply had no honour. They'd proven that time and again. A clenched fist was the only way to deal with them.

"They wanted off the island, as you'd expect," Oscar continued, "but just so they could form up and give us battle. It sounds insane looking at it now, but Byrhtnoð agreed and he was right to. We'd already refused to give them any money, and if we'd just left them to it, they'd have gotten back on their ships and headed elsewhere. If we attacked along the causeway ourselves, we'd be fighting at a massive disadvantage. Agreeing to their offer of a fair fight in open ground was the best option."

Cenric nodded along, humouring the old man despite already knowing much of what he'd just said. In his opinion, there wasn't anything wrong with what Byrhtnoð had done, since one of the biggest problems with fighting Northmen was their manoeuvrability. If Byrhtnoð had declined their offer, they would have taken to the sea again and gone for a softer target. He'd had the chance to face them down in an open brawl, and he'd gone for it. It was just a shame what had happened next.

"And it all looked alright at first," Oscar added. "They came flowing off the island, up onto the causeway and right at us along the banks of the Panta. We were all hacking away at each other for most of the day. I killed a few of the bastards, and then I took an axe in the chest. Nearly ended me, but nearly wasn't enough, as it turned out. Then

Byrhtnoð fell. I didn't see it, but that was it. We broke apart like splintered wood. My mates, those I had left, dragged me out of there, but I don't remember that part. Svienn burned Malduna soon after. Made a right show of it. Murder. Enslavement. Rape. The man's a monster."

"Do you want to know why we remember Malduna so much?" Oscar then asked, his aged eyes unusually bright. "Two points," he said, not bothering to wait for Cenric to answer him. "Two reasons, even. One is that no battle like that had been fought in years. We'd not taken that kind of hammering in decades, maybe even longer. It hurt, in more ways than one. The other is Byrhtnoð himself. He was one of the last links between our King Æthelred and his father. He was a good man. A good influence on the king. So when he died…"

Oscar turned away, gazing out into the darkness ahead. Cenric understood. Their king was a complicated man. The general consensus across the realm, as far as Cenric could tell, was that he wasn't a good ruler, yet not necessarily from wickedness or inaction. He was always so ill-advised, unprepared, or downright unlucky, and in recent years that had destabilised him further, leading to the emergence of a vicious streak Cenric didn't appreciate. He had, after all, ordered Eadric of Mierċe's attack on Hamptonscir and the kidnapping of his Lord Ælfric. Cenric wasn't about to forgive that.

"I understand," Cenric said simply. It was an honest enough answer. Oscar continued in his silence for a while longer, content to let things rest as they were. Eventually, he spoke again, his voice hesitant, like he was afraid to ask for fear of the answer he might receive.

"So now I've told you a story of one battle, would you tell me of another? What happened back there at Canterburie? Is my son dead?"

"He may be," Cenric confessed, not wanting to waste the old man's time with honeyed words. "I'm sorry. I wish I had something else to tell you, but I can't lie. I don't think anyone who was still fighting when I left would have prevailed. Thorkell had every advantage."

"Lord have mercy," Oscar breathed, his eyes moistening with sorrow. "I don't want to believe it…but I know what you say is true. I can feel it. Something is missing…like a flame that had been aglow in my heart is now extinguished. Pray you'll never know what I mean, Cenric. Unless…have you ever lost a child?"

"Yes". He didn't want to say any more than that. Not because he felt no affection for Oscar, but because he didn't think he'd be able to stand talking about it. Some things in his past he just wanted to bury and forget about. His children were one such thing. He'd rather fight a half dozen Danes, right now, than revisit that kind of grief.

"Then you'll know…you'll know…" mumbled Oscar, his eyes still wet. "What pains me now is not just Edwin's fate. What will I do with Cwen and Stefn back there? To have to raise children again at my age…it's a heavy burden. I worry enough that I wasn't a good enough father to Edwin, and I was in my prime then. Now that I'm so long in years, how can I be what they really need…"

His voice trailed off again. He wasn't wrong, and his fears were quite justified. A man his age should be taking it easy somewhere with his wife. Instead, he was travelling a frozen road through a frozen forest at night, with two vulnerable children, a wife, and a particularly high-value target for attack in the form of the Ealdorman Ulfcytel. That was a lot to take on for a man at any stage in life. Raising his grandchildren without their father also made for a daunting prospect. Cenric wished he had some advice to give.

"Ulfcytel is a man of means," Cenric began, hoping to be able to put Oscar at ease. "He's kind and good. I can say with some certainty he'll be grateful for the aid you've given us. When he's up on his feet and aware of your situation, he'll help. You need not worry."

Oscar said nothing, for he was staring straight ahead in alarm. Cenric followed his gaze, recoiling in shock at the flickering of lights in the near distance. It was hard to spot, and the trees were dense enough to have obscured it up until now, but it was there. Flames. Something was on fire up ahead. Something large.

"Stop the horses," Cenric hissed, not wanting them to blunder any closer and alert whoever had set the blaze. Oscar complied, his loyal steeds thudding to a halt at his command, faint trails of vapour emerging from their nostrils into the freezing air. Cenric got down, moving towards the rear of the cart to check on their passengers. Everyone was asleep. Good. The last thing they needed was for anyone to panic and start making noise.

Cenric instructed Oscar to stay put whilst he scouted ahead. He crept onward, avoiding the road, skirting through the naked trees and doing his best to keep silent. The snow didn't help, the "crump crump" of his footsteps making him wince. He hoped any malefactors wouldn't have too keen an ear tonight. He'd left a ridiculously evident trail of deep footprints behind him too. He'd never liked the winter.

He soon heard the crackling of flames, the blaze in all its intensity becoming more visible as the tree cover parted. It was a small settlement, or at least a series of farms and barns, most of which were burning, the ash and smoke stinging his eyes. He moved at a dash, staying low to avoid any onlookers, hoping the night would cloak him whilst he moved closer to the conflagration. There were several dead men scattered about, their forms twisted in pain and shock, each one bearing signs of violence upon their flesh. None of this was an accident. This place had been attacked.

Shouts of alarm drifted in upon the breeze. Survivors were ahead, crying out in anger and urgency from amidst the inferno. They were trying to tackle the blaze, throwing snow and earth into the flames. Cenric wasn't sure if he could really help, but he felt compelled to aid them. He stood up and hurried towards the nearest person. The man heard him and spun around, screaming at the sight of him. Others came, some bearing reaping hooks, at least one gripping a spear tightly and looking like he meant to use it. The tip was coated in something, like congealed red rust. Cenric knew what that was. This man had taken life tonight.

"Do not fear! I'm English!"

He held his hands up and open, trying to project his voice without sounding like he was roaring something before charging in for a fight. They relented somewhat, able to discern from his appearance, manner, and armour that he wasn't one of Thorkell's reavers. The spearman approached, his face haggard and troubled, the others forming around him, each looking as if they'd faced one too many ordeals these past years.

"Who are you?" asked the spearman, his manner gruff despite the emotion in his wild eyes. "Are there others with you? Have you come to hunt them down?"

"Hunt who down?" Cenric asked, feeling a little foolish, considering it was overwhelmingly likely they were referring to a party of Norsemen. "Nobody sent me here," he added quickly, "I'm from Canterburie. The city has fallen to attack."

A collective moan escaped every man's lips. All of them had no doubt heard that Ulfcytel himself was making his stand at Canterburie. It would have given them hope, even if they had not answered the summons themselves. He saw why as he looked upon each of them, their faces fully revealed now they'd come within striking distance. They were all way past their prime, their skin gnarled and pitted like ancient oak, their rough beards long and grey. They were not entirely incapable, but they were certainly of an age ill-suited to marching south to fight in a siege.

"That will explain why they hit us," lamented one. "They'll be moving out all over now that they've got Canterburie. Nowhere will be safe!"

"Let's consider our options," suggested Cenric, speaking more for the sake of getting them to focus on him rather than succumb to panic. "Are you all that have survived? How many Danes attacked you?"

"About a dozen," grunted the spearman. "I don't know where they came from…it was all so fast. They didn't take anything, just set fires, killed anyone they caught and then rode off, to the east, I think. The bastards were enjoying themselves. Laughing at us. I got one of them, though. Stupid oaf thought he'd get off his horse and come at me all man-to-man or something. I speared him as he was dismounting. Can't be taking any chances at my age!"

The others all spoke in agreement, their grey heads nodding in unison. This was a ludicrous situation for them. Men this age shouldn't even be out in this kind of weather, let alone fending off marauding Danes and extinguishing fires. The buildings were well past saving anyway. He had to get these poor souls and whoever else they had with them away from here and somewhere safe. Where such a place could be found, he had absolutely no idea.

"Where are your wives? Your sons and daughters?" Cenric hoped they wouldn't say dead. Everything was falling apart enough already. He didn't want to have to deal with the sight of ravished and murdered women.

"The women are in the trees," said a scrawny-looking chap, his long, thin beard caked in ash. "We hurried them there when it all kicked off. Our sons…"

"All went to fight in Canterburie," interrupted another. "We hoped we'd receive word of them soon enough. Now I suppose we have."

"Is the city really taken!?" the spearman suddenly wailed, his eyes glistening with tears. "All our sons dead?! It can't be true! Say it's not so, please!"

Cenric opened his mouth, gaping like a fish whilst he struggled to think of something to say. The spearman flinched suddenly, his gaze shifting past Cenric's shoulder and into the woods behind him. Cenric turned. Oscar was making his way towards them. With Swet, the children, and Ulfcytel himself.

He was both a humbling and inspiring sight. He was weak, that was obvious, his right side propped up by a large stick that he was using to support himself. Oscar stayed close, allowing Ulfcytel to wrap his left arm around his shoulder as they proceeded.

The old lunatic must have woken up shortly after Cenric had left and demanded to know what was going on. He could imagine what had happened then. He'd insisted they allow him to follow. A foolish move, one that could have gotten him killed if the enemy had still been around and spoiling for bloodshed. Yet here he was, coming closer now, his face straining with effort. The men nearby gasped in amazement and recognition. They knew who he was, somehow. Cenric wasn't entirely sure, but they seemed awe-struck by the emergence of the ealdorman, even in this battered state.

Cenric shared in their admiration. There was something mighty and also paternal about him, striding onward despite his wounds, the two children following eagerly as they kept pace with this limping giant. The flickering aura from the flames washed over him, illuminating the fine, if at times dented and smashed, scales of his battle dress, his huge silver beard seeming to almost sparkle in the dancing light. He stopped about a half dozen paces from Cenric, Oscar standing by in case he should fall. Ulfcytel looked at each man in turn, his eyes reflecting the continuing blaze just beyond. Then he spoke. A simple statement, conveyed with a simple authority.

"This is Witenestaple."

Cenric didn't know if Ulfcytel had indeed been here before, but if he had, that would explain why the others seemed to recognise him. The spearman spoke up, moving closer to the ealdorman as he noticed Oscar, relief spreading across his face.

"It is, my lord," he said shakily, "and it's good to see you again. Thank you for bringing my brother back to us. I'd feared the worst, I had."

So this must be Oscar's brother, Cenric mused, the one they'd intended to stay with whilst Ulfcytel recovered his strength. That wasn't an option now, clearly. He didn't know which house was his because they all looked the same, what with them all being on fire. There'd be little left of Witenestaple by morning, and they had nowhere to go. They were stuck, in hostile territory with nothing but roaming Danes for company. They needed a new plan. But he was stumped if he knew where to begin.

"I'm sorry things have come to this," announced Ulfcytel, addressing everyone. "When I passed through here last year, I told you I would be Thorkell's end if you but sent your fighting men to Canterburie to join me there. We had him, you know. Twice we threw him from the walls of the city. But betrayal was our undoing. I don't know how, and I don't know who, but I promise you this…I won't cease until I find out what happened. I owe it to you. I owe it to your sons."

They looked to each other, the old folk, all confused, saddened, and inspired all at once. Some held each other's hands, grasping and embracing their fellows in dismay and reassurance, the news of Canterburie's fall and now the appearance of the ealdorman proving a lot to take in. Cenric felt a wetness on his cheeks, thinking it to be from the incessant snowfall. It wasn't. He also must have been moved by Ulfcytel's words.

"Are my ships still safe?" Cenric didn't know what Ulfcytel meant by that. Then he remembered. Alaric had told him how they'd stolen several ships from Thorkell's fleet as it lay moored at Gipeswic. A bold move. One that had nearly killed Ulfcytel. But it had worked. Had they made landfall here and then walked south to Canterburie?

"They are, lord," said the spearman. "As far as I know, anyway. We hid them well. I don't see how the heathens could have discovered them."

"Then I have something else to ask of all of you," said Ulfcytel. "There is nothing left here for us, and yet we still have a chance to put things right. If you help me crew those ships and get us into the Temes, we can reach Lundenburg. I have friends in the capital still. I'll make sure you and your families are cared for."

"What will you do in Lundenburg?" Cenric asked, knowing in his heart what the answer was likely to be.

"I didn't want it to come to this," Ulfcytel rumbled, "but I've no option now. The whole realm has no option. I will face King Æthelred. And I will quickly discover the truth of all that has gone wrong for us of late. The rot that assails our land from top to bottom must finally be exposed. He has to listen to me. He MUST listen."

"And if he won't?"

Ulfcytel didn't reply to Cenric's question. He paused, staring into the blazing fires before him, the light still reflecting in his cold eyes. He then began to move forward, slow and unsteady, his wooden crutch trembling under his weight, Oscar doing his best to support him. The others parted around them, following the ealdorman as he made his way through the blazing settlement on what Cenric assumed must be a path towards his hidden vessels. He didn't need an answer. He could guess the situation well enough.

If the king would not listen to Ulfcytel, things would take a darker turn. It would be dangerous to confront him, that was undeniable, but Cenric would remain at his side. Æthelred couldn't just kill Ulfcytel in front of everyone. He was too popular and important for that. Cenric would also slay any man who tried it. He'd remain loyal to the ealdorman, even if called upon to commit himself to the unthinkable. Treason. Treason against the crown. The thought bore a tremendous weight, dark and cold, like the winter's night itself. To think these evil days should be theirs, that they should even have to contemplate such things.

But contemplate they must. And then act. He hoped it wouldn't come to that. But he would if he had to. Their presence in the capital would also present certain opportunities for Cenric. The king had imprisoned his Lord Ælfric, abducting him and his family and using that cur, Eadric of Mierce, to further brutalise the people of Hamptonscir. If they were still in captivity, he would see them freed. If the king had executed them, he'd have his vengeance. There was no other way. It was a dangerous path ahead, potentially more dangerous than the ordeals they'd faced so far. Yet he would not shirk from the challenge. No matter how great the obstacles, they had to succeed. And as dim as their prospects were, he sensed things were about to get very difficult for King Æthelred.

XXI

Edmund had never understood melancholy before. He'd thought it something for weak men or the downright unfortunate; a malady he was simply too strong to ever let rest upon his broad shoulders. He'd been wrong. Sadness could visit a man in the long or short course of his life, if it chose to and for as often as it pleased. There was no resisting it when it came, and only a fool would claim otherwise. Misery and loss could make themselves an unwelcome guest of anyone, no matter their station or disposition. Even an aetheling such as he. He'd know. It was his lot now.

Morcar and Sigeferth had tried to be kind, but he feared their patience was wearing thin. Reminding him of his duties wasn't enough. It would have been in the past, when his responsibilities were less burdensome and he'd at least had somebody to share them with. He had another brother, other siblings, and there was still family for him here in the Five Boroughs and in Lundenburg, too, but none of that seemed to mean much presently. He was empty, like something had hollowed him out from the inside to snatch at his very soul. He couldn't say when or indeed if such a feeling might pass.

His many troubles, sadly, were not going to pause to allow him respite. His father awaited him. Æthelred had written, dispatching messengers demanding news, then imploring, begging even, that Edmund return home. Edmund didn't want to face him. He didn't want to stand there and tell him that Æthelstan was really dead. It was hard enough admitting it to himself. To speak of it to his father could finally push him over the edge.

Playing it safe was easier. He was past glory, weary of it, and he felt like the man he'd been was fading away as sadness and isolation took hold. He'd begun to dwell on it, thinking often of his mother and his uncle, Æthelstan. It was common knowledge they'd shared a bond, and his mother had thought so highly of him she'd insisted Æthelred name their firstborn son after him. And so it was. He'd been kind to his sister's children, proving himself a paternal figure when their own father was either too busy or lost in one of his turbulent episodes. They'd loved him, and he'd loved them right back. Then he'd been lost at Hringmere. And now the brother that bore his name had been lost too.

Edmund began to ponder darker thoughts. His mother was gone, his uncle was gone, the sibling he'd been closest to was also gone. Was this to be his fate, enduring whilst so many others faded, to be trapped with his tempestuous father whilst all those who might help him met an untimely end? The thought troubled him beyond description. If it were to be so, he didn't think he could bear it. To fall in battle as his uncle and brother had would be a mercy in comparison. At least there'd be some honour there. Anything was preferable to the loneliness that now gripped him.

He was sat at what had become his usual spot, gazing upon the not-so-fresh earth of his brother's grave. The snow had blanketed it these past nights, the blizzard flowing in from both the north and south to seal the people of Snotingeham inside their homes. Edmund didn't care. The cold didn't bother him. Nothing bothered him. He was numb, like all was a dream he'd yet to wake from and showed no sign of ending.

The graveyard was an unassuming place, stashed away a little distance from Sigeferth's hall and reasonably secluded from the rest of Snotingeham's streets. Row upon row of stone crosses protruded from the snow here, some elaborate, some not, all of them serving the same purpose regardless of who lay buried beneath. They all looked largely the same from where he sat, the evening's sallow light obscuring further scrutiny. Only one grave mattered to him right now, anyway. He had to be here. He had to keep coming back. He didn't know for how long. He just had to be close.

He couldn't remember much about Æthelstan's funeral or their journey carrying him back here. His mind had refused to focus on what was taking place, preferring instead to keep reliving those same moments in the monastery when his brother had slipped away. Even the companionship of the thegn-turned-monk, Wulfgeat, who had accompanied them to Snotingeham, couldn't provoke much interest, despite his claim to know of the bad blood between his father and many of his nobles. Edmund just couldn't summon the strength to listen to him. Who cared about intrigue and the scheming of sin-addled men at a time like this? Such things had brought them to this point, and Edmund couldn't stand to hear any more of it.

Morcar thought otherwise. He'd pressed Edmund on what Wulfgeat had claimed to know, arguing it was imperative they find out more on the nature of the relationship between the king and this Alaric fellow. Edmund told him to go and ask him himself. He assumed he had. Morcar was curious about all sorts and couldn't resist learning something new. If he'd stumbled upon anything that could help them with his father, he'd kept quiet about it. Edmund couldn't say he was sorry. He respected Morcar, but he needed to understand he just wanted to be left alone. That wasn't too much to ask.

Edmund looked over his shoulder upon hearing footsteps approach. The sound was light and gentle, not belonging to anyone weighed down by weapon or shield. He saw the figure moving towards him with a delicate step, its slight physique well concealed amid a thick fur cloak. Somebody else was present, standing back just at the entrance to the graveyard itself. They were armed, the physical bulk from beneath their thick winter robes suggesting they were a warrior assigned to watch over whoever was now approaching. This was somebody of import then.

He'd worked out who it was long before they were within striking distance. A sliver of wavy auburn hair had escaped their hood; a dead giveaway when one observed the soft, almost hesitant tempo of their movements upon the snow. It was the lady Ealdgyth, wife to Sigeferth. The man standing some distance behind must be her escort. Her husband certainly wouldn't let her wander the town on her own. A woman such as her just wouldn't be safe. He already had a feeling on what she had to say to him.

"Are you all right?" she asked, her face more visible since she'd come within a half dozen paces. She sounded uncomfortable, like the cold weather was getting to her and she'd rather be elsewhere. There was a genuine concern to her tone, though. Everyone was worried about him. He understood that. But he did appreciate his solitude.

"I am fine, Ealdgyth. I just like to be here, that's all. I have to gather my thoughts for what's ahead."

That was a brave way of putting it. He didn't want to admit to her just how pronounced the depths of his grief really were. She'd likely know just by looking at him, but there was still no way he'd come out and speak of it. He had a reputation to maintain. He'd already wept openly enough in front of Sigeferth and Morcar. He felt little shame in it, but it wasn't a display he was looking to repeat.

"We are all so concerned for you," she said, confirming again what he already knew. "This winter has lasted too long already…will you not come inside where it's warm?"

"I will soon enough. It's getting late, I know, but I can't quiet my mind elsewhere. I have to get whatever this is resolved in my head. But I appreciate your concern."

He couldn't tell if she was hurt or not, so obscured was her visage from beneath her furs. The last thing he wanted was to appear rude, but the repeated notion that he should make his comfort a priority irked him. The cold just wasn't an issue to him. Let the soft and the effeminate worry about such things. Edmund was a man and wished to live as such. He would return to the hall when it suited him.

"Sigeferth has news for you," she muttered hesitantly, apprehensive over what she now spoke of. "A messenger came just hours ago."

"And what of it? News of the war? My father?"

"The war, yes. Thorkell has attacked Canterburie. He was beaten back twice, but the city fell on the third assault. We don't know anything more than that."

Edmund lurched to his feet and turned to face Ealdgyth properly. Snow cascaded from his back, the stuff hesitant to let him go after his prolonged stay within its frigid embrace. He hadn't even known Canterburie was within striking distance of Thorkell. Shamefully, he hadn't given his movements much thought. He'd been entirely preoccupied with his brother's death. A mistake. If he were to be king, he should not be so easily moved.

"Why was I not told of this immediately?" he snapped. "You said the messenger came hours ago. I've been here all this time."

"You've told us many times you wanted to be left alone. We can feel your grief, Edmund. We share it too. And in truth, we didn't want to add to it, so Sigeferth decided to hold off whilst he had a meal prepared for you. He's thoughtful like that. He waits for you now, if you'd just come inside."

He didn't bother responding, instead setting off at a determined pace back to Sigeferth's hall. He was irritated they'd waited to tell him, also feeling a little self-conscious that they'd thought him so fragile. Then it occurred to him they'd been right. He had been fragile. They'd all read him like a book; a reality he wasn't remotely comfortable with. He'd have to work on making his emotions more opaque. He'd also have to work on his manners. He'd left Ealdgyth just standing there, as if she wasn't even worth another word. He stopped and waited for her. He shouldn't forget proper courtesy, hard times or no.

Ealdgyth caught up with him, saying nothing whilst she fell into step beside him. Her escort followed, content to remain a few paces behind. Ealdgyth's silence continued as they made their way through the snowy streets, unwilling to prod the still taciturn Edmund into further conversation. He was, in some ways, thankful. He wouldn't have really known what to say to her, and he'd grown tired of people saying how "sorry" they were over Æthelstan. Regret he had in abundance. What he needed was clarity.

They passed onto the main road leading to the hall, an unpleasant, biting wind sending renewed shivers up Edmund's spine. Snotingeham looked to be wilting within winter's grasp, its thatched buildings that were so picturesque last summer appearing to recoil inwards under the ever-thickening layers of snow. The inhabitants were generally making themselves scarce, only leaving their homes on errands that presumably couldn't be delayed, but when they were spotted they looked troubled, the burden of the weather and also something else serving to weigh them down.

Edmund knew well enough what it was. Plenty of families here had been told that their fathers, brothers, or sons had fallen in the same battle that had claimed Æthelstan. It was worse for them, in a way, since most of them had to endure the grim reality that the bodies of their loved ones had been left behind to rot on the field. Edmund should be grateful, he supposed. He'd been able to say goodbye to his brother properly. He also had a warm hall to go back to, where there was no shortage of firewood, food, and ale. That was more than some others had.

Privileged or not, Edmund still hadn't eaten much since the battle. Sadness had stolen his appetite along with his desire for company, but he'd make the effort now for Sigeferth's sake. There was no point in spurning his good intentions.

Despite his newfound resolve, Edmund still looked very much the unapproachable man as he strode into the hall, the chill blast of wind that followed him summing up his mood perfectly. Flecks of snow blew in across the threshold and melted upon contact with the floor, the guard at the door doing his best to seal the entrance rapidly now that Ealdgyth and her escort had returned with their errant friend.

Edmund made his way to the table by the hearth where Sigeferth sat waiting. The whole place was still decked out as if for a celebration and unchanged, more or less, from when he and Æthelstan had sparred here last summer for the entertainment of the assembled thegns. Those were good times for the two brothers. He tried his best to avoid dwelling on the realisation they'd never come again.

He sat down directly across from his friend, still clothed in his damp cloak. Sigeferth stared at him, his deep-set eyes conveying a certain concern. Edmund wasn't trying to be rude, but he simply didn't want anyone else to ask him if he was feeling all right. He'd be happy to avoid the subject of his brother entirely. He decided to take pre-emptive action by speaking first.

"Canterburie has fallen? Is there word then about where Thorkell will strike next?"

Sigeferth took this in his stride, realising Edmund would want to focus on important business rather than his own misfortunes. He himself looked like recent events had been kind to him. He'd lost weight, his paunch much reduced after the exertions of their rapid marching and frenzied fighting. His hairline was higher, though, his long, free-flowing silvered locks having faded to white in places. Stress was behind that. Æthelstan had meant a lot to him too.

"The city has been taken, yes," Sigeferth said, his words imbued with all the gravitas they deserved. "The Ealdorman Ulfcytel, of all people, was there, apparently leading the defenders. Thorkell hasn't moved elsewhere, so we've been told. He's just sat within the walls, reducing it to ruin. Word is he's taken captives for ransom."

This was catastrophic. Canterburie was not only one of the oldest and finest cities in the country, but it was a holy place of considerable esteem. To have it defiled in such a way was simply abhorrent. Depending on whom the hostages were, the king would have no choice but to pay up, especially if Archbishop Ælfheah was among them. He was loved and respected by many. Æthelred couldn't just let him die.

"Why didn't you tell me this as soon as the messenger arrived?" Edmund demanded, ignoring Ealdgyth when she pulled up a chair beside her husband. "I would think it appropriate to inform me, now that…"

"Now that…?" Sigeferth asked, unimpressed with Edmund's complaining.

"Now that I'm heir to the throne." He was. Eadwig might also have designs on kingship, but he wouldn't ever see them come to fruition. Even if he were the elder, which he wasn't, he simply wasn't suited for it. England did not need a scholar to rule it. It needed a fighter. Edmund was that and could be yet more, if necessary. He'd apply himself to any task that came his way.

"You forget your brother, my boy," Sigeferth shot back predictably. "Seniority isn't everything. Eadwig may not have your skills when it comes to brawling, but he has a sharp mind on him. He only needs to build confidence in other areas."

"You and I both know he doesn't want the throne," Edmund persisted. "He has little interest in affairs of state and no zeal for defending what would fall under his authority. He's bookish, withdrawn, and disinterested in others. He doesn't want to be king."

"He told you this?" Ealdgyth asked.

"No. Not directly. We always thought Æthelstan was destined to rule, anyway. But the rest of what I said stands. He's not suited for it. Any of it."

Sigeferth reclined in his chair, his countenance weary. The fire in the hearth nearby was giving off a fearsome heat, the warmth serving to ease the chill from Edmund's bones. One of the stewards appeared to deposit a bowl of winter stew in front of him, followed by a platter of buttered toast and a large cup of mead. Edmund waited until Sigeferth and Ealdgyth were similarly served before he took a sip. The taste was delightful. The stew too. It was a good sign. With any luck, his appetite might be returning.

"I confess, I do understand what you mean about Eadwig," admitted Sigeferth. "Sadly, he's not here to tell us what he wants. He left this morning with Morcar and that monk we brought back with us from Bernecestre. Wulfgeat, that's his name."

"Why?" Edmund asked, suspicious they should have both gone elsewhere with this man who claimed to know so much about his father.

"Morcar has his residence in Derbei, you know this. He wishes to question Wulfgeat there. I don't know why since he has little of any real interest to say, in my modest opinion. It's all about your father taking certain lands from the Church. Courtly intrigue and the like."

"At the behest of this Ælfric of Hamptonscir," Edmund said, thinking aloud, "who is the father to this Alaric whom my own father is so fearful of."

Sigeferth paused, unsure of how to proceed, or so it looked. When he spoke again, he sounded more than cautious, akin to how a man might speak when fearful of upsetting somebody they already thought was close to the edge. Edmund didn't appreciate it. He didn't need anyone to take that kind of care around him. He wasn't prone to unprovoked aggression and never had been.

"Edmund…don't you think it's possible your father might have just dreamed of this Alaric by chance? I mean, he's had dealings with all his ealdormen, Ælfric included, so he would have heard him mention his son, even if they'd never met. Could it not be that his troubled mind is just plucking at things from memory to fuel his nightmares?"

Edmund had never thought of that. What Sigeferth had said was possible, by all means, but his instincts cautioned him against coming to easy conclusions. His father was unstable, and increasingly so, but Edmund didn't think his dreams were entirely random, at least from what he knew of them. He hadn't imprisoned Ælfric and his family by chance, and he wasn't enraged at the mere mention of Alaric just because of a few sleepless nights. There was something deeper and darker at work here.

"I would agree with you, Sigeferth, if it were anyone but my father. And even if what you say is true, I can't afford to just put his behaviour down to his usual eccentricity. Ælfric and his family are still languishing in captivity as far as I know, and none of them were able to give me a proper answer as to why. There must be something to all this that goes beyond an old king's nightmares."

"You visited them?" Ealdgyth asked. "Alaric's wife too? And their son?"

"Æva, yes," Edmund confirmed. "I returned the boy to her after they'd been separated. The woman knew nothing and had done nothing, as far as I could tell. She was completely confused about why my father would have ill feelings towards her husband. I didn't know about Wulfgeat's claim that my father usurped lands from Abbendone at the behest of Ælfric, though. If I had, I would have asked them."

"Then surely that is what we must do," said Sigeferth. "We have at least one piece of this puzzle now. You can return to Lundenburg and ask him…and Ælfric, if he's still alive."

Edmund raised his hands to his head and began massaging his temples with his thumbs and index fingers. This was all very peculiar to him. He didn't care for old claims about who had apparently wronged whom, even when it came to something as astonishing as allegedly manipulating a king into seizing Church assets. If Ælfric had really done that, it would seem he deserved his imprisonment. But why should any of them care about past intrigues? If they lost this war, neither the Church, nor anyone else, would have any lands left. Everything would be put to the torch.

"I don't really see the point," Edmund said tersely. "Even if it's all true and Ælfric is a rat of a man, that doesn't explain why my father is so anxious about his son. And even then, none of this matters when we consider what's going on elsewhere. We're losing our country, bit by bit!"

"So it really is true?" said a new voice, weak and hesitant, coming from the doorway leading to the kitchens behind them. "We've lost Canterburie now, along with my husband?"

Edmund knew the voice. He saw her, his sister, Wulfhild, standing there, even paler than usual. She was dressed as if she'd not bothered to go out all day, her red and gold threaded long-sleeved dress as immaculate as her intricately plaited hair. She must have heard them talking about the recent news. She was entitled to fear the worst. If Ulfcytel had resurfaced at Canterburie to rally the defenders, it made sense to think him dead. He couldn't say that to her, though. He had to find a way to soften the blow.

"We don't know," Sigeferth answered, motioning for her to come and join them. "All we know is that the city was taken and that Thorkell was driven back twice before succeeding with a third assault. Your husband didn't make it easy on them."

"But he's dead," Wulfhild persisted, sitting between Edmund and Ealdgyth. "He was always quick-thinking, but Thorkell won't have been in the mood to let him escape again. He'll have killed him, won't he?"

"We can't know," Edmund ventured, taking her hand in his. "Ulfcytel has a talent for surviving. We also know Thorkell has taken hostages. Maybe Ulfcytel is one of them."

"You think so?"

"It's very possible. He's an important man. Thorkell will know he'll be worth a great deal as a hostage."

"But he could still die then? If nobody pays for him? I don't have enough…"

"The king will pay, my dear," Sigeferth assured her. "He'll pay for all of those taken. He won't just leave them to die."

Wulfhild said no more, although the look on her face said she didn't quite believe him. Edmund knew what she was thinking. There was no guarantee their father would pay for Ulfcytel to be freed or that he'd even survived the siege. It was one thing to pay the ransom of an Archbishop of Canterburie, as holy as Ælfheah was. People would expect that, and it would go some way to easing the pain of Canterburie's desecration.

Ulfcytel was another matter. From what Wulfhild had experienced recently when staying in Lundenburg, it was fair to say there was some bad blood between him and their father. It was for that reason she'd agreed to come with her brothers when they'd left to help Sigeferth and Morcar raise their army to try and confront Thorkell at Northantone. Edmund was glad to have her here now. It was just a shame he couldn't be a better comfort to her.

Sigeferth turned to look at Edmund, his face apprehensive, as if he were again contemplating saying something he suspected he'd dislike. When he spoke, he sounded uncertain, but his words were quite reasonable, even if Edmund would really rather not have heard them at all.

"Do you think now might be the time to try to meet with your father? He's asked you to return to Lundenburg a few times now. With what's happened at Canterburie, you could impress upon him the importance of paying Ulfcytel's ransom."

Edmund liked Sigeferth in more ways than one. He was shrewd, and this was him at his finest. He knew there was no way he could refuse. Wulfhild was sat right there, staring at him with those large, mournful eyes of hers. He couldn't let his sister down by refusing to at least attempt to save her husband's life. Edmund said the only thing he could.

"I will. I've not looked forward to such a meeting. But I don't seem to have a choice now. If Ulfcytel is not ransomed, we'll have lost another hero of our time. We can't have that. It's just not right."

"Are you sure, Edmund?" asked Sigeferth, still concerned. "I know this is a painful time for you. How were things the last time you were there? Did Eadric of Mierċe appear to have any particular disposition towards you?"

"None. If I'm honest, I didn't really interact with him. He was there when we forced our way into father's hall. Emma, you see…she wanted to keep us out. Eadric was there, looking happy about something, or just sinister, it was hard to tell. He never approached us. But it's a given that my father has taken him into his confidence. It was all a waste of time, anyway. He wouldn't listen to us. You know the rest."

"That's what has long worried us," Sigeferth said. "And the warning Morcar and I gave you still stands. Be careful around Eadric. A lot of our present difficulties likely originate with him. He may try to stand in your way now."

"Why?" sobbed Wulfhild, the possibility that somebody might wish to see her husband killed getting the better of her. "Why would he do that when all we want is to see Ulfcytel safe?"

"I can't know for sure," Sigeferth confessed, Edmund noticing that Ealdgyth had taken one of Wulfhild's hands in hers. "I have a feeling, though, and I'm afraid my instincts are often right about these things. Eadric may not be pleased to have a powerful and popular man like Ulfcytel returned to court."

"He'll have to put up with it," Edmund glowered, some of his old fury returning. "I'll not see another good man die if I can help it. I'm an aetheling. Eadric is nothing, just a jumped-up social climber who was made an ealdorman for reasons I can't understand. He'll keep out of my way if he knows what's good for him."

Edmund looked around, wondering why everyone seemed to have fallen silent. Sigeferth was looking right at him, pleased now, like he'd said something truly joyous. Ealdgyth had a slight smile on her face, too, so slight you'd miss it if you didn't know what to look for. Wulfhild, despite the tears in her eyes, also looked different. She was calmed. Relieved, actually. Were his words really that noteworthy?

"There you are, my boy," said Sigeferth, his smile clearly infectious, as Edmund couldn't help but return it. "I was wondering when you'd come back to us. There's the fire in you that I knew hadn't gone out!"

"He's right, Edmund," nodded Ealdgyth, still smiling. "It's good to see you talking like this. Æthelstan would have wished it."

Edmund bit his bottom lip at the mention of his brother. She wasn't wrong. Neither was Sigeferth. He just wished he didn't have to face his father alone. There would be questions. Furious questions, most likely. He'd have to explain his role in the attack on Thorkell's army. He'd deflect as much as he could on the part played by Sigeferth and Morcar. He had to. There was no telling what his father would do if he thought they were entirely responsible. Edmund was safe, though. He couldn't kill him. His father wasn't that far gone.

"Will you come with me, Wulfhild?" Edmund asked. "It would help. He might be more receptive to our request to aid Ulfcytel if you're there."

"But he hates me, Edmund. You were not there to see how he greeted me when Ulfcytel sent me from Noruic. He despises me and my husband. I don't see what I can do."

"Hate is a strong word," Edmund cautioned. "I don't see it in him, at least not towards you. He's just…lost. Now that Æthelstan is gone…I think he might need us. I mean, just how many messages have we received, Sigeferth?"

"Two, not counting the request for you to return that came with the message about Canterburie. I've never known Æthelred to be so insistent. He's grieving. I don't envy the man. It's a terrible thing he's going through. I did, of course, send a rider as soon as I could to inform him that Æthelstan had fallen but the rest of you were safe. His response to that was…peculiar…but I could tell on some level he wants his children back. He's worried."

"What exactly did he say?" asked Edmund, curious about what Sigeferth might have kept from him whilst he'd been struggling with his loss.

"As you'd probably expect, he accused me and Morcar of manipulating you both into attacking Thorkell and assured me there would be consequences. I don't know if he really thinks that, but this just speaks to how important your task is now. This isn't just about Ulfcytel. You have to convince the king we didn't put you up to this. You and your brother are not pieces in a puzzle to be manipulated. We care about you. We never wanted it…we didn't want…"

"I know," said Edmund gently. "You don't need to worry. Æthelstan and I made our own decisions, and we both agreed to attack Thorkell. I will make that clear to my father. I will not allow him to harm you over some delusion of his."

All were quiet, Sigeferth taking the opportunity to steady his nerves. There was no realistic chance of reprisals from Lundenburg, at least overtly. Æthelred had enough to worry about with the military situation. Sparing men to punish the Five Boroughs over a suspicion of his would be foolhardy, even for him. But fortunes were known to change suddenly. If he was allowed to persist in thinking that Sigeferth and Morcar had done him wrong to the point of costing the life of his firstborn son, then dark deeds could only follow. Whether it was from an assassin's blade or an executioner's axe, it mattered not. The two thegns were in danger. Edmund wouldn't have it.

"I'll prepare my horse," Edmund announced, rising from his chair. He'd quite forgotten about the stew that had been placed before him, the weighty conversation requiring all of his attention. He was relieved to see Sigeferth was in the same situation, only now beginning to chomp at a slice of bread after dipping one end into his bowl. Edmund then noticed Wulfhild hadn't been served. He stared hard at Sigeferth, nodding his head towards his sister upon catching his eye. Sigeferth understood. He called into the kitchens for a steward. Edmund wouldn't have Wulfhild going without. They had a long journey.

That didn't mean he could afford to starve himself, either. He put etiquette to one side, reaching down to lift his bowl to his mouth. He drank the contents, finishing it all in seconds and wiping his mouth with his sleeve. He then turned and headed away from the table, his recently thawed boots resounding sharply off the sturdy wooden floor. He'd never bothered to take his cloak off to begin with, so he was well protected when he strode out into the snow again, pulling his hood up close around his face to shield himself from the wind's probing fingers.

The stables were but a short distance away, several dozen yards at most, their ample size providing Sigeferth's household with all the mounts they'd need. The snow had begun to relent, the wind, too, Snotingeham appearing quite pleasant as she sat enveloped in the almost pristine whiteness. He was glad. They'd move faster if the weather stayed halfway sane.

He arrived at the stables, Sigeferth's man on duty guiding him to his horse without a word. Edmund had developed a real fondness for this beast. He'd ridden him in the attack on Thorkell's host, and the faithful creature had also carried his brother's broken body away from the battlefield. They'd bonded since then, or so Edmund felt, and the animal always appeared pleased to see him. This time was no exception. It rumbled and grunted in greeting, turning to face him with its large, shiny dark eyes. It was a deep iron grey in hue but dappled down its neck and across its back with a lighter shade, like it had been decorated with tiny pale beads. Edmund had thus named him Bede. He wasn't venerable. But he was good.

He reached out with his hand and gently caressed Bede's tremendous face, wishing he'd brought something for him to nibble on. If the horse was disappointed, it didn't show, and he began nuzzling at Edmund's palm and wrist as if he might indeed have something tucked away in his sleeve. Optimism. Edmund could do with more of that. Perhaps Bede was, in fact, worthy of at least some of the wisdom of his famous and saintly namesake.

Wise or no, Bede was compliant as usual when Edmund reacquainted him with his bridle and saddle, seeming quite eager to get outside. Edmund also readied his sister's horse; a chestnut mare with an impatient look to her that suggested she'd gotten tired of being indoors. He then led both beasts out of the stable and back towards Sigeferth's hall. They made for quite a sight ambling through the snow, the horses' breath forming trails of vapour whilst they whickered to each other in conversation, if horses could be said to converse. Edmund was surprised to see Sigeferth waiting for him outside, appearing at first unrecognisable beneath his dark-furred cloak and enveloping hood. Edmund brought his four-legged charges to a halt. He had a feeling words of significance were about to be shared.

"What about an escort, Edmund? You'll need good men to guard you and Wulfhild. Are the men you brought with you from Lundenburg around?"

"Mostly," Edmund said, his heart aching a little at the thought of those who were no longer with them. "Some of them didn't survive the battle. Others are too injured to travel. A half-dozen are fit and ready."

"A half-dozen? That's not enough. Take some of mine."

"As you say," Edmund said appreciatively. "More is better."

"There's something else I wanted to speak with you on," Sigeferth continued. "Away from all others, or at least not at the table. It's about your brother, Eadwig. You're not planning on doing anything…aggressive?"

"If you are suggesting I'd take a hand to my own brother, you're wrong, Sigeferth. I'm surprised you would even think that."

"It's not that," Sigeferth protested, "but you have to think on how you appear to others. You would be a better king than he, Edmund, of that I have no doubt…you just can't go around declaring yourself the heir irrespective of your father's wishes. It doesn't reflect well on you. And how others see you will matter a great deal in the days ahead. Arrogance doesn't win trust."

Edmund paused, digesting Sigeferth's words. He didn't see himself as arrogant. Eadwig just wasn't a king in the making, and had never shown any signs of changing. Æthelstan's final words to him had also made it more than clear he'd wanted Edmund to take his place and rule as England's "warrior king". Was it really mere hubris to believe he was better suited to the challenge? Could it really be said that England would do better with a bookish recluse like Eadwig on the throne, in dark times such as these? The answer, at least to Edmund, always seemed so obvious.

Yet he understood that humility was a virtue. Pride was a sin, and for good reason. Humanity had lost its original connection with God precisely through its own arrogance in believing itself to be above the express will of the Father. This fallen world they inhabited was the sorry result. If Edmund were to be a good man, let alone a king, he would need to make humility a part of everything he did. He'd be a servant to all, as well as a leader. He wouldn't have it any other way. It mortified him that others didn't see that.

"The fault, perhaps, really is mine," he said, choosing his words carefully. "I did not wish to appear like I wanted to just knock Eadwig aside. But you heard what Æthelstan said to me when he lay dying. I had his confidence."

"You did," Sigeferth confirmed sadly. "Ironside, he called you. A fearsome name, that. I don't doubt he wanted you to rule. But think of who will ultimately make you king. It's not just what you want, or even what your father wants. It's us, Edmund. It'll be notables like myself and Morcar who will make up a Witan to decide. Don't alienate them by acting entitled. Find out what Eadwig wants. Respect him. Be seen as the dutiful brother. Good will come of it."

"And if it comes to a contest between me and him? Who will you support? Edmund or Eadwig, who has never fought a day in his life?"

"You, Edmund," Sigeferth said forcefully, sounding surprised that he'd even asked. "It would always be you. You are a warrior. England needs that. But far more importantly, you're a good, pious man. In all sincerity, I have no idea if your brother even believes in our Lord. But you have to be seen to respect him. Honour and protect him. Don't conspire behind his back. It's beneath you."

He was right, as usual. Edmund despised those who huddled in the shadows, plotting this and that with their own selfish interests in mind. He wouldn't be one of those men. If he became king, he'd purge the court of such reptiles. England would not be a place for the self-serving and the treacherous. Those ways had led them to disaster, time and again. Only faith and virtue would see them survive long enough to perhaps flourish once more. And could he really call himself a virtuous man if he conspired against his own kin? He had much to think on.

"What you say is true," Edmund said, trying to sound as humble and thoughtful as he felt. "And yet I have to ask you…why has Morcar taken Eadwig and Wulfgeat to Derbei? Why not remain here with them? Is there something afoot here in terms of making Eadwig heir to the throne?"

"There is no conspiracy against you, if that is what you're asking," said Sigeferth. "Morcar believes it's important for Eadwig to experience the world outside of Lundenburg. Broaden his horizons. He can't do that stuck in my hall. Wulfgeat is a curious fellow, I'll admit, and Morcar wishes to get the measure of him. That's all that's happening. Trust me, Edmund."

Edmund wanted to believe him. He had no reason to think Morcar was somehow turning against him or might mean him harm in any capacity whatsoever. But something didn't feel right. This Wulfgeat was more than a "curious fellow", as Sigeferth described him. He was too much of an unknown quantity, like he was accustomed to using honeyed words and dishonest means to get what he wanted. It didn't matter that he was a monk now, or that he'd allegedly ended up that way because of his principled objections to the seizing of Church lands. He was up to something. Edmund just wished he knew what.

Another hour passed as they organised their escort, just over two dozen warriors assembling outside Sigeferth's hall, horses and supplies, too, for the journey south. They looked weary, Edmund thought, each appearing like he was partially slumped in his saddle and uncomfortable under the weight of his armour. All of them would have fought in the battle at Bernecestre, and he imagined all of them had lost a friend there. Such burdens were heavy indeed. Edmund knew that, just as they did.

The snowfall had thankfully dwindled to almost nothing, yet the chill remained, everyone present taking measures to insulate themselves in thick cloaks and furs. Wulfhild was no exception, her well-wrapped figure finally emerging through the hall's double doors, Ealdgyth also accompanying her as she made her way to her horse. Edmund sprang into the saddle of his own steed, Bede responding with an almighty snort that he presumed was a form of salutation. All were ready, or so it looked. They had only to say farewell to their gracious hosts, and they'd set off.

"Your hospitality, as always, is much appreciated," Edmund told Sigeferth.

"There's no need to be so formal," Sigeferth replied, briefly struggling to keep his balance in the thick snow. "It's not hospitality if this is your home. We've come too far, you and I, to pretend otherwise. You will always have a place here. You're one of us."

"He's right, Edmund," said Ealdgyth, her face again almost entirely obscured beneath her winter apparel. "No matter what happens, you will always have the support of the Five Boroughs. You and Æthelstan were like…are like family to us. You'll always have a safe haven here."

"Just don't bring down an entire Norse host on us without sending written warning," Sigeferth chuckled. "But in all seriousness…do send us word. I have a bad feeling. Like we're approaching a critical time. A fork in the road where our next step will determine the fates of many."

"Sounds terribly dramatic," Edmund chided, taking up the reins and patting Bede's mane. "But I hear you. I will write to you of my father's state of mind. I won't just up and leave this time. I have the notion I'll need to remain in the south for as long as Thorkell is there."

"Should I not simply come with you?" Sigeferth proposed, his eyes lighting up. "After all, my presence might…"

"Antagonise my father," said Edmund, cutting him off. "It will, trust me. If he thinks you and Morcar are responsible for Æthelstan's death, I can't say what he'll do. If I am to convince him of the truth and also get him to save Ulfcytel, I'll need him calm. Very calm. That can't happen if you're there."

Sigeferth nodded, his face downcast as he stepped back and away from Edmund's horse. There was little else to say now, and so Edmund and company said one final farewell before moving forward at a trot, the column of horsemen eventually heading out of Snotingeham and onto the road south.

Wulfhild drew her mare up alongside Edmund so they might ride together at the head of their escort. He grinned at her from beneath his hood, the snow-covered countryside stretching out before them. He was happy to be riding forth with her, feeling like he could still achieve much just as long as he had family with him. She returned the smile, looking earnest and energetic atop her chestnut steed, her manner the mirror opposite of the troubled woman he'd found sequestered away in their father's halls just last summer. She was a brave and devoted soul, he thought. Many would have left negotiations to ensure Ulfcytel's release to others, preferring to stay in the warmth and safety of Sigeferth's home. Not Wulfhild. She'd not shirk from her duty and would face her fears. Perhaps she and Ulfcytel were a better match than many had first thought.

Night was fast approaching, what was left of twilight giving way to a blanket of stars. Edmund didn't care for the dark, but tonight he wasn't bothered, the light from the heavens above shining down over their wintery environs as if to guide their way. The frigid breeze tugged at his garments, and he upped the pace, Bede responding to his commands like he was eager to be moving on. Wulfhild matched him, the line of men behind them responding likewise and staying close in case of any sudden danger.

Edmund felt alive for the first time in weeks. Canterburie had fallen, and his older brother was never coming back. His father was likely to be more unstable than ever, with a mind to seek vengeance on those who'd done nothing wrong. The Ealdorman Ulfcytel, perhaps their last hope for real leadership in a time of war, was also in chains or even dead, the latter possibility being liable to break his sister's heart and further fracture his already divided family. Edmund's task was truly monumental in trying to bring some order out of this chaos.

But sometimes, it didn't do a man any good to focus entirely on the troubles he faced. Sometimes it was enough to take to horse and ride out on a night like this, willing and able to face whatever might lie ahead. Sometimes it was enough to enjoy the company of a sister who knew you would always look out for her and would return such loyalty by accompanying you into strife and danger. Sometimes it was enough to know there was a good sword at your hip and a fine steed beneath you, both ready and able to serve you in your own service to God, kin, and country.

It was on this last thought that Edmund found himself feeling particularly grateful. He was useless to everyone when denied the opportunity to serve. When his brother had fallen, he'd felt like he'd failed in his duty to protect him and the king he might have one day become. That feeling had vanished now. He had a task again. To protect the Five Boroughs from his father's wrath and ensure his sister's beloved was returned to her. It was the right thing to do. Heir or not, Edmund would always strive to do the right thing. The Witan would someday see that, and then he'd sit upon his father's throne as a servant and warrior, a friend to all his subjects and a furious terror to those who might mean them harm. Æthelstan had wished it. He would honour his brother's memory by making it so.

XXII

The crackling sound never ceased. It was always there, day and night, a constant reminder of the city's slow ruin as it was consumed in flame. Alaric wasn't certain how long it had gone on for. He knew when it had started, for the Danes had set fires almost as soon as they'd made it inside the walls. Days had passed since then, the heat making it feel like it was the height of summer. It wasn't. The dark, mournful clouds above put paid to that notion. Summer was far off, and Canterburie's sorrows wouldn't be lifted with its coming, if the city even existed by then.

Archbishop Ælfheah wasn't of such a mind. He was still hopeful and praying almost constantly, his huddled form perceivable right now whilst he knelt to again commune with the Lord. He'd been defiant each and every time Thorkell or any of his henchmen had appeared, refusing to submit to them and their demands that he petition the surviving population to give monies to secure his release. It had become heated more than once, the archbishop turning red in the face, his fists clenched as he again denied Thorkell at every turn. The giant had just looked down at him, bemused and unsure of what to do. It had been something to see.

Alaric watched him, curious as to his behaviour. The old man's spirit was incredible, possessing an indomitable zeal worthy of the first apostles and martyrs who'd risked everything to spread the Gospel. Strength wasn't only possessed by warriors, and it was foolish to think otherwise. Ælfheah was fast proving himself to be a very, very strong man, despite the frailties of his body. There was still room for hope. Ælfheah wouldn't let him forget it.

Alaric looked around, taking in his confined surroundings and the company he shared it with. Thorkell had led them out of the cathedral when they'd put down their weapons, the giant surprising some by not simply massacring everyone as soon as he was able. He'd not touched the cathedral, leaving it unharmed even whilst the rest of Canterburie was scorched and plundered. He'd stashed Alaric and several other survivors in this storage shed, the place looking like it had previously been used to house kegs of ale for one of the city's many public houses.

It wasn't built for human comfort, but it was fortunate that the wooden beams that made up its walls were replete with gaps and holes that Alaric could use to observe the grim situation outside. Ælfheah hadn't joined him in doing that, preferring to pray and console the wounded Osbert and Leofwine. Eamon was also present and suitably taciturn, but he was thankfully largely unscathed from the battle and not of a mood to give in to defeat. Osbert spent most of his time resting, and Leofwine tended to slip in and out of consciousness, so serious were his injuries. There were a few others also, men he'd not known before yet had survived long enough to be captured with the rest of them. There should be more, and there had been when they'd given up the fight in the face of Thorkell's terrible threats. What had happened to them, he did not know.

The front door suddenly flew open, the stark light of day pouring in past the towering silhouette of a man standing in the entrance. He saw who it was as he strode over the threshold, the red and black helm of Osmund's killer unmistakable. Red Helm grabbed Alaric by the collar of his torn tunic and hauled him to his feet. Alaric's armour and weapons had been stripped from him days ago, so he was in no state to defend himself, dressed only in his mud and sweat-encrusted undergarments. He glowered at Red Helm regardless, with all the intensity he could muster, defiant and resolving to remain so for as long as he might live.

The brute of a Dane said nothing, instead punching him in the stomach and dragging him outside by the scruff of his neck. He turned to slam the door shut behind him, the shouted yet muffled objections of those within following them into the street. Another Dane barred the door just in time to prevent something heavy from bashing its way out. That was probably Eamon. Like Alaric, his fires were still smouldering.

Alaric blinked over and over, finding the daylight painfully intense now it was coupled with the terrible light of raging fires. The smoke, too, was difficult to bear. Back in the shed, it had been a bitter scent, yet it was overwhelming now he was out in the open, its smothering reek making his brow furrow and his eye water. He still forced himself to take in the situation, hoping to spy some weakness or advantage that could work towards his potential escape. There was nothing like that. Danes surrounded him, their faces twisted in mockery. One of them reached out for him, slipping a noose around his neck and tightening it so much Alaric thought he might be trying to kill him, here and now.

Nothing of the kind was intended, at least not yet. They tied his hands, Alaric feeling a sliver of satisfaction that they feared him enough to make sure he was restrained. He didn't have time to feel too pleased, for Red Helm suddenly began striding down the street ahead of them, the others dragging Alaric by the neck as they followed. He stayed on his feet, endeavouring to keep his back straight and head up, not wanting any of them to get the sense he was defeated. He'd never be defeated as long as he was alive. Red Helm might be acting the victor now, but Alaric knew he'd hurt him in the fight at the cathedral. He could tell from how he moved. There were wounds under that fine armour. Wounds Alaric had inflicted on him. He'd finish the job if opportunity came.

His desire for vengeance only increased when he spotted what was hanging from Red Helm's belt. It was his scabbard, or more truthfully, the silver-studded scabbard the late Æthelstan had gifted him. His sword was still in it, its shimmering hilt unmistakable. He shouldn't have been surprised. It was a fine weapon, but there was something seriously unsettling about it being in the possession of the enemy. Red Helm didn't deserve it, that was certain, but that was a minor irritant compared with the thought of him using the esteemed blade to kill Englishmen. Alaric shuddered to think of it.

The Danes marched further along the street, southward, Alaric thought, and away from the cathedral. He could still see it if he angled his head over his shoulder, its single stone tower rising imperiously over the smoke and ruins below. It had a certain presence to it, like it thought itself immune to the privations it beheld and was unwilling to be cowed by anything as mundane as the malice of foreigners. Alaric hoped it would stay that way. As long as the cathedral stood, Canterburie couldn't really be destroyed. He hoped the Danes wouldn't work that out themselves. He had the feeling Thorkell's decision to honour his word and leave the cathedral untouched wasn't too popular among his murderous brethren.

His attention was soon forced back to what was in front of him. Not everyone had made it out of the city, and the cries and lamentations of the remaining populace served as a sorrowful reminder, day and night, of the terrible defeat that had befallen them. Alaric hadn't been able to see what the Danes were doing to these people, but he'd feared the worst. Now he saw his fears were justified.

He tried to look away, angling his head to the right and downward to spare the woman yet more humiliation. Red Helm saw what he was doing and marched over to him, gripping his head and forcing him to watch as another man forced himself upon the maiden, her protestations a source of amusement for the two dozen heathens looking on. Alaric bared his teeth, closing his eye so that he might blot out the sight. He would not have this imprinted on his memory.

If only he could somehow seal up his ears too. The woman's pleading was heartbreaking to hear. He wished it would just stop. Then it did, abruptly. He opened his eye. She lay dead, her dress ruffled up to her waist and her nakedness exposed, the Dane who'd only just violated her having bashed her head in with the haft of his axe. Alaric looked at him, trying to root his face into memory. He'd kill this monster. He'd see him broken and ruined before his life was done. He took a silent oath that it would be so.

Red Helm dragged him onwards, trying to force him to witness yet more atrocities as his men continued taking the city apart. He saw a man up ahead, in grief and fixated upon the sight behind them. He was calling out to the dead woman like she was wife or kin, the tears falling freely from his eyes. Alaric felt a compelling need to bring him comfort, but he was the only one who felt such sympathy, the Danes instead pushing and pulling at him with mocking contempt. Several barked obscene jokes in reference to the horrific deed they'd just carried out, their guttural laughter rising in intensity to the point Alaric sincerely hoped they'd choke on it. The man tried to break apart from them, begging them to let him pass and attend to the maiden. Alaric didn't know what he thought it might be possible to do for her. Love gave rise to strange hopes, he thought.

Whatever his intentions, they were soon dashed. Alaric was made to step over him as he lay in the street, an axe lodged in his upper back with enough precision to split the spine. He tried to ignore the sickening sound of it being pulled free, desperate for some respite from this sequence of horrors. There was none. Red Helm pulled him on, looking back at him with those cruel eyes of his. He was enjoying every moment. Alaric would remember this and make a full accounting of it.

The next few minutes were pure agony. In truth, Alaric had lost track of time, feeling like he'd been wandering for hours, so harrowing were the sights he was forced to endure. The Danes were brutal, killing for the joy of it, showing absolutely no mercy or restraint. More bodies lay tangled in the streets, the men cut and hewn, the women likewise after being ravished by who knows how many assailants. Others had been strung up and slaughtered whilst they hung, their corpses swaying to and fro whilst their blood pooled beneath them. That wasn't the worst of it. Jagged wooden stakes had been erected in places, and Alaric had wondered what purpose they could possibly serve.

Then he saw the figures impaled on them. Not all of them were adults. He wasn't shocked easily. But this was a level of savagery he'd never thought to see on earth.

More shouts were heard up ahead, some desperate, others gloating. Alaric staggered along just in time to witness an old man being thrown headlong into the flames of what might have been his own house, the Danes responsible acting like this was all done in good humour. What Alaric assumed to be his daughter and grandchild followed moments later, their agonised screams serving to wilt the very soul. Alaric lurched towards them, trying desperately to tear the fetters from his wrists. He had to get to them. He had to do something to help.

It was a fool's endeavour. His actions were from pure instinct, born of goodwill but doomed from the start. Another blow from Red Helm ended his valiant efforts. Alaric sank to his knees and closed his eye, hoping to blot out the screams, his tears streaming down one side of his face. He could smell their flesh on the wind as it was seared and charred, the scent so utterly abhorrent he feared he'd committed some horrific sin just by inhaling it. His stomach heaved, dispensing what little it held onto the scorched earth. The heathens laughed, the sound cold and brittle. None of them were actually amused in any real sense. They were just pleased at his pain. That was all this was. The joy of base savages celebrating the agony of others. They were pathetic, all of them. Not a man among them. Worse than beasts.

He was hauled upwards again, the rope cutting into the skin of his neck. The procession moved on, Alaric following despite his efforts to free himself. He spotted a number of other captives, bound just as he was and looking like they were being herded towards an open area just up ahead.

Serious business was afoot here, and Alaric soon discovered why he and these others had been brought to such a place. The Danes had taken many prisoners, and they were forcing them into this makeshift square and confining them to hastily constructed pens laid out upon the ash-strewn ground. Alaric knew what this was about. Slavery was an unfortunate reality even in Christian nations, and whilst he thought it outrageous, there were hypocrites and sinners aplenty who deemed it right to profit from the toil and misery of others. The Danes indulged in the practice without remorse, and Alaric wasn't surprised they'd seek to profit from the living bodies of those who'd fallen into their clutches here. It was their way.

They called out to him, men, women, and children alike, their faces visible through the wooden slats of their cages, some recognising him, others not, but all imploring him to do something. He didn't know what they expected, bound as he was, but he then noticed a few others looking at him like they didn't want his help, and that hurt him the most. They glared, accusatory in their misery, like they thought he'd failed them. He had. They'd made such a big show of it, he and Ulfcytel, acting as if the siege would be one glorious battle that would finally break Thorkell and his horde of barbarians. It hadn't been so, and now they were lost, the people Alaric had striven to protect either dead or bound for a life of forced servitude.

He felt overwhelmed, his stomach and chest filling with a cold, icy grief that seized at his limbs to send him almost toppling to the ground. So he was to be a slave now? Sold and carried across the waves to serve some Scandinavian notable until his life was utterly spent? He'd never lay eyes on his wife again. He'd never see any of his family, nor Cenric or Ulfcytel or Osbert or anyone dear to his heart. He couldn't live like that. He couldn't endure such a cruel fate. He'd rather die now than be slowly broken in some foreign holding, the memories of his former life fading into obscurity until death finally claimed him. This could not be. It must not be.

Somebody shouted out of the surrounding hubbub, their voice cutting through the chattering chaos like a spearhead through flesh. Thorkell emerged from somewhere up ahead, his strides long and purposeful as he made his way towards them in the company of four fearsome-looking warriors with furred cloaks and heavyset hauberks. Alaric didn't know what to make of it. Thorkell looked intense but irritated and impatient. Had Red Helm displeased him in some way? Were there divisions in the enemy camp? Was this something that could aid him somehow?

"Not this one, Hemingr!" Thorkell rumbled, closing the distance already. "This one is a great warrior, a thegn of value. He stays with the others for ransom."

Red Helm stopped, gazing at Thorkell in silence, his men forming around him, uncertain of what might happen next. Alaric wasn't sure what any of this meant, but he sensed a simmering animosity between the two men that implied their interests were not always in complete accord. It wasn't unusual for savages like these to turn on each other with alarming rapidity, even over something as immaterial as an imagined slight. Alaric sincerely hoped he'd live to witness it.

"He's a nobody, brother," Red Helm replied, Alaric looking on in silence at the realisation that "Red Helm", the man who'd slain his best friend, Osmund, was none other than a brother to Thorkell the Tall. That would explain why they were so rarely apart. He was almost always at Thorkell's side. Alaric should know. It had been this "Hemingr" who'd wounded him so severely back when he'd tried to kill Thorkell in Eastengle.

"That is not true," Thorkell corrected sternly. "He is known to Ulfcytel. His people all looked to him after he fled the battle. He fights too well to be just another Saxon."

"He's nothing," Hemingr repeated sullenly, upset at being contradicted. "He and his people are nothing. We've had our fun now. Time to make what coin we can from them and move on."

"Always thinking in the short term, brother," answered Thorkell. "The English king has noticed what we've done here. He will come, with whatever treasure he still has. He will pay for men of note, like this one. He stays here."

"The king is a snake, he hates you!" snarled Hemingr, his chest inflating as he sought to puff himself up to compensate for his brother's greater stature. "He ambushed us when we came to talk to him in good faith! We'll not be seeing him again. All there is left to do is topple him from his throne and take what he has for ourselves!"

"Again, short-term thinking, my still young brother. There are things in motion that you do not know. King Æthelred has already sent a man to us, asking us what we want to leave the city and return his archbishop. Æthelred will pay for the warrior here too. I know this. He'll need such men. Return him to the gaol, unharmed. Do as I say."

Hemingr turned to glare over his shoulder, his men following suit to stare at Alaric. There was resentment in his eyes, Alaric could see. He was bitter, upset at this exchange, but also angry at Alaric himself for having nearly bested him during the fight inside the cathedral. Alaric stared right back at him, a slight, lopsided smile upon his lips. Let this murderous bastard resent him all he liked. They both knew Alaric would have killed him had their contest not been interrupted. It pleased him to think that weighed upon his mind.

It was also interesting that the king had attempted renewed communication with Thorkell already. Alaric himself had suspected that any "relationship", if one could call it that, between them would be impossible following the battle in Oxenefordscir. It was not so. Perhaps the loss of Canterburie was something even Æthelred couldn't just shrug off, as he was so often inclined to do. Perhaps matters were about to come to a head here, or Alaric might indeed gain his freedom, ransomed as a man of rank.

But would that really happen? Alaric was no friend to the king, not because of anything he'd personally done but because of who his father was, and so he couldn't see Æthelred handing over large sums of money to secure his welfare. If anyone was to be freed, it would be the archbishop. Æthelred couldn't just leave him here. The people wouldn't stand for it. But Ælfheah was also determined not to be ransomed and had refused to speak with Thorkell any further on this. Alaric wondered if the old man would be so stubborn when it came to the lives of others.

Hemingr wasn't concerned by such conundrums, instead turning to face Alaric before once again driving him to his knees with yet another blow to the stomach. Alaric gritted his teeth, exhaling his rage, his hands and wrists twisting feverishly at his restraints. Thorkell turned away, unconcerned at the sight of continued violence, this being nothing compared to the vile abuses meted out to the rest of Canterburie's people.

Alaric was then dragged back the way they had come. Hemingr was angry, and wasn't bothered if Alaric remained on his feet, hauling him on regardless of whether he was on his back or face down on his front. Alaric spat grass and dirt out of his mouth, his efforts to pull himself up continually frustrated by the sheer force of Hemingr's exertions. The bastard hated him. That was fine. He understood. But he knew well enough there was no way Hemingr's hatred could ever exceed his own. He had a hatred born of spite and resentment, yes, but he didn't have the deep, black rage that Alaric felt and would always feel as long as Hemingr remained alive. Someday, not far off, he'd take time to ensure he understood that.

He was soon back where they'd started. Alaric had finally managed to stand up and was wondering if he looked as bruised as he felt after his harsh journey through the streets. Hemingr removed the noose from his neck and unbound his hands, taking the time to also spit in his face for good measure. One of his associates then unbarred the door of the gaol, only for several others to seize Alaric and throw him through it. He crashed to the floor just in front of the still-praying Ælfheah. He hadn't moved this whole time, yet he sprung to life now, rushing to Alaric's side like a concerned father. Alaric was grateful for the gesture. Hemingr wasn't so moved, instead spitting at them both before slamming and barring the door.

"I'm alright," Alaric said, not wanting to appear weak in front of the others lest it give them cause for despair. Eamon rushed over, a rare tenderness washing over his usually gruff features as he beheld Alaric's dishevelled form.

"What happened out there?" he asked. "When they took you, I thought…"

"I know," replied Alaric, wishing to put his friend at ease. "And they were. That clown with the red helmet is Thorkell's own brother. And he's not happy with me, probably because I bloodied him up in the big fight. He was going to sell me as a slave."

"So that's what they are doing?" Ælfheah asked, both he and Eamon helping Alaric to his feet. "They are selling the people? How many?"

"Lots. After all the rape and murdering, that is…it's worse than anything I've seen before. They've…they've killed children. I don't…I can't…"

Ælfheah reached out, placing a gentle arm around Alaric's shoulders. They stood like this for a time, Alaric doing his best not to embarrass himself with tears, although some came anyway, his single eye weeping of its own volition. Eamon remained close, rigid and unyielding, his face like thunder. It was obvious he wanted to fight, to explode into violence, to make the enemy pay in blood for all they'd done and might yet do. Alaric understood. But vengeance would have to wait. For the moment, he had little strength left in him.

He'd have looked a peculiar sight for any stranger who beheld him now. Alaric wasn't as tall or as powerfully built as Cenric or the beast, Hemingr, but he was still of a formidable appearance, frightening even, with his ruined eye and many scars. He cut a different figure now, held in the protective half-embrace of the aged Ælfheah, his sorrow at the sights he'd just been forced to endure writ large upon his bruised, ash-covered face.

"Have they really done that to my people?" asked a strained voice from a darkened corner of the shed. Everyone turned to look, spying the sorrowful form of the reeve, Ælfweard, emerging from the shadows. He looked rough, his normally immaculate hair and beard now ragged and wild, his blue eyes also taking on the likeness of a trapped animal. He wasn't used to battle and death, and he was even less used to captivity. The fact the enemy were now brutalising the people he'd presided over for so long would be difficult for him to bear.

"I won't describe it," replied Alaric, dabbing the tears away from his eye. "Yet it is what you'd expect from these monsters. I'm sorry, Ælfweard, I truly am."

Ælfweard didn't respond, instead angling his head to gaze upon the ground, his expression blank. He then turned away, lifting his hands to suddenly grip at his hair like he intended to tear it from his scalp. He thought better of it, instead returning to his shadowed corner, alone in his despair. Alaric felt completely useless. There were no words he could employ to help poor Ælfweard, just as he had no means to aid those being murdered or enslaved beyond the miserable confines of their prison. His options were few, if he could be said to have any at all.

He moved away from the still concerned Ælfheah to approach the sleeping Osbert. He lay stretched out on the floor, close to the western wall of the shed, the wounded Leofwine lying close by. They were out cold, too drained to be bothered by the unpleasantness of their accommodations, but Alaric could see that at least Osbert had a little colour back in his cheeks. That brought him some relief. Osbert couldn't just pass on like this, in the ruins of a dying city. Alaric had few friends left as it was. He couldn't lose another.

The door suddenly flew open again, a single burly warrior stepping through to hurl a sack and waterskin upon the floor before swiftly withdrawing. Eamon picked it up, offering the water first to the archbishop. He then opened up the sack, retrieving a few loaves of stale, mouldering bread and a clutch of sorry-looking carrots. Ælfheah moved swiftly, kneeling at both Osbert and Leofwine's side to gently rouse them so they might drink. Alaric had seen him test it first with a sniff and a taste. None of them would be overly surprised if the Northmen had urinated in it. Given the things they were capable of, such an affront would be almost nothing to them.

Alaric watched Osbert drink. He'd built up a thirst; a good sign that his body was eager to receive sustenance rather than just give up altogether. Leofwine was a harder patient, initially refusing to drink at all, such was his displeasure at being awoken. Ælfheah persisted, explaining in a low, patient tone how he would not leave until he'd taken at least a few sips. Leofwine soon assented, his manner softening as he took what was offered. Now they just needed to get him to eat. Osbert was easy, but this old soldier was stubborn. He was also more severely wounded. In that respect, Alaric didn't even know if feeding him was such a good idea. He hoped his appetite would return soon. They could do with some good news.

Eamon appeared at his side, offering him a hunk of bread and what looked like one of the more presentable carrots. Alaric went to eat, noticing the bread he'd been offered must be the choicest piece, given the state of the other loaves. Alaric split it in half, chewing on one piece whilst pushing the remainder back into Eamon's unwilling hands. He wouldn't have his men giving him preferential treatment. If the heathens were feeding them at all, the wounded would get the best of it. He told Eamon as such, insisting also he take half of this rather fine carrot for himself.

The afternoon came and went, Alaric eating as little as he could whilst he went about checking on the others to make sure they had their share. They were all filthy, stripped down to not much of anything, the smell inside their gaol barely tolerable as the single slop bucket at the far end continued to gift them with its baleful odours. Alaric had taken to relieving himself as infrequently as possible, so loath had he become to even approach the thing and add to the stench. If they ever got out of here, that bucket would be one of the many things he'd try hard to banish from memory.

Sleep didn't come easily, despite the welcome blackness of night. The ambient sounds of a city in despair rumbled on, the crackling of flames interrupted only by the occasional outbreak of raucous, gloating laughter and the cries of yet another hapless victim. The scum were enjoying themselves still, inebriated, most likely, on good Saxon mead and looking to continue their predations with the advantage of strong drink. Alaric feared he wouldn't be able to sleep like this. His heart ached, a deep, throbbing pain extending out from his very core, of a kind he'd only felt once or twice in his whole life. Wiltune came to mind. That place had been consumed by fire, too. It was also where his heart had been broken for the first, but not the last, time.

He dreamed of his son that night, his mind eventually succumbing to sleep from sheer exhaustion. Alfred was the happy chap he remembered, tiny and joyous as he beheld his father from the safety of his mother's loving arms. Alaric had missed them. He'd missed his wife, and he looked to her now as she stood cradling their son, marvelling at every detail of her face, her skin as fresh and brimming with life and vigour as he remembered.

Her hair was uncovered, free in the privacy of their home, its resplendent flow cascading downward and out across her shoulders like a waterfall of sunset colours. Her dress was of a similar hue, long and flowing yet light, its gold thread embroidery spiralling up from the intricate patterns along her sleeves. Her pale eyes sparkled at the sight of him, yet they conveyed a strange sadness, her mouth also pursed with something akin to regret and words long left unsaid.

He looked about, recognising his old home in all its reassuring splendour. Wiltune had been a more than pleasant town, and their home was the real jewel in its crown, a place of sanctuary and reflection of the kind he'd never found again. He loved this room, paved with smoothed stone that heated up on a summer's day like this, the light pouring in from the window serving to bathe the entire chamber in a gentle radiance. He looked ahead to his front door, noticing how it had come open to reveal the sun-drenched street beyond. Cherry blossom. There was cherry blossom blowing on the breeze. Just like the day he'd left to go and face Svienn.

He heard footsteps off to the left. Brandon appeared and hastened to his mother's side, his gaze drifting upwards to meet Alaric's. He looked at him without comprehension, his brow creased, like Alaric was a stranger in his own home, a home that admittedly did not exist anymore and Brandon had never visited.

"Who are you?"

Alaric went to answer him but couldn't. His voice eluded him, like it was caught in the memory, or what had been a memory until his own insecurities had seeped in to twist and distort his past with the worries of the present. Æva was crying now, her tears trickling down her cheeks with the flow and intensity of genuine heartbreak. Alfred vanished from her arms to be replaced with a bundle of rags, or what looked like a bundle of rags, Æva's arms tightening around it protectively. Alaric reached out to pull at a single piece of cloth, the pressure revealing the face of his dead child, pale and blue, eyes crumpled and dry, his head bloody and broken and marred, dried red fluids encrusting the wound, his skin...

He snapped his hand away, inhaling with shock. Æva was glaring, a look of anger and accusation, like he had done this, like he himself, somehow, had murdered his own son. Brandon stared up at him still, impatient, spitting out his next words like they were poisoned shards.

"Where were you?"

"You weren't even here!" Alaric seethed, alarmed and angry at his "son" and his peculiar impudence. "You're not even mine! A bastard child of a heathen! Don't dare judge me, boy!"

Æva breathed in sharply, the sound giving the impression she'd hissed at Alaric in some kind of warning. The rags fell from her hands, Alfred's battered form vanishing into nothing as they spread across the floor. She then clutched at Brandon, drawing him closer, the lad continuing to stare up at Alaric. There was something in that face. Not hurt, but mockery. Brandon found Alaric amusing. He liked being here, in this home that was never his, Alfred removed, too, his life snuffed out to make way for Brandon's coming. The boy was poison, like whatever bastard animal had sired him. He had to go.

"You failed, Alaric."

What was that? Brandon had clearly spoken again, but it didn't sound right, like the voice wasn't his own and somebody else was somehow speaking through him. Alaric turned, wanting to break eye contact with this bizarre, hateful child and his incessant staring.

He found no rest. Osmund was stood there, leaning against the wall, a flagon of mead in one hand and a hunk of cheese in the other. He was peering off to Alaric's left, into their kitchen and pantry, looking through the sloping archway at what lay beyond. He was always greedy. A man that size needed a lot to eat. Yet something wasn't right. He had an ill feeling from Osmund this time. His presence here did not bode well.

"I said you failed," Osmund muttered, a few flecks of cheese escaping his lips to nestle in his erupting tangle of a beard. Alaric didn't know what he was even talking about, but he had a certain look that mirrored Brandon's, like he and the boy were in agreement. Osmund kept on chewing, mashing his teeth together with all the manners and refinement of a man who'd not eaten in days. He finished off the cheese and took a swig of mead, downing whatever was left in one before letting the flagon crash to the floor. He licked his lips, an unsettling sight, and folded his arms, a second later fixing Alaric with a mocking gaze.

"Failed, didn't 'cha?"

"What are you talking about, Osmund?" Alaric demanded. He got no response, just another strange look, like Osmund thought him a fool or somebody he could mock on a whim. He continued eating, somehow manifesting yet more cheese in his great paw of a hand. It was revolting. He had no shame, stuffing the substance into his mouth as if trying to provoke a response, his entire front now covered in flecks of yellowed spittle. What had gotten into his friend, he did not know. But he'd had enough.

He turned around and reached out, hoping to take Æva's hand so they might depart from these two and start anew. He grabbed her wrist, heaving it away from Brandon's shoulder and stepping forward to hurry them out of the front door. She followed him, their fingers intertwined, both Osmund and Brandon thankfully remaining silent whilst they made their escape. It was time to break away from the sorrows of the past. He needed Æva with him, always, not the sneering contempt of others. Besides, Alfred would be wondering where they were. They had to find him.

The streets of Wiltune were not what he'd expected. Flames were sweeping across the town, clouds of ash billowing upwards to almost blot out the sky. The trees were withering, their blossom combusting all at once, the air unbearably hot. Alaric broke into a profuse sweat, his lips, eyes, and throat itching and stinging as he tried to endure the sudden heat. There were figures in the streets, dark and menacing, hacking away with weapons, axes, he thought, yet he couldn't see who they were supposed to be fighting. The screams, though. He could hear them well enough; frightened, despairing, the sounds a person makes when they know they are truly helpless and hope but a cruel jest.

He looked to Æva. She still gripped his hand, but her frown returned, her eyes finding his to again fix him with that accusatory look. He didn't understand how this could be his fault. He hadn't been here. He'd left to meet his father. They were supposed to unite the fyrds and smash Svienn before he could make it this far. It wasn't supposed to be like this. Or was it? Was it somehow? Hadn't Ulfcytel told him something about his father? Told him something about all this? What was it? Why couldn't he remember? He had to remember!

The flames around them continued to spread, reducing much of Wiltune to a collapsing, smouldering sea of embers. Alaric's reality then shifted and warped, his environs changing physically around him into what looked like another place and another time. The fire and heat remained, as did the screams and sobs, and he soon recognised where he was, this place possessing a certain dread familiarity.

Canterburie. He was in the square, outside the cathedral, but that too was aflame, burning with the rest of the city in one great towering inferno. The heat was still intense, the smoke cloying and suffocating and obscuring his vision. He blinked once, then twice, trying to focus, trying to discern reality from illusion. Æva was still with him, but she'd changed also, her hair ruffled and unkempt, her attire mere rags rather than the delicate finery she'd been clothed in a moment before. She still stared at him, a bruise visible upon her left cheek, like she'd been struck by something when he'd been looking elsewhere. He didn't understand how it was possible, but the bruise was spreading, the contagion slowly creeping across her flesh until much of her face was a sickly, sallow lesion.

"Again you failed!"

Alaric knew the voice. Osmund was here, too, sauntering over like he had not a single worry in the world. He was dressed for war, just as he'd been when he and Alaric had last fought together, but his armour was split, and the bloody shaft of a spear protruded from his chest. If it bothered him, he gave no complaint, standing with his hands relaxed at his side, his face and front coated with dried mud and what could only be the desiccated fluids from his own wounds. He sneered, his beard a ruined mess and his eyes dead and withered.

"Another failure of yours, this. You failed Alfred and Æva at Wiltune. You failed here. And you failed me."

"How can you say that?!" Alaric spat, enraged at the bold, bitter claims from his supposed best friend. "I wasn't even in Wiltune when it fell! And I fought for you! It was that bastard, Hemingr, who cast this spear, not I!"

He gestured towards Osmund's wound with that final sentence, as if he really needed to draw attention to the obvious fact he had a spear embedded in his chest. Osmund looked down at it, his face twisting in mock surprise, unconvinced by Alaric's explanation.

"But this was all on you!" he announced gleefully, his arms lifting up and outward to take in their miserable surroundings. "You came here and preached dreams of glory and resistance to all who would listen. What happened then, Alaric? What happened then? Did those dreams come true, or is this just another smouldering ruin you've left in your wake? Another failure from a man who can't even protect his own family!"

Osmund gestured towards Æva with his filthy hands. Alaric turned back to her, grateful for any opportunity not to hear Osmund's bitter accusations. She was still staring at Alaric, her bruised face somehow worse than ever, the corrupted flesh now covering almost her entire body. For some reason her eyes remained healthy, but they were thick with tears, her look doubly sorrowful as she beheld her husband. She'd raised her hands, seemingly in a pleading gesture, and so he reached for her, hoping to give comfort.

Their fingers interlinked, each gripping the other, but then Æva began to pull away from him, like she'd been seized by some invisible force. Alaric tightened his hold, trying to bind her in place. It did no good. Their hands were gradually stretched apart, both straining to retain purchase on one another's fingertips. Æva opened her mouth to speak just as her grip was finally broken, Alaric letting loose a pained sob at the sight of her accelerating away from him.

A figure emerged from the smoke, tall and broad, and Æva drifted towards him, the force that held her seemingly giving her little option. Alaric had no idea why he'd not seen him before, but he was there now, and he grabbed Æva's hand as if he meant to break it. Alaric went to step forward, intending to wrest his wife from this stranger's grasp and punish him for his audacity. He didn't get far. He didn't even begin. His legs remained rooted in place, some tremendous weight pressing against them from the thighs downward. He felt Osmund come closer, his reek overpowering as he placed a single dead hand upon his shoulder.

"What did you think might happen, a pretty girl like that, left alone in a cell somewhere whilst you were off looking for glory?"

"Just shut up and help me, Osmund!" Alaric bellowed, his mysterious fetters refusing to budge.

"There's another mistake of yours. You see, Alaric, I'm not really Osmund. Osmund died and passed on. He can't help you now. But he's alive. He's real."

Alaric looked to where this Osmund-who-claimed-to-not-be-Osmund was pointing. Red Helm, or Hemingr, stood there, clear as day, the surrounding smoke parting to allow Alaric to identify him properly. He'd been the one to somehow snatch Æva away, dragging her withering body across the muddied stones and into his embrace. He hauled her up into his arms with ease, looking back at Alaric with a cruel grin, daring him to try and follow. Alaric still couldn't move, the force binding him to the spot refusing to yield in the slightest. That wasn't the worst of it. Æva was gazing upon Hemingr like he was some lost saviour, the unashamed attraction in her eyes making Alaric's stomach turn.

"If you're not Osmund, then who are you?!" Alaric barked, turning to find only empty air. Dead Osmund, whoever or whatever that was, had vanished. He was alone, immobile and helpless, watching desperately as Hemingr and Æva turned from him to disappear into the smoke. Alaric blinked back his tears, shouting his protestations, demanding the brute heathen return his wife to him or suffer the consequences. There was nothing, no sign of either of them, the only sound heard the rumble of flames as they continued to consume the ruined city.

Alaric couldn't move at all. There was no escape, and so he did the only thing left to him. He screamed, a deep, roaring bellow of hatred and lamentation, knowing himself to be powerless, knowing himself to be trapped in a place he'd failed to defend and haunted by the spectacle of the family he'd lost. He was alone, no Osmund, no Osbert or Ulfcytel, nobody to aid him, nobody to be his brother, nobody to help him spare his precious wife from the vile touch of the monster who'd taken her. He screamed again, a deep, shuddering howl, his face gradually turning rigid as the force that assailed him spread upwards to seal his lips and make a prison of his own body.

He was stuck like this now, forever, his eye locked open to eternally gaze upon the consequences of his folly. He tried to scream again, calling out for Æva, Brandon, Alfred, his own mother even. It was no good. Nothing did any good, there was no hope, there was nothing that could help him, nothing that could…

"Alaric!"

He sat up suddenly, his back aching from its time pressed against the hard ground. He was wet with sweat, the dampness soaking his linens so much he thought he'd slept out in the open and been caught in a downpour. It was still night, and the shadows obscured much of his vision. Who had spoken? What was happening?

"Alaric, you were dreaming, man. Sounded like a bad one. I thought I'd do you a favour and wake you."

He knew the voice. Osbert. A dream, was it? All a dream! It wasn't real, but who could really say that with any certainty? Was Osmund not dead? Was Æva not taken from him? Was Hemingr not still out there, murdering as he pleased?

"Osbert!" Alaric exclaimed, reaching out to paw at his face. "You have no idea… you…from this point forward, you always have permission to wake me up if you see the need. Don't hesitate."

"That bad, was it?" the younger man sniggered, wincing a moment later in discomfort at his own movements. "And waking up to me is preferable? I find that hard to believe."

Alaric laughed, quiet and subdued, but still a laugh, sweet relief flowing through him in wake of the realisation his nightmare was indeed just a nightmare. "You're a funny man," Alaric muttered, a half smile still on his face. "Osmund would have liked you."

"I thought he did like me," Osbert protested jovially. "I'm the one who introduced him to Bertram, who went on to introduce him to all that food. I deserve credit."

They laughed again, a light yet bittersweet sound, both thinking of the two friends they'd lost and yet how glad they were to have known them. Alaric tried to restrain his mirth, aware that he was in a confined space with several other slumbering men who'd object to being disturbed. If they were, none of them made it known, and all was tranquil, the fading night outside as quiet as could be expected, save for the crackle of flames.

Whatever solace Alaric had found swiftly dissipated when the door crashed open. Several Danes thundered inside almost immediately and hauled the two of them to their feet without care or ceremony. Alaric protested when they dragged Osbert upward, the poor lad wincing and gasping as they manhandled him despite his frail condition. Alaric earned a split lip for that, the fist impacting upon his mouth with such force he felt his front teeth shake in their sockets. He tasted blood, lifting a hand up to test the damage. He'd been lucky. His teeth were still there, and he'd remained on his feet. He took pride in that.

He stared at the man who'd struck him, daring him to attack again. The Norseman ignored him, instead barking at the other prisoners to rouse themselves. Some were slow to awaken, and the Danes began kicking at those who tarried, cursing and shouting for them to hurry. Alaric was about to say something when they began hauling him and several others towards the door, making him fear they would drag him through those nightmarish streets again. He prayed it would not be so. Once was enough.

The air still tasted foul as they were lined up, Alaric and the other prisoners, outside the gaol. Dawn wasn't far off, the spreading glow from the east drawing the eye, and Alaric was glad to hear something approximating bird song coming from somewhere out over the walls. It took a few more moments to assemble everyone, and the Danes insisted on pushing and shoving them to an unnecessary degree, the aged Ælfheah blinking in shock at his incredibly rude awakening. The reeve, Ælfweard, stood with him, offering his arm for support, something the archbishop declined, albeit with gratitude. Alaric felt relieved. Ælfheah's strength had been a great comfort to him these past days. He was glad it wasn't starting to ebb.

Yet if anyone gave Alaric cause for concern, it was Leofwine. He couldn't stand properly, and he'd slumped against the wall, his head hanging low like it were an impossible weight to bear. He had that look to him, that sickly, pale, desperate look men get when they are close to death yet unable or unwilling to come to terms with it. Alaric caught his eye as he tried to ascertain his surroundings. He was struggling all right, his eyes wide and bloodshot, apprehension and anxiety pouring off him like a bad smell. He then realised that wasn't just a metaphor. Leofwine did smell peculiar, in a way he'd not noticed before, no doubt due to the stench given off by that damnable slop bucket. His wounds must be infected. He'd die without aid.

Their captors began barking at them to move, gesturing frantically for them to head up the street and towards the main square outside the cathedral. Alaric couldn't work out what they might have planned, and any questions he asked were met with a threat and a curse. Something was different. The Danes were deadly serious and displaying none of the mocking contempt they'd shown previously. Whatever was to happen this morning was urgent business for them. If Alaric had to guess, he'd say Thorkell had come to a conclusion on what was to be done with them. Only time would tell if it were so.

The walk to the square was difficult. Leofwine could hardly put one foot in front of the other. Alaric tried to support him, deciding to carry him between himself and Eamon, one arm each over their shoulders. They shambled on like this, the Danes shouting and bellowing for them to hurry, but Alaric paid them little mind, knowing this was the only way to get Leofwine to move.

Alaric turned his head upon hearing Ælfheah suddenly gasp. He'd had a feeling something like this would happen, and sure enough it had, for the archbishop was staring at the ruined buildings and charred, hanging, or impaled bodies of Canterburie's populace with an incredulity that was impossible to miss. He began to curse the Northmen openly, denouncing them as "heathen murderers" and "soulless, disgusting savages" who would "face judgement" for what they had done. His defiant rage was sweet music to Alaric's ears, but surprisingly the Danes just marched on, entirely unconcerned with the old man's words. They were not worried for their souls, quite possibly because they'd never had any to begin with.

Dawn had almost fully arrived by the time they reached the square. Alaric had not been here since the battle, and yet it remained a forlorn sight, despite the fact the bodies had been cleared away. Much of the ground looked like it had been daubed in a flaking patchwork of red and black, the melting snow intermingling with layers of soot and blood to create a stinking slurry.

There were yet darker sights. Thorkell was here, his eyes lingering upon the captives as they were lined up against the cathedral's wall. Hundreds, perhaps thousands, of his warriors were gathered around him, raw and menacing, possibly due to being awoken so early with hangovers to endure. There were other persons of interest joining them from the streets beyond, their armour and demeanour setting them apart from these bloodthirsty men. Alaric soon saw why. They were English, part of some kind of delegation. The king must have sent somebody to treat with Thorkell. Things were about to get interesting.

Thorkell wandered closer, Alaric leaning back against the stone wall rising up behind him. The heathen was flanked by two severe-looking guardians, but he didn't need them, especially in the face of unarmed and terrified men. Hemingr emerged from the crowd to his left, looking bleary-eyed and irritable, and began exchanging what looked like equally bad-tempered words with his brother. Thorkell cut it short with a wave of his hand and resumed his course towards Alaric, several members of the English delegation now breaking ranks to join him. Hemingr was angry at this turn of events. Alaric had no idea why, but he had the notion it was important. If there were tensions between the brothers, then they needed to be exploited.

His thoughts were soon disturbed by an outpouring of murmuring and subdued exclamations from his companions. They'd seen something in the crowd, and Alaric followed their gaze so that he might identify what had them so disturbed. His stomach turned to ice when he saw what they were looking at. Abbot Ælfmær was there, accompanied by a few of his dark-robed monks, all of them standing about him as if it were any other day in any other time. So it was all true then. Ælfmær had betrayed them. There was no other reason why he'd be here now, unfettered and unharmed and no doubt still very much believing himself to be a "holy" man with a good cause. Alaric felt sick at the sight of him. He knew he wasn't the only one.

There were other faces present, unknown to Alaric but apparently recognised by Ælfheah, if his protestations at their condition were anything to go by. These were also captives, so it looked, and they were being herded alongside them so they might be better viewed by their bestial observers. A woman was amongst them, apparently untouched, this one being consecrated to Christ and perhaps even an abbess of some import if Thorkell had bothered to take steps to ensure she wasn't mistreated. There was another clergyman with her, also known to Ælfheah, the old man calling out to him by the name of "Godwin" as he came closer. Alaric had no idea who many of these people were, but he was glad to see his band were not the only ones to escape either death or slavery. He just wished he knew what had happened to the other men who'd fought alongside him in the cathedral. Had the Danes only seen fit to spare Alaric and these few others?

Thorkell stopped a few feet from them, his back straight and his arms folded like he were about to chastise them all for some imagined misdemeanour. He looked fierce and capable as he always did, towering over them alongside his predictably shorter bodyguards. Several others moved up beside him, these looking like Englishmen of some standing judging from their escort of armed guards. Alaric peered at them intently, hoping to spy perhaps a glimmer of sympathy from beneath their helms. He didn't discern much, but he liked to think there was something there, some flash of concern from war-weary hearts like his own that, if he could just see it clearly, would help him feel there was still something left of his country out there to protect.

"Thegns…the king's reeve here…Bishop Godwin and the abbess… and your archbishop." Thorkell gestured to them casually whilst he spoke, his manner similar to that of a tradesman showing off his wares to a prospective customer. The Englishman closest to him nodded slightly, his face as yet hidden within the confines of his hood. He was dressed well, his flowing cloak a rich blue, covering all aside from some ornate fur-lined boots that seemed oddly familiar. He stood there in silence, like he was contemplating making a purchase. Then he revealed his face.

Eadric appeared just as he had when Alaric had last seen him. He looked a little tired, but his flowing, rippling blond locks still gave him a hint of the feminine that Alaric now found all the more revolting in light of the revelations about who he was and what he'd done. The skin of his face remained soft and supple, akin to a man who'd been well insulated from the horrors afflicting the realm and wasn't inclined to share in them. His eyes lit up when he beheld Alaric; a predatory glimmer rather than mere recognition.

He came yet closer. His grey eyes, always unlikeable in Alaric's mind, had grown harder, as if the man's soul had become even darker ever since he'd first set events in motion months ago to ensure Thorkell's victory at Hringmere. Alaric still didn't know why he'd done such a thing, but he'd have it known what he thought of traitors. There was no better time than the present.

"Stare all you like, snake! Here stands a man, which is more than I can say of you!"

"Delightful," Eadric replied, a smile emerging across his pale, narrow face. "Yet you must admit, being honest as you are, Alaric, that you're not the man you were."

Eadric gestured towards Alaric's face, his smile broadening further as he beheld his ruined eye socket. Alaric felt no insult. He'd earned that in battle, fighting the enemies of this land whilst Eadric skulked and conspired from the shadows. For an effeminate clown such as he to mock him over his wounds was nonsensical and merely alluded to his own weaknesses.

"You wouldn't understand, manling," spat Alaric, his teeth bared. "Yet do tell me…what happened that night you led Æthelstan and I to Thorkell's camp? Did you kill Æthelstan yourself, or just let him blunder into the trap of his own accord?"

"I let him blunder into the trap of his own accord." Eadric shook his head slightly at his admission, the movement suggesting he thought the answer entirely obvious and his decision completely within the bounds of reason. "Don't take it so personally, Alaric," he continued, his tone patronising. "You weren't even supposed to be there. Ulfcytel was the man we wanted killed. It was just unfortunate that Æthelstan convinced him to remain behind."

"But why?" Alaric asked, emotional now at the mention of poor Æthelstan. "What did Ulfcytel do to displease you so…to displease the king?"

Eadric grinned ruefully, like he was speaking to a boy who needed coddling. "There's a great deal you don't understand," he said. "You live in a world of heroes and saints, of grand ideals and happy endings. That's a child's world. I live in a world of…practicalities. The world as it actually is, rather than how simple people might wish it to be."

"Practicalities!" Alaric snarled, his sorrow swiftly turning to anger. "Practicalities that led you to plot against a good man like Ulfcytel?! Practicalities that led to the death of my best friend?! Practicalities that ensured our best chance of defeating these murderous bastards was squandered on the whim of a backstabbing cur like you?!"

"Best chance?" asked Eadric, seemingly in disbelief. "If you are referring to the slaughter at Hringmere, then I think it again speaks to nothing but your own naivety. There was no hope of victory there. None. Even if all of Ulfcytel's men had stayed loyal to him, you'd still have been swept away. This is the difference between you and I…you see a threat, and you want to smash it, regardless of whether there's a greater danger on the horizon. You and Ulfcytel are alike in that regard. Which is what has led to your current predicament."

"So you admit it then?" Alaric asked, eager to see what else Eadric might let slip. "You set some plot in motion to ensure Ulfcytel's army split and abandoned him?"

"I admit nothing!" Eadric snapped, blushing slightly as he realised he'd said too much. "My point is that your methods are crude, destructive. Not all men are what they appear to be. You can make enemies into friends and vice versa. This is what the king, in his wisdom, has long sought to do. There has always been a worse threat than Thorkell. We need to prepare."

"You're referring to King Svienn?" Alaric breathed, astonished at what he was hearing. "You think he's set to return? And you hope to somehow use Thorkell against him? That's what this new tax is for, isn't it? To pay Thorkell to fight Svienn, even if it ruins the country?"

"I'm not interested in discussing these matters with you, Alaric. They are beyond your capabilities. Just be aware that you…and that lumbering oaf known as Ulfcytel…

have inconvenienced the king greatly, something that you, if you had any sense or loyalty, should never have done. It's always been up to men like me to pick up the pieces after so many so-called heroes have run riot with ill-advised notions."

"Ill-advised notions," Alaric said, repeating Eadric's words back at him. "You mean notions such as the love of country? Love of family? Love of God? To face those who would threaten such things with sword in hand, rather than skulking in the shadows to betray your own for the sake of an alliance that won't ever come?! What madness is this, Eadric? Do you honestly believe it yourself, or is this some grand scheme of yours to simply gain more power?"

"You think this is just me, that I did all this?" Eadric spluttered defensively. "There are men like me everywhere. Men who do what must be done, for themselves and the goals they'd see achieved. Your little notions of there being a static sense of right and wrong, heroes and villains…well, it's pathetic, isn't it? That's not how the world works. That's not how England works. Not anymore."

"There is right, and there is wrong," said Alaric, "and you'd be wise to remember that. Every evil-doer in history believes himself free of such constraints because he's just so magnificent…because he's above such supposedly petty concerns or sees some prideful truth that nobody else can grasp…but it simply isn't so. If you had any humility, let alone wisdom, you'd see this."

Eadric laughed, again shaking his head to step back and away, satisfied that their exchange was over. Alaric called out to him again, demanding to know what he'd done with his family and why he'd taken them. He went to pursue him and force the issue, his hands forming into fists. His efforts were thwarted when one of his not-so-gentle handlers struck him across the face and threw him back into line. Eadric ignored the altercation, instead moving back over to address Thorkell, the latter staring on like he was bemused by their argument and impatient for them to make a point.

"We'll pay you for the archbishop," Eadric said sharply as he faced Thorkell. "The rest we don't need. You can keep them as your guests or…whatever you like."

Thorkell frowned. "The one-eyed Englishman is a great warrior," he rumbled, Alaric feeling unsure of what to think now the monster had described him as such for a second time. "He killed many of us, made us fight hard, defended the city to the last…he even…"

Thorkell reached down, lifting the edges of his mailed shirt to expose his stomach. There was a severe gash running across his midriff, well-treated and free of infection, but a clear wound, all the same. Alaric felt a surge of satisfaction. He'd been wondering if his blade had cut through that armour when he'd fallen upon Thorkell after he'd bested Ulfcytel. Now he knew it had, he felt strangely reassured. The giant was human, after all, made up of yielding flesh and blood like anyone else. Now if only Alaric could make him yield a little more…

"It doesn't matter," Eadric answered. "He's nobody, or he was somebody, but his father is no longer in the king's favour, making him nobody as far as our task is concerned. The king will sleep better knowing he'll remain with you, I can say that with certainty."

Alaric wasn't even sure what he meant by that last comment. What he did know was that Eadric had mentioned his father as if he was still alive. That was an obvious mistake on his part, but a welcome one, since Alaric now knew his father was likely still among the living, and with him, possibly the rest of his family, too. The only downside was that his own life was now in imminent danger. If nobody would pay for him, then there was no point in keeping him alive.

"So you just want the bishop?" Thorkell asked, incredulous. "How much do you offer? And not the reeve nor the warriors? Not any of them? This is King Æthelred's will?"

"It is," Eadric confirmed, "just the archbishop. We'll pay you a considerable sum, exceeding his real value."

"With decisions like this," Thorkell laughed, amused at Eadric's short-sightedness, "it's no wonder your king cannot keep hold of his country."

Whatever Eadric might have said to that would have to remain a mystery. He looked like he'd been thinking of a reply, but it was all conjecture now, as Ælfheah had suddenly stepped forward, his enraged words cutting any further conversation short.

"I have told you already! I will NOT be ransomed! I will NOT be used as a bargaining chip to line your pockets, Thorkell! I have said this to you before, and my mind is not changed!"

Eadric snorted in derision, unimpressed by the show of defiance. Thorkell shook his head, irritated at the outburst and no doubt wishing to avoid another exchange with the strangely brave archbishop. His men didn't feel the same way, the assembled warriors instead hurling a cacophony of angry shouts and insults all in Ælfheah's direction. Alaric had suspected there were tensions in their ranks, and he'd been right. This was a breach of discipline, and from the looks of it, Thorkell wasn't remotely comfortable with the situation.

The Danes began to shout something specific, unintelligible at first, such was their anger and the strange harshness of their accents, but it became clear soon enough. "Give us gold!" they cried, over and over, many brandishing weapons in frustration at Ælfheah and his persistent refusal to allow any ransom to be paid out. What choice did he have now, though? Eadric had come to pay for him, hadn't he? From where Alaric was standing, Ælfheah was just making a spectacle of himself, although he admired his courage, as always.

"I will not!" shrieked Ælfheah, his voice cracking under the weight of his outrage. "I will not give you a single coin, not for me! None of you will profit from my capture, not as long as it's in my power!"

"But it's not in your power," Eadric said, dragging each word out like he thought Ælfheah was slow-witted and needed to have things explained to him. "The deal is done. The king has agreed. We only need to transport the…"

"How much?!" Ælfheah demanded, his hand flailing wildly in Eadric's direction. "How much money has Æthelred offered so that I might go free whilst so many others are in bondage?"

"Forty eight thousand pounds in gold and silver." Eadric cited the amount like it was nothing. It wasn't nothing, not even to an ealdorman like him. That was a vast amount, one of many paid by King Æthelred to a whole sequence of foreign invaders. Alaric didn't approve, but if it freed a man like the archbishop, was it so much of a bad thing? He got a hold of himself. Of course it was bad. Thorkell would only be encouraged by such a bounty.

Ælfheah certainly seemed to agree. He began to berate the Danes with a ferocity that bordered on recklessness, lecturing them on their many misdeeds and again affirming he'd never allow a single coin to be paid for the sake of his freedom. Eadric looked like he found the entire spectacle amusing, enjoying it with that insufferable grin that seemed to be becoming a permanent fixture on his incredibly punchable face. Thorkell didn't seem so assured, instead glancing nervously behind him as his men again hurled insults and threats towards Ælfheah. This didn't look to be going well.

The first projectile missed entirely, shattering at the archbishop's feet and showering him in what looked like either mead or water. Given the unruly temperament of the Danes, mead seemed more likely, a well-founded suspicion considering the abundance of haphazardly thrown objects that followed. Most of these also missed, scattering and breaking at Ælfheah's feet, but a few found their mark, the old man raising his hands up above his head in an ineffectual attempt to protect himself. Alaric rushed towards him, wincing slightly when he saw what looked like a bone from an ox bounce off the archbishop's head. It must have stung, and it drew blood just above his eye, other bones, some with flesh still on them, clattering around them as the deluge continued.

Somebody grabbed Alaric from behind, hauling him backwards and thwarting his spirited charge. The archbishop had by now fallen to his knees and was bleeding from a dozen cuts and grazes, his hands trembling with pain and effort as he persisted in trying to shield himself from the storm of hurled detritus. Alaric gasped when something large and heavy hit him clear on the top of his head, the poor man slumping forward onto his stomach. A great mocking cheer went up from amongst the drunken savages. They were pleased with their handiwork, despite the increasingly loud demands from Thorkell for them to desist.

Alaric spun around just in time to see the reeve, Ælfweard, being wrestled to the ground, his own attempt at rushing to aid the archbishop leaving him with nought to show for it but a bloody nose.

All of the prisoners, minus Ælfheah, were being similarly manhandled, the Danes tolerating no resistance as they dragged, wrestled, or beat them back towards the street they'd emerged from. Alaric protested, worried for the wounded Leofwine, and demanded to know what they intended to do with the archbishop. He received no reply, just growled insults and threats of more physical punishment.

He peered back over his shoulder, hoping to catch sight of Ælfheah. Thorkell was having significant difficulty controlling his men, many of them looking like they'd prefer to kill rather than obey him. Others remained loyal, a few drawing their weapons on suspected dissenters, the entire square looking like it might again descend into mayhem, albeit this time as a battle between the Norsemen themselves. He could see Ælfheah still lying there, motionless and vulnerable within the threatening chaos. Alaric had to do something.

He went limp, intentionally acting like he'd lost consciousness in a bid to burden his captor with the full weight of his body. The Dane's grip slackened, and Alaric took advantage, lashing out with his elbow to catch him in the gut. He stumbled over from the impact, permitting Alaric to break from his grasp, his foot connecting with the Dane's jaw a second later. He fell, his front teeth cracked and broken, his hands reaching up to contain the rush of blood that now spewed forth.

Alaric began sprinting back towards the fallen Ælfheah. He was acting entirely on instinct, his heart overpowering his head in an effort to reach his friend and render him aid. He'd almost made it when persons unknown slammed into him from the side and wrestled him onto his front, his arms held behind his back. Alaric snarled, baring his teeth and rattling out incoherent threats and promises, demanding the "Godless foreign bastards" unhand him immediately.

He felt himself being pressed further into the ground, his chest straining as it took the full weight of whoever was atop him. He could see just ahead if he strained his neck, his chin forced against the hard earth so that his skin began to tear and bleed despite the wiry profuseness of his beard. The archbishop was just a few feet away, his face lit with panic and pain. Their gazes met briefly, yet Ælfheah's eyes barely flickered with recognition, his concussion so severe he didn't distinguish friend from foe. Then the unthinkable happened.

Alaric had not seen or heard him approach, so thunderous was the ongoing uproar and so uncomfortable was his current physical predicament. He was one of the drunker Danes present that day and one very much angered by Ælfheah's recent defiance. Despite his intoxicated state, his axe was both heavy and sharp, and it cut through the middle of Ælfheah's skull with ease, splitting open his head and scattering its contents across the cold stones.

A shocked silence descended, all who'd witnessed the act, foreigner and Englishman alike, appearing momentarily numb in the face of such sudden violence. Then the uproar began again, the enemy camp splitting openly between those who apparently approved of this murder and those who did not. Thorkell was very much among the latter. He let loose a great roar, like he were pained and angered both, and propelled himself over to seize the axe of the man who'd only just killed the archbishop. They tussled in front of Alaric, the murderer unwilling to give up his weapon, even to his own leader, his objections managing to sound slurred, frenzied, and fearful all at once.

Alaric felt the weight on his back shift, and he was hauled to his feet by a pair of scowling warriors, their foul stench of stale ale and staler sweat making his nose wrinkle. They began to drag him backwards, Alaric calling out for his companions in a futile bid to locate them. They were nowhere to be found, at least as far as he could see, which wasn't much, for all around him had turned to chaos. The Danes were openly brawling with each other, lashing out with their boots and fists, some even using their axes and spears to shed blood and take lives. It was all so unexpected, and it was getting worse, the square now appearing almost as it had a few nights back, such was the intensity of the fighting.

Thorkell had run out of patience. He struck his struggling subordinate across the face, doing so again and again until he finally gave up his axe. Thorkell took it from him and got to work, reducing the man to nothing but a bloody mess at his feet, his vital fluids pouring out across the earth to mingle with those of the murdered Ælfheah. Alaric was astonished. He'd known, as did everyone, that the Northmen were a barbarous people and would happily kill each other over mere slights or if there was money at stake. Yet the transformation of this horde from victorious army to fractured rabble had been as sudden as it had been unexpected, and Alaric couldn't help a slight smile upon seeing them now. The enemy's division was his opportunity.

At odds or no, the two men at his side were successful in heaving him back to his prison without incident. They were angry and far from gentle, and Alaric was again hurled through the door without so much as a warning. It hurt, but Alaric couldn't do much other than curse. The Danes ignored him, unfazed by his expletives, and instead pushed the other captives in alongside him before barring the entrance and hurrying off in the direction of the square. They were rattled, and their urgency was a clear sign the mayhem they'd witnessed was not going to just stop on its own.

Alaric got up from the floor, his chest and stomach still tender. He felt his nose again wrinkle in disgust. The air in here was foul. He'd noticed it before, of course, but his brief time outside had re-introduced him to reasonably fresh air, making his return to the shed that much more intolerable. It was the bucket. The smell from that thing was so intense they should figure out a way to use it as a weapon against the Danes.

"He's dead!" Osbert spluttered, his eyes wide with alarm. "Did you see it? They killed him! For what? They won't get paid now, will they?!"

Alaric nodded, also confused over the logic of what they'd just seen. "They won't, no," he answered, suddenly sorrowful at the thought of the archbishop's bloody and unexpected fate. "They were all drunk. They've been drunk for days. None of them are thinking straight. But this is our moment. We can use this."

"Can we?" asked Eamon, who was presently sat with the deathly pale Leofwine, the poor fellow looking like the recent drama might finish him off. "They are out of control, Alaric! And you heard what was said! The king only wanted Ælfheah, and now he's dead! The rest of us are of no consequence! They'll kill us all now if we don't think of something!"

Eamon wasn't wrong. Eadric had been clear enough. The archbishop was the most valuable hostage, and it seemed the king only cared to see him released rather than all the others Thorkell had taken captive. It was a harsh decision and not entirely rational, but the days when Alaric had spent any time trying to understand the mind of King Æthelred were long gone. Let the king do what he willed. They had bigger things to worry about right now. Like how to get out of here.

"We'll need to act fast," Alaric announced. "They'll have forgotten about us whilst they are busy fighting among themselves. This is the chance for escape we've been waiting for."

"What about Leofwine?" Ælfweard asked, his nose still bleeding from the blows he'd taken earlier. "He can't move. We'll have to carry him, but he might not surv…"

"Then we'll carry him!" Alaric snapped, annoyed that the reeve would talk about Leofwine dying whilst the man himself was right there to hear him.

"Don't bother," Leofwine rasped, his voice almost inaudible, so weak had he become. "I won't last. I'm a burden. I won't have you put yourselves at risk just to haul my corpse along."

"Don't talk like that," Alaric commanded, some authority returning to his voice. "Let the heathens betray each other, kill each other…we don't abandon our own. You're coming with us."

"We should have…we should have evacuated the city," Leofwine answered, pronouncing each syllable like it was taking every last ounce of strength he had. "We should have known what would happen to the people here…if we…lost."

He wasn't wrong. Ulfcytel's notion that the men would fight better for a living city than a dead one had been reasonable, but it had involved the assumption they'd actually win. They hadn't, and the misery inflicted upon the innocent people of Canterburie had been extreme. Alaric didn't know if he'd ever forget the terrible things he'd witnessed here, but he did know it wasn't their fault. Only one Englishman was responsible for all this, and that was the traitor, Ælfmær. He hadn't seen what had happened to him when the Danes started fighting each other, but he had a feeling he was still alive. Alive and very much deserving to be dead.

"Did you see Abbot Ælfmær?" asked Alaric, addressing all present. "Did you see him there? Safe and unscathed, like he was one of them?"

"I did," said Ælfweard, his mouth twisting in disgust. "I think we can rest assured we've worked out who let the enemy into the city. He must have riled up some of his manic supporters to get them to help him. No chance he could have just done that on his own."

"He needs to suffer," growled Eamon. "Too many decent people have died because of that man. We have to give them justice."

Alaric didn't disagree, but it was important not to be too hasty. Right now, they needed to work out how to get away before the Danes remembered the king wasn't going to pay to have them back. They couldn't bring anyone to justice locked in here, nor could they if they were all dead.

"Let's think of a way out of here first," he said, hoping to placate Eamon and get him to focus. "Once we're free, we can plan properly on what to do next. None of us can think straight with the stink in here."

Eamon laughed, Osbert and the rest following, even Leofwine managing a smile at the mention of their horrific accommodations. They set to work swiftly, checking and re-checking every corner of their prison, hoping to find some weak spot they could exploit. They'd done all this before, naturally, but there was a real sense of urgency now. Their lives truly hung in the balance, and none felt like dying in such a place as this.

But it was no good. The shed was well built, and despite being intended to simply store ale, it had no vulnerabilities in its construction. The earth at their feet was also solid and unyielding, the recent winter weather hardening it so that any hope of digging through was soon dashed. They were trapped here, at least until somebody opened the door from the outside. Perhaps then they'd be able to overpower whoever came through.

They waited, the morning turning to afternoon and then evening as they skulked, dozed, or fretted their time away. Nobody came for them, no gang of killers looking to dispose of them or sell them as slaves. There was still bedlam going on outside, the sounds of strife reaching them from the cathedral square, making them think Thorkell had been unable to get control of his men. Alaric took to listening intently, hoping he might discern what exactly was happening. There was roaring, protests, objections to this or that, the clash of iron on iron, the screams of men dying. The enemy were actually shedding each other's blood. It was perfect. If only they could work out how to get out of this stinking shed.

It was almost pitch black in their prison when he heard something else outside. There was a sudden thump and a clatter, like somebody had fallen, possibly from drink or maybe a knife through the back. Alaric then heard it again, the same sound like somebody had fallen, but this time followed by a grunt and a cry of pain. There was killing going on just beyond the door. He got to his feet, Eamon, Osbert, and Ælfweard taking up positions with him on either side of the entrance. If anyone was coming in, they were going to have a fight on their hands and no mistake.

They could hear the door being unbarred from without, whoever was responsible going to some effort to minimise the noise. The door then creaked open, and a single male figure, cloaked and hooded, stepped into the shed, a bloodied seax extending outward from his right hand. Alaric was on the intruder before he could do any harm, lifting his arms up and kicking at the back of his legs before spinning him around to smash him face-first into the wall.

The figure grunted with rage and shock. He recovered quickly, throwing his weight backwards to try and slacken Alaric's grip. He could hear the sounds of further struggles behind him as Osbert and the others moved to subdue several more intruders attempting to enter through the doorway. Alaric went to deliver a punch to his opponent's kidneys when he felt a stabbing pain in his own midriff, the man's elbow cracking into his ribs with a force that almost doubled him over.

He stumbled backwards, trying to recover his breath before he fell to that wicked blade. The figure didn't advance upon him, instead pulling his hood back to reveal his face. Black hair, hanging loose, with a similarly coloured beard flecked with silver and grey to mark the approach to middle age. His hooked nose and narrow brow were wet with perspiration, his deep, dark eyes sparkling in their sockets in a way that reassured Alaric there was at least some humanity there. His countenance, whilst clearly irritated at being assaulted, was not overly hostile, nor was it the face of a man who'd come to shed innocent blood. His words confirmed that notion.

"Enough. Stop fighting us. We have not come to harm you, and we are not with the heathen host. We come here as your rescuers, not murderers."

Everyone stopped, the sounds of desperate scuffling easing off. His voice was soft; delicate would be one way to describe it, but there was real authority there, like he was a man accustomed to the necessities of command.

"Who are you?" asked Alaric, straining to stand up straight, what with his aching ribs.

"I am Wulfnoth. You may have heard of me. We must flee this place, now. Both liberty and vengeance await."

XXIII

The streets were packed and filthy. As strange as it was, Westceape had somehow managed to get even worse since he'd last been here; a remarkable feat for a place with an already unsavoury reputation. The people made for a piteous sight, all of them desperate and ragged, imploring him to stop and aid them for the sake of charity. He did what he could, flipping a coin to those within reach, even removing his gloves to pluck the rings from his fingers. Hard times had fallen upon Lundenburg. He knew the cause.

It wasn't just the war. The capital had been overcrowded for years, the population increasing again and again as people flowed in to escape the many raids of Svienn Forkbeard. Things were far worse now. Thorkell had reduced so much to ruin, from Theodford to Northantone to Oxeneford and everything in between, his brute armies sending vast columns of terrified people into a city already fit to burst. It was the walls, the high Roman walls. Everyone wanted to be behind them, safe at least, even if miserably poor.

The heregeld had made it all worse. The new tax, ostensibly to finance a new army, was grinding the people down, taking what little they had until there was nothing left to give. The people looked truly wretched as a result, likely exchanging what few possessions remained just to satisfy their king's demands and be permitted to remain within the boundaries of his once august city. Many could be seen sitting despondently upon the road, not even bothering to beseech him as he rode by, their hearts as empty as their purses and hunger their ever-present companion.

Edmund looked back over his shoulder, hoping to gauge Wulfhild's reaction. She looked uncomfortable, her lips pursed and brow arched nervously whilst she gripped the reins lest some desperate townsmen pull her from her horse. There was no chance of that, given the warriors that rode with them, but he understood her. People were capable of much when pushed to it, and starvation could rob a man of his senses and drive him to acts he'd never thought himself capable of. If all of Lundenburg were now similarly impoverished, then they were in a precarious situation indeed.

They rode on, Bede continuing his spirited pace, and approached the stone bridge that crossed the narrow Walbrook as it flowed in from the Temes. The river here provided some relief, the free-flowing water proving a pleasant distraction from the surrounding squalor. St Mildred's, too, was a sight for weary eyes, its sheer stone walls and elegant flint-tiled roof appearing as Edmund had always remembered. He hoped the monks and clergy within were doing their best to provide alms for the many needy persons now in their care.

They began to traverse the bridge, their horses' hooves clattering across the stonework. They were assailed by yet more desperate people upon making it to the other side, all imploring Edmund and those with him to stop and show mercy. Edmund continued to pass out coins, one for each man or woman, feeling increasingly glum upon realising he was fast emptying his purse. The rings on his hands were also all gone, and the only things of any real value that he had left were his horse and his sword. He couldn't give those up. If a man such as he didn't have a mount and a weapon, he'd be incomplete.

Wulfhild suddenly cried out from behind him. Edmund twisted around in his saddle, drawing his sword without a thought. She was there, still atop her steed, but flustered, her withering gaze settling upon a man of advanced years who appeared to have grabbed at her leg with calloused, rough hands. His eyes were wide with panic, and a spear from one of their escorts had been levelled down to point at his throat. His hands shook as he raised them over his head, hoping whatever offence he'd caused might be forgiven. His eyes found Edmund's. They widened yet further, tears welling up around them upon spotting his sword. He was terrified.

"What happened?" Edmund asked, his question put to the old man and his sister both.

"He grabbed at me," answered Wulfhild. "I thought he intended to pull me from my horse."

"I never meant nothing like that, no, please! No!" wailed the senior fellow, tears flowing freely down his weather-beaten cheeks to soak into his grey hedge of a beard. "I just wanted to get this lady's attention, that's all. I've not eaten in days, my daughter and I…my wife passed on after we came here and…and…"

"Have no fear," Edmund commanded, dismounting from Bede so he might talk with this man face to face. The crowd parted around him, hesitant to come closer now he was on foot and so visibly armed. "Is the whole city like this?" he asked quietly, taking the man's hand in his. "I would have words with my father if it is so."

"Much of it, from what I know," came the response, his hand trembling in Edmund's grasp. "We didn't have much to begin with, and then the heathens took the rest and then the taxes for the army came…"

"I suspected as much," Edmund muttered, shaking his head sadly. He sheathed his sword and reached for the purse at his belt to retrieve another coin. He pressed it into the old man's palm before folding his fingers around it, ensuring his hand was now like a fist gripping the precious coin in its centre. He then placed both his hands on his, holding him gently but firmly until his trembling eased.

"These recent days have not been kind to you, my friend," said Edmund, his voice warm but authoritative. "Rest assured, I will do everything in my power to see our situation improve. I go now to speak with the king himself on what can be done to see his people fed. And yet I would ask something of you first."

"W-w-what would you need from a man like me?"

"Pray for me. And don't stop. I'll be praying for you, on that you have my word."

"Pardon me, sir, but who are you? I don't see like I used to."

"I am Edmund, son of King Æthelred."

The old man nodded eagerly in recognition, a broken smile spreading across his face for perhaps the first time in an age. Edmund couldn't help but grin back, releasing his hand now to again clamber back atop of Bede.

"Pray for me, Edmund, son of the king, and let us pray for each other," he announced, his voice carrying clear and strong across the assembled multitude. "With prayer, the God who sent his only begotten Son to us will hear us in our plight, and with His mercy, we will prevail. Through the good works we do for each other, here and now, He will see that we still hold fast to Him and repay us with His love. I assure you I will see aid and comfort delivered to you before the day is done. You did not survive the merciless heathen only to starve in the street. That is not just. I will not have it."

He crossed himself before stirring Bede into motion, his escorts following alongside the now visibly calmer Wulfhild. She came up abreast of him, a smile on her face, her cheeks still flushed from her scare but pleased with Edmund's compassion. The crowd called after him, some applauding, others crossing themselves when he passed, the odd person even weeping openly at the sight of him. He wondered how many were languishing like this, bereft of even a kind word, shut inside these walls with next to nothing yet fearing to venture out.

That was no way for anyone to live, even in times as trying as these. How could his father just sit on his throne, fixating on politics, when there was such dire need not a few hundred yards from his own chambers? Was that truly how a king behaved, a Christian king, one not just chosen to rule by his people but appointed by God to discharge mercy and justice to those in his care?

It wasn't right. They'd tried to talk him out of this heregeld, Edmund, Æthelstan, and Morcar together, back last summer when Canterburie was still standing and much of the kingdom had not yet been reduced to ruins. They'd failed in that, but their failure then had not been apparent, the future consequences hidden from view.

Now they were there, exposed for all to see and all the more terrible to witness, given their father had seemingly done absolutely nothing to lighten their impact. He had to relent. The people of Lundenburg were unlikely to just quieten down and simply starve to death. Nor should they. Many would take action, desperation driving them to take matters into their own hands. The sooner this situation was resolved, the better it would be for all concerned.

Edmund nodded at the men guarding the outer gates as he and his company approached. They recognised him quickly, heaving aside the great wooden doors to the courtyard of his father's royal residence without question or challenge. The riders went on through, Edmund always feeling the need to duck when passing through the gate, the imposing masonry making him feel like it might collapse upon him at any moment. It didn't, of course, and he didn't need to duck either, so high and wide were the gate's dimensions. This was a fortress within a fortress, if that made sense.

They continued forward and then left, arriving at the stables within a minute or two. Edmund dismounted when several attendants made themselves known, three of them bringing out buckets of cool water to refresh the road-weary steeds. Edmund led Bede over to one of them, the beast lowering his head to drink with enthusiasm. It had been a long trip, it was true. Edmund had not wanted to linger nor slacken the pace. It had been hard on the animals, but it was over now. Time for them to rest and feed.

Edmund had little time for such luxuries himself. Wulfhild approached, looking strangely formidable in her furs and riding gloves, and yet Edmund could see a hint of nervousness in those brown eyes. Seeing their father again would be a hard thing for her. She'd been wondering how he'd react to her following their flight to Snotingeham. Edmund hoped for her sake that the death of Æthelstan may have softened his heart towards his remaining offspring.

He looked around, instructing his men to go and get themselves something to eat in the kitchens nearby. He and his sister then proceeded on foot back the way they had come, turning north when they came within spitting distance of the gate to move up to the main entrance to their father's hall. The twin guards on duty initially went to bar their path, relenting a second later upon recognising their faces. They opened the doors, pushing them back until they swung inwards, Edmund and Wulfhild striding past without a word.

The atmosphere within was better than Edmund had expected. The royal apartments could often be stuffy and oppressive, their winding, labyrinthine corridors making him feel more trapped than protected. It was different now. The place felt fresher and more uplifting, like the burgeoning spring of the outside world was seeping in to dispel old worries and old habits. They reached the king's audience chamber feeling reasonably hopeful, the guards outside permitting them to pass within with minimal fuss. Then his optimism faded.

It wasn't just that the room was crowded. The people seated at the banqueting table looked happy enough, but that was the problem. They were drinking and feasting, Æthelred himself sitting at the head of the table like all was well and his people were not, in fact, starving. Edmund scrutinised them as he approached, Wulfhild walking at his left. They were all thegns and men of good standing, almost all of them from scirs close to Lundenburg with the exception of Beorhtric, the younger brother of the accursed Eadric. He sat there amidst the revelry, stuffing his face and looking pleased with himself, his brother thankfully absent from such gluttony.

Edmund wondered where he could have got to, his eyes narrowing in suspicion the longer he beheld Beorhtric. He looked somewhat like Eadric, being blond and sallow of skin, the same eyes, too, that reminded Edmund of some kind of reptile. He was fuller in the face than his brother and broader in the shoulders, this stemming either from overindulgence or a stronger physique in general. Edmund didn't care for him, but he'd get the measure of him now he was here and hopefully obtain the whereabouts of Eadric so he could finally confront the man. He'd neglected to do so the last time he was here. He didn't want to waste any opportunities now.

Archbishop Wulfstan was seated nearby, nodding in respect when he caught Edmund's eye. The bishop was a busy fellow, burdened with his duties as Archbishop of Euerwic as well as the Bishoprics of Wirecestre and Lundenburg combined. Edmund always thought he was a good if severe man, his past as a simple monk of the Benedictine Order ensuring he put God first and fools second. Edmund considered it probable he'd felt obliged to attend this feast and would certainly be looking forward to returning to his responsibilities elsewhere. Edmund would be sure to try and speak with him later about the refugee situation. If anyone here was to understand the importance of charity, it should be Wulfstan.

Edmund was just turning his eyes back to his father when the old king nearly bowled him over. He'd flung himself at him, enveloping him in a desperate, trembling embrace, his breath ragged as he clung tightly to his son. Æthelred held him like this for several moments, releasing him only to place both his hands upon his cheeks and gaze straight into his eyes. His father wasn't drunk, or at least Edmund couldn't smell much wine on him. Something even more unusual had taken place. He was genuinely pleased to see him.

It got better. He saw Wulfhild, beckoning for her to come closer so he might hold her alongside Edmund. He hugged them both, wrapping an arm around each of them like he was trying to squeeze them together. The whole room had fallen silent, everyone present seemingly fixated on this rare display of family bonding. Their father eventually relented, taking a half-step back before speaking, a hand still placed on each of their shoulders.

"You have no idea…no idea, my children, how happy I am to see you come home to me."

Neither of them knew what to say, so taken aback were they at this almost unprecedented behaviour. Edmund thought to mention Æthelstan, deciding against it lest it bring grief back to the surface and ruin their so far congenial encounter. There was one thing that just couldn't wait, though. Pleased as he was at his father's welcome, he couldn't just ignore the plight of the people he'd seen outside. The fact that everyone here was eating and drinking like all was right in the realm was inexcusable. Words had to be said.

"What's happened to Lundenburg?" Edmund asked. "So many more refugees, and so many of them in such a parlous state. What is being done for them?"

Æthelred blinked several times over, somehow confused by what had been said. He took Edmund by the arm, leading him delicately back the way he'd come to seat him at his right hand, the man who'd been sitting there previously vacating the spot in all necessary haste. Somebody also made room for Wulfhild, yet she was not to sit as close to the king, for the place immediately to his left was occupied by none other than Queen Emma. Edmund groaned inwardly. He'd somehow not noticed she was there. This was not going to be pleasant.

Indeed, whilst his father was unusually buoyant, Emma was her usual self, looking severe and generally unapproachable whilst she simmered in her seat. She was wearing that cream dress again, minus the purple head scarf, her hair this time covered with some kind of gold-embroidered monstrosity that made her look like an eastern princess with a penchant for scowling. She didn't have any of her children with her. That was something. She was always so much more irritating when showing them off to the king's other offspring. He wondered if she'd even been sorry to hear about Æthelstan.

"There is much for us to speak on," Æthelred announced quietly, the rest of their company returning to their own meandering conversations. "So many things for us to consider. Is Eadwig with you? How is life up in the north?"

"Hard," Edmund admitted. "The winter was severe, and we had much to attend to after the battle."

He bit down on his bottom lip in frustration. If he knew his father, he'd be well advised to avoid sensitive topics, and he and Æthelstan leading a surprise and ultimately disastrous assault on the armies of Thorkell the Tall certainly qualified as "sensitive". This was something to mull over when they were in private. He didn't want to risk angering him with so many others present.

"And Eadwig?" Æthelred asked again, unfazed by the mention of the battle. "He is well? But not with you?"

"No," Edmund confirmed. "He remains in Derbei with Morcar."

"Why?" Æthelred queried, the slightest hint of bitterness creeping into his voice. Edmund had to think fast now. He couldn't tell him about Wulfgeat, the monk they'd retrieved from the monastery at Bernecestre who apparently knew oh-so-much about Æthelred's past entanglements. Such a revelation would convince him his sons had been plotting against him with Sigeferth and Morcar all along. He had to make something up. A sin, lying was, and one he didn't care for. He'd be sure to go to confession as soon as he got the chance.

"He's not well," Edmund said clumsily, cringing internally at the utterance of a falsehood. "Morcar offered him accommodation for as long as he needed it. Hopefully, he'll be recovered by now."

"That is not true, you are hiding something," muttered Emma, her green eyes sweeping over him malevolently. Edmund stared at her blankly, trying to think of a rebuttal that didn't involve lying again. Seconds passed by, the pair gazing upon the other, neither willing to break eye contact. Edmund felt awkward. If there was ever a time he needed rescuing, it was now.

"We heard about Canterburie," Wulfhild interjected, saving Edmund at last from Emma's withering stare. "What happened, father? Do we know if my husband is alive?"

"You've probably heard what we heard," Æthelred said coolly, his previous enthusiasm for his children ebbing at the mention of Ulfcytel. "Thorkell took the city. The archbishop is believed to be held captive. I've already sent a delegation to discuss terms for his release."

"But no one else?" Wulfhild pressed. "Do we know if my husband is among the captives? You will pay for him to be freed, won't you?"

"We know no such thing, daughter," said Æthelred, his hands now fidgeting with the remains of the meal still in place in front of him. "He was in charge of the defenders, so I hear, but as to his ultimate fate, I have no idea."

Wulfhild sat back in her seat, her cheeks flushing. Edmund shared her sorrow, but he also felt a flash of anger towards his father. Aside from his initial excitement upon seeing them, his behaviour was exactly how he'd expected it to be. Getting him to do the right thing when it came to Ulfcytel would be an ordeal. Getting him to help the starving populace here might be easier if he could somehow impress upon him the severity of their plight. He'd start with that.

"The people in the streets are in dire straits," Edmund began, hoping Wulfhild wouldn't feel slighted at him changing the subject. "Many are so thin and weak they can hardly walk. This is just wrong, father. We have to do something for them."

"We have," his father sighed, irked at being challenged so much. "There is a rationing system in place. But we have to prioritise. Those warriors we have left come first. There's no point in feeding everyone a little bit extra if those manning the walls are weakened by hunger. We're working with what we have."

"Then what's all this?" Edmund asked, spreading his arms out to take in the whole room. "Where's all this food coming from? Why waste it on a fat bastard like Beorhtric when there are so many others with nothing?"

"That's enough, Edmund," Æthelred warned. "I won't have you disrespecting our friends here."

"And with respect, my dear aetheling, I am not fat. I am just larger than my brother. I have few vices, and overindulging in food and drink is not one of them. As to me being a bastard…well…you're not the first to suggest such a thing."

All eyes shifted to the man who'd spoken. Beorhtric was on his feet, a cup of wine held in one ponderous hand. Edmund had no idea how he'd heard him from halfway down the table, nor why he thought now was a good time to make jokes. Edmund wasn't amused, and the few infantile titters he heard from elsewhere only darkened his mood further.

"Be quiet and sit down. Now."

Beorhtric did as he was asked, Edmund's tone making it clear he would tolerate no dissension. Everyone else fell silent, whatever mirth they'd enjoyed a moment ago vanishing in the wake of Edmund's command. He wouldn't let an insipid clown like Beorhtric address him like that in front of everyone. The man was arrogant, and probably thought himself untouchable ever since Eadric had wormed his way into the king's confidence. Edmund would have to teach them both some humility.

"Where is Eadric, anyway?" Edmund asked, turning his attention back to his father. "And why are all these people here? You're not usually one for company. What's changed?"

Æthelred smirked at that. "You're right, my boy...and yet the situation beyond these walls has caused a great many of our noble friends here to come to me, seeking refuge. I do what I can and suffer what I must."

"And Eadric?" Edmund pressed, wanting a clear answer from him. "Where is he? On some errand? Dead? Missing?"

"He's in Canterburie. I sent him with a delegation to oversee the completion of negotiations with Thorkell. We finally have the money to get his attention after your... disruption...of negotiations last year."

"So that means you'll be freeing my Ulfcytel?" Wulfhild interjected suddenly. "Please, father, you can't just let them kill him!"

"Eadric has instructions to see Archbishop Ælfheah freed," replied Æthelred tersely, his manner again frigid. "Nobody else. We don't even know who else was captured aside from the archbishop. He's my main concern."

"But you can't!" Wulfhild shrieked, her composure finally shattering. "You can't just leave him there or not bother to even find out what happened to him! He's an ealdorman! He's MY husband!"

Æthelred lurched forward, his eyes flashing with aggression towards the despairing Wulfhild. Edmund didn't like where this was going, and he didn't like the smug look on Emma's face either, but it was as he'd expected. The queen liked seeing rifts appear between the king and his children. It strengthened her position, increasing the chances of Æthelred declaring the boy, Edward, his recognised heir. His father was also temperamental, to put it mildly, and he didn't take well to being questioned in front of others. Edmund needed to cool things off before they escalated further.

"Listen to me now, girl," Æthelred hissed, Wulfhild seeming to shrink a little before him. "Your husband is an arrogant, disobedient fool who may, for all we know, be dead in a ditch somewhere. I won't bother wasting money on such a man, and you will not take that tone with me again if you wish to be married to anyone suitable."

"Married?" spluttered Wulfhild, her face flushing with redoubled indignation. "I'm already married! I won't be bartered off like some ageing brood mare just because you've given up on Ulfcytel!"

As if on cue, the doors to the chamber were thrown open, a throng of men forcing their way through at the head of what looked like a sizeable crowd. The guards who'd been on watch outside recoiled before them, unsure of what to do, their spears half-lowered in case of violence. Edmund stood up, his eyes focusing on the burly, limping figure advancing towards them. Others followed, farmers by the looks of them, and all of them of an advanced age. The entire spectacle appeared more bizarre than threatening.

Then Edmund saw him. The limping man, his face like thunder and eyes the colour of flint, his voluminous beard so silver you'd think it was flecked with the precious metal itself. It was him. Ulfcytel. Wounded, no doubt there, and using a makeshift staff for support, a tall, dangerous-looking man also walking alongside him to offer aid should he stumble. But it was him. He'd returned. And brought what looked like an entire village with him.

Wulfhild leapt upright and rushed over to him, a cry of delight escaping her lips. Ulfcytel stopped, unsteady, his face pink with emotion. He then embraced her, Wulfhild almost vanishing within his huge, enveloping arms. Edmund noted how his bodyguard flashed a look of concern when Ulfcytel took his hand off his walking stick. The thing clattered to the floor, Ulfcytel apparently forgetting all about it, the reunion with Wulfhild imbuing him with renewed strength.

If Ulfcytel was growing stronger, then Æthelred appeared to be doing the opposite. Edmund was aghast at his father's changed appearance, the king looking like he'd somehow managed to age even more so within the space of a few seconds. His two formidable personal guards had already taken up position on either side of him, but if he were comforted by their presence, he gave no indication. He instead stood up, his hands on his hips, his following words sounding so bitter Edmund found himself again wondering just what Ulfcytel had done to displease him.

"What is the meaning of this interruption? Not content with bringing ruin and destruction everywhere you go, Ulfcytel, you thought you might bring a riot into my halls?"

"This is no riot, my king," Ulfcytel boomed, having managed to free himself from the doting Wulfhild. "These are your people," he said, gesturing to his aged and weary companions. "The people of Cantwara. Witenestaple, actually. Burnt out of their homes, like numerous others, their sons lost to them, snatched from their grasp by the murderous Northmen."

"Why bring them here?" asked Æthelred, his eyes narrowed. "Is there a reason you think I should see them? I did not lose the siege of Canterburie nor the Battle of Hringmere. You did."

Ulfcytel flinched at the king's remark, as did the tall fellow next to him, their assorted company letting out a single collective gasp at the sheer impertinence of what had been said. Ulfcytel was a tempestuous man and not one for being insulted, but he weathered the situation well, retaining his dignity in the face of such obvious provocation.

"It's true, you did not lose them, my king. You would have needed to be present to play any part in our victory or defeat. But you were not."

That got another reaction, the seated thegns muttering and rumbling to themselves at the ealdorman's rather blunt choice of words. Æthelred smiled, a cold, cruel look this time, his pale lips stretching over his teeth in a manner that left Edmund unsettled. He had a feeling things were about to get out of hand. Whatever Ulfcytel was looking to achieve here, he hoped it wouldn't involve bloodshed. He admired the man, but he wouldn't allow anyone to hurt his father.

"I was not present, that's correct," Æthelred conceded, some confidence returning to his demeanour as the guards from outside fell into position around him. He had four armed men at his back now, and hardly any of Ulfcytel's mob were properly equipped to counter them. The tall one next to him could be a problem, and the same went for the ealdorman himself, but in terms of weapons and armour, things were certainly in the king's favour.

"And I was not present because those battles did not need to be fought," Æthelred continued. "You've always been an impetuous one, Ulfcytel. But you've crossed the line this past year. You failed to march your army out of Eastengle to muster with me and…"

"Abandon Eastengle?" interrupted Ulfcytel. "You'd have an ealdorman abandon his home, his people? What man could do such a thing? And the men that made up my army? You'd think they'd abandon their own families because… what exactly?"

"Because their king ordered it. I am the king. Had you done as I asked, you'd still have an army, and perhaps your lands might not have been ravaged so severely if Thorkell knew we were combining forces. He'd have been brought to the negotiating table sooner."

"Negotiations?" inquired Ulfcytel, his neck craning forward like he genuinely couldn't believe what he was hearing. "You'd negotiate with that fiend? You think you can tame him? You think wrong. These men around me are testament to your foolishness."

Another round of exclamations rattled across the room, the others, Edmund included, feeling more than uncomfortable at the exchange they were being forced to witness. Both contending parties were right, to an extent. His father was correct to think it important to consolidate their forces rather than fight piecemeal, but it was unfair to expect Ulfcytel to abandon his own people for such a strategy.

Edmund couldn't deny his father was also correct to place at least some emphasis on dialogue. He couldn't shake the troublesome notion that he and Æthelstan had been too impulsive in attacking Thorkell's armies. Thousands of men had died because of that, including Æthelstan. That was a heavy price to pay. There were no easy answers as to who was in the right here. The truth lay somewhere between them.

"If you expect to live much longer, you will not address me with such disrespect," said Æthelred, his manner uncharacteristically calm considering Ulfcytel's insult. "You came here with a goal in mind. Speak of it, so we might end this exchange sooner."

"I would have answers," replied Ulfcytel, "and I would also know where that snake, the Ealdorman Eadric, is. He got good men killed, divided my army, ensured our defeat at Hringmere…that man is poison, and you hold him far too close for your own good."

"He's not here," answered Æthelred simply. "And I'm not interested in your paranoid fantasies. If your army failed in battle, that's your affair. I ask again…"

"Wait a moment," Edmund interrupted, unwilling to remain a passive witness. He stood up, troubled and alarmed to hear Ulfcytel's allegations about Eadric. He had no idea if any of it was true, but something told him it was, and he would hear more of it before his father could resume arguing with him.

"You mean to say Eadric came to you before battle and sabotaged your efforts?" asked Edmund. "He demoralised your forces? Killed your own? How?"

"He did," nodded Ulfcytel solemnly. "And I regret to inform you his actions led to the untimely death of your uncle, Æthelstan."

"That's enou…"

"No, father, it's not!" snapped Edmund. "We must know what happened! Uncle Æthelstan was all we had left of mother! What would she say if she were here now? Would she just shrug and dismiss her brother's death like he was nothing?"

"That's not the point," spat Emma hatefully, moving beside Æthelred to take his hand in hers. "You should obey your father rather than listen to this renegade! Your father always knows best!"

"Be silent, woman!" snarled Edmund, his temper flaring at Emma's simplistic mindset. She had no idea, and almost certainly didn't even care, how much he and his brother had grieved when they'd heard of their uncle's death. Edmund had to know what had happened. Ulfcytel must be heard.

"My brother is not here to defend himself against these slanders," wheezed an irate Beorhtric from further down the table. "Eadric is a loyal servant of the king. That is all. Those who judge him otherwise probably have something to hide themselves, like that traitor, Wulfnoth, who if you recall…"

"Shut up, man!" barked Edmund. "Nobody is talking to you, and no one cares for your witless prattle!"

Beorhtric settled down, again chastised by Edmund's outburst. He'd probably made an enemy of him now, but Edmund didn't care. All he wanted to know was what had really happened to his uncle.

"So what happened, Ulfcytel?" Edmund asked, turning his full attention back to the ealdorman. "Please tell me…how did my uncle die?"

"I'll keep this short," Ulfcytel began. "The night Eadric came to us with orders from the king for us to abandon Eastengle…well, he saw we were not willing to do that. I wasn't. Oswy wasn't. Æthelstan wasn't. So Eadric claimed he knew the location of Thorkell's camp from some prior meeting he'd attempted. Said we could sneak in, kill him in the night and end the whole invasion."

"And you attempted such a foolhardy endeavour?" asked Æthelred, his voice a little hesitant now that Edmund had very much seized the moment.

"I was up for it, yes, but Æthelstan wouldn't let me go, saying I was needed to lead the army, which was true. He volunteered along with Alaric to go and…"

"Alaric, you say?" interjected Æthelred. "But I understand Alaric survived this incident? He survived, and Æthelstan did not? Are you quite sure Alaric is not the true source of your woes rather than Eadric?"

"I am completely sure. And Alaric did not survive unscathed. It's a miracle he lived through it. Æthelstan was not so lucky. From what Alaric told me, it sounded like they were lured in…like there was some kind of plan in motion to trap them. To trap me, which would have happened had Æthelstan not insisted I remain behind."

"So this was some ruse?" Edmund queried. "An attempt to get you killed before battle even began? Something that my uncle foiled by chance and got him killed into the bargain?"

Ulfcytel nodded, his eyes mournful. He was telling the truth. Edmund fancied he knew something about men and how to spot a lie. He couldn't detect anything suspicious in what he'd been told. The Ealdorman of Eastengle was famous for his blunt honesty, even in situations where it might be better to be tactful. He wasn't a liar, and hadn't started being one in the past few minutes.

Edmund turned back to his father. He'd sat down again, his head in his hands, Emma kneeling at his side to console him. His reaction told Edmund all he needed to know. It had all been true. Uncle Æthelstan was dead because of some dastardly plot on the part of Eadric of Mierce. And by the looks of it, Æthelred himself had known of it.

"So it's true, father?" asked Edmund, his voice cold and pointed like a shard of ice. "Uncle Æthelstan is gone because of some filthy scheme hatched by that…man…

you hold so close to heart? Did you know he'd done this? You discussed it? Planned it? Talked it over like friends and pondered your next moves? How could you? How could you do that to him?! To mother?!"

"That's not how it happened!" Æthelred sobbed, his hands falling from his face to reveal pallid cheeks streaked with fresh tears. "It wasn't supposed to be like that! Æthelstan shouldn't have even been there! He was always so impulsive, always wanting to act the hero, like you and your older brother! Always charging off with no regard for the wider consequences!"

"But you wanted Ulfcytel gone? You wanted to kill him? For what exactly? Raising an army to fight your enemies?!"

"He need not be our enemy!" Æthelred shrieked. "None of you ever understood that, only Eadric! The Northmen… we can buy them off! Make them fight each other like we did with Olaf Tryggvason! Svienn damn near lost his hold on Norway because of that! We can do it again! Can't you see that? We HAVE to! We can't win when Svienn returns! And he IS coming!"

"So this was all just some ploy, all along, to use Thorkell as a shield?" Edmund countered, unimpressed by his father's theatrics. "You'd have Eadric lie, betray, and murder, all for the sake of bending Thorkell to your will, even if half the country lies in ruins because of it?!"

"It didn't have to be like this! We were talking, he and I, at Bernecestre! Then you and Æthelstan and those bastards, Morcar and Sigeferth, had to storm in and ruin everything! You ruined it all, boy! YOU RUINED IT ALL AND GOT YOUR BROTHER KILLED!"

Edmund stepped backwards, almost tripping over his chair. This was all too much. He couldn't stay. He had to get out of here. His heart hurt. It ached, terribly, like it might split in two. He stumbled past his chair, moving around his father to approach Ulfcytel. With a single look, they'd agreed. They'd both leave this place. There was nothing here but pain.

The tall warrior who'd been at Ulfcytel's side this whole time moved forward to intercept him. Edmund stopped and looked up at him, hoping to discern his intent, his hand hovering close to the hilt of his sword. He didn't have the face of a man who meant harm, at least not at this time, his green eyes possessing a certain gentleness that contrasted with his otherwise fearsome appearance.

"Please forgive me," he whispered nervously. "My name is Cenric, and I am sworn to the Ealdorman Ælfric and his family, who were cruelly snatched by this Eadric you speak of and…"

"They are alive," Edmund said curtly. "They are alive, are they not, father? Ælfric and his blind son, with that woman with the red hair?"

"And why would you care?" snarled Æthelred. "You fancy that woman, do you, boy? You thinking of making her your little wife for the night and…"

"How dare you!" snarled Cenric, his eyes now not so gentle. "This is not just! You sent Eadric to lay siege to our home! Murdered innocent people, children even! I saw it! All so you might take my lord and his family away in chains! And now you speak of the lady Æva like this?! Tell me where they are! Tell me, you damn tyrant!"

Æthelred rose from his chair, his eyes burning with fury despite the abundance of tears that still trailed his cheeks. Edmund wasn't exactly clear about the events Cenric had just spoken of, but he'd crossed a line. Ealdormen and aethelings could and did argue with kings, yet that privilege did not extend to anyone else. Edmund didn't have any reason to think Cenric was wrong, morally speaking, for what he'd said, but he knew his father wouldn't see it that way. Things were about to take another turn for the worse.

The king stepped forward, breaking away from his queen to stand on his own two feet. He drew his sword from its sheath, and his guards fell in around him, their spears lowered to point directly at Cenric. When Æthelred spoke again, all emotion had drained from his voice, his tone as icy as his look as he gave instructions to the formidable men at his side.

"Kill this man."

They all rushed forward, the king's two personal bodyguards looking particularly fearsome in their heavy chain hauberks. Cenric, to his credit, didn't even flinch, instead producing a sword of his own and adopting a defensive fighting stance like it was second nature to him. Ulfcytel also drew his sword and came to Cenric's aid with a bellowing shout, several of the old farmers he'd brought doing the same. This was a bloodbath waiting to happen. Edmund wouldn't have it.

"STOP!"

They did. The guards halted at Edmund's order, confused, indecisive, conflicted between a king's command and that of his son. His father protested, demanded, and then threatened, his voice becoming hoarser and frailer the angrier he got. Edmund positioned himself between them and Cenric, blade in hand, his face defiant.

"We are leaving. We're all leaving, Ulfcytel, Cenric, Wulfhild, and all the others. We'll leave and not return. There is no need for killing today."

"Do as I say!" Æthelred raged, his anger turning to frustration and then impotence as his guards remained rooted to the spot. One of them took another step forward like he was of a mind to make a lunge with his spear. Edmund raised his sword and moved to bar his path.

"Don't test me," he said. "I know you are just following orders. But I will fight you. You must relent. I command it."

The man stopped, his face hidden beneath the metal of his faceplate, except for his eyes. Edmund could see the truth there. They were conflicted. There wasn't a wicked soul behind those. Just a simple man, most likely, in a very difficult situation. Edmund reached out with his left hand so it rested on the tip of his spear. He let it lie there for a moment before applying a gentle pressure to gradually ease the weapon away until it hung loosely at the warrior's side. This was as good as it was going to get. He ushered Cenric and the others away, his sister joining her husband as he limped towards the hall's exit.

King Æthelred howled after them, demanding Edmund stay, even imploring the seated and suitably stunned thegns to rise and seize him. Edmund dissuaded them with a look, each of them knowing better than to try and accost him after his recent display. He saw Beorhtric still sitting among them, looking aghast like the rest, and for a second or two, Edmund considered making an effort to take him with them so they could question him about his brother. He decided against it. They were on a knife's edge here, and if he escalated things with an attempted kidnapping, it would most likely result in bloodshed. Edmund's standing and authority was the only thing preventing total chaos. If he came across as the villain rather than the noble aetheling, then violence could only ensue.

Nobody tried to pursue them as their party passed through the doors and into the draughty corridors beyond. Edmund marched at the head of them, leading the way towards the main entrance and their hopeful escape. He could hear his father's voice for a long time, even after he'd passed from earshot. It echoed, in his mind and in his heart, the sad, desperate, despairing sound of a man coming apart repeating over and over. Edmund had never imagined it would go this badly.

He'd set out wanting to put things right for his friends and secure the release of his sister's husband. Ulfcytel, true to his nature, hadn't needed help to begin with, but a whole host of fresh problems had presented themselves. He'd been forced again to abandon his father. He hadn't wanted to, but it was the only way to avoid violence, and there was no getting through to him now. He was lost, and he feared for him. He was surrounded by darkness, and Edmund wondered if anything in the world could bring him out of it.

"Lord have mercy," he muttered, stepping out of the shadows of his father's hall and into the light beyond.

XXIV

To watch a man die was a sad and curious thing. This wasn't like it was in battle. There it could happen in a split second, a previously boisterous, courageous man falling to an axe or spear without warning or apology. This was different. It was a long, drawn-out process of shallow breaths and whispered words, a fever rather than a blade gradually snatching the life from him as he yet struggled to endure. There was courage there, of a sort. That was always to be admired.

Leofwine had tried to speak. Alaric didn't always understand him, so intense was his delirium, and at times he spoke like he thought Alaric was somebody else in another time and another place. He became intelligible close to the end, his last words whispered into Alaric's ear. "I'm sorry," he'd said. "I'm sorry they got in. I didn't know."

He'd died then, the air easing from his lungs in a long, straining rattle. Alaric had sat back, pondering what he'd meant, Leofwine's cold, clammy hand still clutched in his. Leofwine had nothing to apologise for. He'd fought well, leading his men in the most intense fighting Alaric had ever seen. It wasn't his fault they'd been betrayed, if that's what he'd meant. It wasn't his fault a man as vile as Abbot Ælfmær existed. It pained Alaric that he'd died thinking it somehow was.

They'd buried him in a hurry, the escapees expending the last of their energy in seeing him treated with proper respect. Alaric was exhausted by the time they'd placed the last handful of earth and stone over him, the few words of consolation and prayer he'd managed to muster seeming inadequate, despite their sincerity. Their rescuer, Wulfnoth, had merely observed, perhaps realising it was important they bury their friend through their own efforts rather than rely on strangers. Alaric understood and appreciated that. He'd already done enough for them.

Their flight from Canterburie had been truly remarkable. After Wulfnoth had made it clear they were there to help, they'd made their way through the darkened streets, crouching low and moving with stealth to avoid attention. They'd had to carry Leofwine at this point, so weak had he become, and for a time, Alaric had feared his condition might serve to give them away. They need not have worried so much. The Danes were occupied, the sounds of internecine strife and struggle carrying through the night to gladden their hearts. There'd never be a better time to attempt this.

They'd made it to the eastern wall, its sheer facade of dark, uneven stone serving to dampen their hopes of ever seeing the other side of it. Alaric imagined all the gates were still guarded, regardless of how disunited Thorkell's army might become. Their endeavours now seemed halfway foolish, consigning them to wandering around the city, clinging to the shadows, whilst jumping at every sound that headed their way. No matter how he looked at it, there was no way for them to get up on the wall without being seen, and certainly no way down without being killed.

Wulfnoth had thought otherwise. They'd hidden for a few minutes amidst the charred ruins of what had once been a smithy, waiting for a score or so of Danes up ahead to move off. He'd then led them towards and up a stairwell used to access the battlements above, Alaric wincing with anxiety at the echoing sound of their footsteps. It was cold on the wall, high above the ground, the night concealing much of the countryside beyond. All seemed peaceful out there, and despite Alaric's fears, nobody had yet spotted them, the ambient darkness serving to mask their movements, at least for now.

The city behind them was a different story. Some parts of it were still smouldering, and something was happening around the cathedral; the glow of torches and several larger fires revealing a significant number of people still up and active in the area. Several other lights could be seen moving north, illuminating what looked to be hundreds upon hundreds of men moving as if to leave Canterburie altogether. Were the Danes looking to desert Thorkell? Was this the end of his great army?

Alaric let out an involuntary groan at what happened next. The fires spread, part of the cathedral itself lighting up from the windows like it was aflame from within. Thorkell had promised to keep the place unharmed, but it seemed he'd broken that promise, his deserting kinsmen likely setting the blaze after looting whatever valuables remained inside. Smoke billowed from the entrance, several windows breaking and shattering outward as the flames spread. From what Alaric could see, the fire soon re-ignited the Danes' passion for battle, for the fighting immediately intensified around the cathedral before spreading into the streets beyond. Thorkell must still have some men who remained loyal.

Alaric turned away, unwilling to dwell further on the chaotic sights before him. The others lingered, Ælfweard appearing moved to tears by the sight of his city's ruin. Alaric was just about to try and comfort him when Wulfnoth hissed something, the sound snapping their attention back to the urgency of their predicament. He gestured impatiently, bidding them follow, Alaric and company promptly complying as he led them further south along the wall until they came to something almost miraculous, such was their relief at seeing it.

Several ropes had been tied around the wall's crenellations, their lengths vanishing from sight as they dangled into the darkness. The first of Wulfnoth's men seized one of them and flipped over the wall, commencing a speedy descent into the night beyond. A moment's panic clutched at Alaric. It was one thing for a man with some degree of strength to descend a rope, but a complete impossibility for the now-insensible Leofwine. They'd have to think of something, and quickly. Abandoning him to save themselves just wasn't an option.

They'd somehow got Leofwine to cling to Alaric's back. Everyone else bar Wulfnoth and two of his men had descended, but Wulfnoth had stayed, presumably wanting to ensure all the captives got away without complications. Climbing with a man attached to him was harder than Alaric had thought, but his physical discomfort was nothing compared to the dread fear that Leofwine might fall. They were about halfway down the wall when Alaric began to sense that Leofwine was weakening, his grip around his shoulders and chest starting to ebb. A sudden, sharp wind also began to snatch at them with an almost malevolent persistence, causing Alaric to let loose with a deluge of silent prayer.

Alaric then glanced up, hearing and feeling the rope swing to and fro as it ground against the stonework above. His panic grew by the second, fearing the rope might wear itself out and send them crashing to the hard earth below. He hurried on, his legs braced against the wall like he was walking backwards, his hands burning with effort. Leofwine slipped once, managing to arrest his descent at the last moment, his hands digging into Alaric's shoulders. Then he slipped again, letting go of Alaric altogether to begin his inexorable fall downwards. Alaric reacted fast, twisting himself around and flailing wildly into the dark with his left hand. By the grace of God, he caught something, his fingers tightening around Leofwine's forearm with all the strength he could yet muster.

His shoulder ground and protested, the bones creaking in their sockets signifying their objections. He didn't have long. The will was there, but a body as exhausted as his could only take so much. He let his feet go from the wall and began sliding downwards, the flesh of his palm weeping and tearing against the rough hemp of the rope. At some point, he could take it no longer, and his fingers came free of their own accord to send him hurtling earthward. He hit the ground, landing arse-first on something soft and yielding. Leofwine lay next to him, silent and sickly, unappreciative or at least unaware that their fall had been broken. Alaric leant back, ecstatic over their good luck, only for his hand to slip in something wet. He stood up and turned around, trying to focus on what he'd landed on. All elation left him. He felt sick. His stomach heaved, his chest icing over from the sheer horror of it all.

There were bodies scattered here and there, twisted and decaying, the rich, sickly stench almost overpowering the senses. Locals from Canterburie, by the looks of them, and Alaric had landed on one, crushing the unfortunate man's ribs inward with the combined weight of both himself and the injured Leofwine. Alaric noted with dismay that his lower half and hands were now covered with blood, the dark, stagnant substance sticking to him regardless of how frantically he attempted to clean himself. The man must have been dead for some time, having been hurled from the walls by the invaders within hours of their victory. The enemy was nothing if not sadistic.

He retrieved Leofwine, Ælfweard moving to assist in carrying him to wherever it was they might now go. Osbert looked on, his face contorted in a grimace at the sight of the corpses around them. Wulfnoth finally joined them, scurrying down the rope with ease, the last of his men following as they began to hurry away from the wall. Everyone was tense, and there was a considerable amount of open ground to cover before they could even hope to reach the woodland Alaric knew to be some distance ahead. They might yet be detected.

The night again proved to be a blessing, the darkness enveloping the fugitives to the extent that, even if anyone had been atop the wall, they'd be hard-pressed to see them. Alaric wondered if anyone was up there at all, since the enemy looked to be entirely preoccupied with burning the cathedral and disputing with each other. He chastised himself. Just because they'd gotten this far didn't mean their luck would hold. If Thorkell's men discovered the guards around the gaol were dead, there'd be some kind of response. It was thus imperative they get as far away from the city as possible, and quickly.

Wulfnoth moved up and past him, leading the way with both stealth and speed. Alaric was tired, as was Ælfweard, but they refused the offer from several of Wulfnoth's associates to let them carry Leofwine. He was their friend and their responsibility, and Alaric didn't entirely trust these men nor the motives behind their sudden appearance in Canterburie. If Wulfnoth was THE Wulfnoth he thought he was, he'd have to think fast. From what he'd heard, that man was dangerous and unpredictable, and certainly not one to shy away from drawing the blood of his own countrymen if he thought he'd benefit.

Alaric lost track of how long they'd been moving, feeling like hours had passed with no sounds but that of their feet upon grass and the odd splutter from Leofwine. They'd crossed the old ditch they'd dug months back and hurried into the trees, glad they were at last concealed. The woods soon opened up into what must have once been farmland, the fields unattended, overgrown, or otherwise neglected. He tried not to think on who might have been reaping the bounty from working these lands just last year. For all Alaric knew, he could be the fellow he'd landed on earlier.

They moved into yet another stretch of forest, the tall, slender pines creaking and groaning as if irritated at the sudden intrusion. Their journey carried on and on, Alaric's legs straining and aching, the dry, uneven ground proving difficult to negotiate. His feet felt raw and painful, pricked by the incessant pine needles, but he dared not let up, anxiety about the enemy still very much on his mind.

It was still dark when they finally stopped. Alaric had no idea how much time had passed, but sunrise surely could not be too far off, so long and frantic had their journey across country been. Wulfnoth and company had led them yet further through the trees, taking them down a sudden, sloping decline until they'd reached what looked like the bottom of a shallow ravine. This had been a particularly hazardous area to traverse, and Alaric had almost twisted his ankle at least twice as he shuffled along in the blackness.

Dawn had eventually come, or what passed for a dawn; the cold, faint light inching its way between the bare, spindly trees to reveal the extent of Wulfnoth's well-concealed camp. He had more men here, several dozen, actually, all of them hardy and resolute in their duties, like they'd already seen everything this war could throw at them and couldn't possibly be taken unawares.

The ravine was deeper than Alaric had suspected, making him marvel at how they'd reached the bottom of it in the dark without incident. He could tell why Wulfnoth had set up camp here. It was secluded, and a shallow stream ran right through it, providing fresh water for anyone looking to linger. Alaric had taken to it eagerly, washing himself free of blood and grime, noting how Wulfnoth's men had constructed a number of wood and bracken shelters on either side to serve as places for both sleep and storage.

They'd placed Leofwine in one of these, hoping the enclosure and addition of several blankets might ease him back into some semblance of consciousness. He'd lasted much of the day, yet his fever had gripped him more tightly by the hour, his delirium interspersed with brief moments of lucidity that served only to give them false hope. He'd refused all efforts to give him sustenance, almost choking when Alaric had tried to get him to drink, but they'd had to try. Doing nothing just didn't feel right. Not after what they'd been through together. Not after they'd come so far.

He'd died that evening, trembling and gasping, his suffering finally ceasing after he awoke to apologise for the loss of Canterburie. It had rankled them all to hear it. Leofwine had been a decent man as far as Alaric could tell, one who'd led his men in defence of his home and shown neither reticence nor apprehension in the pursuit of his duty. Alaric should be the one apologising. He'd been the one to surrender them to Thorkell. He could have kept fighting, overruling the archbishop and making a heroic last stand. He'd instead delivered them into shame and captivity. If anyone ought to feel guilty, it was him.

Wulfnoth came to him after the burial. Alaric had been sat by the stream and staring into the flowing water, the sights and sounds serving to partially still his troubled mind.

"Are you alright?" Wulfnoth asked, his voice low and gentle.

"I'm not," Alaric confessed, shivering in the chill evening air, the dying light of day only enhancing his melancholy. "I've seen too much, I think. I've seen battles before. Battles are not the problem. But I'd not seen anything until I saw…"

"I understand," said Wulfnoth, offering Alaric a hunk of bread. He'd undoubtedly seen what Thorkell had done to Canterburie beforehand whilst infiltrating the city to look for survivors. If he wasn't bothered by that, he was either insane or a far tougher man than Alaric. He hoped the memories of what he'd witnessed would fade with time, but something told him he was now changed, the sight of so much barbarism altering him irrevocably.

He took the bread and chewed away at it, its rough texture hard on his gums. He then rose to accompany Wulfnoth to the beginnings of a campfire that was just starting to glow hot, thanks to the persistence of Osbert and Eamon. All the survivors of Canterburie had gathered here, and Wulfnoth sat with them, the men who'd accompanied him into the city joining them also. They'd by this point gifted Alaric and his people with some worn clothes and blankets, the former captives feeling blessed indeed at having some proper boots on their feet. They all ate together, rescuer and rescued alike, the warmth from the fire giving them at least some comfort, despite the ache that persisted in their hearts.

"What will you do now?" Wulfnoth asked after a while, looking like he hadn't wanted to interrupt them whilst they'd gorged themselves on toasted bread and goats' milk.

"I don't know," said Alaric, "I was hoping you could tell us who you are and why you saved us."

"You know who I am, and you can guess why I came."

"I don't, actually. Enlighten me."

"I am Wulfnoth. I'm surprised you've not heard of me."

"THE Wulfnoth?" Osbert asked. "As in the traitor? The reaver? Surely not?"

"Is that what they say about me?" Wulfnoth chuckled. "I suppose they would. I've heard the rumours myself, but hearing it never gets old."

"Well, are you?" Alaric pressed, hoping these "rumours" were fabrications. "Are you him? Did you betray us and turn renegade?"

"It depends on how you look at it, but I'll resolutely deny the claim that I'm a traitor to this country. A dissident, I'll own that title, but not traitor. I've never abandoned the cause of England nor those who are rightfully disposed to rule it."

"That's a very interesting answer," said Alaric, wondering if Wulfnoth might care to get to the point. From what he'd heard, he'd been accused of treachery just as the king was first mustering his fleet to oppose Thorkell two years back. The exact details were unknown to him, but the word was that Wulfnoth had deserted with a force of men to pillage numerous settlements along the south coast, several of them in Hamptonscir. Alaric had seen the damage. It had angered him beyond words to think of Englishmen turning on their own as a foreign invasion loomed.

"And a truthful one," Wulfnoth affirmed with a nod. "People may say whatever they like. It doesn't make it fact. Just because the king chose to believe them doesn't change anything, either. I'm a victim of a long-running struggle that got out of hand at the worst possible moment. Or the best, depending on who you are."

"Did you turn on us?" Alaric snapped, growing tired of the meandering waffle already. "Did you kill your fellow Englishmen to wreak chaos in preparation for Thorkell's landing?"

"No, to all of those things. I did not. The accusations against me are false. Beorhtric whispered poison in the king's ear, and the king was foolish enough to believe him. I fled with what I could. Beorhtric sent people after us. We fought them. I was wounded and needed to recuperate. But I could not just abandon my country. So here I am."

"Rescuing fools like us?" Ælfweard said, bitter in his self-deprecation.

"Saving my countrymen, yes," answered Wulfnoth. "We'd heard Canterburie was under siege. By the time we'd got there, the city had already fallen. I knew they'd want to loot it and ransom whoever was of worth, the archbishop, for certain. So we waited for the right moment and snuck in."

"You were too late then," lamented Osbert. "They killed him. Right there. Killed him for refusing to be ransomed."

"I know, and I'm sorry for the delay…it takes time to get into a city, and getting up those walls was considerably more difficult than getting back down them. That we were able to do it without being seen…"

"They were lax," said Alaric, cutting him off. "They'd thought they'd won. They had won…and then they started fighting each other."

"Indeed," nodded Wulfnoth, unconcerned at the interruption. "We were surprised at that, but we used it to our advantage. We only had to kill a few times whilst searching for you. The bastards were more interested in going after each other than us."

"They're enraged they won't be getting paid as they thought," said Alaric. "Remember that we've not been fighting a single army. Thorkell's force is made up of multiple different warbands from all over Scandinavia. They want money. That's it. That's what they fight for. They wanted the ransom money for the archbishop, and once they thought they wouldn't get it, they turned on each other. Thorkell's greed got the better of him."

"That it has," Wulfnoth smiled. "But I'd venture we've not heard the last of Thorkell the Tall. He's a resourceful man. Unstoppable in battle, so goes the word."

"He bleeds," Alaric muttered darkly. "Trust me. He does. Same for his despicable brother. They both suffer like any other if you strike them."

Wulfnoth leaned back slightly, his eyes focusing in on Alaric. "You're right," he said eventually, "the Northmen have a fearsome reputation that looms larger than life in the minds of many. Underneath all the bluster and renown, they remain but men. And they die as such."

"And you'd know this?" asked Osbert. "Where have you been until now? Wounded this whole time?"

"Not the whole time, but for most of it," answered Wulfnoth. "That storm that rolled in after I fled the king's fleet knocked us off course just as we were nearing the Isle of Wit. Beorhtric's men caught up with us shortly after."

"And then what?" pressed Osbert still. "Word is you attacked him without hesitation and wounded him in personal combat."

"Yes, and he's a liar, like his brother," said Wulfnoth. "His men had already killed some of mine without cause, so we ambushed them as they struggled to come ashore. There was a fight, that's true, but Beorhtric wasn't even there. Where he was, I cannot guess. But there was no duel between us, that I can confirm. I didn't raid any settlements either."

"I saw the damage…" said Alaric.

"And I tell you it wasn't me," Wulfnoth replied sternly. "There's plenty of raiding going on, has been for years, but not by me. Believe it. For all I know, Beorhtric did some reaving himself just to blame it on me."

"Beorhtric is brother to the Ealdorman Eadric, yes?" asked Alaric, putting the issue of "reaving" to one side for the moment. "Eadric was in Canterburie, you know that? He came to negotiate for the archbishop's release. He abandoned the rest of us, though. We were not worth saving."

"That doesn't surprise me," said Wulfnoth. "He's a rat. Acting on the king's orders, probably, but having fun with it too. I suspect Beorhtric was his proxy when it came to accusing me of treason. Eadric is the sharper one out of the pair of them, and he stands to benefit the most from my disgrace."

"Why?" asked Ælfweard. "Who are you to him?"

"Me? Nobody. Eadric cares nothing for anyone. It's who I'm close to that irks him. It's a hard thing when a king remarries to sire yet more children from another woman. It creates tension between the bride and his sons from his previous marriage. That's the case here. I'm loyal to the aethelings, Æthelstan and Edmund. Either of those would make a fine king. Others would rather not have it so."

"Like who?" Ælfweard asked. "And you know Æthelstan is dead? He was killed battling Thorkell in Oxenefordscir."

Wulfnoth's reserved persona faded a little, and for a single instant, he appeared as if he were either about to weep or fly into a rage. He regained his composure almost immediately, but it was clear enough to all present he'd not known of Æthelstan's fate and that the pair of them had been close.

"Who says this?" he asked quietly. "Who says he's dead? What happened?"

"We're not completely certain on all the details," replied Ælfweard, "but there was a battle, a large one, south of Bernecestre. The king clashed with Thorkell and was supported by a force from the Five Boroughs. Æthelstan and Edmund were a part of it."

"And Edmund? He's alive? Please say it's so!"

"It is," Ælfweard confirmed. "As far as we know, he was able to retreat with the thegns, Sigeferth and Morcar, and head back north. The king, of course, retreated to the capital and has remained there since. How many men he even has left, I know not, but since he made no effort to defend Canterburie…"

"He'll make no effort to defend anything!" Wulfnoth growled, his eyes flashing briefly, "…but I grieve for Æthelstan. We've lost a good man, a future king, no less. I know Edmund will be grieving too."

"So is this why you were targeted for slander and accusation?" Alaric asked. "Because you were close to the two brothers? Who would not want them to be king? The queen?"

"You are correct, Alaric. She loves her children and would no doubt prefer it if the king had never had any children before her. That's perhaps to be expected. The problem is her ambition and envy aren't all we have to contend with. Eadric himself wants the king's adult offspring out of the way. They are too headstrong. Independent. And good. Definitely too good. Children like Edward are easy to manipulate. Easy to control and mould."

Everyone pondered for a moment, each man taking time to properly think on Wulfnoth's words. Alaric stretched his legs out closer to the fire, the flames warming the soles of his boots. An owl hooted from the swaying trees above, and the flames continued to crackle to themselves, the gentle burbling of the stream making its way past causing Alaric's eyelid to feel yet heavier. Sleep beckoned. But not just yet. There were things he would know.

"So you maintain Eadric had you accused of treason to weaken Æthelstan?" he asked. "Remove an ally of his from court? That would strengthen Eadric's hand and that of the queen, yes?"

Wulfnoth nodded several times, his eyes now levelled towards the campfire. "The queen is irrelevant to him, though," he muttered. "She fancies herself a player in this game, but she's not. She's vain, greedy, jealous, and petty, and she has trouble controlling her emotions. She's easy to read. Eadric can read her like a book. And manipulate her desire to see her children take priority."

"Are you suggesting that Eadric and the queen…that they…" Alaric didn't want such a thought in his head. It was bad enough, all this treachery and intrigue, but to throw lasciviousness and adultery into the mix was truly revolting. In Alaric's mind, an adulterer was the lowest of the low. To take an oath before God to love and protect a spouse was a sacred moment, one that was not to be defiled or abandoned for the sake of temporary lust. Those who willingly embraced temptation and did harm to those they were honour-bound to cherish were beneath contempt.

Wulfnoth shook his head slowly before speaking. "In truth, I wouldn't be surprised," he admitted, "but I still doubt it. Eadric isn't that stupid. If he seduced the queen, he'd be at a disadvantage. It'd be a weakness, a vulnerability for him, something that could be exposed and then lead to his death. If you ask me, his ultimate goal is to isolate the king and control his young children. That way, he controls the throne, regardless of who is sitting on it."

"But he can't control Edmund," Osbert thought aloud. "Couldn't control Æthelstan. They are men. Fighting men. So he'd have to weaken them both before moving against them. Hence the accusations against you?"

Wulfnoth nodded again and smiled. It was a sad-looking thing, barely a smile even, but it served its purpose, confirming that Osbert was right in his hypothesis. Alaric had never heard any talk about such matters until now, but he didn't doubt there was something to this. Eadric had directly admitted to him just days ago that he'd intended to kill Ulfcytel prior to the Battle of Hringmere. With that revelation, it was abundantly clear the man was actively seeking to eliminate powerful figures that could oppose him. Wulfnoth was just another victim in his grand designs.

Sadly, none of this was of much use to them in the short term. They were hidden and safe for the moment, but Alaric didn't have any real idea about where they were and what they might do next. Danger seemed to lurk at every corner, and even if Thorkell had lost control over his men, there was still no certainty it would stay that way. He was a man of authority and reputation, and his capabilities as a warrior were beyond dispute. He'd always be a threat, and the setback he'd suffered might not last long.

He also couldn't forget the sights he'd seen in Canterburie. Much of the population had been brutalised and killed for sport, that he knew, but many had been imprisoned instead and bound for slavery. The sight of them stuck in his memory like a sliver of ice, their faces piteous and desperate, each of them knowing with dreadful certainty what awaited them. Alaric had nearly suffered such a fate only to be saved by the word of Thorkell himself; a bizarre and unexpected favour if ever there was one. But what had become of those less fortunate?

"What else did you see when you got into the city the other night?" Alaric asked Wulfnoth, eager to hear if he'd spied anything that might give them cause for optimism. "Did you see the pens they'd constructed with prisoners? Slaves?"

"I saw the pens. They were empty. If they were gathering people there to sell, then they've moved them already. We saw as much just days ago after the city fell. Captives on the road, guarded, of course, but all heading north and east to the coast. I'd say they'd be transported by ship for sale elsewhere."

"Where?! Where do you think they were headed?!" If what Wulfnoth had seen was accurate, then they might have a chance to free some of them. There was no way the Danes could hurry that many people along the roads in quick order. It would be a slow and ponderous affair. There could still be hope.

"Just let me think," sighed Wulfnoth, his eyebrows pressing downwards into a frown. "If I had to guess from their movements, they could have been moving towards Remmesgate, or thereabouts."

"That's not too far!" Alaric exclaimed, well aware that he didn't actually know where they were. "If we set out now, we might yet catch them! What do we have…about forty men altogether? Enough to make a difference."

Wulfnoth's eyebrows plunged further, this time with irritation. "It is a distance, Alaric, and one not traversed lightly. We don't know how many foes we might encounter either. They won't have set up a staging area to transport slaves and just left it unguarded."

"But we have to try!" Alaric insisted, his words supported by mutterings and nods of approval from his companions. "What else are we going to do? There's still a war to fight. We can't just stay here in this bleak forest."

"We won't," Wulfnoth assured him. "But we need sleep first. It's a difficult and dangerous journey, and I…"

"We have to hurry!"

"No, Alaric, please listen." Alaric fell silent, unsure of what to make of the edge he detected in Wulfnoth's tone. "You've been beaten, malnourished, held captive," he continued, taking Alaric's silence for an opportunity. "I admire your tenacity, but I won't risk myself and my men by going into battle with allies who have likely barely slept in the best part of a week. Get some rest. We can leave at dawn so we'll at least be able to navigate our way out of the woods and spot anyone best avoided. That's my only offer."

Alaric nodded, his cheeks flushed after his chastisement. He wasn't used to being spoken to in such a manner, but Wulfnoth was right. It didn't make sense for them to go blundering off into the darkness in pursuit of people he didn't even know were still there. Yet he wished Wulfnoth had not given him such a dressing-down in front of the others. He was worried they might begin to question his judgement. He already questioned it himself. He didn't need anyone else to follow suit.

They soon retired for the rest of the night, Alaric slinking off to lie down inside one of the bracken shelters that had been put together along the stream's banks. It was still cold inside, the passing of the worst of winter doing little to raise the temperature above that of an ambient chill, but it was dry and out of the wind. Eamon crawled in after him, claiming correctly that there weren't enough shelters to accommodate everyone without sharing. Alaric didn't mind so much, thinking he could do with the company until he realised Eamon had fallen asleep almost as soon as he'd lain flat on the ground.

Alaric was not so fortunate. He was one for brooding, or he was now, and a part of him was afraid to go to sleep. That wasn't because he felt unsafe, doubting very much anyone hostile would be able to find them here in this secret encampment. It was the dream he'd had whilst in captivity that bothered him. He'd had some disturbing nightmares in the past, but that was something else, the images of his family and the destruction of both Wiltune and Canterburie distressing him beyond words. They'd also reminded him of another matter he had to attend to. His wife was still in captivity, as far as he knew. He had to get back to her, even if he had absolutely no idea how to go about securing her rescue.

It occurred to him then that this had been bothering him for some time. It wasn't just that his family had been seized, but that he felt completely powerless to do anything about it. He was better on the battlefield with a weapon in hand and foes to face. To Alaric, killing was simple and always had been, not as a means towards sating some lust for bloodshed but because it had to be done and he was the man to do it. There was a simplicity there, something that certainly wasn't present when it came to understanding the relationship between his father and their vengeful king. He had no notion of how to proceed on this, and that in itself troubled him.

Darker thoughts came upon him from that point on. He wondered if he was being neglectful, abandoning his family to pursue the slavers because that was the easier option. He didn't know what to make of that since he'd never intended to abandon his family to begin with, but the idea perturbed him. His life had been out of control ever since he'd left his father's army to do a forced march into Eastengle to join up with Ulfcytel. Some might call it an adventure, but he was starting to wonder how much he could take. If they were successful in their endeavours tomorrow, he had to put serious thought into infiltrating Lundenburg and freeing his people. He'd been delayed long enough. They'd waited long enough.

Alaric began to drift, his thoughts dwelling on Æva and their past together. She'd always stirred strong emotions in him, making him feel like he was walking on air when she was happy and devastated when they argued. He'd been told that was usual for young people still inclined to become lost in the strength of their passions, but with Alaric it had never faded. His wife had always had a hold on his heart, and the passage of years had revealed no sign of it weakening.

He'd often thought of the Book of Jeremiah in that regard, suspecting that, just as the Lord had known Alaric before shaping him in the womb, he'd known Æva also, intending for them to be together in their journey through this life and beyond. He'd never gotten around to telling her that. He'd make a point of doing so when he saw her again. He finally fell asleep, thankful for the happy thought and observing with considerable relief when he awoke that the nightmare had not returned.

He scrambled outside, taking care not to make too much noise lest he wake the still-slumbering Eamon. The ravine was now lit up with a strange, grey light, giving the impression the night that had just passed was resentful at the intrusion and was struggling on for as long as possible in the face of the breaking of day. Wulfnoth was out here, sitting by the charred embers that had been their campfire, his attention fixed on his seax as he worked its edge repeatedly along an already well-worn whetstone. Several of his men sat with him, tending to their weapons in a similar fashion. Alaric approached, thinking the camp felt strangely deserted and vulnerable. It would be best to move on soon.

"Are you alright?" asked Wulfnoth without looking up, his efforts still focused on sharpening his blade.

"Is everyone else asleep?" Alaric inquired, placing his hands on his hips whilst he surveyed the campsite. "It's a risk, if so," he added. "Men have been killed whilst resting in places like this without adequate precautions. I know. I've killed them."

"I have people on watch in the woods," Wulfnoth snorted, amused by what Alaric had said. "You can't see them as they don't wish to be seen."

"So you and yours have been living like this since this all started?"

"Since what all started, Alaric?"

"The invasion. Thorkell. The accusations against you."

"Yes," Wulfnoth admitted with a sigh. "It's good practice. Gets us ready for what's ahead."

"Practice? What do you think lies ahead?"

"War," said Wulfnoth, finishing with his weapon and placing it back into the short scabbard at his belt. "This will be the way we fight for some time."

"Why?"

"Set battles don't always suit. Our enemies have proven too numerous, and they are about to become greater still. This is how men fight when their backs are to the wall. They hide out in the forest, looking to strike when their enemies are vulnerable. They become Silvatici."

"They become men of the woods, the forests, the green?" queried Alaric, unused to hearing such a word or pondering the strange images it conveyed. "And this is who you would become? A Green Man, a Silvaticus, lurking in the wilds and ready to punish your enemies when they let their guard slip?"

"I AM that man," Wulfnoth said darkly. "Believe me, Alaric, I am not one to cross. I have been wronged, as have you, I'm sure. I remember my friends, and I remember my enemies. Lies may have been spread about me, but I and my followers remain loyal to our country. We may be few, but England's forests protect us. They give us the means to fight back. It will be like this for Englishmen for generations."

"Generations, you say? So even once we defeat Thorkell, we'll still be struggling against one foreign oppressor or another? Still having to be Silvatici?"

"Can't you feel it, Alaric? I can, and it gives me no pleasure to admit that. This life hardens a man, but that hardening has its uses. Men accustomed to ease and comfort would not have been able to break you out of Canterburie. Men accustomed to ease and comfort would not be able to do what we're about to do."

"What are we going to do?"

"What you said last night," Wulfnoth laughed, like he thought Alaric was being intentionally forgetful. "We make for Remmesgate. If the Norsemen have ships and captives ready to sell, then we'll pay them with their own entrails for ever thinking our people were fit for slavery."

Wulfnoth's fearsome words stuck in Alaric's head. They inspired him, imbuing him with a rare energy he'd not felt since Canterburie had fallen. He awoke the rest of his men, Wulfnoth doing the same for his, all of them gobbling down a quick and easy breakfast of dry bread and stream water before arming themselves for the journey ahead.

Wulfnoth's people were well-supplied considering their situation, gifting Alaric and the others with a variety of spears, seaxes, and axes. Alaric chose a spear and a deadly-looking seax, light but razor sharp. He looked forward to testing them.

The rest of the morning was uneventful, its stark greyness eventually subsiding as the clouds parted to reveal the sun in all its glory. They left the ravine, breaking camp to begin their journey to Remmesgate and whatever awaited them there. Alaric picked his way through the pines cautiously, Wulfnoth and company doing the same whilst they scuttled onward.

Wulfnoth really was a Silvaticus. He flitted from tree to tree with ease, his men leaving precious little trace of their passage. They must have been expert woodsmen even before Thorkell's invasion, hunters and trackers by profession, all now putting their skills to good use in serving their country. And yet, despite their nobility, there was a coldness to them, Wulfnoth in particular. He was hiding something. He'd saved their lives, and Alaric would never forget that, but he still couldn't bring himself to trust him entirely.

Afternoon came, the sun shining down through the spindled branches of the forest. Spring was not far off, and Alaric could see through the trees that the countryside beyond was starting to recover from the bleakness of winter. It was a far cry from the flourishing meadows he'd ridden through in Eastengle last summer, but it was a start, and it gave him some hope that as the land recovered, its people might do the same.

They continued on their path, the men keeping low, and advanced through a seemingly endless stretch of tall grasses, the soft, pliant soil here suggesting a bog was close by. They came within sight of Remmesgate about an hour or two later, or what was left of it. The town hadn't been entirely destroyed, but several of its buildings had been set alight in the past few days, the blackened stones and charred wooden beams of a church spire catching the eye as it rose defiantly over the blasted earth.

Nobody was home, unless you counted the flock of chickens and the several pigs sleeping contentedly in an open shed. It was a mystery what they were even doing here, since if the place had been hit by Danes it stood to reason they'd have killed or at least taken the animals with them. There was a horse left, too, in the stables; a lonely-looking thing but a horse all the same. Alaric made a point of rubbing its nose in greeting. Its eyes lit up, overjoyed at the prospect of company as it grunted and slurped at his hand. He'd made a friend here.

"This is a strange one," Wulfnoth said quietly at his side. "The enemy has been here but must have abandoned their onslaught before the entire place could be ransacked. It's unusual that they've left the animals. Thorkell must have recalled his raiding parties."

"Because of the infighting in Canterburie?" Alaric wondered aloud. "We've not found any bodies, either. The people must have gotten away."

"Or they were captured and sold," Wulfnoth said, a frown once more upon his brow. "We'll need to sweep the coast. Follow me."

They hadn't needed to cover much ground. Just a few dozen paces north east of Remmesgate was a grassy rise, one that obscured the view for anyone standing on the outskirts of town but provided a commanding vista once it was surmounted. Alaric could see far out to sea here, the wind tugging at his cloak with a frenetic urgency, but the scene a short distance further east was what truly held his attention. Pens, constructed from local timber, each wide enough to hold dozens of people. They were similar to the ones he'd seen in Canterburie. The ones full of slaves. They'd found what they were looking for.

And yet it was too late. They were all empty, just as the entire area was also empty of any hostile foreigners. They could tell from the shingle on the beach that several ships had been pulled ashore here, most likely to take on cargo. Alaric gritted his teeth as an image came to mind. Hundreds of people, herded from their holding pens and forced towards the water, each one baulking in fear at the sight of the fearsome Norse longships. He could see the trail they'd left with their passing, the stones and sand alike having parted under the weight of so many footfalls until all trace vanished beneath the lapping of the tide. There was nobody here.

Alaric sank to his knees, the sharpness of the shingle of minor concern. Osbert and Eamon stood a few feet behind him, staring out to sea, the crashing of the grey waves upon the greyer shore only adding to the feeling of desolation. There was no trace of the ships, and the horizon was as clear as could be. There was nothing to be done. They'd failed.

Something stirred in his heart, the sensation black and raw. Hatred. He hated the enemy. He always had, but after the past few days it had changed, the feeling growing in intensity until he thought of little else but killing Danes. They'd done so much wrong, over and over, to the point Alaric had ceased to even think of them as human. There was no compromising with such beasts. Each and every one of them deserved to meet their end on the point of a sword.

But Alaric no longer had his sword. Hemingr had it, just as he'd taken Æthelstan's wedding ring from him, the same ring Alaric had taken from his murdered corpse so that he might return it to his widow. He'd failed in that, and this was another failure now, one that stung him upon this blighted shore in a manner far worse than any sharpened stone or icy wind. Osmund, or whatever had been pretending to be Osmund in his nightmare, had been right. He was beset by failure. For years it had gone on. Sometimes he feared that for years it would continue.

He stood up, ignoring the ache in his knees. Wulfnoth said nothing when they rejoined him to trudge slowly back towards Remmesgate, everyone in their group looking as wretchedly miserable as Alaric. Spirits were lifted a little when they obtained a dozen eggs from the town's resident chickens, Osbert and the others eagerly making a fire outside the church so that they might cook something. Things got even better when Wulfnoth discovered several pots and a multitude of spoons in an abandoned cottage close by. Boiled eggs it was then.

They were delicious, although not without hazards of their own. Alaric burnt his fingers on one, finding himself so eager to eat he'd forgotten to allow it to cool off. Osbert peeled one and bit into it, yet for some reason the yoke was still soft, leaving him with a streak of bright orange running through his beard. Wulfnoth and his people killed a few chickens and set about plucking them, the surviving birds keeping a wide berth as they clucked indignantly from the deepening shadows of the dying afternoon.

Alaric bedded down in the church after supper, his stomach unusually full in contrast to the meagre days he'd just endured. Night had fallen in a hurry, the moonlight spilling in through the unfortunately shattered windows to bathe much of the interior in a soft glow. It was uncomfortable on the floor, but Alaric wasn't inclined to rest in the stables as several others had. He wanted to be close to the Lord tonight. He needed some resolution, some kind of insight, anything to tell him what to do next.

He slipped into a dreamless sleep again, his fervent prayers granting him some solace as he repeated the holy name of Jesus Christ. He awoke some hours later, the moonlight fading with dawn's approach, the air still and peaceful despite the chill. He stood up and made his way outside, endeavouring to keep the noise of his passing to a minimum lest anyone else had decided to sleep in the church without his knowledge.

The air was freezing, its icy touch seizing at his hands and face and almost burning his lungs with the breathing of it. He could still hear the rumbling of waves from here, finding the sound oddly alluring whilst he made his way up the grassy rise he'd stood upon just yesterday. The view was as he'd expected, the night hiding much of the horizon, but there was something majestic about the sea now. He couldn't tell why, but he felt the urge to remain here, watching the dark waves crash and hurl themselves upon the shore.

He sat for a long time, gazing out across the sea, the rising sun failing to lift his spirits. Remmesgate looked particularly mournful, bleak and ruined and empty, the beach appearing so grey and jagged Alaric felt there was something vaguely menacing about it. He stood up and again looked towards the horizon, thinking he'd caught sight of something moving far, far out upon the waters. Hope seized him. The slavers could be returning. They might have unfinished business. With any luck, they could ambush them as they came ashore. Some good might still come of this.

It wasn't just a single ship. He spied one, then another and another, a dozen now coming into focus and a dozen more following. It wasn't long until Alaric could see the situation for what it was. There was an entire fleet out there, made up of hundreds of longships, their colourful sails billowing outward and their oars heaving through the surf, each and all filled with warriors attired for battle. This was another invasion. This was what they'd been fearing. They'd had a respite from him, but they'd all known he'd return someday, ready to finish what he'd started. It could only be…

"King Svienn Forkbeard," a voice said behind him. Alaric spun around to behold Wulfnoth. It was alarming how he could move so silently, but that was the least of his troubles now. They had to get word to Lundenburg before the city found itself under assault.

"I told you our foes were about to become more numerous," said Wulfnoth, moving up alongside Alaric. "This was always coming. But it'll be different this time. He'll have seen how we struggled to hold off Thorkell, and will have worked to turn all this to his advantage. This won't be the Svienn we've fought before. This is something else."

"What is it then?" Alaric asked, turning to again look upon the distant ships. They didn't have time for riddles. Wulfnoth had best get to the point before he lost his temper.

"An occupation army. They don't come here to raid, pillage, and retreat like they have before. Now Svienn intends to stay. To break us when we are at our weakest and force us into submission. To topple our ill-counselled Æthelred from his throne. To make himself King of England."

XXV

"So how many men does he have left?"

"Not as many as we'd hoped. It won't be a vast army ready to unleash upon our enemies. More like an auxiliary force. Highly experienced and capable, but not overwhelming."

Æthelred sat down, reaching up to his collar to scratch strenuously at his neck. "And what does he want for them?" he asked, suspecting correctly that his fevered scratching had left a sequence of red claw marks upon his throat. "The offer was for him and his army, not him and…how many does he have under his authority?"

"Enough to fill forty-five of his remaining ships," Eadric answered. "I got the notion as soon as I arrived that he'd sustained heavy losses taking Canterburie. With the outbreak of fighting in his own ranks and the desertion of so many others…we're looking at just over two thousand men."

"So how much gold?"

"Same as before, my king."

"That's a vast amount of money, Eadric. A vast amount, even for an intact army. For just Thorkell and two thousand men…"

"I understand," Eadric assured him, "but it's more than just that. This is Thorkell the Tall. His renown is beyond compare now. And he'll be yours. With his most loyal and battle-hardened killers. It will still have been worth it. The money will be worth it."

"Including the price I had to pay to get it?" asked Æthelred, more a rhetorical question than anything. "The alienation of so many thegns? The possibility of rebellion? The people's impoverishment?"

"Temporary setbacks," Eadric answered coolly. "Settlements can be rebuilt, and coffers refilled. Dead men have sons that grow to replace them. The price is worth it, my king."

Æthelred leaned back in his seat and exhaled, stretching his legs out under the table. The warmth from the hearth helped put him at ease, the embers from last night's fire still giving off a pleasant glow. He hadn't slept well again, the dastardly dream returning as usual, and he had aches and pains aplenty from his body's longstanding inability to relax. Eadric also looked worse for wear, sporting a shining bruise across his left eye, his well-worn travelling garb suggesting he'd moved with some haste back to Lundenburg following the conclusion of talks with Thorkell. From what Æthelred had heard, he was lucky to have escaped with his life.

They were once again in Æthelred's audience chamber, the table littered with the remains of yet another nocturnal feast. The air was heavy with the scent of roast meats and strong drink, enough to unsettle his stomach and make him seriously consider choosing another venue for this meeting. He'd eventually decided against that. He liked to hear Eadric's reports here, where his authority was more apparent, and there could be no dispute about where the real power lay. He might look and feel a little unsteady after last night's revelry, but the sight of his throne was reassuring, at least to him.

He'd decided not to sit upon it this time, preferring to remain by the hearth whilst Eadric stood to attend him. There was a subtlety here that he'd grown to appreciate; the act of compelling Eadric to stand whilst he sat reinforcing his authority without overawing him from the throne. There was a time, not so long ago, when Æthelred would have enjoyed doing precisely that, but not now. Besides, his legs ached, and he enjoyed his seat at the table.

It was a shame the table itself did little to impress. Dirty plates and dishes lay scattered across it, the plethora of empty cups alongside them giving off that sickly, rich reek of stale wine that further served to turn his stomach. His wandering thegns had still not thought it safe to return to their lands, and so they'd settled in with him here in Lundenburg. He wouldn't mind so much if he didn't have to act the gracious host, each night inundating them with food and company as was to be expected of a man in his lofty position. He'd never enjoyed such things and increasingly hated it and those involved, especially after the embarrassment of his recent public altercation with Edmund and that bastard, Ulfcytel.

And it was embarrassing. Distressingly so. They'd all seen it, most painfully how Edmund had defied him so that his own guards had refused his orders to kill that mouthy tall stranger who'd openly insulted him. His authority had been undermined to a catastrophic degree, by his own son, no less, and Æthelred had no inkling of how to respond. He'd kept his guests well supplied with wine from that point on, hoping the grape might rob them of any undue recollections. It probably wouldn't work. There would be gossip and rumour over all this. He hoped that's all there'd be.

Certain distractions had thankfully made themselves known. Just a day after Edmund's dramatic departure, Eadric had sent word that he was returning to Lundenburg. Æthelred had thought to go and search for Edmund and Wulfhild, fearing the impact the poisoned words of Ulfcytel might have on their young minds. He'd instead sent some men out into the city to look for them, preferring to remain here so that he wouldn't miss Eadric when he arrived. His instincts had been right. Eadric had indeed brought astonishing news. Thorkell was ready to come over to his side. He hadn't expected it. But the events that had unfurled in Canterburie made for a remarkable tale.

"Tell me once more, Eadric, how you came by that unsightly mark on your face?" Æthelred smiled inwardly at Eadric's discomfort. He wasn't entirely trying to be cruel. Eadric's account of the past few days was quite fascinating, and it didn't hurt to ask him to share it again. Not too much, anyway.

"It is as I said, my king," Eadric began, the fingers of his right hand again dabbing at his face self-consciously. "A particularly drunken Dane decided I might be fair game once the fighting had started. He struck me. My men deterred him from further foolishness, and I escaped the city. Thorkell was eventually able to get control of the situation and treat with me properly."

"But this would be after most of his people abandoned him? All because of Archbishop Ælfheah?"

"That's correct, my king. The archbishop was not of the opinion that he should be ransomed. I suspect he'd made a nuisance of himself before I'd even arrived. The enemy...the Northmen...had drunk a considerable amount that night and morning both. They had no patience for his theatrics."

"So they murdered him? They murdered him because he wouldn't be ransomed, even though he himself had no choice in the matter? We had the coin ready. It would have been a simple exchange."

"I know it makes little sense to us…as I said, they were incredibly intoxicated and had quite likely been looking for an excuse to harm him and loot his cathedral. Thorkell's commands could only go so far in the face of their greed and bloodlust."

"Why had they not attacked the cathedral?" pondered Æthelred, to himself as much as anyone. "It would be full of relics, full of treasures. I'm right in assuming the building is now in ruins?"

"Yes, they burned it," Eadric confirmed, "or made as good an attempt as possible since so much of it is made of stone. Thorkell told me why he'd spared the place and had wanted to see it untouched. This Alaric fellow…the word is he put up considerable resistance during the siege. Wounded Thorkell, even. He only relented when Thorkell cut him a deal: surrender and the cathedral will be spared, or keep fighting against impossible odds and see the place desecrated."

"That's quite a deal," said Æthelred, "and one I had not expected to be struck. So Alaric, in addition to pestering me still in my dreams, has also left an impression on Thorkell? That seems strange to me."

"Why?" Eadric asked flatly.

"We at first thought Ulfcytel might be the real threat to my throne…a charismatic man with both reputation and armies. But who is he now? He's racked up another defeat for his record, got himself wounded, and lost his men into the bargain, unless you count all those refugees he flooded in here. Could Alaric be the real threat? Is that why I dream of him?"

"You dream of many others, though?" asked Eadric. "The living and the dead?"

"I do," Æthelred affirmed grimly. "The living and the dead…the ungrateful, the disloyal, the best forgotten…all of them. But you saw Alaric? In Canterburie?"

"Yes, as I said earlier; Thorkell wanted to sell him back to us along with the reeve, Ælfweard, and some others I didn't recognise. I think Thorkell thought that anyone brave enough to fight him as long as they had must be of some value. He thought we'd want Alaric. He actually seemed to respect him and was confused that we only wanted the archbishop. Of course, Ælfheah himself objected…then he died, and the fighting started."

"So Thorkell still has Alaric in custody, or was he killed when they realised we would not pay for them?" Æthelred had to know. He'd tried to assure himself in recent months that this Alaric was irrelevant and his appearance in his dreams nothing but coincidence. After the renown he'd earned at Canterburie, he wasn't so sure. He couldn't think of any other Englishman Thorkell had ever singled out for admiration. That didn't bode well.

Eadric's eyes narrowed in thought, the two greyish-blue orbs seeming to flit from side to side as he struggled to recall what exactly had taken place. "I had some words with him," he finally said, "just before the chaos ignited. It was nothing…just insults, really. He hated me. He'd worked out what our plan was for Hringmere…"

"How intelligent he is," Æthelred snapped. "Now, please tell me…is he alive?"

"I…"

"Just tell me how it is, Eadric. Don't worry so much."

"I confess I did not see him die. I recall he was led away after taking a bruising from his minders. He tried to save the archbishop, you see. A foolish move, but that's him. Thorkell did not mention him again to me when we talked properly. I admit I neglected to ask him about Alaric, specifically."

"Why would you not ask?" Æthelred could feel his temper rising, the bile from last night's repast gurgling uncomfortably in his stomach. He wasn't in the mood for excuses, despite the assurances he'd just given.

"It just didn't occur to me…Thorkell is the main issue…Alaric is a nobody…"

"He's not a nobody!" Æthelred roared, his fist slamming down onto the table with such violence that a nearby dish flipped and crashed to the floor. "What did I just tell you? Why do I even bother sharing my thoughts with you? Am I of such little import that they just fall from memory?!"

Eadric flushed slightly, his cheeks again developing that rose-tinted sheen that made him look akin to a petulant child. He wasn't fazed otherwise, instead locking eyes with his king and waiting patiently for his rage to subside. He'd grown used to him, Æthelred could tell. He only hoped he hadn't learned to stop fearing him. Æthelred had given up trying to inspire affection in his people a long time ago. Fear was how respect was maintained. Eadric would need a sharp lesson in that, should he continue to prove himself forgetful.

"If the notion pleases you, my king," ventured Eadric finally, "I believe it probable that Thorkell disposed of Alaric regardless. The sole reason he was alive was for ransom. I can't fathom why Thorkell would bother holding such a man just for the sake of it. Chances are he's headless in Canterburie, somewhere."

"But you don't know that," cautioned Æthelred, his manner less tempestuous. "He's survived peculiar situations before that he didn't have any business enduring. I…I can't rest until he's gone, Eadric. I can't…there's something about all this that troubles me. And now Thorkell…what? Admires him? Respects him for his tenacity? If he provokes admiration in the enemy, just think of what effect he has on our own. A dangerous man. Very dangerous."

An uneasy silence fell, broken only by the occasional shifting of ash as the fire in the hearth continued to burn itself out. The sun gleamed in from the tall, narrow windows just behind Æthelred's throne, the afternoon outside shaping up to be a pleasant one. Æthelred continued to sit, his mind fixed on Alaric's as yet unconfirmed fate and what any of it could mean for his reign.

If he were alive, he'd be more ill-disposed towards him than ever, especially after he'd effectively refused to pay for any of the captives aside from Ælfheah. He'd also no doubt be irate over the imprisonment of his family. Æthelred had still not decided what to do with them, his not-so-recent exchange with the lady Æva achieving nothing other than to make her hate him even more. He'd had her sent back to her cell after that and separated from her son; a cold but necessary move following Edmund's strange decision to reunite them. He wouldn't afford his enemies any comforts. That was not how it worked.

If he were honest, he enjoyed having them here. Ælfric was a snake who deserved execution, but Æthelred felt a perverse satisfaction in keeping them all guessing as to their ultimate fate. After all Ælfric had put him through over the years, he owed him that discomfort, and whilst Æthelred would likely kill him at some point, it pleased him to make him languish in captivity for a while longer. Some would call it cruel, especially when he was of a mind to take the life of Æva and Ælfgar along with him.

But traitors like Ælfric deserved no mercy, and it made no sense to leave their families intact so that they might seek revenge.

This was another reason to ensure Alaric really was dead. It wasn't just about his fearful dreams now. If Æthelred went ahead and had his family killed, then Alaric would come looking for him, and by the sounds of it he wasn't the kind of man who could be stopped with any ease. They all had to die, him included. It was the only way to be safe.

The twin doors to the chamber began to grind open, slow as usual, their great metal hinges protesting at the strain. Ecgberht, the commander of the Lundenburg garrison, strode forward, still very much the dutiful warrior in his long chain hauberk and hardened leather breecs. His face, too, was as soldierly as always, his skin tough like animal hide and his flowing dark hair and beard giving him an almost feral appearance. He looked particularly intense today. He clearly had business to discuss.

He was followed by four of his men, all of them armoured like he was, their faces hidden beneath worn iron helms. As they came closer, Æthelred could see there was a sixth person in their party walking directly behind Ecgberht, his hands bound with rope and his movements watched by the four men alongside and behind him. He couldn't identify much about him yet, hooded as he was in a mud-splattered grey cloak, but he had a bearing similar to the men around him. He was a fighter, also.

Ecgberht stopped about a meter away from Eadric. He flashed him a look, partly disgust and partly apprehension, before turning to Æthelred, a quick bow following before he spoke.

"I apologise for intruding, my king, but I bring you news that is of vital importance to the country."

"What is it?" Æthelred asked. "And who is this with you? A messenger from Thorkell?"

Ecgberht shook his head and turned to pull down the hood of the mystery figure waiting patiently behind him. Eadric suddenly jerked upright and stepped back and away, his hand reaching for his sword. Æthelred surged to his feet, the ache in his legs the least of his worries as he beheld the man now staring back at him.

He didn't look entirely as he'd expected. His face had been marred, several bruises and cuts giving credence to the notion he'd been sorely treated. His left eye was gone, the flesh around the socket pinched shut like a closed purse, a great scar also running from there to the side of his head before his dark locks obscured it from view. The man was staring at him intently, in a way that seemed too familiar. He'd seen it before. Just last night, in fact. His dreams didn't lie.

"Alaric," hissed Æthelred. "You lived through it all then."

Alaric frowned and shook his head slightly, whether dismayed or confused, he could not tell. Ecgberht also had a perplexed look, if only for a moment, perhaps surprised by his king's familiarity with the prisoner.

"He came through the gates an hour ago," Ecgberht said, "and accosted several of my men on duty, claiming Svienn Forkbeard himself was returning at the head of an invasion fleet."

"And is he?" asked Æthelred, his gaze still pointed directly at Alaric. "Are we beset by yet more foes, just as we've turned one to our will?"

"So it's true then," Alaric said, his voice sharp yet deep. "You do wish to buy off Thorkell with this tax you've foisted on the realm. It's too late now, though…we killed throngs of them at Canterburie, and then they started fighting each other…all you've done, in your foolishness, is hire the scraps. Svienn's force is vast. Thorkell won't be much help."

"Watch your tongue, or I'll have you killed immediately." There was no anger in Æthelred's voice. It was a simple statement; a fact he wished to convey. This man had vexed him for months now, and he wouldn't tolerate further insolence. He'd put up with too much from the likes of him. Ælfric, Ulfcytel…they were all irritants, but they didn't terrify him like Alaric did. Æthelred still couldn't explain why that was, but now he was here, he wouldn't allow him to insult him. He'd have the respect he was due.

"How on earth did you escape?" asked Eadric, the slightest hint of admiration creeping into his voice. "Last time I saw you, there was no chance, no hope…you were barely dressed, unarmed…stupid, as you remain, but not one I'd guess to be capable of miracles. How do you do it?"

"I will not share words with this creature," said Alaric to Æthelred. "He is the source of many of England's woes; a traitor and a grasper, for certain. I only came here to tell you I spied a mighty fleet just a day or so ago. Svienn's fleet. You're all in great danger."

"Why come as you are?" Æthelred demanded. "Alone and without friends…how did you even escape Canterburie? And now you come here to warn me, a man you haunt at night? For what purpose?"

Alaric sighed slightly, his eye drifting over Æthelred like he both pitied and despised him. He flexed his shoulders, the joints cracking disagreeably, for a brief instant giving Æthelred the impression he intended to force his hands from their restraints.

"I am alone," he affirmed, "but not without friends. I have no desire to converse with you, but I will tell you…"

"You will tell the king whatever he wishes," intoned Eadric. "You owe him obedience. Tell him how you escaped."

"I will not answer to you, Eadric. You are not a man. But since the king did ask me, I will tell him. The Lord Wulfnoth took advantage of the chaos when the Danes started fighting each other after their damnable murder of the good and holy Archbishop Ælfheah. He broke in with his men and saved me and many others."

So it was true. Æthelred had wondered for months what had happened to Wulfnoth and why he'd turned against him. And now he'd resurfaced to aid a renegade like Alaric. He wasn't surprised. Beorhtric, Eadric's own brother, had been right to warn him of Wulfnoth's treason. What other schemes had he set in motion since?

"And where is he now?" Æthelred demanded. Seconds passed, followed by yet more. Alaric had heard him. He just wasn't answering. This wasn't acceptable. Æthelred inclined his head towards Ecgberht. "Make him talk," he ordered. Ecgberht clenched a mailed fist and turned to Alaric, then hesitated. He opted for words instead. "Answer the king!" he bellowed. Alaric continued his silence. Æthelred was about to order him struck when he finally spoke.

"I won't tell you where he is. You'll seek vengeance upon him for whatever misdeeds you believe he's committed. He's done me a great service. I won't betray him."

"You're a tool in events of which you have no understanding," Æthelred shot back. "This has always been the problem with you petty thegns. You won't cooperate with higher authority. You think you know best, despite knowing nothing of the broader situation. Hence our disunity. Hence the calamity. Will you not do as you are asked, Alaric? Just this once? Tell me where Wulfnoth is!"

"You may be right," Alaric conceded, "but it's not like you've ever put any effort into convincing us petty thegns, as you call us. A king should be a friend and protector to his people. Yet you simply demand. You demanded Ulfcytel abandon his own in Eastengle and then had this rat," Alaric nodded towards Eadric, "hatch a plot against him when he refused. You demanded a ridiculous new tax for a new army…but there was no army, and the tax, I venture, was to pay off the very people who came here to harm us. And now you demand I betray the man who saved me from those same invaders? I will not. Never."

"You've just demonstrated you yet remain the fool," sneered Eadric. "We kept the nature of the heregeld a secret to avoid further disunity. We couldn't have the realm splinter apart over misunderstandings. And Thorkell has agreed to come over to us. It's done. The strategy was successful."

"At what cost?" asked Alaric. "Just how much of the coin you've squeezed from the weary hands of the people does this barbarian want? Will there be anything left for them now their bellies are empty? What about the widows? The orphans? Will there be anything left for them?"

Eadric glowered, unsure of what to say, his mouth then twisting into a wry smile. "Let me kill him now, my king," he asked. "Such insolence is unacceptable. You've wanted this man dead for a long time. Let me do you a service here."

"Hold, Eadric, I have a question," said Ecgberht suddenly, moving himself into position as if to shield Alaric from harm. "This heregeld… that wasn't for an army?"

"What would you have from me, Ecgberht?" Æthelred asked, annoyed that the man felt he was somehow owed an explanation. "You were, if you recall, at Bernecestre when Thorkell and I discussed bringing him and his men into my service. Now it's done. He's agreed. And the kingdom will be all the better for it."

"But just how much is he getting?!" Ecgberht asked, shocked and dismayed. "After all he's done…after all he did, and all the men who died that day beneath that blasted hill…you'd still look to sweet-talk him and give him whatever he wants?"

"Remember you're talking to your ki…"

"Shut up, Eadric!" shouted Ecgberht, his cheeks flushing red. "I never liked you! No man of honour does! What hand did you have in all this? What do you stand to gain from the impoverishment of others?"

"Enough! All of you!" Æthelred bellowed. "Thorkell has got what he wanted, and his services have been secured! We now have an elite force and the most ferocious man in the world to lead it. That should give Svienn pause."

"It won't," Alaric said quietly. "You can't trust Thorkell. And Svienn's army is vast. He must have recruited every able man in Denmark, such is their number. We made Thorkell suffer in taking Canterburie. He doesn't have the men to stop him."

"How much money is Thorkell being given?!" Ecgberht again demanded, his rage still fresh despite Æthelred's chastisement. "I am the commander of your forces, my king! I have bled for you! My men had died for you! I will have an answer from you!"

Eadric said something, quiet and low, like he was embarrassed to speak but felt compelled to do so. He named the sum, yet to be paid, but agreed upon already with Thorkell himself. Æthelred winced, annoyed to hear it out loud. It was a truly vast amount, sure to drain the treasury even with the additional funds secured through taxation. Alaric's eye hardened further. Ecgberht just stood there in shock, visibly trembling at what he'd heard. Alaric then spoke.

"So after all this hurt and loss, you'll loot the kingdom for the sake of a foreigner and a murderer? And then kill me, too, for daring to resist?"

"I'll kill you as it must be done!" cried Eadric, stepping forward and to the side in a bid to avoid Ecgberht and strike at Alaric with his blade. Ecgberht spun to face him, grabbing Eadric with his right hand around the collar of his tunic. His left shot forward to hold the wrist of Eadric's sword arm, his steely grip enveloping and crushing it.

"You would murder this man who did nothing but come here to warn us of an approaching army?!" shouted Ecgberht, his face so close to Eadric's that he showered him in spittle.

"The king wants him dead!" whined Eadric, unable to resist Ecgberht's superior strength. "I do as he wishes, as should you!"

Æthelred could see the situation was spinning rapidly out of control. He breathed in deeply, trying to settle his nerves and resist the urge to succumb to an emotional outburst of his own. He'd humiliated himself in front of people all too recently, and it wasn't the first time, either. If he wanted to retain any sense of authority, he had to handle this well. Ecgberht was the commander of his forces here and a brutal warrior in his own right. He was also very popular among the ranks. He couldn't afford to alienate him. The results could be disastrous.

"Hold a moment!" he commanded, raising his right hand into the air in the hope of conveying some measure of strength. "Ecgberht, you will release Eadric! Eadric! Once he does so, you will sheath your sword and take no hostile action. I am your king, and I command it be so!"

Ecgberht shoved Eadric backwards, allowing him to stumble away. Eadric bared his teeth, the look giving him the likeness of a frustrated child rather than a warrior, but he, too, did as he'd been told and placed his sword back within its scabbard. Æthelred nodded slowly and placed his hands on his hips, content at least that his wishes had been respected. Now that just left the problem of Alaric.

He stood there still, defiant as always. The little weasel was, no doubt, pleased that he'd sown division among his captors. He deserved death for that, but Æthelred couldn't shake the feeling that if he were to have him killed, he'd lose Ecgberht. If that happened, he'd forfeit the obedience of the warriors he still had left. It didn't matter if he'd secured Thorkell's loyalty. He'd need all his forces if he were to resist Svienn. As much as it displeased him, Alaric would have to remain alive, at least for a time.

"Ecgberht, I want you and your men to escort Alaric to a cell. He is to remain there, under guard, for as long as I wish. No harm will come to him."

Ecgberht looked at Alaric, the two seeming to share a moment of understanding before he again turned to face his king. "I will do as you ask, Æthelred," he said, the king frowning slightly at the fact he'd addressed him so informally. "But I will have it known this situation is unjust. The false heregeld…the scheming and plots, and now the measures taken against a man who did nothing but try to warn us…"

"I understand," soothed Æthelred, doing his best to keep him calm. "I know this is a great deal to take in. Your loyalty is always seen and valued, Ecgberht. You do your men credit."

Æthelred hoped his words would have the desired effect. He didn't mean any of them. Ecgberht would need to be replaced at some point. He didn't appreciate his disrespect, nor did he favour his undisguised sympathy for a dog like Alaric. But there was a time and a place for everything, and to act in such a manner now would see yet more enemies rise up to oppose him. He'd bide his time.

"What about Svienn?" Ecgberht asked. "If he's on his way, we'll need to prepare."

"Then prepare for a siege," said Æthelred. "And send out riders… and ships to the mouth of the Temes. I'd have an accurate picture of what we're up against."

Ecgberht nodded, this time neglecting to bow as he led Alaric away, his men following. "So I'm to rot in a cell, like my father?" shouted Alaric, his head twisting back over his shoulder so he might still face Æthelred. "For how long will you play at this, king? Lundenburg is starving, and you don't have the men to defend her! Svienn will storm this city and take your throne! You have to…"

His voice was cut off, the heavy doors to the chamber closing with their usual resounding boom. They were alone again, he and Eadric, the silence an unexpected joy in the aftermath of such turbulent proceedings. It wasn't to last. Eadric, predictably, began talking again, his self-satisfied tones even more displeasing to the ear than usual. If he didn't have such a fine mind, Æthelred would be glad to be rid of him. It was a thought that still occurred to him on occasion.

"To think a man so unappealing has survived so much. It must be the devil's work that saw him escape Canterburie. And the men I hired to dispose of him, for that matter."

"You sent men to kill him?" asked Æthelred. "When?"

"Before the siege, it was," replied Eadric, sounding even more pleased with himself, if that were possible. "It was no secret that Ulfcytel's appearance in Canterburie was a big affair for the locals. I made a few inquiries, curious as to whether Alaric was with him since Edmund had confirmed he was alive. I then took steps to ensure he ceased being alive as soon as possible."

"Which failed, obviously," said Æthelred irritably. "Just how many men did you send? And did they know they were facing such a formidable opponent?"

"I wouldn't describe him as formidable. Just lucky. And I sent a fair few. What exactly happened, I am still uncertain of."

"Well, he killed them, of course!" Æthelred snarled, wishing Eadric would leave him now to his thoughts. "Did it not occur to you that Ulfcytel would always be close by? That man can cleave skulls with a flick of his finger. No wonder your men are dead!"

"I sought to act on a situation. It's regrettable that it didn't work out, but I think it was the wise thing to do at the time. Besides, had they succeeded, would you have missed him?"

Æthelred didn't answer. He rubbed his temples, hoping to curtail the headache he knew was about to wash over him. He wanted Alaric dead, but Ecgberht's behaviour had confused him. He didn't know why loyalty was such a hard thing to come by, but he'd made the right decision in holding off on Alaric's execution for the time being. Making an enemy of Ecgberht in their current situation would be a serious error.

Yet it would be doubly foolish to just do nothing. Everything now hinged around obtaining information on Svienn's army. If it were as big as Alaric was saying, then they'd be in trouble. Lundenburg's defences were impressive and a major obstacle to anyone with ill intent, but they needed manning, and the English forces inside the city were no longer numerous enough to do that with any degree of proficiency. Thorkell's men would help considerably, but their numbers were not what they were. He needed other options.

"How many people do we have in the city now?"

"Uncertain, my king. Too many. The people go hungry but are too afraid to leave. If Svienn is indeed set to entrap us here, the situation will worsen."

"Then we need to thin their numbers before he can besiege us. We can't hold out with extra mouths to feed like this."

"What would you have us do?"

"Get rid of them. Anyone who isn't a native or property owner in this city is to leave immediately. There will be no exemptions. I cannot tolerate a surplus population, not now. We either do this, or the city will fall to famine before Svienn Forkbeard has even made his first assault."

"Anything else?" Eadric asked, his tone thoughtful, like he was contemplating the task ahead.

Æthelred's next words were hard to get out, the effort straining him to the edge of physical discomfort. Many would object to this, finding his actions loathsome and his motives questionable. It didn't matter now. Things had to be done if they were to survive, if he and his wife and children were to remain safe. One day people would understand.

"Have word sent to the treasury. They're to prepare Thorkell's payment for when he arrives. All of it. If we're to hold this city, I'll need to focus on doing just that. I can't be fretting about Thorkell's loyalties. I need him content with our arrangement and willing to fight."

****

The king moved from his table with those final orders and made his way over to the double doors to leave his chamber. Eadric noted, with some satisfaction, how he had to wait for the guards beyond to help him, so heavy were the doors and so clearly beyond the physical strength of the ageing king. Eadric knew in his heart that he, too, had difficulties with them, but he didn't let that bother him. He enjoyed watching others struggle. It made him feel better about himself.

He sat down, his back to the still glowing hearth. He rubbed his thighs with both hands, soothing the ache that had come from standing upright for so long. He resented Æthelred's myriad attempts to exert his authority over him, but he endured them, knowing the king would always have his eccentricities and that the rewards for forbearance were greater than the perils of defiance. Eadric was the real power in England now, or would become so. Æthelred was just too addled to realise it.

He took further stock of the situation. A lot had gone right, and a lot had gone wrong. Despite some initial grumbling, delays, and even the odd threat, a fair number of the remaining thegns and ealdormen of the land had more or less cooperated with the king's heregeld. That was a surprise, and it had denied Eadric the opportunity to isolate the king further, yet it had provided them with the means to placate Thorkell.

Æthelstan and Edmund's surprise attack at Bernecestre had been potentially disastrous, but the death of the king's eldest had sweetened the pot and permitted Eadric to blame Sigeferth and Morcar. That truly was a blessing, and it was likely Æthelred would take action against them. He'd further encourage him to do so if need be.

The recent drama with Edmund and Ulfcytel was also useful. Eadric needed Æthelred away from anyone who might try to help him, and Edmund was certainly one of those. Ulfcytel's bizarre stunt had also further antagonised the king, making it more than probable he'd be pleased should Eadric's men manage to find the ealdorman and put an end to him. This left Æthelred more dependent than ever on his queen, who was quite clearly a dunce and open to manipulation, especially through her children. This was a far easier situation for Eadric to control, one that wouldn't be the case at all if any of Æthelred's grown male offspring were still present and able to interfere.

There were a couple of points that still troubled him, however. Wulfnoth's survival was unexpected. He was a popular man; a dashing figure that had been a natural ally to the Aetheling Æthelstan. Beorhtric had done well to frame him for treason, but he'd failed to bring the matter to a close by allowing Wulfnoth to flee from grasp. If Wulfnoth was alive, it didn't bode well, but as long as he was kept away and the king remained cut off from Edmund, the situation should prove manageable.

That just left Alaric. Eadric couldn't understand the man. When he'd first met him in Eastengle, he'd taken him for an idealistic, God-fearing buffoon with delusions of heroism. But somehow, he kept surviving everything fate saw fit to throw at him. It was some relief that he'd been at least imprisoned, but Eadric was rapidly coming to the conclusion that Alaric was more of a threat to him than all the Sigeferths and Ulfcytels and Edmunds of this world combined. He'd press upon the king to have him executed as soon as possible, along with the rest of his family. He'd look forward to seeing his red-haired bitch of a wife die. He still remembered how Æva had insulted him from atop the walls of Porteceaster. He wouldn't take that. Not from a woman.

Eadric stood up, his hands restless. He found a half-empty cup of wine adjacent to the remains of some kind of stew, and he lifted it to his nose, the smell predictably stale and unpleasant. He set it down, a smirk on his face as he contemplated the foolish debauchery that was now commonplace here. Svienn would put a stop to that, or at least the threat of him would. Everyone would be on their toes now, afraid of the Forkbeard and yet also of the beast Thorkell that walked among them as a supposed ally.

Fear was good. Frightened people were easier to control. With any luck, they would weather the storm of this new invasion, and by the time it was over, Eadric would have strengthened his hold over the king to the point it would never slacken. He'd be indispensable. And when the old madman died, Eadric's influence over the royal family would remain. Emma did not have the wit to oppose him. She also hated Edmund, so would herself prove useful should the aetheling make a bid for the throne. Her own children were also too young to know much of anything, and so could be shaped by their kind "Uncle Eadric" as he saw fit.

He'd have to befriend them first, though; an endeavour he wasn't looking forward to, but it'd pay off, of that he was sure. No matter how he looked at it, the future was bright. For him, anyway. And that was all that mattered.

XXVI

He slipped off the street, doing his best to ignore the scenes of impoverishment, and ducked into a narrow side alley. There were refugees almost everywhere, desperate and dangerous, the precious bag he clutched under his cloak making him a real target for those in want. Easter wasn't far off; this time of Lent normally calling for a period of fasting and repentance before the blessed celebrations to mark the Lord's rising. Many were fasting, that was true. They had no choice, and it didn't seem likely anyone would soon be in the mood to celebrate. A bleakness had settled upon Lundenburg, its smothering melancholy impossible to shake.

He hurried down the alleyway for about a hundred yards, relieved yet hating himself for being glad he no longer had to gaze upon the sorrowful sights of human misery that flooded the main roads. He turned left at an intersection, his feet splashing through the puddles left by last night's showers, and eventually came to a door marked with a single incision across its breadth. He'd seen this before. He knew what to do.

Four knocks were required, slow and purposeful. Something then moved on the other side, a scraping, sliding sound becoming audible as the door was unbarred. It opened, the motion smooth and silent despite the door's evident age, the man within peering out at him with suspicion until recognition dawned. He let him pass, closing the door behind him and barring it once more. Secrecy was paramount. The city was no longer safe for any of them.

They moved through the dimly lit antechamber, brushing past a pair of tattered curtains that marked the division between the building's entrance and what lay beyond. It was hard to see in here, since the windows and their shutters had been sealed up with pine wood. The place felt stagnant and claustrophobic despite the safety it promised, and it was crowded also, the two men doing their best to avoid stepping on any of the slumbering forms as they passed by. There was nothing for these people to do, he supposed. They'd had a hard time of late, and none of them were young. They deserved a rest.

They turned to the left of the chamber to head down a stairwell, their footsteps echoing across its narrow walls. Darkness soon covered them, although a faint light began to shine from the depths, acting as a convenient guide whilst they descended. They finally reached a basement, the light they'd followed turning out to be a single torch pressed into an alcove across from the stairs. The place was strewn with barrels, some open and empty, others sealed and filled with contents unknown. A single door lay ahead, solid and imposing, its surface illuminated by yet another torch ensconced in a slender metal brazier.

He knocked without ceremony this time, and an elderly gentleman, his face lined from the passing of seasons, opened up. He nodded once in greeting and stepped back, gesturing for them to enter. They did so, taking in the view before them.

Another cellar, spacious and draughty, with several corridors branching off to either side and a single door towards the rear. There was somebody else in here, sitting at a rickety table pressed against the eastern wall, their stocky, powerful frame and flowing beard difficult to miss.

"How goes it, Edmund?" the man asked. "Have your father's men given up the chase yet?"

"It looks clear," Edmund answered, revealing the bag he held as the old man who'd opened the door, Oscar, he thought his name was, took the cloak from his shoulders. "I couldn't see any trace of them or anyone acting out of the ordinary anyway," Edmund added. "Just starving refugees. They grow more numerous. But nobody looks to be of a mind to come and kill you yet, Ulfcytel."

The man himself smiled, a strained look, yet not without humour. Edmund had been out on the street often in the past couple of days, keeping watch for signs of the men his father had almost certainly sent out to search for them. He'd known he wouldn't give up looking just like that, not after what had happened. He didn't fear for himself. They wouldn't hurt him due to his status, and as unstable and cold as his father was, he wouldn't want to see either Edmund or his sister come to harm. The same could not be said for Ulfcytel after his recent and dramatic intervention in Æthelred's own halls. It was a minor miracle Edmund had been able to get them out unscathed.

Edmund turned to face the man who'd let him in from the street and escorted him down here. He seemed both a strange and impressive figure, his aged yet powerful physique commanding respect. Ulfcytel afforded him a genuine affection, despite his brash words before the king that had resulted in Æthelred ordering his death. Edmund had needed to think fast to save him. Even as moved by emotion as he was, it had been profoundly ill-advised to speak to his father like that. If Edmund knew Æthelred, he wouldn't just let that go. He'd have perhaps taken the insult from an ealdorman or some other notable, but not a commoner like Cenric. Things would have gone considerably easier if he'd kept his trap shut.

Edmund sat at Ulfcytel's table, Cenric vanishing without a word to resume his post guarding the entrance above. Edmund placed the bag on the table before opening it with almost tender care, revealing the precious treasures within. Two loaves of barley bread. Three large onions. A few carrots and a decent-sized wheel of cheese. He'd really had to haggle to get the cheese, but he'd done it. They could make a meal with this. Given the situation in the city, that was as luxurious as things would get. He felt almost decadent in contemplating it.

Ulfcytel grunted in approval. The door towards the rear of the chamber then eased open, a shadowy figure emerging to eventually reveal itself as Wulfhild. She moved up alongside Ulfcytel and placed an affectionate hand on his mountain of a shoulder, her husband returning the gesture by placing his hand over hers. She looked tired, Edmund thought, and she was still dressed as she had been during their ride down here from Snotingeham. He had not yet had the opportunity to ask her how she felt about the confrontation with their father, but he imagined she'd been troubled by it. She was fortunate in other ways, though. Neither of them had expected such a dramatic reunion with her husband. In that respect, they'd been truly blessed.

"So you got food?" asked Wulfhild, her voice quiet from fatigue. "I thought we had some in storage already? Surely such a feast as we have here would be of better use in feeding those on the streets."

"We don't know how long we'll be here, and the stuff in storage is good only if you like eating raw barley," Ulfcytel said. "Don't worry," he added, his eyes on Wulfhild, "we'll see if we can give what we can to those that need it…but I don't know why what's-his-face hadn't done that already. It's like he'd forgotten about this place until Cenric convinced him to let us use it."

"An innkeeper, isn't he?" asked Oscar, ambling over after hanging Edmund's cloak up with the others. "Runs the Hanged Man, close to the king's compound? I suppose he was using these rooms to store all sorts of things that over-spilled from his cellar."

"And now he's got an overspill of two aethelings and a crooked ealdorman!" laughed Ulfcytel, the table shaking with the force of his mirth. "And a bunch of old folks from Witenestaple! I bet he thought he'd been drinking too much of his own brew when he saw us!"

Edmund sniggered, Wulfhild and Oscar laughing so much Edmund feared Oscar might succumb to a coughing fit. Their situation was undeniably absurd. Edmund didn't know how Cenric had persuaded the innkeeper to turn this building over to them, but he'd been very grateful, although worried about whether the man could be trusted to not reveal their location.

"My father won't give up," Edmund said, the humour leaving him as quickly as it had come. "He'll keep looking for me and Wulfhild. And he won't be gentle with anyone else he finds."

"Aye, I understand," sighed Ulfcytel, rubbing at his mouth with his sleeve. "We should leave the city as soon as we can. There's nothing for me here, and I won't be separated from Wulfhild again." He turned to look up at his wife, a hint of concern in his eyes. "Unless you'd rather stay? I can't be the man to tell you to abandon your own father, as much as I loathe him."

"I will go wherever you go," Wulfhild answered with a squeeze of his shoulder. "I spent months shut up in those halls when you sent me from Eastengle. He doesn't care for me, and I'm tired of his coldness and instability. I just want a peaceful life. I hate the way he's come to hate you. I don't understand it."

"That makes two of us," Ulfcytel mumbled sadly. Edmund couldn't stomach speaking the truth of the matter out loud. He suspected Ulfcytel had already worked it out for himself. His father despised him because of his popularity and persistence in defending the country rather than blindly following whatever callous scheme had most recently hatched from the mind of Eadric. It was depressing to think of it in such terms, but it seemed to be the truth. As hard as it was to bear, the only way to stay in the king's favour was to submit to him entirely, even if he was totally wrong. Ulfcytel wasn't the kind of man to do that. Neither was Edmund.

Their morose thoughts were interrupted by a disturbance from upstairs. Somebody was hammering on something, a fist upon wood, the sound urgent and unrelenting. Edmund felt a flash of anxiety. He'd done his best to avoid detection, but it sounded like somebody had followed him here. He stood up when he heard footsteps thundering down the stairs towards them, wondering if he may have to defend himself here and now. They all turned anxiously, the door leading in from the staircase creaking open to reveal a worried-looking Cenric. He'd moved seriously fast to get down here in such a short space of time. He soon explained why.

"My lords, somebody is at the door, and they have not used the signal. I can't see who it is, and they won't desist. What shall I do?"

Ulfcytel got up, his look determined, like he thought to storm out into the street and make whoever it was depart by force. Edmund raised a hand to placate him. If he went charging off to confront the newcomer, he'd only advertise his presence here. If it were his father's men upstairs, then there was also a chance they'd try to kill him. Edmund had a dark feeling about this, and he was sure Ulfcytel's brute force approach wouldn't help them.

"Sit down, and I'll go and investigate," Edmund pleaded, his eyes darting towards his sister in hope of gaining her assistance.

"He's right," she said hurriedly. "Let Edmund and Cenric go and try to talk to them. They won't harm him."

"But they'll recognise him!" Ulfcytel countered gruffly. "If they see he's here, they'll work out the rest of us are nearby and do what they've come to do. Neither of us can be seen!"

"Cenric can open the door then," Edmund said, retrieving his cloak and putting it on. "I'll keep my face covered and stay out of sight. It might be somebody I can reason with if need be."

"Are you sure you were not followed?" Cenric asked, his green eyes still wide with worry.

"As sure as I can be. I'm not used to all this sneaking around, so I can't be certain. But I tried. Let's go."

They turned and left, Cenric and Edmund rushing up the stairs to enter the upper room. Edmund waved to the inhabitants to reassure them, hoping his presence might keep them at ease or at least prevent them from doing anything foolish. They then passed through the curtains leading towards the entrance, the hammering at the door continuing on and on without pause. Whoever it was seriously wanted a response.

Edmund stood back from the door, his cloak pulled tightly about himself and his form partially obscured in shadow. He nodded to Cenric, who unbarred the door and eased it open just a few inches. He paused, holding the door as if to brace himself upon it, assuming anyone out there with hostile intent would attempt to rush him and barge their way inside. Nothing of the kind took place. Cenric peered out, Edmund still motionless in the shadows.

He heard a voice, a familiar one. The person outside was known to him. They were not going away either, and Cenric's efforts to convince him he was merely the caretaker of a warehouse were falling flat. The exchange was going nowhere, but whoever it was had not attacked him nor threatened him with such an outcome. Cenric bid him wait, easing the door shut and turning to Edmund.

"He says he knows you!" he whispered. "I didn't confirm anything to him, but you must have been seen…he says he wants to help and has vital information for us! What do I say?"

Edmund decided to act. If this fellow had seen him enter the building, then there was no point in getting Cenric to keep up the ruse. He pulled his hood back and stepped forward, his hand reaching for the door. He heaved it open, ready and willing to deal with whoever lay beyond.

Edmund gasped with relief, his grin broad and sincere in the face of the man standing before him. He could tell it was him even without his armour, the faint scar running the length of his neck and up into his wedge of a beard giving his identity away. Ecgberht. Commander of his father's armies, or what was left of them. And he'd come alone, dressed as a commoner, his simple, long-sleeved grey kirtle, breecs, and cloak making him look like just about anyone else in a crowd. Edmund opened the door all the way and stepped back. Ecgberht took the invitation and slipped inside.

"What is it?" Edmund asked softly. "Why come here? Good heavens, man, I've not seen you in ages! What have you been doing with yourself?"

"It's a long story," Ecgberht whispered nervously. "Your father…he's lost, Edmund. It was all a lie. All of it. The heregeld. It was just a means to pay Thorkell!"

Edmund nodded, Ecgberht's revelation coming as no surprise, given his past doubts and suspicions. Cenric wasn't moved either, instead barring the door and turning to face Ecgberht like he was still some kind of potential threat.

"What do you come here as, Ecgberht?" Edmund asked sternly. "As my father's man, or my friend?"

"Your friend! There are things that weigh on my conscience…things that I have learned and that you must hear, but…" Ecgberht paused and looked around, his expression curious. "You've been hiding here the whole time?" he asked. "What is this place? Is it just you and your friend here?"

Edmund didn't answer, instead peeling back the curtain behind him to usher Ecgberht and Cenric into the adjacent room. The inhabitants recoiled at the sight of the stranger, uneasy and nervous to see somebody unknown pass freely amongst them. Ecgberht gazed upon them in confusion, likely wondering who these sorry-looking people were and why they all seemed so long in the tooth. Edmund walked past him with Cenric following, the three of them then descending the steps to make their way to the cellar.

Ecgberht stumbled in the darkness, Cenric clutching him by the shoulder to prevent his headlong plunge down the stairs. He righted himself, turning to thank Cenric before he continued following Edmund's lead. They finished their descent, passing through the storage area before opening the door to the main cellar.

Ulfcytel stood up and away from his chair upon seeing them, his broad arms folding threateningly across his broader chest. Wulfhild remained at his side, her expression cold as she spied Ecgberht stepping through the doorway. Oscar stood a little distance away, a nimble-looking axe clutched in his right hand. He had the bearing of a warrior, Edmund thought. He'd not seen it before, but now it was as clear as the day outside.

Others had emerged from the chamber beyond. Oscar's wife, whom Edmund had only heard referred to as "Swet", was now present, her two grandchildren clinging to her skirts apprehensively. There were several others, too, all of a ripe age and looking markedly disturbed at the presence of Ecgberht. They were probably still awed by what had happened the other day. Chances were few of them had even been to Lundenburg before, and yet their benefactor had ushered them into the king's own halls to witness a confrontation. That would have made an impression. No wonder their nerves were shot.

"You bring one of your father's men down here, Edmund." Ulfcytel wasn't asking a question, and his statement did nothing to dispel the mounting tension.

"He's not here as my father's man," Edmund said, approaching the table and pulling a chair back so that Ecgberht might sit. "He's come alone. He brings information about the heregeld, and more."

"I have," said Ecgberht, still on his feet, his manner guarded. "And with God as my witness, I mean no harm to any of you. I've been lost in doubt this past day and night, my heart troubled beyond endurance by the things I've seen and heard. The heregeld isn't for a new army, Ulfcytel. The king has purchased the services of Thorkell and what's left of his horde."

Ulfcytel grimaced, displeased yet not surprised. "I got that impression from my last little talk with him. He's done this kind of thing before. Why come here to just tell us that?"

"Because the cost is too great. It will take virtually everything we have. There'll be nothing left once Thorkell gets his agreed sum. The country is in ruins, the people starving…this will break England."

"Why does he do this?" asked Wulfhild, her head shaking mournfully. "Why does he always resort to this? Have they not had enough of English gold? It will only encourage them more. They'll always be back if they think we'll pay."

"My wife is more than correct," Ulfcytel said with a grim smile. "And here I fear lies the heart of my disagreements with the king. I would fight the enemy rather than pay them. If they'd had it made clear to them that England was a land of warriors rather than wealthy fops with no appetite for resistance, we'd be in a different situation now."

Edmund took a seat, hoping his actions would encourage the others to do likewise and end this tense stand-off. Cenric remained as he was, but Ecgberht took the hint and sat down, flexing his arms and placing his elbows upon the hard wooden surface of the table. Ulfcytel joined them, settling himself on the opposite side so he might face everyone directly. Wulfhild remained standing just behind him, her hands again on his shoulders, Oscar and the others also looking on.

"What do you suggest we do, Ecgberht?" Ulfcytel finally asked. "And what else can you tell us? We've all known for some time that Æthelred might try this. Tell me…how ever did you find us?"

"I have many men under my authority," replied Ecgberht. "And I know Edmund. He made a great display of himself the other day when he came here and pretty much gave all he had to those who needed it. I thought he might be out on the street again soon enough. And I was right."

"So you were seen, Edmund!" Ulfcytel said. "I told you this would happen. You're too recognisable, even when you're all dressed up like that. If Ecgberht and his boys can spot you, then so can Eadric or whoever else wants a beef with us. Thank heavens Ecgberht hasn't told the king."

"I have not, and I will not," Ecgberht assured them all. "It's not my business, and from what I've seen of the king, I'm not surprised you've fallen afoul of him. The man has been poisoned, in his heart and in his mind. I don't trust him to weather the storm that's coming. And that Eadric…he's likely the culprit…he grows in power by the day. And he's been given yet more authority, of a sort he will only abuse."

"What do you mean?" asked Edmund, wondering if he really wanted to hear this.

"The king has given Eadric the task of depopulating the city," announced Ecgberht, his expression heavy. "I've refused to give him any of my men to help him do it. I don't trust him, and what they propose is merciless. They've decided there's too many people here…that they'll eat too much of what little we have left and leave us vulnerable to what's coming…like I said, I've refused to give Eadric command of any of my men, but I can't hold out long. If the king directly orders me to hand my people over…"

"A cold plan," Ulfcytel rumbled. "Those people have lost everything and have nowhere to go. But you said something was coming? What could that be?"

"King Svienn has arrived with a great host," Ecgberht elaborated, his words making the hairs on Edmund's neck stand on end. "His fleet was spotted off Remmesgate a couple of days ago. My people have confirmed he's landed already at Sandwice. He has thousands of men, and we got word before I came here that it's not just him we have to worry about…apparently, he's been active in the north already, rowing up the Humbre and demanding all submit to him. Rumour is the Ealdorman Uhtred has pledged obedience."

"Already?" Ulfcytel scoffed. "He hasn't even seen much of the fighting yet, and he just capitulates like that? The man's a snake. Another creature the king's content to let writhe at his feet. He'll regret that now, I expect. The loss of Norþanhymbre will be a real blow."

"It is, but we have other concerns," continued Ecgberht. "Svienn's main force is making its way west, so my scouts say, obtaining the submission of anyone that will bow to him. I also received a report this morning indicating he may already be heading this way. We'll be under siege soon, and we don't have the strength to repel him."

"Who alerted you to all of this?" Edmund asked, concerned about the possibility of misinformation intended to panic the populace. "Was it one of your own men who saw Svienn's fleet at Remmesgate? I was under the impression all of Cantwara was in ruins now."

"He wasn't one of my lot. He stormed in here yesterday, riding a gaunt horse and looking half-starved and beaten. He was bellowing at my men on the gates, saying he had to see me, saying Svienn had returned. I saw him. I believed him. I took him before the king…"

"And?" Ulfcytel prodded, eager to hear more.

"The king knew who he was! Recognised him on sight! Gave him a proper earful, too, Eadric also acting all high and mighty towards him. Eadric wanted to kill him, but I wasn't having it. So they had me lock him in a cell. That was his reward for warning us! It's not just."

"What is his name?" Cenric demanded suddenly, moving closer to the table to loom over the proceedings.

"Alaric, I think," answered Ecgberht, his neck twisting slightly as he turned in his chair to answer. "Grim-looking man, he was. Just one eye. Smelled bad, too. Like blood and death. Been fighting for a while, I'd suspect. That's why I believed him. He looked too damn tough to be dishonest."

Edmund frowned, concerned at the expressions now on both Ulfcytel and Cenric's faces. They had somehow managed to look surprised, relieved, and horrified all at once, Cenric, in particular, appearing downright emotional at what had been said. In truth, Edmund could remember meeting Alaric some time ago, and he'd also met his wife, Æva, shortly after she'd been imprisoned. He felt almost guilty that he'd then largely forgotten about either of them, the battle at Bernecestre and the loss of his brother taking up much of his mind. Judging from the reaction from Ulfcytel and Cenric, however, it seemed this Alaric was still very much a person of interest.

"So he made it," Ulfcytel whispered, awestruck. "He actually got out. How in God's blessed name…"

"I've prayed for this," said Cenric, a slight quaver creeping into his voice. "On the journey here and after, whenever I had a chance, I prayed for God to give us some sign that there was yet hope. This is it. And now I hear it, I can't quite believe it."

"What's there to believe?" asked Ecgberht, his eyes darting from Ulfcytel to Cenric in bewilderment. "Who is this man to you? Family?"

"He is to me," answered Cenric firmly. "I've known him since he was a boy. Trained him. Saw him grow and became proud of the man he is. And yet now he's imprisoned like the rest of his family…I cannot let this go. I can't."

"The rest of his family? Who? So the king has reasons for all this?"

"No, or at least none that are any good," said Ulfcytel. "Alaric helped lead a sneak attack on Thorkell himself just days before the fight at Hringmere. He somehow survived all that and joined me in our attack on Gipeswic and escape to Canterburie. After the big fight there…I thought he must be dead. I thought…I should have…"

"You were not conscious, my lord," said Cenric. "Alaric ordered me to take you out of there, and so I did. There was nothing you could have done at that point. You'd been wounded twice over."

"This Alaric certainly has a way of finding himself in strange situations," said Edmund with a shake of his head. "I encountered him by chance when I was on the move with Æthelstan and Morcar. He looked like a hardy enough sort, but I'd have never thought he'd have such a capacity for surviving. God must have plans for him."

"It's his wife, too," said Cenric. "He cares for her with a passion and dedication I've rarely seen. He'll fight through just about anything to get back to her. And now, in a way, he is back with her."

Edmund contemplated telling them of his conversation with Æva when he'd reunited her with her son. He decided not to mention it, feeling sorrowful for not doing more for her and just leaving her to her fate whilst he waged war in Oxenefordscir. He had intended to again question Alaric's father, the Ealdorman Ælfric, on the information he'd uncovered about his alleged efforts to convince the king to embezzle Church property, but he'd failed in that, his father's latest episode forcing him to hide out with Ulfcytel in this dank cellar.

But that didn't mean he would just sit here, nor could they all vacate the city to plan afresh from a distance. Edmund had an ugly feeling his father would become even more vindictive now he had Alaric in custody. He could even seek to kill him. That would be a harsh fate and an undoubted tragedy for the wife and child he'd leave behind. They couldn't allow that to happen. For their sake and for the sake of his father, he had to act. Murder was a terrible sin. He couldn't permit that to weigh upon his soul.

Edmund sat up, his eyes brightening as ideas ran through his mind. "How long until Svienn's army reaches us?" he asked, knowing it would be far easier to flee the city with Alaric and his family if it wasn't already under siege.

"Not long," answered Ecgberht. "Now that he's gained the submission of the north, there's not much left for him to do but attack us here. I'd say we'll be hearing from him within a day or two."

"What are you thinking, Edmund?" Ulfcytel had narrowed his eyes, the slight smile creeping across his lips suggesting he already knew the answer to his question.

"I'm thinking what you think I'm thinking," said Edmund, smiling back. "And it's not just out of sympathy with Alaric. I take your word for it that he's a good man. But I fear for my father, too. He's been obsessed with him for months. I feel something terrible is about to happen, and we can prevent it by getting Alaric as far away from here as possible."

"And the rest of his family?" Cenric didn't need to ask, but he had. It would make the entire enterprise a lot harder, but it had to be done. They couldn't just leave the rest of them there. The king would take it out on them if he realised Alaric had escaped alone.

"Have no fear, my man," Ulfcytel assured him. "We'll get them all out. Now we just need to think on how."

"I can help," said Ecgberht. "Many of the warriors stationed within the king's halls will do as I ask as long as Æthelred isn't standing right there to contradict me. I can reduce the guard around the gates and the prison tower and order those on duty to let Edmund pass unhindered. That shouldn't arouse too much suspicion. After all, you remain an aetheling. Anyone who sees you will assume you wish to reconcile with your father."

That was very workable, Edmund thought. The difficulty now lay in actually getting to Alaric and freeing him and his people. It would look incredibly strange for Edmund to be seen just walking with them. Even those most loyal to Ecgberht would think it wrong for an entire family of prisoners to come wandering out of the tower. They'd have to think of a diversion to draw off prying eyes. As it stood, he had no idea what that might be.

There were other problems, too. If Thorkell really was now in the king's service, then that could mean a massive amount of coin was about to be delivered into his possession. England could not resist Svienn if it were bankrupt. They needed money, and not only for the military situation. The people needed relief, particularly in terms of food, and they might not get that if Thorkell made off with all the coin required to pay merchants to bring it to them. The bastard had already brutalised them beyond endurance. It was incredibly unlikely he'd spare a thought for them going hungry.

"We'll need to get into the treasure vault somehow," Edmund announced suddenly, ignoring the surprised look on Ulfcytel's face. "Like I said, it's not just about Alaric. If Thorkell is paid what Ecgberht thinks he's getting, then it will be another disaster for us. We have to get our hands on at least some of the money."

"And do what with it?" Ecgberht exclaimed, dismayed at the prospect of further complications. "We can't just ride in and load up a cart with chests of treasure and then amble off with a bunch of prisoners. And where would we stash the money?"

"Snotingeham," Edmund answered without hesitation. "The Five Boroughs. You all know Sigeferth and Morcar will take me in. They'll take you all in, too. We can work from there, building up a centre of resistance against Svienn…and Uhtred in Norþanhymbre. Overthrowing him should be our priority. We need the north with us, not subjugated under the rule of a man who capitulates at the first sight of a forked beard."

Ulfcytel snorted at the mention of Uhtred, sounding partly amused and partly derisive. Edmund found himself wondering why Ulfcytel might have taken such a dislike to the man. As far as he was aware, they'd had no heated disagreements in public or much to do with each other at all. Then he recalled what Sigeferth and Morcar had told him about the murder of Ælfhelm and the subsequent expansion of Uhtred's authority over all Norþanhymbre. He didn't know if Ulfcytel knew about all that, but he'd bet money he had suspicions and just didn't trust Uhtred as a result. That was fair enough, he supposed. Ulfcytel prided himself on a certain rough and robust virtue, something that just wasn't compatible with the courtly intrigue associated with Uhtred and many other so-called notables.

Ulfcytel sat in thought for a moment, his face doubly serious. "So you already have a great campaign laid out for us?" he asked, as if resenting Edmund's proposals. "We need to focus on one thing at a time," he then added, "for although I would see Alaric freed, there's no sense in complicating things further. A raid on the treasury is more than complicated. I don't like complicated."

"I understand," replied Edmund, "but if Ecgberht can use his influence to minimise the guard, we can free Alaric and still ensure we have some money to resist Svienn. It's either that or allow Thorkell to just take everything. That's not an option. I need that money if I'm to…"

"Become king?" Ulfcytel asked, his voice now laden with cynicism. Edmund didn't like that. The ealdorman was becoming suspicious of him, and it wasn't right. He'd saved his life just days ago. It wasn't fair to suspect him of anything here, and he wasn't in the mood for a lecture on how he had to consider the wishes of his brother, Eadwig. He'd already had that from Sigeferth.

"You know my advice is sound," Edmund said evenly, refusing to back down. "Alaric isn't just one man. His imprisonment is just a single part of a whole sequence of bad decisions my father has made. Understand that. We won't win here if we don't look at the big picture."

Ulfcytel didn't reply, instead staring at Edmund like he'd said nothing at all and there was nothing to consider. Edmund was about to speak again when he heard something. A dull roar, or a multitude of such things, like a great and angry crowd was somewhere above them. Ulfcytel could hear it, too, his face straining with concentration as he tried to identify what it was.

"You hear that?" asked Cenric, gazing up at the ceiling. "It's like there's a mob out there. I'll go and look."

He turned to leave, Edmund rising to accompany him. "I'll go with you," he said, not wanting to be left behind with an argumentative Ulfcytel. Ecgberht also joined them, and they began vaulting up the stairs, unwilling to wait for anyone else. Ulfcytel remained behind, thankfully, but that seemed to be largely because Wulfhild had engaged him in another argument about why he had to stay out of sight. He was a stubborn one. Edmund would be sure to thank Wulfhild for her intervention. The last thing he wanted was for Ulfcytel to get over-excited at the spectacle of drama and accidentally reveal himself to any potential assassins. The man was about as subtle as a drunken ox at times.

They reached the upper room, the noise from outside now so loud they were almost sure some kind of riot was taking place. Cenric paused to reassure the room's occupants, who were all alarmed and a little frightened at both the disturbance and the continued presence of the stranger, Ecgberht. They passed through the curtain barrier, Cenric in the lead as he opened the door a tad so he might peer outside. He looked left and right and stepped out, Edmund and Ecgberht following, the noise increasing all the more now they were in the open air.

Whatever it might be was nearby, most likely out on the main street. Edmund shut the door behind them and broke into a light jog so that he might keep pace with Cenric, who had begun to move off towards the disturbance. His feet again splashed through puddles as they turned to the right, each moving in single file to navigate their way back along the alley providing access to the street. The noise seemed to get louder with each step. It was either a riot, or the citizens of Lundenburg had grown bored with their predicament and decided to vent their frustrations with a shouting contest. Edmund thought the former more likely.

Cenric slowed in front of him, crouching low whilst he approached the intersection that would take them out into the open. He glanced around the corner, Edmund noting how his eyes widened as he took in whatever was happening. He stepped out into the street, motioning back to Edmund that he should raise the hood of his cloak. He did so, begrudging himself for being so forgetful. Cenric had raised his hood before he'd even stepped out of their hiding place. If he were taking such precautions, it was doubly imperative that Edmund do the same. If there really was a mob on the rampage, there was no telling how they might react if they saw an aetheling in their path.

It wasn't quite that dramatic. The alleyway they'd just emerged from abutted a wide thoroughfare that led in from Billings Gate on the south eastern edge of the city. It was broad, well-paved, and largely straight, one that could easily allow a reasonably large column of men to march on through without having to reform their ranks. That seemed to be happening now, but the local citizenry were outraged, screaming obscenities at the approaching force and sporadically pelting them with stones. Other warriors were moving around the column in a bid to keep things peaceful, but they were having a hard time of it, and the mob's fury grew by the second.

Edmund didn't understand. He scratched his beard, thoughtful yet concerned, Ecgberht's next words only adding to his confusion. "I'm sorry, Edmund," he said bitterly. "I wish there'd been a way to avoid this. I…I'm sorry."

Edmund looked back at him, his brow creased in a deep frown. He turned just in time to see the banner, the image upon it and the approaching men who bore it clearly visible now they'd advanced further towards them. Ravens. There were ravens on the banner, black and glossy and glaring out from the fabric with a life of their own. They were surrounding something; a horrifying, one-eyed figure that seemed half human and half beast, the birds at times perching upon its massive shoulders. Not a Christian image, and the same went for the men beneath it. No wonder the crowd was so agitated. These were Norsemen. In Lundenburg! His father had actually done it. The sheer nerve! The outrage! After all the blood and misery Thorkell had inflicted on them, here he was, marching in with his force of killers like he owned the place!

Edmund soon caught sight of him. A giant of a man, riding a grey, heavily-muscled horse, an unnecessarily large axe strapped to his unnecessarily broad back. His armour sparkled and shone like it were wet; the recent downpour probably catching him as he crossed the Temes to demand entry to the city he'd thus far failed to take by force. Those behind him looked worse, muddied and damp, some bloodied from some prior engagement. They still looked fearsome, regardless, possessing an air of savagery that spoke to an abundance of cruel deeds they'd yet to answer for.

Edmund was rooted to the spot, his every instinct screaming at him to either run or fight. He saw now that those attempting to hold back the crowd were Englishmen from the garrison. Theirs was a thankless and humiliating task, one that would certainly earn them the enmity of those starving commoners now screeching their frustrations upon the uncaring ears of their foreign tormentors. Edmund sincerely hoped they'd ultimately succeed in keeping the two sides separate. If anyone was foolish enough to rush Thorkell's men, there'd be bloodshed in no time.

Thorkell was about two dozen paces away when their eyes met. Edmund felt a jolt of something pass up his spine, the sensation so cold and sharp he almost wondered if he'd been struck. There was something massively unwholesome about Thorkell, his eyes appearing as glassy, blank portals to something absolutely horrifying. If Thorkell was similarly unsettled by the sight of Edmund, he gave no indication, merely holding his gaze for a few seconds before looking away, his expression blank.

Several other mounted warriors were present, one a younger man with an ornate scabbard and a similar set of ring mail, the other a burly-looking monster in a helm painted partially red. Edmund didn't know the significance of either, but he fancied he sensed Cenric flinch at the sight of the latter, as if he, too, were struggling to suppress some innermost instinct that was screaming for violence. The tension didn't ebb with their passing, and the rest of Thorkell's men marched on after them, the thunderous scraping of their boots harsh and discordant upon the stones.

And there were many of them. Despite whatever difficulties Thorkell had encountered before and after taking Canterburie, it looked like a great number of his men had survived and remained loyal to him. There must be hundreds of them here, possibly more, all of them following their fearsome leader north into the city in the direction of his father's halls. That made perfect sense. They'd be wanting payment, or at least to see the money before swearing loyalty, not that the word of a Dane meant anything to anyone halfway sane. But therein was the problem. His father's mind. That had always been the issue. And now, just as before, Edmund had no notion of what to do about it.

He stepped away, taking Cenric's arm to usher him back into the alley they'd come from. Ecgberht paused a few seconds, his head bowed low in sadness before joining them, their footsteps quick and sharp as they hurried towards their hideout.

"This complicates everything," Edmund said aloud. "It was one thing to rescue Alaric from my father as planned, but we now have hundreds of savages in our way. If we ever needed a miracle, we need it now."

"Then let us pray for one," Cenric answered. "Because come what may, I will not abandon Alaric. I had to desert his kin once before in the hope of finding help. I won't do so again. If we do nothing, they'll all die, either by the king's hand or Svienn's, if and when he takes the city. I will not allow that. I mean it, Edmund. In a few days, they'll either be free, or I'll be dead. You can either help me or leave me to it. But I will not be denied this."

XXVII

He tried to blink. Nothing. All was blackness. He lifted his hands to his face, recoiling in pain at his touch. They'd really done a job on him. He wished he could say he'd stayed strong. Defiance in the face of evil was always to be admired. But few people who'd judge him now would have ever gone through what he'd just endured. It was easy to talk heroic when there was no call for heroism. He'd done it himself in the past. Now he understood how cheap such boasts truly were.

Alaric heaved his legs up and back, using the rear wall of his cell to prop himself into a sitting position. He breathed, slow and steady, trying to calm and soothe his racing heart. He could now see just a little out of his eye, swollen as it was, his dim surroundings coming into focus the more he concentrated.

There was a flimsy chair several feet away, and a narrow but solid oak door about six feet after that, bolted and sealed shut on heavy iron hinges. There was also a bed, or at least a shabby approximation of one, just over to his left, looking more like a single ragged blanket atop a sack of mouldering straw. About five feet up the wall at his back was a narrow opening, not even a half-foot across in width or length, that served as a window to the outside world. He couldn't see much out of it even before he'd been beaten senseless, and he wasn't going to try and take in the view now. His cell was otherwise unadorned, the bare stone walls largely featureless and almost hostile in their starkness.

He'd known Eadric was a cur, but he'd had no idea just how much he was capable of. He'd come to him shortly after he'd been imprisoned here, getting one of his lackeys to tie his hands so that Eadric, of course, would remain safe from any attempt on his person. He'd questioned him over and over, always on the same point, demanding to know where Wulfnoth was. He wouldn't tell him. The effeminate fop would have to do better than simply raise his voice if he were to get anything from him.

Then something truly astonishing had happened. A figure he'd not expected to see had stepped into the room, fully armoured and muddied from the road, his expression one of triumphant, undisguised malice. Eadric had gloated, pleased at the sight of Alaric's apprehension and voicing his pleasure at "bringing old friends together."

He'd prattled on like that for some time, stating glibly how this new arrival had "not forgotten" him and was looking forward to "repaying you for the wounds you gave him in Canterburie". It was all tedious, sadistic waffle as far as Alaric was concerned. This was how a weak man spoke when he believed himself to have the advantage, and there was nothing weaker in all the world than a sadist. Eadric was certainly one of those.

The armoured man had then spoken after retrieving something from a coin purse at his belt. "Do you recognise this, Alaric?" he'd asked, showing off the ring before slipping it onto the third finger of his right hand. Alaric had glared. The ring was Æthelstan's, the one Alaric had retrieved after he and Osmund had discovered his corpse back at Thorkell's camp in Eastengle. This sneering fool had no business wearing it, and the same went for that sword and scabbard that still hung from his waist. Alaric would have them both returned.

"It's not yours, Hemingr. What is this? You're proud of the fact you're a thief as well as a murderer and slaver? The man who bore that ring was…well, he was a man. Not a mindless beast. Which do you think you qualify as?"

Alaric hadn't minded that first punch. He'd probably confused him, since there was a good chance the stupid bastard had assumed the ring was Alaric's own wedding band. Hemingr had probably looked to take some kind of perverse pleasure by striking him whilst wearing it. The ring had indeed made the blow sting all the more, but he'd gotten under Hemingr's skin, and that was always something to be happy about.

It was the blows that had followed that were hard to bear. It had gone on and on, and Eadric had kept repeating the same few questions: "Where is Wulfnoth? How many men does he have? What does he have planned?" over and over, Hemingr rarely giving Alaric a chance to spit an insult in his direction before the battering resumed.

He'd felt fear. His face had gone numb, as had his stomach, the fluid remains of his last meal splattering out across the floor. There'd been blood in his vomit, and not just a pinch either. Hemingr hadn't let up, showing absolutely no mercy as he continued to rain down more and more blows, his expression gleefully manic. Alaric did not want to die. He never had. He wanted to get back home, to how things had been before he'd marched to Eastengle and somehow changed his fate for the worse. He'd held up his hands in a pleading gesture, his bloodied, split lips parting to form words. Hemingr had then paused. Eadric had looked pleased. Alaric had spoken.

"H-he's h-heading west. He intends to…seek refuge in Wiltunscir and…wait to see who wins here."

"And how many men does he have?" Eadric snapped.

"N-n-not many. About a hundred. They only saved me at Canterburie…as as as he th…thought I'd be worth a ransom. I was more trouble for him…than I was worth."

Of course, it was all nonsense. Wulfnoth had commanded about thirty men in his camp east of Canterburie, which would bring his number to just over forty once you included Osbert and Eamon and the other survivors from the siege. He also wasn't heading for Wiltunscir, but Eadric would have to waste time and effort seeing if any of that were true. He'd no doubt suitably punish Alaric once he found out he'd been tricked, but that could be weeks from now. A lot could have changed by then.

"You wouldn't lie to me, would you, Alaric?" Eadric had taken on a certain expression; blank yet menacing, his eyes dark and hollow so that he barely looked human. Alaric had thought it unwise to lay emphasis on his honesty. Eadric would have seen through it, and the beatings would then recommence. He'd instead opted for something more realistic.

"What do you think, Eadric? I d-d-despise you and would see you dead…yet I don't want to die here…and Wulfnoth…he and I have no high regard for each other. Run yourself ragged chasing him. Leave me out of it."

It was an ordeal even to speak, but he'd managed it. Eadric had nodded his head just once in acknowledgement, accepting what was, in actuality, another half-truth from Alaric. He did very much want Eadric dead, but everything else he'd uttered was fiction. Wulfnoth had saved him, and he wouldn't betray him just like that. Yet he was ashamed at his own weakness. He'd always thought he'd be able to endure an interrogation without fear or fragility. He'd been wrong. But at least he'd bought himself some time. Eadric must have thought him sincere on some level. He'd actually cut the rope around his wrists before leaving.

Alaric had made himself busy leaning back against the wall. This was serious business, since after the hammering he'd taken, sitting upright was an achievement in itself. He didn't know how long he'd stayed like that, but it was getting dark by the time he managed to open his eye properly. It would swell further in time, he suspected, but for the moment he at least had some sight back.

There sadly wasn't much to look at. His cell appeared as uninspiring as before, the deepening shadows doing nothing for his already dark mood. Looking out of the opening above might help, but that was all dependent on him having the physical strength to stand up. He tried once. He landed straight back on his arse again. A second time sent him almost toppling forward so that he was compelled to shift his weight backwards to slam back against the wall. His third attempt proved lucky. He was upright, palms flat against the wall for support, but still upright.

He was facing the opening, the cool air of another spring evening washing over him to sharpen his senses. They'd placed a couple of bars across the gap, as if somehow otherwise it might be possible for a prisoner to squeeze through the narrow space and go on to survive the considerable fall into the courtyard below. Alaric wasn't such a man, nor was any other he'd met. You'd have to be the size of a dog to be able to escape like that. If anyone existed who was of comparable dimensions, Alaric had never seen them.

He inhaled deeply, filling his lungs with fresh air. It felt good, but his body reacted badly; a sudden cramping of the stomach leaving him dry heaving against the wall. Hemingr had given him possibly the worst beating he'd ever endured, and he could tell from the metallic taste in his mouth that his nausea was most likely caused by his own bleeding. He didn't know if it was possible for him to bleed to death internally, but he felt it wise to try and think about something else. Scaring himself wasn't a sound plan right now. He had enemies enough to do that for him.

He tried to focus on what lay in front of him. From the view, he guessed he'd been confined to some kind of prison tower within the fortified compound that served as the king's bastion in the capital. The daylight was fading, but he could still see out beyond the gate from here, the densely packed buildings of the rest of the city huddling together as if anxious in the face of the coming dark.

There was something on the wind, a sound as well as a smell, both of which he somehow knew were connected. Angry voices. Lots of them. Some kind of disturbance, further out in the streets. A crowd perhaps, or more likely a mob, enraged and looking for trouble. Something was burning somewhere. Wood and thatch, not on the scale of Canterburie, but unmistakable all the same. He'd had enough of that smell for a lifetime.

He got to thinking, his breath slow and steady, his eye still fixed on the darkening skyline. Try as he might, he could not keep troubling notions at bay. Was this the end for him? Was he to die in this cell, bleeding out from the blows of an enemy he'd almost bested just weeks ago? Or would he survive this only to then fall victim to the unstable machinations of King Æthelred; a man who hated him for reasons unknown? Was that fair? Was that justice, after all he'd been through? Why would God, in his wisdom, ever permit it?

Alaric knew from experience that he didn't like to think on such matters. When misfortune struck, there was always somebody who claimed it was "God's will", as if God was entirely capricious in his judgements and enjoyed bestowing random agonies on His people for generally unfathomable reasons. That had never made a lot of sense to Alaric, and neither had the claim that God "allows evil" for certain purposes; a notion that seemed to imply the death of a child or the loss of a cherished friend was some grand lesson for the betterment of all. Alaric had rapidly learned to avoid those who talked like this, realising they were more interested in shocking others and appearing overly pious than helping anyone.

Besides, if they were such good Christians, they'd be more concerned with alleviating the sufferings of others rather than looking for reasons to justify them. There were no justifications to be had in many cases. Bad things happened sometimes, and there was indeed such a thing as bad luck. A man might trip and fall one day, or discover that his child was not his after all. God didn't will such things, nor did He just shrug at the sight of them like the misery of His children was of no real consequence. That wasn't the God he knew. That wasn't the Christ that had come.

Yet a seed had been planted. Doubt crept into Alaric's mind, tying his lonely fate to the possibility of divine judgement. It wasn't right. He didn't deserve to suffer like this. What had he done? He'd tried to be a good man, a good Christian, his whole life. He'd wanted to march to Eastengle and help fight Thorkell. He'd been aware of the possibility of defeat and death, but he'd never expected things to turn out as they had. These past months had been a sorry story, of the type he'd not want to even hear, let alone participate in himself. To have it end like this, trapped as the plaything of a grasping Eadric and a deranged king, was too much. That wasn't just. He'd not deserved this.

Anxiety crept up on him, mingling with his bitterness to spur on yet more troubling thoughts. Much of his life hadn't been fair. He'd lost his home in Wiltune and then had to endure the ultimate humiliation; his wife impregnated by another man. The dream he'd had in Canterburie had been right, speaking to fears he'd long suppressed. Brandon wasn't his, and he couldn't stand that. There was no point in denying it any longer. He couldn't raise the child. He'd be rotten, just like he had been in his dream. It might take years to become apparent, but he was sure it was only a matter of time before the boy showed his true colours. He had the blood of savages in his veins. Alaric was a fool for thinking himself noble in attempting to father such a creature.

Brandon would be sent away, to a monastery or somewhere, Alaric cared not. He would not tolerate this stain on his honour, and Æva's inevitable objections were nothing when it came to something as precious as honour. He then wondered if Æva had even enjoyed watching him suffer as he played the father. Perhaps she hadn't been forced after all. She could have lain with the Dane willingly, lust lighting up her eyes just as it had in his dream when she'd beheld Hemingr. He hadn't had the vision for no reason. It was trying to tell him something. He knew that now. He'd been betrayed all this time, a cuckold and a fool. This would not stand.

He gritted his teeth, a torrent of fresh, hot anger rising up from his stomach. He could still hear the sounds of a disturbance outside, the angry cacophony escalating into a generalised outpouring of primal rage and indignation. He could relate to that. That was his world now. He might be powerless, but he'd always have his hatred. He'd nurture it, holding fast to his black fury no matter what was thrown at him. They could take everything away, but his hate would never leave him. It was his, the only thing he had left, a weapon that would never desert him and always stay true and potent until his last breath.

He was breathing fast now, his lungs heaving in great hissing breaths from between his bared teeth. He couldn't stop the thoughts, the memories of every hurt and dishonour he'd ever experienced playing out before him. He'd get even. He'd right this wrong. He'd be a man again, and damn the consequences. He'd kill every foreign bastard on English soil, and then he'd kill more of them for the sake of it, brutalising his enemies, heathen or otherwise, until every slight had been answered for.

A low, continuous growl began to emerge from his throat, the sound reverberating within the hard walls of his prison. A dark and terrible malevolence took hold, its black energy seeming to course through his veins to gift him with renewed strength. He snapped his head up, his bloodied eye fixed straight ahead and out across the city, his mouth opening wide to unleash a single, undulating scream of anger and despair. Like his growl, his furious shout echoed within his cell, his own fury repeating in his ears, over and over, long after he himself had fallen silent. He wished he could say he felt better. He didn't. Only righteous retribution would slake his thirst now. Let those who'd heard him come. They'd find a man here whose desire for violence would always exceed their own.

"Who's there?"

A voice, uncertain and wavering, feminine and familiar. His anger ebbed a little, another emotion stirring within to push it from prominence. Yet more memories stirred, and the hate left him, spiralling down and down whence it had come. He shuddered, his hands still pressed against the wall, every ache in his body reminding him of his sorrowful predicament. He knew who it was. He'd know that voice anywhere. He was sworn to her, body and soul.

"Æva."

"Alaric?"

It was her. He breathed out, relief flooding his limbs. His vision clouded over, forcing him to blink back tears. He tried to ascertain where her voice was coming from. It was somewhere above him, on another level in this damned tower, her cell no doubt as spartan as his own. She'd heard his scream, probably rushing to an opening in her cell just like the one he now stood at. It didn't matter. All he needed to know of was her safety.

"Are you alright? Where are you? Have you been here all this time?"

"Yes!" she cried, sounding both elated and relieved. "I feared you dead! I waited so long, I've been so alone, but you've come!"

He paused, feelings of shame replacing his last vestiges of anger. He'd come close to falling. His hate had threatened to make him a beast of a man, one turned against all humanity, his wife included. Alaric had never felt such a cascade of sheer foulness in his entire life, nor had he thought himself capable of such. But he was. The remarkable thing was Æva had snapped him out of it just through the sound of her voice. She had absolutely no idea what a gift that was.

"Where are you? Is Brandon with you? How did any of this even happen?"

"I don't know why," she said. "But Eadric turned up with hundreds of men, shouting something about treason. We fended him off, but he started…he started killing people he'd seized elsewhere, trying to shock and shame us into surrendering. We slipped away by boat but were betrayed in Suthhamtunam."

"I heard all of this from Cenric. He found me in Canterburie."

Æva fell silent for a few seconds, as if surprised Cenric had managed to do such a thing. "He's a brave man, isn't he?" she finally said. "So where is he now? Why were you in Canterburie?"

"I don't know where he is," Alaric confessed. "I ordered him to take the Ealdorman Ulfcytel away from the city after Thorkell wounded him. As far as I know, he got away, but that's all. Everything was so chaotic. I was captured and..."

"Thorkell?" Æva said the name with some considerable anxiety. "You saw him? He came to Canterburie?"

Alaric sighed. His wife really had been in captivity for a long time. He couldn't imagine how hard the winter had been on her, if her cell was as uncomfortable as his. It was a testament to her resolve that she'd made it through. It occurred to him, though, that she'd as yet failed to give answer on the location of Brandon and the rest of his family. He needed to know.

"Yes, he came," said Alaric. "There was a great battle. But Æva... what of Brandon and my father and brother? Are they safe?"

"I have not seen them since I was thrown in here," she said sadly. "The king wasn't making sense when we saw him. He thought Ælfric had betrayed him somehow and that it wasn't the first time. I didn't understand it. They took Brandon from me, but then Edmund, the aetheling, brought him back to me! Then Edmund went away...and they came and took Brandon again...that was months ago, I think..."

Her voice faded. She sounded sad but also erratic, akin to someone having trouble marshalling their thoughts. It was no shame, given the length of her imprisonment, but it was difficult for a man to hear. She must have been half-crazed waiting for him to come to her, and now he finally had, he was powerless to give her proper comfort. To think the king would do this to her and the rest of them, too, all because of the alleged crimes of his father...Alaric didn't know what to think, but it all amounted to yet another injustice perpetrated by a man who had long lost any credibility as a monarch.

"So Edmund came to see you?" he said slowly, wanting to settle things in her mind as clearly and gently as possible. "Why did he do that? Did he want something?"

"He wanted to know about you. I don't know why, but the king is obsessed with you. Something about a dream. Something about him killing his brother, or you thinking he did. I couldn't tell Edmund much then. The king had me brought to him one night and..."

"And what?" Alaric asked urgently. If he'd laid a hand on her, he didn't know what he'd do. He felt the rage rising again, building up within him. He'd never heard of Æthelred favouring the wives of others, but if it were true in this case, he'd remove his manhood before this was over. It was bad enough that he was a vindictive and incapable fool. To be a sexual predator also was beyond the limit.

"He struck me," said Æva bitterly. "It was cold, it was always so cold, and he had me dragged to a garden of his and he ranted at me and hit me. Then they threw me back in here. It's always so cold, Alaric, and I...I don't know what I might look like now...I hope..."

"If you're suggesting that I may no longer be pleased by the sight of you, then put such thoughts out of your mind. Put them far away, Æva. And then bury them. Burn them first. Then bury them. Then dig them up and throw them into the sea. And never speak of them again."

He heard a sound from above, light and delicate, something he'd not heard in almost a year. He'd missed it, only realising now how much he'd yearned for it. She was laughing, a faint sound, for sure, but there it was. That was his wife. She was still there, regardless of what had been done to her or how heavily the burdens of captivity yet weighed on her. She was there, and he loved her for it.

"I lost an eye." His mouth dropped in surprise at his admission. He hadn't thought to say that, but he had, like he'd been somehow spurred on to admit it in the face of her own fears on her appearance.

"How?" she asked without hesitation.

"Fighting," he said bluntly. "The blow would have killed me if I'd not been wearing my helmet. That was when…Æva …Osmund is dead."

"How?" she asked again, sad now rather than just worried.

"We were betrayed. It's complicated. But they killed Osmund. They killed everybody. I only just made it. It's been a hard journey, Æva. I'm sorry all this happened. I'm sorry you got caught up in this."

"It's all right," she soothed gently. "It's not your fault. But how did you come to be here? Were you going to petition the king for my release? Is Cenric with you?"

"He is not." Alaric didn't know what to say aside from that. He'd already told her he didn't know where Cenric was. If he also told her that Sviens Forkbeard himself had again invaded England at the head of a great host, it might push her over the edge. It was bad enough being imprisoned like this, but to tell her there was an army of Danes on the way would be massively ill-advised. She'd be terrified. He couldn't do that to her.

He'd been a fool to come here himself, he realised. They should have sent Osbert or Eamon to warn the capital of what they'd seen. Alaric hadn't been thinking, instead just leaping upon that horse and riding for the Temes. He'd told Wulfnoth to head for Offetuna in Eastengle and wait for him, ignoring all appeals to slow down and think things through. Now he was paying for his recklessness.

Yet, in some ways, he knew why he'd done what he had. He'd wanted to get to Lundenburg. He'd needed to get closer to Æva. Emotion had blinded his reason, and now he was a prisoner, too, unable to do much of anything. If he'd thought himself capable of hatching some kind of escape plan in the spur of the moment, then he'd been wrong. His only hope now rested with this Ecgberht fellow. He'd appeared sympathetic to Alaric and more than alarmed at the prospect of Thorkell entering the king's service. He'd also stopped Eadric from killing him. Was it too much to ask for a good man to do a little more? Was there any chance at all Ecgberht might again be his saviour?

Æva had continued to talk whilst Alaric was lost in thought. She sounded chaotic, the words tumbling from her mouth in a hurried babble to further demonstrate she'd been entirely alone for longer than was natural. She sounded close, likely just a single floor above his own. That did him no good in his present circumstances, but it was valuable information in the event he found himself outside his cell. He'd bury that little piece of knowledge somewhere safe for later use.

"…and that's when I knew he'd been bottling it up so we wouldn't worry."

"What?" Alaric hadn't been listening. He felt shame for that, but he had much to think about.

"Your father," Æva replied. "He'd been grieving in secret, just as I had. We thought you were dead, but he knew he had to appear strong. I had no idea you'd survived the battle until Edmund told me."

"I wasn't in the battle," Alaric said hurriedly, regretting his words already since they were likely to only confuse her. "I was recovering from my head wound. A priest found me and took me to his church in Offetuna."

"How were you wounded then, if not in the battle?"

"There was more than one. We had a plan, you see. Or we thought we did. We thought we knew exactly where Thorkell was. So we set out to kill him in the night."

"Oh? That sounds a bit..."

"I know it does, but we had little choice. I'd kill an evil man in his sleep if it meant saving others from harm."

"I suppose." She didn't like it. He could tell. He didn't begrudge her for that. War was a terrible thing, and it pleased him that she'd not been hardened by witnessing it.

"So Edmund saw you after?" she asked, changing the subject. "And that was in Offetuna? Or somewhere else? You sound like you've moved around a lot."

"I have. We saw Edmund on the road, me and a friend I made. We didn't talk for long. His brother gave me a gift. A sword. But I lost it."

"That's a shame," she said. "Do you think Edmund and his brother will want to come and help us?"

He hesitated again. There was no need to tell her Æthelstan had been killed, and he certainly didn't want to tell her how he'd lost his sword. The horrors he'd seen in Canterburie would hopefully rest deep in his memory, undisturbed and unmentioned by either himself or any other. Yet her question was otherwise a valid one. Edmund was known to be just, and Alaric had no reason to question that. He might indeed hear of what had happened and decide to intervene in their favour. It was a slim hope, but hope all the same.

"Alaric?" Æva sounded quiet, subdued to the extent he could barely hear her.

"Yes?"

"I love you."

A tremor began in his shoulders, spreading to afflict his hands and legs as he stood propped against the wall. It wasn't from physical effort. Æva's three short words had hit him like a hammer. They were the complete antithesis of everything he'd been about this past year, their sweetness akin to a sudden torrent of fresh water dispersing amidst a pool that had hitherto been stagnant. The darkness that had overcome him earlier finally left him, its talons releasing whatever hold it had on his heart. Æva's words settled in to take their place, soothing and nourishing, restoring him to the man he was. He'd almost forgotten what this felt like. He was grateful beyond expression. He said what he could, knowing he could never truly convey the significance of his feelings for her.

"I love you too."

A sudden sound shattered the moment, harsh and unwelcome, the key in the lock of the door behind him seeming to crack and grind against the cool hardness of the surrounding metal. The door flew open, its hinges protesting, a single figure then stepping forward into the cell.

King Æthelred looked fit and well, in a severe, unsettling sort of way. His face looked like it belonged on a man of his age, but there was an energy to him here, like he'd been buoyed by purpose and could not rest until he'd seen some kind of completion. He was dressed as befitted his position, his heavy robes, scarlet tunic, and gold-threaded breecs conveying a stark and unmistakable impression of royalty. His crown added to the spectacle, the golden, jewelled circlet stating a sure and simple message: I am the king. I am authority.

Alaric leant back against the wall of his cell, the tenderness stirred from his exchange with Æva receding before this sudden intrusion. Æva had said something else, but it was muffled now, for her voice was only really audible when he pressed his head close to the barred opening. He had a feeling she could wait. Whatever was about to happen would require all his attention if he were to survive it.

"Alaric," Æthelred said, his robes parting slightly to reveal the sheathed sword at his belt. "I think it's time we talked."

XXVIII

He felt a strange sensation when he looked upon him, his bloodied and indeed horrifying visage stirring something akin to pity. He forced the emotion into submission, crushing any hint of sympathy before it could take root. This man was dangerous. He didn't know why, and he didn't know how, but something told him he remained a threat. This was not a time for weakness. Let the self-indulgent and the soft-minded talk of mercy. He was a king. And kings couldn't afford the niceties so often enjoyed by others.

"You're hurt."

Æthelred wasn't intending to ask Alaric a question, and the statement was an obvious one to make, considering the state of him. Eadric had worked hard on him, wasting no time in finding out the location of Wulfnoth and those who might yet be in his company. Æthelred wasn't convinced Alaric had been telling him the whole truth when he'd broke, but from what he'd heard, there was a limit to how much punishment he could take. Eadric had done what he did for a reason, but his methods were only good for one kind of result. Æthelred had other things in mind, and he felt it best to now try his own approach.

"It's nothing," said Alaric dismissively, making no effort to bow, kneel, or otherwise acknowledge the royal presence standing just a few feet from him. One of Æthelred's guards had entered the cell with him and taken up a position on his left, the other remaining outside in case Alaric somehow got past the first if he were to launch an escape attempt. Æthelred turned and closed the heavyset door behind him. It would help deter such notions. It would also provide them with some privacy. What he had to say wasn't for just anyone.

"Your hands are unbound," commented Æthelred casually. "That should not be so."

"Eadric cut them loose before leaving," Alaric countered. "I know not why. I doubt it was for the sake of mercy."

"Your doubts are well grounded," said Æthelred. "I will ask you plainly now…do you intend to kill me?" Æthelred felt it was important to ask. His fear of this man up to this point was partly over the suspicion he wanted him dead. The dreams had to mean something, and the possibility they were warning him of yet more enemies seemed reasonable enough.

"Why would I want to do such a thing?"

Æthelred frowned, moving to settle himself down upon the cell's solitary chair. It was uncomfortable, its flimsy frame creaking under his weight, his regal robes billowing out over its arms. That wasn't what perturbed him. What struck him as odd was that there was no malice in Alaric's question. That surprised him, considering how he'd treated him thus far. Was he just adept at hiding his emotions?

"You tell me," Æthelred asked. "You've haunted my dreams incessantly for months now. Always with the same look. You always stare…but with two eyes. I wonder if you'll have just the one eye when the dream returns tonight."

Æthelred laughed quietly, the sound dry and bitter. Alaric stared at him like he didn't know what to say, eventually managing to breathe out a single question.

"You had a dream that I intended to kill you?"

"More than that," Æthelred affirmed. "You stand there with all the others, everyone else who turns up to glare at me, always as my brother, Edward, lies dead behind me upon the altar. A chapel, you see, the same one where I laid eyes on him for the last time before we buried him properly. His killers didn't afford him such dignity."

"I don't understand," Alaric confessed. "I tell you, truthfully, I don't know what you want from me."

"It only comes during a time of crisis," Æthelred went on, unworried by Alaric's lack of comprehension. "When the land is at peace, it goes. When the enemy returns…so does the dream. Some famous faces appear in it, dead and alive. Byrhtnoð you'll have heard of. He died before your time. Bishop Ælfstan, also. He always disliked me. Favoured my brother, you see. I'm not surprised he appears in the dream to accuse me."

"But I have not accused you," said Alaric. "I came to warn you. I've never intended you harm."

"Would it pain you further to know you've wasted your time?" answered Æthelred. "We received word just earlier that the Ealdorman Uhtred has already capitulated to Svienn. Apparently, Svienn turned up in the north before coming here. You needn't have rushed here as you did. We'd have found out about Uhtred's treachery in any case and been made aware of Svienn's force shortly after. You risked your life for nothing."

"Uhtred's cowardice is his own affair," said Alaric, a little irate now. "I came to do what any loyal man would do. I saw a threat to my country, and so I acted. Kill me, if you will. What's one more unjust act to a king like you?"

"What would you do in my position?" asked Æthelred. "You mean me harm. I know it. The dream only comes in times of trouble. Everyone in it, including your father, was or is an opponent of my reign. What else can it be but a warning? You, my enemies, you gather in the chapel to mourn Edward and accuse me of his death. It's crystal clear what it means. It's crystal clear that you are a threat."

Somebody called out, appealing for something or someone. Æthelred glanced about, unsure of where it had come from. Alaric looked back towards the opening in the cell wall, his face saddened.

"My wife is in the cell above us," he said glumly, turning back to Æthelred. "She's wondering why I fell silent, most likely. Is she one of your enemies too? A dangerous woman needing to be shut away lest she come for you?"

Æthelred ignored his impertinence. "Your wife was with your father when I had him arrested," he said quietly. "You should be thankful I have not simply killed both of them. It's been some time since they were brought here. But I had a feeling you'd show up sooner or later. I wanted to have answers from you before I made any…final decision."

"Whatever you do, king, remember the state of your soul. I have heard of the bad blood between you and my father, but my wife is innocent. Of all of us here, of all of those involved in whatever it is that troubles you…she had nothing to do with it. Show her mercy, as is proper for your station."

"I'll judge what's proper for my station!" he snapped, irritated at Alaric's assumption that he could offer him counsel. "This is a time of crisis, and that woman is an associate of those who sought to wrong me! I may be a hard man, a hard ruler, but I will not be considered a fool!"

"You've failed incessantly and allowed your people to be butchered from Oxenefordscir to Westseaxe and Eastengle and beyond. In light of the sheer devastation that has taken place during your reign, calling you a fool is the bare minimum."

Æthelred's bodyguard jerked upright, his shoulders filling out. He took a heavy step forward, his large fists clenched, turning to his king now to seek approval before he physically punished Alaric for his damnable tongue. Æthelred gestured for him to remain as he was. It wasn't out of compassion. He'd enjoy seeing Alaric pay for that remark. He just feared if he took any more damage, he might expire before their conversation had really got anywhere. That would be a shame. He'd waited a long time for this.

"I care nothing for your petty insults," said Æthelred calmly. "You are not privy to what I know and what I have had to deal with. You only possess knowledge of a tiny fraction of the concerns and calamities I've contended with. Remember that."

Alaric nodded weakly and slowly lowered himself into a sitting position underneath the window. He pressed his back against the wall behind him and drew his legs up to his chest, holding them in place by gripping his knees with the palms of his hands. He looked defensive, perhaps fragile now he'd been corrected over his ill-advised words. Æthelred decided he'd again put him to the question.

"Do you think I killed my brother, Alaric? So that I might be king?"

"That was before my time," he replied wearily. "And no, for what it's worth, I don't see how you could have killed Edward. You were too young to wield a weapon or plot an assassination."

"That is a fair hypothesis to make," Æthelred said eagerly. "So, who do you think really did it? What do you make of those who blame me for it?"

"I've never heard anyone claim it was you. Nobody knows what happened. How could we? We were far removed from such things."

"People do talk, though," pressed Æthelred. "And what do they say about it all? Somebody must have killed Edward."

"I believe I've heard it said your mother was displeased when Edward ascended to the throne before you," conceded Alaric with a shrug. "Or that she simply didn't like him. Or that she wanted you to rule, as you had more of a right since she was a formally consecrated queen and Edward's mother was not. That's what I've heard. I know not the truth of it."

"You must favour one particular argument over the others. Which do you think is more likely?"

"The notion that your mother thought herself slighted or somehow threatened by Edward and his supporters makes some sense. That's all I'll say."

"So you're accusing my late mother, a Queen of England herself, of murdering a boy?"

"Like I said, it was before my time. I'm in no position to judge the queen's character or motives. I don't have much interest in gossip or idle conjecture. I prefer to focus more on what's happening now."

"And what would you say is happening now?" Æthelred probed. "I came to you here to find out your intentions and shed light on why you haunt my dreams. What's the real reason for that? Some dark spell? Or perhaps you're lying to me now? Is that it? Do you know why you might appear in anyone's nightmares, let alone those of a king?"

Alaric broke eye contact, his face thoughtful, like he was putting some genuine effort into Æthelred's question. "I'll be honest with you…many would assume you were mad for obsessing over such matters. I think differently. Visions and dreams as such have been recurring themes throughout the history of our faith…"

"I don't want a history or a theology lesson, Alaric," Æthelred interrupted brusquely. "I just want you to answer the question."

"You say the dream only comes in a time of crisis?" asked Alaric, his gaze drifting back up to meet Æthelred's. "When your people are at risk and the land threatened?"

"That's right. A warning, I always thought. The Lord alerting me to dangers in my midst so as to strengthen me."

"Are you quite sure you've not misinterpreted them?" Alaric looked enlivened, like the spark of an idea was beginning to take shape in his mind. "Some things within dreams are harder to explain than others," he continued, "but think about who is present. My father, the Ealdorman of Hamptonscir…well, the south is devastated now and had put up with Svienn Forkbeard's raids for years prior. Ulfcytel, too, once your friend, but now estranged from you, with his lands ravaged also…"

"Get to the point, Alaric."

"What I'm saying is…perhaps we don't come to accuse you. Perhaps the dream is saying something else. That we needed you. We were suffering. We suffer yet still. You are our king. And we needed you."

Æthelred took a deep breath, unsettled by what he was hearing. He'd always assumed those that appeared to him were there to accuse him. The fact the dream always took place in a chapel that hosted the body of Edward seemed to attest to that notion. And yet many of those present were long dead, so why they'd be there to seek his aid wasn't clear. Alaric seemed to just be thinking aloud. The poor fool knew his life was on the line and was hoping to buy himself some time. It was understandable.

"All very interesting," muttered Æthelred, "but not that convincing. Many dead men appear in my dreams alongside you and the others. Byrhtnoð, for instance…and the Ealdorman Thored, too. All looking at me as I attend to my brother. Why would dead men want me to protect others? And why would Edward's corpse be there?"

Alaric still had that look, like he fancied he'd hit on some truth that couldn't be denied. "I can't say for sure," he said. "I've never had to interpret a dream before. But I don't see why anyone would accuse you of murdering somebody when you were not yet a man. The timing of the dream says something. It's like you're being reminded of both a danger and your responsibilities. The dead men, though…Byrhtnoð, you say? And Thored?"

"That's correct," answered Æthelred, "and many others beside them. Enough to fill the chapel. All staring. With you."

"Byrhtnoð died fighting Svienn Forkbeard so that your reign might go on. Thored was your father-in-law. Both were good men, as far as I know. Both of them would care about you and England. It makes perfect sense they'd stand to warn you rather than judge."

Æthelred nodded slowly. Alaric's last point actually sounded halfway convincing.

It was true that Byrhtnoð had always been a fierce advocate for both English unity and the general well-being of the people. For him to seek to warn Æthelred of imminent danger was plausible. The same went for Thored. That man had always gone out of his way to be an almost fatherly figure to him. It was of some relief to Æthelred that perhaps he really wasn't wishing him ill after all. The thought had upset him greatly.

"Then why is Edward there?" Æthelred finally asked. "And why a chapel? My mother, too…she appears towards the end. I can never hear what she's whispering, but she always looks set on reaching Edward. I don't know what this could mean. I don't know if it means anything, really. Why dream of such things at all? Who is really warning me? Spirits from the grave? God?"

"I would say God is more plausible," Alaric said without hesitation. "Despite what some might say, the Lord has not abandoned us. Perhaps this is a way He's chosen to remind you of your duties as king. The chapel might signify such a thing. I don't know why your brother or mother make an appearance. They could signify something that needs resolution. Your own conscience…"

"My conscience is clear!"

"You may say that, King Æthelred, but we both know it's not true."

Æthelred eased back in the chair, the crude pinewood creaking under his shifting weight. Alaric was right, of course, but he didn't want to admit it, at least not to him. A thousand and one things bothered him, and sometimes he didn't know what was worse; his own guilt or the feeling others were standing in judgement over him. That was always how he'd interpreted his dreams beforehand. Perhaps he really had made a mistake. Perhaps his fear and self-loathing had caused him to misunderstand the message that was being conveyed.

"Then why are you in the chapel?" he asked. "You only recently appeared in my dream, and we'd never met. I still have little idea about the man you are, and you're nobody special. The son of an ealdorman, yes, but part of a disgraced and mistrusted family, which makes you nobody in the grand scheme of things. Why would you suddenly take your place in the chapel with all the others?"

Alaric was glaring at him now, insulted and also apprehensive at the mention of his family. "God puts us on strange paths, King Æthelred," he said. "And I have suffered so very much over the years. If my interpretation of your dream is correct, then I'm not surprised God is using my image to reach out to you. I lost a son, a baby, at Wiltune. They killed him, the heathens…took him right out of my wife's arms and then violated her…and now my best friend is gone, thanks to the treachery of your Eadric. I didn't think I'd make it out of Canterburie alive…all that's left to me is…"

That noise again. The woman calling from above. She must have been conversing with Alaric before Æthelred had come here. They'd not spoken in months, perhaps longer. Æthelred wondered how he'd feel if he was in Alaric's situation. If he were ever separated from his queen, he didn't know what he'd do. Emma was one of the few people he truly loved, and…that's enough. He mustn't start thinking like that. He shouldn't give in to sentiment. Alaric and his family were justly imprisoned. Comparing himself to them wouldn't help him attain clarity. They were nothing alike.

"You love your wife." Æthelred wasn't asking a question. The statement was true and indisputable. She loved him, too, and it brought Æthelred no satisfaction to see Alaric affirm his statement with a nod, a single tear then sliding down his bruised cheek to vanish within his beard.

"I love my wife also," Æthelred continued, "and I'm sorry it came to this. But I would still have a clear answer from you…why do you appear in my dream now and not before?"

"I can't say," Alaric said quietly. "Through no intention of my own, I've somehow found myself at the epicentre of events in this war. I think perhaps I'm here to remind you of something. That England bleeds, and I've bled with her, not just from the actions of the Danes…but from your own."

"You think that highly of yourself, Alaric? You think God Himself is using you as an example to me of how England suffers under my rule?"

"You tell me," glowered Alaric, his look suddenly fierce. "I lost my son…then my best friend…now I've lost my home and family. I've endured hardships because of the enemy AND you. So perhaps I really do represent the people of England here…long-suffering but still striving, beaten down by your own hand and yet still wishing you'd aid us in our plight. We needed you. You understand that, king? We always needed you, at Hringmere, Canterburie…Wiltune …I needed you! Your country needed you!"

"It's interesting that you keep mentioning Wiltune," said Æthelred, feeling of a mind to ignore Alaric's anger for the moment. "I'm afraid you have your father to thank for that defeat. I'd ordered him to raise his forces in Hamptonscir and march to Wiltunscir's aid. Of course, at the critical moment, he again acted out, claiming some unknown malady had assailed him and rendered him incapable of giving battle."

"I heard something of this recently," admitted Alaric. "If there is any mercy in you, king, tell me the truth now. Did my father really do this? Is he really responsible for Wiltune's destruction?"

"Yes," Æthelred said bluntly. "And more, too. I should have dealt with him years ago, but things were different. He could have made trouble for me. Not so now, with the south so ravaged. Partly his fault again, of course. All he had to do was rally his men to join me when I came south to face Thorkell and…"

"That's not true!" Alaric whined, his frustration giving Æthelred the impression he'd had this argument multiple times in the past. "I don't know how this story came to be or who spread it, but it's not true. You must have been misled. You must have been ill-advised. Tell me, truthfully…was it Eadric who told you my father had not readied his fyrd and that you had best retreat?"

Æthelred paused, his jaw tightening at the realisation it was indeed Eadric who had done such a thing. He wasn't about to let Alaric know that. The man was looking for an opening here, probably as a means to undermine him and ferment discord and distrust. Alaric's father was a known liar, even before his latest outrages. For that reason, he'd continue to place his confidence in Eadric.

He decided to cut this exchange short in as pleasant a way as he knew how. "I understand you feel obliged to exercise loyalty towards your father," he said carefully. "I would do the same in your position, I think. And yet the situation is what it is. I thank you for this…conversation. Now I have other matters to attend to."

The king rose from his chair, the flimsy thing creaking in relief at the lifting of his modest bulk. His guard turned and opened the door to the cell, heaving it back on its hinges as they again groaned in protest. He then stepped into the corridor beyond, Æthelred moving to join him until Alaric suddenly called out.

"Remember what I said. Your dreams are not telling you that your people plot against you. They are reminding you of your duty. But it's too late now."

Æthelred turned, his hands lifting to place themselves on his hips. "What do you mean it's too late?" he asked. "Are you saying I can't make amends for whatever it is you think I've failed at?"

"That's it precisely," Alaric said, his certainty quite palpable. "You've failed at too much, and now Svienn is here. And even with Thorkell and his bastard brother in your employ…you won't be able to hold this city against him. Others need you now. Look to those closest to you. Your children…your queen. Don't let them die here, Æthelred. Don't linger to fight a hopeless battle just for the sake of wounded pride. It's all over for us."

"It doesn't have to be," declared Æthelred. "The walls will hold. Svienn will hurl himself at them as he's done before and be…"

"No," Alaric said plainly. "You'll run out of food, if you have not already. He has the men to block the roads and ships to prevent you offloading supplies from the river. Nothing will get in or out without Svienn's say-so. Things will deteriorate, and quickly. The people will rise up, and the garrison will be caught between them and the enemy. You already have so few men, and nobody trusts Thorkell. I'm serious. Think of the dream. Think on what it really means. Think on who needs you now. Your family. Be a father. You might yet succeed at that. You're lost as a king."

Æthelred stopped, his feet frozen in place at what he'd heard. Moments passed, Alaric's words repeating over and over in his head. He finally broke free of whatever spell had held him, turning to slip out into the corridor. He took the key from the guard and locked the door, placing undue emphasis on every movement, as if wanting Alaric to somehow know it was Æthelred himself who was sealing him in. He then made his way to the stairwell with his escort, the three men descending the numerous narrow steps towards the ground floor and their exit from the prison tower.

Cuthbert almost bumped into them on the stairs. He'd been running, the sweat beading on his already pale face, a piece of parchment clutched in his trembling hands. It was a message, for Æthelred, of course. He took it, allowing Cuthbert to catch his breath whilst they stood somewhat precariously on the steps. Æthelred recognised the crude writing. It was from Alwin, one of his spies in the south. Eadric wasn't the only one who employed such people, and Æthelred had been content to allow Alwin to enjoy a certain freedom in pursuing his objectives, knowing he'd always get results. He had done so again, but the news was otherwise catastrophic. The Ealdorman Æthelmaer of Dæfenascir had submitted to Svienn. With Uhtred also on his side, Svienn now had relatively little to worry about. All that was left to take was Lundenburg. Æthelred was finished.

Alwin went on at some length, claiming Æthelmaer had met with Svienn's forces at the old Roman town of Bade, of all places, to offer his surrender. That was confusing. He knew Svienn had appeared in Norþanhymbre to force Uhtred's hand, but Alwin's account would suggest the enemy was moving fast across the entire country and encountering little to no resistance. This either highlighted a flaw in Æthelred's spy network, or heavily suggested everywhere outside of Lundenburg was now more or less lost to him. This was his single place of refuge. It wouldn't last. Svienn would be coming for him now. Nobody would be looking to help them.

Æthelred's soul was beset. He continued down the stairs, his escorts following, and tried to work through this new information. This latest news made Alaric's perspective on his dream considerably more compelling. If the dream's purpose was to remind him of his duties, then it stood to reason those duties couldn't be confined to his role as king. He was a father, too, and as painful as it was to admit, Alaric was also correct about their chances of defending the city. If Æthelred could no longer protect his capital, then he still had a responsibility to protect his heirs. Some may be scattered or even dead, but those he had under his care needed him now. He'd have to make preparations. It had to be done. Because as much as he hated it, Alaric was entirely right. Æthelred had misjudged the dream. He just knew it in his heart, as if something had clicked into place to reveal a final piece of a long-unsolved puzzle. He knew what he had to do. The only thing he could do.

They finished their descent, some seconds later passing through the tower's heavily guarded entrance to emerge into the spacious courtyard beyond. The evening was coming on rapidly, the cries of swifts carrying on the air as they took up residence in the nooks and crannies of Lundenburg's winding streets. A light rain had begun, largely unnoticeable were it not for the way the raindrops pattered across the surface of the still numerous puddles from last night's shower. Æthelred stopped, craning his neck to look up at the tower.

It was an impressive building, raised way before his time by architects unknown. It had long served as a means to house the enemies of Æthelred and his father before him, its dark stone walls rendering it immune to both fire and storm. Tonight it didn't look so formidable, and Æthelred couldn't shake the feeling there was a vulnerability to it. There was a vulnerability to everything. Lundenburg might not be the bastion it once was, and if that were true, then nowhere was truly safe anymore.

He ambled through the courtyard, passing the stables and the smithy on his way to his main place of residence. Yet another messenger was waiting when he passed within, the young man handing him what he claimed was a written message from Ecgberht. Æthelred snatched it from him and read it as he walked. It conveyed a simple assessment of recent events.

"Riot contained. Two buildings off Cornhill set alight. Three fatalities among the common folk. High chance of further disorder. Food situation critical. Svienn's forces again spotted. Considerable numbers. Siege imminent. Presence of Thorkell's Danes within city DEMORALISING GARRISON."

Æthelred had always liked a terse man, and Ecgberht was certainly one of those. He didn't appreciate the capital letters, but his concerns were well-founded. They should have prepared for the chance the people of Lundenburg, overpopulated and malnourished, would react badly to Thorkell's entry into the city. He understood their anxieties, but he wouldn't tolerate violence from his own. Someone would have to answer for that. Examples had to be set. The men on the walls wouldn't be able to endure a siege if there was bedlam in the streets behind them.

Eadric would be able to find out what had happened. He'd have people in his employ who would have heard things and be able to point out any ringleaders. A swift sequence of executions would cow any further troublemakers. It was grim work, but they had a city to fight for, and disorder wasn't something he could afford. Besides, he had other things to attend to. He had to make preparations. They couldn't assume victory would come their way. The worst-case scenario had to be considered.

Æthelred headed for his garden, knowing there was a high chance his beloved and their children would have opted to spend the afternoon there. The place was coming into bloom, as was only proper, the newly emergent flowers looking strangely forlorn in the fading light. There was no trace of his family, although the shuffling form of Osbern, his old gardener, was here. He was working diligently as he always did, his mind seemingly at peace and fixated on his task regardless of what troubles assailed the realm elsewhere. They spoke, Osbern answering his questions with all due courtesy, claiming he'd seen the queen and her children just recently, only for the rain to have driven them indoors. That was all Æthelred needed to know.

The queen did not favour his audience chamber or the table there he generally used for dining. She believed it a coarse place, too often frequented by men she despised, preferring to take her meals in a smaller chamber that partially overlooked the garden and the undoubtedly impressive views beyond. He found her there now, their children with her, Edward, Alfred, and Godgifu, all seated at her table and eating heartily of whatever repast had been provided. A single armed attendant stood nearby, watching the entrance carefully as Æthelred made his presence known. He bowed. Æthelred ignored him.

"Your father is here," Emma said excitedly to the children. Edward, his eldest, must have shared her excitement, as he quickly got up and ran over to hug him around the waist. Æthelred knelt down, his knees creaking in protest, and placed his hands upon his son's shoulders. He was growing strong. He had a noble look to him, green-eyed and handsome, like his mother, and from what Æthelred had been told, he was fairly advanced in his letters and learning. He was pious, too, praying every morning, afternoon, and evening, and knew virtually all the saintly feast days of the year by heart. He'd be a Godly, scholarly king, so his tutor had suggested. Æthelred loved him. He wondered if one day he'd find the words to tell him that.

Alfred was a different story. He was the youngest of Æthelred's children, and was more withdrawn in temperament than his brother. Sometimes he seemed to ape the worried mannerisms of his father despite his youth, and yet peculiarly, Æthelred felt close to him because of that, hoping to somehow guide him so he wouldn't succumb to the insecurities that had always beset his own mind. He was failing. There was never enough time to spend with his children. Alfred otherwise seemed happy his father was here, but he didn't come to him, opting to remain seated at his mother's side.

His daughter, Godgifu, did the same. She'd been born a year after Edward but had little in common with either of her brothers, preferring to remain aloof from them like she was caught in a perpetual daydream. She also looked like her mother and had inherited her beauteous auburn hair, but she was growing to be a strange child, less worried than Alfred but also disinterested in anything other than spending time with Emma. Æthelred didn't understand her, but he didn't understand any of his other daughters, either. That could explain why he'd always been so eager to have them married off as soon as possible. He had enough worries without having to scrutinise the inscrutable.

He realised he was being unfair. Some fathers might be disappointed at the birth of a daughter, but Æthelred was simply lying to himself if he tried to pretend he'd met such an occasion with anything other than joy. He just had trouble relating to them once they were of age, but then that could be said of any number of his male children, most emphatically his rebellious son, Edmund. Perhaps the fault was his own? Maybe he could have tried harder, rather than marry his daughters to whoever might prove an ally.

Eadgyth entered his mind. He missed her, in particular. She'd not wanted to depart from him, but Eadric was an ealdorman, and it was appropriate he marry a woman of suitable standing. She'd objected, shouting and crying, claiming she didn't like Eadric and that he wasn't a kind man. Æthelred had been hard on her, and when she'd departed for Mierce, they'd not been on good terms. He'd not seen her since. Her absence weighed heavily upon him now. He wouldn't be so harsh with Godgifu.

Æthelred broke from Edward's embrace and drew himself back up to his full height, his knees cracking and clicking. He turned to his wife's attendant, commanding him to take the children elsewhere. Æthelred stood and waited until it was done, reaching out to pat each of his offspring upon their heads when they filed past him. His wife stared at him, a worried look on her face, the remains of the meal in front of her untouched since his arrival.

"We have to make preparations to leave."

She frowned, her emerald eyes flickering like they were reflecting some hidden light source. She looked beautiful, as always, her purple and gold cyrtel accentuating the slenderness of her figure. Her hair was tied back and plaited to reveal and exaggerate the almond shape of her face, but it was always her eyes that Æthelred found himself drawn to. There was something in them that had ensnared him the very day they'd met. He'd never broken free since. He didn't want to.

"Do you not trust Thorkell to defend the city?"

The question was a good one, even when posed in Emma's peculiar, almost languid accent. She'd never lost the mannerisms of her Norman brethren, and her disdain for English ways and their comparatively hard, rumbling speech patterns was no secret to those that knew her. Æthelred had once asked her if she regretted coming to England. She'd said no, but he'd detected the slightest hint of hesitation before she'd answered. He'd spent the rest of that day even more miserable than usual. He'd go anywhere with her if it meant she was safe and happy. He just wished his responsibilities were not of such a nature as to always complicate that simple wish.

"I don't trust him," said Æthelred candidly, "but he'll fight anyone we point him at now he's rich at our expense. And yet I'm afraid he won't be able to fight Svienn alone, not if the reports I've seen are anything to go on."

"Then what of your own men?" Emma exclaimed. "You English always pride yourselves on how fierce you are, despite all the battles you lose. Will your people not fight to defend their homes?"

"Calm yourself, and let me explain." He didn't want her getting upset. When she was upset, he felt unbalanced, which was one of the primary reasons he tried to avoid discussing politics or strategy whenever she was around. He needed her calm and coherent, for his own sake as much as anything.

"We took significant losses at Bernecestre," he said carefully. "My English-born warriors do not trust Thorkell's men for self-explanatory reasons. The people are starving, also. We're overpopulated here. Massively. And when the siege comes, we'll run out of food. The people will riot again. We'll have a fight on our hands from outside and within."

"Then what was the point in any of this?!" Emma wailed. "I thought everything depended on getting Thorkell on your side? You've done that. But now we are defeated so quickly?"

"We are not defeated," said Æthelred sternly. "I am simply preparing for the worst. We were warned about Svienn, but we did not expect him to return so soon and with such numbers. I'm doing what I can. People need me, and whilst I may have lost much of my kingdom, I can still do my duty to those in my care. Starting with you and our children."

"You're sending us away?!" Emma sounded more panicked than ever. These were hard times, the hardest Æthelred had ever contended with. He didn't blame her for being fearful of leaving what had, up until now, seemed like an unassailable city.

"I will go with you. I will always be with you, Emma. And think on it…my alliance with your brother still stands, at least formally. He will have to give us sanctuary. We're family."

"Richard does not take the alliance with you as seriously as you think, husband. You know one of the conditions of our marriage was that he'd close his ports to the Northmen. He has not always done this."

She was right there. Æthelred didn't actually like Duke Richard, finding him cold and aloof and difficult to trust. The close relations that had come with his marriage to Emma were also a mixed blessing, as Svienn Forkbeard himself had intentionally attacked the Norman presence in Execestre in 1002, sending a message through blood that their alliance wasn't worth the parchment it was written on. Richard had done absolutely nothing to help, and as Emma had just reminded him, he'd also been slow to close his markets to the Danes, allowing them a haven to sell the loot and slaves they'd only just snatched from English hearths. Æthelred had hated him for it, and their relations over the years had soured accordingly.

But Richard wouldn't turn away Emma or his nephews and niece. It was one thing to play politics and duplicity when it came to Æthelred and England, but doing the same with his own blood just wouldn't be a good look for him. Richard would take them in, of that he was sure. He'd make sure Emma understood this.

"He's your brother, Emma. He won't deny us in our hour of need, unless there is a darker side to him you're not telling me about. Would it not also benefit him to have a king and queen of England take up residence in his court?"

"A king and queen in exile!" she cried. "What benefit would that prove? We'd be objects of pity, at best. I could not bear the humiliation."

Æthelred frowned, annoyed that Emma's main concern was how she might look in front of others. "We will bear what we must," he said sternly. "If this city falls, I will do everything in my power to see our family safe. And so I will act in preparation. You are to ready yourself and the children for a journey to Normandy. Tell them we're to visit their uncle. It's true, and they'll like that. Do not tell anyone you don't have to. I don't want word to get out that we're thinking of escape."

"But how are we to escape? If Svienn's on his way here, then how many of the roads are safe enough to travel on? We keep hearing stories of brigands and bandits all over…and if Svienn has ships, won't he block the river? We'll be caught and…"

"I have a solution." He didn't like interrupting her, but this was starting to get irritating. She was full of problems, preferring to fixate on the negatives than think on how to be of assistance.

"There are tunnels under the city," he continued, quieter now. "The Romans built this place well. They built the walls tall and sturdy, but they didn't intend to become trapped by them. There is a means to escape under these very halls."

"I have never heard of this. Why tell me only now?"

"Because there was no need. The entrance is hidden. And they are old and ill-maintained. Hardly anyone remembers them aside from a select few. They run under the city, connecting to the sewers and beyond for some distance. If we're in danger of being overrun, we can make our escape and rendezvous with a ship…"

"One of Thorkell's ships!" she exclaimed, hammering the table with a small yet determined fist. "He has a fleet, yes? You'd trust him to take us to my brother? More likely, he'd take us captive and sell us to the highest bidder! Our children, too!"

"We still have ships, Emma. And yes, I'll keep Thorkell with us. He'll be of use in exile, as will his men. We have a means to escape. I suggest you get yourself ready."

"What use can he be now that so many of his own have abandoned him?"

She wouldn't let this go. She was normally a force for calm whenever he was upset, but tonight it was her turn to be on the brink of losing control. He could somewhat understand. It was one thing to try to assuage his worries when it was just him who was troubled, but something else altogether when it came to the safety of their children. It was inevitable she'd want to cover all possibilities. That last question was strange, though. He'd not told her of the rebellion in Thorkell's ranks after he'd taken Canterburie. How did she know?

"Who told you that? Answer me, Emma. I can't have information like that circulating freely."

"It's just what people say," she answered sullenly, her bottom lip protruding slightly like she were a child facing chastisement. "…after all his fighting, he's taken losses, and plenty of his men deserted him after they killed your archbishop. That and Ulfcytel is said to have attacked his fleet as it lay moored months ago. Who knows what damage he did to the ships."

Æthelred was temporarily lost for words. Perhaps he'd been mistaken in thinking her incapable of understanding much outside of courtly life. She certainly had a mind on her, and it was a sharp one if what she'd just said was anything to consider. But her fears were still somewhat misplaced. Thorkell had more than enough men and ships left to be of use to them.

He was, however, quite irritated at the way she'd mentioned Ulfcytel. She'd sounded like she almost admired him. He felt some satisfaction knowing that if Ulfcytel was still in the city, he'd almost certainly be unable to escape now. Death or captivity would be his lot; a fate well deserved considering his incessant defiance. If Edmund and Wulfhild had any sense, they'd abandon the foolish ealdorman and come back to him. Æthelred couldn't just leave them behind. He hoped sincerely that he'd receive word of their whereabouts soon.

"We have enough ships, my dear, and that's the end of the matter," said Æthelred with finality. "It's your job now to prepare yourself and the children. Do not fear. I will do whatever it takes to keep us safe. You just have to trust me."

He turned to leave, a little flustered at how forceful he'd had to be with his normally cooperative wife. Emma called out to him as he opened the door.

"What's happened to you? You seem different. Like you are certain of something you were not sure of beforehand."

She could read him well. He was impressed. "I had a good conversation just earlier," he said, not bothering to turn back and face her. "That dream of mine…I think I was wrong about it."

"Oh? You don't think it's about your enemies and this…whatever his name is? Aldric?"

"Alaric," corrected Æthelred. "And it was about him, but not how I'd thought. It's too late for him now, as interesting a man as he is. Some people are just unlucky. A shame. He doesn't seem half-bad once you actually talk to him."

He stepped through the door and closed it, leaving Emma alone in her confusion. He wasn't willing to discuss Alaric with her. She'd not really understand, and he didn't want her to see his ruthless pragmatism. Part of him felt sorrow for Alaric. He'd fought well and was undeserving of the fate that had befallen him. But he couldn't be left alive. That would mean Æthelred would have to spare his father, and if he did that, Ælfric would escape justice and go on to remain a thorn in his side in any way he could. If he killed Ælfric but spared Alaric, then the son would come after him regardless. It was the way of things. He'd seek to avenge his father's death, as was entirely natural.

So all of them must meet their end. Alaric, Ælfric, and the blind Ælfgar, also. Æthelred thought to spare Alaric's wife, Æva, or whatever her name was, but something turned him against it. A woman like that could work wonders on the minds of men, manipulating them into quarrels and feuds that might ultimately see Æthelred pay dearly for her husband's death. He shuddered at the thought. He could tell she had it in her. There was a fierceness there, clear as day.

He'd arrange their executions then, all of them, at once. Normally, he would oversee such a thing in person, but he had too much to prepare for, and, in truth, it was a task he would rather put off for as long as possible. He'd send some men when he was good and ready and hopefully far away from this place. Eadric could do it, or perhaps that brother of Thorkell's. They'd clear out the prisons and then join them later. There would be no ceremony or drama. He'd take care of his enemies quickly, leaving nothing and no one behind to note his passing. Sviern could have his city if he could fight his way inside. Æthelred would have his family and his vengeance on those that had betrayed him. In time, he hoped, he'd have vengeance upon Sviern, too.

He was halfway to the gardens when he remembered. Alaric and Æva had a son. He'd ordered the child separated from Æva when Edmund had reunited them, allocating him to one of Emma's gossiping friends to be fostered here within the confines of his halls. He'd forgotten all about him since. What was to become of him?

The sight of his own children settled it for him. As expected, his wife's attendant had taken them to the gardens, knowing through habit their father would almost certainly come looking for them here. The man stood close by, watching them attentively to ensure they didn't fall victim to mischief.

The children were happy. The rain had eased off, and they were playing at some kind of game that involved the clashing of pebbles, the blossoming cherry tree they huddled under seeming to arch its branches up and over them protectively. Æthelred approached, noting the stars just beginning to become visible in the faded sunset skies above, the evening breeze tugging at his robes as he sat down amongst his offspring. His bones again cracked in protest, but he made it, reclining awkwardly against the base of the tree so as to partake in the game. The children came closer so he could reach, flattered that he'd taken such an interest. There was nothing to it. You just took turns knocking one pebble against another. They found it entertaining. That was what mattered, he supposed.

He decided there and then he'd let Alaric's child live. It was right in more ways than one. Æthelred had done some grim things in his time, but he'd never ordered the death of children. He might be up to his elbows in blood, through his own actions or the commands he'd given, but he'd never committed himself to such dark and shameful deeds yet. He didn't want to ever go that far. Despite the man he'd ultimately become, he still wanted to go to his grave knowing even he had lines he wouldn't cross.

Alaric had also done him a great favour. It was not enough to mitigate the threat he and his father posed, but a favour was a favour. He'd fretted over his dreams for years, always thinking he understood them as warnings about potential plots and accusations over his brother's murder. He'd not wanted to believe Alaric's interpretation, not at first, but something told him he was right. The dreams were about his people. How they suffered. How he'd failed them. It had lifted a burden. He owed him for that. Sparing his son seemed like a just recompense.

They'd have to take him with them. Leaving him alone in the capital would be a strange mercy, especially with a hostile army set on conquering it. Emma would no doubt want to bring her closest confidants with her, so bringing the boy along was eminently possible. He was still of an age where he'd likely forget his parents, or at least the exact look of them, preferring instead the emotional bonds he'd build with his fosterers. He'd have a good enough life. He'd perhaps be married to some Norman lady of modest standing and have children of his own. Æthelred could secure the match by making it known he was the son of an English noble killed during Svienn's invasion. That wouldn't be a lie. Nobody needed to know he was the one who'd killed him. The boy could be happy with such illusions. They all could.

Æthelred leaned his back further into the tree to let it take his weight. He might yet be defeated here, losing his last bastion to his long-term rival, but he could turn that defeat into something workable. He'd rid himself of many enemies, their deaths easily blamed on the chaos of war. He'd also secure his family's safety, and with the likes of Eadric and Thorkell at his side, he'd be a force to be reckoned with, even in exile.

Then it was just a case of planning his return. Svienn couldn't keep all of England down, and Æthelred had an heir that would look to take back what was theirs. As grim as the present might be, for once Æthelred couldn't help but remain optimistic. He'd long felt the urge to flee from his duties, the burdens of rule proving themselves an irritant he'd often desired to cast off. Now he might be being given just such an opportunity. A rest could be what he needed. And he'd have his family with him, too, or at least those that were still obedient.

That, of course, brought Edmund to mind. He had a feeling he'd not be seeing him for some time; a thought that made his heart ache with a severity almost beyond words. But knowing Edmund, he'd find a way to make life difficult for Svienn. He'd prove himself, as he had done already. He had an indomitable spirit, and even with defeat staring Æthelred in the face, he had a feeling his son would move heaven and earth to turn things around. King Æthelred might fade into obscurity, but he had a premonition that history would remember Edmund and that Englishmen would forever draw strength from the example he'd set. A foolish, prideful thought for a father, perhaps. But he knew it to be true. Edmund would make his mark. He could do nothing less.

XXIX

The Ald Gate was always a sight to behold. It was a landmark as well as a military strong point, and for travellers heading into Lundenburg from Eastengle, it was a welcome symbol of order and civilisation after the perils of the road. Ancient and strong, the Romans had built the gateway to stand the test of time, its towering stone walls a potent reminder to anyone with ill intent that any attack on the city would be a bloody and unprofitable affair.

Unfortunately, Svienn Forkbeard had apparently not thought as much. When Edmund had been informed of the Danish king's arrival on the north and eastern side of the city, he'd set out from his refuge, ordering Ulfcytel and the others to stay put lest they be spotted by his father's men. He was expecting to observe the enemy from the battlements, comfortable that their position atop the walls was at least secure whilst he made his own assessment of the besieging force. He'd not made it that far. As he hurried along the unusually spacious confines of Fenchurch Street, he'd seen what awaited him in all its terrible drama. The Ald Gate was wide open. And Svienn's men were charging through it.

There could be only one response to that. Edmund mounted a charge of his own, his legs pounding across the muddied stones and a roar shaking from his throat. Other men were joining him, the local garrison streaming in from all directions, the question of how the gate had been opened now postponed until the more immediate task was completed. They had to push the enemy back. They had to win here. To fail would cost them everything.

Edmund waded into them at speed, the hundred or so men alongside him doing likewise. The foe had already cleared the entrance into the city by a stone's throw, the Danes that made up the vanguard of this night-time assault looking truly terrible amidst the flickering glow of torchlight. They were eager and overly so, each of them likely aware how critical this location was if they hoped to ultimately take the city.

Ecgberht was already in the thick of it, fighting with a spear in one hand and a sword in the other. His helm was spectacular, its faceplate hiding his whole visage aside from his eyes, the metal so expertly wrought it was like he had a second face fashioned from burnished bronze. His skill at arms was also something to behold, his spear impaling enemies from a distance whilst his blade hacked down any who dared get too close. His men followed his example, tearing into the invaders with a bravery that spoke of desperation. They knew what was at stake. If Lundenburg fell, all was lost.

Edmund narrowly dodged a thrusting spear, almost losing his balance and falling backwards into the men behind him. He found his feet and also found the man who'd just tried to kill him, this time slicing open his throat before he could get any more ideas about trying to impale him. The English were grinding forward as a human wave of flesh and mail, their advance inexorably pushing the enemy back towards the narrower confines of the gate. Edmund caught another Dane raising his axe to attack, putting his boot into his stomach with such force he collapsed to the ground. The English advance pushed on over him, crushing the now screaming Dane under the armoured weight of a dozen and then a dozen more. A sad fate for anyone. But that was war.

He lashed out again, this time using his sword as a lever to prise the shield down and away from an enemy's grasp. It clattered to the ground, a look of panic on its owner's face upon realising his vulnerability. Edmund took the opportunity for what it was and impaled him through the stomach, the Dane's expression turning to anguish and agony as he was disembowelled with brutal efficiency. The man was dead, or would be soon, but there were plenty more behind him and more after that.

It was a risk for Edmund even being here. He wasn't dressed for it, for he was attired in the very same riding clothes he'd been wearing when he'd set out from Snotingeham with Wulfhild. When Ecgberht had sent word to him that Svienn's army had arrived and was encircling the city, he'd had to come, feeling an urge to again look upon the enemies of England with his own eyes. He hadn't expected to have to fight so soon. Something had gone wrong here. Somebody had either made a serious mistake in leaving the Ald Gate unsealed, or they'd been betrayed. He hoped it was the former. Human error was understandable and forgivable. Treachery was not.

His eyes lifted to behold the gate above him. There was fighting up top, spreading out across the adjoining walls, Svienn's Danes leaping over the battlements to grapple with the defenders. Not all of them were making it, and from the looks of it, the attackers were incredibly vulnerable as they struggled to dismount from the tops of their scaling ladders. A few who'd survived and fought their way clear were now trying to raise a banner directly atop the gatehouse itself. Edmund couldn't make out what was depicted on it, but something told him they should not be permitted to do that. It could be a sign for something, although what exactly he knew not. He had to stop them.

He broke from the fighting, doing his best to make his way over to the right of the gate so that he might access the adjacent stairwell. It wasn't easy, and the sea of men slowed him, but he made it, dashing up the steps to find himself atop the wall and just a few yards from the gate's eastern tower. A Dane was climbing over the crenellations before him, his face etched with pent-up rage. Edmund reacted like lightning, gripping his sword in both hands and slicing his head from his shoulders in one single devastating arc. He leaned forward, peering over the wall's edge with grim curiosity at the headless body falling to the earth below. It was a good kill.

His elation was short-lived. More men were climbing up behind the one he'd just slain, each moving with such haste their scaling ladder had begun to shake unsteadily under their weight. Edmund sheathed his sword and gripped the top of the ladder, pushing with all his might to fling it backwards and send his adversaries toppling into the darkness. It was too much. It wouldn't move, the weight of those ascending keeping it fixed to the wall. Strong as Edmund was, he didn't have the physical power to push back against what looked like at least a dozen men clambering towards him.

An idea formed. He gripped one single edge of the ladder and heaved to his left, hoping to provide enough leverage so the enemy's own mass would cause them to slide over at an angle. He had to put his back into it, and for a moment he feared his head might burst from his exertions, but it worked just as he'd hoped. The Danes cried out and clung on all the tighter when they realised what was happening, Edmund again looking down at them as the ladder slid over to begin its deadly descent. They went with it, screaming whilst they fell, the desperate sound cutting short when they hit the ground in a mangled mess of splintered wood and shattered bones.

Edmund looked to his right, taking in the length of the eastern wall and what lay upon it. He couldn't see much in the darkness, but he could tell there were more ladders braced against the walls. The Danes were flocking to them, unconcerned with their fragile construction and scrambling upwards to get to grips with the defenders.

One Dane completed his climb only to cry out upon coming face to face with several Englishmen, the silly bastard appearing so alarmed it made Edmund wonder if he'd been told there would be nobody atop the walls to oppose them. He took a spear in the chest and then the face, his body falling back and down with such velocity it carried away the two men climbing up after him. The English jabbed downwards at the remainder, laughing and challenging them to continue climbing so that they might receive a proper welcome. The survivors lost their courage and made a hasty descent.

But it wasn't always so. More and more Danes were making it to the top of the wall, aided in large part by the relative thinness of the garrison here. The fighting was thus still in the balance; the battle below also undecided as the outnumbered English did their best to push the enemy back and seal the gate. Edmund had wasted enough time. He turned to his left, spying the three Danish warriors who had by now successfully raised their banner atop the gatehouse. They howled with triumph, a thunderous deluge of cries answering them as the night outside lit up with thousands of torches. Sviennn's entire army was out there. It broiled and seethed with aggression, its gargantuan mass surging forward at the signal. They were heading for the gate. The open gate. All of them. This was it. Either they got that gate sealed in the next few minutes, or they were all dead.

Edmund charged the men with the banner, heaving his sword up and down to cut the arm from one of those holding it aloft. The Dane howled and fell backwards, his two comrades letting the banner drop so they might turn and face this new threat. They circled him warily, each aware that yet more Danes were scaling the walls with each passing moment. One made a lunge for him, but Edmund deflected it with ease, his counterattack costing the Dane a hand and then his life.

The third and last of the Danes was a real bruiser, of an age that said he'd been fighting and killing since before Edmund had even been born. They duelled, Edmund noting his skill, and he was just about to go on the offensive when he saw several more Danes approaching, axes held ready. They must have clambered over the walls whilst he'd been distracted here. It didn't matter. He'd kill them too.

It wasn't easy. They acted fast, one howling like a madman as he made a downward swing for his head. Edmund barely dodged it, but he did reward his attacker by striking him at the elbow, half-severing his forearm. The Dane fell onto his arse, clutching his arm and shrieking at the copious amount of blood splattering outwards across the stones. It looked painful. Edmund would give him a quick death when he had a moment.

He didn't have the luxury. Somebody grabbed him from behind and heaved him into the air, their foul breath washing over him. Edmund didn't bother struggling, instead gripping his sword with both hands before flipping it downwards and back to impale whoever held him. They dropped him in a flash, Edmund landing comfortably on his feet to leave the now expiring Dane to mewl and paw at his own spilling guts.

His next opponent was not so easily disposed of. He was good, and he was angry, undoubtedly because of what he'd just seen Edmund do to his countrymen. He bellowed as he came on, aiming strike after strike towards Edmund's neck, his persistence giving the impression he intended to decapitate him and take his head as a prize. Edmund parried one blow and then another, but a third swing was fast – almost too fast – causing him to again nearly lose his footing.

The Dane, by this point, had grown irritated by the contest. He reached out, again alarmingly quick, and grabbed Edmund by the scruff of his tunic to heave him closer. He then smashed his armoured forehead directly into his face. If Edmund had been wearing a helmet, this wouldn't have been an issue. Against his unprotected head, it was an absolute disaster. He'd fallen over, he could tell from the ache in his rump, but apart from that, he was unable to discern much of anything. There was blood in his eyes, and his head was ringing, his vision all shadows and what looked like tiny stars flickering in and out of existence. Somebody was roaring something, and another was laughing, the proximity of the sounds making him think his opponent found his situation humorous. He had to get away from this man. If he couldn't stand or even see, he was dead. He might be anyway, even if he did manage to escape. Given the size of the Norse host outside, it would only be a matter of time before the resistance below collapsed altogether.

Heavy footfalls and then yet more shouting sounded at his back. Somebody had run up the stairwell and launched themselves into the melee. Edmund's vision cleared slightly when a body hit the ground close by, a second soon following and a third falling headlong over the front of the gate. The man Edmund knew as Cenric stood amidst it all, his every blow drawing blood and his every step heavy with purpose. He was still dressed in the armour he'd been wearing when Edmund had first seen him. The same armour he'd worn at Canterburie. Whatever he'd faced there had not broken his spirit. He was relentless.

The surviving Danes began to cry out, alarmed at the skill and ferocity of this man that had so suddenly come upon them. Cenric killed and then killed again, the stones around them turning slick with gore, and before long only the Dane who'd felled Edmund remained. He fancied his chances, putting up a courageous struggle and doing his utmost to split Cenric's skill. The fight became close, too close, the Dane managing to grapple Cenric and turn their exchange into a question of both weight and strength. They tussled like this, Cenric looking like he might yet prevail until he slipped upon the blood he'd only recently shed. He fell backwards, becoming wedged between the rocky crenellations along the wall. His opponent wouldn't let up, placing his hands around his neck and pressing down, intending to crush the life from him.

Edmund lurched upright, staggering like a drunkard, his head spinning. He did what he could, hefting his sword upward and then forward to impale the Dane before he could finish Cenric. He fell short, in his befuddled state managing only to stab at the man's right thigh, but it was enough, buying Cenric precious time to recover and launch himself at the Dane's waist. He tackled him, knocking him backwards several steps, both men struggling to retain their footing whilst they wrestled. It was clear by now that Cenric was at a disadvantage in physical strength, but not in his wits, as he suddenly leapt upward to smash the top of his head into the Dane's jaw. He did this once, then twice, a third and final action resulting in an audible crack as his assailant's face started to fracture. He weakened, yielding several more steps backwards, the undoubtedly unbearable pain corroding his resolve. Cenric didn't play any games with him, instead planting a boot in his stomach and kicking him off the gateway to plummet into the desperate fighting below.

And it was desperate. Frighteningly so. The English were gradually losing ground, their numbers thinning, the Danes mounting yet another charge. Edmund had to do something. He couldn't stand up here, looking down at the fighting. He needed to be a part of it. He could make a difference. With the beast known as Cenric at his side, he knew it for a certainty.

He then saw something happening further down the street. Figures were advancing, dark and fast, the sound of their heavy footfalls clear and audible despite the frenzied clamour of battle. Hundreds of men, over a thousand, perhaps, were running towards them, each letting loose a bellowing war cry that almost drowned out all else. Edmund saw it now. They were Thorkell's men, coming from somewhere within the city, and he was leading them from the front with that red-helmed warrior at his side. There was only one reason for them to be here. They were going to attack the English from behind and open up the city for Svienn.

Edmund and Cenric moved quickly, both men leaping down the stairs to rejoin Ecgberht and his warriors. Edmund cried out to them, pointing towards the advancing horde and screaming for them to take heed. All of this had been so foolish. Thorkell was probably working with Svienn. They'd both hatched a plan to take advantage of his father's desperation so that Thorkell might get into the city at the critical moment. If that's what was truly happening, there was only one thing left for Englishmen to do. They'd die fighting. Honour was all they had now, and Edmund would rather be dead upon the bloodied ground than turn and flee.

Thorkell's men stormed into them, Edmund's eyes widening in surprise as not one single Englishman fell to their axes. They weren't attacking, at least not them, these savage warriors instead flooding into the gate to begin driving Svienn's men back into the open ground beyond. They fought like brute animals, their great axes hacking and hewing, each tearing into their own Norse brethren without hesitation. The English surged after them, cutting down any hostile Danes within reach, the fight for the gate turning decisively in their favour.

Such a dramatic turn of events might all be for nought if they didn't get the gate properly sealed. The enemy was surprised, but they'd soon recover their confidence, and Thorkell's men were not numerous enough to take on the vast army outside the walls. He'd bought them time, nothing more, and if they failed to use it, they'd still be defeated here.

It was to this task they now applied themselves, Edmund and the others using the space won from Thorkell's assault to push the gate's great oaken doors closed. Thorkell saw what they were doing and began to move his men slowly back, not wanting any of them to be left stranded on the other side. It was difficult, since the size and weight of the doors was tremendous, requiring many men to use their full strength. Edmund's legs, back, and arms were soon trembling with effort, but their now mixed English and Scandinavian force did an effective job of keeping the gateway clear long enough for them to make a start. It wouldn't be long now. Soon they'd be safe.

Perhaps inevitably, Svienn's forces quickly realised what was happening and began to hurl themselves forward with renewed urgency. Thorkell's men fought back, doing their utmost to hold out long enough for their English allies to finish what they'd started. One of Svienn's men grabbed at Edmund, roaring and gabbling incoherently, only for Thorkell himself to bring his axe crashing down upon his shoulder. The man squealed and wept whilst he was dismembered, what Edmund presumed to be cries for mercy falling on callous, uncaring ears. He looked away, focusing on his task whilst Thorkell and his men went about their own bloody business.

A great boom sounded when the doors were finally shut. Nobody friendly looked to have been trapped on the other side, so they set about piling everything they could into a barricade, using old barrels, bales of hay, and even corpses to ensure that even if the gate was again breached, the enemy would struggle to break into the streets beyond.

Edmund stepped back to survey their work. The enemy screamed like madmen from the other side, and there was still some fighting up on the walls, but the city had been secured. Thorkell's men had performed well, their frenzied bloodletting drenching the stones around the gate with gore. Edmund wondered if this place would soon be renamed the "Red Gate" as a result. It would be fitting, what with the horrifying sights he beheld now. The stench was repellent.

Thorkell's mob didn't wait around, instead spreading up and out across the walls to cut down any enemy warriors still attempting to scale them. Ecgberht and his men watched them go, apprehensive in the face of their new allies and wary for any sign of trickery. They could not be blamed for that. They'd been fighting these men for months prior to Svienn's arrival. It didn't feel right to have them here, even considering their actions in winning them this battle. Thorkell was acting in his own interests and could just as easily turn on them at any moment. It was in his nature.

Cenric looked aghast, his eyes darkening with contempt whenever a Dane got too close. They gave him a wide berth, likely sensing he was a warrior of tremendous capability, but there was otherwise absolutely no interaction between them and the English. They were still two peoples standing apart, even if gold and the payment of it had temporarily brought them together. The English hated them, and rightfully so. Edmund dearly hoped the day would come soon when they'd take their revenge upon Thorkell and Svienn together.

"That was something," said Ecgberht, his breath hurried and rasping from beneath his faceplate. "I've never seen anything like that. To be saved by such men...I don't know what to think."

"It is what it is," said Edmund. "They want to live to collect the payment my father has gifted them. They can't do that if the city is breached and Svienn moves his entire army through here. They put gold before everything, even their own kin. We've always known that."

Ecgberht turned back to his men, barking several commands for them to take up position atop the walls to deter Svienn from any further attempts to surmount them. Edmund couldn't tell from here how effective Thorkell had been in securing the battlements, but he imagined it was a fairly easy task. From what he'd seen, it was only really possible to climb and dismount from a scaling ladder if there were so many of you doing it the defenders could not keep up. If there was a man waiting for you up top with killing on his mind, it looked almost impossible to survive, and Thorkell's men certainly intended to kill. They decided to see for themselves, Cenric joining him as they followed Ecgberht back up the stairwell, the three men moving atop the gate to gaze out at the enemy beyond.

The walls were clear, and every scaling ladder in sight was now ruined and broken upon the ground, clutches of dead and wounded Danes visible amidst the wreckage. Svienn's army was retreating back across the broken turf, their enraged cries rising up into the night sky. More fell as arrows planted themselves in their backs, the English on the walls firing into them whilst they fled. They should have had archers up here before, Edmund thought. They should have made sure the gate was sealed, too. Just what exactly had happened?

"I trust you'll ensure the other entry points are secure? This was a potential disaster that should never have happened." Edmund hoped he didn't sound like he was chastising Ecgberht. He wasn't an incompetent man, and this wouldn't have been his doing. Something else was afoot here.

"They are," he replied soberly. "I don't understand it either. I ordered all the gates to be sealed and manned at the first sight of the enemy. I'll need to speak with those who were here. I have a bad feeling, Edmund. I fear treachery was almost our undoing tonight."

"Who from?" asked Cenric. "The Danes? Some in Thorkell's lot probably having second thoughts about fighting with us?"

"It's possible, but that's not what I was thinking," Ecgberht said. "Neither of you have been out much among the people of late, for good reason, I'll admit. There's an ill mood. There was hardly any food before, and now we're under siege, there'll be none. The people are restless. They want this brought to an end. They want Svienn."

"Surely you can't be serious?" Edmund gasped. "They want him as king? He's a murderer! A foreigner! A savage!"

"He is that," concurred Ecgberht. "But in my experience, it takes a man of real character to put his principles before his stomach. The people are sick of war. And if I may be honest, Edmund, they are sick of your father. There have been gatherings. Assemblies of citizens, if you will. Many are calling for us to allow Svienn to take the throne. Thorkell's appearance didn't help. It gave the impression the king was never serious about opposing him. So why oppose Svienn?"

"It's a hard thing to consider," chimed in Cenric. "This whole city is like some slumbering beast just waiting to awake and attack. I'd say the people won't allow themselves to just starve to death whilst we hold the walls. If they want Svienn to sweep in, they'll find a way to make it happen. We could end up fighting on the walls and behind them."

"What makes them think Svienn won't just burn the place down?" mused Edmund, still unsettled at the idea of Lundenburg's inhabitants actually wanting a Danish king. "He's shown little restraint with that kind of thing in the past. Do they think he'll at least feed them first before putting them in the ground?"

"I understand, Edmund," said Ecgberht. "Yet remember, I was with your father at Bernecestre when he tried negotiating with Thorkell. He'd ordered me away, irritated that I'd dare tell Thorkell what I thought of him. I'd obeyed, as was right, but heard later of what they'd discussed. Svienn isn't here to burn. He's here to rule. He has a son, Cnut. He's out there now. This army is for him, and Svienn will use it to take Lundenburg intact so that Cnut might rule it."

"So this is it then," Edmund said wearily. "We're caught out. Surrounded and starving with a hostile population to contend with. What do we do? I'm serious…what do I do?"

Ecgberht removed his helm and turned to face him, his appearance troubled and dark now they'd left the relatively well-lit environs of the gateway. "We can still do something," he said sternly. "You can still save your friend…Alaric, was it?"

"That's the name," confirmed Cenric.

"Then think on this, both of you," Ecgberht continued. "I've had to pull more warriors from your father's compound to defend the walls. Those left have been instructed to obey you, Edmund, should you make an appearance, and Thorkell's men won't be in your way either. There's never been a better time."

"What good will it do?" replied Edmund sharply, irritated at his companions and their lack of understanding. "We're besieged. There's no point in freeing Alaric just so he can walk about on the walls and perhaps fight with us as we all go down. If we had some means of escaping the city, it would be…"

His voice faded into silence, both Ecgberht and Cenric peering at him out of the darkness with an eagerness that compelled him to speak further. He took a deep breath, hoping the secret he was about to reveal would be the lifeline it appeared to be.

"There are…tunnels. Under the city. Ancient things. Roman things. One leads from my father's hall to the banks of the Temes."

"Then we can use it!" Cenric exclaimed excitedly. "We can free them all and make our escape!"

"Not I," said Ecgberht. "Somebody has to hold the enemy back. I won't abandon my men, unless you want Lundenburg to fall whilst you're trying your daring rescue. And remember, some of this is my fault. I refused to give Eadric any men to move refugees out of the city. I thought it was a callous plan…but now we're stuck, with the people trapped and still wretched in their plight…I accept responsibility for that. And so my place is here. I can't just let Sviemn walk in unopposed. It's not right. Not after all we've suffered."

Edmund glowered a little, irked by Ecgberht's insistence on finding fault with himself. "If you'd done as Eadric had asked, the people you moved out would just have been attacked outside the walls," he said. "This was always a difficult situation. Unavoidable, some may say. Don't begrudge yourself, Ecgberht."

"All the same, I feel some responsibility. I won't shy away from that. If need be, I will give my life for this place and those within it. That's just how it is now."

Edmund stared at him, lost for words. They'd long been friends, but he wasn't sure if Ecgberht had ever looked as magnificent as he did now, marred from battle, yes, and half-concealed in the surrounding darkness, but magnificent all the same. If they had more men like him, England's troubles might altogether be of a lesser nature. It was sin and the treachery of the ruling orders that had brought them to this sorry point. There were too many corrupt men in positions of power, and they'd all preyed on his father for far, far too long. Eadric was the worst, yet he wasn't alone. The most ill-suited of men sought power, Edmund thought, whilst the best did as Ecgberht did. They did their duty for the sake of others.

Edmund briefly wondered what that said about him. He wanted to be king. Despite Sigeferth's advice, he couldn't tolerate the notion that his brother, Eadwig, would or should take the throne. Did his ambitions make him a hypocrite in this regard? Was he no better than Eadric, deluding himself with talk of nobility and virtue whilst actually only thinking of himself? He decided to ponder all this later. Right now, there were more important things to be getting on with.

"Then I suppose it's settled," Edmund said softly. "If what you say is true, Ecgberht, and I don't doubt you, it should be easy for me to get Alaric out of his cell. But this is about more than him. We'll have to get more people out, including Ulfcytel and my sister, and they won't leave without all those people they brought with them from Cantwara. We'll have quite an entourage."

"Then that's what we'll do," Cenric said firmly. "You're an aetheling, Edmund. We'll look strange wandering about your father's halls with all those people, but if the men stationed there have already been expressly told to obey you, we can't go wrong. Then it's just a case of freeing my lord and his family and escaping."

"To do what?" asked Edmund, suddenly unsure of himself. "What will we do? What will I do? Am I an aetheling? Truly? Will the people follow me now they've grown to hate my father? And what about him? Do I leave him to his fate? I cannot abandon him."

Ecgberht sighed and shook his head, but there was no derision there, only sympathy. "You'll have to make some hard decisions," he said. "I've done what I can. The opportunity is there for you. You can leave this place and survive and do what you do. I know you, Edmund. You'll not let us down. You'll be our king someday."

"Ironside."

"What?" asked Cenric.

"It's what my brother called me before he died," Edmund said sadly. "He told me to go on and be a king. Made that joke he often did about how it was like I was made of iron. Called me Ironside."

"Edmund Ironside." Both Ecgberht and Cenric had spoken as one. "It's a good name," laughed Cenric. "A great name, and there's truth in it. I don't know if you've given it much thought, but you did just get head-butted by a man in a full helmet and still managed to get up and carry on fighting. That was something."

"I agree," Ecgberht said. "And it's good to know that's what happened to your face, because all this time I was thinking you'd just fallen down the stairs like a right clumsy bastard. You look absolutely terrible. Ironside or no, you need to get yourself washed and bandaged."

Edmund wanted to laugh, desiring nothing more than to join his two friends in just the briefest moment of levity. He couldn't manage it, the dull throb in his head and the view stretched out in front of him giving him pause for thought. Svienn's army was still moving, recoiling from the walls and scurrying back towards its camps to the north east. They were spreading out, the flanks of their army and sizeable detachments of cavalry moving fast to secure every road and possible trail that might lead into the city. Lundenburg was to be strangled into submission. Svienn couldn't take it by force, so he'd starve them instead. Edmund found it pathetic. But it would still be their undoing.

He squinted his eyes, trying to focus, trying to identify who was out there. He'd never seen King Svienn before, let alone this Cnut, but he liked to think they'd witnessed this battle tonight and experienced the sting of defeat firsthand. By all rights, they should have won here. They'd had every advantage, whatever had happened at the gate ensuring they'd gotten inside with far greater numbers than the defenders. Thorkell had certainly played an important part, it was true, but Edmund knew the sheer tenacity of their own troops had helped win the day. Lundenburg might yet hold out, if starvation and civil unrest were not additional enemies to contend with. When those were factored in, their situation was indeed dire.

"I need to wash and think," Edmund muttered, turning back to his friends.

"I'll come with you back to the safe house," Cenric said reassuringly, the older warrior acting like he was concerned for Edmund's safety should he walk alone.

They set off back the way they had come, moving away from the gate and onto the broad length of Fenchurch Street. Ecgberht had called after them, saying he'd come to them in a few hours after he'd "investigated" the situation and spoken with his men on precisely how the enemy had surprised them this night. Edmund had nodded and walked on, Cenric quiet at his side. The city was far from restful, despite the lateness of the hour, the occupants of every home they passed seeming to eye them nervously from their doorways. He shouldn't be surprised. Everyone within earshot would have heard the fighting. Their fear was justified.

"Why did you come?" Edmund finally asked, breaking the silence that had hung over them like an unwelcome guest. In the mad frenzy they'd just emerged from, he hadn't thought to ask Cenric why he'd made an appearance. There was every chance Edmund could have been killed had he not. He owed him his life. He hoped to repay him somehow.

"Your sister was worried for you," came Cenric's answer. "As was Ulfcytel, also. After you left, he again wanted to march down here himself to get a look at the enemy. You know it's hard convincing him to stay put. I only just managed it. I can't have him out on the street. He's too recognisable. That and he roars like an enraged bear when he fights. Everyone would know it was him just from the bloody racket!"

"It's for the best," agreed Edmund. "I mean, just imagine if he and Thorkell had laid eyes on each other."

Edmund wasn't trying to be funny. Ulfcytel had not taken the news of Thorkell's arrival well. He'd simmered like an overdone pot of stew on a campfire, hissing and spitting and pacing up and down. He'd called Thorkell every name under the sun, seeming to forget Edmund and Wulfhild's presence by openly cursing the king, also.

He'd calmed down, eventually, but when they'd got word of Svienn's army appearing at the walls, he'd been predictably eager, wanting to march out and take charge of the defence. It took a great deal of effort to convince him the king was likely still looking for him. Edmund had then assured him he'd go and investigate what was happening. It was just as much out of a desire to shut him up as it was genuine curiosity.

"Trust me, Edmund, we don't want Thorkell anywhere near Ulfcytel," Cenric warned. "It may sound obvious, but Ulfcytel would try to kill him on the spot. He's a proud man. He's been defeated on the battlefield twice by him now and bested in single combat once. Ulfcytel had taken an arrow to the knee before they fought, sure, but I know he doesn't see that as an excuse. He'll lose control if he sees him. We need to remember that when planning our escape."

"How so?" Edmund asked. "Do you think we'll encounter Thorkell in the prison tower? I think my father has better uses for him than guard duty."

"Not Thorkell himself, perhaps, but we can't be sure all of his men will be assigned elsewhere. Some of them could be around, and Ulfcytel will want to kill them wherever he finds them. I understand him. I feel the same. I'd never been in a battle like at

Canterburie before. I'm glad I didn't see the aftermath. I think it's fair to say Thorkell was less than gentle with those who fell into his grasp. I'd kill him just for that a thousand times over!"

Edmund nodded, impressed with Cenric's resolve. "And what of Alaric?" he asked. "He got away from Canterburie somehow. Do you think he was captured and managed to escape?"

"That's the only explanation I can think of. Ulfcytel confessed to me earlier that he was saddened only Alaric had escaped. He feels guilty, particularly over a young fellow called Osbert, who I fear wasn't as fortunate. Again, I can understand him. I commanded men at…"

Cenric had fallen silent, as if he'd forgotten what he was saying. Somehow Edmund doubted that was the case, but it still seemed peculiar. "Forgive me," Cenric finally said. "I can't recall the village in Eastengle where we faced Thorkell. Hametuna, was it? I know not. But it was hard fought. We were late for Hringmere, you see."

"So Hamptonscir responded to Ulfcytel's initial call for aid?" asked Edmund, finding it remarkable that a place so far away would do so. "That strikes me as…"

"Strange, yes," Cenric said, finishing his sentence for him. "But that's Alaric. He wouldn't leave it alone. Said we had to march. Said Ulfcytel would be seen as a beacon for resistance and that all true Englishmen had a duty to rally to him. And he was right. Yet, if I'm honest, sometimes I wish he'd stayed home."

"Why?"

"Alaric's arrival at Hringmere was a catalyst, I think. Everything got worse from then on. Osmund died…you wouldn't know him, but…let's just say I'm a bit apprehensive about seeing Alaric again. I first met him when he was a lad and had the privilege of seeing him grow into a fine man. I wonder if after all that has happened…"

"You're scared his experiences have changed him?" Edmund knew this fear well. He'd felt it before, for himself and others. He worried at times he'd lose himself, either through exposure to the kind of power he held through accident of birth or the general harshness of life in a fallen world. Sometimes he felt it more keenly, having the notion his heart was hardening against his will to leave him a cold, unfeeling caricature of the man he was. It was a horrifying prospect. And one Cenric was right to be afraid of.

"That's it," Cenric confirmed. "Alaric isn't an old man…not exactly young anymore, but not old…he's already suffered a lot in his time. I hope whatever he saw after Canterburie fell was not too harrowing, but I fear that's a foolish thought. He'll be different. But that doesn't change my duty. Damaged or not, I'll see him freed."

Edmund said nothing, and the two of them walked on in silence. Their surroundings had become somewhat ominous, the light from the braziers at the gate receding further and further as they approached the intersection leading to the Billings Gate and the river-crossing beyond. By the time they'd reached it, they were having trouble seeing, the inhabitants of this part of the city apparently content to remain slumbering and without need of lighting their homes. Edmund was thinking he was glad that at least some people were relaxed when he heard something. The sound of a crowd. An angry one. These people had not been sleeping. They were simply not at home. Trouble was afoot.

His suspicions were soon confirmed. At a market square just off from St Donis' Church was a gathering of people, hundreds strong, the light of one single intense bonfire thankfully serving to illuminate them and a great deal else. Edmund, at first, couldn't make much sense of it. Some of these people were armed, mostly with staffs and cudgels of one type or another, but also the odd spear and hand axe, making him wonder why they hadn't rushed to their aid during the fight just earlier. He could spot the refugees from the regular Lundenburgers as he came closer, the former looking more dishevelled and possessing a wild look, like they were close to the edge. He supposed that was to be expected. They'd fled war, and now it had followed them here. But none of that explained what they were doing.

A figure emerged from somewhere ahead of them, his mere presence provoking a flurry of adulation from the growing crowd. He ignored them, instead climbing up atop several stout wooden crates to get a better look at his audience. Edmund and Cenric stood back from the multitude, observing warily, this entire spectacle continuing to give them an ill feeling.

The man was portly and better dressed than most others, his breecs and tunic well-dyed in an assortment of greens and tans. A long seax hung from his waist, the ornate scabbard it called home marking him out as a man of at least some means. Edmund had no idea who he was, but he already had a very real notion he wasn't going to like what he had to say. And so it was.

He began by making a sequence of dramatic statements, his hands waving in the air whilst he prattled on about "King Svienn's terrible army" and "our king's continued refusal to protect us." Edmund couldn't entirely disagree with him, but when he started to preach treason it was too much, and his argument that life under Svienn's rule might at least get them fed was a little peculiar given the dimensions of his waistline. He certainly wasn't going hungry like so many of his admirers.

He had a feeling about the kind of man this was. A merchant, and an important one in the world of commerce, but a nobody to those who actually had a say in governance. That rankled his type. They thought money entitled them to rule somehow, as if spending your life accumulating metal tokens was a mark of "success". And here he was, and who knows how many more of his kind, making his own little bid for power upon the backs of desperate people. Edmund would have none of it. He began to make his way through the crowd, Cenric following, both eager to shut this man up.

The people parted around them, some appearing to recognise him, others not, but all of them keeping their distance upon seeing his bloodied face and the grim and imposing figure that was Cenric. Edmund looked up towards the makeshift stage again. He found it strange that so many people would assemble at this hour to hear such a man shoot his mouth off, but there was every chance the fighting had woken them up, the hunger in their bellies also likely ensuring sleep remained elusive. If they wanted to do something productive, they could volunteer to man the walls. Dissent was one thing. Treasonous yap was another. Somebody would pay for this.

The crowd, however, was getting more animated, the fat man's words continuing to find their mark. He'd brought up Thorkell, jabbering something about how the king had "paid murderers and rapists to take up residence amongst us", a statement that was sadly true, despite the objectionable conclusions he drew from it. King Æthelred, so his argument went, was a "failed king" who had "lost the right to rule", which somehow meant it was logical to open up the city and allow Svienn to walk in and take his place. Edmund's gut twisted in anger at the thought of it. They were close now. He made his move.

"What say you about my father?!"

Silence fell, the man atop the stage looking down at him like he was both mad and dangerous. Edmund clambered up to him, a few moments later enjoying a new perspective as he again took in the crowd. Hundreds of people. Tired and famished. Edmund would have to win them over somehow. He'd done such things before and could do so again.

"I know you are hungry," he began, his efforts to project his voice apparently successful since everyone continued to stare at him attentively. "But allowing this city to fall is no solution. My companion and I have just come from the Ald Gate. You'll all have heard the fighting. I'd venture that's why you're awake and so many of you are armed. But we won. We fought them off. We can do so again."

"We'll starve, all of us," objected the well-to-do man beside him. "We're past promises of glory. We've given all we can. Lundenburg is surrounded and without food. It's time somebody else was in charge…even if that means Svienn. And who are you anyway? Who are you to offer us advice?"

Edmund shot him a menacing look, the man falling silent in the face of it. He then turned back to the crowd, puffing his chest out just a little before revealing his identity. "I am the Aetheling Edmund," he announced. "I have slain many a Dane, here and elsewhere. They are not unbeatable. And I tell you, now is not the time to despair. If we despair, we are lost. With courage and prayer, we can overc…"

The entire crowd was mute. They'd not reacted in the slightest, his revelation that he was of royal blood making absolutely no impression on them. Edmund faltered. He felt like the biggest hypocrite he could think of. He planned to escape the city with his friends. He planned to save himself so he could lead some heroic struggle to reclaim his kingdom. And here he was, lecturing a horde of half-starved commoners on why they had to believe in him and keep up the fight. His cheeks flushed. He felt shame. The crowd sensed it.

It started with a few dismissive murmurs, these first trickles of dissatisfaction gathering strength until they were a veritable tsunami of indignation. He couldn't consistently make out what was being said, but they seemed enraged that he'd dare ask more of them, the years of war, ruin, and now starvation taking its toll to the point they'd grown to hate his father and him, by association.

"You shouldn't have come here," leered the fat man into his ear. "You can't expect these people to warm to you just because of who your father is. It's not like that."

"I can," Edmund snapped, trying to think of a retort. "They'll remember who I am. They know I care for them… why only days ago I…"

"I know," came the rather smug reply. "I was there. I saw you. Quite the show you put on with that old man your fancy sister thought had tried to grab her. Very charitable. Noble. And they've all forgotten about it."

"What are you talking about? Who is to say what…"

"Don't try and argue your way out of this, Edmund," he sneered. "I'm an expert at this. You were good at acting all heroic and Godly…but when people are starving, they focus purely on what works, not what looks or sounds pretty but has no substance."

Edmund didn't have a mind to listen to this. He'd heard this kind of prattle several times before, and always from the manner of merchant who, like this one, seemed to assume his financial abundance was indicative of some kind of right to rule. He couldn't work it out, probably because there was nothing to really understand. These were men of pride and greed, the two vices growing steadily as their purses grew yet fatter. Edmund didn't want to hear it.

The merchant took advantage of his silence to address the crowd again. "You see here how the promises of Æthelred and his ilk ring hollow," he cried, his palms open and held in front of him like he thought he was balancing some great wisdom there. "They ask and then demand, using flattery and dishonest words to make us sacrifice ourselves when we've already given up all we have. Whether it's war…taxation… and now empty bellies…we've given and suffered enough for them. Now is the time for change. Now is the time to petition good King Svienn and…"

Edmund kicked outward, incensed that the savage who'd only just now tried to butcher his way into the city could be considered "good". His foot connected with the fool's ample rump, prompting him to slump forward under his own weight until he fell off the crates to land face-first in the mud below. Edmund laughed. The crowd didn't find it funny. They cried out, the sound raw and hateful. Edmund had a feeling they were moments away from trouble. He wasn't wrong.

Cenric scrambled up onto the stage, several men clambering after him. Edmund didn't want to harm any of them, but he had to do something, for the once silent crowd now looked like it were about to turn into a frenzied mob. He kicked at one of them, stamping on the hand of another, Cenric grabbing a third man and hauling him up and backwards so that he fell atop several others.

Edmund felt more than foolish. He'd had a chance here to speak to the people, and he'd ruined it all simply because the rich paunchy bastard at his feet had stolen his thunder and insulted his honour. He should have started with the tunnels. He should have offered them the chance to escape with him. They'd have loved him then. He'd have given them hope. Instead, he'd begun to make some grandiose speech of the kind they'd all heard before.

The mob was now doubly enraged, their ire growing with every attempt he and Cenric made to defend themselves. They had scant seconds before they all charged, this great mass of people rolling up onto them to crush them to jelly. Edmund turned and grabbed Cenric by the arm. He then jumped off the back of the stage, pulling Cenric with him, the horde at their backs letting loose a great roar and surging after them. They got up and ran, heading into some side street Edmund hadn't seen before, the darkness failing to hide them as the furious crowd gave chase.

They ran faster, desperate to escape, ashamed and angry over the fact they were fleeing. The street twisted and turned, growing narrower and darker, their every move somehow matched by their pursuers as if they knew where they were heading. Of course they did. This was their home. They knew every backstreet and dead end and could navigate in the pitch blackness if need be. Edmund and Cenric had no such advantage.

Edmund cried out when he was tackled from the side, whoever it was seeming to spin him around and direct his trajectory towards the mouth of an adjacent alleyway. Cenric was also accosted, two men pushing him alongside Edmund in a bid to get them both off the street and into yet darker confines. Cenric lashed out at one of them, his efforts causing a third man to push him from behind so that he staggered forward. Edmund struck the figure closest to him, the resulting grunt of indignation prompting an appeal for reason from the man next to him.

"Don't fight us, Edmund! We'll all die here if you do! Trust us!"

He didn't know who this fellow was. He couldn't really see his face, nor any of them, since they were all concealed in dirty, hooded robes that masked almost everything aside from their breecs and boots. These gave something away, at least. They were made from good quality leather, of a type generally used for making light armour. These could be soldiers. And they knew him by sight. Edmund allowed them to duck him into the alley entrance, Cenric following a moment later.

They rushed onward, running single file, the howling and raging ebbing slightly from behind them. Edmund had been wrong. Perhaps the people back there didn't know the area that well, or they were just in such a rage they'd lost the use of reason and were unable to work out where they'd snuck off to. One of the strangers tapped Edmund on the shoulder reassuringly, presumably to let him know he remained a friend and that he and his companions were not about to stab them to death now they were out of sight. Edmund was grateful, in some sense. He didn't want to die like this.

They took a left and then a right and then a left again, the bedlam behind them receding yet further. They were not out of danger, and their new associates were not of a mind to slow down. Their pursuers, too, whilst no longer at their heels, were still around and ill-disposed towards giving up, if the racket they continued to make was any indication. The man who'd spoken earlier then suddenly brought them to a halt, Edmund straining his eyes fiercely whilst he tried to see what he was doing. Someone opened a door somewhere, the noise of the lock and creaking of the hinges sharp and clear in the blackness. Edmund's eyes eventually adjusted, spying a faint light beyond a now-open entryway. There must be a fire within. They could get out of the open air. They could be safe.

Everyone bundled inside, the door closing with a faint groan. The room they now occupied had seen better days, its stale odour and soot-stained walls suggesting it hadn't been properly occupied for some time. There was a fire, or at least a grate with some embers in it, over in one corner, its sombre light revealing a set of chairs and a table adjacent to a wooden ladder leading up to a second level. An archway led off towards the back and to the right, the deep shadows obscuring whatever might lie beyond.

Edmund felt paranoid. There could be yet more men waiting through there or up the ladder. If he and Cenric hadn't been murdered in the alleyway, it could just be because their supposed rescuers had wanted to get them here where they were certain not to be disturbed. Edmund's hand drifted down towards his sword. He wouldn't go out like this.

"It's not like that," said the man who'd spoken before. He'd pulled his hood down, as had the rest of them, each still a stranger to Edmund. They all looked typical of the fighting men of these times, bearded and tough with skin like leather, their eyes dark and hard in a way that told him they'd seen more than enough violence in their lives and would never be quite the same because of it.

As formidable as they looked, none would be of any use if the mob chasing them somehow got inside. It was still around, screaming into the night, its rage yet unspent. One of Edmund's rescuers barred the door, giving them a little security, and they all then waited, becoming as still as statues. They stayed like this for what felt like hours, motionless in the faint firelight, their breath hushed with trepidation lest the slightest sound give them away.

Nothing came of it. The bastards outside made a huge fuss, their frustration echoing through the dark whilst they rushed from street to street in the hope of picking up their trail. The sound of their passing gradually eased off, their fury dispersing with the knowledge that their quarry had eluded them. Edmund hoped they'd be satisfied with the mischief they'd caused. The city did not need another riot on its hands.

One of their new friends turned to Edmund, apparently satisfied that the danger had passed. He looked the most senior of the bunch; his pockmarked skin, salt-and-pepper beard, and straight greying hair implying he was either getting on in years or had lived a harrowingly stressful life. He stared at Edmund for a few moments, his sharp eyes possessing a quality bordering on gentleness. Was that respect he also saw there?

"I know what you must be thinking," the man said softly, his hands rising up slowly, palms outward, in what looked like an attempt to placate. "Don't take this the wrong way, but we've been looking for you. When that crowd went berserk, we saw an opportunity to get you somewhere so we could talk."

"And where is this?" Edmund asked testily, gesturing at their surroundings. "And who are you? I would have your name."

"I am Wilfrid." He bowed once, deep and genuine, his men also lowering their heads. "I serve your father, the king. He wants…"

"You wanted to find me and kill Ulfcytel." Edmund wasn't in the mood for any of this. He didn't like being followed, or spied on or whatever these men thought they were doing. He'd have honest words with them.

"I'll confess we were told to do that," Wilfrid said regretfully. "I'll also confess I pondered ways to achieve only the first part of my orders and leave the second entirely unaccomplished. I'm loyal to your father, but he…"

"I know, I know," Edmund sighed, weary at the prospect of yet another person thinking he was something special because he'd noticed his father was prone to making bad decisions.

"…and I fought alongside Ulfcytel years ago after Svienn burned Noruic," Wilfrid then added. "We got his attention that day. I'm sure you heard all about it."

Edmund blinked. He could tell these men were fighters by how they moved, but to realise at least one had been with Ulfcytel when he'd famously fought Svienn to a standstill seven years back was quite something. No wonder he wasn't willing to kill him. Sometimes loyalty was owed. Other times it was earned. Edmund fancied the latter often created a stronger bond. Thus it was with many who spoke Ulfcytel's name. Edmund was envious. But this showed that Wilfrid was a good man.

"I know all about recent history," Edmund said bluntly. "What do you want from me?"

"We were to bring you home, but I'll not force you. I think if we did, your friend here might have something to say to us."

Cenric glowered from his position by the doorway. If Wilfrid was trying to be funny, he'd made little impression. He continued speaking all the same: "Your father wants you back. He has a plan to leave the city. Hardly anyone knows of the tunnel network 'neath the ground, but I reckon you do, Edmund. Your father intends to use it. He's convinced all is lost, and all he can do is save his family. He wants you and Wulfhild back with him."

So they'd both had the same thought. His father intended to escape the siege through the tunnels under the city. Edmund felt contemptuous of such a scheme until it occurred to him yet again that he was quite the hypocrite. He'd been planning to do precisely the same, albeit with more than just his family in tow. There had to be some way to get as many people out as possible. He wasn't like his father. He couldn't save only those known to him. They had to think of some way to get the word out that escape was still an option.

"But he has Thorkell now," Edmund scoffed. "Wasn't he worth all that money? He just threw Sviern back not even an hour ago. Can't this great and mighty… murderer…hold the city on our behalf?"

Wilfrid paused, his lips parting and closing again as he pondered what to say. He had the bearing of one who had something of import to present but didn't quite know how to go about it, perhaps fearing a hostile reaction or confrontation. Edmund tried to calm himself. He knew he was being difficult. Considering the scare they'd just had, he liked to think he could be partly forgiven for that.

"I hope you will not be angry with me for what I'm about to say," Wilfrid half-whispered. "But the treasury is now being emptied. Thorkell has a hundred men moving his payment through the tunnels, where it will be loaded upon several ships further up the Temes. He's then being sent ahead with the rest of his force to secure the estuary. The king and his household will follow soon after to rendezvous with him at Beamfleote to make the passage to Normandy."

"Normandy!" Cenric said through a sudden bark of laughter. "I see the old man has entirely fallen to his wife's influence then. Perhaps we can't blame him. He'll be safe there. Anywhere is safer than here."

"But he's robbing us," Edmund said with a slow shake of his head. "It was bad enough levying a new tax to pay a cur like Thorkell…but to allow him to still take payment when all they are doing is abandoning the country…it's a fool's move. Sviern has ships in the Temes right here, and there's no guarantee there won't be more downriver."

"I know," said Wilfrid patiently, "and I know this must be hard news to hear. He'll leave England an impoverished and ruined land. But those are his wishes, and I must obey him. But he wants you with him. Will you not go?"

"I will not!" thundered Edmund, his anger rising once more. "Our people have suffered too much for me to just turn and flee because my father would rather live the rest of his life in comfort! If I escape Lundenburg, I will remain in the country and make Sviern pay in blood for even THINKING he's fit to call himself our king!"

Wilfrid nodded, his men also acknowledging his bold words. They liked what he'd said. He could use that. "Will you not aid me in this?" Edmund asked, making sure he made eye contact with each of them. "I will need good people if we're to escape this city and rally others to me. I can't do it alone."

The men responded all at once, Edmund missing the particulars of what each was saying amidst the deluge of affirmations of loyalty and respect. Wilfrid was smiling when he next spoke: "There's your answer," he said happily. "I must confess to being conflicted… but you are right, and going with your father will not help our people. We'll stay with you. I never liked Normans anyway. But there is more you must hear."

"Yet more?" Cenric asked sarcastically. "What's next? I mean, how can this be any more of a betrayal than it already is? Can our plight really be any worse?"

"It's not for me to say," replied Wilfrid. "But we have an unusual… guest at the prison tower. He came from Canterburie and the recent fighting there. Fierce-looking bloke. One eye. But it's believed he's the one who convinced the king to go into exile.

You'd think that'd save him, but Æthelred has given orders to have the tower cleaned out after he leaves. Everyone there is to die."

"And who will perform this evil deed if the king and Thorkell have already left?" Cenric had a point, Edmund thought. Just who could his father trust to perform such a merciless act once he was gone?

"I can't pronounce the man's name," admitted Wilfrid, "but I know of him. He's believed to be Thorkell's younger brother. It's also believed he has some kind of vendetta against our new prisoner and volunteered to assist with his interrogation…"

"Torture," murmured Cenric bitterly. "Let's be honest…he'd have volunteered to torture Alaric…probably for having the wits to escape them at Canterburie…and for all the Danes we killed defending the city to begin with."

"You're way ahead of me, my friend," said Wilfrid. "If what you say is true, then that'd be reason enough for him to want to hurt…Alaric, was it?"

"Yes," Edmund and Cenric said in unison.

"Well, there we go then," said Wilfrid. "And this is Thorkell's brother we're talking about. Evil will be in him, no mistake, and he'll want to cause hurt for the sheer sake of it. I'd say Alaric and the other prisoners don't have long left."

"Wait," Edmund demanded, "just when does my father plan to leave? I had the impression from what you were saying that we still have some time before he's gone."

"Not at all. Your father will likely be away come the morning. After daybreak. He was desperate we bring you his request to join him. He'll be mortified that I told you everything else. If he knew, he'd punish me and…"

"Fear not," Edmund said. "You are in my service now. Just let me think a moment…"

He began to pace back and forth, hoping the movement might help him attain a little clarity. They had to get back out onto the street. They had to accelerate their plan to get into his father's compound and free the prisoners before they were all killed. That meant they couldn't round up half the city to conduct an orderly evacuation through the tunnels. Time wouldn't allow it. They had to move. Immediately.

"Cenric, my man," said Edmund finally, his pacing easing to a stop so that he might stare into those green eyes. "Did you mean what you said to me just days ago? That you would free your lord and his family or die in the attempt?"

"I did."

"Then let us get to it," said Edmund. "We'll move with all haste. Let us first gather Ulfcytel and my sister and all those with them and march on my father's halls. If Ecgberht's orders are in force, the men left there will obey me. We'll rescue Alaric and his kin and be away from this place."

"And then what?" Cenric asked, raising a single eyebrow quizzically.

"We will head north. To the Five Boroughs. This city may fall, but England does not fall with it. Not whilst we're alive."

Nobody said anything. Not Cenric, not Wilfrid, nor any of his men. Just as Edmund was about to inquire what the matter was, he heard something outside. A low, continuous roar, some distance off but getting closer and closer. The others had all been distracted by it as he'd been speaking, but there was no mistaking it now. It was the mob. It was back. Something had happened. Worse than before. Far worse.

Wilfrid moved with haste, checking the door and pressing his ear to a crack in its edges. He turned to Edmund, a look of pronounced alarm upon his face. Edmund went to speak, but Wilfrid was again in motion, ushering him and Cenric towards the single ladder leading to the mystery upper level. Cenric went first, then Edmund, making the climb somewhat awkwardly, Wilfrid and the rest of his men following with practised athleticism.

It was dark up here, the light from the fire below falling short. Edmund's eyes gradually adjusted, the place they now occupied turning out to be little more than a long-neglected but spacious attic. There was a window, at least, sealed and shuttered but likely easily opened if he put some force into it. He tried. The shutters unfurled outward with a slight groan, the fresh air caressing his face as he stared out over the troubled city.

The riot outside was intense. He had no idea how it had started. Perhaps it was the same mob from before, albeit far larger. Perhaps its anger had spread, stirring others up in desperation to new acts of wanton violence. They'd never know the truth of it, but as dawn broke, it looked like the streets from Cornhill to St Ethelburga's were in a state of total anarchy. Men and women both were rampaging about, hacking and burning, their guttural cries splitting the air. Multiple fires had already been set, the flames reaching up to cast a pall of acrid smoke over the northern and eastern approaches to the city.

Edmund could understand it, in a way, for every great and terrible event has a catalyst. Years of frustration, defeat, and misrule had taken a toll on the people of England. Now it was all coming out, the years of resentment and fear boiling over as they found themselves trapped within Lundenburg's walls, starving and desperate. It made his heart ache to see it.

Not everyone was so possessed by madness. Some were resisting, others attempting to secure their homes and fend off the fury and chaos that simmered and frothed outside. They were not always successful. Edmund spotted a man being accosted, a gaggle of persons dragging him from his home and beating him to death. He worked out why when several of his attackers dashed into his house only to reappear with armloads of vegetables, bread, and even a keg of mead. Word had clearly got out that the now deceased fellow had a supply cache of his own. He'd paid with his life for his foresight.

Similarly bloody incidents played out before his eyes, all tragic, all unnecessary, all speaking to their failure to prepare for the worst. The rioters used whatever they could, attacking others with weapons, implements, or their bare hands, all somehow instinctively knowing who was with them and who was not. Skulls were smashed on the stones, those attempting to flee finding no refuge as they were run down by the terrible weight of frenzied bodies. It was both brutal and tragic, and it kept on and on, the chaos spreading outwards with the break of day to envelop yet more souls in its manic embrace. Lundenburg was dying, its walls still unconquered, its downfall instead wrought from within at its own desperate heart.

"Why do we bother, Cenric?"

"What do you mean?"

Edmund shifted to the side, allowing Cenric to take a look out of the window. He watched for his reaction, Cenric's battle-worn face giving little away whilst he gazed out at the carnage. He looked back at Edmund, satisfied he'd seen enough, his features blank and his heart seemingly unmoved.

"Some say that an animal is at its most dangerous when mortally wounded, or at least believes death to be imminent," he said. "This city is such a beast. There is no reasoning with these people. They believe the end is near…and in their hysteria, their actions are hastening it. We can't evacuate them with the rest of us, Edmund. They'll tear us apart. We have to make it into the king's compound and hope the doors hold against this mayhem long enough for us to do what we intend."

Edmund looked into his cold eyes, hoping there might be some glimmer of warmth there. There was nothing, and the longer Edmund looked, the more he realised this was why Cenric was such an impressive fighter. It wasn't just his skill at arms. He had a heart of stone if he willed it, evaluating situations quickly and coolly regardless of how harrowing and threatening they might be.

It was a strength, and as much as Edmund admired it, he was glad he did not possess it. People were suffering out there, their broken minds and broken hearts causing them to destroy themselves and all they held dear in one final act of madness. Edmund felt for them. Cenric was completely right in his assessment, but there was a detachment there that he'd never want for his own.

"We have to get through them somehow," Edmund announced, his words intended for everyone present. "And we have to do it fast. If Ulfcytel gets the notion to try and intervene, he could put my sister at risk, not to mention all those old folk he brought from Cantwara. I don't…I don't want to think of it."

"Be still, my lord," Wilfrid said gently. "You're too close to this. Leave this to me. We're experts at getting into places without being seen. We'll get you to Ulfcytel and your sister. And then we'll get you all where you need to go. You've impressed us with your words tonight. We'll help you put those words into action. You have my oath on it."

XXX

They'd watched the city burn all morning. Neither of them knew what to make of it, the scale and ferocity of the chaos rising up from the streets catching them off guard. The gate to the compound was holding, and so they remained safely locked in their tower, but everything else looked like it was fair game. This wasn't an enemy army that had overcome the walls to burn and pillage, as armies do. This was their own people, driven mad by hunger, poverty, and the incessant ineptitude of a failed king. But these were reasons, not excuses. There would never be an excuse for such self-defeating savagery. Alaric felt sick.

"Did you hear the chanting?"

Alaric nodded in response to Æva's question, only then realising she couldn't actually see him and he'd best reply. "I did," he said, his face pressed to the opening in his cell, this being the only way to see outside and communicate with his wife imprisoned on the level above. It was a small mercy. Speaking with her again had brought such comfort, despite the misfortunes that had befallen them both. It was a torture of its own kind not being able to see or hold her, but this was far better than being locked up alone. He didn't know how she'd managed to take that for so long. She was stronger than he'd thought.

But he had indeed heard the "chanting", as she put it. The rioters beyond had not become mindless animals overnight bent solely on looting and fighting. They cried out at times, cursing Æthelred and demanding his head. Soldiers from the garrison would sometimes appear, making attempts to disperse the treasonous rabble, but it never did much good. There were too many looters and not enough men available to quell the disorder. Most of them had to be on the walls, facing off against the Danes. How long they could do that with such violence at their backs remained to be seen.

The mob also called for Svienn. Alaric couldn't always tell why or what they were doing, so inadequate was his view from up here, but he'd definitely heard Svienn's name being shouted through the streets. "The Forkbeard", they kept calling him, and if Alaric's ears were hearing it right, they wanted the gates opened to him. They wanted him as king.

This hurt him most of all. He'd spent years of his life fighting Svienn and Thorkell both, always thinking the true threat lay in the hearts and minds of such men and never from his own. Eadric had taught him a bitter lesson there, showing him firsthand how England's greatest liability was the corruption of its own nobles. But he'd still never thought to see the common folk behave in this way. To watch them tear at the heart of their own country for the sake of a mouthful of bread was painful beyond measure. He wondered what the men who'd died fighting at Hringmere and Canterburie would make of it all. Something told him they'd be as sickened as he was.

Æva was of like mind. She'd endured captivity and maltreatment at the hands of Æthelred for months, but she wasn't insane enough to somehow think inviting the

Danes to take the throne would change much. Svienn's entry into the city would be a disaster for those calling for it. He'd never taken a settlement in the past to apply a gentle touch. He'd never shown mercy. Lundenburg would burn like any other place. Or so Alaric thought. There was always a chance there was something else afoot that he wasn't aware of. He was locked in a tower, after all.

"Something isn't right."

Alaric didn't know what Æva meant by that. There were quite a few things that weren't right, and none of them would be addressed, let alone solved, by being intentionally vague. "What is it?" he asked. "The people outside? Can you see something I can't?"

"No, in here," she replied. "Nobody came in to give me breakfast, and it's nearly midday. The guard usually knocks around now to ask me if I'm all right."

"Why does he do that?" Alaric chided himself for the spark of jealousy. The guard was most likely just trying to be charitable. There'd be nothing in it. Not everyone in this world was base and evil. Besides, Æva would have told him by now if she'd suffered from unwelcome attentions.

"He's old," she said. "I think he had a daughter at some point and feels sad. He's the only human contact I've had before you came. It helped."

"I've not been in this fine establishment for long, Æva. I don't know how it works. So we get regular meals?"

"I wouldn't really call them meals," she said grimly. "But it's food. Breakfast and dinner. No exercise. No visitors. Just the cold and the view from here."

"And me now."

"And you," she said softly. "But I can't touch you. Sometimes I wonder if it would have been better to not talk to you. It hurts me to hear you down there and not even be able to touch you."

"You can't mean that."

"I suppose not. Yet it does hurt. If I reach, I can just about get my hand outside…can you do the same?"

Alaric tried it. His hand was larger than Æva's, but it slipped through the opening fairly easily. He held his palm upwards, facing the sky, thinking perhaps that Æva intended to drop something to him. A foolish notion. She'd have had to be able to see downward to risk doing something like that.

"It makes me happy to think our hands are sort of close," she said. "Like you could take mine in yours if you were able to reach up. I don't know. I'm silly."

"If you are, then so am I," Alaric said mournfully. "You know how I feel about you. I'd tear this cell to pieces to get to you, had I the strength."

"Then let's just stay like this for a while and pretend."

"Good idea," he said. "Let's pretend…perhaps somebody will see, and…"

Alaric's cell door flew open, the echoing crash of wood impacting on stone painfully loud. Hemingr stormed on through, his strides long and powerful as he closed the distance to grab Alaric by the neck. They struggled briefly, the contest frantic but short, Hemingr's abundant strength proving more than enough to subdue the weakened and wounded Alaric.

By the time their altercation took them into the corridor, he had Alaric in a headlock, the hard scales of his mailed sleeve pushing into his throat. Alaric tried protesting, even aiming a blow with his elbow towards Hemingr's guts, but it did nothing, merely striking the metal of his hauberk to no real effect. Hemingr laughed in his ear. His breath stank. Alaric told him. He laughed even more. Alaric saw the bastard still had Æthelstan's sword at his hip. If he could just reach it he'd have a chance.

He'd have to wait. Hemingr began dragging him down the stairs, laughing still as Alaric's legs kicked and whirled about in an effort to find some purchase. The tower was built around a single stairwell, and a fall down it from their level could prove disastrous. Hemingr didn't care, hauling Alaric down each step like a sadistic child pulling at a doll, the sounds of his laughter and the heavy tread of his feet echoing in all directions.

Alaric gave up resisting and instead put his strength into trying to breathe and remain somewhat upright. He thought he heard Æva cry out somewhere up above, his attempt to answer her failing before it had begun, such was the strength of Hemingr's hold on him. Something was going on below, for there were sounds of activity rising up to meet them, suggesting the entire tower was being emptied of occupants for some unknown purpose.

They made it to the ground floor, Hemingr releasing Alaric to begin shoving and pushing him towards the main entrance. When Alaric had first passed through here, there had been English guards on watch, a door leading off to the east providing barrack space for those assigned to duties here. Those men were gone entirely and had been replaced by Danes, who by the looks of it were herding another batch of dishevelled prisoners outside. They were frightened, and their minders were not gentle.

Alaric nearly fell as Hemingr gave him a shove to take him out of the tower and into the daylight beyond. He looked about, his eye blinking in the brightness. He remembered this courtyard, situated just under the southern wall of the compound, with what he assumed were kitchens and stables off to the north west. The main hall of Æthelred's residence was a little distance to the north east, and the gate into the city was then just a short dash to the south. Alaric pondered his chances. If he could just get a little room between him and Hemingr, he might make it. Then he remembered the gate was most certainly still shut against the carnage raging beyond in Lundenburg's streets. He couldn't leave Æva, either. They'd been separated once. Not again.

Hemingr pushed him into a clutch of Danes, each laughing in his face in what he assumed to be an effort to intimidate him. There were well over forty of them, all with a certain fierceness and looking very much like those merciless warriors that had wrought such devastation on their forces during their defence of Canterburie cathedral. They shoved Alaric towards the other prisoners, these men possessing a wild, frantic look that spoke to their obviously fearful state. Then he recognised one of them.

"Father!"

He'd cried out involuntarily, Ælfric's eyes widening in surprise upon hearing it. Imprisonment had not been good to him. He looked old, older than his years, his back slightly bent and his beard long to the point it reached his chest. Alaric gasped again upon recognising the man next to him. His elder brother. Ælfgar. Hunched like his father, dirty and very much worse for wear in his appearance, but it was him. He stared at Alaric, angling his head in his direction, his ruined eye sockets exposed and gazing sightlessly towards him. Alaric called out to him, excited and yet fearful over this sudden and unexpected reunion.

"Brother! They got you too? What's happening?!"

"I thought you would have a better notion, Alaric. After all, you've been rushing around the country whilst we've sat in chains." Ælfgar's voice had lost the confidence it once had. It was almost a whimper, similar to that of a nervous child expecting a rebuke. He still had a bite, though, which was annoying since Alaric was genuinely concerned for him.

"Don't start bickering now, please!" Ælfric implored, addressing his sons. "They are just moving us, it has to be that…" He paused, his face lighting up in dismay at the sight of Alaric's destroyed eye. "My poor boy," he said softly, reaching out with his gnarled and pallid hands to touch his face. A Dane slapped them away and pushed him back. Ælfric hissed with anger, frustrated at his own helplessness.

"Just tell me what happened, Alaric," he pleaded. "What happened to your face? In God's name, where have you been?"

"The enemy happened," Alaric said wearily. "Or if you want a quick explanation… that bastard, Hemingr, killed Osmund and smashed my face in before I could remove Thorkell's head. That's about it."

"Indeed," rumbled a voice from behind, "and at first, I did not remember you. At the time, I thought you were just another dead Englishman who didn't know it yet. But after Canterburie…my memory stirred. You put up a good fight wherever you go."

Everyone turned to stare at Hemingr. He was stood there with his hands on his hips, his head bare and lacking his customary red helmet. Alaric couldn't get over just how much he looked like Thorkell. They had the same face, almost, plus the same brutal physicality across the chest and shoulders, although Hemingr was younger and nowhere near as tall as his bastard sibling. He continued to glare at them awhile, unaware of Alaric's musings, his men spreading out to form a circle around them, their great axes held ready and their expressions cruel.

Then Æva appeared. She put up a struggle, the Dane dragging her by her hair looking like he found her efforts mildly amusing. Alaric screamed a curse at him, barking a threat also about what he would do to him if he did not relent. Hemingr slapped him across the cheek, the sting bringing tears to his eye. Alaric blinked several times and pawed at his face, recovering just in time to be almost knocked down by Æva as she was hurled into the circle with them.

He didn't let her fall. He held on, some desperate strength allowing him to arrest her descent and heave her upright into his arms. Her hands reached to her face, brushing aside the mad red tangle that had become her hair. She looked around, panic-stricken despite the presence of her husband, her eyes wide with terror when they spotted Hemingr. Something was wrong. She recognised him. And her expression told him she was not recalling fond memories.

"It's him, Alaric!" she whispered, embracing his neck, seeking to cling on lest she be snatched away.

"What do you mean?" he asked, trying to stay calm and hoping the effect might somehow rub off on her.

"At Wiltune," she whispered, "he was there…he killed Alfred and…hurt me."

Alaric stood dumbstruck. Æva had no reason to lie, and she'd had no reason to encounter Hemingr during his time in Lundenburg. If this was the first time she'd seen him here and she did indeed recognise him among every other Northman present, then there would be good reason for it. There were also no grounds to presume he'd not cooperated with Svienn Forkbeard's previous campaigns in England if he'd thought he stood to profit from it. If he also didn't appear to recognise Æva, that was most likely because she was just another woman he'd violated in a long and doubtlessly shameless list of similar deeds.

Alaric's stomach turned at the thought of it. He felt his rage return, simmering in his chest, the black, bitter fury seeking to consume him just as it had days earlier in his cell. He began to shake, his very soul clamouring for him to let go and lose himself in violence. He took a deep, shuddering breath, imploring Christ Himself to calm his spirit. He had to see how this played out. He couldn't get himself killed seeking vengeance now. He needed to save his family. He needed to find his son, who was actually Hemingr's son, but that didn't matter. Brandon remained innocent, and on that score, he'd still do what he could for him.

"Now we are ready for some entertainment!" Hemingr roared, the circle his men had formed around them leaving no doubt in Alaric's mind that he was most likely to perform this "entertainment" for their benefit. His men bellowed and thundered with mirth, Alaric wondering if they were genuinely amused or simply attempting to mock him. He suspected it was the latter.

"Where is Brandon, you revolting foreign pustule?" he snarled, his arms still wrapped tight around Æva. "What have you done with our son? Bring him to me so we might not be separated again."

"You're in no position to make demands on me, you one-eyed Saxon turd. I didn't even know you had a son until you just mentioned it."

"So he's gone?" Alaric asked, incredulous. "Where is the king?"

"Gone too."

"What?"

"Your good and honourable king has decided to be remembered as a coward," smirked Hemingr. "My brother and your Eadric go on ahead of him with our forces to secure his flight. He follows with his family and all those weak little men he had around that kept eating all his food."

"So he's abandoning the capital?" Ælfric piped in, the old man looking like a little strength had returned to him after witnessing his son reuniting with his beloved.

"He is. And we still get paid. That's all taken care of. We all leave rich. You don't."

"You intend to murder us?" Alaric had a feeling he knew where this was going. Hemingr just looked too damn pleased with himself for it to be anything else. The question was why he hadn't done it already. He could have snapped his neck in his cell rather than drag him down here for the sake of spectacle. Did he want them to witness each other's deaths? That was very possible, and after what Alaric had seen him do in Canterburie, he suspected something dark and cruel was afoot.

"You die, yes," he affirmed. "All of you. But let's be fair. My brother thinks you're a great warrior, Alaric. He's impressed by that sort of thing, even in his enemies. So let's see you do it again."

Alaric frowned, half wondering if Hemingr was challenging him to some kind of duel. The odds would be with him if so, since Alaric was weakened by hunger and bruises, but he had a feeling Hemingr wouldn't risk it. He knew what Alaric could do when he had a proper weapon in hand. The evil bastard might be a brute animal, but he wouldn't risk getting killed by a prisoner in front of all his men. That wouldn't be much of an end for a man who no doubt wanted to be remembered in whatever passed for history among his murderous kind.

"You fight him," Hemingr said, pointing over Alaric's shoulder, another Dane passing Alaric a small hand axe. Alaric released Æva from his embrace and turned, fully believing he was to do battle with one of the intimidating warriors surrounding them. He'd thought wrong. Ælfgar stood there, looking awkward and out of place, a similar axe to Alaric's held weakly in his skeletal grip.

"I can't fight him," Alaric protested. "He's my brother! And he can't see!"

"Indeed!" Hemingr thundered, barely able to contain his laughter. "Clever, isn't it? You do my job for me and also keep us amused! I have a feeling the blind one might even draw blood. I get a good feeling from him. I think he wants to hurt something."

"I'd hurt you, Dane, if I were able," sobbed Ælfgar, pawing at his axe with both hands. "Of all the things you could dream up…making brothers fight…and when one is as wretched as I!"

"I won't do it!" Alaric shouted. "Give me back that sword of mine, if you dare! We know how our little encounter in the cathedral would have gone if your brother had not saved you! Fight me again, you disgusting monster, and I'll…"

Hemingr moved fast, stepping forward to knock Alaric onto his back and deliver a savage kick to his ribs. Alaric gasped, the breath fleeing his lungs. Hemingr then heaved him up and hurled him in the direction of his brother. Alaric hit the ground, rolling to a stop at Ælfgar's feet, the man frowning in confusion at whatever he thought was taking place.

He rose, his breathing hoarse and his guts burning. Hemingr wasn't finished. He grabbed Æva by her hair, hauling her in front of him and placing his hand around her throat. He held her like this, her back to his chest and facing Alaric, her breath a panicked, rhythmic wheeze as his hand gradually increased the pressure.

"You'll fight him," Hemingr grinned, "and you'll do it now, or I tell you, I will choke the life from your lady here and then violate her before dismembering the rest of you!"

Alaric was speechless. An old feeling returned, akin to the helplessness he'd felt in his dream when in captivity at Canterburie. Æva's eyes were again wide with panic, her hands clawing at Hemingr's gnarled paw in a desperate struggle to slacken his grip. The bastard laughed in her ear, sadistic as always, but he then leaned closer and whispered something to her that only intensified her struggles. It did her no good. He was a towering brute of a man. Cruelty was second nature to him, and Alaric didn't doubt for a moment he'd follow through on his threat and enjoy it, too.

He looked to his father. Ælfric was on his knees, his face bloodied and his hands pressed to his nose in an effort to stem the flow. He hadn't seen what had happened, but the two towering Danes behind him looked pleased with themselves, which told Alaric his father had just attempted to intervene. It was brave of him. But unarmed heroics would do them no good. He turned to face Ælfgar.

His brother, perhaps fortunately, had only a limited notion on what was happening. He was scared, you could tell that from the way he stood, but he had no tears to spare, such were the sightless ruins that were his eyes. Alaric wondered if that would make this easier. If his brother had never been blinded for whatever crime he'd apparently been guilty of, this might be even harder. If he had to look into his eyes and tell him he had to kill him, Alaric didn't think he'd be able to take it. As it stood, all he had to do was swing his axe once. Ælfgar might barely feel a thing.

But then he'd be a murderer. Not only that, he'd have killed his own kin; a sin he didn't think he'd ever be able to wash clean even with a lifetime of contrition. It then occurred to him he was missing the point. He wouldn't have a "lifetime" for any purpose, even if he killed his brother. Hemingr had been perfectly clear. He meant to kill all of them, Æva included. He'd likely violate her anyway after slaughtering the rest of them. They'd done much the same in Canterburie. He'd seen it. They'd made him watch.

Clarity settled on his mind. He was dead. They all were, but he still had some control over how this might play out. If he killed his brother, Hemingr would have won, and he'd then dispose of the survivors after formulating some other sadistic spectacle for his men to enjoy. Alaric wouldn't go to his grave like that. He'd keep his honour. The fools had given him a weapon. With any luck, he could kill at least one of them. He took a deep breath, his hand tightening around the haft of his axe. It was time to go to work. He prayed God would grant him the honour of a noble death and a speedy passing for the rest of them.

"Unhand that woman and stay where you are!"

Alaric glanced about, the others, Saxon and Dane alike, all visibly alarmed by the sudden interjection. The voice was loud but clear, imbued with anger but also an unmistakable authority. He looked for its source, his eye finally resting upon a bizarre procession of men, women, and even children hurrying towards them from the gate. He recognised the man at the head of them. He'd seen him before, a fair while ago, but he knew him. It was the Aetheling Edmund. And he had Ulfcytel and Cenric with him.

"Do as I say!" Edmund bellowed again, drawing his sword from its sheath to add further menace to his words. Cenric had done the same already, as had Ulfcytel, this trio of deadly warriors looking like they were up for tearing through these Godless savages regardless of what was said in reply.

Not everyone in their company looked so formidable. Alaric had no idea what they were doing here, but it looked like Edmund had decided to recruit a small force of elderly men and equip them with shabby spears and the odd axe better suited for chopping wood. A few among them seemed somewhat competent in a fight, and he could see the odd smattering of younger men who looked to be warriors, but the majority were clearly out of place and knew it too. Were these refugees of some kind that the aetheling had taken pity on? But why bring them here?

The commotion was drawing others. Warriors from elsewhere, perhaps the ones who'd allowed Edmund entry to the compound, came running at a jog to fall in alongside him, their shields raised and spears pointed outward. A group of commoners was also gathering to the north, their attire suggesting they worked in the nearby kitchens. They gazed at the Danes in disgust, looking fearfully over to Edmund from time to time as if worried for him.

"Who are you to tell me to do anything?!" Hemingr barked, squaring his shoulders in defiance. He still held Æva, and his hand was still clamped to her throat, her fearful wheezing cutting into Alaric's heart. He contemplated throwing his axe, then dispensed with the idea since he'd be liable to hit Æva instead. If the rest of his men would just back away towards him a bit, then Alaric might have a straight line of attack through which to charge. Hemingr would then be forced to let her go in order to defend himself.

"I am the Aetheling Edmund, in the company of the Ealdorman Ulfcytel of Eastengle and Cenric of Hamptonscir. In the name of my father, King Æthelred, I demand you release that woman and disarm yourselves. Now."

That prompted the reaction Alaric had been waiting for. Hemingr's men fell into position around him, abandoning their circle to stand in line alongside their leader and face off against Edmund. There was now nothing between Alaric and his foe. With one single mad dash, he could reach him. He'd almost gathered his courage when something at the back of his mind bid him wait. He'd been planning to attack as a last resort. The appearance of Edmund had given him other options. He'd wait and see where this exchange went.

"Your father is gone," rumbled Hemingr. "And I am here acting on his orders. We are to clear out his prison and remove his enemies before following him."

"That woman is harmless, you damn coward!" Cenric bellowed, his face flushing with anger, the scar tissue that marred both his cheeks looking like it was glowing through his beard. "Let her go now, or I'll kill you all, just as I put down plenty of you at Canterburie!"

A murmur rippled out from Hemingr's men, some spitting on the ground in contempt. The mention of the losses they'd taken in Canterburie was undoubtedly a sore point for them. Alaric would have laughed, were he not so worried for his wife. She'd turned alarmingly pale, and her struggles were growing weaker. She didn't have long left.

"Like I said," snarled Hemingr, "I have the authority here. Put aside your weapons and speak with me, Edmund. I know we can come to an agreement."

Alaric wasn't sure what happened next. Somebody's nerves snapped, possibly Cenric's, a sudden dash forward prompting all of Edmund's men to break into a charge. Edmund and Ulfcytel ran with them, the kitchen hands who'd been watching from a distance also charging in to attack the Danes with nothing but carving knives and rolling pins. The Danes reacted swiftly, as was their forte, and they rushed to counter Edmund's charge with one of their own. The previously tense atmosphere now finally shattered under the weight of hammering footfalls and competing war cries. Bloodshed was imminent. And Alaric, Ælfgar, and their father were set to be caught right in the middle.

Hemingr had let go of Æva, no doubt realising it was ill-advised to charge into battle whilst dragging a woman just for the sake of it. She'd fallen, but then Alaric had lost sight of her when the Danes ran forward, their stampede blotting out much of anything that now lay behind them. Ælfgar stood as before, axe in hand and head angled towards the ground, frightened yet also unaware he was seconds away from being crushed between the two incoming groups of men. There was only one thing for it. Alaric made a grab for him.

He at first found Ælfgar heavy, and for a split second Alaric felt terrified, fearing with good reason that his efforts to rescue his brother were about to ensure they both perished. Somehow he was able to speed him away, some desperate strength allowing him to carry Ælfgar on his shoulders and deposit him up against the curtain wall of the compound. Alaric looked up and saw his father, his face marred from his beating but still very much alive.

Ælfric went to speak, but his words were cut off by the sudden crash of shields impacting on shields and the clash of iron on iron. Alaric turned, seeing the fight had begun in earnest, and he stumbled into it, his axe flailing wildly, hoping to cleave his way to Hemingr and finish him for the sake of Osmund and, if Æva was right, several other crimes he found too terrible to think about.

He couldn't see Hemingr, so intense was the fracas, but he could deal with some of his curs as they tore into Edmund's ad hoc company. And they needed the help. These men really were getting on in years, and it was testament to Edmund's leadership that they'd followed him at all, let alone into a situation where they'd be fighting the elite guard of Thorkell's remaining army. They were brave, but the enemy were hacking through them with ease, their heavy axes smashing them to pieces with each brutal swing.

Alaric dealt a little justice, cutting the hamstrings of a man who'd just finished splitting the skull of one heroic but very dead Englishman. Alaric didn't wait for him to fall, instead hewing away at him like a tree in need of felling before cleaving his face in two.

One of Hemingr's men leapt forward with a shout, his own axe rising up to smash Alaric's aside. They fought, each man wary of the other yet determined to kill, Alaric finding the going difficult in his weakened condition. Fighting with an axe was a relatively new experience for him. It was a very different weapon than the sword and one he didn't particularly care for. It was too imprecise; any hit he felt he might score lacking the exactitude he'd grown accustomed to. It did serious damage when it did hit, though, as was demonstrated when he managed to demolish half of the Dane's face with a wild swing to the jaw. Perhaps the axe did have some good points, after all.

Alaric fought on, killing another Dane by hacking his legs out from under him and then splitting his chest and head into a grisly, red ruin. He turned, his throat trembling with the strength of his war cry, and put his axe through the back of a Dane struggling with none other than Edmund himself. The aetheling finished him with an almost casual savagery, hacking open his throat and then decapitating him with a sequence of heavy, deliberate swings of his sword. Just as Alaric was about to speak, they were set upon by fresh foes, the necessity of battle compelling them to fight first and talk later. Alaric didn't mind so much. From the looks of it, his vengeance might soon be at hand.

Hemingr had been closer than he'd thought. He must have been seeking Alaric just as Alaric was seeking him, withdrawing from the front ranks to find him and finish him. They flew at one another, Hemingr the stronger combatant, Alaric admittedly quicker without his armour but still vulnerable due to his physical frailties. It was these disadvantages that proved decisive, and as determined as Alaric was, it was all over in seconds. Hemingr used his axe in a rather unexpected fashion, slamming the head of it into Alaric's stomach like it were a blunt, heavy spear. He collapsed, blood trickling from his mouth, his breath once again elusive.

If Hemingr thought he'd won, he was sorely mistaken. Somebody tackled him from the side, their hands frantically reaching for his to hopefully break his hold on his weapon. Hemingr threw them off, his sheer strength knocking Ælfric onto his back with an audible crack. His father had made a brave move there. Alaric was grateful. Despite everything he'd heard about him, he still clearly cared for his sons. The thought brought him relief. And strength. And strength would come in useful now.

He sat up, his body protesting and his stomach again twisting in pain. Hemingr towered over his still prone and winded father, his axe raised above his head to split him in twain. He'd used that weapon in an unusual way to fell Alaric, and now Alaric would return the favour. He threw his axe, from a sitting position with both hands, an enraged bark bursting from his throat. It was a shoddy throw, inaccurate and clumsy with a weapon that held both those qualities. But it still hit home. Hemingr's surprised scream left little doubt of that.

It hadn't seemed likely, but somehow the axe had embedded itself in Hemingr's elbow, its heavy yet keen edge cracking through the links of his mail to plant itself in the tender flesh and bone beneath. Hemingr dropped his own weapon and commenced squealing, his face contorting like he couldn't decide whether he was angry or had just been given the most tragic news of his life. He clawed at his wound with his free hand, each effort he made to remove the axe prompting another bout of agonised mewling. Alaric had never seen him look so vulnerable.

He launched himself at him, hands outstretched in a bid for his throat. They rolled together, Hemingr howling each time their weight pressed down upon his arm, the axe eventually snapping itself free with a sickening crack. Hemingr screamed like a newborn, the sound upping in pitch and intensity as Alaric's fist hammered into his face. Certainty had settled in his mind. He knew Æva had been telling the truth. It had been Hemingr that had killed Alfred and then raped her out of sheer spite. He owed him a reckoning, and he'd repay his debt in full.

Alaric split Hemingr's lips, smashing his nose to ruin and hammering his now bloodied and weeping eyes with heavy, crushing blows. It seemed he was back outside Gipeswic, fighting to escape the camp with Osmund and the others. He'd just snatched a spear from Hemingr's hand, and it was a good thing, too, as he was quite sure he'd been about to hurl it at Osmund. He'd then wrestled him to the ground, bruising and battering the cur's face to the point death couldn't be far off.

He looked up, his vision focusing on a single warrior tearing his way through the fighting. Osmund was roaring like a madman, his twin axes, one in each hand, cutting down every bastard Dane within reach. He was a giant of a man, physically and in other respects, his bravery and skill an inspiration. It was good to see him. Alaric paused, staring at his friend whilst he fought, his heart glad with the witnessing of it. With one final effort, they could escape and all would be…

Alaric snapped back into reality, Hemingr's oversized fist leaving him little option when it ploughed into the side of his jaw. He had no idea what he'd been thinking, finding his sudden descent into fantasy almost as alarming as the ferocious blows he was now taking. Hemingr successfully knocked him down, his boot lashing out to catch him on the forehead whilst he struggled to his feet. Alaric still somehow managed to get up, unsteady and unarmed, his mind whirling. Hemingr drew his sword, or what was in actuality Alaric's sword, a cruel grin of reddish, broken teeth erupting across his ruined features. He'd enjoy killing him with that. He had to think fast.

Somebody knocked into him, sending him flying further back into the grinding melee. The brawling mass seemed to swirl and flow with an energy of its own, and Alaric snarled upon realising he and Hemingr had been separated. He looked about, catching sight of the warrior responsible. He didn't know the man, thinking he must be one of Edmund's lot, and he'd collided with Alaric by accident in an attempt to avoid his current opponent cracking his skull. The two men, Saxon and Dane, kept on, both hacking at the other, Alaric feeling helpless as he desperately searched for a discarded weapon. He eventually found one, heaving the spear up and then forward to impale the raging Dane through the midriff.

The Englishman nodded to him in thanks, his cordiality, unfortunately, ensuring he failed to spot the incoming axe that severed his jugular and almost his entire head along with it. He dropped, dead before he hit the ground, or so it looked, his long and menacingly keen seax clattering to Alaric's feet. He reacted fast, snatching it from the earth just in time to avoid the same axe now swinging for him. The bastard wielding it did not relent, roaring like he was possessed, Alaric now fighting with both spear and blade to keep him at bay.

The seax soon proved its worth. The Dane kept on at him, bellowing still like he was trying to shout him to death. He then stumbled, slipping on someone or something, and Alaric made his move, burying his newfound blade between his ribs. He repeated the action, slamming the sharp iron into already torn flesh over and over, eventually deciding that this heathen maniac was no longer among the living. He caught his breath, trying to fill his lungs with as much air as possible whilst he evaluated the situation.

Despite being outnumbered, the enemy were making a frightening mess of the English. He couldn't see Edmund or any of the others, but Hemingr's men were proving their mettle as the more experienced combatants. If anyone was holding out, it was the few warriors Edmund had managed to call to his side, but even they were hard-pressed. Edmund's attack had bought them time, but ultimately this messy, unpleasant affair would only be resolved with Hemingr's death. Alaric sincerely hoped he'd be the one to do it. After everything the man had done, he'd feel cheated if somebody else were to rob him of vengeance.

Ulfcytel emerged up ahead. He was a distance off and fighting bravely, his tremendous strength and thick, heavy blade cutting into the foe with great sweeps of his arms. Alaric soon lost sight of him, but he'd seen enough. It was like Canterburie all over again, with one exception; this time he would not be defeated. This time he could not be coerced into giving himself up. This time he would kill them all.

He started by spearing the first Dane within reach, twisting and thrusting so that the sharpened tip bored through his mail to split open his back and ribs. He carried on, his seax taking another life and then another, his old fury returning to embolden his heart and strengthen his arm. If he failed here, his wife was dead. His father and brother, too. His son, wherever he was, also likely dead. He'd not allow this. He'd come too far. Everything he'd fought for had led up to this moment. He couldn't fail now.

Despite his wounds, he felt unstoppable, his fatigued and battered body committing itself to a swirling dance of lethality that pierced stomachs and opened throats with deadly precision. He began to shake, blood oozing from his mouth, his battle-lust overflowing even as his limbs turned numb and his joints ground in protest with each killing blow. He was doing it. There would be no escape for Hemingr and his men. He'd dispatch them all and settle scores long overdue. He'd win this battle on his own if he had to. Given his kill count, he just might do that.

The sword arced towards him, its silver-plated workmanship catching the light, had he been able to see it. As great a warrior as Alaric was, and as much as he'd compensated for his handicap under the tutelage of Ulfcytel, his vision was still much reduced following the loss of his eye and could only work to his disadvantage. He thus failed entirely to spot Hemingr when he caught up with him on his blind side; a misfortune that now saw him collapsing to his knees as Hemingr hacked into his ribs with one shattering blow after another. Alaric looked down, his eye wide with alarm, the sight of his own blade embedded in his side shocking him to the core. This wasn't how it was supposed to be.

Hemingr snarled and continued his bloody work, his bashed and weeping face terrible to behold. Alaric tried to thrust his spear toward him, but Hemingr stepped aside and then split it in half. His laugh echoed in Alaric's ears, but that was the least of his worries. Blood was pouring out of him in torrents, his left side looking like it was collapsing in on itself. Miraculously, he somehow managed to stay upright, some hidden reserve of hate and rage pouring into him to stave off unconsciousness for a moment more.

He glared up from his knees, scrutinising every detail of Hemingr's face whilst the fiend readied his stolen sword to slam it point-first through his chest. The bastard then spoke, the words sounding fluid and sickly as they flowed from his ruptured mouth.

"As it was at Hringmere…as it was at Canterburie…as it always shall be."

He shouldn't have said that. He shouldn't have gloated. There was only one answer to that, and Alaric was still of a mind to give it. He thrust his right arm up and forward, using his broken spear in one last frenzied attack before his strength gave out altogether. They impaled each other, Alaric silent in his agony as the sword tore through him, Hemingr, by contrast, bellowing in surprise at the jagged length of splintering ash now embedded in his groin. Alaric's heart gave out, rupturing and tearing under the weight of silvered metal, his last single ounce of strength going to his right arm to force his shattered weapon deeper into his enemy's flesh.

He fell backwards, impacting hard upon the bloody ground. His vision clouded over, his eye giving up along with the rest of him, and strange and unexpected images rushed through his mind, chaotic and discordant. There were faces and voices, like everyone he'd ever known was addressing him at once. He couldn't focus on any of them, and they were talking so quickly, each sounding like they had something of the utmost importance to tell him.

The vision faded into shadow, a welcome silence following with it. A red-haired woman then appeared out of the darkness, dressed in the colours of a widow in mourning. Her shoulders were slumped in grief, and she was all alone, lost in this void with nothing and no one to comfort her. Alaric could see it was his beloved. He could see it was Æva, and his soul ached with remorse upon realising he must leave her. He wanted her with him. Needed her. He couldn't let her go. He loved her too much.

She vanished, and all was again blackness, although Alaric was not alone, for there was something in the silence; powerful and yet gentle, of a real substance and yet impossible to grasp. It formed words, but the silence remained undisturbed, somehow, and it began telling him he'd see his wife again, telling him to be still and know that…

The voice went as suddenly as it had come. He had no idea who had spoken, for the sound was entirely unlike anything he'd ever heard. It was quiet but somehow impossibly loud, reverberating through him whilst possessing a gentleness that defied description.

Other images swam into view. A small boy, not yet a decade old, sauntered up to him and stopped, a slight smile on his face. There was something familiar about the lad, and the more Alaric stared, the more he felt they somehow looked alike. Was this some vision of himself as a youth?

He had company. Alaric's mother, Aefre, stepped forward, her face beaming, and took his hand. The boy did the same, reaching up to grip his left palm. Alaric looked at the pair of them, unable to fathom who this boy was or how he'd come to be with his mother. She'd died so long ago, when Alaric wasn't yet a man, but she looked as he remembered, her black hair still waist length and a gentle smile still upon her face as her wide, hazel eyes drank him in.

More came into focus. They were in a field, green and lush, the summer's day receding to the horizon, the sweet song of swallows returning to their nests carrying on the breeze. Church bells pealed from somewhere, and the sound of happy parishioners making their way home began to echo across the fields.

He could see some of them. One turned to look at him, those whom he presumed to be his family also stopping to gaze in his direction. Alaric's eyes widened upon recognising Osmund, his giant, almost crimson beard unmistakable. He went to cry out to him, but surprise and emotion snatched his voice away. It didn't matter. This was the real Osmund, not the malevolent apparition from his dream in Canterburie, and he looked well, like nothing was out of the ordinary and he'd never suffered a violent death. His wife was at his side, as was a child, no older than eight, that Osmund currently held in his trunk of a left arm. He smiled at Alaric, raising his right hand to wave to him, a great toothy grin upon his face. None of this made sense. Ealhswith had taken her own life after their child had died suddenly at six months of age, leaving Osmund all alone in the world aside from Alaric. Yet here they were. A family again. Osmund wasn't about to explain, instead turning to amble off, his final gesture towards Alaric suggesting he expected him to follow.

As if in response to the bells, a dove appeared, coming out of the deep expanse of blue on high. The day's fading light seemed to gather around it, leaving a shimmering, golden trail wherever it flew. It settled on Aefre's shoulder, his mother and the boy both still calm and content whilst they looked on. Then Alaric felt it. A feeling of peace, beyond his understanding, extending outward and over him, the sensation building within until he felt like he was glowing from the inside out. The boy then spoke, his voice gentle and affectionate, his words dispelling any lingering doubts on who he was and where they'd all ended up.

"It's all right, father. His peace He has given you. It's all over now. It's time to rest."

XXXI

Something was wrong with the enemy. It was difficult to put into words, but anyone who'd been in battle before would know it, these things having a certain subtlety operating purely on the level of instinct. It was true now, and it was true of the Danes, for only moments prior they'd been winning, their terrible, brute forms tearing through the English ranks like wild, monstrous beasts from some overblown saga.

Then it had all changed. The foe was wilting before them, their strength and resolve collapsing suddenly and undeniably. He had no idea why, and in the immediacy of witnessing it, he didn't much care. All that mattered was their defeat, and if these foreign dogs had lost their nerve, he'd be sure to take full advantage.

Edmund began by hacking an arm from the man in front of him, severing it at the shoulder and ensuring his already bloodied axe wouldn't be taking any further lives. He put down another, this one already wounded from some previous exchange, and split his head upon the stones, blood and brains both rupturing outward like fluid from a smashed egg. Edmund thundered forward over the corpse, his people following, their cries jubilant. The Danes were falling. Glory was within reach.

Then he saw the reason. The enemy were a strange people, brave but inclined to rally around their leaders in accordance with the ferocity of their reputations. If that was questioned or they proved wanting, any Norse warband was prone to demoralisation and fragmentation. Now he saw their leader was on the ground, defeated, his life's blood pouring out from him. It was this that had decided the battle. It was this that had brought them victory.

Edmund looked down at him. He was broad, strong, heavily armoured in what was undoubtedly skilled metal work, yet whatever presence he'd had when he and Edmund had confronted the other just earlier had faded. He was whimpering, sobbing, his chest rising and falling rapidly, the blood continuing to seep from his bruised and broken face. A spear looked to have been rammed into the soft flesh just above his manhood, shattering his mail and everything else as it splintered and snapped its way deep into his groin. Whoever had dealt this wound must have possessed a rare strength to inflict such considerable damage with nought but a broken wooden shaft. The pain must have been excruciating. Death could not be far off.

There was something in his hand. It was a sword, which wasn't unusual for a man of his standing, but there was something about it and how it caught the light. He recognised it. Something triggered in his mind. A memory. Of better times.

"That looks familiar," growled Edmund, bending low and retrieving his brother's blade from the enemy's weakened grasp. He studied it. There was no doubt about what it was. This was the sword Æthelstan had given Alaric when they'd met him months back upon the road from Snotingeham. Anger swelled in his heart. This heathen that lay dying here had used his brother's own weapon to shed English blood. Something had to be done about that.

"This does not belong to the likes of you!" Edmund bellowed, observing how the man flinched and mewled at the sound of his voice. He stepped on his stomach, yet more blood erupting from his wound under the cruel pressure, the heathen squealing like a frightened child as Edmund loomed over him.

He then noticed another body, dressed in the plain, dirtied white of the prisoners they'd seen earlier. He stepped closer, forgetting the weeping, dying fool at his feet. This other fellow had taken more than his fair share of punishment before death. He was a mess, bleeding from multiple points in his side and face, a huge puncture wound on his front suggesting this had been the killing blow. Another glimmer of recognition stirred. This was Alaric. That red-haired woman he'd seen being accosted earlier must have been Æva. This wasn't good. This was a tragedy, in fact. Somebody had to answer for this.

Quiet finally came upon them, the sensation strangely jarring when contrasted with the furious cacophony that had only just passed. The battle was over, and England had prevailed, the last of the Danes lying broken and defeated at the base of the prison tower. They'd not gone lightly. Edmund's force was much reduced, and many a man had fallen to the enemy's cruel axes. At least it was over now. They'd bring some good out of this situation and…

Edmund lost his train of thought when Æva rushed over, her face frozen in horror, and knelt to cradle Alaric's head. Her hair was dishevelled, her skin unnaturally pale, the months she'd spent in captivity looking like they'd taken a toll on her health. That was a minor inconvenience compared to what she was going through now. She wept, rocking back and forth whilst she cleaved to her husband, the sound quiet yet heartrending. Edmund was at a loss. He had no idea what to say. But he had to say something.

"I'm so sorry," he mumbled, thinking his difficulty in this situation rather peculiar considering the savage deeds he'd only just performed. Ulfcytel approached, as did Cenric, the two men freezing on the spot when they realised who'd fallen. Ulfcytel began to draw in great heaving breaths, his hands and lips trembling. Edmund had never seen him suffer such a reaction before. Knowing Ulfcytel, he was struggling to keep it together for the sake of appearances. Judging from the tears welling up in his eyes, he was failing.

Cenric was a similar story. He'd fallen to his knees beside Æva, his left arm around her shoulder so that he might steady her. He'd taken one of Alaric's hands in his, as if his touch might somehow stir him to life. Like Ulfcytel, Cenric was struggling to hold his emotions at bay, but his despair was obvious, and it took only a few seconds before his face crumpled under the weight of it, his tears flowing thick and free.

Edmund recognised the enfeebled, hesitant form of the Ealdorman Ælfric shambling over to join them. His face was cracked with a combination of age, weariness, and now abject misery, the old man kneeling at his son's side to paw at his face in silent lamentation. Snake or no, Ælfric was truly suffering, and whatever crimes he may have committed in his time did not warrant the terrible pain he'd now bear for the rest of his life.

What was doubly distressing was the sight of his other son, Ælfgar. Edmund didn't know much about him, but he was possibly the most sorrowful looking of all of them, not because of his tears, but because of the lack of them. Ælfgar was incapable of crying, such was the damage done to his eyes years back, and so he was unable to join his father and sister-in-law for that same reason. He just stood there, hunched and alone, his head shaking slowly from side to side, grappling with his own private turmoil.

Edmund heard a commotion behind him and turned in time to see a scowling, blood-soaked Wilfrid hauling the Norse leader to his feet. One of Wilfrid's men rushed over to assist, and together they held the Northman between them, one arm each so that he could be questioned. Edmund strode over to gaze into the bastard's bloodshot eyes, noting how he continued to whine and whimper through his split and broken lips. This man might have once led armies and inspired his barbarous kind to greater acts of savagery, but he'd been laid low now, of that there was no doubt. It pleased him.

"What is your name?" Edmund demanded, his own sword and the sword he'd just reclaimed gripped in each hand.

"Hemingr," came the whispered, pained response. "Br-brother to…Thorkell."

"You had orders to clear out the prison before joining my father and your brother in escape?"

Edmund had already been told as much by Wilfrid. He just found it remarkable his father was so vindictive he'd assign such a man as this to do it. What was the point? If he wanted to flee, then flee. Why compound his many sins by slaughtering those he'd already punished with imprisonment?

Hemingr gurgled, a deluge of red-hued spittle leaking forth from his mouth and into his beard. His eyes were rolling in their sockets, and his nose looked like it had been shattered in multiple places. Even his ears were bloodied and torn, and so Edmund didn't think they'd get much out of him, the wound in his groin leading him to conclude it was remarkable Hemingr was even able to cling to this sorry semblance of life. All the same, he eventually managed to speak, his words falling from between struggling, wheezing breaths.

"Yes…English king doesn't want enemies left behind… my brother went on ahead to make safe the way…he'll kill you when he discovers what you've…done…"

"Let him try," sneered Edmund. "But am I right in thinking your wounds have been caused by the man we now grieve over? Did you kill Alaric?"

Hemingr actually grinned; a broken, brutal, and terrible sight, his gleeful malice undiminished, even now. Ulfcytel saw it. And he reacted as was typical. He went berserk, baying like an animal, his charge almost knocking Edmund over in his bid to get to grips with Hemingr. Edmund tried to restrain him, but it was like wrestling an avalanche, and before long the ealdorman's hands were clamped around the Northman's throat.

"Tell me, brother to Thorkell!" roared Ulfcytel, his voice like cracking thunder. "You'd have been there the night Alaric and Æthelstan attacked your camp! Was it a trap?! Had Eadric plotted with Thorkell in the hope of killing me?!"

Hemingr looked like he didn't want to answer, although in all fairness, that may have been because Ulfcytel's grip upon his neck was ensuring his silence rather than facilitating the breaking of words. The ealdorman saw it and relented, releasing one hand to reach down and grasp the bloodied, splintered spear that still protruded from Hemingr's flesh. He twisted it, growling menacingly for him to speak, Edmund feeling almost sorry for the heathen as he hissed and yelped in agony.

"It's true!" he spluttered. "I was…it was as you say…we'd been told by Eadric… to expect you…kill you."

"And where is Eadric now?" demanded Ulfcytel, still unwilling to release his hold on him.

"G-g-g-gone! With my brother! Ahead of your king! They'll be to their ships soon and then to N-Normandy…"

"What else do you know?" Edmund asked. "My father flees with the queen? Anyone else?"

Hemingr's knees buckled, an agonised grunt following as he collapsed to the ground. Wilfrid and his companion still held his arms, but they were of no help in holding him aloft now his legs had finally given up. His strength was spent. He was dying. These were the last few moments they had with which to get any information from him.

"It would be easy to end your suffering," said Edmund, his twin blades twitching eagerly in his hands. "Yet I would know…do you feel any sorrow? Do you regret living the life you lived? Do you feel any remorse?"

"What about my son?!" Æva suddenly shrieked, leaping up to accost the dying Northman. She clawed at his face, her teeth bared, demanding over and over that he tell her where her child was. If Hemingr had seemed entirely spent, he proved them wrong. He spoke again, his voice thick with mocking contempt, like he enjoyed the woman's heartache.

"He's with the king, along with all the other useless people who do nothing but eat. You'll never…you'll never…"

Edmund had been sure he was about to expire. Instead, he reached out to grip Æva by the throat. She resisted, tearing his hand from her before snatching a discarded seax from the ground and burying it in his neck. She stabbed him, and then again and yet again, continuing in her fury until she had reduced his throat to a mess of shredded, weeping flesh. She was gabbling something, fast and accusatory, Edmund rapidly getting the impression this man had done more than kill her beloved husband. Was it possible to wrong a woman even more than that? Whatever the truth of the matter, Edmund felt he'd somehow managed it. And he was paying for it now.

She eventually rose from her bloody task, her face blank and her vengeance having left her numb and empty. Cenric went to her side, taking the blade from her hand and again placing an arm around her shoulders. She didn't react, her energy spent, stress, sadness, and now fury taking its toll. Edmund looked down upon her victim, this once great scourge of Christendom now nothing but a broken corpse upon the bleeding earth.

He lay there, finally still amidst his own butchered brethren, his marred visage almost peaceful now his malevolent soul had departed. He was Hemingr. Jomsviking. Brother to Thorkell the Tall. Murderer. Rapist. Slaver. And now dead. Very, very dead. The world was better with his passing. Of that there could be no question.

"So it was all true," Ulfcytel murmured. "We were right. Eadric really was behind it all."

"You were there when I put my father to the question on this, Ulfcytel," Edmund said, his hard gaze still on the dead man at their feet. "That was all I needed to know as to whether Eadric was involved. Yet to hear this…monster… admit to it so casually…"

"You have to find my Brandon," Æva suddenly said. "You brought him back to me before. You have to bring him back again. Please, Edmund, please do this."

Edmund had known indecision in his life. He didn't feel it now. This was beyond politics, beyond the schemings of men like Eadric and the tragic blunderings of his father. This woman had just lost her husband after enduring incessant misery in the solitude of her cell for crimes that had nothing to do with her. For her to lose the only part she had left of her Alaric would be catastrophic. There'd been enough injustice. He knew what he must do. For her sake. For mercy's sake. For the sake of Christ in Heaven, it must be done.

XXXII

He'd had enough of tunnels. When Wilfrid had bundled him and Cenric down some hidden entrance to Lundenburg's ancient sewer system, he'd been curious, the terrible riot in the streets above meaning they'd had to find other ways to reach Ulfcytel and then infiltrate the royal halls. Edmund had found it quite interesting for a time, his thoughts occupied with just how extensive and stable the underground network truly was. By the time they'd collected their compatriots from the safe house and emerged behind his father's walls, he was quite tired of them, thinking the sewers dark, claustrophobic, and unhygienic. He'd dearly hoped he'd never have cause to frequent them again.

Wilfrid's opinion was quite the opposite. He was enamoured with them to the point of eccentricity, stressing their utility for those looking to move about in secret. He seemed to almost want to give Edmund a history lesson, arguing it was a mistake for the Romans to have left and lamenting the state of the city now the English had ceased to use the subterranean infrastructure bequeathed to them. Edmund found that perplexing. To him, the smell was evidence enough the English were indeed still using the sewers, and very much in the same spirit as the Romans. He'd been almost overjoyed when they'd finally made it out, despite having to then hack his way through a horde of malevolent Norsemen.

He was, for that reason, loath to descend into the tunnels he actually knew about, fearing the atmosphere within to be much the same as the main sewer system. For all he knew, they were somehow connected, and whilst as a boy he could remember thinking the old passageways might harbour all kinds of majestic secrets, it seemed possible now they were just a means towards the disposal of waste. He didn't know the truth of that, and he didn't have time to investigate now. His father, the king, had gone this way, and judging by the multitude of footprints heading east, he'd not been long in passing. He had to hurry. It wasn't an exaggeration to say Æva's life might hang in the balance. People could do strange and terrible things to themselves when brought low by despair. He'd avoid that tragedy if he could. They'd had enough for one day.

Edmund broke into a run, knowing he'd best make haste. The air in these tunnels was different, he had to admit, the sewers proper being stuffy and moist compared to the drier, fresher environment here. He suspected that was most likely because these tunnels seemed larger and purposefully built for human traffic, providing an ideal means of escape for anyone wanting to circumvent a besieging army and slip away undetected. He prayed Svienn didn't somehow know about any of this. If he did, he'd be able to capture anyone attempting to flee this way with relative ease. After all the stress he'd been through lately, Edmund didn't want to have to rescue his own father. He would, of course, if he had to, but only him. Eadric and Thorkell could remain in chains.

He reached an intersection, his eyes straining to pick up the trail he'd been following amidst the light cast by his stuttering torch. He saw it again, the mess of prints quite stark as it continued its way east, the sheer abundance of them suggesting the evacuation may have involved quite a considerable number of persons indeed. Of course it would have. Thorkell had most likely moved his entire army through here. The men they'd fought only just now were the rearguard, or at least those tasked with ensuring none of his father's enemies somehow lived to see Svienn's ultimate conquest of the city. He hoped they'd got all of them. If any had somehow escaped the recent fighting, they would have fled through here to try and warn Thorkell himself. That would prove disastrous when Edmund caught up with them. He hoped it wasn't so. He didn't fancy his chances fighting on his own.

As he ran further east, he wondered what his companions up above might be thinking. Out of all of them, only he and Wilfrid knew about these tunnels. They were a long-held secret - an option of last resort - and their existence was well beyond the purview of anyone not in the confidence of the royal family. He'd left Wilfrid close to the entrance, ordering he stand watch and not tell the others of what he had planned. They'd only complicate things. There was already too much grief and heartache to share around. Edmund didn't want them adding to it.

It wasn't their fault, of course. The death of Alaric had shaken all of them, but there was one person, in particular, who could be very dangerous when in a state of emotional upheaval. He appreciated Ulfcytel's loyalty and bravery, but he could act impulsively, especially when pushed to it. The death of his friend had rendered him unstable, and Edmund couldn't be sure he wouldn't simply attack Æthelred if they crossed paths again.

That wasn't acceptable for two very important reasons. The first was that Æthelred had Brandon, and that meant they would need to engage in some delicate dialogue to secure his release. There was nothing about Ulfcytel that was delicate, especially in his current state. He'd be a total liability and had to be kept away for that very reason. The second was that Edmund simply didn't want anyone to hurt his father. Try as he might, he couldn't bring himself to hate him. Family mattered to Edmund, even if such values were not necessarily in vogue elsewhere. He'd do this his way and without interference from anyone else.

He stopped briefly, leaning against the tunnel wall to catch his breath. Sometimes he thought he'd heard something behind him, like a boot scraping on stone, but it was nothing, the silence that enveloped him remaining undisturbed. He looked up, holding his torch aloft to scrutinise the ceiling, the tunnel roof appearing reassuringly solid despite its advanced age. He had no idea how the Romans had built like this, the architectural remnants they'd left in Britain sometimes appearing as if they'd been created via magic rather than the hands of men. He knew he wasn't alone in thinking that, and he'd even heard that some of the common folk had developed their own myths about them, thinking giants or demons had built such things before Christianity had arrived to dispel them.

Edmund liked to think he was wise enough to know there was often a good reason why people came to hold such beliefs, even if they were ultimately wrong. There was great humility in admitting that some things were or should be beyond the capabilities of men. Whereas this didn't justify descending into the world of make-believe, it did show a certain willingness to refuse to become caught up in a kind of collective hubris that might lead one to think it was humanity's destiny to achieve absolutely anything it set its mind to. There was danger in such sentiments, he thought. Human endeavour always had to remain fully human. That meant being constrained by both reason and the moral boundaries that made men authentically men. To think anything was within one's grasp, or perhaps should be, was the path to evil and madness. In that sense, Edmund would rather have his myths about giants than any number of supposedly learned persons who felt their knowledge put them beyond what was right and what was wrong.

He broke into a run again, following the well-trod trail, his path always taking him further east towards the eventual exit. He'd only come this way a couple of times in his life, and they'd never spent long down here; their visits always prompted simply because his father wished to show them how this area might be of use if the worst came to the worst. Edmund had thought it strange at the time, thinking no situation could possibly arise that might see Lundenburg fall. He'd never thought the day would come when he'd fully realise how foolish those assumptions had been.

It occurred to him then that Ecgberht was still out there, defending the walls against Svienn whilst the rest of the city tore itself apart behind him. It was a hopeless task, but Ecgberht wouldn't even consider fleeing with them. Edmund felt guilty thinking of it. He should have tried harder to convince him. But would that have done much good? Without him leading the garrison, the city would fall immediately, and then all escape would be rendered impossible. Ecgberht was giving them the time they needed to fashion some good out of this mess they were in. He just wished it were different. Perhaps by some miracle, Ecgberht might survive and join them later. Stranger things had happened, and Edmund felt he was owed some good fortune.

He turned a low, sloping corner, the tunnel he was now facing trailing off in a long curve towards the north east. He could see torches swaying and bobbing up ahead, their bearers looking like stooped shadows trudging ever onward towards their destination. These must be his father's men. They'd not detected him, which was fortuitous given the amount of noise he'd been making. Success was within reach.

Edmund paused, pondering what to do. He'd thought everything would become obvious if he made it this far, imagining he'd simply be able to talk to his father and get him to make the right decision of his own accord. Now that he could see what looked like his entourage, he wasn't so sure. There were at least thirty of them, not counting the six or so armed men that comprised their escort, and they gave off a certain foreboding air, as if their path was one of intense regret they'd not be dissuaded from. He didn't want to stop them. He just wanted them to give up Brandon. Then it occurred to him he didn't even know what to say to bring about such an end. Was all this just a fool's errand?

He stopped himself there. His task was a noble one, and he'd told Æva he'd return her son to her. There'd been no hesitation, and he'd gained the respect of all by agreeing to it; a boon he might lose if he just gave up now simply because he was alone and unsure of how to proceed. It was also clear that he'd been quite lucky in reaching his quarry so quickly. He'd been right to run, but his father's party hadn't been anywhere near as far ahead as he'd feared. He could see why. Plenty of the shuffling figures were burdened under the weight of trunks, chests, and sacks of what could only be the personal belongings of various thegns. As the city burned above and the enemy charged the gates, these supposed noblemen had been counting coins and fretting over heirlooms. It was contemptible. But he wasn't all that surprised.

A voice cried out. Somebody had spotted him. Two guards began to advance on his position, the rest of the party stopping to stare, wondering perhaps if the enemy had already overwhelmed the walls and somehow made their way down here. Edmund stepped out into the torchlight of the approaching warriors, his own torch held out and above to reveal himself further. He must look an absolute mess. He'd not changed his clothes since he'd arrived in Lundenburg, and they were certainly worse for wear after his escape from the riots and the savage butchery in the shadows of the prison tower. He'd never considered himself a handsome man at the best of times, but his visage presently must be pretty harrowing, and he could feel how his hair and beard had become matted with a hardening layer of sweat, grime, and blood. At this rate, they might indeed mistake him for a hostile Dane. He'd have to do something about that.

"It is I, Edmund," he called aloud, his voice echoing down the tunnels and out into the surrounding darkness. Something stirred from within the group, their ranks then parting to reveal his father. He seemed well and was clearly excited to see Edmund, a look of undisguised relief on his face as he made his way towards him in the company of what could only be Emma and their children. Two additional guards flanked them, their arms and armour easily identifying them as Englishmen, born and bred. That was good. The presence of Thorkell or any of his Danes would only complicate things.

"So you came," Æthelred said, stopping a few paces away from him. He really was pleased, appearing as one who'd just had a great weight lifted from their shoulders. Wilfrid had been truthful then when he'd told him his father wanted him with him. That was something. Hopefully, this would mean he'd be inclined to listen.

"I did," Edmund began cautiously, knowing he had best choose his words carefully if this were to end well. He wanted to scream at him and demand he account for the death of his uncle, that he explain every hurt and neglect he'd suffered over the course of his life. It would be foolish to do so. This wasn't just about him anymore. Others were relying on him. He kept that in mind when he formed his next words.

"I have a proposal for you, father. But before I give voice to it, I must know…where is Eadric? And Thorkell?"

"Approaching Beamfleote, if all is going well," replied Æthelred. "Why do you ask? Do you have news for me? Where is your sister?"

"She's up above with her husband," Edmund said, doing his best to ignore the look of distaste upon his father's face at the mention of Ulfcytel. "She's safe," he continued, "and Wilfrid led us through the sewers to get back to the hall so we didn't get caught in the riot. I had no idea you had such skilled men looking for us, father."

"Well, I do," Æthelred said simply. "And I suppose Wilfrid is not with you either? I have the feeling I'm not going to like your explanation."

"They're safe, don't worry, but not all are unscathed. You shouldn't have left a mad dog behind to clear out the prison. He had to be…put down."

"So Hemingr is dead?"

"He is," nodded Edmund gravely. "And so is Alaric. It's what you wanted, I suppose. They killed each other, or at least Hemingr would have died of the wounds Alaric gave him if somebody hadn't hastened his end further. It was quite a brawl. One that didn't need to happen."

Æthelred began rubbing at his temples, his look implying he was both somehow relieved and yet irritated by Edmund's account of the battle. "This is another headache for me, my son," he said wearily. "If Thorkell finds out you had something to do with the death of his brother, I won't be able to restrain him. You've put us all in danger with your recklessness."

Edmund bit his tongue, his temper rising at his father's lamentable hypocrisy. Nobody had made him hire such a beast, and nobody had made him assign him to murder his enemies as he scurried away to safety. Hemingr would have always been a liability along with his brother. If there was anything positive about what had happened, it was that at least one of them was now dead and unable to cause further harm.

"I'm not here to argue," Edmund finally said. "But I'm not here to come with you."

"Then why come? The city is under siege! You must leave with me, and your sister, too!"

"Father, I need you to show mercy. The boy, Brandon …he is with you?"

"He is," confirmed Æthelred, his eyes narrowing with suspicion. "And why would you ask me this?"

"I don't have time to give you every detail. Lundenburg is falling, father, you know this. I ask you now, for the sake of charity, to give Brandon back to his mother. She's without her husband. Don't take her son from her, too. There's no need."

"So the red-haired woman is alive? Alongside who else? Just how much did you interfere with Hemingr's task?"

"I don't care to repeat what happened," Edmund said, his patience beginning to wear thin. "Suffice to say, many lives were lost, and it was always going to be so when a monster was let loose to do as he willed. Just let me bring something good out of all this. Please."

"And what kind of life would the child have with just his mother?" Æthelred countered. "He'll be safe with us and fostered to a good family. England under Danish rule will be no place for him. And his mother is…troubled. It's better this way."

Edmund scowled, feeling more annoyed than ever. "His mother is troubled because you locked her in a cell and had her husband murdered!" he said angrily. "In the name of God, father, will you not admit to your part in all this?"

Æthelred didn't reply immediately, instead turning to gesture towards the rest of the group still waiting behind him. Edmund thought he saw a figure come forward, its hand placed upon the shoulder of what looked like a child walking nervously alongside. They entered the light, revealing a woman Edmund didn't recognise, Brandon himself lingering at her side like he were fearful of being snatched away into the dark. Edmund gave him a small, sad smile, hoping he'd recognise him. If he did, he gave no sign, his brow instead creased with worry as he glanced about.

"Can you really say he will not be cared for, Edmund?" Æthelred asked. "Both Emma and Cathryn here will take good care of him until something more permanent can be arranged in Normandy. He'll live his life in…"

"He'll live his life away from his family in a foreign country," Edmund interjected testily. "That's no way to live, and you know it. He belongs here with his mother."

"His mother?" asked Æthelred, seemingly rhetorically. "His mother…who has nothing to offer him and is beside herself with grief? Is that any way to…"

"Brandon is all Æva has after you had Alaric killed!"

Edmund immediately regretted his words. They'd been ill-chosen, stupid in fact, his irritation at his father's coldness provoking him to bluntness. He winced as he looked at Brandon, hoping beyond hope he'd somehow not heard him. He had. He was staring right at him, his bottom lip trembling, his eyes glazed over with tears.

"Who was killed?" he whispered nervously. "My father's name is Alaric. But he's been away a long time."

Edmund paused, at a loss for words, until he noticed his father looked like he was about to lean down and speak to the boy on the quiet. That wouldn't be right. The child couldn't be told the whole truth, and if Æthelred was set on doing that, it was imperative Edmund interrupt him.

"Nobody is dead, lad," Edmund said hurriedly. "I've come to take you back to your mother. Like I did before, if you remember. But this time we won't have to stay in that tower. We can go wherever you want."

"I'm afraid that's not so…"

"Enough!" Edmund shouted, his anger finally breaking free in the face of his father's continued intransigence. His ire echoed outwards across the surrounding stonework, those around him flinching in shock and apprehension at this sudden display.

"You will give me the child, father, and then leave!" Edmund continued, his voice still booming. "You will do me this small mercy and then be gone from here! And take your murderous foreign mercenaries with you!"

Æthelred scratched at his head, his likeness thoughtful rather than alarmed. "Or what?" he asked quietly. "You're alone, and if you hope to force my hand…"

"Then you and I end here," Edmund declared. "Wulfhild too. She'll support me. We will be family no longer. You will have lost us both because of your callousness. You will flee to Normandy with what little you have left…but I tell you I will fight Svienn without ceasing for the crown I know belongs to me. And when I have that crown, I will still not acknowledge you. You will be dead to me. I will have no father, and I will never claim to have had one. I will make it so we never knew one another, and if you return, I will not see you."

Silence drifted in, broken only by the flickering of flames as their torches continued to burn away in defiance of the dark. Minutes went by, or so it felt, his father appearing to look sadder and frailer the longer this went on. Edmund had never wanted to say such a thing in his life. It hurt him, but if it caused him some pain, it must be doing yet more to Æthelred. He could tell that just from looking at him. He'd gone pale, or paler than he had been, like somebody had taken a pin to his chest and deflated him so his very life energy was now in danger of being extinguished. It was a sad sight. But he'd left Edmund no choice.

"You would do that?" he whispered. "You'd no longer call yourself my son?"

"I would," replied Edmund firmly, "unless you show yourself capable of mercy. Be a father again, rather than a king. Imagine if you had passed years ago and somebody had taken one of us from mother! Do you think she could bear that? Please do as I ask!"

Æthelred turned away slowly to look down upon Brandon. He then took him by the hand, leading him gently towards Edmund before releasing his hold on him. The boy reached out and latched on to Edmund's cloak, partially concealing himself so the band of watching thegns further back could no longer see him. He must feel quite safe with me to be able to do that, Edmund thought. Chances were he did remember him, and knew he meant well.

"So this is it then, my son?" Æthelred said with a quaver. "You will stay here and do what? You can't stay long in Lundenburg. Why not gather your people and come with us?"

"I think I can imagine more tranquil and considerably less violent scenarios than Ulfcytel, Thorkell, and Eadric all in one boat together, father. Our paths separated a long time ago. You go as you will. There's nothing I can do. But I will do what is in my power. I must."

"You think you can defeat Svienn where I failed?" Æthelred didn't sound like he was questioning him. There was no mockery in his voice. His inquiry was genuine. "You can't hold the city, Edmund," he went on, "and it's death to try it. Don't throw your life away. Come with me."

"I will try my utmost to defeat him, that's all I can say. I won't stay here, either, nor will Wulfhild. We'll be safe. But we cannot come with you."

With those words, Edmund turned away, taking Brandon by the shoulders so he might walk slightly ahead of him. He gritted his teeth, resisting the urge to turn and take one last look back at his father. He stayed true to his course, focusing on the child and his surroundings, wondering just how long it would take to get back to the halls now he was not free to run.

"Edmund!"

He turned at the sound of his father's voice, his heart aching at the sheer anguish he heard there.

"Promise me, Edmund, that you'll find some way to think well of me. Promise me. And if you have children one day and they ask after their grandfather…please try to remember me as I was in better times. Not as I was in evil days. Not as I am now. Not for my failings."

"Your failings?" Edmund breathed, astonished he'd admit to such a thing. "So now you realise, with Lundenburg aflame and your whole kingdom in ruins, that…what? You should have listened? You should have listened to us? To those who loved you rather than those who sought to use you?"

"I do," Æthelred sobbed quietly. "I know I failed. I understand the dream now. It wasn't a warning. Alaric didn't plot against me. He helped me see it. I spoke with him before…he said my dream was about my people…our people. How they needed me. And how I failed them."

Edmund's initial hunch was to dismiss what his father was saying altogether. He'd wondered about his dreams and fixation on Alaric, but until this moment, some part of Edmund had always feared they were just a symptom of madness rather than anything more profound. This felt different. He'd never seen him like this before. If Alaric had managed to trigger some kind of change in him, he felt it best to inquire further.

"What do you mean?" he asked. "How have you failed them?"

His father laughed, the sound soft yet bitter, his manner suggesting Edmund knew the exact answer to his own question and it was foolish to pretend otherwise. "Let's just say I now know what I have to do," he said. "The time for me to sit upon my throne and command others has passed. I've squandered…so much. I squandered the right to call myself king. Yet I remain a father. And my family needs me to remain as such."

"I don't know what to say," Edmund admitted. "None can know how your reign will eventually be judged. You endured one crisis after another…but if you feel all that's left to you is to adhere to your duties as a father…"

"That's exactly how I feel," Æthelred confirmed. "Because it is true. And I'd ask you to come with me again…but I sense your mind is made up. I'm not surprised. You always were…stronger than me. You and your brother both."

"Not so, father. We just were…are…what we had to be. I have to do what I'm about to do. I have to stay. I have to fight Svienn."

"I know, Edmund. And if you drive him from England, you'll make a good king. Just don't make the mistakes I made. Don't give in to…"

"Bad advice?" Edmund suggested dryly. "Turning on your own people at the behest of a villain like Eadric? Killing the man who aided you because…well, why did you kill…why did you kill the man who helped you?"

Edmund felt awkward, fearing his father somehow wouldn't work out he was referring to Alaric. He'd already mentioned his death right in front of Brandon, and he wanted to spare the child as much as possible before the time came when he'd have no choice but to learn of his father's fate. Fortunately, Æthelred had been listening well.

"I did not want to," he said. "But his father's crimes were too great. If I left either of them alive, unfinished business would follow me wherever I went. I did not want to leave any loose ends behind that might later trip me up."

"You're still thinking like Eadric," Edmund said sadly. "I hope and pray that man does not lead you down any even darker paths. Because what you've done here may trigger a reckoning, regardless. Besides…if I ever see Eadric again, I'll have him seized. You value the venomous snake too highly, thinking it frightens your enemies…but in doing so, you hold it too close to your chest."

"I know you think of yourself as a political man, Edmund, but…"

"I mean it, father. That man will be your undoing."

Æthelred nodded slowly, his expression blank like he hadn't really come to one conclusion or another. He'd begun to turn away and head back towards Emma and the rest of his escort when he stopped. He spun around to face Edmund again, his chest rising and falling rapidly as if suddenly anxious in the presence of some long-feared adversary.

"You don't hate me, do you, son?"

"No," Edmund said weakly. "We never did. Not I, nor Æthelstan, nor Wulfhild. None of us. You just never let us love you. Not since mother passed. Maybe even before."

It was a moment of perfect clarity between them. Neither had ever known anything like it, the two men, young aetheling and despairing king, finally seeing eye-to-eye for the briefest instant of their last meeting. They'd both loved Ælfgifu. They all had, and for a time she'd been the bond that had cohered them into some semblance of a family. When she'd passed that had been broken, and the endless strife and incessant invasions had pushed Æthelred further and further from his children until there was precious little left to salvage. Unless they remembered. Unless they remembered Ælfgifu.

Edmund took Brandon's hand in his before slipping away into the surrounding silence. He wanted to leave it there. If he stayed, there was a chance they'd begin to converse on other, less pleasant memories and those questions between them that were still left unanswered. Edmund didn't want to spoil anything. He might never see his father again. He'd treasure this last meeting as he left it, with a gentle truth and the memory of someone they'd both cared for.

He passed from sight, retracing his steps to take him back to the surface. There were trials that must be faced, yet he found it hard to decide who had the harder part in them, himself or Brandon. Within an hour, the boy would discover the truth of what had happened to his father; an experience that would sear itself into his memory and fundamentally change the person he'd been. Edmund had not been far-off his age when he'd lost a parent. He hoped he'd receive the care he never did.

Edmund looked down at him whilst they walked hand-in-hand. He squeezed his palm gently, smiling to himself when the lad squeezed back, Edmund making sure to keep his pace slow and steady so that the young man might walk alongside him in comfort. That small mercy was all he could give for now. He'd do more if he could. But he feared Brandon would soon have to walk a path where he'd be very much alone.

XXXIII

She'd taken him inside, stripping him down and bathing him so that he might be made presentable. She didn't know why she did it; trapped and desperate as they were, the idea of giving Alaric a proper funeral sounding faintly absurd in their situation. The man they called Ulfcytel had helped her carry him, as had Cenric and Ælfric, the three men heaving the body through the king's empty halls until they'd found a suitable supply of water. Æva had then insisted they depart. She was grateful to them for all they'd done, but she needed to be alone now. She needed to just be with her husband.

She'd eased him into the tub herself, its spacious confines easily accommodating his body. There were several others like it laid out on either side, this chamber serving as a washroom where the servants of the now absent King Æthelred had busied themselves with the mountains of clothes, linen, and other sundries that routinely piled up in the midst of life within a royal hall.

There was thankfully no shortage of water, an adjacent archway leading to a pool that looked like it was being supplied by a source Æva could not physically locate. She moved back and forth between the pool and the tub, emptying and then refilling a large and cumbersome bucket she'd spotted mouldering in the corner. She stopped when the water just about covered Alaric's shoulders. It was cold, and Alaric was filthy, the grime and gore clinging to his pallid skin like it were a second layer to him.

Æva had cleaned him halfway, her hands lingering on each and every bruise, cut, and scar he'd picked up since she'd last known him. There were so very many. He'd suffered through so much. She felt like weeping all the more because of it, had she any tears left to give. She'd run out some time ago.

Memories stirred. She'd bathed him before in the not-so-distant past, helping him to relax whenever he'd been overburdened with work, study, or training. She'd helped put him at ease, rubbing his temples in a way that always calmed him into drowsiness. She did it now for old times' sake. He mouthed no word of appreciation. She carried on anyway.

Yet washing him now was more difficult than she'd expected. He had a hole in his chest, and part of his side below the ribs simply wasn't there anymore, making it nigh impossible to clean him given his body's insistence on bleeding in apparent perpetuity. She'd eventually given up, heaving him from the tub with considerable effort and depositing him on the floor. She'd sat patiently with him whilst he dried, wrapping his chest and side with a shredded linen cloth she'd recovered earlier. She then wrapped him in a sheet from the neck down, binding him tight so that he could be carried without risk of his limbs protruding outwards.

He looked halfway decent, considering what he'd been through. She tied his hair back and did the same for his beard, fastening it with a band at its mid-point so it hung relatively neatly from his jaw. She caressed his face delicately, her fingers noting the patchwork of brutal scar tissue that spilled out from his right cheek. There were teeth marks, of a size that suggested a human had done this. She had no idea what had happened here, and she'd never know now. She wondered if she'd really be able to relate even if he had survived to tell her all his stories. She'd never dared presume to know what it must be like to be a warrior, compelled by oaths of duty and kinship to fight and kill in the name of your king. But she'd give anything to hear him talk about it. Just a few words, one last time, before she made do with her memories.

He didn't speak. Silence was his way now, his body stiff and cold to the touch, his jaw shut rigid as he lay upon the floor. She'd closed his single eye some time ago, finding it difficult to look at when it was open. She'd lost herself in his eyes so many times in the past, but now it was different. She could tell his soul had departed. She'd honour his body as was appropriate, but the true essence of the beautiful man she loved was elsewhere. He'd be waiting for her, and they'd see each other again in a better place and a better time. God's abundant mercy would see it done.

The door began to open, creaking inwards to allow Cenric to step through. He was another man who could benefit from a bath, as could that Ulfcytel and even Edmund. They were quite pungent, possessing the appearance of men who'd been fighting non-stop for months. Then she realised that perhaps wasn't far from the truth.

"Edmund has retrieved Brandon."

That was all he had to say. She hastened out into the corridor, shutting the door tight behind her and following Cenric. She'd wondered where Edmund had gone to, finding the explanations of this Wilfrid fellow a bit difficult to comprehend. She'd been shocked he'd vanished on his own. She'd wanted to go after him, but Wilfrid had insisted he didn't want anyone following, wherever that was. If it were anyone else, she'd have been angry, feeling as if she'd been tricked following his assurances to bring her son back to her. But he had done precisely that before. He'd proven he was a man who meant what he said. In times as treacherous as these, this was a quality that was truly precious.

Cenric led her on and on, hurrying through corridor after corridor until they finally passed under a stone archway and into an expansive garden. She knew this place. The king had brought her here one night. She'd not really been able to appreciate it then, dark as it was, and the king had made for disagreeable company, but it was quite a sight now. She wasn't here to gather her thoughts amidst the trees, though. The person now running to greet her was her sole object of concern.

Brandon gripped her around the waist, clinging to her tightly and shaking like he feared for his life. Æva knelt and held him close, a few whispered assurances ensuring his trembling gradually began to ease. She spied Edmund watching from ten paces, his look one-half relief and the other soldierly restraint. Wilfrid stood with him, as did Ulfcytel and several others she'd not been introduced to. They'd been discussing something, and as much as Brandon was the most important thing to Æva, she did not imagine that these men of war and authority had been talking exclusively about him. Something was afoot.

"What is it?" she asked, standing upright, Brandon detaching himself from her arms. Generally, the child knew better than to speak when Æva was conversing with adults, but this time he did, giving voice to the subject the others had been discussing.

"The king is gone. He wanted to take me away, but Edmund argued with him. Now England has no king."

Æva stared down at him, detecting no trace of a lie in those sapphire eyes of his. She glanced back at Edmund, wondering what he'd said to Æthelred to get him to give him up. "Why would he take him?" she asked. "What goal of his would be served by escaping with my son?"

"We should discuss that in private," Edmund said gently. "My father had his reasons…which were typically questionable, but reasons they remain. What we have to do now is prepare to make our own escape."

"So there's some kind of tunnel under these halls?" asked Æva apprehensively. She'd never been underground before. The notion did not please her.

"There is," Edmund confirmed. "Extensive ones, across the city, but that doesn't concern us now. We need only travel through a few, but for some time. The same my father now travels."

"But won't we just bump into him?" she asked, alarmed at the prospect of another confrontation with the violently eccentric Æthelred. "Didn't he have warriors with him? More Danes, too?"

"We need not worry," assured Edmund. "He'll have probably reached the Temes by now. He'll then move on foot to Beamfleote and take command of what's left of his navy and Thorkell's own fleet. Then he's away. He has no more interest in us or being our king."

"I still find it hard to believe," said Ulfcytel, his burly, scarred arms crossed tight across his broad chest. "He's been our king for so long and endured so much, for better or worse. Why doesn't he try and raise another army and make a fight of it?"

"I wondered the same," confessed Edmund. "But from my conversation with him, it would appear your husband, Æva, made some kind of impression on him. Were you aware the two had met whilst he was in captivity?"

"As luck would have it, his cell was directly below mine," she answered. "We could hear each other and talk if we pressed ourselves to the window. He did go silent for a time. I feared he'd been moved, but then he started talking again. Said the king, of all people, had visited him."

"And what else?" Edmund pressed.

"He didn't admit to much," she replied. "If he did somehow convince the king of anything, perhaps he wasn't even aware of it himself. He was still locked in a cell, after all. And the king still ordered his…"

"I know," Edmund said sadly, his gaze drifting downward towards Brandon. "I think you and your boy may need to discuss recent events. I'll leave that to your discretion. In the meantime, I'll have somebody find you some proper clothes to wear and something to eat. You'll need it for our journey."

Æva had been dressed in rags for so long she'd almost forgotten she once wore anything else. She looked down at herself, her dirty, grey dress stained with sweat and whatever else had accumulated during her seemingly permanent incarceration. She probably stank something terrible. The offer of cleanliness was welcome.

Edmund let her leave, saying he'd send Wilfrid for her within an hour or so. Æva and Cenric wandered back the way they had come, Brandon's pace measured and easy as he walked at her side. They stopped at the door to the washroom. She couldn't do it. The child had to find out about his father at some point, but presenting him with his corpse, one-eyed and scarred, was not the correct way of going about it. She needed to finish tending to him. Only then would she perhaps allow the boy near him.

She left him with Cenric, giving the latter instructions to find something for him to do whilst she finished up in here. She shut the door tight, not wanting Brandon to come barging through in the possible event of him sneaking away from Cenric. Alaric was as she'd left him, and his wounds had slowed in their bleeding, leaving him looking reasonably presentable, if a little bloody. Fortunately, there were more sheets available, stashed away in a cupboard, and she used a few of them to wrap Alaric's entire body until he was almost completely subsumed in white. Only his head was visible, his face gaunt yet oddly serene.

She held his face in her hands, leaning down to kiss his lips for the final time. Tears suddenly came, her sobbing increasingly bitter when she began to wrap his head in cloth, each movement laden with regret as yet more of his face was obscured. Her heart stung with every inch of him that vanished from view, knowing full well this was the last she'd ever see of him. She let out another sob upon finishing, her tears pattering off the stone floor like raindrops. That was it now. She'd never see his face again. She observed her handiwork. It could be anyone in there, wrapped tight and ready for burial. Nobody need know who it was, and Brandon would be left to wonder until she found a way to break the news.

Both Wilfrid and Cenric came knocking soon enough. Wilfrid had obtained for her a set of travelling clothes properly suited to a lady well accustomed to riding. Æva took them eagerly, changing in the washroom and noting with some considerable satisfaction how novel it was to be wearing shoes again. The same went for her new undergarments, and the grey kirtle she wore over them proved both functional and decorative. The fur-lined cloak was an absolute luxury, if a little large, but it would serve her well, undoubtedly.

She emerged into the corridor, feeling more confident in her new attire and doubly pleased to see that Wilfrid had managed to find a platter of bread and cheese for them. She'd not had anything but watery porridge in months. She wondered how she'd ever become indifferent to something as joyful as the taste of bread. She tried to hide her enthusiasm. It didn't work.

They met Edmund in the gardens soon after. The sun was rapidly going down, yet the city was not any calmer for it. They could see much of it from here, for the gardens were situated upon an incline that elevated them so they could look southward towards the walls.

The sounds of strife echoed out across the entire capital. She couldn't tell where it began or ended, but her ears told her all she needed to know. This wasn't a mere riot now, nor was it anything as directed as an uprising. This was a city that was dying, consumed by its own fury, its people reduced to the level of base animals tearing at the other. What was even sadder was that there were still warriors out there, fighting on the battlements, resisting the invaders even as everything they fought for fell to ruin just behind them. She couldn't make any sense of it. She imagined they couldn't either.

And yet not everyone in the streets could be held responsible for the self-defeating actions of the mob. She'd suggested to Edmund they announce to the people that they knew of a means of escape, believing it selfish of them to just slip away and leave everyone to Svienn. Edmund had confessed he'd been of the same opinion until the riot had started last night. It was too dangerous now, and she could see for herself the disorder was showing no sign of ceasing. If they opened the gates to let people in, there was every chance they'd just bring the violence with them. They couldn't have that. They couldn't risk it. And from what they could hear, many of those out there actually wanted Svienn as king. It was hard to believe. But a truth was still a truth, regardless of how bitter and unexpected.

Æva looked around at her present company. All the survivors of the battle with Hemingr had assembled here. There were few of them left, just a clutch of old men and some warriors from the hall, the rest of their group looking like it was made up of women and children and a rather striking, dark-haired lady who apparently was none other than the sister of Edmund and wife of Ulfcytel. There were some walking wounded with them, and at least three men who had to be carried by their friends, such were their injuries. There were also at least a dozen servants who had been left behind when the king had taken flight, but for what reason, Æva had no idea. What mattered was that Edmund wasn't abandoning anyone if he could avoid it.

Brandon remained close, gazing sadly in the direction of the great bear that was Ulfcytel. He was a sensitive and astute child, for Ulfcytel and Cenric carried a wicker frame between them upon which lay Alaric, unrecognisable in his tight-fitting and impromptu shroud, but Alaric all the same. There was absolutely no way Brandon could know that it was indeed his father, but he kept looking back at him regardless, some instinct telling him that whoever that was had meant something. Perhaps she was reading too much into it, Æva thought. The boy had probably just noticed that she herself kept looking mournfully over towards her husband. That would have given him the impression something tragic had happened.

Such a notion was further reinforced from a quick look at those who carried him. Ulfcytel had insisted that he bear the burden of Alaric's body, Cenric likewise announcing he'd help him, given he was apparently "strong enough to carry" the ealdorman himself. Æva knew not why Cenric would have cause to make this boast, but they were sincere in their desire to help. They'd handled her husband with an almost delicate care as they lifted him up between them. She'd been moved to see it.

But it was a lot to take in. Æva had never met Ulfcytel before in her life, and yet the man seemed almost in awe of her, adopting an air of deference and respect that Cenric claimed was born of his great admiration for Alaric. Æva wanted to speak with Ulfcytel at length when she got the opportunity. She wanted to hear of the final months of her husband's life. She wasn't the only one who loved him, and it touched her to think others had come to care for him despite the relatively short period in which they'd known him. She knew she'd feel comforted by their company.

Edmund addressed the gathering, telling them of the necessity of their flight and the prospective journey underground. Many in the crowd shifted uncomfortably, Æva feeling gladdened that she wasn't alone in her apprehension at what lay ahead.

Edmund looked like he was about to carry on speaking when a great booming sound suddenly echoed across the gardens, repeating again and again with mounting urgency. The mob was at the gates. Æva could hear them shouting, demanding the head of the king. Edmund stated the obvious, telling them all to hurry and stay close.

Nobody questioned him as he led them onward, their party leaving the gardens through a sequence of archways leading to a long corridor that sloped partially downwards. Æva and Brandon stayed just behind Edmund, thinking the cobwebs and musty atmosphere a sure sign this part of the compound was not often frequented by those in residence. The air in here felt cooler, and she thought she could hear water, a slow, ponderous dripping sound emanating from somewhere up ahead. They couldn't hear the mob from in here, but that didn't mean they were safe. She'd only feel better once they got some serious distance between them and the city.

They kept on and on, hurrying lest undesired company catch up with them. Their path was eventually blocked by a pair of remarkably large and aged double doors. Everything about them spoke of neglect and the passage of time, making Æva wonder if it were even possible to open them.

Cenric lit a torch, illuminating the corridor, the doors appearing even more decayed when inspected in the light. Edmund probably knew all about this place, but he remained silent whilst he fumbled with the doors, intent on proceeding with all haste. He eventually managed to get them open, their rust-covered locks and hinges clicking and scraping as he pushed them both inward to reveal another passageway. They all followed him when he passed within, waiting patiently for him to seal the doors behind them before continuing. Wherever they were going, he didn't want anyone to follow.

This place was as they'd expected, save for the atmosphere. There was a stale, lifeless quality to the air here, giving one the feeling it wouldn't be wise to linger lest you eventually suffocate. The stones were also odd, as if entirely drained of colour, although by what she could not tell. They pressed on in a hurry, a winding, spiral stairway eventually revealing itself to their right. It was damp and decrepit, its pale stonework marred with slimy growths and puddles of stagnant water. Edmund lit his own torch and began his descent, Æva and everyone else doing their best to stay close. The stairs eventually flattened out, their path taking them down a wide, sloping tunnel roughly hewn through the surrounding rock.

Æva guessed they were heading east, their hurried footsteps echoing over and over, this main tunnel looking like it were host to multiple others branching off at random intervals. Nobody spoke as they walked. Everyone felt uneasy, even Ulfcytel, the torchlight reflecting in his wide eyes giving him an oddly nervous look. Only Edmund seemed confident, his head lowered and torch held aloft, following the mess of footprints that trailed on ahead of them. This must be where the king's party had passed, Æva supposed. If they followed, they'd find the exit he himself had used. It was just as well. She doubted any who didn't know this place could find their way otherwise.

She felt anxious at the thought. She moved away from Edmund, falling back through the straggled line of followers so that she might mingle. She was fearful but didn't want to speak of it, knowing full well there was every chance she'd make things worse if she gave voice to what everyone else was most likely thinking. It was perfectly reasonable to assume they were not out of danger, and if the king had been vindictive enough to send Danes to massacre everyone in the prison tower, he might see fit to take steps to prevent anyone from following him. She wasn't sure what such contingencies might look like, so she held her tongue, thinking with good reason that to babble anxiously about things she wasn't even certain of would help no one.

Æva moved alongside a grey-haired couple, a man and a woman with two children, a girl and a boy, hoping Brandon might be comforted by the presence of his peers. The girl, Cwen, introduced herself, but the lad named Stefn kept trying to interrupt as if vying for attention. The older fellow, who called himself Oscar, eventually told him to pipe down and remember his manners. He seemed like a good man, and he and his wife, "Swet", as she was apparently called, had fled Canterburie with their two grandchildren. Æva was sorry to learn that their son and father to the children was not with them, nor was their mother, but she was amazed to hear of their escape in the company of Cenric and Ulfcytel.

Their story became even more dramatic from there. They'd travelled by ship, using a vessel Ulfcytel had somehow stolen from Thorkell. They'd then confronted the king himself in his own hall, eventually fleeing his wrath to hide out in the city with Edmund. Æva was rightly astonished, but her feelings turned to regret when Oscar revealed the wound he'd taken to his chest and side in the battle with Hemingr. It had been bandaged well, but she still felt sorry for him. She hadn't wanted anyone to get hurt on her behalf, let alone a man clearly as gentle and aged as Oscar. She'd be sure to pray for him and for the well-being of his son, wherever he was, dead or alive.

She took her leave, moving with Brandon back to the head of the column and the company of Edmund, Cenric, and Ulfcytel. The last two still bore the body of Alaric between them, each man keeping up a brisk pace even as their arms must surely be aching with effort. Both also looked on edge, ever alert for unseen threats, perhaps thinking the exact same thoughts she'd had about the king leaving unpleasant surprises. Edmund was the only one who didn't seem bothered. He pressed on, eyes still lowered and following the tracks, his twin swords dangling at his waist.

The atmosphere had begun to feel more smothering than ever. Brandon started to complain, saying he couldn't get his breath and didn't want to be down here again. Æva assured him they would be out soon, hoping their speedy progress would prove her right. Just as she'd begun to formulate some new words of comfort to placate him, the air changed, and a refreshing breeze washed over them from somewhere up ahead. Edmund began to hurry, picking up his pace, everyone else endeavouring to match him, the prospect of freedom and the open sky spurring them on.

It must have been another half hour before they were finally free, the tunnel seeming to phase out naturally to emerge from the side of a smooth cliff face. The ground here was sandy and crisp, like chalk mixed in with gravel, and there was a breeze blowing in strong from the south east. She turned to face it, letting it flow through her hair and fill her lungs. Night had fallen, and the ground immediately ahead was lost in shadow, but she could see the Temes, perhaps a half mile away, rippling potently upon its course, the scant moonlight reflecting gently off its choppy surface. The wind was getting stronger, and the trees hissed and sighed with its touch, the sound a welcome one after so long in captivity. She only wished Alaric was here at her side to experience freedom with her.

Everyone was out now, breathing heavily and with much relief, some sitting within the sand-strewn opening to rest their aching legs. A new optimism was in the air. They'd escaped the tunnels, and there was no trace of the king or any of his foreign hirelings who might wish them harm. Æva gazed back the way they had come, finding it a marvel as to just how hard it was to notice anything there. The tunnel seemed to blend with the cliff, looking like a perfectly natural opening that was of no real depth and thus of absolutely no interest. This whole area looked secluded, the cliffs immediately behind and the trees to the east and north concealing them from prying eyes. Nobody would be likely to notice anything out of place here, let alone stumble upon a passageway that would take them underneath Lundenburg itself.

Svienn evidently hadn't spotted it, and neither had Thorkell before him, although he certainly knew about it now since he'd apparently passed this way himself not so long ago. Æva couldn't shake the feeling they'd all come to regret that. The king had often confused her from afar, but his sudden success in wooing Thorkell to his side was downright bizarre. She'd heard of wars where combatants had switched sides once or even multiple times, but she just couldn't bring herself to think of Thorkell as an ally. He wasn't. He was a murderous beast who only served himself. It was just as well they were getting out of here. Once he found out what they'd done to his brother, he'd come looking for them. She doubted the commands and promises of Æthelred would restrain him then. He'd want his revenge. Of that they could be assured.

She approached Edmund. The young aetheling was in conversation with Ulfcytel, who had, for the moment, put Alaric down on the ground so he and Cenric might rest their arms. There was some confusion, as if nobody had thought this far ahead and had little idea what to do once they'd escaped Lundenburg. She listened intently, not wanting to interrupt, feeling relieved when Ulfcytel had stressed the need to get away from the city and Svienn's army before they made any concrete plans. Edmund had readily agreed, looking a little chastised in the face of Ulfcytel's common-sense planning.

She kept Brandon close when everyone again set out, their path taking them north and east, the trees and darkness giving them some much-desired cover. Æva occasionally looked back westward, hoping to spot Lundenburg's walls and the army that assailed them. She could see nothing, the landscape behind them appearing as a broken, shadowy expanse topped by an equally inscrutable layer of dark, fast-moving clouds. The Temes itself was also featureless, snaking its way west without effort or outcry, as if it had never known the disturbance of man-made vessels heading upriver for the sake of war and plunder. They were safe. She hoped it would stay that way.

They stopped to rest just a few hours before dawn, the ambient stillness interrupted only by the creaking and swaying of trees buffeted by the still persistent winds. Brandon was fast asleep, resting contentedly in a bed of leaves. Æva was stretching out her arms, trying to coerce the ache from her muscles, when Cenric sauntered over to offer her a drink of water and several torn slices of bread. She ate eagerly, surprised still at how good proper food tasted. She went to share with Brandon but thought otherwise when she saw how deeply asleep he was. There was no need to disturb him. She'd make sure he got something to eat when he woke up.

"We need to bury my husband," Æva said softly. Cenric nodded, his eyes suddenly sad. He moved away, exchanging a few words with Edmund, who then peered in her direction like he'd been told she knew something of import. He walked over, Cenric at his side, his look sympathetic. She had a feeling she knew what he was going to say.

"I would give Alaric a proper burial," Edmund said quietly. "But we are pressed for time. I cannot spare anyone to take him back to Hamptonscir, and I have already spoken with his father on this, who is of the same opinion as I. If you know of anywhere nearby where you might like to lay him to rest, say it now."

Æva thought on it. She'd not spoken with Ælfric or Ælfgar just yet, and her dislike of her brother-in-law still felt fresh despite his prolonged absence. She really had no idea what to do with Alaric, believing perhaps it might be best to simply bury him at any spot they came across that might appear suitable. Just as she was about to suggest precisely that, she remembered a conversation she'd had just recently. Alaric had mentioned a priest. In Offetuna, if she remembered right. He'd apparently saved him when he'd been injured. And he wasn't too far away. If anyone should preside over a burial, it should be him.

It was easier to convince Edmund than she'd feared. Ulfcytel was also amicable to her suggestion, the prospect of returning to his own holdings in Eastengle pleasing him. She didn't know how anyone else really felt, and Edmund's subsequent announcement about where they would be going made little impression on them. It involved a lot of walking, though, and the going started to get hard on Brandon and the other children in their company. The old folks, too, began to suffer, the cross-country journey wearing them down despite their great efforts to avoid complaining. She helped where she could, but she'd started to fatigue also. No matter how much she wanted to avoid admitting it, her health had suffered in captivity, both physically and mentally. She longed for some respite. She hoped Offetuna might somehow provide it.

It was fortunately all over within a few days. The weather held, turning neither hot nor cold, some rain clouds appearing on the second day to shower them for the best part of an hour before thankfully heading west. Eastengle was strangely deserted, the roads empty and the villages they passed through depopulated and partially ruined. Ulfcytel was visibly troubled and kept muttering of revenge upon any "heathen" that might dare show himself. Edmund was passive in the face of such talk. He had other things on his mind, she assumed. Like how they might acquire the numbers to help them in any pursuit of vengeance. A smattering of aged farmers and a few tired warriors just wouldn't suffice.

If Offetuna had been inhabited when Alaric had been here last year, then things had certainly changed. It was all ruins, the farmhouses charred black and the fields choked with weeds, a small church also besmirched with soot and ash following what could only have been a prolonged effort to set it on fire.

They found Alaric's priestly saviour upon the steps leading up to the entrance. He'd been dead for some time, a spear pinning him upright in a sitting position as if he were still of a mind for prayer. He looked strangely tranquil, his expression suggesting he'd met his fate knowing precisely what awaited him, his conscience clear of the troubles that might assail less virtuous men.

What was curious was the figure that lay close by. It was another corpse, but this one had the likeness of a Dane, his thinning blond hair and angular features setting him apart from the other man. He'd lost a hand at some point, but it had healed well, and he was dressed in the attire of a monk, the simple wooden cross around his neck making his allegiance to Christ and Christianity clear enough. He'd been fighting, a simple spear gripped still in his single remaining hand, like he'd attempted to defend the church against whoever had come calling. Æva didn't know what to make of any of it, but she had the feeling something truly tragic had happened here.

The good news was that the church had some supplies left intact. Æva thought that whoever had raided this place would have taken them, but it looked like they'd been in a hurry and missed things they'd normally spot with ease. There'd been a fair number of them, since they'd left a muddied onslaught of footprints sweeping up from the south and then heading off eastward towards Gipeswic. Edmund said they were likely to be renegades from Thorkell's army attempting to get back to their ships after abandoning their leader in Canterburie. Æva couldn't say if that were the truth of it, but she wasn't surprised by the thought of such men behaving as savages, even when in retreat. It was their nature.

They retrieved as much food as they could carry before retreating into the forest at the rear of the church. It was good stuff, especially when the vegetables were chopped into a stew and cooked over a campfire. Æva lay down after eating with Brandon, the warmth from the fire and her full belly compelling her to rest. She fell asleep, the sound of crackling flames and the wind through the trees easing her into a deep and satisfying slumber. It didn't last. Somebody cried out. Something was awry.

Every warrior had rushed for their weapons, Edmund, Ulfcytel, Cenric, and Wilfred all standing tall to greet whoever might emerge from the dark. A figure had appeared, walking slowly towards them with his hands raised as if to signal he meant no harm. Edmund had then laughed, genuinely amused, like he recognised who it was. He'd embraced the stranger, Ulfcytel too booming with laughter when several others and then yet more emerged from the trees. These men were known to them. There was nothing to fear.

The leader of the newcomers was named Wulfnoth. He looked like a dangerous man, cold and sharp like a fine seax, yet the others trusted him, liked him even, which gave Æva at least some reassurance. Edmund, in particular, appeared very close to him, and the two shared some sincere words about the fate of Edmund's brother, Æthelstan.

Wulfnoth then claimed Alaric himself had told them to meet him here after he'd left Remmesgate with news of Sviennn's fleet. Æva immediately wanted to know why he'd been allowed to depart alone. A young yet hard-looking man called Osbert gave some explanation, claiming Alaric had taken the only horse left in the stables and raced off before any of them could argue with him. Ulfcytel, who seemed familiar with Osbert, had taken him at his word, as had the others. Æva felt helpless. She then realised she was just looking for somebody to blame for her husband's fate. It wasn't fair. These men were not responsible for that, and they were genuinely distressed to hear of his death.

She soon began to feel a little better. Wulfnoth's men were armed and capable, and their presence was a welcome addition to their now not-so-vulnerable group. Æva sat up with them alongside Ulfcytel, Cenric crouching some distance off as he watched over Brandon. There were other newcomers who also claimed to have known Alaric. Eamon was one. He was a formidable-looking warrior, dark and serious, who told her about how he'd watched from a ship when Alaric had plunged into the waters of the river Arewan to save the life of the Ealdorman Ulfcytel. Æva listened intently, knowing in her heart his dramatic tale was all true. Ulfcytel sat with them, concurring at his recollection of events, his great bearded face solemn and mournful whilst he listened. Osbert also softened whenever Alaric was mentioned, his previous harshness ebbing slightly as the first hints of grief sprung up across his features.

Dawn had come, and they were still awake, talking about where they might go and what might be done now that King Æthelred had abandoned them. Somebody mentioned Eadric, the name hateful to all present, only for Ulfcytel to suddenly leap to his feet. He then snatched up Alaric's body and heaved him over his shoulder, his great strides taking him some distance east before anyone could react. They followed, yet Ulfcytel did not relent and remained content to ignore their demands for an explanation. Æva moved to his side, beseeching him to at least tell her what was on his mind. He looked down at her, his eyes wide with emotion.

"You'll see," he said gently. "I'm taking him back to his friend. Trust me."

There was something in his voice that allowed her to do just that. They'd been walking for hours when they came across it, the battle site disturbed by little but the passage of time. They moved closer, the morning light revealing what she was told was an old fortified camp Thorkell had used in his attack on Eastengle. They claimed Eadric had led Alaric here last year after tricking Ulfcytel and Edmund's uncle, Æthelstan, into attacking this place in the hope they'd be able to kill Thorkell himself. Æva had heard some of this from her time speaking to Alaric in captivity, and Hemingr had more or less confirmed it when he'd lain dying after the battle in the courtyard. It was a well-fortified place, the palisade that encircled it still looking formidable, but it was absolute chaos as soon as they stepped inside. Many bodies – or more precisely skeletons – lay about, the flesh of these fallen warriors having long since rotted away to nothing. If Alaric had lost a friend here, there would be no identifying him.

Ulfcytel had come to a similar conclusion. He was frustrated, looking through the tangled mess of armour and bones in the hope that repeated scrutiny might yield something. Æva asked if he was looking for a man named Osmund, as from what she could gather, this was more than likely to be the "friend" he'd mentioned. Ulfcytel nodded enthusiastically at the name, but it didn't really help them find anything. If Osmund were here, he'd look like any other of the Saxon warriors, albeit larger. Then Edmund called out.

They hurried to him, finding him knelt over yet another body, this one missing a forearm. He'd found something around its neck, some form of pendant or token, that had been enough for Edmund to decide this was, in fact, his uncle. He stayed as he was, hunched over in sadness, everyone stepping back to allow him this private moment of mourning. Ulfcytel then began rummaging in his own belongings feverishly. Within moments he had it, revealing a single gold ring he then pressed into Edmund's hand.

"Alaric kept this throughout our travels," he said. "He retrieved it when he found your uncle here that night…he was too late to save him, but he'd wanted to return it to his widow. I feel that you should have it now."

Edmund stood up and began examining the ring with some intensity. He finally nodded, satisfied that it was as Ulfcytel had claimed. "How did you get this?" he asked. "I find it hard to believe Alaric was somehow able to keep it after my father had him imprisoned."

"That beast, Hemingr, was wearing it," Ulfcytel answered. "He'd taken Alaric's sword, too, but I see you retrieved that yourself. I almost missed the ring, so small and inconspicuous it was, but I took it from his dead hand for safekeeping. I didn't want to announce it to anyone there and then. We were troubled enough without reminding you of your uncle and his fate."

"So why bring us here?" Æva asked, her son hovering anxiously on her left. "Is this where you would lay my husband to rest? The place where he was betrayed and so many died?"

"That is precisely what I would do," confirmed Ulfcytel. "He would understand. I know he would. These were his men that he fought and bled and almost died with. And Osmund will be around somewhere. He has to be. We can bury every Englishman here just beyond the palisade. They'll be together, in dignity, with the honour they deserve. We owe them that."

Æva wasn't sure. This was a harrowing place, even in the sunlight, and everyone here had died as a result of Eadric's treachery rather than some honourable defeat in defence of the kingdom. She was about to say something when Osbert came running over, his hand gripped around a weapon he'd just retrieved from the surrounding debris. Æva recognised it almost immediately. So did Ælfric, who hurried over as fast as his ageing bones could manage. He asked Osbert if he might hold it. The young man passed it to him, allowing him to grip the blade in his trembling hands.

"It really is true," he whispered. "Alaric's sword, the one I had made for him."

"I do recall he was lacking a weapon when I met him further north," Edmund said quietly. "He must have lost it here when he'd been wounded."

"We should get to work," Ælfric said. "We'll bury your uncle and everyone else here, aside from the Danes, of course. We'll turn this place from one of treachery into honour and remembrance. My son can be buried with his sword and…"

"No," Æva said, surprised at herself for her interruption. "He'd have wanted the sword given to his firstborn son… I…just please let me have it. I will think on what to do."

"We'd best do as the lady says," growled Ulfcytel, his withering gaze silencing whatever objections Ælfric seemed about to make. "Since Alaric's firstborn is gone…I think you owe it to her, Ælfric, to do as she asks."

Ælfric's eyes lit up in hostility. He tensed visibly, spine fully erect, his hands and arms trembling as he held his son's sword out, point-first, towards Ulfcytel. Edmund suddenly stepped between them, his hand reaching to press on the flat of the sword so that Ælfric might be compelled to lower it. He did so, but didn't lose the venomous look in his eyes. Edmund then turned and whispered something to Ulfcytel. Æva did not understand, but was grateful when she was finally given Alaric's blade. It was heavy, but she held onto it, reassured by its weight and the thought of him grasping it with his strong right arm.

They set to work, Ulfcytel and Ælfric content to let their animosities simmer elsewhere whilst they dug a sequence of open graves just beyond the camp entrance. It was hard going, and they lacked proper equipment for it, but the ground was soft and yielding, the earth shifting with relative ease under the leverage of spear shafts and whatever else they had to hand. Hours passed, every man putting his back into it, Æva herself insisting she be allowed to help.

By the time dusk was upon them, they'd managed to sort the English dead from the Danes and prepare their remains for burial. It hadn't been easy, and the work was as unsettling as it was arduous, but they'd finally done it. Alaric was the last to be put to rest, his body lowered into the ground by Osbert, Eamon, Cenric, and a well-spoken man called Ælfweard.

Everyone gathered, gazing downwards into the grave at Alaric's well-wrapped body. Brandon had by this point sensed the shrouded man was indeed his father, and had begun to weep, Æva's efforts to console him proving futile in the face of such a frantic deluge. She wouldn't try and provide false comfort by lying. He had to find out sooner or later, and it was already burden enough keeping his true ancestry a secret. He could never know who his real father was. That man would rot back in Lundenburg, his throat opened and a spear through his innards, forgotten and unmourned. It was what he deserved.

Ulfcytel stepped forward, taking position at the head of the encircling crowd before addressing them. He spoke softly, telling them all of how he'd first met Alaric after he'd rushed into Eastengle to offer his assistance with just a couple of hundred men. He then took them through how he'd thought him dead following his attack on this very camp, and how surprised and pleased he'd been when Osbert had reunited them in time for their assault on Gipeswic.

His recollections were full of heroism and violence, all of which were very believable but still left something out as to who Alaric was and what had set him on the course he'd followed. She was thus pleasantly surprised at Ulfcytel's final words. Alaric wasn't just a "man of England", he said. He "was England", in the sense he "personified the hope and spirit of every true Englishman in these troubled years, where the love of family, faith, and country is kept alive, despite the betrayals of our own rulers and the mercilessness of our enemies."

Æva had not expected a warrior like Ulfcytel to be capable of such depth. He'd evidently grown to know her husband well. They all had, judging by the reactions of Eamon, Osbert, and the rest. They all grieved for him, and she with them.

But as true and inspirational as they were, Ulfcytel's words only conveyed one side of the man he sought to honour. Æva did not know Alaric as the brave and furious warrior that had been described. She'd never seen him as a man clamouring for battle, although she'd not doubted there was such a side to him. She'd remember him first and foremost as the husband and lover he had been. The gentle man, who'd set out to raise a child that was not his own, regardless of how much it might hurt him to do so. The man who'd mumbled his words the first time he'd tried to speak to her and the man who'd ultimately given his life trying to protect her. That was her husband. And that was how she'd always hold him within her heart.

A light rain began to fall, the drops pattering off the grass and freshly dug graves that now hugged the tree line immediately adjacent to the ruined camp. They had no priest, so Edmund led them in the recitation of the Lord's Prayer. Æva then dropped the first clod of earth upon her husband's body, Ulfcytel and the others bending low to fill the grave until there was nothing left to do but fashion a makeshift cross and secure it in place. Brandon continued to protest, and there was nothing Æva could do to console him. Cenric put a hand on his shoulder, his presence a reassuring one as Æva knelt to embrace her son. It seemed to work. He eventually stopped crying, yet he wouldn't be moved from the grave, nor would he eat. Æva didn't mind. She felt the same way.

Her thoughts briefly turned to Osmund, wondering what had really become of him and whether he had indeed died here at this battle site. In truth, they had recovered his remains, but the passage of time had rendered him as unrecognisable as the others, his large frame and the manner of his death leaving him as just a tall skeleton with a spear through its ribcage. Yet by some twist of fate, he had been buried close to Alaric. Nobody would ever know for certain, but the two friends were now resting together, as close in death as they had been in life. Æva, perhaps through some kind of intuition, had a feeling this was true, and she liked to think of the souls of the two best friends being reunited, the violence and pain of their deaths all forgotten amidst the rekindling of brotherhood.

Night came on, and most of the others departed to seek refuge in the trees and a good meal by a campfire. Cenric stayed with her, as did Ulfcytel. Ælfric and Ælfgar had also left for the sake of nourishment, leaving Æva with an ill feeling. The recent tension between her father-in-law and Ulfcytel was a strange and unexpected thing. She had kept Alaric's sword, and it rested now in the grass at her feet, but something told her she'd created a divide between herself and Ælfric by doing so. There was some as yet hidden issue here that nobody was willing to explain. She deserved to find out.

"What was the problem between you and Ælfric?"

Ulfcytel almost jumped at the sound of her voice, as they'd been so quiet for the best part of an hour now. He turned to look at her, his eyes sparkling and wet, taking a deep, shuddering breath before answering.

"Did Alaric not tell you anything of his father, when you spoke to him in the prison tower?"

"He didn't," she said. "Or nothing out of the ordinary. You know each other then, you and Ælfric?"

"We do," sighed Ulfcytel, in a manner that implied he'd rather not have this conversation. "I spoke of these matters to Alaric in Canterburie not long ago…and I'm afraid if I speak of them again here, I will only add to your burdens. So you'll have to forgive me…but you must not ask me anything of this now. Soon…but not now."

"But what…"

"I believe the Ealdorman Ulfcytel is quite correct," Cenric said gently. He'd been standing behind her and Brandon for some time, silent and strangely comforting. "Trust me, Æva, when I say you don't need to hear such things," he continued. "For your own sake…wait until the pain of your loss has eased a little."

"It's true," Ulfcytel said reassuringly. "When I told Alaric of his father's past, he was devastated. That was hard enough for me to bear then. I would not see you so afflicted. Please…think of it as a kindness towards me. A favour to an old man and friend of your husband. Wait a year or so for the heart to heal a little. Then I will tell you, if you'll still ask."

She sat down in the grass, tucking Brandon into her lap and wrapping her cloak about him. At any other time, she'd have felt impatient or even irritated over Ulfcytel's cryptic warnings. This was not just any other time, though, and the note of caution from both him and Cenric struck her as well intended. Her curiosity could wait, as great as it was. She had other things to prioritise. Like staying strong for her son. If Ulfcytel knew something that could further break her heart, she didn't need to hear it now. If she were alone in the world, she might press him on the subject, but not now. She had a grieving child to think of. She'd wait. And then she'd face the truth when better disposed to hear it.

"Will you not come and eat with us?"

Æva looked to the right across the gravesite, spying in the darkness the outline and familiar countenance of Edmund. He was caked in mud, blood, and perspiration, looking more like a common brigand than an heir to the throne, but his voice was still noble, such was the depth of concern within it. Ulfcytel grunted in affirmation, making his way over to the trees just ahead and the flickering campfires that beckoned. Cenric followed, looking back towards Æva as if asking permission to join the others. She gave him a nod, prompting his departure, his steps brisk and hurried so he might catch up with Ulfcytel. She sat alone, her son asleep in her arms, Edmund standing nearby across the freshly dug earth like he was expecting something. An owl hooted in the near distance, the stars casting a faint glow from on high.

"I can't leave you out here alone."

Edmund sounded almost nervous. He was afraid to come between her and her solitude, she supposed, and they knew from the fate of Offetuna that this region was still far from safe. She'd not do herself much good lingering out here in the dark, away from the safety of strong arms and sharp spears. Yet she couldn't face company, even if it was well-meaning. She needed to remain here for just a little longer. She needed this time with Alaric. So did Brandon. They had to sit with him as he slept, if only for a little while.

"Can I bring you something then?" Edmund persisted. "Or perhaps arrange a guard so you can keep vigil here?"

"Do you intend to make yourself king?" She thought she'd be as direct as she could. There was no other way to ask such a question, really.

"Yes. Men will follow me. Others elsewhere have already submitted to Svienn. I will remind them of where their loyalties should lie."

"You sound very sure of yourself." She didn't mean it as a point of criticism, but he did have a great deal of confidence, like he felt he was born to rule. Perhaps he was, but she'd learned that overly-confident men were prone to pride, and from that, nothing good could grow.

"It's not arrogance," he insisted. "I know this land and how my father has long neglected it. I have two choices. Let it fall or act. I choose to act."

"And where does this conviction come from? Forgive me, but I can't imagine your father instilling it in you."

"You'd be right," said Edmund. "So let me just say this ...a good friend of mine commanded Lundenburg's garrison. He refused to leave with the rest of us. I know he would have stayed with his men until the end. If he's truly gone, I owe it to him, and those like him, to again make a nation of this land. That will be my way of honouring them."

"And your father?"

"He'll be what he'll be. He'll continue to make mistakes and consort with the wrong company. He has his own burdens, just as I do. It's how we choose to deal with them that matters. He made his choice to flee to Normandy. I made my choice to stay."

"Just what did he want with my son anyway?" She knew as soon as she'd asked the question she'd best leave the subject alone. There was every chance the boy might wake up and hear. He didn't need to relive past traumas. She was sure his time with the king and his court had been a confusing one.

"I don't rightly know," answered Edmund. "My father had the notion he was doing him a service. Alaric, too. He'd grown to admire him somehow, but he still wanted you all..."

"He wanted us dead. I worked that out for myself. Would you, Edmund, actually do something for me?"

"I will."

"Become king."

"I intend to."

"There's more," she insisted. "Become king, and create a kingdom where somebody like me can visit their husband's grave without fear. Where horrors like what we've just gone through are never repeated. Where a child like mine can always rest easy…where all the children now and yet to come can rest easy…and a boy like my Alfred can grow up in safety, free and happy at his father's side and not…"

"I think I understand," said Edmund quietly.

"Well, can you do that? Can you do that for us? And not just for us, but for all others who would look fondly on you and call you their king? Can you do that, Edmund?"

She looked right at him, his blunt, soldierly face half-shrouded in the dark, those expressive eyes gazing back as he pondered her question. When he spoke again he was brief, but he had his usual conviction, and then something else along with it. He meant what he said. And he believed it. He believed in himself. What he said was true. She felt it with him.

"I can."

XXXIV

The wind was blasting across the water, its icy touch inescapable upon the woefully exposed deck. Æthelred winced as he pawed at his hair, hoping to wrest control of his thinning locks to prevent them from being blown about by the irritatingly intense gale. Sea water sprayed up and over the outer hull, half-soaking the fifty or so oarsmen huddled at their stations. They nonetheless continued to row, their strong arms and even stronger backs ensuring their ongoing course through the increasingly rough waters.

Emma and the children sat just behind him, huddled close and taking advantage of their relatively shielded position up against the stern. Æthelred didn't want to join them. Despite his discomfort, he wanted to stand for as much as possible, observing the surrounding seas. He couldn't explain why he felt the urge, but something didn't feel quite right.

He turned eastward, taking in the three dozen vessels spaced out in a lazy formation about a hundred yards away. These were Thorkell's lot, or about two-thirds of his surviving fleet, rowing steadily with their sails fully unfurled as they guarded his flank. Æthelred had been well aware that Thorkell's navy, like his army, was much reduced, his other ships regrettably suffering destruction or seizure by those men who'd rebelled against him in Canterburie. They'd reputedly then taken flight from England for parts unknown, leaving Thorkell with a rump flotilla. It was an unfortunate turn of events, but Æthelred was grateful for what he had.

And that wasn't all. To the rear and starboard both were the remnants of Æthelred's own navy, battered but still very serviceable despite the steady losses they'd taken after years of war. They all made for an inspiring sight churning through the raging waters, each defying the worsening weather and the heaving, blue-green depths that assailed them.

It was easy to tell who was who. The Norse ships were lighter, narrower, and more agile, their colourful sails and bizarre hull patterns marking them out even at a distance. The English ships were plainer in appearance but also heavier, with thicker hulls to smash into any hostile vessels should the situation require it. They were highly effective if used correctly, but that depended on whether they could find the enemy to begin with and come close enough to either ram or board. They'd been the terror of the seas during his father's reign, but those days were long gone, and the times of hardship that followed had ensured his once mighty navy was a mere shadow of what it had been.

Despite that, their present situation was still of note. This was an allied Anglo-Scandinavian fleet powering its way forward as one, the clashing waves and the buffeting wind powerless to stop them. What warriors he and Thorkell had left were crammed aboard, the men either lending their strength to the oars or pacing impatiently up and down the wind-swept decks. There had been minimal friction between the two groups, and Æthelred had wisely refrained from encouraging them to mix. He knew his own men hated the Danes and always would, and Thorkell's mob retained that arrogant callousness towards other peoples that was the hallmark of their kind. He didn't want things falling apart now. Not with his family at risk.

Their flight from Lundenburg had gone smoothly. It remained a source of great sorrow to him that he'd been unable to convince Edmund to come, but the boy had to follow his own path. If times had been different, he would have shouted him down and done everything possible to bend him to his will. Æthelred wasn't sure what had changed. Edmund's threat to cut off relations with him had been a surprise. He normally wouldn't have taken such a thing seriously, but he could tell he'd meant it. He might try to deny it, but the thought of his own son despising him was too much to bear. He couldn't have that. He'd already lost his mother and several of his siblings along the way. To have a son turn on you and deny your very existence was too harrowing a prospect. He'd had to relent. He'd given up the child, Brandon. It was a small price to pay, considering the alternative.

The trek to Beamfleote had also gone without major incident. The myriad thegns and hangers-on who had been loafing around his court for months had proven exceptionally annoying, and their complaints and backbiting had given Æthelred reason to consider leaving them all behind. He hadn't, of course, and when they'd arrived at the fortress their mutterings had ceased, each of them presumably feeling a little safer now they were at least away from any immediate danger.

It had gotten better from there. Thorkell and his men were well prepared, with their ships already assembled and ready to depart. The remnants of Æthelred's navy had been a little late, but when they'd finally come their commander had been more than cooperative in allowing the garrison from Beamfleote to board. It had been a speedy operation. Nothing was to be left behind for Svienn to take for himself, and as luck would have it, his own ships failed to detect them entirely, although for what reason Æthelred was unsure. He wouldn't question good fortune when it came calling. It was a rare enough visitor.

And yet one person hadn't shown up, and his absence was a mystery that refused to be unravelled. Eadric was supposed to have accompanied Thorkell as part of the advance force to secure Beamfleote. According to Thorkell, he'd been with him for much of the journey, only to suddenly vanish about an hour before they made contact with the garrison. Thorkell was emphatic that his men had not killed him, nor had there been any other dishonest antics on his part, stressing over and over again that the "man of Mierċe" had simply disappeared.

Æthelred hadn't known what to say. If Eadric had just gone missing, then they couldn't waste time looking for him. Lundenburg could fall at any moment, and for all they knew, Svienn's ships might be about to row back up the estuary to engage them. He couldn't risk thousands for the sake of one. They'd had to move. Eadric's fate would have to remain unknown for the time being.

Thorkell himself had become quite emotional, putting on a display that convinced Æthelred he was indeed telling the truth. His brother, Hemingr, had, of course, been killed by Edmund and his men, and his failure to appear in time for the evacuation had made Thorkell visibly disturbed. Æthelred wasn't stupid. He wasn't about to tell Thorkell what had happened. If he discovered that Hemingr had been murdered, he'd leave them or become violent as part of some misguided attempt to get even with Edmund. Æthelred would feign ignorance for as long as it took. But the experience had been helpful to him in some ways. He'd learned that Thorkell had emotions other than bloodlust and greed, and that it might be possible to manipulate him. If Eadric were here, he'd no doubt be capitalising on that as much as he could. It was his way.

But he wasn't here, and despite his best efforts, Æthelred felt vulnerable without him. Eadric had been a loyal advisor to him for years, and in that time he'd rarely left his side, preferring courtly life to frequenting his own holdings in Mierce. That was unusual. Ealdormen were generally quite independent, only attending their king when required. Eadric's behaviour had thus been a novelty, one Æthelred had been grateful for. In his darker moments, when all others had seemed to fly from him, save his wife, Eadric had been there. It wasn't right that he'd been left behind.

Not everyone felt that way. Eadric was hated by many. Æthelred wasn't always sure exactly why, and for a long time, he'd put it down to simple jealousy over his remarkable rise from humble beginnings. And yet he couldn't forget what Edmund had said to him just recently. He'd claimed Eadric would be his end. He'd heard far worse, but there had been something in Edmund's voice that suggested he knew more than he was letting on.

Æthelred didn't know where his son was getting his information from. He'd never really spoken to his children about Eadric, nor had the man himself made a habit of mixing with his family. His suspicions naturally fell upon Sigeferth and Morcar. They knew of Eadric's history, just as they knew of some of the troubling episodes in Æthelred's own life and how Eadric had been of assistance in resolving them. Æthelred regretted some of the things he'd had to do as king, but it had all been necessary, and Sigeferth and his ilk did themselves no favours by spreading rumours. They'd always shown too great an interest in his sons. The same went for that damnable Wulfnoth. Æthelred felt he understood intrigue and the role it sadly played in the politics of his realm, but he truly resented people attempting to use members of his own family to further their ambitions. Wulfnoth and Sigeferth were certainly guilty of that. He'd taken action against the former. It remained to be seen how he'd one day deal with the latter.

And yet vengeance would come. He'd always hold Sigeferth and Morcar personally responsible for Æthelstan's death. They'd encouraged him and Edmund to attack Thorkell at Bernecestre. Defeated as Æthelred was, he'd still find a way to get even. He had wealth, most of England's wealth, in fact, for he'd seen it loaded aboard his ships just yesterday. He also had some influence, even if confined to the court of his brother-in-law in Normandy. Sigeferth and Morcar were fools if they thought he'd just forget about them and what they'd done. Blood would be shed.

Eadric would have come in useful for that. He knew how to set things in motion, just as he knew how to apply brute force and even command troops in the field if he had to. It had been he who had captured the traitorous Ælfric, and the death of Ælfric was perhaps one of the few good things to have come out of recent developments. He'd enjoy the peace of mind that it brought.

But something still troubled him. He wasn't sure if he was just being paranoid, but Edmund had confirmed only that Alaric was dead, rather than his entire family. Would it be logical to assume the rest of them had survived? Æva certainly had, so what about Ælfric and Ælfgar? Would Hemingr have somehow managed to kill the fearsome Alaric, only to fail to execute an old man and his blind son? That would be a strange turn of events if it were so. For the moment, Æthelred didn't need the additional stress. If Alaric was dead and it was Hemingr who'd killed him, then it was fair to assume he'd killed the others. None of them were anywhere near as capable as Alaric had been. That man had seemed truly blessed in his capacity to fight his way through monstrously difficult situations. Sadly, few things lasted forever, and Alaric's luck had run out.

 He was surprised at just how ambivalent he felt over it. He'd wanted him dead for so long, fearing him without really knowing why. It occurred to him now that he wouldn't even be here if it were not for Alaric's words. It had been Alaric who had convinced him he'd been wrong, not just about his dream but in his actions as a ruler. The dream was a means to an end, sent by God or something else, it mattered not, but he now truly believed it had been intended to alert him to a situation he'd failed to comprehend. He'd festered in paranoia for years, neglecting his duties just to fixate on the treachery and politicking of others, and England had suffered for it. He couldn't say he was entirely to blame. Troubled times had always been his. Yet it had been Alaric who had made him realise how blinded he'd become. With his city surrounded and starving, he'd still not understood until he'd spoken with him. Then everything had somehow become clear.

 His time as a ruler was over. His armies had been ground down to almost nothing, and most of his kingdom was in ruins. He'd failed as a monarch, but he wouldn't fail as a father. He hoped his children would see that. He wouldn't have them suffer the fate of his firstborn, used like a pawn in someone else's game until they sacrificed themselves for no good reason. He'd take them far away from it all, where nobody could hurt or manipulate them. They'd be safe.

 He stood back from where he'd been observing the other ships, turning instead to look to his family as they sheltered from the weather. One of his men stepped over to hand him a cloak that was more animal hide than fashioned attire. He took it with a brief nod of gratitude, draping it over his shoulders and head to properly insulate himself against the continuing deluge. It had been unwise to allow himself to be soaked to the extent he had. He was an old man now. He couldn't afford to take risks with his health. But he often found the cold to be invigorating. It spurred the mind, compelling it to sort through its old burdens so fresh insights might be attained.

 He moved over to join his queen huddled under the furs with their children. He sat down next to them, pulling his excessively thick and heavy cloak about himself. This time last year, he'd never have thought he'd be in this situation. The very first night Alaric had appeared in his dream, he'd assumed he was just another traitor in need of killing. He'd set Eadric upon that task, and by mere chance he'd failed. Æthelred couldn't have imagined then how his position would unravel and how he'd be partly to blame for it. He'd been drunk on notions of power, imagining himself ruling England with an army of Norse mercenaries at his back. He'd obtained some of those men, that was true, but he'd forfeited his throne regardless. Perhaps if he'd encountered Alaric sooner, this might have been avoided. Perhaps if he'd been more eager to listen rather than simply react, he could still call himself king.

 But why should he ever have met him? Alaric was of noble birth, true, but he'd been a rarity in a land riddled with the prideful and self-serving. The barbs of a hundred times a hundred plots, schemes, and dubious undertakings had hardened Æthelred's heart so that a virtuous man seemed almost mythical to him. But he'd met one. Alaric could have just spat bile at him from his prison cell, as would be understandable after the ill-treatment meted out to him. Instead, he'd told him the truth so that he might yet save what was most precious to him.

Æthelred held that thought and squeezed Emma's hand. She didn't stir. She was asleep, but Edward wriggled his way over to him and tucked his head underneath his arm. The boy was at rest in moments, safe and content beside his parents despite the harshness of their environs. Æthelred stared at him awhile, jealous at his capacity to fall into slumber with such remarkable ease. His own eyes grew heavy with the pondering of it, and before he knew it his head had dipped forward, his chin upon his chest, his eyes closing as he drifted away to a place long familiar.

The chapel. The dream had come, the wind howling outside, the rain battering against the darkened windows. His half-brother, Edward, again lay upon the altar before him, still and lifeless. He was truly a king, even at such a young age, and a far cry from the haggard, miserable apparition that was Æthelred now. Fate had dealt them both a cruel blow the day he'd been slain; Edward through the loss of his life and Æthelred through being forced to take a path he was ill-suited to walk. It hurt him to realise that. But it was true. And he was sick of lying to himself. He was sick of lies entirely.

He knew what would happen next. He turned around, knowing the audience he'd have and well prepared to take in their piercing looks and silent accusations. That was how it had always been, and yet tonight he didn't see things quite the same way. They were all assembled, looking right at him, familiar faces all. These were his people, alive and dead, yet he knew now what they'd always wanted. They wanted him to act. They wanted him to help them.

Alaric was still there, but he looked different from his appearance on past nights. He was deathly pale, his face scarred, one eye socket ruined and closed like it had been when they'd met in person. A few other things had changed about him since then. He bore a chest wound, open and obvious, like a spear or the tip of a sword had been rammed through him with some considerable force. The prison garb he wore was also stained with both blood and sweat in abundance, suggesting he'd not gone quietly or easily when it came to his death. Of all those assembled, he was looking upon him differently. There was accusation in that single eye of his. Bitterness. He hated him for ordering his execution. Æthelred felt despair once more. If only there had been another way.

"I'm sorry," he said abruptly, his voice rough and wavering. He looked down at himself, his aged and calloused hands drawing his attention. He'd always been as a boy in the dream, but not now. This time he was a man, as he was in reality. He couldn't guess why. He'd long failed to understand much of this, and he wouldn't do himself any favours trying to work it all out now.

"I said, I'm sorry," he repeated, addressing all those gathered before him. "I know you needed me. You deserved better than me. Please don't blame me for my shortcomings. I did as I thought best. It just wasn't enough."

He blinked. The hall emptied. Everyone had vanished, Alaric included, whatever task they'd set themselves now completed. A burden shifted from his shoulders, its absence permitting a dimly remembered sense of purpose to take hold of him. He was no king, and the people of England no longer needed him in light of his failures and final confession. He felt strangely at peace, this rare strength filling him with the realisation that he was now free to settle other matters. He knew what was coming. He could hear it. Footsteps upon stone, and something else. He turned to look.

His mother was attired as she always was, her mourning dress dragging across the draughty, hard floor. She moved closer, whispering to herself incessantly, her lined, hollow face barely visible beneath her veil. She moved up and to his side, her gaze drifting down towards Edward in his otherwise peaceful slumber. Something was wrong. Æthelred would always wake up by this point, driven to hysterics by the baleful presence now standing right next to him. He didn't feel scared. That was unusual. In life as well as death, she'd terrified him. Now it was different. He knew not why.

She leaned down close to Edward, those withered, vascular hands reaching out for him. She took his hands in hers, the motion gentle and maternal, her lips continuing to move as she whispered over and over. Æthelred found his courage. He leaned in, holding his ear closer to her mouth so that he might finally understand her.

"Forgive me."

Æthelred pulled away, drawing himself to his full height as he spun to face her. She did the same, releasing Edward's hands to lift back her veil. He saw those hateful eyes, so often filled with reproach, disappointment, and any other type of poison she'd seen fit to inflict upon him. It wasn't so tonight. They were wet with tears, blinking slowly, sad and sincere and desperate for conciliation.

"You forgive me, too, Æthelred. Please. Please forgive me."

He woke up, inhaling enough to fill his chest twice over, his lungs straining in protest at the cold, biting air flooding into them. It was dark, and the seas had calmed, the deck of his vessel merely damp instead of saturated. His family was asleep next to him, Emma twisted over to embrace Godgifu, Alfred clinging to her for extra warmth. Edward was still entangled in his father's arm, his face a picture of peaceful contentment. Æthelred began to cough, the sound brittle and sharp. One of his nearby guards heard him and thundered over across the hollow wooden decking, his heavy, metal-clad physique remarkably fast despite his obvious burden. Hereward was his name. Æthelred had kept him close ever since he'd saved his life at Bernecestre. He was loyal and decent.

"Are you all right, my king?"

He settled himself, catching his breath and taking a few seconds to adjust. He wasn't sweating, and it wasn't just because it was cold. In the past, the dream had always frightened him, his mother's appearance startling him out of his sleep as a matter of routine. He'd not expected that to change. But it had, and in a way he'd never thought possible.

Admitting his failures had given him the strength to finally face his mother as she, too, sought to confess and be forgiven. It had been she who'd arranged Edward's death, as many had suspected. He couldn't tell anyone it had come to him in a dream, but he knew in his heart it was so. It was good to finally know the truth. A weight lifted from his heart, one so heavy and long-endured he'd forgotten what it was like to be without it. He looked up at Hereward, noting the concern in his eyes. He actually cared about him. It was wonderful.

"I am fine," he said, coughing again to clear his throat.

"Is there anything I can get you?" Hereward asked, always helpful.

"No. I...I think I'm all right. I think...I feel..."

"How do you feel?"

"Free," Æthelred said. "I feel free. A terrible weight has been lifted."

"And what does that mean for you?" Hereward was humouring him out of politeness, but Æthelred still appreciated it. The poor man had no way of knowing what he was talking about, but it felt good to give voice to his thoughts.

"It means I can start living rather than just reacting," he said, his eyes flitting affectionately to the still-sleeping Edward and then back to Hereward. "I've lost everything, almost, but truthfully I think I'm happier now than I've ever been. I'll be all right, my friend. You can go about your duties now. You have yours. I know I have mine."

XXXV

His heart was pounding, his breathing ragged as he was caught up in the human avalanche pressing in upon the walls. Horns were sounding, the signal clear and undisputed. The gate was falling. This was the time to attack. They'd hit the English here and take their city by storm.

Cnut was dressed for the occasion. He'd tied back his flaxen, almost waist-length hair, hoping to keep it out of his face lest he be blinded in his efforts to prove himself. He'd trimmed his beard somewhat, preferring a neater look than the wilder, unkempt facial hair of many of his compatriots. His armour, predictably, was of the finest quality, but it was heavy, the shaped metal scales of his hauberk feeling as if they might press him down further into the mud. His helm, too, was a hefty one, resting uncomfortably upon his scalp like a cold, dead weight. He almost yearned to remove it. He couldn't. The English kept firing arrows and throwing rocks from the walls. He wouldn't chance dying a fool's death. Not when glory was so close at hand.

They charged the gate. It was huge, bigger than anything he'd seen in Denmark, its sheer construction casting long, imposing shadows out and over them as they ran towards it in a bristling wave of axes and spears. The towers on either side kept up a steady stream of arrows, the men on the walls adjacent to them content also to hurl stones and spears into their ranks with distressing regularity. A warrior close by fell, an arrow protruding from his eye socket. Somebody else screamed from somewhere in their midst, the sound half pain and half anger. Others raised their shields higher, presenting a barrier of wood and iron to protect them whilst they advanced. Cnut wisely did the same, lifting his own ornate rönd into place with the men next to him. It was a fortuitous decision. Something smashed into it almost immediately, the tip of an arrowhead appearing a moment later as it split the wood in a bid to reach him. Luck was with him. He could have easily taken that clear in the face if it were not so.

They continued onward, Cnut peering over the rim of his shield at what lay ahead. This whole endeavour would be suicide were it not for the fact the gate had been smashed open. It had taken awhile, and Cnut could see the remnants of the now discarded ram just off to his left, but it had done its job, and for that they could all be glad. The enemy had managed to set it on fire, of course, but it hadn't burned quickly enough, and the Danes had simply kept on ramming, breaking through even with their hair singeing and the sweat running in torrents from their bodies. They'd then fallen upon the English, Cnut and the rest of the army rushing after them to capitalise on their success. Cnut couldn't see clearly how it was going, but given that he and those around him were still surging forward, he could only assume victory was at hand. The English resistance was finally breaking. They'd been fools to try to hold out, but in a way, Cnut was grateful. If Lundenburg had surrendered as easily as the rest of the country, his father's conquest wouldn't have been much fun at all.

He made it through the gate, leaping ahead to traverse the detritus of shattered timber and scorched masonry. The English looked like they'd tried to erect a barricade here, but the flames from the ram had spread across it rapidly, destroying just enough to allow a breach to be made. He followed the warriors charging through ahead of him, the smell of smoke thick and raw in his nostrils. He could see the fight up ahead. It was glorious; a surging mass of men, enough to entirely block the main street leading in from the gate, all of them hacking at the other as blood and bodies fell thick and fast. Cnut pushed his way into the vanguard, wanting more than anything to join the melee. He knew his father would be angry, thinking him reckless for taking the risk. Cnut didn't care. He'd endure his harsh words if he had to. Right now, he wanted his share of glory.

He saw his first Englishman, or the first one he'd seen in full battle dress up close. He was fearsome enough, his helmet decorated with flowing gold and silver, the metal of his faceplate looking like it had been shaped to give the likeness of a stout moustache and a heavyset brow. Like Cnut, his armour was made of shimmering metal scales flowing downward towards his knees, and he was fighting bravely, wielding both spear and sword to cut down any Dane that came within reach.

Cnut couldn't help but feel a flash of admiration. This man was a commander, that was clear, and his fellow Englishmen were rallying to him, inspired by his bravery in to making a final stand against overwhelming odds. As glorious as it looked, Cnut knew his people would not be stopped by this. They were thousands, and the English were mere hundreds, and it was only a matter of time until this thin line of metal and flesh was overcome. Cnut knew that for certain. He'd do it himself. He'd start with their leader.

He made a move straight for him. He sensed victory, picturing his triumph before it had even happened. He'd split this man's head, breaking open his ornate helmet and taking his blade for himself. His men would see him do it, knowing he'd secured the victory, and the surviving English would turn tail and flee. It would be perfect. He was nearly within reach. He dropped his shield to grip his axe in both hands, heaving it up and back so as to hew it downwards to split armour and bone alike. He bared his teeth, his low growl cascading into a gleeful roar as he closed the distance. Now was the time.

He ended up flat on his arse. The Englishman had moved fast, smashing Cnut in the forehead with the butt of his sword and somehow sweeping his legs out from under him. He'd then killed the man next to him, his spear thrusting in and out of his chest with a rapidity that seemed almost impossible. Cnut's head rang, the ache in his skull intense, despite his helm remaining intact. Somebody pulled him up, and when Cnut looked his opponent was gone, as were many of his ilk, the defenders pulling back. Cnut grimaced with frustration. Numbers were winning it for them here, not skill and heroism. Where was this man who had bested him so easily? Who was he? He'd have his blood on his axe before the night was spent.

They pressed on, their force fanning outward beyond the gate and into the city's streets. More men followed behind them as the breach widened, their army forcing its way into Lundenburg like some vast, malevolent tide that would no longer be kept at bay. Cnut looked behind him. His father was following, far back where it was safe, but still following. King Svienn had entered the city. He wouldn't have entered if he wasn't sure of victory. Everyone knew that. The men saw him and roared in triumph, their massed cries reverberating into the night. To Cnut, it was exhilarating. This was life. This was life as it should be.

He killed a man. He wasn't as well-dressed as the fellow he'd seen earlier, but Cnut killed him all the same, splitting his shield with his axe and then doing the same for his head. His skull made a strange sound as it collapsed inward, letting rip with a sharp crack, but wet rather than dry, like the axe had caused something to burst inside. Cnut paid it no mind. He killed again, hoping to hear that sound once more. It wasn't quite the same. He didn't really care.

The warrior next to him fell. He was known to him as a veteran of many battles, but he'd been careless here, thinking, like the rest of them, that victory was already at hand. The Saxon who'd killed him was raving incoherently, he and those with him possessing an air of desperation generally displayed by men who knew death was almost certain. They were right, but they still fought on, killing and being killed until there was nothing left of them but bloodied, ruined flesh. Cnut made a point of walking over their corpses as they swept forward, deliberately pressing their remains into the stones. So it was with these men. So it would be with England.

The fighting suddenly stopped, the only sound heard the groans and splutterings of the injured and dying scattered at his feet. There were no more English here. All had been killed or had fled further into the city, leaving the gate and interior in their well-deserving hands. Svienn approached, slow and bulky in his armour, his crown sparkling in the light of a dozen fires burning up ahead. Cnut found that perplexing. They'd not set any additional fires, as far as he could tell. Were these English tackling an accidental blaze before they'd even been attacked? Surely no people could be so unfortunate?

Figures emerged from the streets. Regular people, the citizens of Lundenburg, fear and apprehension heavy upon their shoulders. They gazed at them, not wanting to move closer, a leader of some sort emerging from their ranks with his hands raised above his head. He looked like a man of wealth, dressed in furs and fine fabrics. A merchant then, rotund and clearly not a warrior, yet he considered himself worthy to address them. King Svienn headed towards this envoy as if they might parley, and so Cnut hurried to his father's side. He wanted to hear what was said.

"The city is yours, gracious king," said the Englishman, or merchant or envoy or whoever he was. "King Æthelred has abandoned us, to where I know not. We did not wish to resist you further, but certain villains within the garrison sought to defy you. We apologise for your trouble."

"Who?" His father's voice had a low, rough quality to it, like gravel being poured over stone.

The envoy looked confused, his eyes darting nervously from Svienn to Cnut and the multitude of warriors around them. "I'm not sure I understand," he said timidly.

"Who are these villains?" Svienn clarified. "Do you have them? Are they still in the city?"

"You killed most of them," he said, gesturing towards the bloodshed behind them, "but we have the ringleader and…"

"Bring him to me here."

The fat man didn't argue, instead turning to walk briskly back to his brethren and engage in a prolonged bout of intense whispering. Just as Cnut was beginning to lose his patience, their ranks again opened, revealing a group of men that now advanced towards them, a single bound figure held fast in their grip. Cnut recognised who it was. This was the warrior who'd knocked him down earlier. He'd enjoy this.

"This is the commander of Æthelred's remaining forces in the city," said the envoy hurriedly. "We...apprehended him...and present him to you in the hope you will take note of our good faith and willingness to cooperate."

Cnut stared at the one in their clutches. He wasn't moving, and the others looked like they had to hold him up, so limp had he become. He was bleeding, a steady trickle of red emerging from several rents in his armour. Svienn reached out and removed his helmet to get a better look at him. Dark hair. A beard of a similar colour, like a wedge of bristles attached to a jaw that was a tad too large. Rough, scarred skin, almost sickly in hue, with a hefty, wide nose that looked like it had been broken a few times and not set. Englishmen were ugly, Cnut decided, and this one was no different. They all looked very practical. Boring, perhaps. But for all his mediocrity, there was something in his eyes, burning outwards towards them. He wasn't afraid. This was hatred.

"You fight us even as all hope fades for you. Why?" Cnut grinned at his father's question. Æthelred was the worst of weaklings. To think he'd not even put in an appearance to defend his own walls was astonishing. He didn't deserve the loyalty of men like this.

"I fight you because you're a heathen and a killer!" There was some real venom there, despite his evident frailty. His voice was otherwise shaky and wet, like he had too much fluid in his throat and couldn't get rid of it. Cnut looked to his father, curious whether he'd taken offence.

"We are Christians," Svienn said in reply, his voice even and flat. "You have no..."

Laughter. The man was laughing at him. A bad choice. Cnut might have thought it pleasant to let him live, had he been wiser and not taken to mockery. He was a good fighter. Cnut could always humble himself and learn from him. It was too late now. He shouldn't have laughed at his father.

"Tell me your name before I dispatch you to hell." King Svienn was angry. Cnut knew he was disturbed by few things. But being mocked was one of them.

"My name is Ecgberht, and that's all you'll get from me. I may have been betrayed by this rabble behind me, but I'll not treat with a murderer and a heathen with delusions of piety. Kill me and be done with it, for you are no Christian and no king!"

Cnut heaved his axe back and down, splitting Ecgberht almost to the base of his neck in one fluid motion. Blood sprayed outwards over the envoy and his companions, these already frightened men scattering like startled birds. Ecgberht's ruined corpse collapsed to the ground, and so Cnut hacked at it several more times, heavy and deliberate, reducing the body to a pulverized mess of tattered flesh. He stepped back, turning to his father. Svienn looked at him. He nodded. He approved.

Everyone was kneeling. Not their own warriors. They stood as they were, their breath heavy and laboured after their assault on the gate. It was the English who were kneeling, in their dozens and then hundreds, more and more people appearing from the streets and buildings to prostrate themselves before the invaders. So many of them looked terrible. Encrusted with mud, filth, blood...some barely dressed at all, their ribs visible and protruding 'neath the skin as if half-starved. They were starved. They were wise to submit.

Svienn and Cnut proceeded through them, brushing past the cowering rabble to lead their army further into the city. They marched on and on, their boots heavy and purposeful upon the stone and gravel streets, the populace pleasantly frightened and subservient in the face of them. From the looks of it, the city had been gripped by famine, and these dishevelled, pathetic people observing their passage had thrown their lot in with obsequious cowards like the "envoy" they'd encountered earlier. This Ecgberht whom Cnut had just slain had been one of the few who'd been of a mind to continue resisting. He'd been betrayed for it, and by his own kind, but in his deeds he was at least worthy of being called a man. Cnut couldn't say the same for the others here.

They'd also fouled their own nests. So much of the city looked to have been ransacked or set alight, the charred and broken remains of many a home or place of business greeting them in sorrowful resignation. Some were still burning, the flames lighting up the night, the shadows of their men dark and ominous as they filed past. It looked like any building believed to hold food or wealth had been attacked, the people tearing them apart in the hope of subsisting for one more day. Cnut would have preferred to think they'd defeated the English through skill and bravery, and so it jarred his pride to realise they'd merely caught them at a disadvantage when they'd gone mad with hunger. At least some had offered resistance. There'd been honour in overcoming it whilst it lasted.

His thoughts were premature. Sounds of battle erupted as another portion of their army made contact with what was left of the enemy. The meandering streets and those buildings still standing hid it from view, but his ears did not deceive him, and he dearly wished to rush off and again prove himself through the shedding of blood. His father ignored it, and Cnut dared not do otherwise himself. He'd taken enough of a risk in leaping ahead to charge in with the first assault. He'd been seized by the moment, and didn't want to try his luck a second time. Svienn might not stand for it.

In any case, he could see others from their procession rushing to investigate. Cnut could imagine how it was. The last of Ecgberht's warriors were likely being slaughtered. Chances were they'd been weakened by hunger. There wouldn't be much more they could do. They were all doomed men, and whatever fighting was left to be done would only result in their deaths. They'd know it, too.

The night soon grew quiet, the shouts, screams, and echoing clash of metal on metal subsiding into a pained silence. More brave souls had fallen. There was nowhere for them to go ever since the city had been surrounded, so sporadic last stands like this were to be expected. Only the cowards lived, choosing to greet their conquerors on bended knee. Cnut hoped it wouldn't always be like this. He didn't want to rule such people. He didn't think he could stand it. There had to be more out there who were worthy.

He heard something behind them. The "envoy" had pursued them, breathing heavily under his excessive weight, and was skirting around their heels like he hoped to be noticed. Cnut glared back at him, wondering who he thought he was, but his father was content to let him remain. The fat man took note of this, eventually finding his courage and moving to his father's side to dare speak to him. He was to act as a guide, so it appeared, ushering King Svienn to a destination in the northern quarter of the city. Cnut didn't like him. He whispered to his father, saying as such. Svienn looked back at him, his expression disdainful. Cnut felt his cheeks flush with embarrassment. It wasn't fair. He didn't think he'd said anything out of turn. The man couldn't be trusted. He'd betrayed his own. There was only one proper response to that, and it didn't involve talking.

They carried on, marching in the night, the ambient flames lighting their way. More survivors watched them pass, many huddled in doorways or peering through shutters, unwilling to come out into the street and debase themselves like so many had. A few others appeared defiant, remaining on their feet and glowering like they thought looks alone could make a difference. It was better than nothing, Cnut thought. Even when defeated, you could still retain your pride. These few had. Many had not.

A ruined gateway loomed before them, leading into a wide courtyard adjacent to what could only be King Æthelred's own hall. As they moved closer, he could tell he was right. The places where kings chose to dwell were often the same, as spacious as they were imposing, and here was no exception. What was curious was the state of its surroundings. The gate looked like it had been battered in, not by a single ram but by the force of hundreds, like a great horde had assailed it with anything they had to hand. The courtyard beyond was scattered with bodies, each of them bearing the marks of deadly violence. From the arms and armour in evidence, some of these men were Norsemen. Cnut had heard Æthelred had finally won over Thorkell the Tall. These must be his people, although how they'd come to meet their end here was a mystery. Had the English suddenly turned on them?

His father gave them a brief look, a faint, familiar smile creasing his aged features as he gazed down at one particularly burly fellow with a spear shaft protruding from his groin. Cnut winced at the sight of it, and matters were not helped by scrutinising him further. His face was a bruised, scabby mess, and somebody had destroyed his throat, rending it into pieces with a cold and deliberate fury. Cnut had seen some grim sights in his still young years, but whoever this man was, he'd not enjoyed an easy or glorious death. He'd died hard. Very hard. The warrior responsible must be formidable indeed.

Fortunately, there were no such sights to be found inside. Æthelred's home was a sprawling, complex affair, and their babbling envoy didn't really know his way about, despite his frequent mention of himself as a "man of means". Much of it was draughty, cold stone, all passageways and corridors leading to chambers and halls of various utility. The study was of interest to Cnut, but it held no real meaning to his father, and somebody looked to have vandalised it, scattering the shelves and books across the floor. Cnut picked one up. He couldn't understand it. It was written in some language that was entirely unknown to him. He thought it wise for a ruler to learn such things, but if his father thought the same, he made no mention of it. Cnut made a point of keeping the book with him. He wanted to look at it in private.

As messy as the study was, the view from the window was impressive. Svienn took it in, gazing out to observe the mournful city beyond. Cnut stood with him, the envoy stepping back, realising it was wise to give them a wide berth. Lundenburg had certainly seen better days. Smoke still hung over it, like a dark, smothering blanket, its substance so black and heavy it was quite visible even in the night. The damage was extensive as far as he could see, the famine-induced riot looking like it had led to some kind of civil war within the city. He could still hear the sounds of fighting ever so faintly upon the wind, but his father didn't look concerned. Their army was sizeable. Once they were through the gates, it was all over, and the English knew it. It was only desperation and honour that had led some to continue to resist. They'd pay with their lives, but keep their dignity.

Despite this, they could still see people milling about in the streets below them, their manner suggesting they were apprehensive and yet curious about their new rulers.

Some would be wondering why they were still alive, thinking quite correctly that their decision to submit had saved them. It was true that Svienn had not been kind in his previous expeditions to English shores. Back then, he'd come as Viking, and Cnut had never tired of hearing him speak of it, finding the stories of war and fortune exhilarating. He was old enough now to know this was a different kind of undertaking they'd embarked upon. Everything before had been leading up to this. England had needed to be bled - and thus weakened - before his father's final plan could be set in motion. And now they'd done it. They had the prize, but it was one to keep and rule over rather than destroy. They had plans for this place.

They both turned away to leave the study and head towards what they were assured was Æthelred's throne room. Cnut was surprised. The throne itself didn't look like much. Neither did his father's, come to think of it, but he'd expected a man possessing a kingdom as rich as England to have something more memorable. The whole chamber had a sad air to it, the few tattered banners looking like they were nothing but mournful reminders of more vital days. The banqueting table was annoyingly vast, its surface still littered with platters and cups, the forgotten mess making Cnut wonder what exactly had been happening here. Had this so-called king spent his time entertaining guests when he should have been giving battle in defence of his realm? If so, the country would do well without men like that leading it.

His father settled into the throne. He took his time, like he was testing its dimensions, removing his cloak beforehand and passing it to one of his jarls. A rumble of approval then sounded out from all present. King Svienn of Denmark was finally seated upon the throne of England. He looked happy. Few would be able to tell, but Cnut knew him better than anyone. He had little signs that indicated his mood. He was pleased. And the throne was a good fit. As if he were meant to sit there. One day Cnut would, too. He was counting on it.

The next few hours were beyond tedious. Their men had searched the halls, finding absolutely no trace of Æthelred or any of his people. Oddly, Svienn wasn't troubled by it. He'd find Æthelred at some point, and Lundenburg itself was now secure with their army firmly ensconced within it. He then decided to start accepting personal oaths of loyalty from any well-to-do-city folk willing to attend him. And plenty were. Dozens of them, each one as spineless as the next. This "envoy," who was actually called Osgar, was the first to do so, making a truly revolting display as he knelt before the throne and swore to "honour and serve my king until death renders me incapable of fulfilling my vow". Cnut didn't believe a word of it. He'd betrayed the last king, and no doubt had a hand in the chaos that had afflicted Lundenburg during their siege. He'd certainly been involved in capturing this Ecgberht who'd been brave enough to try and fight to the last. That made Osgar's vow entirely empty as far as Cnut was concerned.

They kept on coming, men just as unappealing as Osgar, and his father kept hearing them, aloof and menacing from atop his new throne. The lateness, or perhaps the earliness, of the hour dissuaded no one. They all wanted to see the new king, and they all knew how important it was that they make themselves known to him. Cnut knew his father wanted to include at least some Englishmen in the administrative apparatus he'd set up to replace the old order. He'd choose the best from those that presented themselves to him. They'd reward loyalty as and when it was given, and punish defiance and treachery on the same grounds. But for the moment, Cnut found the whole process incredibly boring.

He left the chamber, whispering his intentions into his father's ear so as to not prompt undue irritation. Svienn fixed him with a look that said he was mildly disappointed but was still free to do as he willed. Cnut took it for what it was. He'd come here for glory, and they'd had that when they'd finally overcome the defenders. This procession of subservience wasn't to his taste. Those Englishmen who were worth anything were dead outside. He'd not waste time on these petty men with petty hearts.

He found himself outside, the double doors almost making him jump when they slammed behind him. He stared back at them, wondering how the reputedly aged King Æthelred had ever managed to tackle such things without breaking his own back. The thought reminded him of the book he'd taken from the king's study. He took it out again, drumming his fingers across the hidebound cover and flipping the delicate pages with his fingertips. He couldn't understand a word, but he'd learn. His people had never been scholars, but the English were immersed in knowledge. There was a strength there. One that he'd have for his own.

Cnut began striding back towards the study, waving off several warriors who tried to escort him. He didn't need protection. He was a man now and a fighter, too. He'd shown everyone that when they'd taken the gate. Nobody could deny he'd killed men and done it well. The blood on his armour was proof of that. He'd get cleaned up soon enough. But first, he had to check on something.

The study door opened with a jarringly high-pitched creak, Cnut wondering if it were somehow objecting to his presence in this place of refinement and learning. He kicked it once he was within, playing with the notion of breaking it to his will like it were just another defiant subject who needed a lesson. The door slammed shut, the crash of wood on stone soon fading into the heady bliss of profound silence. He understood why Æthelred might have favoured this place. Cnut had always preferred the quiet. He could think clearly, and when it was as deep and undisturbed as this it was like a soothing balm upon his mind. Those men now dripping insincerity upon his father had made an awful babble. They were men of noise, waffle, and bluster. Given a choice, Cnut would always be found here rather than in their frightful company. His aching head wouldn't allow anything else.

Cnut bent low, gathering the books that littered the floor and arranging them into neat piles. It was difficult to see, and he'd not sent for a torch, but the night sky had begun to clear enough for some moonlight to intrude from the open window. His mind wandered whilst he worked, thinking on the difficulties and joys that might lie ahead. Once his father was done with those idiots from the city, they'd arrange a formal ceremony with the people who really mattered. The thegns and ealdormen who'd already submitted, and there were a good many of them, would need to be summoned to make a formal display of subservience. It shouldn't be a problem. Uhtred in Norþanhymbre had been one of the first to switch loyalties away from Æthelred, and as far as Cnut understood, he'd been reputed to be among the king's most steadfast of men. With him on their side, the rest would surely follow.

The books were now all arranged as he'd intended, but he couldn't do much for the shelves, not at present, since he had no tools with which to repair them. It looked like somebody had physically torn them down, but he'd see them mended and this place restored. He'd need it, the day he became king. He'd need the quiet.

The window was beckoning, drawing Cnut towards it. The streets were now largely empty, the people opting for the safety of their homes rather than hanging about in the dark on the off chance of spotting their new king. Cnut found the view mesmerizing. Denmark didn't have anything like Lundenburg. They had towns and fortifications of their own, sure, but a prize such as this, with the means to defend it, was a rarity he'd not witnessed before. To think it now belonged to his family made him almost giddy.

It was for this reason Cnut failed to notice the door opening behind him. Whoever it was must have known this place well, for he knew just the right amount of pressure to apply to ensure the door frame didn't make a sound. They crept up behind, observing Cnut whilst he gazed outward. Several moments passed. Then they made a noise. A simple clearing of the throat. It had the desired effect. It caught his attention.

Cnut spun around, his hands finding the haft of his axe with instinctual ease. He held its edge to the intruder's throat. They said nothing, instead lifting their hands, slowly and deliberately, to peel back the hood of their cloak and reveal themselves. Blond hair, wavy and girlish in appearance. Grey eyes, lifeless and unnerving, and cheeks like he was accustomed to staying indoors rather than facing the bite of the wind. Another man of means, then. Cnut couldn't wait to be rid of him.

"It was foolish to come here," Cnut said. "I could have killed you. I still might."

"That would be a wasted opportunity." There was something about how the man spoke. He was very sure of himself, this one.

"How so?" Cnut asked, lowering his axe slightly but not entirely. The man wasn't afraid of him at all, or if he were, he was expert at hiding such things from the naked eye. Impressive, really.

"You are Cnut, yes?" He'd ignored his question. That was irritating, and Cnut saw no reason to reveal himself to him if he wasn't already sure of his identity. For all he knew, he could be an assassin looking for confirmation of his target's identity. He should kill him now.

"Don't presume to ask me anything," said Cnut through bared teeth. "Tell me who you are and why I shouldn't take your head."

"My name is Eadric," he finally said, like he attached some considerable weight to the claim. "And you are Cnut. I can tell. You show promise. If you were like the others, you wouldn't be here, not now. You and I should talk. We have much to discuss."

"About what?" Cnut spat, exasperated by the ambiguity.

"Your future," Eadric replied. "Your future as king."

Milton Keynes UK
Ingram Content Group UK Ltd.
UKHW020746181223
434584UK00017B/1485